# Tontine

## The Scales of Justice

by
Brian Darr

# Tontine
### The Scales of Justice

This is a work of fiction. Names, characters, places, and incidents are either the product of the author's imagination or used fictitiously, and any resemblance to actual persons, living or dead, business establishments, events, or locales is entirely coincidental.

Library of Congress Control Number: 1-4398802741

ISBN-13: 978-1542734042

ISBN-10: 1542734045

10 9 8 7 6 5 4 3 2 1

First Edition United States

This book is dedicated to two of my best friends,
who I also get to be related to:
Jason and Roxy Darr.

"What goes around, comes around."
                                    -Unknown

# *Chapter 1*

## 1

Six months passed and nothing happened.

After Richard's death, a number of things took place, but no one's mind was on the money or Victor Stone. The world slowed down for a while and the remaining beneficiaries reflected on the events that had taken place. The neighborhoods of Los Angeles were filled with signs endorsing a vote for Bernard Bell or Royce Morrow. A heat wave struck the city that started in May and as June approached, the stress and discomfort left the citizens of the city in a foul mood. Crime was up, the sidewalks were crowded, and construction on every major highway jammed the traffic into a new level of frustration. It was the typical Los Angeles cycle and for thirteen surviving beneficiaries, life moved past the will. Most found themselves in different places, while for others, life kept moving as usual. It was inevitable that temptation would resurface eventually and someone would do something drastic, but the spark that rekindled the fire didn't come from the remaining beneficiaries. It was someone on the outside of the group that couldn't take it anymore. He'd been humiliated. He'd been scared out of town. But after the dust settled, he quite simply couldn't move on. The course of actions that followed the return of Sal Blovik to Los Angeles, were ultimately what started it all over again.

Sal wasn't the most intelligent person in many groups. He'd murdered his wife and did enough time to harden him a bit, but he lacked the motivation or passion to be of much value or danger to the world. His ex-wife certainly was impacted by his existence, but not too many other people. The last anyone saw of Sal was from his waist up as he stood in a river, looking up at the bridge where Toby O'Tool and Adlar Wilcox laughed at his misfortune. His plan was to catch up to them and kill them, but when he parked outside Toby's hideaway, he spotted two police cars at the end of the block. They probably weren't there for him, but it made him take pause anyway. If Sal were to get so much as a parking ticket, he might be dragged in and treated brutally. He was lucky to be out of jail and he preferred to keep it that way. Sure, he'd planned on a killing spree to prove something to Toby and make a hefty amount of money in the process, but killing Toby and Adlar had no real gain. Revenge was never a good reason because police always find the enemy of the dead. Sal was dumb, but he had enough good sense to walk away. Not only did he walk away, but he got as far away from the city as possible. He decided to forget the money, forget Victor's will, forget his friend William Lamone, forget his ex-wife, and try to find a piece of happiness.

What he found was Las Vegas, and that was fun for a while, but he couldn't take advantage of the nightlife without a source of income, and he wasn't qualified to do anything but minimum wage jobs. He lived on the outskirts of the city and fell in with a group who loved to play board games. Between each member, they had over three hundred games, and they met nightly to play. Sal liked that for a while, but he was a hothead at times and a stickler for the rules. The group played for fun and didn't follow unimportant rules when the general consensus was that it wasn't a big deal, but Sal didn't allow anyone in the group to fortune off blurring the rulebook and sometimes raised his voice to a decibel that scared them. One night, he sensed his relationship in the group had changed and they were no longer enthusiastic about having him around. He thought he saw looks and eye rolls exchanged behind his back. Instead of saying anything, he quietly finished out the night and never returned.

It was the next day that he stopped and asked himself why he was in this position. He followed the trail of events backward and always ended in the river, Toby and Adlar laughing at his expense. Toby had been abusive and hurt his feelings so many times in the course of a few days. He couldn't control his hatred, and as he worked his monotonous factory job every day, he kept telling himself I hate Toby O'Tool and soon he caught himself saying it out loud. He said it in the mirror every morning and when he closed his eyes to go to sleep. One day, he woke up and after saying he hated Toby O'Tool, he stared at his ceiling and told himself he couldn't go to work. He didn't have the energy to keep going to a boring job and trying to find friends that would ultimately see him as an oaf. He didn't want to live on the outskirts of the city, knowing he was a few miles away from people enjoying themselves and burning through money like it was meaningless. Life had to be more than waking up, working, trying to find a social life, and going to bed—all with the backdrop of Toby O'Tool constantly in his head.

He took a bus to the heart of Las Vegas and stayed all day and the following night. He walked from one place to the next, people-watching and wishing he could be a part of it. He was approached multiple times and handed papers that advertised escorts. He wanted to call the number but he had no money. He wanted so badly to just have something there was no way he could have. He'd had that chance, but Toby took it away.

And then, finally around midnight, as the lights began to blur and the streets began to really fill with the crazies, Sal closed his eyes and said "screw it" out loud to himself. He knew who some of the beneficiaries were and remembered some of the names. In that moment, a plan developed—not a very good plan, but a plan. Go back, kill someone, tell Toby and see what happened. Toby always tried pounding it in his head that they needed to be careful, so Sal would be careful, but he wanted in. He couldn't take revenge but he could have another chance. Six months had passed. He could convince Toby he was a changed man, and maybe he was. It didn't matter. He mulled it over for a few days, and when finally decided he was going to do it, grew excited. He went to the bus station and bought a ticket on the next bus to Los Angeles. When he boarded the bus, he fell into a seat toward the back, and rested his head on the seat. He was asleep within minutes. He dreamed about one of the beneficiaries and when he woke in Los Angeles, he decided she was the one he was going to kill…

*…Aileen Thick stood in her wedding dress at the end of an aisle, looking out into a small crowd of mostly men in suits. They were strangers to her, and didn't look happy. She wanted to go to the courthouse, but Victor Stone insisted that if they were going to get married, they were having a real wedding. There was no chemistry, and it wasn't the ideal life she'd dreamed of when she was a child, but it beat living with physically and emotionally abusive parents. In fact, for the first time in a while, she felt safe.*

*After the wedding, they sat in the back of the limo, far apart from each other. It was awkward, but Aileen thought in time, that gap would close. In time, maybe they'd grow to love each other. Their unborn child was the key to making that happen. She turned to Victor and managed to sound sincere. "Thanks," she said.*

*"For what?"*

*"Doing this."*

*"All I ask is you keep your word," Victor said.*

*She nodded. "I will. I promise. This is for the baby."*

Victor turned away at the mention of the baby and Aileen looked down with shame. She hated that the child would come into the world with such an unhappy parental arrangement. She'd agreed to get married, have the baby, and when they could create a stable environment, she'd move out. She was allowed to live in a guest room in his mansion for a year. Afterward, Victor told her he'd make sure she was taken care of, but they would have a clean split without drama or controversy. It was all for show. Everyone was to believe the baby was born out of love and brought into the world with true intention. Afterward, they were free to live their lives apart. As long as the baby was taken care of, everybody won.

She started crying for no reason. She was overwhelmed. The direction life took was unexpected and so surreal that she didn't know how to respond. She was appreciative of Victor. He'd taken her away from the hell that was her life before, and she would be set for life, but she didn't know if she could travel the same path she'd been on before.

"What's wrong?" Victor asked. He managed to seem so concerned, as if he was protective—maybe cared about her.

"This isn't what I expected," she said.

Victor nodded silently. He had no words to make her feel better. He never did. Usually he'd display a gesture here or there to prove that he cared, but if she needed a shoulder to cry on, Victor wasn't the guy. "What can I do Aileen?" he asked.

"Nothing. I just...I wish he could grow up with a normal childhood."

Victor frowned as he took in what she said.

He.

"Is it a he?" Victor asked.

"I'm just calling him a he."

"I don't want a boy," Victor said, matter of factually. He looked so serious that Aileen wondered what would really happen if she were to give birth to a male.

"That's not really up to you."

"I know."

"We should give the baby away," Aileen said. The idea had been on her mind for a while, but she finally managed to speak it out loud.

Victor sat next to her and folded his hands in his lap. "I didn't expect this either," he said. "Please understand that I make decisions based on what's best for business. Believe it or not, my public persona affects everything."

"Isn't this more important?"

"I think you're assuming that this child won't grow to be healthy and successful because we're not in love."

"I just want him to be happy."

*"Please stop referring to our child as a boy."*

*"Why don't you want a boy?"*

*"I was surrounded by boys in my youth and as an adult. They're destructive, greedy, ruthless. We hate our fathers but carry on the very genes we hate. Women defy the flaws they see in their parents. They go their own way. I don't want a second generation millionaire spoiled boy, who one day feels everything I have is his. I suspect if I have a girl, she'll run away and be better than me."*

*Aileen laughed, but didn't object. It was the very story of her life. Unfortunately, calling her baby 'he' wasn't a premonition. It was wishful thinking.*

*"Victor?" she said, softly. He turned and their eyes met. "Do you think there's even a possibility that this can work between us?"*

*Victor gave the question serious thought before shaking his head. "Our lives are headed in different directions Aileen. The only glue that holds us together is the baby, and even that we don't agree on. We weren't meant to be..."*

...Six months before, on the day Richard Libby died, Aileen decided to keep her name on Victor's will. She did it to make a point to Toby O'Tool, but every day after, she regretted it. It would have been nice to have rid Victor of her life once and for all, but she was given an out, and she refused to take it. After the funeral, there was silence from the others. She hadn't seen or heard from anyone since that day, and began believing she never would. After she learned Tarek Appleton saved them all, she watched his late night talk show, but that was canceled after a month and the rumor was that Tarek had gone into rehab. With Tarek off the air, she had no way of keeping track of what anyone was doing. With those connections lost, she felt no danger, but wished she'd removed herself just so she could detach completely from Victor.

There was a time when she believed her personal life couldn't get any worse, but somehow she found a new rock bottom. She stopped dating completely and lived in her apartment. She watched television and smoked cigarettes most of her days, but started running out of money. She dug into her savings, but depleted that too. When she got her eviction notice, she tried calling Jason Stone, but his old number was disconnected and she no longer had a way.

Many times in Aileen's life, she thought about hurrying along the inevitable. She always saw it coming, but tried holding out. She'd worked in strip clubs, dated wealthy men, even found one night stands in bars, just so she'd have a nice place to rest her head, but life never got any easier. Instead, it eroded, and without much skill in anything, she knew she'd one day be on the streets. She tried putting an ad in a flier once, an advertisement for a full body massage, but she only got a response here and there, and the work scared the shit out of her. The life of a prostitute wasn't appealing at all. In the movies, they were portrayed as women headed in better places and hooking until they got there—women with a heart of gold who were just waiting for the right man to save them. Aileen knew better. There was nothing glamorous about Santa Monica. The street was dark and the women weren't friendly. They certainly didn't like when a newcomer started showing their face, especially a newcomer that was as pretty as Aileen, but Aileen hadn't fully committed to the idea yet.

On the day that she admitted defeat, she took a walk in the area, scoping it out and testing the water before she jumped in. She passed a group of women, kept walking to the end of the block, and ran into a neighborhood where she crouched down on the sidewalk and began sobbing uncontrollably. Memories of her life flashed before her eyes: An emotionally abusive mother, a physically abusive father, sitting in her room and doodling and discovering she was good, impressing her classmates with drawings far ahead of her years, drawing whenever she could because it was the only positive attention she got, being beaten, being berated, focusing on a career in art, making friends, crying at night, running away from home, returning when she realized she had nowhere to go, meeting Victor...

Her tears flowed freely and she grabbed at the concrete under her, desperate for something to hold onto.

"Are you okay?"

She looked up. The voice was compassionate, but Sal scared her the moment she found his eyes. She quickly forced herself to her feet and dismissively nodded and turned.

Then, his voice wasn't as passionate. "Hey!" Sal shouted. "I asked you a question."

He'd remembered her name. He remembered Aileen Thick when she married Victor Stone. It was on the news and in the paper and Sal remembered seeing her and being astonished by her beauty. He'd made a comment, and his wife—who he later murdered—shook her head in disbelief. In Sal's short-lived partnership with Toby O'Tool, he'd listened as Toby discussed the names with William and Henry. When he heard Aileen Thick, he'd smiled to himself and secretly hoped his assignment would be similar to Henry's: Meet the girl, date the girl, bed the girl... that's as far as he'd gotten. Aileen was an old fantasy that was cast into his life and Sal couldn't let the opportunity slip. If only Sal had gotten to the point where Toby trusted him enough to give him anything to do, he might have suggested Aileen as an assignment.

I hate Toby O'Tool.

"I just want to be alone," Aileen said, her voice wavering.

"Yeah, but you were down there crying."

"I don't talk to people I don't know about personal shit," she said. She turned and started walking. Sal followed her, keeping the pace.

"Maybe you should," he said. She was already afraid of him. This wasn't going to go as he had planned, but it was going to happen.

She felt his presence behind her as she walked and she knew he wasn't just a stranger concerned for her well-being. She walked faster, but heard him increase his pace. She turned quickly, which brought Sal to a halt. "Stop following me," she said. Then Sal did something unexpected, something that told Aileen he wasn't there as a coincidence. He smiled at her. His smile made him look even uglier and his eyes were fixated on her with something that looked like infatuation.

This is what I get for coming here. This is where it ends.

Aileen turned and ran.

Sal took off after her and though Sal's frame was large, he moved with grace, closing the distance quickly. Aileen changed direction, making a sharp left at the corner, trying to get back to Santa Monica, but Sal would catch her before she got there. She kicked off her high heels and sprinted, but the ground was hard and sharp corners pierced the balls of her feet as she ran, which caused her to stumble and slow. Then, Sal's meaty hands were on her shoulder, pulling her to the ground. She tried to scream but his hand reached around and covered her mouth. Her eyes went wide and she tried to wiggle free, but she fell to the ground instead as his body barreled down on her. He grabbed her legs and held her down, and suddenly he was undoing his belt. Aileen's eyes darted from side to side, but he'd cornered her between a wall and a dumpster. The best chance she had was to move between them, but then what? She'd come out the other side with Sal waiting to finish the job. She wriggled and kicked anyway, and managed to slip through his grip. Sal swore and gnashed his teeth at her. He began moving on hands and knees toward her as she backed between the wall and dumpster.

This is it. This is what I deserve.

Her hand nudged a beer bottle, which rolled to the side as Sal's hands were on her again, pawing at her ankle, up her leg, to her thigh...

She was completely cornered now. The only way out was if the large man were to walk away, or if someone would come to her rescue, but neither seemed likely. There was only one thing left for Aileen to do, and even as she believed her life was coming to an end, she was unsure she had it in her. The man's hand surfaced with a large hunting knife and he raised it toward her throat with a toothy grin.

Now or never. Live or die. Find it within…just do it.

She reached out and grabbed the bottle and with one swift motion, smashed it against the dumpster. Before Sal could react, she took what was left and jammed it up into his neck.

Sal's eyes went wide and his hand moved to the pain. He tried to cover the blood flow, but only succeeded in making the pain worse. Aileen pushed herself backward and watched in horror as Sal's eyes went wide in shock and the realization that the glass in his throat was fatal. He suddenly forgot about Aileen and tried saving himself, but as he tried to back his way out from behind the dumpster, he couldn't find his balance. Instead, he just pushed the ground with one hand in an effort to steady himself, and held the other to his neck. He looked up at Aileen, who backed away slowly until she'd cleared the dumpster and got to her feet. She watched his eyes gloss over before his eyelids fluttered and he fell to his side.

Aileen Thick watched the man die with tears in her eyes.

## 2

"Do you take this woman to be your lawfully wedded wife, to have and to hold, til death do you part?"

Henry smiled and looked into Maria Haskins's eyes. "I do."

Those two words changed everything. Henry had never been married and he'd always told himself he never would be. He didn't believe you could love one woman for the rest of your life, and as he verbally committed to Maria at the county courthouse on a Friday afternoon, he realized that he'd crossed a new line. When the time came to follow through with his plan, Maria would either be dead or unable to recover. It was hard for Henry to pretend this was the happiest day of his life while alarms were going off in his head. He reminded himself to follow through and do what needed to be done. He'd spent the last six months with Maria, and in that time, he'd grown sick of her. She was too attached, too loving, too accommodating. It made his assignment easier, but he wanted to be done with her so he could move on.

Toby had kept everything at a standstill, but he wouldn't tell William and Henry why. He simply forced them to get closer to their targets, but didn't say much else. Henry and William talked instead, and both began to doubt the plan, but carried on. They'd even created a side bet on who would be dead first: Brian or Maria, but Henry sensed the same thing in

William that he felt in himself: Guilt.

They were real people and they'd gotten to know them on such an intimate level. The whole game had changed, but as Henry stood at Maria's side and slipped a ring on her finger, he knew there was no other way out. Just the plan.

They left the courthouse and got in their car, where they'd packed their suitcases and were driving straight to the airport to fly to Oregon. Henry wanted something tropical, but Maria ooed and aahed over trees and nature.

"I'm glad to have that over," Maria said, and then confessed something that had been bothering her. "I was afraid we would see that judge."

"What judge?"

"Proctor. He was at The Coop."

"Yeah? Why wouldn't you want to see him?"

"I don't know," Maria said. "It would be awkward."

"The way I see it, everybody won that day," Henry said. "I never believed in what they were doing."

"Someone died," she said.

"Not because of the will. Maria, you're going to possibly profit someday. I'm not saying you'll inherit blood money, but you may outlive them."

"Is that what you hope?"

"Of course. Your life will be set."

"Our life," she said, correcting him.

Henry made note that he'd have to make an effort to use verbiage that made it seem as if there was a long run with Maria. "Our life."

"I don't necessarily agree," she said, "but I'm happy you feel that way, because I had the choice to remove my name."

Henry cocked an eyebrow. "What do you mean?"

"I never told you this, but we were one person short and that judge didn't just say we lost. He said we could volunteer to have our names taken off if we wanted."

Henry's face went blank. He stared at the road and registered this and how he was supposed to react. If Maria had removed herself voluntarily, he wouldn't have had to spend another second with her after that day. He wouldn't have had to move in with her, marry her, sit in the car with her now. She wouldn't have to die. It enraged him that she didn't remove herself, but he couldn't show it. It would contradict everything he just said. He did it anyway. "Why the hell didn't you remove your name then?" he asked with disbelief.

She turned to him with a double-take. She tried to read his face, but it made no sense. He seemed upset. "Um, because you didn't want me to.

The main reason I kept my name on there was because I thought of you and what you wanted."

"I…" He stopped himself before he could finish. He'd just finished telling her he wanted her on it. "You said you didn't want to be on it though. That's the whole reason you were there. Don't tell me you decided to keep your name there for me. Don't put that on me."

"I did. Sorry."

"Yeah, but…" He let out a deep breath. There was no excuse that could justify his response. He was visibly angry. He should have known this and Toby clearly withheld it. Probably because Toby knew the same thing Henry knew: Maria didn't have to die, if only she would have taken her name off. Henry was still working an assignment that was a simple nay vote away from her life being spared.

"Why are you upset?" she asked. "It's the same thing you wanted. We didn't win, which was good. The judge offered another solution and I kept myself on there. I did it for you."

"Did you ever consider you're putting your life in danger?"

"You didn't care about that a minute ago."

"Fuck…" Henry said out loud, but didn't follow up. He needed to drop the conversation now or he'd put himself in the corner. With great effort, he changed his expression and normalized himself. "I just don't want you making decisions because of me," he said. It was the best he had, but it wasn't bad. Henry's wedding day couldn't get worse.

"I didn't just do it for you. One of the guys there, he supposedly had been doing things to some of the others to manipulate them and he clearly wanted us to take our names off, so some of us agreed to only remove them if he did, and of course he didn't." She smiled proudly as she reflected on the moment that the group got the best of Toby. If she'd turned to her side, she would have seen Henry's face was bright red.

## 3

"Guy's name is Sal Blovik," the officer said. "He was released from Kern about a year ago. Murdered his ex wife. You're lucky."

Aileen nodded, shakily, as she sucked on a cigarette and watched officers take pictures and work the crime scene. "Do you know Trish Reynalds?"

"Afraid not. Who is she? A cop?"

"Yeah, but probably not in this area."

"I can look her up and give her a call if you want."

"Sure."

The cop nodded and left her there, wrapped in a blanket, exhaling smoke and staring at the blood behind the dumpster.

When Trish arrived, she didn't hurry over to Aileen. She watched from a distance and slowly approached and stood at her side. Aileen turned, relieved to find a familiar face, but Trish seemed different. She was rigid and had no concern for Aileen. She only stared at the dumpsters.

"What happened?" Trish finally asked.

Aileen relayed the whole incident and Trish followed up with questions, but neither was satisfied when all was said and done.

"I'll look into whether or not this guy could be attached to anyone on the will."

"You think that's what happened?" Aileen asked. "You think he was supposed to eliminate me?"

"I don't think so. It's been pretty quiet since Richard died. It seems like everyone just agreed to forget about it."

"Yeah, but…"

"Aileen, you're walking around this neighborhood. You're putting yourself at risk. You said he was trying to rape you."

"He was going to kill me. I know it."

"You need to make better choices," Trish said, bluntly. "You're lucky."

"Clearly, I know how to defend myself," Aileen said.

"If you hadn't been able to find a weapon, or it had been out of reach, or if he'd injured you, we wouldn't be talking. That man was twice your size."

"Okay, sorry," Aileen mumbled.

"What are you doing out here anyway?" Trish asked.

"Nothing. I was walking through. That's all."

"You don't look well Aileen. Where do you live?"

"You know what? Forget I asked for you."

"You need to take care of yourself."

"What are you? My mother?"

"I'm looking out for the group. Prevention of possible outcomes."

"I'm the last person who's going to be a problem," Aileen said with a laugh as if to say that was an understatement.

"You should have removed your name Aileen. You should have let the judge take your name off and everyone else would have too."

"Is that what your problem with me is?" Aileen asked.

"This isn't a game. I heard what happened. A bunch of you rallied against Toby O'Tool and it was your idea."

"Toby O'Tool's a prick."

"And you endangered yourself to get the best of him? It wasn't smart Aileen. And if anything were to happen to those who followed you, that would be on your head."

"Oh, whatever. The will would have been invalid if you hadn't walked out. You were the one that left and shorted us one."

Trish opened her mouth but found she had no way to dispute that. Aileen may have endangered four people, but Trish endangered everyone. "I just want you to be responsible. Not just because you're one of the group, but because I know you and I think you're better than this.

Aileen laughed again. "You got me all wrong," she said. "I had nothing to be proud of before. Now, I killed a man. I'm about as…"

*"…useless as they come," Aileen's mother said, staring straight ahead at Victor. Aileen's father, Eugene, was at her side, but contributed nothing to the conversation. They looked out of place in a conference room in Stone Enterprises. Victor wore a suit. The Thicks wore tank tops, tangled hair, and looked as if they never groomed themselves.*

*Victor was taken aback by Aileen's mother. He knew they had problems at home, and part of the reason he'd invited the Thicks to meet him was to get a better grasp of Aileen's situation. When the baby was born, he needed to know what to do with her. It seemed family was out. "Excuse me," Victor said. "Are you talking about your daughter?"*

*"Hey, I'm just being honest. The girl does whatever the hell she wants."*

*"I was under the impression she was doing well in school."*

*"Well, what's she doing carrying a baby if she's got it together?"*

*"Mrs. Thick, I didn't call you here to talk about her decisions. I want to know what will happen moving forward."*

*"What's that supposed to mean?"*

*Victor leaned back and crossed his legs and fearlessly addressed them. "Aileen may want to go home and if she does, I will need to know that you will be a good influence for the child. I'm helping Aileen out substantially. I prefer you allow her to detach."*

*Eugene let out a grunt which contained a hint of a laugh. "What will that be worth to you?" Aileen's mother asked.*

*"It's not worth anything. It's a request."*

*"I'll do whatever I please. She's my daughter."*

*"I apologize for being so blunt Mrs. Thick, but even you should know you won't be receiving any parenting awards for the way you raised her. Considering her circumstances, my opinion is that she turned out fine despite the parents she was unfortunate enough to have."*

*There was a long silence as they digested what Victor said. Finally, her mother leaned forward with a sneer. "If you want me to stay away from your baby and keep my mouth quiet on your charades with my daughter, then it won't come free."*

*"What are you asking?"*

*"I think it's worth millions, but we'll settle for…" she pretended to think, "…a hundred thousand."*

*Victor nodded slowly, never taking his eyes off her. "What exactly am I buying?"*

*"Aileen can't handle herself out in the world. All she knows is where she was. She has no money, no sense of how to conduct herself, she can't even do the laundry. She'll do what I ask. You can give her anything you want, but if I tell her to come home, she'll come home. And I'll have her take that baby from you. You can get your big fancy lawyers, but we'll raise such a stink for you and you'll feel it. Ain't that right, Eugene?"*

*Eugene grunted.*

*"And what happens if I do give you what you're asking?" Victor asked.*

*"We stay away from you and Aileen. Let you live your life. You can toss her aside, do what you want, and we'll stay out of it. Probably won't even stay in the city. Hell, a hundred K is pocket change for you. I'd say everybody wins."*

*"Except Aileen."*

*"Oh, please. That girl got herself in this mess. We don't want her. If you're so concerned, you can keep her."*


*Aileen walked through Victor's home, staring in awe at her surroundings. It was beyond any place she ever expected to live. She knew it was temporary, but found it motivating. She'd never live in a mansion, but she found a second wind for a better life. A baby wouldn't necessarily hold her back. She still had Victor—a man who would make sure their child and she was taken care of. They wouldn't be a happy family, but they'd function without drama.*

*She was sitting in the kitchen bar, popping cherries in her mouth when Victor came home. It was late. He'd probably been out with a woman. Sometimes he brought them home. Sometimes he came home late. She preferred the latter.*

*He walked through and grabbed a bottled water from the fridge. "You're still awake," he said.*

*"Yeah, I was thinking about sketching."*

*"Well, make yourself at home."*

*"I need to get supplies."*

*"We may have something in a box in the cellar."*

*"That's okay. I'll run out tomorrow."*

*Victor nodded. "Will Aileen Thick still become an artist?"*

"*Maybe. Probably not. When the baby is old enough, I'll probably go back to school, see if I can pick up where I left off.*"

"*I'll take care of that. We'll find a care provider and you may do as you wish.*"

"*Victor, I'm going to have to afford an apartment and work a full-time job and take care of a child. It won't be that simple.*"

"*I already told you I would make sure you're taken care of.*"

"*But I don't want that. If you're giving me money to start out, you'll see every dime back. I promise. I know you don't need it, or even want it, but I'm not going to have you take care of me just because I'm the mother of your baby.*"

"*You can do that after you go to school then.*"

"*I can't ask you for that. You're just going to confuse things.*"

"*This is all very simple for me.*"

"*It's not for me. You have all these options. Pay for me, pay for my baby, pay for daycare, college...but if it were you, if the situation was reversed, would you want that?*"

*Victor found her eyes.* "*Then why are we having this baby?*"

"*I want him,*" *she said.*

"*You lost a career, ended up in a loveless marriage...*"

"*It's just a bump in the road. I'll get back to my life. It will be hard, but I'll handle it.*" *She suddenly grew emotional and sniffled as she wiped her eyes.* "*Is this completely loveless?*"

*Victor took a long moment as he thought about the answer.* "*I care about you and I care about how our daughter turns out.*" *She broke into laughter and shook her head.* "*We're mismatched Aileen. Our marriage isn't loveless. It's just not what it's supposed to be. I'm not the right guy for you and if we tried to force it, we'd hate each other in the end...*"

...Aileen stood outside Sal's home for five minutes, afraid to knock on the door. Sal's mother already knew her son had been killed and when Aileen finally did knock, she was certain his mother would want her gone. Instead, a short pudgy woman with coke-bottle glasses and curly gray hair, took one look at Aileen and motioned her inside. She was neither sad nor irate. Aileen got the impression that Sal's mother had expected this for some time.

"You can't choose what kid you get," Val Blovik said. "Every parent has this picture perfect idea their kid will be a lawyer or an astronaut, but you get what you get. I did my best with Sal. Gave him everything a kid needed, but he was so angry all the time. Punching holes in the wall and yelling at me and running away all the time. He started bow hunting and buying guns. When he killed his wife, I was in disbelief, but I suppose the progression added up. Nothing surprised me after that. If I were you in that situation, I would've done the same thing. I just hope you're okay dear."

Aileen wanted to cry. Val didn't know her well enough to understand that she was nothing special, but on the day her son died, she'd shown more concern for Aileen. "I'm okay Ms. Blovik, but I don't know what to do about this."

"Do about what?" Valerie asked. "There's nothing you can do. He's gone. He didn't leave much behind. Me. A couple bar friends."

"I want to know who he is and I guess…anything I can about him."

"Ever since he got out of prison, I haven't seen him much. I knew he was in town but I had no idea where he was living or what he was doing. I didn't want to go through the disappointment." Aileen nodded and thought about Jason. It seemed their scenario was the opposite. "Only friend of his I knew was that William Casey, one of his friends from long ago."

"Really? Is he in L.A. too then?"

"I saw him a month ago working downtown."

"Do you mind if I ask where?"

"Not at all. Restaurant called The Wasp. Went in for lunch but don't think that Casey boy recognized me."

"Thank you," Aileen said.

"Mind if I give you a piece of advice before you go on down there? You might be looking for something human about my Sal so you can feel guilty about what happened, but you needn't bother. I can tell you all kinds of good things about that boy, but in the end, he enjoyed ruining things more than he liked fixing them. You think you need to get over what happened, then the best thing you can do is something my late husband was told once. He accidentally left a burner on and burned down his house. His girlfriend at the time died because of it and he was all torn up until his friend told him that he needed to live life for two people now…like living extra to make up for it."

Aileen felt better when she left the house, but constantly relived the attack in her head, trying to remember everything that was said. She kept thinking about the look in his eyes, a look that said he was on a mission. He was going to rape her, but he was there to kill her, and he wasn't discreet about it. He didn't coax her into a car or quietly sneak up on her. She felt there was something more to it.

She pulled into the parking lot of The Wasp and observed the building, unable to move.

"Care if I have the fifth off Van Dyke?" Guy asked.

Brian pretended to think for a moment. "Go ahead and put the request in. If no one else asked off already, I'll approve it."

William worked at his side, silently. All passion for the job and his assignment was gone. He'd helped Brian break out of his shell. He'd given him the push he needed to stand up for himself, and six months later, Brian was assistant manager. He was also thirty pounds skinnier. He was still a pushover, but Toby had William in a holding pattern and while nothing happened, William got stuck cooking in a shitty diner, being friends with a guy he didn't care about. He missed his friends at the bar. He missed picking up girls and playing poker and X-box. He couldn't take much more of the nothingness. There were twelve beneficiaries to oust and Toby was frozen in time.

"William!" Eve shouted as she approached the window. "Girl in lobby wants to see you."

William was happy to hear this initially. He could use a night out. When he looked into lobby at the girl who was waiting, his forehead wrinkled with confusion. "Her?" he asked.

"Yup," Eve said, and walked away before William could ask what she wanted.

"I know her," Brian said, staring at Aileen. "How do you know her?"

"I don't. How do you?"

"Victor Stone's ex wife," Brian said.

All at once, William grew sick. This was it. The whole scheme was about to ignite. "Weird," was all he managed to say before dragging himself into the lobby. Once there, he motioned Aileen to follow him to a booth in the corner, so he'd be hidden from sight.

Aileen followed at a distance. William had a strange look on his face. She wondered if he knew what happened to Sal and what her part in it was. Most importantly, she wondered how good of friends they really were.

William fell into the booth but Aileen stood, afraid to trap herself in a seat. "You're William Casey, right?"

"Yeah, do I know you?"

"My name is Aileen Thick."

"What can I do for you?"

"Um, well…" She slowly sat and looked down into her lap. "You knew Sal Blovik?"

He felt sicker. Sal must have done something. He must have told someone. He realized that six months ago, before Toby got rid of Sal, they'd spoken openly about some of the beneficiaries. He had no doubt Aileen's name came up. He wanted to get up and run, but the only thing that kept him there is that he hadn't done anything wrong yet. He could blame Toby. He could apologize profusely. He could…

"He died this morning."

William let out a breath of relief.

4

Sam Smith Auto was unusually packed for the occasion. Forty men won the honor of competing to win a Mustang, compliments of Sam Smith. Forty men stood with one hand on the car, ready to outlast everyone else. Their friends and family came for the occasion, rooting for their own to be the last standing with their hand on the car. After four hours, three men had already been eliminated. Not one of them walked away exhausted. They'd all been coerced or enraged because one man worked his way around the car, antagonizing them.

Sarah Trask was number four, when she couldn't take any more and suddenly used both hands to shove Toby O'Tool. His hand stayed planted on the car and Sarah was eliminated. "Asshole!" she screamed, realizing he'd gotten the best of her.

"Can someone get this lady out of here?" Toby said, looking toward the judges. "She's trying to shove me off the car."

A guard approached and the woman willingly stormed off while the crowd politely applauded her effort.

Toby looked at her replacement, a gawky teenager, who smiled awkwardly.

Toby smiled back. "Good luck with that one," he said.

"Who?" The kid asked, confused. "Me?"

"Yeah, she didn't give you her number?" The boy shook his head slowly. "She said you were hot. I assumed she gave you her number or something."

The teen was suddenly torn between the attractive woman, who was walking through the parking lot. "Are you being serious?" he asked with desperation. Toby nodded. "Did you get her name or anything?"

"No, but…"

The woman was entering her car. Before Toby could finish, the gawky teen pulled his hand off the car. "Screw it," he said and hurried toward the parking lot. Toby was pleased to have knocked two out within a minute.

"You're unbelievable," a voice said, approaching him. Toby turned to find Henry standing there, shaking his head.

"Here to watch me win?"

"No, I'm here because you're an asshole."

"I wish I had a dime for everyone who said that to me today."

Henry ignored him. "The day Richard died, in the diner with the judge, did he give everyone an opt out?"

Toby's face changed as he thought about the world of shit Henry was about to go through. "Yes," he said, bluntly.

"How could you not tell me that? How many people wouldn't have had to die?"

"It wasn't something I planned or could have prevented. I didn't tell you because I knew you'd be up in arms. I tried talking them into scrubbing their names off that thing. No one bit."

"And you're okay with this?"

"I'd rather not have it this way, but it was up to them. Not me. I was just relieved that the whole thing was still on."

"Unbelievable."

"Just calm down."

"Calm down? Who's out there in the trenches, spending months with someone they have to watch die, while you're here trying to win a car? And then you've got nothing but criticism for everything we do."

"I don't see how this changes anything Henry."

"There's a lot of weight on this thing already. Knowing it didn't have to be this way…"

"Look, ever since that incident…"

"Stop calling it an incident Toby. You say it in the same way that people call Vietnam a conflict—not a war. People are dying!"

"Which you knew would happen when you signed on."

"I didn't know I'd have to be this close for so long. I see her every day. I sleep in the same bed. Most of these people are decent people. I married this woman for God sake!"

"Congratulations by the way. Did you get my gift?"

"Yeah, I threw it away. You're not funny."

"How's a toaster supposed to be funny?"

"This whole thing is too much. I thought I could handle it, but she thinks we're in love. It's beyond dishonest."

"Are you kidding me? Amid all the dishonesty in the world, con artists are among the most honest."

"What is it with you and your speeches condoning horrible things?"

"All we are are masters of rationalization, but only because it's part of the game. In the end, we admit our chosen profession is anything but honest. Your ability to rationalize is an invaluable skill."

"That's your problem. You could make a case for Hitler's beliefs if you wanted to. Doesn't make it right."

"I'm trying to tell you that everyone does what we do. Don't be fooled by the amateur status of our society's semi-honest citizens. Many of them pull off at least one good scam in their lifetime. The thin line that separates our activities from legitimate business practices now exists only in theory. Lawyers lie and win cases. Politicians lie and win elections. Advertisers lie and make money. Parents like to win control of their children. Lying, which makes deception possible, is an everyday event and no longer shocks my senses. All I'm doing is polished deception of what everyone else is doing."

Henry shook his head, his eyes sad. "I can't do this to Maria."

"What? You love her now?"

"Her father's dying."

Toby opened his mouth, but it snapped closed. After their spat that morning after the wedding, Maria received a call and immediately packed for Nebraska where her family was from. She didn't invite Henry, which surprised him. His wishy washy demeanor was pushing her away, and he thought that was for the best. He wanted Maria to fall out of love with him and kick him to the curb, but he wasn't sure that was possible. The funeral was his opportunity to use her emotional state to his advantage— to convince her that he wasn't the right guy for her.

"Then why are you here?" Toby asked.

"I can't," Henry said, running his hand through his hair, visibly stressed.

"What if I cut you in for a third?" Henry shook his head, unable to think straight. "You're not going to end up with her either way. You can't undo what you've done at this point. I'm asking you to stick with her. It's great that you're having some hangups about this. I liked Richard, but we're all ashes anyway. If she hasn't left yet, get your ass home and go be with her. Win a gold star for the day."

"You really are an asshole Toby," Henry said, completely serious.

"I'm way too desensitized by that word."

"How you gonna cut me in for a third?"

"I just will. Even if it's out of my share."

"It's not necessary. It goes four ways. We're all at equal risk."

"See that? You're a good guy Henry. You're going to have to learn to tone that down though if you wanna get through this. You think you're gonna miss Maria? Wait until I have you sleeping with Royce Morrow."

"Alright, I'm going back."

"Good man."

Henry walked away feeling a little better having vented. He'd always told himself to detach from his emotions if he was going to do this. It had been easy in the beginning, but after seven months with Maria, he'd invested too much time. She was still too attached though. Without Henry in her life, she'd fall into a depression. All he could tell himself was that

Maria wasn't someone who even seemed to want to live—at least without a constant ego boost at her side, and it seemed as if she would never have that anyway. He walked slowly to his car, ready to go to her, comfort her, meet her family in Nebraska and pretend to grieve with her when her father passed away. He closed his eyes tight when he got to his car, talked himself into moving forward with the plan, and drove home.

"Planning on winning?" a well tanned blond haired man with buck teeth and a cowboy hat said, looking at Toby.

"No, of course not," Toby said. "I really want to lose."

The man laughed. "Well, I reckon you will. I plan on taking this puppy out of here with me. Girls go wet for a guy in a Mustang."

"You know," Toby said. "I heard babies conceived in the back seat of a Prius have IQs thirty points higher than those conceived in the back seats of conventional gasoline powered cars."

## 5

After Aileen relayed the story to William, he sat silently for a long moment. He felt guilty for being so relieved that Sal was dead. William and Sal just kinda fell in together in college and William had always been unable to get rid of him. When Sal ended up in prison, William moved on and hoped to never see him again. Then, Sal was released and came knocking on William's door. When Toby told William about the will, he decided Sal could be utilized, but misjudged what Toby was looking for by a long shot. After Toby ran him off, William wondered if he'd ever show his face again, and when he did, how would he do so? Toby was right: Sal was a liability, but William never stopped believing they wouldn't see the last of Sal and according to what Aileen was saying, Sal came back with every intent of helping them through their list, but Aileen killed him first.

"We weren't that close," William said. He didn't want to seem close to a man who almost murdered the woman sitting across from him. "He used to be a better guy before the thing with his wife."

"Why did he kill her?"

"It goes back long before her. Sal was always a big guy and he had that thing where half your face muscles are dead and so he was uneven, with a lazy eye, and a giant body. In college, while everyone else was hooking up, he was getting nothing. And he'd try. He seemed to think he was a catch and when he got turned down, he'd just be angry about it. He grew this deep-seated hatred for women. Well, then he met one who liked him back. They rushed into a marriage, but rumors were floating around that they weren't getting along at all and she was talking divorce within a month. She was seeing this other guy at the same time and I assume Sal figured that out and killed her. Or maybe he never figured it out and killed her. It actually didn't surprise a whole lot of people."

"So you knew he killed his wife, but you were his friend?"

"That's an overstatement. I wasn't a fan, but he was chummy with me and he knew I was a single bar-goer, so I didn't have an excuse to get rid of him, other than to tell him I just don't like him, but he already scared the shit out of me."

"I see," she said. "Well, I talked to his mother and now you, and no one seems to mind that he's dead."

"The buck stops here cause I don't think he had anything else in the world. I pitied him a little. I wish I could say the world will miss him, but I'd be lying. I doubt anyone will attend his funeral. Can you imagine that? No one at your own funeral…"

Aileen looked down. She'd imagined it many times and wondered if that would be her fate. "It's strange to think of a person as completely bad," she said. "I guess…I don't mean to sound like a drama-queen, but I don't do a lot of good and I guess I thought this was something else I would regret forever, but…"

"But what?"

"I guess I killed an evil man. And that's a good thing?"

"No one is made evil, but I guess the guy had the misfortune of some bad genes and circumstance. At some point, he embraced it. He knew the world saw him as a monster, so what would be the point of being anything else?"

Aileen appreciated William's words, but couldn't help but ask herself the same question after she left. She wondered how the world really saw her—a whore, a broke nothing, an ex-gold-digging lowlife who no longer had a roof over her head. It began to grow dark and she considered her options. She scanned a list of her exes in her head but came up with no one she could call and hope for a place to stay. She'd forgotten her circumstance throughout the day, but when all was said and done, she had nowhere to go.

The world saw him as a monster, so what would be the point of being anything else?

She wanted to bring herself to tears, but couldn't manage. She was too exhausted. As she wandered through the streets, she stopped as a television sounded through a pornography shop. The story relayed the incident of that morning. Sal's face was plastered to the screen and the story only referred to her as a "girl working nearby." She stared through the window at the screen, where the face of pure evil looked back at her.

Sal Blovik…pure evil. Who knew what he was capable of? She may have even saved lives by ending his. It was the first thing that brought a smile to her face, but then the sun completely set and with nowhere to go, she was only left to face the inevitable. She walked to the same street she'd been the night before. There were less prostitutes in the area. They'd been scared off by the police that had been around all day. The few remaining pierced her with their eyes as she walked past, searching for an area to call her own. The reality of her decision hadn't quite hit her. She knew it would the moment a car pulled up and the window rolled down. She was disgusted with herself, but she knew what she was and there was no point in delaying it any longer.

Within ten minutes, a car pulled through the street slowly and came to a slow stop where Aileen stood. She watched from a distance. It wasn't too late to back out now, to never go through with it.

Then the window rolled down and a familiar face stared back at her.

Her eyes went wide in fear. "You…" she said, numbly…

*"…Me?"*

*"Yeah," an officer said, giving Aileen a sympathetic look.*

*"Did I do something wrong?"*

*"We'd like you to come outside so we can talk."*

*Aileen was still in her robe. She reluctantly joined them outside. "Ms. Thick, are you Aileen Thick who previously lived at 3240 Maplewood, Lot 30?"*

*"Yeah…," she said slowly. "My parents live there now."*

*The officers exchanged a look before going on. "This morning police were called to that address because the postal carrier thought he smelled fumes and the mail had piled up for a week. Police responded to the call and found Eugene and Vicky Thick dead from carbon monoxide poison, which had been leaking into the trailer for days."*

*"What?" Aileen asked, growing numb. "Wait…no, wait…they're both dead?"*

*"I'm afraid so."*

*She didn't go into shock and she didn't start crying. Instead, she unexpectedly grew angry. Later, she'd realize it was because of all the things left unsaid—everything they'd gotten away with and she'd never gotten the best of them, never grew into a mature adult so she could one day turn back and laugh in their faces for her success when they only endorsed her failure.*

*"I need to be alone," she said.*

*She realized later that she really did want to be alone—not just from the police or those who would be calling to tell her they heard about her parents, but alone from the world. When reality set in and Aileen was able to see life without her parents, she realized there was only one thing she knew she wanted to be: A mother. She could one day be an artist, and she'd figure that all out, but Victor Stone suddenly felt like a third wheel. He offered security and a place to hide, but ultimately, they were just roommates. They were an arrangement, but there was no love. They couldn't even agree on the sex of the baby. Victor would forever resent her for forcing him to be a family man, and one day, she knew she'd resent him too.*

*Aileen took a cab to the mansion and asked the driver to wait at the curb. She packed a box and a suitcase and left a note on the counter that read: Victor, thank you for all that you've done, but I'm asking nothing more from you. I can take care of the baby alone and I will never ask for anything from you. You're free to live your life and please know that I'll be able to take care of myself. I'm not one for charity and I have my own path to follow. Thank you again. Please know that your son will be in good hands.*

*She smiled a little and knew Victor would too. Maybe it would be easier for Victor envisioning Aileen giving birth to a boy. Maybe Victor would be relieved by her decision, and as she closed the cab's door and drove away from his home, she thought about Victor, and she thought about her parents, and her dreams, and her unborn baby, and only felt relief...*

"...Tarek?" she asked, staring into the eyes of the man who once owned late night TV.

It took a few seconds for Tarek Appleton to register who he was staring at, but when he finally realized who she was, he managed an awkward smile. He was busted by the very woman he aimed to pick up. Hookers weren't usually acquaintances of his, and it changed the game completely. "You need a ride?" he asked, hoping she'd think he was just a naive guy who gave scantily dressed women rides home at midnight.

"Sure," she said, before she realized she didn't really want a ride home. Whatever Tarek was feeling was magnified in Aileen. She'd never officially sold herself yet, but once word spread, from Tarek to god-knows-who, she'd forever be known for standing on that corner in that moment.

They drove in silence for a few moments before Aileen forced a conversation. "Where are we going?"

"I can take you home," he said.

"I don't have a home," she said. "That's why I'm out. I was just evicted. I don't do what you think."

"I never said you did. How about a hotel?"

"I don't need you to put me in a hotel. I can take care of myself."

They sat in silence awhile, and then managed to talk about the weather and other forced lines of conversation. Finally, Tarek asked if Aileen had seen any of the others since Richard's funeral.

"Other than Royce Morrow in the news constantly, I've only seen that bitch cop and that was this morning," Aileen said with a sneer. She then relayed what happened to Sal and when she finished, Tarek sat in a long silence.

"You really don't have a place to stay?" Tarek finally asked. She shook her head. "I've got a guest room. I won't take no for an answer, so don't bother fighting me on this. It's too dangerous out there. That guy could be another who wants the money from Victor's will. You get the full story on the guy with the bomb?"

"I only heard you saved everyone in The Coop that day," she said, finding his eyes.

"Yeah, well don't call me a hero. In the end, I got fucked by that mess."

"How?"

"I felt good after that…at least in the moments after, talking to the police. But Stanley Kline went to jail and he haunted me all day every day. I couldn't focus after that. I kept having this feeling like the guy was behind me all the time. I was walking through my house once and just felt him behind me and I turned, knowing he was there, but it was ridiculous because I knew he couldn't be. I recognized how crazy I was but I couldn't turn it off. And I carried that with me to work and everything fell apart. I was too fucking paranoid all the time."

"I heard it was other things," she said, slowly.

"That was my cover. The truth was too complicated, so we played up the partying unprofessional at work angle. The truth is that I quit. I wasn't fired. I couldn't handle it anymore. I remember being onstage and looking into the audience and I always felt like he was out there."

"Do you know what happened to Anthony Freeman?" Aileen asked.

"He left. He wanted to get far away from people. He said he could have a stroke or heart attack at any time. He was afraid to sneeze because he said it temporarily stops the heart, but who knows? He just wanted to make sure that if it ever went off, no one was around, so he isolated himself, but I don't know where. Other than that, it's been quiet for me too, but if someone tried to kill you this morning, you're safer with a roof over your head. I have security, and you can be free to come and go."

"Why would you do that? You don't even know me."

"In the coming days and weeks, you're going to relive that attack. It probably hasn't all hit you yet. I've been there. Those of us that are still alive from your ex-husband's will, we need to keep the peace. Two of us are dead, and that's unnerving enough. I don't need to know you. I know you won't rob me, and even if you did, oh well. Being a guest in my home is barely a sacrifice for me. Trust me."

Tarek pulled his car into the driveway and Aileen looked up at the mansion in front of her. Tarek was afraid she'd relive the attack, but the sight of the mansion took her back even further, to a time when she lived with Victor and entered a place not much different from this every day. That had turned into a disaster, but as far as she could tell, Tarek was a nice guy.

"So what happened?" Tarek asked.

"What do you mean? With what?"

"Why does Victor hate you? I'll tell you if you tell me."

"Because he blames me for taking something from him."

"What's he think you took?"…

*"…Doctor will be right in Miss Thick," a nurse said, prepping a tray at the side of Aileen's gurney before exiting the room, almost running into a man on his way in. The nurse sidestepped Victor, who slowly entered and sat next to her bedside. She felt his presence and closed her eyes without turning.*

*"Before you say anything…" Victor said, "…I want you to know that I admire your decision. It's not only your decision to make though."*

*"You don't even want this baby."*

*"I never said that. I don't believe I want this baby any more or less than you do, but I'm a part of it."*

*"I can't just be in a loveless relationship, living in your home…"*

*"That's not what I'm asking. I'm asking you to take this one step at a time. Let's get through this appointment and figure out the next thing."*

*"I'll tell you what I'll do," Aileen said, "I'll let fate decide. When the doctor tells us the sex, that will make my decision."*

*"If it's a girl?"*

*"I move back in with you—at least until we know the next step."*

*"I assume if it's a boy, you're gone?"*

*"I see how you react whenever this comes up. It's not just a preference with you. You just don't want to raise a boy."*

*Victor nodded, unable to deny her claim. "You really believe this is the best way to make a decision?"*

*"My parents once told me I was a coin toss away from never seeing this world. And sometimes it seemed like they wished that coin had*

*landed heads up."*

*"I apologize to be insensitive due to their recent passing, but they're not the best models for decision-making."*

*"Maybe not, but my life is already off course, Victor. It's already out of my control. I can't make this decision because it's an impossible decision. If it's a girl, we will try to keep going. If it's a boy, I'm gone."*

*"The possibility of a future is no option?" Victor asked.*

*She slowly shook her head. They sat in silence until the doctor came back and took them through the motions before the sonogram exam. They spoke in one word answers and the doctor couldn't help but notice their lack of enthusiasm. They weren't the first couple who were bound together by a baby, but there was something more to them—a glimmer of hope. For Victor, it was the hope of a sign—perhaps a girl. It wouldn't just mean he would have a baby girl; it was a chance to buy time so he and Aileen could find common ground. She didn't believe they could ever work together and he could never convince her if she walked out now.*

*The doctor smiled as he examined the screen. He looked up. "Do you know what we're looking at here?"*

*Both Aileen and Victor squinted their eyes at the screen trying to make out the screen.*

*"Can you tell if it's a boy or a girl?" Victor asked.*

*"Sure can," the doctor said. "Do you have a preference?"*

*"A girl," Victor said, meeting Aileen's eyes.*

*"Well, I've got good news and bad news," the doctor said. "The bad news is you're having a boy."*

*Victor looked away and closed his eyes, frustrated beyond what he could express. Aileen nodded slowly, her mind made up. She wasn't sure what she wanted to happen, but she was officially on her own in this world, with a baby boy in tow.*

*"What's the good news?" Victor asked.*

*"You're having a girl," the doctor said with a smile. "What you're looking at here, is twins."*

## Chapter 2

### 1

Maria's eyes snapped open suddenly and the vision faded. She sat up in bed and looked out the window for an indication of the time. The sun was setting, but the day was far from over.

The vision...she saw the whole thing. It was a girl who she shared Geography with and the girl had been by the river after school, and suddenly she was being chased by a man and the girl was clumsy and lost her footing in the river. The man grabbed her by the jacket and...

She tried to shake the vision but it was too vivid and she saw the face so clearly. It was the post man who chased April Lovelace. His last name was Chowder. It was stitched on his uniform. Maria had always found his name funny before today. Chowder, like the soup, she'd say with a giggle and her mother and father would pretend to laugh.

The Chowder guy murdered April Lovelace...today...after school. Maria didn't even consider the possibility she'd had a daydream or her imagination was running free. Somehow, she just knew it was real, and when the distant sound of sirens sounded throughout the town, she sunk in a chair in the living room, trying to figure out how it was that she had a premonition so randomly and so real, but most importantly, so right.

The body of April Lovelace was found quickly, but it was two days later that Maria realized no one had been arrested. The police chief held a press conference and swore justice would be served, but nothing was said about the Chowder guy and when she saw him delivering mail two days later, a skip in his step and a tune on his lips, she suddenly knew it *was her who had to lead the police to the guy.*

*She thought about her plan throughout the school day. It was simple, really. Just go to the police and say she knew who killed April. But how would she explain how she knew? And what if the police went to the Chowder guy's home and he simply said he didn't do it and there was no proof? She thought about telling the police she witnessed the crime, but they'd likely disprove that and what she knew wouldn't be taken seriously.*

*The truth.*

*I'm psychic.*

*She smiled at the thought. She'd never been a particularly interesting kid and she'd never stood out or had a talent like most kids. She was plain-Jane, nothing to write home about. But that was yesterday's news. A more up-to-date subscription displayed itself in her imagination with a large headline: Maria Haskins, age 10. Psychic!*

*She tried to remind herself that April's death was a tragedy, but something good was stirring inside. Something told her she was special. Suddenly she was anxious to share her gift with the world. After school, one week after the day April was killed, Maria marched into the police station, approached the counter, and told an officer that she knew who killed April. They took her in a room and asked dozens of questions but she didn't have the answers. She only said she saw the Chowder guy. They wrote in their notebooks and eyed her suspiciously, and finally, one officer asked if she actually witnessed the crime.*

*She smiled a peculiar smile and looked into the officer's eyes with confidence. "I wasn't there, but I had a vision...a dream." She corrected herself so she wouldn't seem crazy. She'd wait until after she was proved right to spring the "how" on them. They approved a search warrant and Maria waited at the station while four officers went to Matthew Chowder's home. After a thorough search, they came up with nothing and apologized to the man. They then called Maria's parents to pick her up and sat her down for a serious conversation.*

*"What are you? Nine or ten?" the officer asked.*

*"I'm ten," Maria said.*

*"Well Maria, I'm going to go easy on you because you're just too young to know better, but what you did actually wastes a lot of time and resources that would best be used elsewhere."*

*"How do you know it's not him?"*

*"It's just not. He doesn't fit the profile and there's no link between Matthew Chowder and April Lovelace. To top it off, we searched his home and came up with nothing. I'm afraid you're going to have to let the police handle this one."*

*Maria closed her eyes and concentrated hard. The officer watched her curiously and looked up with a smirk to share amusement with another officer. Then, she suddenly opened her eyes. "He has a storm shelter in his backyard. It's covered with grass. The Chowder man buries in his yard."*

*The officer might have sent her home then and there, but her face was all serious, and something about Chowder's demeanor had been unnerving. The officers went back to Matthew Chowder's home, less enthusiastic about the prospect of finding a killer this time around. They flashed their search warrant and as three officers walked to Matthew's yard, the fourth kept his eyes on Matthew. Before they uncovered the storm shelter, the officer knew it was coming. The fear was plastered to Chowder's face.*

*In Matthew Chowder's underground room, the police uncovered clothes, knives, and the decomposing bodies of six girls...*

"...That's disgusting."

Maria awoke from her nap to find the source of Henry's remark. Along the side of the winding road was a raccoon spread five yards across the pavement. Maria's heart broke as she thought about the animal. He was probably just crossing the road—another day in his life—and only realized for a split second that it was over. She almost cried thinking about it.

She turned to Henry, whose eyes were focused on the road. He finally turned to her. "So tell me what the deal is with your dad."

"What deal?" she asked.

"Sounds like he didn't even know you were married. You've hidden him and your siblings from me. At least until now, but only because he's dying."

"It's no secret. We weren't close."

"Why not?"

"He doesn't approve of my path."

"See, I don't get that. He was there when you were a kid, right? When you did what you did?"

"Yes."

"So what's the deal? Does he just not believe you? Does he think it was a trick?"

"No. I got a lot of attention for helping them catch Matthew Chowder. He just thought it wasn't something I could always do. Or he thought I dreamed it. I don't know."

"Is he right?"

Maria fell silent. She thought for a long moment. "You've always believed in me."

"Sure," Henry said. "I've always believed in what you do, but can you do anything? Can you take my hand and see what's in my head? Can you see anyone's future or past? Can you read my life by pulling tarot cards?"

She took a deep breath. "It's hard to explain Henry."

"Try."

"Some people have vibrant personalities, or they go through monumental changes in their lives. When our auras are strong, whether by personality or circumstances, I feel it. Most of us live mundane lives and do the same things over and over and if I sit with someone who lives in a circle, I will feel nothing. For some of us, there is a storm on the horizon, and I can feel this if they are receptive and open. I must be allowed in by the recipient."

"How much does this even mean to you? Let's assume you can look into the mind: Should you? Do we need to be steered or should we just go with the flow and let life unravel?"

Maria seriously considered long enough to give Henry satisfaction. His mission was simple: Cast doubt. Make Maria walk away from everything she knew. Create an environment where Maria has nothing—only Henry to rely on.

"I think you should sell the place," Henry said.

"What do you mean?" she asked, slowly.

"I make enough money to support us. Pretty soon we're going to want a kid. You can stay home while I work and that will be stable. It wouldn't work the other way around—not with kids in the picture. We take what your shop is worth and we invest that money. We'll probably turn a nice profit, but if we don't, we'll still have my income and each other."

"How can you ask this of me?"

"Because I don't think you enjoy it Maria. I think you do it because you think you're supposed to—because once upon a time years ago, you helped the police with your vision, but tell me Maria, other than a flash here and there, has anything happened since? Anything significant? Where were you when terrorists flew planes into our buildings? Where are you with the fifty to hundred active serial killers, or thousands of missing kids? There are stacks of files of cold cases just waiting to be solved, but you're sitting and waiting for people to walk through the door so you can tell them whether or not their careers or relationships are favorable or not. And even then, I see your self-doubt. So where's this headed? Are you trying to prove something that you may never prove, or are you going to start taking our lives together seriously at some point?" *Toby would be proud.*

Maria stared into space for a long moment and then turned to Henry lovingly, as if she was playing their life in her mind—Henry and Maria, three kids, a nice home and two kittens. No more burden. She smiled to herself and finally spoke. "You know, I've thought about this before," she said. "Even before I met you. And I've almost stopped doing what I do but I always am pulled back. Maybe that's in my head, but I feel as if I'm not the one who steers people. I feel as if I'm steered; as if there's something I'm supposed to see that I'm not seeing. When we were supposed to meet, on the day that Richard Libby died, I could have removed my name. There's this guy on the list who was being vulgar and cold—most of the others who were still there were just trying to get under his skin, but when I decided to keep my name on the list, it's because I felt like I was supposed to—like there was something more to see and if I removed myself from that group of people, it would be forever lost."

"If you ask me, there's nothing to see. I mean, yeah, Victor's idea was interesting, and probably some of you don't care about the money and just want to be a part of it, but you ignore that there's a very real and dangerous implication behind that."

"I know…"

"I think you made a mistake keeping your name on there, and I think you're making a mistake if you think that someday, what happened to you when you were a kid is going to happen again. You had a moment. I don't know how to explain it. I even looked it up and sure enough, you were the real deal, but that was forever ago. We're adults now. I think we need to move past that so we can build our lives together."

Maria turned away from Henry and stared out the window as the trees passed by with a blur. Henry stared at the back of her head and smiled to himself. *This is it. This is going to be the trip—back to her family, to face her childhood, to face April Lovelace. This is going to be the trip that will finally accomplish my mission.*

2

Jacob Wallace was found dead in his apartment by his landlord. The rent was a week late and it raised his landlord's suspicion. It looked as if Jacob just collapsed on his floor, but police procedure had them searching for foul play, which they didn't find. Only one detective, Manny Quinny, searched between every toe, behind the ears, throughout the scalp.

An officer whose name read Avis approached. "Detective Quinny, nice to see you. I assume your presence means this is more than influenza?"

"I was in the neighborhood and thought I'd take a look. You have any witnesses?"

"Guy's girlfriend said she thought he had an envelope filled with money in his sock drawer. Made me wonder if this was a robbery, but there's no signs of break in or struggle."

"She thought there was an envelope or knew?"

"Said she thought."

"Don't make something out of nothing. There's no case here. Just a guy who didn't eat enough veggies."

After wrapping up at Jacob's apartment, Manny made his way to his car, looked over his shoulder out of habit, and drove to a brick building which served as a massage parlor. In the basement of the building, Adlar Wilcox sat waiting, only it wasn't Adlar the slob or Adlar the Gothic rebel. It was a neatly trimmed Adlar who didn't slouch and who had no interest in gaming.

"Do you know how I did it?" Adlar asked simply, leaning forward.

"Thallium."

Adlar fell silent, disappointed that it had been so easy. He retraced the steps in his mind. He was sure this time he could pull off a kill without Manny detecting the method. "What makes you think that?" Adlar asked.

"Thallium will make your hair fall out. Ran my fingers through the vic's scalp and voila. Found an empty water bottle in the trash and ran a residue test. Found high concentration of potassium in the body. All that would have been acceptable because no one would have known to even look, but I figured it out because I knew to look. The police think he just keeled over. When you really screwed the pooch is when you robbed him."

"What do you mean?" Adlar asked, but his voice went higher an octave.

"Money from the sock drawer. Where is it?"

Adlar stormed off and came back with a crumpled bag. He tossed it to Manny, who turned it over in his hands and contemplated his next move. "You know what the first question police ask when they have a body? Who had motive? Forget evidence. First and foremost, who wanted to kill this guy? Let's say I give you what you want. Let's say I let you have Charlie Palmer. What do you think the cops will find?"

"Not if I'm doing it the way you taught me."

"Except you're not, because if you do everything the way I tell you, but you take a dollar from their pocket, a soda from their fridge; if you so much as change the channel on their T.V., someone will find out, and that will is going to essentially be a list of suspects and you'll be the shadiest character on it. Taking money from a sock drawer raises a question: Was it murder? From there, motive. From there, suspects. If a crime hasn't been committed, the police will never travel that road."

"I get it."

"You've got a shitty learning curve."

"I just got greedy."

"Well, the longer it takes you to get on the level Bedbug was, the longer you wait for Palmer."

"But I'm ready. The only reason you catch me is because you know what to look for. You even said so."

Manny ignored him and straightened the room. "Pick up your trash Wilcox," he said, tossing a soda can into the recyclables.

"Why can't you just work through the list since you know what you're doing?" Adlar said. "Cause if we have the money sooner, then we don't have to even do this."

"Whether we have the money or not, you work for me now."

"But why would you keep doing this? You wouldn't have to."

"I like thinning out the population of this city. It's too damn big."

"Oh…" Adlar said, hanging his head. He didn't notice Manny backtracking to think about what Adlar said. It wasn't long after Adlar called Manny and accepted Royce's debt that he took Adlar into his home and learned the history between Adlar and Royce. After he knew of Victor's will and Charlie's part in the whole charade, it was easy to put the puzzle together. He was no longer angry about the situation. Instead, he saw potential. In the end, Victor's money would be easy to gain. He could have had it by now if he was ever in a hurry, but he still believed in the principle of paying a debt, and Adlar would carry out Bedbug's assignments until Manny was satisfied. The longer he worked with Adlar, the more potential he saw. His learning curve was slightly slower than average, but he'd put enough time into the boy and he had finally come to embrace him. Lately, as Adlar perfected the art of murder, he grew more anxious and felt more ready. He kept asking about the will, specifically Charlie, and Manny rejected him repeatedly, making a point to stay in charge, but Adlar was just about as polished as he could be. The job on Wallace had been pretty good, aside from the theft, and there was merit in what Adlar had said: Manny was looking for Adlar's prints. Any other cop would have never found a trace.

He turned to Adlar, who was reclined on the couch now, looking up at the ceiling. Retirement did sound good. He hadn't thought about what he would do with endless options until recently. He wanted to get out of the city and live in seclusion somewhere. Retiring had never even been an option, but the older he got, and the more he grunted when he moved, the better it sounded. He could kill twelve people in twelve days, Adlar could pick up their cash, and he'd say his final farewell and good riddance to Los Angeles.

"I've got another name for you," Manny said. Adlar's eyes lit up. "You can do it whenever you want and I don't want to know when, but do it like you've been doing it, don't leave a shred of evidence, and Palmer will be next, followed by that list of names, but it's going to all be you."

"Why me?"

"Because that's how I know I can trust you. I've gotten you to a point where you can do this successfully. Your job is to do it. All I ask is for my share. If you need help changing your identity or getting to where you want to go, I'll give you all the help you need, but let's not talk about that now. Focus on getting this job done."

"Who is it?" Adlar asked, eager to start.

"Guy named Sean Bentham" Manny opened a drawer at his desk and pulled a small stack of papers with a single staple. He tossed it to Adlar. "There's everything you need to know. Kill him clean and without a trace and you're in charge. Good luck."

## 3

Maria and Henry didn't receive a warm welcome when they arrived. It had been over a decade since Maria had seen her brother Nelson, but all she received from him was a "nice to see you" and the door held open. Henry carried a suitcase behind her and shook Nelson's hand and introduced himself. Nelson forced a smile that said he didn't approve of any man who bothered to be with his sister.

Inside the house, friends and family gathered, prepping food and paying their respect. It was crowded, and most were faces Maria didn't recognize. Those she did were only traces of a younger profile she'd long forgotten. Henry stayed at Maria's side as she made her rounds in the hopes she'd be recognized or that someone would strike up a conversation with her, but she was oddly out of place, as if no one even knew who she was.

"Are you sure you want to be here?" Henry asked.

"The funeral's in two days," Maria said. "He was my father."

"I feel like you might have downplayed the issues between you and your family."

"I don't know how much they've grown to hate me over the years."

"We're at least getting a hotel, right?"

"I don't know. I'll talk to Nelson."

"Doesn't seem like he wants to talk."

"I know. Let me try. Do you mind if I leave you here for a moment?"

"I'll be outside," Henry said, uncomfortable to be left in the house alone. He gave her a kiss and wandered off while she tracked Nelson down and waited for him to be alone. She finally caught him coming out of the bathroom and stood in his path.

"Do you need help with anything?" Maria asked. He gave her a blank stare and she wondered for a moment if he even remembered her.

"No, thank you. All arrangements have been made."

"Are you okay?"

"As okay as I can be."

"I left as soon as I heard," Maria said. "I'm sorry I didn't make it in time."

"No need to apologize to me. Dad's the one who didn't see you for the last twelve years."

"Did he say anything before he passed?"

"About you? No. I'm pretty sure he knew there wasn't a lot of hope he'd see you."

"It's a long drive."

"It's not a long flight."

"I can't fly."

"You know your odds of dying in a car are a lot higher than a plane, right? Or is this one of those things you decide because of dreams."

Maria's eyes fell and she almost broke down in tears there and then. Nelson had been there when they were kids. Nelson had seen what she was capable of. "You can't be angry because I chose my own path," Maria said.

"No, just that you left everything behind based on the fact that…

"*…you got lucky once.*" *Officer Raymond Burkette stared across his desk at Maria who stood before him with a newspaper in hand.*

"*What I did wasn't luck.*"

"*We used three quarters of the force and searched a five mile radius from where you told us the body would be, even though it was an area far from where we believe she is. You wasted our time and taxpayer's money.*"

"*You must have listened to me for a reason.*"

"*Yeah, because I know your name and what you did with Matt Chowder, but after our search, I looked further and with all due respect Miss Haskins, you seem to have been a one hit wonder. This needs to stop. You come to the station again, we won't give you the time of day. If you have concrete evidence of a crime, we'll take a look. Your visions won't be taken seriously here again.*"

"*I believe if you go back and look closer, you will find the bodies of both women. I know what I envisioned.*"

*Raymond sighed and finally looked up as if he had a confession to* make. *"You need to talk to your father about April Lovelace. That's all I can say."*

*"Talk to him, why? Did you talk to him?"*

*"I gave him a call. He had some insight as to what happened. I can't tell you more than that."*

The last time Maria saw her father Emrich Haskins, was when he flew down to see her after she called him that day. He told her they needed to talk in person and flew out to Los Angeles that weekend. She picked him up at the airport and showed him the sights; the walk of fame, the Hollywood sign, the Chinese Theater. She finally took him to her shop and smiled as she watched him scan the area with his eyes, seemingly impressed.

*"You really went all the way with this, huh?"* Emrich said.

*"I was called to it."*

*"How did you afford this?"*

Maria told her father about Victor Stone and how he'd discovered her and confided in her for the last year. Instead of being impressed, her father seemed disturbed by the news. *"I think you're walking a dangerous line,"* he said.

*"He's one of the most successful people in the city and he believes in me."*

*"And what is it you see when he asks you to look inside?"*

*"I see his aura. I know his heart. He will walk a path and will struggle and I will see his aura weaken. I offer guidance."*

*"You're in over your head if you're offering this guy advice. You're playing with fire."*

*"How can you say that?"*

*"What will you do when you tell him the wrong thing? Or when he finds out he's known all along who he is and used you as an excuse because he can't trust his own decisions?"*

*"I always tell him the right thing,"* Maria said. *"He's come repeatedly because he trusts in me. He sees in me what you can't."*

*"You can't build your life around one incident Maria. You're mistaken if you don't remember the April Lovelace incident well enough to see the whole picture."*

*"Then tell me what you've flown all this way to tell me,"* Maria said.

Her father sat and took her hand. *"Maria...you didn't do what you think you did that day..."*

...Henry sat on a swing that he barely fit into. Children of the family played on the jungle gym outside, ignoring the man as he talked to

William Lamone over the phone. They talked about their assignments and progress. They were both at a defining moment in bringing their beneficiaries down, and both were suffering the psychological ramifications. Henry asked William to tell him about Brian, more eager to listen than to talk. After William recounted the last few weeks, Henry asked him a deeper question. "Do you like Brian?"

"He's alright. He's funny in that way that you're not actually funny, but funny to watch because he's so naive."

"But do you like him?"

"I guess. I mean, he's not that deep and the thought of him dead doesn't feel so tragic, but it kinda sucks. Something about knowing the guy is spending all his time with the guy who is going to end him…it messes with my head sometimes. I try to see his bad side, but he's innocent and clueless and I feel like absolute shit about this."

"I hear you. Maria's in love with me. I'm constantly thinking if she only knew the truth…"

"All you can do is try not to like them. I think about how needy Brian is and how he's so influenced by everything and I think 'what's he really going to bring to this world?' I think that's all you can do."

"I tried doing that too," Henry said. "I use the psychic angle. The woman is about nothing else. It's all psychic, all the time. You know the key to winning her over? Say you believe her. That's it. I've given her no other reason to like me, but she's in love cause I support her belief. It's creepy for a while, but this woman is genuinely trying to cling onto this belief that she has a gift and it's all she has. And my job is to take that hope away and I'm so close, but no matter how pathetic I think she is, I ask myself what's so wrong about someone so content in having that one thing to hold on to?"

"You've gotta just think of the money."

"Is it worth it?"

"I don't know, but it's too late to turn back."

"Toby made us go after the weak minded first. Here we are, half a year later, still working the weakest and still no victims. How can we possibly do this another five or six times? I don't know if I'm going to do this. After she recovers from her dad's death, I think I'm breaking it off and going my own way."

"You've come too far to do that."

"Toby wants me to talk her into dropping the business, lose all her money, lose the roof over her head, lose me…William…this could possibly be the shittiest thing anyone's ever done. This isn't who I want to be. I don't know what I was thinking."

"I know, but…look, I have to go. We can talk when you get back. My break is over, so I have to go. Can you believe I was employee of the year here?" Henry chuckled as William went on. "I need this money because I've got nothing else going for me, and I'm currently sucked into the restaurant business as a con—I'm not even really here. I just fake it. I get frustrated when I'm supposed to make an over easy egg and break a yolk. I'm not faking this life anymore Henry. I'm living it. When I started here, I was stealing eggs. Last week, I ratted out a waitress for time theft. This sucks, but it can't be for nothing at this point. Someday, you can use all that money to do some good, donate a few million to a few charities. We can more than make up for what we're doing to Van Dyke and Maria. They're two people who are miserable anyway. We'll put them out of their misery and compensate later."

"Yeah…" Henry said, thinking William was probably right.

"Just get through your trip and do what you're supposed to do. If when you get back, you still want out, talk to Toby and get out, but you'll be passing up a good thing."

They ended the call and Henry walked back to the house, hoping Maria had already talked to her brother and was ready to go. Before he got inside, Maria stormed out the front door and walked past and down a dirt road at a pace that Henry didn't even want to bother to catch up with. Nelson stepped out of the house and watched her disappear into the forest.

Nelson turned to Henry. "Maybe you should go get her, talk her into going back to L.A."

"Her father died. I'm not going to tell her to do anything."

Nelson laughed to himself and shook his head. "Whatever boss. You just like her?"

"What do you mean?"

"You think you're psychic too?"

"No."

"You one of her clients?"

"What does any of that matter? She makes a living doing what she does. It's not that dishonorable."

"It's disgusting. If she knew how much our dad disapproved, she wouldn't be here."

"I suppose you guys would be okay if she was a meter maid or a traffic cop, ticketing people all day and pissing them off. Or maybe if she worked for a big bank with corruption at the top and peons at the bottom, widening the gap between the rich and the poor."

"This is a little different."

"Maria may not be legit, but there's always people who feel lost who just want someone to give them some optimism. That's what she does, and it's not because she sees a bright future. It's because telling people that everything is going to be okay creates a placebo effect. People like to hear it. And sometimes, it's all that has to happen for everything to be okay. You're a logger, right?"

Nelson nodded. "Yup."

"Aren't there whole groups of people who hate you guys for the environmental impact you have?"

"Sure are, but…"

"You eat meat?" Nelson fell silent. "I'll bet animal rights activists and vegans have something to say about that."

"If you don't like…"

"I love meat and I can't think of anything I care about less than saving trees, but those shitty organizations who are up in arms over everything everyone does: That's you Nelson. You're an asshole who's out to ruin the dreams of harmless people. A lot of people make themselves sick with anxiety, stress, paranoia… It's always those people who get sick and die early. I've always thought that if feelings of physical and mental distress damage the body's chemistry, then wouldn't positive thoughts rehabilitate it? Is it possible that love, hope, faith, laughter, confidence and the will to live have therapeutic value? That maybe chemical changes don't only occur on the downside? Yeah, the psychic thing could be a scam, but it's one designed to help people. I guess I don't find that as easy to hate as you do."

"No one cares about what she does," Nelson finally said. "We care about what she doesn't do. She tell you she didn't come home when our mother was dying either?"

"She didn't."

"I wanted to go out in the world and do something else too. You know why I'm a logger? Because she left me to take care of them. I gave up a life to be at her bedside. Dad's too. She wouldn't budge. Always thought the world needed her and she doesn't even know everything she thinks she does. She's selfish. She only sees her own shit."

"And what is that?"

"She's frustrated at life for coming up short. She's not complete, like a parasite feeding on almost anything: A passing compliment, control, power, even fear. She's consumed with what she lacks, what she thinks she's owed, and what else she needs in order to be complete. She's endlessly searching because her quest is never satisfied; forever one more thing…one more compliment away from happiness. She seeks temporary hollow refuge of immediate gratification and gives in to impulses instead of rising above them. Surely, you must know this by now."

"Hey, we all punish ourselves in ways disguised as pleasure. She just wants acceptance. If she ever felt she had that, she wouldn't do those things."

"She doesn't need love. She doesn't love herself and to fulfill the emotional void she turns to the world for approval. Interpersonal conflicts…if the world ever respects her, then she can respect herself, converting their adoration and praise into self-love. Her self-worth is a direct reflection of others' opinions. Her mood is vulnerable to every fleeting glance and passing comment. She's an emotional dependent needing the whim of the world to nourish her, but she's never satiated. Little reality comes through and what does can't be retained because she has no solid vessel to hold it, like pouring water into a cup with a hole in the bottom. It feels good as long as it's being filled, but when it stops, it's empty again. We boosted her ego for a long time and she never snapped out of it. You seem like an intelligent guy, and I'm sure by now you know exactly what I'm talking about. If you really want her to be your personal project, that's your problem. It doesn't have to be ours anymore."

"Then tell me how you've been boosting her ego all these years. Tell me what she doesn't know about April Lovelace."


4


Adlar didn't waste any time planning his attack.

He was proud of how much he'd learned but tired of training. He felt he was polished and Manny was just stalling because he was unwilling to admit Adlar was a good student. Adlar had been a mess when he called Manny. He'd just murdered Romey for ruining his life at home. He had nowhere to live, no friends or family. He only had one option and so he called Manny to see what he could get for turning Charlie in. Instead, he accepted a debt, unsure of what that even meant. Twenty four hours later, he was in Manny Quinny's home, sitting across from him in his living room in a rocking chair. Manny made a simple statement: Adlar was a target, but Bedbug was caught in the cross-hairs and someone had to pay.

Adlar spilled all the details of what had happened and when Manny heard of Charlie Palmer,'s vendetta his eyes grew dark as he realized how events had unfolded on that rooftop. Adlar had mentioned another name: Trish Reynalds, and Manny pieced together his encounter with her. When Adlar finished recounting his story, Manny simply told Adlar he would take the place of Bedbug and get paid handsomely for it. When he was strong enough to take care of himself, they would work the list, take the money, and do whatever they wanted for the rest of their life.

Adlar jumped through every hoop and listened to everything Manny had to say, but eventually, there was nothing left to learn. Adlar's last four targets had been easy. He'd taken some money from his last hit, but he didn't need to be told it was a mistake. He knew and did it anyway because he was feeling courageous.

One thing he'd learned was that he had to be innovative. Manny taught him everything, so Manny knew what he was looking for, but Adlar knew his way around the net, and decided to effectively fool Manny, he would have to use a method of his own—something he hadn't been taught. The first objective was to familiarize himself with Sean Bentham, find if he had any allergies or medical issues. It turned out that Mr. Bentham was a world traveler who took phosphates for chest pains. Adlar settled on using a parathion, a highly organophosphate pesticide, a highly toxic drug that produced symptoms similar to malaria—useful for a world traveler because it wouldn't arouse suspicion. He had the address, the plan, everything he needed to execute. He just needed a date. What Manny surely wouldn't see coming was for Adlar to do it immediately. Usually they let a week pass between hits for education and mental preparation, but Adlar wanted to make a statement. He wanted to show Manny how efficient he could be and how easy it was for him. All he had to do was be careful not to leave a trace of his presence behind.

That night, after Manny fell asleep outside in his patio furniture, Adlar walked out the front door, walked four blocks to a bus-stop, and hitched a ride to the part of town Sean Bentham resided, and scouted it out from across the street. Sean wasn't home, but would be soon. Unless he happened to go out after work, Adlar had no problem waiting. He always waited from a distance and eventually approached the house, looking for an opening. Sean made it easy by having a window with a simple latch. Adlar pried it open and waited inside. He walked through the house and looked at all Sean's belongings, careful not to touch a thing. When he grew bored of waiting, he pulled out his phone and played on-line, his feet sprawled out on the hardwood floor, holding his cell above his head.

It wasn't until shortly after two in the morning that Sean returned. As the headlights shined through the curtains, Adlar hurried to Sean's bedroom and pulled a small spray bottle from his inside pocket. He sprayed a good dose on both sides of the pillow—enough to be fatal, but not noticed. Sean would sleep ingesting the parathion. The next day, he'd wake up with a headache, and maybe start vomiting. If he wasn't dead within 24 hours, Adlar would give him another dose and that would surely do the trick.

When he was done in the bedroom, he descended the stairs into the basement, where he'd propped a window open for escape. He'd waited too long for Sean and he wanted to be there when the man fell asleep, if only to see to it that everything went well. Adlar waited at the bottom of the stairs as footsteps creaked above him. Sean made a trip to the bathroom and the kitchen before finally walking toward the bedroom. It was there in the hall, right above Adlar when he heard a large crash. Adlar grew confused as he listened to the noises directly above him. There was coughing and wheezing and something slid across the floor—probably his cell phone. *Did Manny get to him first?*

Why would Manny do that? It made no sense. Sean hadn't even ingested the parathion and he was upstairs on the ground, struggling to breath. And he was alone. Adlar was sure of it. The wheezing slowed and the ceiling stopped creaking. Adlar waited another half hour anyway. He abandoned his plan to escape through the window, instead ascending the stairs. The lights were on, but it was silent. Sean's cell phone sat in the middle of the dining room.

"What the…" Adlar said to himself as he slowly turned the corner. Sean lay on the ground, his eyes open, but no movement. His eyes were bloodshot and his face was white. He was clearly dead. Then Adlar had a thought—something that made him laugh to himself and realize that somehow fate had stepped in and fooled Manny. Manny might have figured out Adlar's method before, but he certainly would never guess how Adlar killed a man who'd just had a heart attack.

5

Henry found Maria two hours later. He followed the river downstream, ducking under tree branches and forcing himself through the tangle of weeds at his feet. The sun was setting and he was thinking about turning back when he spotted her sitting on a rock by the river. She looked as if she was ready to lean forward and plummet into the water.

*Would that be such a bad thing?*

As he started to consider the notion, Maria suddenly turned, as if she'd sensed he was there. She found his eyes and stared blankly into them, as if afraid of Henry. Her eyes were red from crying. Her hair was undone and she'd taken her button up shirt off and only wore a tank top underneath.

"I'm going to get a cab and go to the airport," Henry said. "Stay as long as you want."

"Why can't you be here for me?"

"You just ran away Maria. I just trekked through a fucking jungle to find you. I don't know anyone back there. Are you kidding me with this shit?"

"Then go," she said, and turned back to the river.

Henry was losing her. Maria was supposed to be vulnerable, but her spirit was completely broken. If there was ever a time to earn her trust, now was it. Or he could turn around, go back to the airport, fly home, and tell Toby he was done. Neither option was good.

"Tell me what happened back there," Henry said.

"Nelson just had to tell me what he thought of my life."

"Yeah, he told me too. He told me a lot. Some of it was about April."

"I've already heard it."

"And you don't believe it?"

"No."

"It makes sense Maria. It's the same thing that happens to soldiers traumatized in combat: selective memory. You were here, probably in this spot, playing by the river, and you saw it happen. You ran home and fell into your bed. When you woke up, you reported it as a vision, but the truth is you saw it happen. You were an actual witness."

"No…"

"Authorities later looked at your shoes and found evidence of where you'd been. You were young and no one bothered to tell you the truth. You never had to testify because Chowder confessed to the whole thing and there never was a trial. That was your true psychic moment and it wasn't even a vision. Just your memory."

Maria looked down. She'd heard it before. She'd heard it from her father, her brother, she'd even suspected it herself. But she'd never let go of who she was. "It wasn't just the murder," Maria said, softly. "There's been so many things. Some have been so vivid. I believe in a sixth sense and I believe anyone can open themselves up to tap into it."

"Fine, you can believe that, but we need to go back to what I asked you earlier: When are you going to take us seriously?"

She turned to him and they connected again. *I have her where I need her. This is the beginning of the end for Maria Haskins.*

"Put the property on the market. We'll invest, or open a restaurant, or I don't care what. I don't want to be the husband of a woman who constantly questions herself—who constantly puts herself in this position. Your superstition is about making a greater, deliberate effort in some kind of hope that it will increase your control over a situation you're powerless against."

"You don't know what I've been through."

"Yeah, well I've boosted you long enough, but you're forever one compliment away from being satisfied. Isn't it enough that in 3.8 billion years, in time older than mountains and oceans, every single one of your ancestors on both sides have been attractive enough to find a mate, healthy enough to reproduce, and sufficiently blessed by fate and circumstances to live long enough to do so. Not one of them was squashed, devoured, drowned, starved, stranded, or otherwise deflected from their life's quest of delivering a tiny charge of genetic material to the right partner at the right moment in order to perpetuate the only possible sequence of hereditary combinations that eventually, astoundingly, and all too briefly, ended in you? Can't it be enough for you that you're just lucky to be here? Do you need to be so goddamn special too?"

Her eyes fell and filled with sorrow. Henry watched her from a distance, sure he had her where he wanted, and guilt-ridden. He told himself he was an evil person doing one of the most despicable things to have ever been done, but carried forward, because he'd gone too far. *I'm going to let fate decide. That's how this is going to play out. She's not the real deal, but there's that fraction of a possibility and if that goes against me…*

He extended his hand to her. "Read me," he said. She looked up suddenly and frowned. It was no secret she'd never asked Henry for a peek in his head, though she likely wanted to. "To show you that I trust you, I want you to read me."

"Why?"

"Because you're either going to see nothing, or you're going to see that I can take care of us. That you don't need this anymore." *I sure as shit hope she doesn't see anything because this is a hell of a bluff you're pulling Henry.*

"I can't. It wouldn't be right…"

"If you see nothing, then I'm asking you to throw in the towel, because I'm not going to do this anymore. We're not children and I'm tired of watching you try to measure up when there's no reason to."

Maria stood and stepped toward Henry. She looked in his eyes and reached for his hand. She thought she saw him try to conceal a hard swallow but she wasn't sure. She took another step forward, taking his hand in her own, and closed her eyes…

*…Victor Stone saw Maria at least once a month. At some point, she realized he'd stopped coming for advice or visions. Instead, he came just to sit and chat. It took a lot of pressure away from her, but she missed the moments when Victor would believe what she said and tell her he was impressed. It seemed the novelty of who she was had worn off and in its place, she'd become just a friend. She wondered why Victor wanted a friend like her, when he was surrounded by so much success, but she didn't give it much thought. She had her shop. She was making steady income. She'd managed to rid her life of all the people who cast doubt on her. She ignored her father and brother's phone calls.*

*She'd almost completely rid herself of her past when one day, the bell above her door rang and she looked up and saw a ghost from her past. Though she recognized the face immediately, it didn't register immediately, and when it did, she realized it was no accident he was there. Matthew Chowder had come to see Maria and if he was the same man she'd helped capture, this could be the end for her. Her eyes darted to the phone on the wall and Matthew followed them.*

*"Don't bother," Chowder said. "I'm not going to hurt you. May I?"*

*She nodded slowly as he took a seat. Instead of sitting across from him as she usually did, she stood against the wall.*

*"It didn't take me long to find you," he said, as he ran his hands over the table, his every move calculated.*

*"Why are you here?"*

*"You know everyone in town trusted me? Knew my name? At Christmas, they baked cookies and bread for me. No one saw that side of me. Only you."*

*"How did you get out?"*

*"Early release. Parole board said I was ready. That a problem? Me being out?"*

*"You traveled far to see me."*

*"I like the city. I may stay."*

*"Please tell me what you want."*

*"I wanted to meet the woman who changed my life."*

*"You made your choices. You only have yourself to blame."*

*Suddenly, Chowder stood and took a step toward Maria. If she wanted to run either direction, he'd be able to grab her. "You were lucky," he said. "You're lucky I didn't see you there that day, or you would have shared a space with that girl."*

*"If you hurt me, you'll just go back to jail. Please just leave."*

*"I'm not here to hurt you. I'm a customer. Are you going to turn away a customer?" He sat again. "How do we do this? You have a crystal ball or something?"*

*She stood still for a long moment but after some thought, she took a seat. If he wanted to hurt her, he could have by now. Maria couldn't resist the offer. A chance to possibly relive the moment she saw April's death. Everyone had been telling her she'd been a witness, but she knew better. She knew it was a vision. She didn't get a read off everyone, but this man was different. This man was such a monumental force in her life that there was no avoiding it.*

*"If I do this, you will go?"*

*"Of course. At least for today. I may just like the product and come back."*

*She relaxed her arms on the table and extended her fingers up for him. He laid his hands in hers and soon, their hands were held together on the table, a murderer and the woman who brought him down. Her eyes closed, but it took some time to find her focus. Every twitch of his hands made Maria think he was about to lunge across the table. Eventually, she found her peace.*

*And then, nothing happened.*

*She didn't dwell on the development for too long. She opened her eyes to find his eyes were open, staring at her hungrily. "I saw nothing," she said.*

*"Then you're not trying."*

*"You will not owe me anything. I would like for you to go. Please don't return."*

*"Well, what the fuck are you offering here if you can't see anything?"*

*"There's nothing to see."*

*"Nothing to see, huh? You claimed you saw me with that girl, but you didn't see all the others."*

*"What are you telling me?"*

*"All the other girls before April Lovelace. The girls after."*

*"You went to jail."*

*"Now I'm out. So tell me how you can't see what I've done—what I'm all going to do..."*

*"I can call the police."*

*"I don't think you'll get far unless you've got something to show for it."* He walked to the door and turned back. *"I'll come by after I bury another...see if you can't find the body. Maybe I'll come by after each one. You're a hero Maria. You outsmarted me once. Surely, you can do it again."*

*Maria tried to speak, but her breathing was too heavy—she was barely able to control herself. She tried to ask him to leave, but her throat was dry and nothing came out. As if he heard her thoughts, he gave her a smile and a nod and walked out. She wanted to call the police, but there was no crime to report—only words—barely a confession. She paced around the room quickly, stopping to lean against the wall so she could catch her breath.*

*The bell above the door rang and her breath caught in her throat. She turned, and breathed a sigh of relief.*

*"Good morning Maria," Victor Stone said.*

*"Victor..." Maria said, her eyes pleading, "...I need to talk to you..."*

"...She's giving it all up," Henry said, holding his cell phone to his ear at a rest stop. "She's a hundred percent reliant on me."

On the other end, Toby leaned forward, unable to give Henry a hard time. He'd proved himself enough—more than William had. "Okay, then I guess the next time you and I talk, she'll be gone."

"Yup, I guess so," Henry said. "If this is really what you think we should do."

"Of course it is. We didn't do all this for nothing."

"If Maria really does take her life, are you prepared to deal with your role in it?"

"Let's do a thing where you have this conversation with a wall from now on."

"Yeah, I get it," Henry said, unsurprised that Toby didn't see the problem with what they were doing. He watched Maria exit the restroom and walk to the car without a care in the world. Having given it all up seemed to have taken a weight off her shoulder. "I have to go."

"Call me again when it's done."

"Yup." He shut the phone and took another long look at Maria as she used the rear view to fix her hair. He'd had a moment of fear in the forest by the river—a moment when everything had been so quiet and Maria hadn't moved at all, as if she was seeing something inside him. He was sure her eyes would snap open and she'd ask him why their whole relationship had been a sham, but instead, she'd opened her eyes and said they could leave. After they got in the car and started driving, she said she'd put the shop on the market immediately—that she never wanted to think of her career again. There hadn't been any tears and she didn't ask for any pity. Instead, she sang along with the radio as if she'd just been freed.

Henry got in the car and started it up. "Ready to get out of here?" he asked.

"Yeah, let's go home," she said, then turned to him and with sincerity, said "I'm sorry Henry."

"Don't be. I get it. Everyone wants to be important. You just have to know that you already are."

"I love you."

"I love you too." *I'm an evil bastard.* "Thank you for being honest. I was afraid you'd make something up or say you saw something but couldn't make sense of it."

"I saw something, but then I realized that it's not a vision. It's just what I choose to think about. I usually would convince myself it's significant, but I know now it's just something that had been on my mind and it came back to me."

"Your father?"

"No, that guy I told you about."

"What guy?"

"The guy from the day with the judge—Toby. Please don't take this wrong, but I tried to look into you and I only saw him."

# Chapter 3

## 1

Charlie Palmer's father always called it bad juju when life suddenly hit a brick wall before dive-bombing into chaos. There were the good times or times of normalcy, and then there was bad juju. When bad juju hit, it was a curse that would last far past its welcome and the world would often crumble before normalcy returned. That was Bobby Palmer's belief and Charlie adopted it as his own long before his father passed away.

When Charlie finally decided to forget Adlar Wilcox, his life hit a stride. He accepted Abby's death and his role in it. He stayed with Mindy. She'd been offered a job in Phoenix and asked Charlie to come along. He searched for a job and found one fairly quickly. His reputation had opened doors and he was on a hot streak again. He'd been called the Miracle Man because he'd operated on three patients who ended up with impossibly positive outcomes. It was easy to get over Abby because ever since she left, his life had improved ten-fold. He knew he was no murderer. It was Adlar that broke into his home. His hadn't even fired the shot that killed Bedbug. He was near the danger for so long—danger Abby got him into—and now he had a chance to start over without the drama. New city, new family, a new start. His home was on the market, and Mindy had already talked to her realtor who was getting offers on the house. They were two weeks away and that time couldn't come faster. Once he was gone, all the bad juju of the past would be gone for good. All he wanted was to avoid any confrontation with the other beneficiaries between now and then.

It was on the day that one paid him a visit that everything changed.

"You're on a roll Charlie," Dr. Chip Harmony said as they pulled their scrubs off after surgery.

"Miracle man," Another said, giving Charlie a shoulder squeeze.

The prestige was wearing off. Charlie was aware that at any time, the kudos could transform into jealousy and he could be hated for being so good at what he did. Especially as other surgeons made mistakes and struggled to measure up to the bar he'd set. He'd already been approached about having a feature article about him in the Journal of Neurosurgery, but he declined, mostly out of fear that rocks would be turned and questions about Abby would surface. In his upcoming start over, the past would be buried.

*Two weeks.*

Charlie exited surgery and rounded a corner, nodding at the staff as they passed and greeted him respectfully.

"Charlie Palmer?"

Charlie turned and smiled awkwardly at Royce Morrow, who extended his hand toward him. They'd never talked one on one, but he was well aware of Royce. First from the will and then from the constant campaigning in the city and signs that said "For a better toMorrow." He even liked Royce and as someone who was completely against Bernard Bell, intended on casting a vote in Royce's direction.

"Mr. Morrow…to what do I owe this visit?"

"Is there somewhere we can talk?"

"No need to waste your breath. You've got my vote."

"You and I share the same enemy," Royce said. "Maybe you already know that and maybe you don't, but I believe we stepped on each others toes in trying to remedy a situation and we made it worse."

Charlie waived Royce toward a room and they entered together. Charlie closed the door and shut the blinds. With two weeks left, he'd simply wanted to avoid seeing a beneficiary. Now, he had one at his doorstep and by the looks of Royce, this wasn't good news. It was very likely that Royce would be able to fill in all the blanks that Charlie never knew though—like why he was shooting at a stranger in Adlar's apartment. Until now, he wasn't even aware that Royce had issues with Adlar.

"What do you mean by that?" Charlie asked.

"Adlar Wilcox came into my home. This was weeks after the reading. He tried to rob me and pointed a gun at my wife." Charlie felt sick. Adlar had a habit of walking into a home and ruining families. "He walked away that day with some personal information that I desperately needed back. I turned to the wrong person as a solution and that person was going to end Adlar's life. Then, you shot him."

"I think you have me mixed up with…"

"I've had a lot of time to think about the course of events since that day and how much Adlar has changed. When your wife died, I never believed anyone else was responsible, and you haven't acted like a man who wants to catch whoever was responsible. You don't have to admit it to me if you don't feel comfortable, but I believe you knew who murdered your wife and I believe you wanted vengeance."

"That's…" Charlie swallowed hard. "That's a strong accusation."

"I'm not judging you Mr. Palmer. I hired a contract killer. We both played a part in this."

"What do you want?" Charlie said.

"We need to finish what we started…"

*…When Charlie Palmer got through medical school and was given a white jacket, he and Abby celebrated with two bottles of wine and made love twice that night and once the next morning. Their relationship was headed places and so was his career. Abby had stuck around for a full year, and Charlie began to wonder if she was the one. Their relationship had been surreal in the beginning. She was too good to be true, but they'd remained a couple.*

*He began looking at rings because Abby started talking about the future and always included Charlie in her vision. She spoke of vacations, kids, a house and never spoke as if there was any possibility Charlie wouldn't be in the picture. Before he eventually made up his mind, one day he found himself putting a down payment on a ring. He held onto the ring for two months without a plan. There was no need to rush and it was nice to know that if an opportunity ever presented itself to propose, he would have everything he needed.*

*The year had just started. People were talking about resolutions. Charlie hoped to eat a little better and give up soda. He'd gained ten pounds and he decided to rid his life of sugar. Abby just started working at Banner General and was toying with the idea of doing some personal training on the side. She had already been asked by one of the meat-heads at the gym if she wanted a job. It bothered Charlie that while she was at the gym, she was being approached by men and offered jobs. It didn't seem to him that her qualifications mattered. Men just pursued her, but she chose Charlie. No matter who she met or where she went, she always came home to Charlie. It baffled him, flattered him, and scared him to death. He feared the day that she'd realize she was out of his league.*

*That day appeared to Charlie in the form of Baxter Welsh, the ex-boyfriend before Charlie—the man that towered over him when they met for the first time in the waiting room of Banner. Charlie caught Abby chatting with him in the lobby and conveniently wedged himself at her side to make himself known. Abby introduced them and their hands shook. Baxter's grip was solid and his broad shoulders and barrel chest caused Charlie to back down when face to face.*

*He wanted to ask why they broke up. It seemed as if there was never a reason. There seemed to be no hostility between Abby and Baxter and they were able to hold a conversation as if Charlie wasn't there, discussing events Charlie had never heard of in all the time he was with Abby. Then, with a laugh, Baxter volunteered the reason for their breakup; "I took a job in Pismo," he said. "Biggest mistake of my life." He caught Abby's eye.*

*"The job?" Charlie asked, secretly begging for the mistake to be the job—not losing Abby.*

*"Pismo doesn't have the same feel as LA. It looks good on the outside, but it's a bunch of retirees."*

*"What's wrong with that?" Charlie asked, trying to prompt Baxter to say something insensitive.*

*"Wasn't any fun," Baxter said with brutal honesty.*

*"What are you doing here?" Abby asked.*

*"Stomach pains," Baxter said. "Just a long lingering pain that won't go away."*

*Abby turned to Charlie with a hopeful look. "Charlie…what could that be?"*

*"A stomach ache."*

*"Be serious."*

*"I'm a surgeon Abby. I can't sit in the lobby and try to diagnose the walk-ins."*

*Baxter laughed agreeably. "It's nothing Abby. Let the man do his job."*

*Charlie hated Baxter. For a moment, a string of obscenities and insults flowed through his head, frame by frame, all to describe Abby. It was as if she was oblivious to the circumstance—to the obvious awkwardness that the ex encounter carried.*

*"I just thought maybe he could ask some questions and narrow it down."*

*"I'm sure the doctors will do their jobs just fine," Charlie said. He turned to walk away without saying goodbye but a grunt from Baxter stopped him in his tracks. He turned in time to see him double over, holding his gut and vomit on the tile below. Before either could react, Baxter hit the ground…*

"…I wanted revenge at one time," Charlie said. "I won't say more than that, but I will tell you that I've put it behind me. I've got a life now, and getting sucked back into this group of people sounds like the worst idea in the world. Whatever you want, you're on your own."

"You can turn me down, but you may not be able to walk away from this so easily," Royce said. "The man who is teaching Adlar Wilcox to be a killer is also a cop, and the last time I checked, they have the ability to cover their tracks well."

"If Adlar was going to come after me, he would have by now."

"No, he wouldn't have, because the man training him is a perfectionist and six months ago, Adlar was too amateur to let loose, but they've been working together awhile, and I've paid attention to the obituaries. There have been some influential people who have passed away lately—all filed as unknown reasons. How long before he and Adlar work the list?"

"The money?"

"Absolutely. Why not?"

"Because they would have done something by now."

"Manny talked to me of debts. He's a man of principle and balance. He wouldn't be the one to do the killing. He'd teach Adlar to do it. He's the teacher. He doesn't get his hands dirty. That's how he works."

Charlie ran his hand through his hair and raised his eyebrows quizzically. "Even if I thought that's what was going to happen and even if I wanted to help, there's nothing I can do. I don't know where he is and if he's working with a cop..."

"I'm not talking about confrontation Mr. Palmer. I'm talking about trapping them and exposing them—possibly without even knowing it was us. That's how Manny does things and that's what it will take to outsmart him."

"You said he'd just use Adlar…"

"Not if we draw him out. He was going to kill me himself because of what happened to Bedbug—even knowing I didn't pull the trigger. Like I said: A man of principle. This is reality. Adlar Wilcox isn't always going to be a desperate fearful kid. He has real guidance now and eventually. He's going to come out of hiding and he's going to be smart enough to know that if a killing spree starts, few people will know with certainty who is behind it. You and I are the only people who understand the extent of which Adlar has gone."

"Then talk to the police. I've dealt with enough. Losing Abby was like driving through a plate-glass window. I didn't know what was there until it shattered, and for months after, I was still picking up the pieces, down to the last fucking splinter. I'm different now. I'm aware of what I have and I'm not going to lose it by getting involved in this mess. You're a pretty powerful guy Royce. I don't know what you think you have to gain by being at my doorstep anyway."

Royce fixated on Charlie's face. He could see that he meant every word. The most he could hope for was that Charlie would eventually come around. "I don't have anything to gain by coming to you," Royce said. "I came to you because you and I are the right people to do this. I could find someone who might be invested, but Manny is right about one thing: There has to be a balance. We have to make right our mistakes and I think you and I have made quite a few. If Manny and Adlar were to be locked away forever, then a lot of lives will be saved. I don't know about you, but I have to find a way to tip the scales and do something good to make up for some poor decisions I've made. Tell me that you can't sit home with your new life, leaving what happened to your wife without closure. Tell me that in five years…ten years…fifty, you're not ever going to wake up with regret and carry it the rest of your life because the person who killed Abby is walking around ruining more lives. Tell me that you can live pretending this isn't happening and I will walk away forever."

Charlie gave Royce enough of a pause to convince him he was lying. "I can live with myself," Charlie said. He diverted his eyes as Royce nodded, accepting what he knew to be a lie.

Finally, Royce extended his hand and they shook. "Then best of luck to you Mr. Palmer."

He turned and walked away.

*2*

Two paramedics, followed by two cops, wheeled the body of Sean Bentham out of his home. As they passed, Manny Quinny squinted his eyes and searched the room again, running a dozen theories through his head every five seconds. Sean was found by his housekeeper the next morning, who called 911. Police and medics responded immediately to find the man sprawled out on the floor. Manny's first thought upon seeing the man was that the kill was a sloppy job, but his death was determined natural and Manny could find no signs of tampering. In fact, the man had seemingly crawled on the ground attempting to reach his phone. He had been alive. He understood what was happening to him. Adlar knew better than to allow a mark to live so long—giving them an opening to find help —but somehow, Adlar had carried out the plan and fooled the police.

Manny couldn't allow himself to be fooled though. His ego was too big and he wasn't ready to let Adlar take on the beneficiaries just yet. He searched the body—behind the ears, between the toes, and through the scalp a dozen times.

Nothing.

He stood akimbo as the medics took the body and began examining the home. It took half an hour before he found evidence that Adlar had been in the basement, but what would be the point of that? To wait? To listen as whatever poison he'd used did its damage? How did he inject it? He examined the fridge and traced Sean's movements from returning home until the moment he bit the dust. Whatever and however Adlar did what he did, he did it quickly.

*This makes no sense.*

He knew Adlar would try to be clever, but he anticipated the ways in which he would. Each scenario mismatched the scene.

Adlar watched Manny enter his home, keeping his eyes down as if he didn't know Adlar was sitting in the recliner. He closed the door, keeping his eyes at the floor as if searching himself for the words. His pride would surely take a hit if he so much as asked Adlar about the kill. If he tried to pry for information, Adlar would know he'd at least impressed him. The smarter side of Manny told him that he needed to know what Adlar did— just in case he made a mistake. The method used could possibly need covering, even if it was invisible before.

"You did a pretty good job on him," Manny finally said, picking his words carefully.

"Yeah?" Adlar asked. "Did the police think anything went on?"

"Foul play? Nah…but they're not looking for that anyway. Maybe if they were looking for it."

Adlar slouched. Manny never easily approved but Adlar sensed there was frustration radiating from his mentor. He sensed Manny had no idea how Adlar did it. He surely needed this approval. When Sean died without intervention, it was as if fate stepped in and gave Adlar an opportunity to stump an unstumpable man. He hoped Manny wouldn't force him to reveal his trick, and had made a decision to stay stern.

"Good thinking doing it so fast," Manny said. "I thought you'd wait a few days and do some plotting."

"Thanks."

"I did find quite a bit of evidence that you spent some time in his basement," Manny said, exaggerating.

"So do you know how I did it?" Adlar asked.

"I have some theories," Manny said. I sure as hell hope nothing shows up at the morgue though."

"It won't."

Manny eyed him suspiciously, but changed his tune a moment later. "I may need to know what you did. I'm worried about this whole thing."

"If you don't know, does that mean I can start?"

"You're not ready."

"But you said if I killed him and you didn't know, I could."

"Half a year isn't enough time…"

"But you know I did a good job. You don't know what I did."

"Until I know, I'm not sure you're in the clear. If they decide to do a toxicology…"

"I didn't use poison," Adlar said.

Manny was baffled. He was positive it had to be some sort of poison, which would have been careless, but untraceable initially. "Look Wilcox, I said you did good and maybe I didn't expect you to, but if this is dumb luck, then setting you loose would be a huge mistake. You were a six yesterday. You didn't go from a six to a ten overnight."

"But what's the difference between killing that guy and just killing one of the people on the list? Why can't that be my test? Wouldn't it be the same?"

"Who would you kill?"

"It would probably have to be Charlie."

"You think you have it in you? You already took the man's wife."

"Yeah, I can do it. I don't care."

"You used to."

"I know, but you convinced me not to."

"So you carry no feelings of guilt or attachment to this man?"

"No. It's just a job. We'd get paid a lot. I think we should do it."

"There is no we."

"I know. I'll do it. And if I mess up, you can just tell me."

Adlar's offer sounded enticing, and he even managed to sound as if he meant every word he said. He probably even did. Maybe Adlar wasn't as amateur as he thought. Maybe he learned fast. No matter what was happening with him, the thought of finishing off that list and taking some money to an easy retirement sounded good.

"He's all yours," Manny said.

Adlar suddenly sat up, alerted by his words. "Seriously?"

"A few stipulations to this. One is that Bentham better be covered up well. I don't want to find out you royally fucked up later and regret this. The same goes for Palmer. Quick and clean. I don't want suspicions raised by this other group of people on the will. Lastly, if any suspicion is raised, if anyone asks you questions, if you end up seeing the inside of a courtroom, if anyone even brings up my name, you will pay the price, you got that?"

"I know. I know this is on me."

"There's one thing you can't avoid when this group of people starts dying: Motive."

"I know."

"Make a list. A logical progression of their deaths one by one. When this starts happening, it has to happen fast, and the last to die has to be the slowest to react. Number two has to be the quickest. The whole thing will be done in a week. I'll make sure I have tabs on each one and know where to find them. When it's over, you collect your inheritance and we hold our deal."

"I know."

"I've been at this for twenty years, and these deaths will be my final twelve. Don't you dare ruin my run of luck or you will regret it."

"I know."

"Palmer dead...by this time tomorrow."

"Fine," Adlar said, with complete confidence, as if he'd forgotten that Sean Bentham was a fluke...that maybe he couldn't go on the killing spree he was challenged to.

Later, Adlar sat alone in the living room watching television. He realized he hadn't heard Manny for a while and walked to the sliding door to look in the backyard. Manny lay passed out in a lawn-chair by his pool, a bottle of Makers Mark at his side. Adlar smiled to himself. Manny was a hard-ass but he'd always believed in Adlar and somehow, the two of them completed each other. Manny needed a killer and Adlar needed a mentor. When they had the money, Adlar didn't know where they'd both go, but Adlar knew he would be the one to walk away victorious. He was once the weakest in the group but somehow found his way to being the real deal. He was dangerous, just like the baddies in the Westerns his father and him used to watch.

Adlar turned off the light and lay in his bed. He fell asleep to visions of Charlie and Abby and replaying the night he murdered Abby and secured his fate forever. It had been a long terrible road, but the end was near.

He woke up the next day refreshed, ready for action. Manny was already at work by the time he woke up. He grabbed a jacket from the closet and headed straight to Charlie's neighborhood.

## 3

Charlie woke up to the smell of waffles.

Mindy had made breakfast intending to surprise him but it pissed him off. She often made unwanted gestures that Charlie had to turn down with a reminder. "I'm good. I have a routine."

Charlie Palmer was most definitely a creature of habit. He woke up at the same time every day, showered, stopped at the gas station for a frozen burrito, worked, went to the hospital gym instead of eating lunch, returned home at night, and made love to Mindy if she was in the mood. When Mindy tried to sidetrack his routine, he grew frustrated. He was a busy man. He tried to be efficient. Unwanted waffles were a distraction and he did his best to turn her down without insulting her, but most of the time his irritation was hard to hide.

"You always eat gas station food," Mindy said. "It's not good for you."

"Newsflash…waffles aren't either."

"Okay, well, maybe someday we can have breakfast together?"

"Sure thing," he said quickly and gave her a kiss on the forehead before exiting for the day. He hurried to his car, though he wasn't running late, and drove to the corner gas station, eager to move on to step 2: the burrito.

The moment Charlie stepped out of the car, something felt off. The colors of the world around him were askew. Everything suddenly felt off balance, though nothing really looked different at all. It was that sense of doom that Charlie sometimes got for no reason at all.

He carried it into the convenience store and before he approached the oven which housed the burritos, he knew the problem. From a distance, he saw the hot case was off and under repair. He approached an attendant who was mopping the floor. "You guys have more burritos coming out?"

"Not today, sorry," the worker said. He didn't bother to give him more explanation.

"I come here every day," Charlie said. "You're never out."

"Sorry sir," the worker said. "Got the cold ones in the cooler."

"People eat them cold?"

"No sir. Just microwave it. You want some help with that?"

"I'm fine," Charlie said, and dismissed the worker. He turned back. "Can you make sure you have them tomorrow?"

"Yeah, I'll bring it up at the next meeting," the worker muttered. Charlie saw he'd probably helped the man have a bad day of his own. Instead of pushing it further, he walked to the counter to pay for gas.

"Twenty on pump four," Charlie said and handed the clerk a twenty.

The clerk glanced at the screen. "Says twenty and eight cents."

"You can't spot me the eight cents?" Charlie asked, as if the man didn't have a choice.

"My register would be off."

"Eight cents?"

"Yeah."

"You don't have one of those penny things for people who pay over?"

"People abused it so we got rid of it."

"Well, I don't have eight cents."

The attendant mopping the floor was near enough to hear the

commotion and suddenly chimed in. "How were you gonna buy a burrito then?"

Charlie shook his head in disbelief and pulled another ten from his wallet. He'd been busted by a couple convenience store clerks, and still didn't have his burrito. In fact, he'd probably never have a burrito again because he could never come back here. He waited as the clerk rang him up. Silence filled the area until the clerk counted back nine dollars and ninety-two cents. Charlie stuffed it in his pocket and exited, never turning back.

He was suddenly very stressed, and not because he didn't have something to eat. He would hit the hospital cafeteria instead. It wasn't a problem. The problem was that there was bad juju in the air. His day had shifted into something different than every day before. He felt like...

*"...an asshole," Charlie said, his surgical mask muffling his words. The team who was working on Baxter looked up, waiting for an explanation. "He's one of Abby's ex boyfriends. Before this happened, he was trying to cut in line ahead of everyone who'd been waiting."*

*"Now he's here with a busted appendix. He should have been front of the line."*

*"Look how long it took the guy to come in," Charlie said. "The moron was walking around in pain, too much pride to see a doctor. He deserves this."*

*Most docs in the room looked up over their surgical masks, observing Charlie as he worked expertly, unaware of how insensitive he sounded. His colleague and mentor, Dr. Emmanuel, was the only surgeon in the room who kept his eyes pinned on Charlie. Charlie looked up momentarily and did a double take when he caught Emmanuel's eyes on him.*

*"Dr. Rodgers," Emmanuel said. "Take over for Dr. Palmer please."*

*"Why?" Charlie asked. "This won't even take another hour."*

*"I only need a minute."*

*Charlie gave up the lead and exited the room with Emmanuel. When they were out of range, Charlie shrugged and stared at his mentor, confused. "Did I do something wrong in there?"*

*"With the procedure, no, but I need you to stop sharing your opinion of everyone who is on the table."*

*"No one seemed to care. The guy made a bad decision. I think we all know that."*

*"I don't care who did what. You rip on every gunshot victim, overweight patient, elderly..."*

*"I don't endorse self-inflicted problems."*

"*You're not a counselor, or a priest, or a psychiatrist Dr. Palmer. You're a surgeon. You have one job, and that is to fix what is broken.*"

"*I may have the best record in this place,*" Charlie said, exasperated. "*Who here is putting in the effort I do? These people want to be fixed. They don't need an ego boost or a best friend. We're in surgery for hours at a time. I listen to Dr. Bloom talk about recipes and Hark talk about his kid's soccer game. It's not the most interesting shit in the world, but I listen.*"

"*You can talk about paint drying for all I care. Hell, form opinions about everything under the sun, but not the person whose life we're trying to save.*"

"*Why not?*" Charlie asked, challenging him.

"*Because you're minimizing their life and sometimes, you're implying they don't deserve our service.*"

"*Yet, I always fix them.*"

"*You may think that's all it takes to be a great surgeon, but I don't just want great surgeons. I want great human beings, and your bedside manner sucks.*"

Charlie tried laughing it all off as nothing. "*The guy's unconscious in there.*"

"*Charlie, just listen,*" Emmanuel commanded. Charlie shut his mouth. "*You've got a good career ahead of you. You're dating one of the nicest people I've ever met. You're young, good-looking, and well respected. Don't throw it all away because you're angry.*"

"*I'm not...*"

"*Just listen. You're angry Charlie. You think you're above the very people who have helped to create your reputation. The people you seem to look down on still have to face themselves and their choices, and I don't think many of them like what they see when they look in the mirror. Whether they never know you have an opinion or not, they don't need their doctor kicking them while they're down. If you want to be a great doctor, have some compassion. If it were you on the table, you would expect the same.*"

"*If it's me on the table, it won't be because I made a mistake.*"

"*The chief of medicine at Banner asked about you today. She wanted to know what your plans were next year.*"

"*Yeah?*" Charlie asked. "*What did you say?*"

"*I said you were a fantastic surgeon. Sharp as a nail. Of course, I didn't want to sound like we had perfection among us, so I gave him a criticism as well. Do you know what I said?*

Charlie shook his head "no", waiting curiously.

"*His bedside manner needs work. I assumed you'd agree. There have been patients you've failed to comfort and even offended. Patients and family who feel comforted in their darkest hours...they suffer less, are physically more capable, and better able, for a longer period, to interact with others. Moreover, after the patients pass, their family members are less likely to experience persistent major depression. In other words, people who had substantive discussions with their doctor about their end-of-life care are far more likely to die at peace and in control of their situation, and to spare their family anguish."*

*"You know, I just think if they're looking for comfort, they don't need a doctor to feed them empty platitudes. People die here, ya know? If I can save them, I do and I tell them that. If it's me, ten times out of ten, I'm going to take the guy who's capable over the guy handing out hugs and kisses."*

*"You don't believe you can be both kinds of doctor?"*

*"I don't believe it's honest. Every time I tell someone "we're going to take good care of you", I feel like I'm just telling them what they need to hear. There's such thing as a hopeless situation."*

*"I just thought I'd share my verbal evaluation with you Dr. Palmer. I believe there's merit, when you're as great as you are at what you do, in becoming better."*

*"I can work on it. I'm always honest though."*

*"And you should be, but it comes down to the simple idea that you should treat people the way you'd want to be treated. Especially when they're in their darkest hours. What goes around, comes around. Our decisions catch up to us in the end. Junk food, cigarettes, alcohol...pick your poison. It all catches up...*

...A patient named Marty Robbins looked up at Charlie and blinked his eyes, which were glossed over. "Are you saying I could lose my sight?"

"It's a possibility. You need to be aware of the risks. Discoveries in neuroplasticity have shown that brains of any age can change their structure and function in response to experience. Even in the visual cortex, which you'd think is pretty hard-wired, can switch from processing sight to touch if you're blindfolded for five days."

"What's that mean?"

"It's a small risk, and one you can afford to take."

"If I don't have the surgery?"

"You'd die," Charlie said, expressionless.

Marty leaned back and weighed his options. "Then I don't have a choice."

"You'd be in very good hands."

"Would you do the operation?"

"I'd assist."

Marty buried his head in his hands and let out a muffled sniffle. Charlie waited patiently, letting the man grieve. Charlie raised his eyebrows and waited, but Marty's sobs only escalated and after a couple of minutes, Charlie grew annoyed and sneaked away. Charlie hated watching people react to bad news. He never understood why a person would sob uncontrollably when they could be spending their time plotting the next move to fix the problem. Marty Robbins had a fixable problem, one that Charlie knew he could repair, but Marty didn't want to talk about it. He wanted to cry.

Charlie wanted to move past this conversation and try to get his day back on track. His usual routine was being thrown off at every turn. The vending machine trail mix he typically bought was empty, the men's room in which he spent twenty minutes sitting on the toilet and reading the news was closed for repairs, and every time he was called for a consultation with a patient, he grew irritated at how unfocused they were. He'd given up on the day, and wandered aimlessly in hopes that it would hurry up and finish so another could begin—a day that would begin the way every other day began and the bad juju could come to an end.

He killed an hour filling out charts and talking to co-workers. He was approached by an associate who told him that Mr. Robbins needed to talk to him. Charlie rolled his eyes and passed the message that he was busy and searched for something else to do. Then, an opportunity crept up on him. He'd been dodging Trish Reynald's calls and making excuses, but he'd been wanting to take another look at Shiloh's charts. He did as promised and looked in on her once, and what he found was nothing short of miraculous. But Trish and Shiloh had been in and out of Banner and it was no secret that she wasn't doing well. For Charlie to check in meant opening a door he'd wanted to keep closed. Royce already tried to reopen it, but now he was bored and standing next to a room that Shiloh was sitting in with her mother.

Charlie walked to the lobby and nonchalantly searched for her chart, but it wasn't there.

"Where's Neomin?" he asked a nurse and she directed him to the fourth floor. Charlie tracked him down, relieved just to have a way to kill time. He found Neomin staring out the large glass windows in a hallway that provided a view of downtown Los Angeles. "Dr. Neomin," he said.

"Dr. Palmer," Neomin said, snapping out of a daze. "How are you?"

"Great," Charlie said, dismissively. "Where's Shiloh Reynald's chart?"

Neomin pretended to think, and feigned placing the name. "Shiloh is my patient."

"I'm a family friend."

"I'll grab it first chance I get and get it to you, but I'm perfectly capable…"

"I took a look months ago. She was having a remarkable recovery."

"Based on what?" Neomin asked, growing angry.

"Based on tests I ran. I couldn't find a thing. So what's happening now? Is the tumor back? Are we looking at surgery? If so, when?"

Neomin was at a loss for words. "You ran your own tests?"

Charlie nodded.

"On who's dime?"

"My own."

"Are there records of this? Does the hospital…"

"Like I said: She's a family friend. She didn't even know I did it."

"You realize you'll lose your license over this…" Neomin said.

Charlie was so busy trying to corner Neomin, he hadn't fully realized he'd put his ethics into question in the process. He'd assumed Neomin would have an explanation and would be willing to help, but he was defensive. He was dodging the question. "We can cross that bridge when we get to it. I'm interested in where Shiloh is on her treatment."

"We've tried an experimental drug and it's had some highs and lows."

"And after six months, you're still pushing this thing? If the tumor is back, we need to operate."

"Ms. Reynalds doesn't have the insurance…"

Suddenly, they both stopped as a scream came from outside and a man passed the window on the way down. A moment later, he hit the pavement below, but Charlie and Neomin turned away before it happened. Charlie had only seen the man for a second, but realized in that time that it was his patient, Marty Robbins. A dozen people rushed below to help, but the impact killed him when he hit the ground. Charlie stared in shock and didn't notice Neomin hurry away with the crowds.

Charlie assumed Mr. Robbins was just emotional, but there were clearly deeper issues at hand. He could have had mental problems, or financial problems, but whatever the case may have been, it was likely that Charlie could have intervened. "Holy shit…" Charlie said to himself as he shook his head in disbelief. He'd never made a mistake that killed a person on the operating table, but this could count as one he may have been able to prevent off the table. He didn't know what to feel, other than to detach the blame. The man had a problem…a problem that would catch up to him sooner or later, whether Charlie Palmer intervened in his life or not. But most importantly, what started out as a bad day because he couldn't eat the breakfast he'd wanted, was now a bad day because someone died in front of his eyes…someone who very likely was asking for Charlie so he could set his mind at ease or help him through whatever emotions he was experiencing.

Charlie took the stairwell back down to the first floor, his mind blank the whole way. Later, he wouldn't even remember anything between when Marty hit the ground and when he was approached by the chief of medicine in the bathroom as he was splashing water on his face.

"Are you okay?" the chief asked.

"Why wouldn't I be?"

"He was your patient."

"I'm fine."

"Go home Dr. Palmer," the chief said. "You've seen enough trauma today."

Without argument, Charlie walked out of the bathroom, through the hallway, and exited Banner.

4

Adrenaline pumped through Adlar's veins as he made his way to Charlie's neighborhood on foot, careful not to leave anything behind that could later be used to track him. Even this precaution was unnecessary since Adlar was going to administer a lethal dose of the same toxin he planned to use on Sean sprayed onto Charlie's pillow. As long as he could enter and exit Charlie's home without leaving a trail, all he'd have to do was wait.

He was two blocks away and he began growing nervous. He couldn't believe this was really happening. He'd made a similar journey to kill both Palmers at one time, but he was reckless and afraid then. Now, he was confident he could get away with it, and when he did, he'd work his way through the list just as easily and be free from the responsibilities and burdens of life. As he thought about these things and focused on walking a straight path to his destination, he didn't see someone approach from the side.

"Adlar?"

He jumped and almost fell. The sound of a voice nearly gave him a heart attack. It was so unexpected and was even more surreal when he found himself face to face with his ex-girlfriend. "Dawn?" he said.

"Adlar Wilcox," she said with a smile and wrapped her arms around him as if their last encounter had been a good one.

"Why are you here?" Adlar asked.

"I live here now," she said, pointing behind her to the home she'd walked out of.

*Great...a witness...*he thought, and considered calling it off, but her presence would ruin nothing if the rest of his plan went smoothly. If she was new to the neighborhood, she very likely didn't even know Charlie, who lived over a block away. All would be fine, but he wanted to get rid of her. She'd broken a confident stride he'd been gaining.

"Cool," he said. "Well, good seeing you."

"That's it?" she asked.

"Well, we broke up."

"Yeah, but I just feel bad about how things were left. I mean, what you did was wrong, but I get why you did it. I guess you didn't really have a lot of options and I was pressuring you."

"You didn't have to call the police on me."

"I know. I wish I'd talked to you first. I was just mad, ya know?"

"Yeah. Well, okay…" he said.

"After I cooled down, cause sometimes a girls just gotta cool down, I got to thinking about you again and it wasn't like you changed while we dated. You were the same guy I met when we broke up, and so in a way, it was my fault because maybe in some weird way, I got together with you thinking I'd mold you into my idea of the perfect guy. I never really dated much, so I was just happy a cute guy liked me, but you weren't my type Addy. Not even in the beginning. So I shouldn't have expected so much from you."

"Well, I'm not as bad as you think."

"Oh, I know," she said, putting her hands on his arm. "Please don't take this the wrong way. If anything, I was the idiot. It's not you or me at all. We're two people who weren't compatible but thought maybe we could be and we should have just recognized it to begin with. It shouldn't have gotten to that point, and when it did, I shouldn't have just called the police, because I do see how that was you trying."

"I have to go," Adlar said with a shrug.

"Okay, I don't mean to keep you. I just wanted to say sorry. And call me sometime if you want."

"Alright," he said.

"What are you doing here anyway?" she asked, trying to think of a reason Adlar would possibly have in the neighborhood.

"I mowed a lawn for someone," he said. The excuse had been in his head since he saw fresh grass clippings along the sidewalk three blocks ago. He didn't think he'd have to use it, but he was glad it was stuck there, or he would have found himself a stammering fool. "I get paid to do that sometimes."

"So you're working?" she asked, with hope.

"I really have to go," he said.

"Oh, sorry. Sorry."

He kept walking and didn't respond when she shouted that she was glad to see him. After a few moments, he turned back, but she was out of sight. He let out a breath of relief.

Breaking into Charlie's house had been as easy as it was the first day he did it. A strange feeling of deja vu crept over him, but he recognized the difference in scenarios. He'd walked in desperately with a gun in the middle of the night the first time. He'd ran and hid immediately after, afraid for his life for months. This time, he'd waltz in during broad daylight, leave a drop of toxin on Charlie's pillow, and exit easily, with only a wait ahead. It felt like he'd lived a whole lifetime and changed bodies between visits.

Adlar walked through the house slowly and kept the vial of toxin securely in his palm with his fingers wrapped tightly around it. He wanted to move quickly and avoid any unexpected problems. He slowly walked up the stairs, careful not to leave a scuff mark or shoe print on the wooden steps.

When he reached the top, he walked to where the bedroom was and flashed back to the night he entered the room in the dark and fired a single shot into the lump on the bed. He wondered how differently events would have played out if he'd finished the job that night. It had been such a pain in the ass that Charlie survived and made his life hell. This was his chance to close the book on the Palmers and finally rid himself of the fear he'd always felt in knowing someone was out there who wanted him dead.

Adlar wandered through Charlie's home, taking in his surroundings. The fridge was covered in invites and the walls were covered with plaques and pictures. Part of him wanted to sift through the boxes in the closets and the basement and look for something to rob her of. He reminded himself of what Manny had always told him. Everything, no matter how small, could tell a story. A box filled with dusty books could tell a tale if the top one was moved a couple centimeters in any direction. The shifting of dust, the placement of where it once was and where it was now.

It had all made sense to Adlar and he'd told himself in the heat of the moment, he would do it right, but in the midst of his mission, temptation always got the best of him. The house could be filled with treasures that no one else knew about, and he could only focus on what he was there to do.

There was a small piece of Adlar that was buried deep within that was sad about what he was doing. First, he took Charlie's wife. Then, he threatened him. He could certainly understand why Charlie was angry, but it was his actions after the fact that made this easy. Adlar didn't expect Charlie to mourn forever, but he moved on fast. The newspapers mentioned him a lot, having been a part of something or other. He'd sponsored little league teams, donated items to charities, saved lives. Now, he lived in a nice home with his new woman—a woman beautiful like Abby.

Adlar wondered if Charlie knew how lucky he really was. Guys like Adlar would never have a fraction of the luck that guys like Charlie had. What was left for guys like Adlar was what he was now. He was that part of the world that couldn't find a place and had to find ways to survive, illegal and immoral as they were. What was the difference between him and Charlie? Charlie used his gifts and Adlar used his. It just turned out that Adlar's gifts were frowned upon by society, but in the end, both were doing what needed to be done to have a meal at the end of the day, and Charlie still came out ahead.

Beautiful women would never love Adlar. He'd never be called a hero or a saint. He had the right to find happiness. Everyone else did.

He reminded himself that he could have anything. He could have the world. Victor's money could buy him a complete life makeover. New identity, a new look, a new everything, anywhere he wanted to be. When Richard died, it dawned on him that someone really would have the money one day. They'd all naturally die if they weren't killed first, and one by one, they'd better the odds for the remaining. It was very real and it was going to happen. He couldn't stand by and so he aggressively pursued an education by a man who had just that to offer.

Manny was rough around the edges, but he had a lot of knowledge and Adlar was confident he could have the money within half a year if he was really ambitious. He'd waited for Manny's blessing. He didn't want to burn the bridge that could help him to freedom, but as he'd gotten smarter, his frustration had grown. Finally, Manny gave permission and this was it. To screw it up, to move the book in the box or treasure hunt would be stupid after everything he'd been through.

He turned off the temptation just like that, and instead walked through the house, searching for the bedroom. A drop on a pillow and it was over for Charlie. There would be no pain or suffering. He'd never even know what happened. It was as clean and optimistic as it got. There was no need to be creative or think about revenge or safety or have the last laugh. It was simple: Charlie needed to go quietly.

As he rounded a hallway, he could see at the end was the bedroom. He reached in his pocket, but that was as far as he got before he heard a car pull into the driveway. He backed up and looked through the curtains and his heart stopped as he saw Charlie Palmer in the driver's seat, oblivious to the intruder in his home.

Adlar turned and ran through the house, searching for a room the least likely for Charlie to walk into. The last thing he planned on doing was leaving. The odds of a sloppy kill increased ten-fold but Adlar didn't care. He'd worked too hard to back out now. He found a door that led to the basement and hurried down. Basements were always dark with lots of hiding places. It would give him time to think and plan and wait for the right opportunity.

He cursed Charlie for coming home. He'd paid attention to his schedule and he had no reason to be here. It was too late for Charlie just to be on a lunch break and the hospital was too far. Adlar cursed again, this time for being so unlucky.

His eyes rolled up as he listened above at the sound of the front door opening and closing, followed by footsteps through the home and the sound of banging cabinets. Charlie sounded angry. Adlar wondered if he had a bad day or if this was the real Charlie. Lucky Charlie Palmer, who didn't know how lucky he was and stomped around on a warpath. Suddenly, Adlar wanted him dead more than he ever had.

He waited in the basement until all noise stopped. Another half hour passed and Adlar slowly made his way back to the main floor, careful not to make any noise, until he reached the top of the stairs and stood silently in the door-frame.

He slid his feet across the floor, careful not to take steps. He wasn't sure where Charlie was, but his car was still in the driveway. He hugged the walls as he walked, taking a look through every open door in the hopes of detecting where Charlie had gone. As he slowly walked to the hall which ended with Charlie's bedroom, he heard what he'd hoped he'd hear: snoring.

Adlar held a breath in his chest as he pressed his back against the hallway wall and slowly moved toward Charlie's room. He slid a hand in his pocket and felt around for the vial until he had it between both fingers. One drop on the pillow, right under his nose or mouth, and it was curtains for Charlie.

He slid one foot through the door way and held his arms at his side motionless, careful not to make a sudden movement. He floated through the room, disturbing nothing and hoping that Charlie wasn't a light sleeper. As he moved to the foot of the bed, from outside, a dog started barking.

Adlar froze, and without question, he knew Charlie would be startled awake by it. Adlar didn't move his head—only his eyes darted toward where Charlie's face was buried in his pillow. Instead of turning toward the barking, Charlie seemingly sensed his presence. In the same moment his eyes opened, he turned toward the foot of the bed, his eyes wide open, but glossed over as the world around him came into focus.

5

Charlie's first instinct was to commend himself for being right.

Bad juju was a concept he'd preached many times, always receiving laughter and doubt in response, but it was real. From the moment he woke up, he knew his day would be a disaster and it had compiled until it toppled.

Adlar Wilcox was the definition of bad juju for Charlie. Seeing him in his bedroom brought back a swarm of memories and trauma and though he hadn't realized it until now, it dawned on him that he'd always known he and Adlar hadn't parted ways forever. Somewhere in the back of his head, he always knew it would come to this.

"What are you…" was all he could say before Adlar turned and ran, slamming the door behind him.

Before Charlie was out of bed, he heard a large thud on the door, clearly a sign that Adlar was trying to barricade him inside. Whatever it was, it would hold Charlie back for seconds before he caught up to Adlar and…

*And what?* he wondered. He couldn't kill him without exposing his own secrets, but as long as Adlar was alive, Charlie would always be in danger and Abby's death left unavenged.

Charlie ran to the door and pulled it open, expecting a small barricade to could shove out of the way, but the bookshelf had wedged itself perfectly between the hallway and the door-frame and couldn't be moved. He tried to go under, but there wasn't enough space. He put his shoulder against it and pushed, but it only wedged itself tighter. Adlar must have used all his strength to knock it over. He'd probably hung from the top, using his full body weight to pull it down and somehow managed to wedge it perfectly in position to keep him there.

He heard movement throughout the house—frantic movement that traveled from room to room but did not exit.

"What are you doing?" he shouted

What Adlar was doing was searching for a clean kill, but he'd already done too much damage. He'd also come too far to go back. Being seen was the absolute worst thing that could happen, and there wasn't much that could cover his tracks at this point, but there was one last desperate act that could possibly cover his tracks and kill Charlie in the process.

He ran to the kitchen and pulled the stove out from the wall, quickly disconnecting the gas and letting it leak. He then ran back to the living room to watch the bedroom door to be sure Charlie couldn't get out. The sound of Charlie shoving it from the other side could be heard, but the bookshelf had neatly fallen and landed diagonally right in front of it, welding itself in another door-frame around the corner. Charlie wouldn't be walking through the door, but the sooner he realized he had to exit through the window, the worse for Adlar. He waited for Charlie to stop pushing at the bookshelf to light it up.

In his pocket, he wrapped his fingers around his zippo. He stepped forward toward the door and though Charlie hadn't stopped shoving, he knew he had to keep him where he was while he waited for the gas to fill the house.

"Dr. Palmer..." he said, somewhat loud, his voice trembling as he spoke. The pounding stopped, as if Charlie was listening closely, unsure if he heard Adlar. Then it commenced, but Adlar spoke louder.

"Dr. Palmer..."

"What are you doing?" Charlie yelled.

"I came to talk," Adlar said. "I'm sorry. I got scared."

"I left you alone!" Charlie shouted. "I thought we had a mutual understanding! You just ruined that."

*Oh no I didn't,* Adlar thought. *I'm finishing the job.*

"I know!" Adlar shouted. "I'm sorry." He realized he somewhat meant his apology. He was sorry to have to finish the job, and sorrier that Charlie was aware of what was happening—not the way Adlar had planned, but it would have to do.

Adlar suddenly caught a whiff of the gas and decided it was time. He couldn't stay and talk to Charlie. It was too intense for his taste. He needed to get out. While Charlie was still yelling through the door, Adlar pulled the lighter out and ran for the front door.

Charlie heard the door slam and paused to listen. He took a moment to evaluate the situation. Adlar was there and gone, standing over him while he slept, Royce Morrow had warned him that Adlar was in cahoots with Manny. If he'd listened, he might not be stuck in a room with Adlar in his home.

*I gotta get out of this house.*

And as the thought crossed his mind, he smelled the smoke.

Anger filled him as he changed direction and hurried to the window. Why had Adlar targeted the Palmers? What had Charlie or Abby ever done to him to deserve this, and when all was said and done and somehow behind them, how had Adlar come back to take the little he'd left Charlie the first time around? Now, his home was on fire, his life was on the line. Adlar would never quit until Charlie was gone because what

Charlie failed to remember was that his own life was the lifeblood to Adlar's bad deeds. Only Charlie had fully known what Adlar had done and that could only die with Charlie.

He tried prying the window but it was set in place, long ago painted to the wall and wedged between the frame. He changed his strategy and hit his elbow against it, rattling the window without luck. Then, he smelled the gas and went into full drive, searching the room for something solid to break the glass. It occurred to him that it was harder than expected to find a solid object in a bedroom filled with their belongings. Shoes and clothes wouldn't cut the mustard, but when he spotted Mindy's jewelry box on the dresser, he found his escape.

He cursed Adlar's name as he held the box high, ready to smash the window in one swoop, but it took two. The first sent a crack nearly corner to corner and the second shattered the whole thing. He used the box to clear the edges, careful to clear every piece, so as not to cut himself on his way out. He stuck his head out the window and from the outside, the danger wasn't present. Except for a stream of smoke billowing out the door, all was quiet in the neighborhood. A woman walked her dog in the distance and the neighbor kids were shooting hoops. Nothing about their home stuck out.

His mind traveled through the house, and though it wasn't probably true for Mindy, there wasn't much there he cared to salvage. This wasn't so bad. This was a reminder—that the job had to be finished—that bad juju was just a sign in disguise—a nagging reminder that some stones could never be left unturned. He should have never given up on Adlar. He should have stayed on the offense instead of allowing Wilcox the upper hand.

It would never happen again.

Charlie reached through the window to grab onto something to level himself before he pulled through.

Just then, the walls burst inward and the blast sent Charlie flying into darkness…

*"…He's alive and well," The chief told Charlie, without his usual enthusiasm. "Nice work as usual."*

*"Thank you," Charlie said and wanted to say more, but his boss turned and walked out before he could. Charlie wandered the hospital, thinking through his day. Something about it all felt surreal, as if he'd been awakened to something he didn't know about himself before— something big and undoubtedly true.*

*He didn't know what it meant—if anything. He was brash and cynical, but he felt no need to change. He was good at what he did. He fixed* people—sometimes allegedly miraculously fixed people. They came to be healed, and Charlie repaired injuries with the best of them. He used to think perceptions of him were high, but people were too sensitive, too easily offended, too...weak.

Charlie felt his phone buzz and looked at the screen. Abby had sent a message—to meet on the roof. They met on the roof often after shifts, to sit in lawn chairs and look at the stars. Sometimes they'd talk for hours, listening to the traffic in the distance and once in a while watching as a patient was flown in by a helicopter on the landing below. '

Tonight, he dreaded going to the roof. He hadn't seen Abby since this morning and he suspected she'd heard about surgery, but even if she hadn't heard, Charlie felt he had to confess to her—but he didn't know what. Something was off. There was a divide...a difference between them that couldn't be contained forever. He'd faked being nicer than he was for a long time, but one day, Abby would inevitably see him for who he really was. He wasn't ashamed of that person, but he also knew Charlie wasn't truly compatible with such a nice woman.

He took the stairs and when he walked out onto the roof, he saw Abby had changed her clothes. She wore a black dress that complimented her figure and her hair was done. How convenient, Charlie thought. The same day her ex is here, Abby looks her best.

He forced the thought from his head and met her where she stood.

"How was your day?" she asked, and he sensed she was testing him.

"Not bad."

"But not good?"

"I don't have good or bad days. Just days."

He expected her to point out what a pessimist he was but she smiled instead, as if she found him endearing.

Maybe she's the problem, Charlie thought. Maybe she just has blinders on when she's with me.

"You saved his life," Abby said. "I mean, I know what you do and that this is a normal day for you, but it never really occurred to me until today that you're a hero Charlie. You save people."

"I fix them, and I get paid well to do so."

"You can't put a damper on this one Charlie Palmer," Abby said, stepping closer, her body almost touching his. "You can't deny your talent."

"Maybe not," Charlie said, taking a deep breath. "But saving lives doesn't automatically make me a good person."

"What do you mean?" she asked, stepping back.

"I'm not a nice guy," Charlie said, simply. "I generally don't like most people, I get frustrated, impatient...I'm not a nice person."

*"You are too a nice person."*

*"Do you just not pay attention to anything I say or do?"*

*"Yeah, but that's your personality."*

*"And you're an optimist. You're always happy. How do I not irritate you?"*

*"What are you trying to say Charlie? What do you want?"*

*"Why are you really with me?"*

*Abby was taken aback but took a few seconds to consider before answering. "You're handsome, you're talented, thoughtful, passionate..."*

*"...but not nice..."*

*Abby thought about it for a moment. "You're nice to people you like. But all those frustrations you express, I figure it's not a big deal— certainly not big enough to ignore all your good qualities. No one's perfect Charlie, and so for every bad thing about you, there's a good thing. It's just strengths and weaknesses. Everyone has them. You're normal Charlie, but I know you're an amazing man and I know you're a hero. I see in you what you don't see in yourself and I really hope that changes someday, but if not, you're not going to get rid of me just because you think you're mean."*

*He closed his eyes and digested what she said. Abby would never give up on him, no matter who he was or what he did. Somehow, she'd believed him compatible and maybe they were. Maybe there was something Abby knew that Charlie didn't. His rooftop conversation would have stayed with him the rest of the night, but to his surprise, as he reviewed Baxter's charts, he made a discovery and before he knew it, he stood at the foot of Baxter's bed, staring at the man who had seemed like such a big threat earlier, but only looked weak and helpless now.*

*"Hey, it's Dr. Palmer."*

*Baxter fell silent, unsure of what to say.*

*"You have a tumor which formed just above the pituitary gland which is a small organ at the bottom of your brain. It grew into nearby tissues, including the pituitary gland and optic nerves."*

*"What's that mean?"*

*"It will affect your vision."*

*"I might not be able to see?"*

*"Probably not." As an afterthought, Charlie added, "But we're going to take good care of you."*

*Baxter rested his head back against the wall in defeat, distraught by the news. He reflected, and spoke quietly. "About three years back, I was gonna try out for the Dodgers. I was in pretty good shape, but back then, I got to thinking I could nail it in a year if I worked out hard. Said that three years in a row. Always sayin this was the year that I man up...like I was gonna have potential for the rest of my life. Now, just like that, I know that will never happen. I thought one day I might get cancer. Everyone in my family does. Thought maybe I'd get in an accident and injure something, but my sight? Doctor...tell me you can do something."*

Charlie stared at Baxter for a long moment and managed to feel sorry for him, but under it all, he believed that somehow, Baxter deserved this. Somehow, he'd lose his vision because too many things went well for Marty in his life and karma would always balance the scales.

"I'm sorry," Charlie said. "I can't make that promise..."

...Hundreds of noises blended together and formed a loud rumbling sound mixed with screams and sirens and voices with a roaring in the background. Then, he felt the pain and piece by piece, the noises made sense, but he could barely remember what happened. He remembered a burrito, and his patient jumping from the roof, but nothing else.

He tried to force his eyes open, but couldn't control his body. His arms were restrained and his lower body was too painful to even consider moving. He finally jerked his head back and his eyes shot open instinctively. A man stood over him, seemingly shouting in his ear, but he couldn't make out the words. All he could see was behind the man, the fire and the smoke, which whited out the scenery all around.

He wanted to ask what happened, but only a long sustained "wuu" came out. A line of drool fell from his lip and stung his neck as it trickled down. It was then that he remembered Adlar, and for a moment, he was sure it was a dream, but the pain was real, and the heat from the fire burned his face. He was able to separate the noises and realized the man was with the fire department and he was strapped to a gurney.

"Sir, can you understand what I'm saying?" the medic said.

Charlie only moved his eyes and tried to nod his head, but it shook instead.

As his memory came back and the world began to become clear again, only one thing was unclear and though he was afraid of what he'd find if he looked, he couldn't help but lift his head and look down at his lower body. He hadn't been able to feel a thing below his hips and he suddenly could see why. One leg was nearly severed all the way through and the other was completely shattered.

"No no no no..." he started to say and it was followed by a long string of 'nos' followed by pain, and finally he passed out.

# Chapter 4

## 1

*The boardroom on the seventh floor of Stone Enterprises was filled with the most powerful men in the business. They sat and listened to a cost cutting analyst give them a pep talk designed to motivate ideas, but the most powerful minds in the building were tapped. At the end of the day, they had done everything in their power to cut costs and the business was still bleeding.*

*Victor Stone wasn't as visibly worried as Bernard Bell and Cory Owens, but his mind was in many places. The bottom line came a distant second to the investigation against him that Adlar had warned him about. Then there was Adlar, who had been many things to him. First, he was just a subject matter expert paid to do a favor. Then, he'd blackmailed his foot in the door, only to be proved hard to get rid of. Then, he'd been compromised, but turned his loyalties to Victor, who now couldn't decide if he needed Adlar or hated him.*

*Adlar certainly wasn't forgettable and that day, the meeting brought him back to the topic of conversation, bewildering Victor further.*

*"What you need is people who think outside the box," the financial analyst said. "I've been looking at all your business decisions and most of it is generic cutbacks. It's all necessary, but if you want to save yourself, you need to dig a little deeper."*

*"Do you have ideas we haven't thought of?" Bernard asked.*

*"We'll get there," the analyst said. "I like what the guy on sixth has*

done with the fonts. That's what I'm talking about when I say outside the box."

"What guy on sixth?" Bernard asked.

"Wilcox," Victor muttered, and everyone fell silent, as if this was a hot topic. "What did he do with the fonts?" Victor asked.

"He's cut the cost of paper, toner, and ink, which quickly adds up. You see, programs like Microsoft Outlook will default to Arial, but a thinner-lined typeface like Century Gothic requires less toner to form its characters. Switching can save eighty dollars per printer per year. We have one hundred thousand dollar print-supplies bill and can reduce it by ten percent by making that simple change."

"Wilcox said this?" Cory asked, fuming inside.

"He didn't say it. He did it. Ink and toner is very expensive and people still print a lot, and there's a lot of variance between fonts in how much ink they use."

"I had no idea," Bernard said, seemingly fascinated.

"The guy on sixth is a joke," Cory said.

"It was still a good idea," the analyst said. "You might want to see what else he has."

"He's got nothing," Cory said, sure of himself.

"He actually showed me another trick," the analyst said. "If you cover the tiny window in toner cartridges with a piece of tape, it fools the optical sensor into thinking that the cartridge is always full. You can actually squeeze an additional two months of life from a supposedly empty toner cartridge before the first streaks appear on printed pages."

"This is ridiculous," Cory said. "No one asked him to change the font. He doesn't have the right to make changes like that."

Another board member held up a memo and studied the font. "I would have never noticed," the man said, impressed. "Century Gothic is just as easy to read. What's the guy on six's job title?"

Cory rubbed his temples throughout the remainder of the meeting, and the first chance he got, he took the stairwell to the sixth floor to give Adlar a talking to. He caught Adlar in the act of holding a kitten down and trying to pull a piece of tape from its paw. It struggled and he proved unsuccessful at grasping it.

Adlar looked up and noticed Cory. He started to hide the kitten under the desk, but stopped when he knew he was busted.

"What is this?" Cory asked. "How did you get that in the building?"

"I think he came through one of the windows or something," Adlar said. "I found him wandering the hallway a couple days ago."

"Well get rid of it. No animals are allowed in the building."

"I'll take him out then," Adlar said.

*Cory didn't accept the solution and quickly scooped the kitten with his hand and brought it to the window."*

*"No, just put it on the ledge," Adlar said, afraid of what Cory might do.*

*"These things always land on their feet," Cory said.*

*"Still, please don't."*

*"Why not?"*

*"Cause he didn't do anything to you."*

*The simplicity of the statement surprised Cory, and instead of letting it fall, he dropped it back to the floor. "Get rid of it," he said.*

*"I will."*

*"So we talked about your font changes."*

*"Yeah?"*

*"We're allowing it but if you're not qualified or educated in economic thinking, Mr. Stone would prefer if you stay out of the way and keep your ideas to yourself."*

*"I didn't think anyone would notice. I know you guys are trying to save money, so..."*

*"That's another thing. How do you know that? Stay out of the system where you don't belong. Just because you can take a look, doesn't mean you should."*

*"Fine."*

*"Just work on the thing with the investigation."*

*"I've been reprogramming all week."*

*"Then it should be done."*

*"No, because it takes time. Like a lot."*

*"What are they saying over there?"*

*"Who?"*

*"Your contact with the agency."*

*"They want evidence. They want me to hurry."*

*"And what are you telling them?"*

*"That it takes time."*

*"Funny. You're telling both sides the same story."*

*"I've been disclosing everything. What more do you want?"*

*"What I want is to be a fly on the wall when you're with them, just to see what's really going on."*

*"What do you mean?"*

*"I think you're playing both sides Wilcox. You're seeing what they have to offer...what we have to offer...and you're trying to see which way you come out ahead."*

*"No, I've been covering up you guys' mistakes all week. You don't know anything about reprogramming and hiding all this. I'm basically*

*rewriting history. It's not easy, which is why hardly anyone can do it."*

*"So we just go on your word then, huh?" Cory asked.*

*"I told you guys about them on my own," Adlar said.*

*"Yeah, well maybe you were looking for a little respect. Hell, if you're approaching our financial analyst about font changes, you must be feeling awfully comfortable around here."*

*"Well, if you don't think I'm working on it then you can give it to someone else and I'll just tell them I can't get anything, but it will still be there and they'll get it eventually."*

*Cory walked to the doorway without a response, paused and turned. "No more animals at work." He walked away without another word...*

...At three in the morning, Adlar Wilcox sat with Manny in front of a television and watched coverage of the explosion at Charlie's home, which reported one man as critically injured. Manny rubbed his eyes, expressionless, but Adlar knew him well enough to know that Manny wanted to tear his throat out.

"You've got balls being here," Manny finally said.

"He'll still die," Adlar said. "Yeah, it will be arson, but it won't come back to us."

"Palmer is in surgery. He could still pull through. And if you had to resort to this, I don't even want to know what else you left behind. This is sloppy. There's bound to be witnesses...something."

"I know his schedule," Adlar said. "The plan was good. He came home early. That's all."

"And as soon as he did, you should have walked out and planned for another day."

Adlar had no rebuttal. He knew it was true. In fact, it was something they'd been over multiple times. When the heat is on, you walk away. "All you have to do is cover my tracks," Adlar said.

"I'm not an arson investigator you dummy. My presence on the scene would raise questions. I've helped you all that I can."

"So what do I do?"

"You need to finish the job."

"No way," Adlar said. "He's in the hospital. I'll be caught for sure."

"You'll be caught if and when he wakes up. This is your best bet, and I'm telling you this as a favor because you and I are done Wilcox. Cover your tracks and get out of my house. You're on your own."

"Wait, why?" Adlar said, pleading. "If I can fix all this..."

"You don't have a choice."

"But we can work together, cause if not, I can still finish the list and then you got nothing."

Manny considered for only a moment. "We've got a deal, but here's what you need to know: You don't come back to see me until we're one hundred percent certain that no one's looking in your direction. You're not going to be able to stage this as an accident, but what you can do is make certain that there's not a trace of your presence at that house. When I know you're safe, we finish the list and go our own ways, but you're going to need to take care of Palmer as soon as humanly possible, cause if you don't, it won't matter what you do. He's going to put this on you and your life will be over, and the last thing I need is you in custody because I just know that one day my name will come up. So rest assured, if Charlie Palmer wakes up, you're a dead man."

Adlar agreed and went on his way, his thoughts scattered as he frantically considered his next move. There were probably too many rescue vehicles at the house, and Charlie was going to be in the hands of doctors for a while, so he was left with one lingering problem that he had withheld from Manny, and it was a very real problem for him.

If Charlie were to die and if the fire destroyed all evidence of Adlar, then he could be in the clear, but there had been a witness, and though he hoped he would never have to confront her again, it was clear to him that his ex-girlfriend would see the action in the neighborhood and quite possibly remember her unexpected encounter with Adlar shortly before it all happened.

He felt around in his pocket for the vial that was supposed to kill Charlie quietly, and felt comfort that it was still there as he headed to Dawn Bradshaw's house.

## 2

Donovan Willis hadn't thought about Christian Dent in months. When the warden forbade him from interacting with Dent, he swallowed his own pride and fought every bit of temptation he had to exact his revenge. It wasn't easy in the beginning, but eventually, other inmates had surfaced that he wanted to target and Dent was forgotten. Then, one night as he was sitting in his barcalounger watching late night TV, he connected two threads that had been there for him to see for quite some time, but his mind had never gotten around to putting two and two together.

It was a story from entertainment TV which talked of rumors of a Tarek Appleton sighting, with none other than Aileen Thick, the ex-wife of Victor Stone. It was an odd coupling, but what really nagged at his mind was that Tarek had been in the news because of the infamously rumored will Victor Stone had left behind. Donovan was one of the many who'd awaited Tarek spilling the names of the others on that will and in the end, Tarek had led everyone astray and announced the names of many of the who's who in the media. Shortly after, it was the media who was under attack as those who believed him began to dig into their lives and it turned out, most of the names Tarek mentioned had skeletons in their closets that were later revealed. Tarek's revenge had been sweet, but it also had boosted him into a limelight that wasn't good for the show. Suddenly, Tarek was a lot of drama and monologues and guests no longer cut the mustard. The Victor Stone thing came and went and when Tarek didn't continue to ride that wave, viewership dropped until one day it was announced that Tarek's show was no more.

For Donovan to see Tarek with the ex-wife of Victor was strange, and though the will had always been a rumor, the coupling granted some validity to the whole situation, and if there was validity to the will then…

His mind spun as he tried to remember where else he'd heard of the will, and it wasn't long before he remembered a desperate Christian Dent, begging not to be thrown back to the hotbox with a claim that on the outside, he was worth billions of dollars. It sounded like the ramblings of a desperate maniac, and Donovan never even considered potential truth to the claim, but the more he thought about it, the more he could connect the dots in such a way that if a will really did exist, there was a strong chance Dent would be on it. After-all, the murders that eventually wound Dent in Kern were those of two of Victor Stone's top associates: Cory Wilson and Jones Mitchell. If the will existed, then it wasn't for Victor's friends, and if it was for Victor's enemies, then who better than the man who murdered two of Victor's top trusted guys to be on it?

Donovan scribbled a time-line onto a notebook and tried to spin truth into the theories. A lot of things happened around the same time which actually went in favor of the will theory. Victor Stone died just days before Dent was captured. The will hadn't even been read yet when the handcuffs were slapped on his wrist. If the will was real, Dent learned of it after he could do anything about it. A smile crept across his face as he thought of Dent's misfortune.

But what did it all mean? There really was a list of names with Dent among them, and they were walking around alive until the money could be collected. And Dent was maybe the most dangerous, but also, the safest of all. If there were other sour apples on the list, Dent was untouchable behind bars.

Donovan spent the next couple of weeks in thought. Knowing what he knew didn't benefit him in the least. Dent wouldn't be able to obtain his fortune one way or another. If someone were to help him escape, he couldn't collect the money. That would require walking into a bank with

identification. Even if he could collect, he wouldn't give a dime to
Donovan, no matter how much help was extended his way. Donovan
certainly wanted the money though—or a piece of it. He hated his career
and was cornered at Kern. There were no promotions down the line and it
was too late in life to seek another profession. He hated being a prison
guard from his very first week. He knew how to put the scare into the
convicts, but it was a matter of time before he pissed off the wrong
person or some crazy got the best of him. For a moment, he thought Dent
had been the guy that would end him. That was what made Dent so
important—not just that he was positioned to inherit a fortune, but that he
might actually be driven enough and smart enough to win.

All that was left was for Donovan to find where he could fit into that.

Donovan wasn't the smartest man alive, but he was a pragmatist and he
was smart enough to know that approaching Dent would be pointless.
Dent could approach him though—if he wanted it bad enough. First there
would have to be trust. Donovan wished he could start over with Dent,
but the next best thing was to swallow his pride and look out for the man
—enough that Dent noticed. He'd play a humble card, say he was sorry,
say he was saved by God and was making amends with his enemies. Then
he'd play it cool for a while until one day, when Dent trusted him, he'd
ask for help.

Christian Dent sat alone in the sun, looking out past the gates toward
the distance where the sun was rising in the sky. Every other day,
Donovan would have avoided him, but today the healing would begin. It
was when his shadow covered Dent's body that Dent turned, but there
was no reaction. He turned back to where he was facing as if he'd
expected Donovan, or just didn't care. Inside, it enraged him but he kept
it buried deep.

"Dent," Donovan started, "You've been in my head for a while now.
For a long time, I figured I'd bury you eventually, but I realized I'm not
going to be able to do that."

Dent turned again and stared up, curiously.

"I mislabeled you is all. Now, don't get me wrong. I have no love for
your type, but most of these fellows are a dime a dozen. You almost got
out of here. You got me off your back. You've done some pretty eye-
popping shit since you arrived. I ain't gonna bury you cause you're the
one shithead in here that I can't predict and I need that. You might get out
of here one day. You might even be the end of me, but shit boy, I'll admit
that you got the little bit of respect out of me that I reserve for the scum
of the Earth, so if anything comes at you or you have any trouble in here,
let me know."

"I don't need your help."

"Sure you do Dent. You need me here cause we're stuck together in this cage. You got friends here. I got friends here. Without enemies though, what makes any of it interesting?"

Donovan suspected Dent would challenge him or force his way into Donovan's mind and find a motive, so he forced a nod and turned and left him there to digest what he said. Then, he let two weeks pass, and though he thought he could play it cool and wait for Dent, he noticed in that time that whatever drove Dent before was no longer there. Every day, Dent just sat on the ground, getting older and doing nothing. It wasn't a game and Dent couldn't be played because he'd been defeated. He'd accepted his fate.

That was when Donovan took a more blunt approach.

"Where you want to be Dent? Kitchen? Crafts? You name it."

"Warden wouldn't allow shit," Dent said, and Donovan realized it was probably true.

"You hear anything I said to you when we talked?"

Silence.

"Alright Dent, I'm not gonna bullshit with you," Donovan said, making a last second decision. He didn't have the patience to win over a man who probably couldn't be won. There were other carrots he could dangle in front of Dent. All he could hope was that Dent would set aside their hatred of each other in the name of wealth and freedom. "You said something to me about money when I threw you in the hotbox. I thought maybe you were just talking but I believe you. You and I will hate each other for the rest of our lives, but without you, I'm stuck in Kern doing a shit job forever and you're just stuck in here. The way I see it, I have what it takes to get you out and you have what it takes to keep me secure in life."

"I don't know what you're talking about," Dent said.

Donovan shook his head in disbelief. "You said it Dent. You denying that?"

"I don't remember what I said."

"But you know it's true. And so do I. I've been paying attention and the people who revolved around that rich guy have had some drama to deal with. You know Tarek Appleton?"

Silence.

"He's one of em. He was supposedly kidnapped by what the news was calling a deranged fan but Appleton wouldn't spill the details. You heard of Anthony Freeman? The author?"

Still silence.

"He famously had a problem with Victor and he was stabbed about a year ago and almost died. People are trying to get this Dent." Donovan talked as if they were in on this together—as if there was something mutual between them and all he had to do was talk Christian into it. "So I don't care what happened between us. This is bigger than us. Much bigger. We can either be in here hating each other, or we can be out there hating each other. But if we're out there, we won't have a care in the world. You could go anywhere and I know I would. Let's do this Dent."

Christian took a moment to consider. The offer was enticing, but Donovan had a way of trying to trap him and he couldn't trust the man. He wondered what could possibly come of him if he could. "I'm just trying to do my time," Dent said.

"Bullshit!" Donovan said, stepping into Dent's face and forcing him to meet his eyes. "You wanted out of here bad enough to gas the whole staff of Kern. You stabbed yourself to get me off your case. Your old cellmate...Ira Moore...you sent him on a killing spree and he failed. You think I can't connect the dots? I connected em all and I know what's out there. If you need some time so I can prove to you that you can trust me, then take it. I'll get you any damn thing you want. I'll even put in a good word at parole time. We'd have to get you out of here legally. An escaped con can't collect. You see? I've thought this through. I'll apologize to you. I'll beg you. Whatever it takes. I'm off your back. No one will touch you with my protection. This is a big win for us both. You think on it Dent. Just don't bullshit me about serving time because ain't no way you want to spend another minute more in this shithole. Think on it."

When Donovan walked away, it wasn't long before Dent decided the man was genuine. He was big and tough, but he wanted out. If Dent asked for his help, Donovan could probably even deliver. The only thing that held Christian Dent back was his hatred for the man. There was no way in hell Donovan would ever see a dime of Christian's inheritance. But in the meantime, for the first time in six months, he had something to think about.

3

Dawn Bradshaw hadn't put two and two together, and she probably never would have. Crossing paths with Adlar had been just what it seemed to be in her mind. Most other witnesses would have called Adlar a suspicious character in Charlie and Mindy's neighborhood, but Dawn knew him to be awkward. His nervous demeanor was normal behavior to her.

Adlar had decided it was better to be safe than sorry, but killing Dawn was a level he'd never known. Manny's assignments were all strangers to him and the Palmers were people he knew but felt detached from, but Dawn…he'd spent time with her, and though he was never as fond of her as she'd hoped, the thought of ending her life made him miserable. If it hadn't eaten at him so much, he might have just stuck her with a needle and called it a day, but upon seeing her pull into her driveway, he pocketed the needle and instead, followed at a distance. It was a job that had to be done, but she deserved to know—she deserved some kind of closure.

Manny had given him a Colt service revolver to keep in case of emergencies. What Manny had meant when he gave it to him, was if Adlar was being chased by the police, he would put it to his temple and squeeze the trigger, but Adlar never understood that. He kept it in his glove compartment with a different kind of emergency in mind, and he hadn't even thought about it until tonight.

When Dawn disappeared into her home, he considered his options. He could break a window, pick a lock, or any of a number of break-in methods that he knew so well, but everything about Dawn was different, and in the end, he walked up the driveway and knocked on the door. When a stranger died, a gunshot in the night would suffice. Adlar didn't even need to be in the home when his victims took their final breath. When it was personal, they deserved more. They deserved to know why.

Adlar listened as footsteps approached the door and stopped, undoubtedly confused as to why anyone was outside her door at one in the morning. She probably had her cell phone in hand, ready to dial the police, but Adlar breathed a sigh of relief when through the door, he heard her say his name.

"It's me Dawn."

"Why are you here this late?" she asked, her voice muffled.

"I wanted to see you."

"You have nowhere to go, right? You're just trying to use me again."

"I have my own place," Adlar said. Though it wasn't necessarily true, she'd missed the mark with her assumption. The last thing he wanted was a place to stay. "I just wanted to talk because I felt bad about things I did in the past."

On the other side of the door, the sound of a lock clicking was heard and the door was pulled open. He stared at Dawn, who looked tired, but was seemingly relieved, as if she'd waited for this a long time. "Come in," she said.

He'd had his hand on the gun, but left it in his pants and under his jacket. She was welcoming and it felt good. It was something he hadn't known in a while. There were times he missed his mother, how she'd ask about his day or have breakfast ready in the morning. He hadn't realized it at the time, but those were comforting things—things that when they disappeared, he no longer felt home.

"Did something happen Adlar?"

"For a while now," he said, and then, it was suddenly no act at all. He found himself spilling things that he didn't even know were on his mind. He talked about how he ran away from home, how he made an enemy of a guy whose life he ruined, how he lived with and looked up to a man as a father figure, who ultimately didn't care about him at all. And then, he told her he was in trouble. He didn't need money. He didn't need a place to stay. He'd just taken things too far.

"How far?" Dawn asked.

"That fire down the street," Adlar said. "I did that."

"What?" Dawn asked, her face going white. "Why would you do that?"

"It was an accident. I mean, I wasn't there to do that. I was there for something else, but he saw me."

"You're not making sense Adlar. Start from the beginning."

"I had to kill him," Adlar said, his eyes squeezing closed to suppress tears. "I don't have anything else I can do. I just had to. I never wanted to."

"Tell me you didn't actually kill someone," Dawn said, her voice shaking.

Adlar realized then that he'd said enough. There was a time he could have backed out, but not anymore. Now, he had no choice. Maybe, he'd told her it all deliberately, as a safety net in case he couldn't go through with it, but what was done was done. "I used to work for Stone Enterprises," Adlar started. "Victor Stone didn't like me. For sure he hated me in the end. He had a lot of money and he said he'd let me have it if I'd kill certain people."

"He told you this?"

"It's everything he has Dawn," Adlar said. The tears finally made their exit as he knew the inevitable was closing in. "I've always been a loser. I can't work or network with people in the real world. I don't know how. I tried and I sucked at it. Maybe some people can do really good with jobs and meeting people, but I can't. You know I can't. You even said so."

"Addy…"

"So I had this way that I could just…do what I had to do and I could have that money. I didn't want to. I never would do that for another reason. But it was that or…I don't know…I'd be nothing forever. Live with my parents and be a loser. So I tried to do it."

Dawn suddenly spoke very quickly and Adlar noticed her hand near her pocket, ready to grab her phone if he said the wrong thing. "Adlar Wilcox, did you murder someone?"

"That's not what I mean." It was exactly what he'd meant, but all he could do was buy time.

Then, her phone was out. A moment later, his gun was out. Her hands froze.

"Drop that," he said. "I don't want to do this, but drop that. It's not as easy to explain as you think."

She shook her head in quick motions and let the phone fall to the counter. She swallowed hard with a lot of effort and tried to stay on her feet, though she wanted to faint. "Please…" was all she could manage to say…

*"…I like the new fonts Adlar," Holly Flowers said as Adlar passed her in the lobby of Stone Enterprises. He managed an awkward smile and carried on toward the exit. He was halfway through the parking garage when DII Agent Lawrence Curtolla stepped out of the shadows. Adlar was displeased to see him so near to Victor and his crew, but Lawrence had been pressuring him to finish the job lately and he'd expected some aggression sooner or later.*

*"Aren't you worried they'll see you?" Adlar said.*

*"Wouldn't bother me if they did. I'm just a guy in the area."*

*"But they might see us talking."*

*"Ah, right. Wouldn't be good news for you if Victor Stone saw you with a fed."*

*"Yeah, so what do you want?"*

*"I'm just out of patience with you," Lawrence said. "I really am."*

*"Why?"*

*"Because I've seen your profile and I don't believe there's anything encrypted enough for you to spend more than a day on. You're stringing this along and I've allowed it long enough, but I've had enough."*

*"I'm having trouble finding anything."*

*"A month ago you said there was evidence."*

*"I was wrong."*

*"Wrong or confused?"*

*"Wrong. I misread some things. I don't understand receipts and records is all."*

*"How about you get us what we asked for and we can be the ones to decipher the numbers?"*

*"No, cause they're not doing anything wrong here and if I did that, I could lose my job."*

*"Are our offers not enticing enough for you? You know Adlar, we have four subject matter experts working with us who are employed strictly because they were experts in crime. Prisons are overcrowded and*

*forgiveness isn't handed out easily these days, but these four people were somehow so good at breaking the law that we saw more use in keeping them with us rather than locked away. You could be number five, and if you pass on that, you're going to sit in a cell someday and regret that decision. No one gets a free pass like that in life after doing the things you've done."*

*"I haven't done anything."*

*Lawrence stepped forward. "Maybe not, but you're knee deep in it and when you turn your head to a crime, that's just as good as committing it. In due time, Stone Enterprises will be thoroughly combed and every employee with their hand in the cookie jar will be serving time. That includes you. This moment in time, standing here with me now, is your best shot for any kind of future. So tell me why you still show your face there every day and hide from me."*

*Adlar let the words sink in but refused to believe that the things he was a part of and his role in the company could ever allow him to be punished. He couldn't understand how big the whole ordeal was. What he knew about Stone Enterprises was very little—some books that were cooked and some secret files that were only gibberish to him anyway. There was no way he could pay for having taken a peak.*

*"I just think you guys are wrong," Adlar said. "I really can't find anything. You keep threatening me and I don't know what to do because I don't think they did anything illegal."*

*"And you know what Adlar? If you played dumb in a courtroom, you would probably sell it, but I have a trick or two up my sleeve, and I'm going to be visiting you very soon and I'm going to ask you whether or not you regretted your decision and you're going to tell me you can provide me with more and try to cut a new deal with me, and you know what I'm going to say? I'm going to tell you I have everything I need and hand you off to be someone else's problem. Decide here and now if you want to be a rat on a sinking ship, or my own personal hero."*

*Adlar walked back to the building shortly after, as if searching for a reason to hate Victor. He needed an easy choice, but other than the likes of a few of Victor's associates who would never like Adlar, people were starting to be nice to him. The cute receptionist kept smiling at him when he entered and exited for the day, a few of the chummier guys were high fiving and fist bumping him. He was finding a rhythm. Not only would he hate to see it go, but to undo all the progress he'd made would have been tragic. The days of blackmail were long behind him. If Victor had wanted him gone, he would have been gone, but that didn't seem to be the case anymore.*

*There was still only one course of action remaining, and it would take a bold move on his part. He walked into Victor's office and asked for time with the man. Victor studied his face and saw the weight of the world on his shoulders, and invited him in.*

*"What can I do for you Adlar?" Victor asked.*

*Adlar liked that he was now Adlar…not just Wilcox like it had been in the beginning.*

*"I need to know about my future here," Adlar said. "I need to know if I'm going to be able to move to this floor and if Cory is ever going to stop bugging me. I just want to know if I'm still here because I matter or if it's cause of…" he faltered, "…how I made you guys hire me."*

*Victor nodded slowly and contemplated. "You make your way Adlar."*

*"I don't know what that means."*

*"A lot of people were impressed with the font idea, but to me, that's just a computer geek who knows a few things. You can't ask me what you're going to be. You have to decide what your story is."*

*"I don't know."*

*"Do you still play interactive video games?"*

*Adlar nodded.*

*"When you start a new game, do you build an avatar?"*

*"Yeah."*

*"What does it look like?"*

*Adlar fell silent.*

*"Is your avatar exactly like you, or do you give him sharp clothes, some muscle, a hairstyle that you wish you had?"*

*"I kinda do that."*

*"That's a nice deal, isn't it?" Victor asked. "Every time you start a new game, you get to make decisions about, literally, who you get to be. You package yourself, pick a look, a name, state your status, not unlike a storyteller creating a character or a publicist positioning a client."*

*"I guess."*

*"The personality eventually becomes the persona Adlar. You package yourself however you want, and at the end of the day, if you're valuable to me, you have a place. If you're not, you don't. But you're not valuable because you come into my office and ask me if you are. You're valuable if you're worth more than the trouble you put me through."*

*"I was visited by that agent," Adlar said. "I refused to give him anything. He still thinks he's going to get you."*

*"He needs you or someone like you to do it."*

*"So you're not worried?"*

*"Not at all. Few people could give him what he's looking for."*

*"He wants to take me down too…for refusing."*

*"Do what you need to do, but you understand he's trying to scare you so he gets what he wants, right? If he didn't need you, he wouldn't be coming to you."*

*"Yeah, I figured."*

*"Let me give you some advice. If you want to do well here and if you want to make a big decision like this, play to your strengths. An independent hacker is theoretically capable of creating a degree of chaos, but I suspect you are who you are because you've been bored by life. Boredom usually welcomes evidence for the presence of thought and reflection, but for you, being civil is rarely fun. It requires patience, forethought, and some willingness to tolerate tedium. For overstimulated people, civility feels like submission, but you need to do yourself a favor Adlar, and the sooner you do it, the sooner you'll find your place in this world."*

*Adlar leaned in as if hypnotized by Victor giving him advice and even before the advice came, his mind was made up and he knew where he belonged.*

*"A computer can only manage things that can be expressed in binary code," Victor continued. "It can play music, but it can't write it or explain its beauty. It can store poetry, but it can't explain its meaning. It can allow you to search every book imaginable, yet it can't distinguish between good and bad grammar. It's superb at what it can do, but it excludes a great deal of what the human mind is capable of. It's a powerful and seductive tool, but it operates using a logic that lacks other, more complex, elements of reason. It focuses ruthlessly on things that can be represented in numbers, but it also seduces people into thinking that other aspects of knowledge are either unreal or unimportant. There are things you won't find sitting behind your keyboard Adlar."*

*Victor raised his eyebrows as if to tell Adlar it was time to leave, and Adlar left, but not before destroying every last piece of evidence he'd collected against Victor...*

...He had a firm grip on the trigger, but his mind wouldn't allow him to squeeze the trigger.

"You don't have to do this," Dawn said, her eyes wet with tears. "I'm not going to say anything."

"I already know you will," Adlar said.

"You're not really like this. I know we fought, but I always knew the real you was good."

"No I'm not," Adlar said. "It's like with games. You never liked that I played them, but one time my dad got me this game because he thought we'd both like it and it was a city and you had to build stuff and take care of the people like you're the mayor. And he played it and was really good but when I played it, they always shut the city down. That's dumb because I don't know how you shut a city down, but it always happened."

"It went bankrupt."

"Yeah, something like that. And I played the game a bunch and every time, same thing."

"I don't get what you're saying," Dawn said.

"That was a game where you had to take care of people. My dad one time saw me buy a shooter game and I beat it in hours. It was all blowing things up and killing people. You know what he said? He said now he understood why I wasn't good at the city game. I know how to destroy but not how to build."

"That's not a good reason to kill people."

"When I killed the guy's wife, it reminded me of a game. It was point and shoot. I think I forgot it was even real while I was doing it because I did the same thing so many times and it was so easy."

"So you're desensitized. That's why you have to snap out of this and start doing better things."

"Maybe, but now it's too late. But I liked it too Dawn. I felt all this adrenaline and it was like being alive on another level. People do the same things every day and then they die, and then it's nothing forever. I did something big. I did something that changed something."

"No, Adlar," Dawn said, starting to bawl again. "Anyone can destroy. That's why those games are easy. You just fire weapons and throw grenades, but doing good things is harder because most people destroy. What if you saved a life or made someone's life better? Would that move you at all?"

"I can't even stop the town from going bankrupt."

"Adlar," Dawn said, shaking her head in disbelief. "That's just a game. You can reset it and start again. In real life, you can't do that. If you kill me, you're going to live with that. Maybe not right away, but someday you will wish you'd made better choices. And if you're incapable of feeling regret, then you need to just turn the gun on yourself, because if you don't have a soul, then you need to put yourself out of your misery before you really start hurting people."

Adlar blinked rapidly and considered. He had no plans to kill himself, but wondered if he really had a soul and if this moment would be something he'd always reflect on.

He lowered the gun and stared at Dawn, searching for a reason not to kill her. Alive, she could put an end to Adlar, and as he stared at her wet face, he realized he felt nothing. He didn't even really like her all that much.

"I have a soul," he said. "I might regret this, but I can't go to jail. I'm not glad this all happened. I don't want to do this, but I have to Dawn. I could have done it so you never knew, but I'm here face to face so you know why."

"I didn't need to know why," she said, a pause between words as she gasped in horror. "This is the worst. You should have done it so I never knew. You're a monster. I wish I never met you. Just." Gasp. "Do." Gasp. "It."

Adlar raised his gun and tried to find something to say, but she'd already given up and was facing down, waiting for the end to come at any moment. If they started talking again, there may not be a better time. "I'm sorry Dawn," he said and closed his eyes.

4

Dent wasn't happy Donovan was back in his life, though he still preferred the Donovan who kissed his ass over the one who wanted to kill him or throw him in the hotbox. He was even less thrilled that Victor's will had resurfaced as a topic of conversation. After Dent's escape attempt, he'd given up all hope of ever getting out of Kern, and even if he were to, he had no desire to live a life on the run. Now he had the backing of a man who actually could help him get out and was forced back into the will's vortex.

As if by coincidence, that was the day Wayne approached again. His old cellmate had kept a distance ever since their near escape. Wayne had spent two weeks in the hotbox, which wasn't enough in Christian's opinion. Wayne had ruined the whole plan and killed Ziggy in the process. Dent's best hope was to one day earn early release for good behavior. If not for that fact, he would have stuck a fork through Wayne's head six months ago. Instead, Wayne would turn direction every time he saw Dent.

"Donovan's asking for a confession," Wayne said out of the blue, as if there was no bad blood between them.

"Get the fuck out of my face," Dent said and stepped toward the man. Up close, he wasn't sure he'd have the self-control.

"I will, but I need to know why he's coming after me now. What'd you say to him?"

"I don't talk to the guards."

"I was looking at another 8 years tops Dent. I only went along cause I didn't have a choice. And what happened to Ziggy..that was self-defense. But after shit went down and the warden was too busy trying to cover up the fuss they threw when they thought you were gone, we took what they gave us. Weeks in the hotbox, no privileges. But I've done what they asked and I've been good, so I need to know what Donovan is after."

Then Dent did something he wouldn't have expected of himself, but knew it would get under Wayne's skin if he knew the truth. "Outside these walls, I'm worth a lot of money," Dent said. "I'm not talking millions. I'm talking hundreds of millions. Maybe more. Donovan learned that fact and has gotten soft on me. He's probably coming down on you to take the alleged escape off my file."

Wayne was speechless.

"Now go away," Dent said. "I'm not doing you any favors."

"You owe me everything," Wayne said. "You dragged me along to something I didn't want to be a part of. You've added at least a decade to my sentence. I wasn't ready yet."

Wayne continued to take his stand, but Christian walked away. He had plenty of plates to spin and the last thing he needed was Wayne in his business. Opportunities were surfacing constantly though. Too many to ignore. If Wayne was going to take the wrap for the escape attempt and Ziggy's death, Dent was in the clear. He'd have the full cooperation of Donovan at his disposal and could be looking at an early release. Just as he'd thrown in the towel, it seemed the world was throwing it back at him, letting him know that he wasn't yet a man lost.

"You having a problem with Wayne?" Donovan asked him later, as he stood in his cell.

"You watching me now?" Dent asked.

"I am. I wanted you to see just what can be accomplished with me on your side."

"Alright," Dent said, hopping down from his bunk and standing face to face with Donovan. Donovan didn't flinch and Dent hated that. "Play this out then. You think there's money waiting for me outside. How do you manage to get me out of here?"

"I get you access to any job you want here and I turn my head when you tell me to."

"And what makes you think I won't just up and leave and never see you again?"

"Did you know that some of those other people on the list have been trying to kill each other?" Donovan said. "You're safer in here than anywhere else. They're going to get the job done while you're locked up, and then I'm going to get you out. You're not jumping a wall or digging a tunnel Dent. You're laying low while they knock each other off, and while that happens, you've got my protection and the protection of all the guards. You'll have full privileges and your enemies will be my enemies. As to whether or not I'd trust you when you collected…I want to say no but I think you just might be a man of your word. Don't think we won't be drawing up a contract though and don't think you'll be walking into that bank without me by your side."

"If I'm a free man, I don't have to do anything with you."

"That's why I'll make sure you're not a free man until I've been paid. You see Dent, for us to have a win-win here, we both need to do each other a favor. You think the sequence of events means freedom then money. Here's the hard truth: It's money, then freedom."

"And you and I sit here and rot while we wait for the deaths of the remaining. How many are left?"

"I don't know the full list, but I have an ace up my sleeve. We'll be splitting the money three ways when all is said and done."

"Who's the ace?"

"A man who isn't listed but knows of the will's existence. He allegedly has, get this: Wired an explosive device inside one of the others. He was working through the list but was arrested for kidnapping and attempted murder but he's set for release in two months because we're overcrowded and I have leverage. He's our insider and his record is twisted, but he's our fall-guy. I get him out of here with your promise of wealth and we let him finish what he started. Every death will be on him and you won't have to worry about getting caught doing anything illegal. You see Dent, I can get you out of here a free man. You wouldn't be on the run and you'd have everything you needed to retire. I would too. Our fall-guy does in the remaining on the list and you and I work together to get out of this place."

"Does he know we exist?"

"Not yet, but he's being transferred to Kern tomorrow and he'll be your new cell-mate until his release. His name is Stanley Kline. You're going to cozy up with him and see to it that he finishes the job for us. Gain his trust, promise him a cut. I'll promise him protection. When he's free, he'll finish the job. Who gives a shit if he's caught or not? If he is, we take the inheritance and run. If he's not, we give him a cut. I'm sure you'll agree that there's too much money to complain about a third guy."

Dent considered. "If I don't do this?"

"My plan is perfect Dent. There's no possible way we can betray each other. If you don't want to go through with it, then I guess we go back to what we had yesterday, and we're trapped here forever."

Dent said nothing and Donovan couldn't read his face, so he offered a gesture instead. He reached his hand out. Dent looked over his shoulders. If another con saw him shaking a guard's hand, his life would be hell, even with Donovan's protection. The cell-block was quiet and they were surrounded by dark—exactly the environment Dent preferred to deal in.

"I'll think about it," he said.

5

The gun didn't fire. Adlar opened his eyes to see why and discovered he hadn't really squeezed the trigger. He'd intended to. He believed his mind was made up, but his hand disagreed and stayed suspended in air, his finger frozen.

He found Dawn's face and her lip was quivering. He'd never seen someone so afraid. "I caused this," Adlar said to himself.

Dawn opened one eye slowly but held the other closed. She appeared surprised to be alive, but saw the conflict in Adlar. It was the one ray of hope she needed. She was suddenly standing tall and held her hand out. "Please just let me go. I won't tell anyone."

"I think I have to kill myself," Adlar said.

"No…"

"I don't think I'll be able to get away with all this. I can't go to jail."

"Just walk away and start over then," Dawn said.

Adlar frowned. She'd made it sound so simple, but it wasn't. "I'm going to have two people who will want me dead," Adlar said. "Probably more. I don't know. I've just pretty much pissed off people."

"Then stop."

"Easy for you to say."

"Okay look, I get it. You've probably done a lot and that kind of stuff is going to probably make you feel guilty, but that's a good thing, because if you're feeling guilty, that means there's good in you. You just have been on a bad path for a long time Adlar. That's all. Just turn back."

"I can't."

"Yes you can. You just fix your mistakes. And the stuff you can't fix, you compensate for. At the end of your life, you're going to have done some good things and some bad things, and some of those bad things might be really bad, but what will matter is what you're doing tomorrow. Not yesterday. Don't be a monster just because you think you're a monster. If you want to be good, then go be good."

"I don't know how."

"Start by fixing your mistakes. Go apologize to people or serve time or whatever it takes to balance you out."

"I can't be balanced out. Some things are too big…"

"Adlar…in a thousand years, no one will know anyone in this neighborhood existed or anything any of us did. Stop thinking you changed history. You're just a guy and you're not as awful as you think. You just made some mistakes. Clearly doing what you've been doing hasn't been good for you and you know that. So go fix your ways. I'm not going to tell anyone that you were here. I'm not angry with you. But you're scared Adlar, and if you kill me and if you go kill other people, that fear and guilt is only going to grow inside."

Adlar realized the gun was at his side. A few minutes ago, it felt so powerful in his hand. Now, it felt like a burden. "I wouldn't know where to start," he muttered. He felt a buzz in his pocket and checked his phone to find he'd received multiple texts from Manny asking if it was done yet, followed by texts that asked why he wasn't responding, and finally, a text that read as a very bad ending to a very bad day.

**Fine. I'll do it myself.**

Adlar closed his eyes and fought back tears. His world was closing in and he had nowhere left to go. He couldn't run or hide. He couldn't be arrested. He couldn't face Manny. He forced himself to consider Dawn's words: To fix what he broke and to do the right thing. He thought backwards: Manny going to kill Charlie…Charlie in the hospital…Adlar blew his house up while he was inside…Adlar ruined Charlie's life and now, because of Adlar, Charlie was about to lose his life.

Fix what he broke…

Adlar took a deep breath and closed his eyes at a realization that he couldn't believe had come into his brain. "I have to save Charlie…"

*…the receptionist at Stone Enterprises had her eyes on Adlar a second after he walked through the door. She pulled him to the side to chat and though she tried to make it seem unplanned, the whole conversation was contrived. If Adlar were capable of recognizing flirting, he might have been smoother, but instead, he acted put out and tried to pass her to get to the elevators.*

*"You just don't have any idea what a difference the font makes," she said. "Can you believe you can look at something every day and not even realize how much one little change can make such a big difference? It's easier to read and saves money. And all this time, no one thought to do it until you came along."*

*"I guess…" Adlar said.*

*He started to move around her again but the the lobby was suddenly filled with agents swarming through the front doors and flashing warrants at the proper authorities. Adlar turned and grew numb at the sight of the DII agents led by Lawrence, who had a large smile on his face upon seeing Adlar.*

*Adlar tried to hurry to the elevator, but Lawrence caught up with him and grabbed his arm. "Where you going Wilcox?"*

*"If I'm not under arrest, you can't touch me like that."*

Lawrence let go of his arm. "*Of course you're not under arrest. You're with us, right?*"

"*Yeah...*" Adlar said, but knew the comment was mocking him. The agents had begun to ascend the stairs and were hitting the elevator buttons. It didn't make sense. Adlar hadn't given them anything.

"*I'm glad to hear it. Come with me then.*"

Adlar followed as if he had no choice, but started wondering if he had the option to run—to escape from the crossfire. In the moment, there were too many things to be afraid of and it all hit him at once. He could be arrested, Victor could be arrested, Victor could see him standing with Lawrence...

That was when he realized what Lawrence was up to. He tried to turn back, but Lawrence had him by the arm again and pulled him up the stairs forcefully. "*We couldn't keep waiting on you Wilcox, so I attained what I needed without you. The problem with playing for both teams is that at some point in time, you have to make a choice. You see, I wear a DII badge and that makes me an agent. Bad guys fear me. Good guys work with me. I know my team and I know my enemies and that means I'll never have to betray or disappoint. I wear my badge on the outside son. Now you...you're a different cut of meat. You're with us...you're with Victor...but you can't be with both, because you can't stall forever and eventually, you're going to have some explaining to do. I'm going to make it easy for you with the DII. I'm not going to charge you with a damn thing, and the offer to work with us is off the table. After today, it will be as if we never met. So there you go kid. I'm letting you off the hook.*"

"*What about Victor?*" Adlar asked, trying to pull away from the agent's grasp.

"*I can't speak for Victor. My side let you off the hook. I don't play for his team.*"

They reached the seventh floor landing and only a door stood between Adlar and a room filled with agents arresting a quarter of Victor's staff and reading them their rights.

"*Please don't,*" Adlar said.

"*Too late for favors. I warned you this was time-sensitive. You thought you could play me. That's what gets me the most. I don't care that you wanted to be on their side, but that you thought I was so dumb that I didn't know what you were doing.*"

"*Just let me go home.*"

"*You'll have nowhere else to go after we're done here.*"

Suddenly, Adlar was shoved through the door, and the timing was spot on. He stumbled to a stop and looked up to find the likes of Cory Owens,

*Jones Mitchell, Bernard Bell, and Victor Stone, all being led out in handcuffs. Cory and Jones were pitching a fit, but Bernard and Victor went quietly…as if they had every confidence they'd be back to work by the end of the day.*

*Adlar tried to divert his eyes, but it was too late. Victor looked directly at him, then to his side where Lawrence stood proudly, and back to Adlar. Victor looked like he was grinding his teeth and suppressing the urge to lunge toward Adlar. Instead, he held himself together and was cooperative with the agents. Victor was wise enough to see the process move smoothly, but Adlar would hear about this later. Or maybe he wouldn't, as Lawrence had stated: He'd have nowhere to go but home. It was pointless for Adlar to even go to his sixth floor office. As far as he could tell, when the arrest was over, he was free to leave, but then what? Back to gaming? The thought actually sounded good. Adlar had cornered himself in a world he should have never been a part of. He was lucky things played out the way they did, and if he walked away now, he knew it was possible he'd never see the likes of Lawrence, the DII, Stone Enterprises, or Victor ever again.*

*As if reading his mind, Lawrence entered the elevator with Victor and his crew, gave Adlar a nod, and the doors closed.*

*He'd lost a large opportunity and his cozy position all in one day. He'd lost all the respect he'd gained and he could never cross paths with Victor again; unless one day, Victor came after him. He knew Victor was vengeful…that he'd never be forgiven. He knew this wasn't over…*

…Charlie Palmer was safe for now. All reports put him in surgery, and though Manny was good, he wouldn't be able to get to Charlie while the whole staff of Banner was checking in to see how Charlie was. Adlar realized that it would be some time before Manny could get to Charlie. If Charlie lived, he would point the police in Adlar's direction. If he died, the Palmers would haunt him forever. There was no winning scenario, but Adlar preferred to see Charlie live. He knew it was the more difficult path, but it was simply time to pick a side. Adlar had looked out for himself for most of his life, and it had only gotten him in trouble. Going against Manny was scary and would probably be the death of him, but Adlar felt revived.

He left Dawn with only the hope that she'd let him go without a word. Adlar knew his days were limited but before it all came tumbling down on him, he had to fix his mistakes—or get as close as possible to fixing them.

With Charlie tucked safely away, that left Manny to deal with. When Adlar arrived at Manny's home, the lights were off and Manny's car gone. Could he really have gone after Charlie after-all? He dismissed the notion. Manny was too meticulous to try. Adlar tried his key in the back door, half expecting the locks to have been changed but Manny didn't have the time. Adlar knew Manny would be angry, but wondered if he'd still take Adlar back under his wing if he asked. There was a time not long ago that Adlar would have begged for another chance, but that road no longer had appeal. Adlar had looked up to Manny like a father, but Manny would have abandoned him in a heartbeat. Adlar had looked up to Toby and received the same treatment. It seemed he was drawn to criminals. For the first time in a while, he missed his real father. He tried to remember why he'd always hated him but he couldn't come up with a reason. In fact, Gary Wilcox had always been pretty accepting, a good provider, nice to his mother...

"I'm the problem," Adlar said to himself. He'd realized it to be true when he almost ended Dawn's life, but as he inventoried the people and events in his life, they all had one thing in common: Adlar was bitter toward every one of them. Now, none of it seemed bad at all. His father, mother, the kids at school, Dawn, his cousins and grandparents and everyone he'd ever shunned...they seemed to have the formula in life. They were content. They chased happiness. Adlar chased misery.

As these thoughts settled inside him, his guilt for the things he'd done increased. He'd killed people. For the first time, he couldn't believe it was really him who'd carried out the deed. He'd helped Manny kill people for money.

Adlar grew nauseous and bent over to throw up, but only coughed.

When he recovered, he set out to work, starting his computer, then Manny's, sending file after file of evidence of Manny's moonlighting work to a secure storage site. He also sent copies to his email and built a folder which would be released all over the Web if he didn't sign in for over twenty-four hours straight. That would at least prevent his own death and if Manny were crazy enough to kill him anyway, at least Adlar would take him down in the process.

He was about to break into Manny's closet for physical files when he heard a voice behind him. "What do you think you're doing?"

He turned to find Manny standing there with a gun in hand, pointed at his head. He hadn't even heard him come home. He froze and his body weakened upon staring at the barrel end of a gun.

"You can't shoot me," Adlar said. "I have all your secrets in the cloud and if I die, they'll be released."

"Bullshit."

"You know I would do that," Adlar said.

"Why are you forcing me to do this?" Manny asked.

"You don't have to do anything."

"Palmer's going to pull through. He's going to say your name. You're going to say mine."

"No, I'm not. Just let me go."

"You'll be in jail and I can't bank on your silence. Especially given your history."

"You don't have a choice anyway," Adlar said. "I told you: If I die, you're going to be caught too."

"Sign into your computer and undo what you've done."

"No."

Manny released the safety and held the gun high, a squeeze away from a gunshot. "I'll do whatever it takes. I know you won't be able to withstand much pain, but that's what it will come to. You're not going anywhere until you've cut all ties to my name."

"Alright," Adlar said, his hand creeping toward his own gun, which was stuffed in the back of his jeans. He wondered if this was it. In the end, it would be Adlar and Manny in a shootout. Manny would surely beat him, but Adlar had only one thing in his favor, which was the element of surprise. He waited for Manny to divert his eyes and let his guard down in some way. He sat at the keyboard and began typing, but he only went through the motions. His mind was on how he could quick draw at an opportune time. With his back to Manny, he assumed the gun was lowered, but still in his hand. One thing Adlar knew was that he would not remove Manny's work from the cloud. He knew this was the end of the line for him, but it wasn't all going to be for nothing. It was a relief really. He no longer had to run or hide or worry about Charlie coming after him or the look in Charlie's eyes when he finally confronted the boy who took everything from him. It was the end of the line for certain and the only thing left that mattered was that Manny go with him.

He typed slower, with only one hand on the keyboard. He still typed faster than most, even with one hand, so Manny didn't notice. He also didn't notice that Adlar had been rewriting the script on the computer's solitaire file. It all looked the same when you broke it down to binary. To Manny, Adlar was just repairing what he broke—but instead was buying time so he could mentally prepare. He wouldn't be able to buy very much before Manny grew suspicious.

He quickly mapped the property in his mind. He wasn't going to run for the street. He was planning a move for the back door. He'd run into the woods behind the house where he could hide in the shadows and move up-river until he felt safe. There would be at least one gunshot— probably more. He thought it all through and when the plan was in place, all that was left was to take a shot. A surge of adrenaline shot through him and he felt more alive than he ever had.

He was ready.

With a swipe of his foot, he hit the power button on the surge protector and everything shut off. "Damnit," he said, for effect.

"You did that on purpose," Manny said. "Plug it in. Start over. I've got plenty of time. But if it happens again, I'm going to start cutting you."

Adlar crawled under the desk and hit the power source. As he backed out, he had the gun in hand, his body blocking Manny's view.

He took one last breath.

He turned and aimed.

He was relieved to see the gun was at Manny's side. He had plenty of time to beat the shot. Where the shot landed was crucial, but in his position and under pressure, Adlar wasn't sure he'd have the focus he needed. Still, he pulled the trigger without much thought and the next thing he knew, an explosion sounded from the gun and tore a hole in Manny's shoulder. It wasn't where he'd wanted to hit, but it caused Manny to drop the gun. Adlar fired twice more, but both shots hit the wall. Adlar didn't stick around to try again. He slid the back door open and ran for the woods.

Within moments, he passed the tree-line and safely ran deeper in, his heart pounding with every step.

He heard shouting in the distance and stopped to hear the voice. Manny was somewhere off to the left, angrily yelling his name.

*Damnit. He's alive.*

Adlar stayed in the shadows, trying to stay low and move as far away as possible. He went deeper into the woods toward the sound of the river in the distance. He wanted to hide near the riverbank and work his way upstream in one direction. Manny would eventually need medical attention. He just needed to buy time.

He felt movement in his pocket and pulled out his cell. It was Manny calling. For a moment, he considered ignoring it, and then realized *why not?*

"Yeah," he said, upon answering it.

"Where are you?" Manny asked. It was just like Manny—direct and demanding.

"You were going to kill me."

"I never said that," Manny said. "We're both in a river of shit right now. You shot me Wilcox. You've got leverage. Okay, I get it. You want to see this through. It's not too late. We just need to talk."

"No. I'm not dumb."

"You're dumb if you run. Tomorrow, every cop in the county will be after you. This all goes away if Charlie doesn't wake up. I can make that happen and I'll finish the list. Let's just finish what we started and walk away."

"I know you won't do that," Adlar said.

"You don't know anything."

"I know you're obsessed with the debt…with making someone fill Bedbug's shoes. But he's dead, and no one wants to, and it was all an accident, so you just need to drop it."

"Son, the reason we're not animals is because we live by rules. I've simply been following a contract that I promised I'd honor when I started. Bedbug served a purpose and when Bedbug died, someone needed to fill his shoes to restore balance."

"What about all the people you killed? Should you be filling in for them?"

Manny laughed. "You got me kid…you got me."

Suddenly, a shot rang out…much closer than Adlar expected. He heard the bullet zing past his face. More bullets began flying and as Adlar realized he'd been spotted, he instinctively ran downhill, letting his feet get ahead of his body at a decline he knew he couldn't keep up with. Suddenly he was rolling, shoulder over shoulder, branches and leaves stabbing his body as he barreled toward the river. At some point, he'd been hit by a bullet, but he wasn't sure where. He felt the sticky wetness of his blood all over his shirt as he continued to turn on his way down the hill. Finally, he was careening for the river, but as he fell, he managed to grasp some roots and hold himself against the riverbank. His gun and his phone were long gone. All that was left was Adlar Wilcox, stuck to the wall of an incline, half a tree hiding him in the dark.

A minute later, Manny stood far to the right, staring down into the river. He doubled back, covered some ground, but kept coming back to the river.

Adlar closed his eyes and kept his breathing steady. Manny knew he shot Adlar. He knew he'd rolled down the hill. He wasn't shouting to get his attention. Instead, Manny mostly stood looking downstream.

*He thinks I'm dead.*

Adlar prayed to himself as a last ray of hope filled him. He stayed positioned under the roots for hours before working his way upstream, far away from Manny. By now, Manny had surely gone to the hospital or started tending his own wounds. Adlar had taken a shot that had only grazed his skin a little, and a bit of the flesh underneath. He still had the evidence he needed to bring Manny down, but had nothing to his name. No clothes, tech equipment, not a dollar. To Manny, he'd be assumed dead. To the rest of the world, he was off the radar. He'd been here before, but never with the mentality he had now.

*I'm one of the good guys now but my days are numbered,* he thought. *Charlie will wake up. Everyone will want me arrested or dead. It will happen eventually. Before it does, I have to kill Manny.*

He fell asleep on the riverbank, the flow of the water calming him.

# Chapter 5

## 1

*Twenty years ago, Christian Dent believed himself to be invincible. Sitting on the shores of Miami with all the protection a man could possibly have, he was unstoppable. He had layers upon layers of protection. If someone wanted to take him down, they would barely be able to penetrate the layer of men who knew men who knew men, who worked for Dent. He'd partnered up with Mitch long ago and having been a part of the operation since he was a small boy, he was young, strong, and knowledgeable. He was the perfectly qualified drug-runner, who stood atop the pyramid and oversaw everything, with only Mitch at his side.*

*They lived in a mansion placed on a hillside, a stone's throw away from the shore. The house was owned by a man named Hector Valdez, who was a day-trader who'd invested in computers right before the World Wide Web took off. Hector leased his mansion out to Timothy Dyer, who was the on-line presence of Mitch's crew. The locals and the police in the area likely knew what was going on in their fortress, but no one asked questions. It was assumed that all their paperwork would be in order and they'd all have solid stories. Besides that, half the Miami police were on the take. What Mitch had was a strong impenetrable operation, and Dent was his right hand man.*

*In that time period, Dent took the name Chris Benjamin and the boy who had been taken from his home as a child was no longer present in him. He'd been hardened by the life he led. Every day, he'd been consumed by drugs, women, and money. He'd stood in when deals went south and he'd seen men gunned down, others who had their throats cut. Some were still teenagers. Most were scared and in over their heads. His crew didn't discriminate in business. The only thing that existed was honor. If the bags were a little light or if they were watered down with a cheaper quality to substitute a fraction of the load, the deal was off, and no one walked away from a bad deal.*

*Dent had seen it all, but had participated in very little. The last he'd checked, he was still a cold case. To look up his name was to find he was still the victim. Kidnapped and never returned—presumably dead. He'd grown fearless, violent, and self-destructive, but above all, Dent was smart. He was the eyes of the operation and was the voice of concern when he suspected someone was trying to swindle them. He owned that role. He embraced it. And when Mitch told him he was no longer coming along on pickups, it sent him into a rage.*

*"It's getting dangerous," Mitch had said, though Dent couldn't be deterred.*

*"For me and everyone else. You're not cutting me out."*

*"Your cut will be the same as it's always been. You're just not coming along anymore."*

*"Why not?"*

*"The feds are getting smarter. So is the competition. And everything's going digital, which is bad news for us. Used to be trade secrets were easy to keep. Nowadays, people are connected and even criminals are able to access anything they want."*

*"We've had no problems yet. We need to keep doing what we've been doing."*

*"That's not good enough anymore," Mitch said. "A habit, good or bad, is just the brain's way of conserving energy. It would require too much energy to think about which hand to use every time you answer the phone. But in business, where innovative thinking is necessary, you have to learn to move beyond habit. Everyone else is one step behind us now, but they know it, and they're going to find an way to surpass us down one day."*

*"What's that got to do with me?"*

*"I need you around if things go south for me. You're the grandmaster."*

*Dent hated when Mitch called him that. They had been playing chess about a year before and Mitch had told him that on the surface, it appeared that each player has about twenty potential opening moves, but they in fact had many fewer because most of these moves are so bad that they quickly lead to defeat. The better you are at chess, the more clearly you see your options, and the fewer moves there actually are available.*

*The better the player, the more predictable the moves. The grandmaster plays with absolute predictable precision—until that one brilliant, unexpected stroke comes along. Dent was their ace, which meant people would try to outmaneuver him, and someday, someone would if he wasn't careful.*

*"Not me," Dent said. "You taught me everything. You built all this. You're the guy."*

*"That's what I'm worried about. My name is known. I'm on their wanted lists. There's a hundred guys who would put a bullet in me if they ever recognized my face."*

*"What and you think I want that?"*

*"No, I want you to cut and run when I'm gone. They're closing in on me. Trust me...some things are just inevitable. I've got lung cancer eating me inside. Doctors give me new drugs but the bacteria develops resistance. You can't stop the inevitable. You beat it for a little while, until it finds a new way to come back at you. I've been reading about that karma shit Chris. It's all real and it's all catching up with me. Doesn't matter how smart you are cause if you keep sinning like we have, someday you'll pay, and I'm not talking about the feds or our competition. I'm talking about the universe saying enough is enough."*

*Marlena Fitzgerald was a beautiful Latina woman who fell for Dent with an hour of meeting him. They'd been at an outdoor pool party and waded too close to each other in the water. Their eyes locked and without having to say a word, they came together in the center of the pool and Marlena put an arm around Dent's neck and looked into his eyes. Half an hour later, they were in her suite and he was inside her.*

*They'd been seeing each other four months and the relationship hadn't gotten past the infatuation stage. They spent their nights dancing, drinking, and making love. Marlena asked no questions about Dent's empire and it didn't bother her when other women would try to pick him up. Sometimes he'd even leave with them and he'd turn back to see Marlena just smoking a cigarette and staring peacefully in the distance without a care in the world.*

*It was all platonic until the day Marlena told Dent she wanted to move out west.*

*"Why?" Dent asked.*

*"Because there's opportunity."*

*"What? You don't have enough here? You have everything you could possibly want. You go out there and you're going to have to find a job. You won't be in the movies Marlena. You'll be a waitress."*

*"So you don't believe in me?"*

*"It's not easy like you think. You're hearing success stories, but for everyone who took a chance and succeeded, a thousand failed. Don't be naive."*

*"What's it to you if I stay or go?"*

*"Nothing. I don't care. But you're stupid. You're pretty, but you're not that special. You're not going to light the world on fire."*

*Marlena shook her head in disbelief, bundled up her clothes in her arms, and disappeared through the door. Dent knew she wasn't going to leave. She'd told Dent she was leaving in the hopes he'd offer to come along, or finance her dreams, or use his influence with other important people on the west coast. He wasn't going to give her that luxury. He meant what he said too. Marlena was good-looking but she was also past her prime and the constant drug usage had worn down her features enough to be noticeable.*

*He fell back into bed and lit a joint, staring at the ceiling as smoke swirled above. He thought about Mitch and what he'd said. If everything ever fell apart, Dent wasn't sure what he'd do. He had an emergency backup plan which was just a yacht filled with money, a week's worth of food, and a fake ID. If shit ever hit the fan, his plan had always been for he and Mitch to sail off into the sunset and land on an island to live the rest of their days. He'd never considered life without Mitch in the picture, but something had put the scare into Mitch and though in the past, he'd tried to talk Dent into going home, this time, something had been different…*

…The man who'd entered Dent's cell that morning was bigger than Dent expected and he looked mean. If Donovan had been telling the truth, Stanley Kline really could be a man who, on the outside, could eliminate the list. He looked like a killer. He felt like a killer. Something in his eyes told Dent that Stan wasn't completely there. His body was, but someone else was steering. It would be harder for Dent to explain that he had no interest in any plan set forth by Donovan…that Dent was only going to be working alone from now on because it was other people—people he was forced to depend on—that fucked everything up all the time.

When the other guards left, only Donovan stayed behind and stood in the cell as if the three of them were old college buddies. Maybe that was his hopes. The scene was out of place behind the walls of Kern. Donovan had once been a bully who attacked unprovoked and buried convicts because they looked at him wrong. Now, he seemed like an eager puppy, dying to be included in the group. Dent hated him more than ever and wanted nothing more than to stick a fork in his neck.

"Christian Dent, meet Stanley Kline. You boys will be spending some time together so I don't want any trouble between you. You hear me on that?"

He was giving his usual speech for effect, but it sounded fabricated in tone and under it all, his eyes were darting between them as if there was a mutual understanding in where their interests really were. Judging by the look on Stanley's face, he already knew why he was there and was in.

When Donovan realized no important conversations were going to happen in his presence, he left them there, but Dent still had nothing to say and Stan approached the topic lightly. "The guard said he told you about me," Stan said.

"I know who you are," Dent said. "I don't know why you're here."

"I worked for Victor Stone a long time ago. I know his will is real and I know most of the people on it. You're one of them."

"And I'm spending the rest of my life in a place where money counts for nothing."

"The guard said he'd see to it that you were released at parole-time and I've only got two months left."

"I told Donovan that I'm not interested in the money, and between us, you don't want to be in bed with the guards around here. Especially that one."

"You tried getting out of here," Stan said. "Heard all about it and I thought to myself that you're brilliant. I'm the same way brother. You know why I'm in here? I put an explosive device inside one of the others. My plan was kill them all in one place and it would have worked, but something just got in the way. But the bomb's still there. Before, my problem was finding someone who'd team up with me. Well, you're here Dent and you're probably safer than everyone, especially if the guards are protecting you. When I'm free, I'll take care of everything for you. You'd have to do nothing brother. Just sit and wait and be generous when you're given all the money. I wouldn't even be greedy. I just want out of here. So does the guard. So they get you your freedom and more money than you ever need and you split that with your partners. I can't think of a better fairer deal."

"In theory," Dent said. "But you can't trust them here. Everywhere are people who can get us what we want if they want something from us, but no one gets what they want because most of what you're being offered is bullshit. Donovan wanted me dead one moment. Then, he has something to gain and wants to protect me. That's self-preservation—you can't trust that kind of person."

"So what?" Stan said, in disbelief. "Who gives a shit if he has honor or not? That's not your problem. I don't understand how none of Victor's list understands tit for tat. It's this simple Mr. Dent: You, that guard, and I hold three pieces of a treasure map. We need to put it together long enough to get our treasure. Then we split it up and go our own way. I don't care if you're a pedophile or if you killed your own mother. There's only one objective in all of this and there's one way to get to that."

"Am I going to listen to this for two months?"

"Not at all," Stan said. "Because the guard isn't just protecting you. He's got my back too. And if you're not on-board, your life's going to be a living hell in here. There's no middle ground Dent. We all get everything we want and get out of here rich, or no one does. And if no one does, then your life is over."

2

Tarek Appleton stretched his arms as he entered his living room and upon taking in the scene in front of him, he let out a deep sigh. Aileen Thick slept on the couch, her hair flowing in all directions and one leg hanging off, nearly touching the ground. On the dining room table, an empty pack of cigarettes was tossed and a nearly empty bottle of wine, but no glasses.

"Unreal," Tarek said quietly and walked to the bathroom.

Kicking Aileen out hadn't occurred to him. He actually liked her company in the evenings but couldn't stand what he saw in the mornings. He'd hoped by now, he'd have been able to boost her ego, but she was completely broken and until he had a real reason to kick her out, he was just giving her a place to land. Maybe she'd get it together or maybe she'd force his hand. The truth was that Tarek enjoyed her because it gave him someone to talk to. She'd proved herself to have been a fan of his for a long time and when he talked about his glory days and his struggles, she listened intently. She rarely talked about herself and he could see her shame when she did. She hated herself and though Tarek had always believed in himself, there was something in her he identified with. It was a need to be important. Where they differed was whether they believed they deserved it or not.

*This is unhealthy,* Tarek thought. *What am I doing with her here?*

He'd grown protective. If not for him, she'd be on the streets, a low price prostitute. She'd probably be getting abused and treated like scum on a nightly basis.

*Don't toot your own horn pal. You're getting just as much out of this as she is. Maybe more.*

That was the reality. Tarek was lost—trying to find himself again. Celebrity was a short-lived concept. People love you until they love someone else. Hollywood was always talking about replacements as if there could only be one of everything. For a while, Tarek had a pretty good sitcom, but that was canceled when a better one came along. The same could be said for his show. Fan loyalty was overrated. Eventually, there was nothing more a person could do to impress. Eventually, all celebrities become yesterday's news. Longevity existed, but not for comedians whose range was being themselves in all things—sometimes with a different name.

Tarek wasn't an actor. He never had the ability to step outside himself and become a character. Even when he dealt with puppets, he couldn't bring himself to be anything other than Tarek Appleton in his acts. He'd always just been himself. He wasn't a goofball with accents and impressions. Maybe that was the problem. Maybe he needed to learn to step outside himself.

As he stared at Aileen, he thought about greatness. Most people wanted a legacy, but most didn't find it, and then one day it was too late. For Tarek, a career of standup, followed by a failed sitcom, followed by a failed talk show, was the end of the line. There was nowhere left to go other than a stint on Hollywood Squares and a "Where Are They Now?" feature in People magazine in ten years. By then, Tarek would likely be fat and have struggled with drugs, alcohol, or all of the above.

He spent the day walking in the village, entering shops and browsing, but leaving with nothing but his hands in his pockets. He spent some time in a Starbucks and had lunch at Village Pizzaria, but otherwise kept his day as uneventful as all the others. He tried to schedule a meeting with his agent, but he was booked until next week.

He missed his stage. He missed the studio. Mostly, he missed his writers. Even Tony, who'd betrayed him, he missed. He wondered what Tony was up to, if he had any projects in the pipeline. When he learned that Tony had helped Stan almost get everyone killed, he hadn't yelled or told him off. He'd simply walked away without a word, but suspected now was the time to reunite and talk about what had happened six months ago. He'd been held hostage by a deranged man who Tony had helped. Stanley Kline was now in Kern and Tarek was safe, but things had gotten out of control for a while and Tarek had barely allowed himself to reflect, but today he did. He replayed the events in his head. Anthony Freeman and the bomb...Tarek in the hotel, forced to push the button. And he didn't. It was heroic, but he didn't feel like a hero. He felt like too many things had gone wrong and then one of the people on Victor's list had died—swept into the ocean that day.

He didn't know why it had all happened. The seas eventually calmed and what was left was a man who was very lonely. He had nothing left except for a girl on his couch who he couldn't save any more than he could save himself. She seemed to be what was left of his fan-base.

*My God, is that why I like having her there? She's my only fan?*

Surely, there were still fans, but the overall perception of Tarek was as a has-been.

"Tarek?" a voice at his side said. He turned to find Christina Harold, who was a daytime talk show host there. She'd been on Tarek's show once and he'd been on the morning show twice. She'd always been professional on air but had a reputation as a lush and Tarek had seen it firsthand. She was a flirt, and though she was married, rumor had it that more than once she'd visited her guests in their dressing rooms for a quickie before the show.

"Christina," Tarek said. They hugged.

"I thought you left this town," she said.

Tarek told her what he'd been up to and downplayed how desperately he wanted his career back. Finally she asked what was next for him.

"Just laying low for now," he said.

"And fending off stalkers."

She laughed but Tarek shifted uncomfortably. Stanley was hardly a stalker but that was how he was perceived after he'd taken Tarek. "That situation was blown out of proportion," Tarek said. "Stan Kline was wanted on other charges and happened to cross my path. That's all."

"Well, we're all glad you're safe," she said. "You should come on the show sometime."

"I've got nothing to promote."

"Come on for fun. We'll do a morning bit or something."

"Will do."

"You ever thought about doing movies?"

*Every day. It's not up to me.*

"Not at all," Tarek lied. "Once you've played yourself, there's just no turning back. I'd rather not embarrass myself."

"So you'd like to?" she asked. "You just don't think you can?"

"Maybe when I started out, but I've had a good run. I'll make a comeback in a decade or so when people start wondering where I went."

"Don't assume you'll fail Appleton. Most of these people who embarrass themselves don't realize they were never talented in the first place. You're perfectly capable. You just have to make sure that when the cameras are rolling, no one sees Tarek Appleton."

"And how does that work in your opinion?"

"Find the role that is everything you're not."

"And if it doesn't exist?"

"Make it exist."

She spoke so simply that Tarek was almost convinced she was right.

"Why you so interested?" Tarek asked.

"I'm a fan, like everyone else. You always had a certain energy, but you were pigeonholed. Yeah, that's hard to come back from, but you can. Comedic actors turn dramatic all the time and it works if they embrace the role. It means letting go though."

"What are you?" Tarek asked. "A drama teacher?"

"Believe it or not, once upon a time, Christina Harold wanted to be an actress. I studied under some of the greats, but didn't have quite the right look for the good roles. I looked, quite frankly, like an anchorwoman, so that's what I became. Then, onto the morning circuit. It's a great gig, so I'm not complaining, but don't assume I don't know a little something about the business. Find the role. Create the role. Bring it to your agent instead of waiting for your agent to bring it to you. How about we discuss this more over drinks?"

There was the rub and Tarek was tempted to go, but she'd actually spoken words to think about and that's exactly what he wanted to do.

"Just a drink," she said, when she saw the conflict in his eyes.

"And where does it go from there?"

"Whatever you want," she said with an eyebrow raised.

"Aren't you married?"

"Haven't you been caught with hookers?"

Tarek reconsidered leaving with her, but didn't want to lose his fire for change. Tarek had always stayed in a comfort zone and if stepping outside himself meant going against his instincts, then meaningless sex was the last thing he wanted. He wanted to be alone so he could try to find something different—some kind of darkness. Tarek had always been the likable, funny guy. He never wanted to tell a joke, wink, or bask in applause again. He didn't want to be the nice guy anymore.

*Respect. I need respect.*

He spent the rest of the day home online and researched top films over the last century, studying the quality of film, the type of characters played, and the path each actor took in getting there. Some had started out in less than serious roles and evolved, but Tarek had never pictured himself submerged so deeply in a role.

"What are you doing?" Aileen asked, standing behind him with a cup of coffee. She wore no makeup and her hair was a mess. Poor sweet Aileen, who had no ambition in life other than to sit on someone else's doormat.

"I'm looking for movie auditions."

"Really?" Aileen asked, lighting up, and Tarek found her quite beautiful in that moment. "You'd be great in movies."

"What makes you say that?" Tarek asked.

"You just would."

"What about in actual good films?"

"Of course. Why?"

"You've never seen me do anything serious."

"How serious?" Aileen asked.

Tarek gave the question some thought before answering. "Dark," he said. "Dark enough to consume me."

*3*

It wasn't long before Dent realized that Donovan's protection extended to all the guards on his block. It seemed everyone in Kern was now afraid of Dent. The sheer power that Donovan had there was unbelievable. Dent didn't even think the warden could have pulled this many strings.

Only Wayne shifted his eyes at Dent and the man who'd always been a coward suddenly looked very hate-filled. He seemed as if more than ever, he wanted Dent gone, and more than ever, there was nothing he could do about it. It gave Dent a satisfaction he cursed himself for having. Favor from the guards was the last thing he wanted in Kern. He wanted to be a con and maneuver the valleys of life in prison in the same way everyone else was forced to. In Kern, it was hard to tell who the good guys and the bad guys really were. He'd seen the guards do unspeakable things— things that were probably worse than why half the population was behind these walls in the first place. He'd seen men who'd been busted for a singular pot offense get cracked over the head with nightsticks and never wake up. The punishment was a harder crime than the crime had actually been.

That was life and Dent was prepared for it, and if he had to be here, he'd deal with problems like Wayne on his own, but his unwanted protection was everywhere, and even though he'd known Victor was worth a lot of money, he'd realized the full extent of the position he was in. There were a dozen people on the outside that would still have to die, and the man who could collect was locked away for life. It still wasn't enough to deter men like Donovan. Dent was somewhat invincible as long as his name was on the list.

In the yard, Stan approached and stood at his side like they were permanently bonded. Stan had never been to prison and should have learned the same way everyone else did, but stood under the same cloak of protection Dent did, and it angered Dent. No one would have an easier ride than Stan, and who was he? Just an outsider who knew of the will.

He wasn't even part of the club. He wasn't invited to play the game. His presence was unfair to the whole thing and only drove Dent further from the temptation of Donovan's offer.

"I worked with the guys you killed," Stan said, squinting in the sun. Dent turned to him—it was news to him. "They were once associates, but also, good friends. Cory Wilson and Jones Mitchel…" he said the names as if they brought him back to memories of the time they spent together.

"You worked for Stone," Dent said.

"I did, and that's how I knew all this in the first place. I had a good deal of intimate knowledge. Cory, Jones and I…we were the guys behind the scenes…cept for…well I was the real behind the scenes guy. They made a lot of calls and did a lot of the plotting, but I was the bullet most of the time. They had a purpose within Stone's company…a purpose other than what we did in private. But not me. I was all behind the scenes. So when the heat was turned up a bit and Stone was under scrutiny for some of his shady shit, who do you think was disposable?"

"You."

"Me. And that's what I knew. I'd been doing it awhile. I made great money. I took care of my family. My budget revolved around the life Stone had provided me. Without that, I couldn't get better than minimum wage anywhere else. I asked Stone for something else. He could have made space, but he didn't. I guess he didn't want me on the books at all, so years of employment were just erased. No audit would even turn up that I worked for him."

"Why you telling me this?"

"Because this is fate Dent. You can laugh or mock me for saying that, but this is fate. Those guys you killed…they deserved to be punished. Not me. But they got away free. I was punished, and I've been punished since. And I don't know your story, but if you killed them, I'm sure you had a reason and they deserved it. But we're still paying because what? Because we're a couple of guys who were dealt shitty hands and did what we had to to survive and society doesn't like us. Tell me something Dent: Ever been falsely accused? Ever had mistakes made by the authorities that buried you, that predetermined where you'd end up? We're at the mercy of a system who has all the power and uses it against us, because they like to see guys like us far away from society. But we've got real power in here now. We have a chance to take what's owed to us Dent. And all you've gotta do is sit and wait."

Dent considered Stan's words before crouching to the ground and running his fingers in the dirt. After a moment, he wiped his hands on his legs and stood. "You know Stan, we're talking about a reward that we would get for ending the lives of a dozen people. We're both no strangers to that, but for you and I and Donovan and anyone else to co-exist, to work together, we have to put our trust in each other while we're faced with the knowledge that we'd all stop at nothing to have that money. We'd end lives for it and that takes a special kind of person, but that's not a person you can trust. You shouldn't put your faith in me anymore than I'll put mine in you because we both know we have no limitation to our own preservation. You'd stab me in the back first chance you got, and you better believe I'd stab you too."

"Not if we need each other."

"We need each other up until a point. After that, we don't. I've been here before and the takeaway every time is that you can only count on yourself to get a job done."

"Except you can't do this by yourself."

"When did I say that?"

"You tried and failed and you quit."

"If I decide I want the money, I'll take the money."

"You're crazy Dent. You're going to have to knock down a hundred impossible barriers to get there. This was arranged for us and no one man can have that money. Not in your position. Unfortunately for you, it takes a village. You may not trust anyone, but you're going to have to. This isn't just going to go away. The guard will kill you if you don't cooperate."

"I know."

Stan stepped close and his eyes burned into Dent's. "Then I guess that will eliminate one more." He turned to walk away but shouted over his shoulder. "If you're not in, I'll find someone else…"

…"*There is no one else I want with me.*"

*Dent looked up at Marlena, who was nearly in tears. "You know I can't leave anyway, so why we even having this conversation?"*

*Marlena sucked on a joint and exhaled as if she needed a hit. She started pacing back and forth. "I'm going crazy here."*

*"You're more fortunate than ninety-nine percent of women your age. You want to go be a waitress, go ahead. Don't assume I'll be waiting for you when you realize how fucking stupid you are."*

*"Baby, we're in limbo here. Why can't we take what we have and just go somewhere else? Just the two of us? We live with fifty people. Half of them I don't even know. They come and go and steal your stuff."*

*"I can afford new shit."*

*"I've seen cops asking questions."*

*Marlena finally had Dent's attention. "What kind of cops? Feds or police? And who they talking to?"*

*"I don't know. I just see them drive past a lot and they stop in town and I see them at the clubs talking to bouncers."*

*"And what's that got to do with me?"*

*"You assume I'm stupid. I don't care what you do and never have, but if you go to jail, what good is any of it? With what you have now, we can move to the other side of the country and start living different. I don't want to have to be afraid."*

Dent took the joint from her hand and inhaled. He fell back on the bed and stared at the ceiling. With Mitch and Marlena trying to persuade him to get out, he finally took the time to consider. He couldn't live a normal life when half a world away, Mitch was running the operation alone. Mitch always had counted on Dent but also wanted him gone. They'd grown into something that resembled a father son relationship and if Mitch wanted Dent gone, it was to protect him. Lately, more often than not, Mitch wanted to go on runs without him. Dent had also noticed the increase in law enforcement in the area, but crime and violence was up on the streets too—which was just a byproduct of their trade. Eventually, everything would lead back to Mitch's crew. Mitch seemed to have accepted this outcome, but wanted Dent far away when that day came.

*"I'll give it some thought,"* he said.

*"I'm leaving day after tomorrow."*

*"That's too soon for me and I never agreed to go to LA. That's you. I've got other things in mind."*

*"Okay,"* Marlena said, *"I'm open to anything. Just something safe and not here anymore."*

Dent needed to have a long talk with Mitch, who would be thrilled to hear Dent was even considering leaving. What he really wanted to know though, was whether or not Mitch would consider going with him. Marlena was okay. She was the closest Dent had ever found to love, but he'd found he had a shelf life with all people and Marlena had grown old to him. Another couple of months and he'd want her out of his sight forever. There was merit in what she'd said though and Dent didn't have the luxury of being naive. The days of invincibility were disappearing. They were too big now and were likely on someone's radar. Cutting and running wasn't a bad idea and Dent was tired of his living situation too. What Marlena said was true. There were many colorful characters coming and going and most of them took what they could before disappearing. Dent had grown to hate most of the company he was surrounded with.

*"I'll talk to Mitch and see what he says."*

*"You said he wants you to go."*

*"He's always said he wants me to go but I've always said no and he*

*knows I'll always say no. If I say yes, it's going to be a different conversation, but it's one we'll have to have."*

*"What do you owe him?" she asked, bluntly. "I know he cares about you now, but he took you away from your home. The guy's no saint."*

*Dent suddenly backhanded Marlena. She let out a quick yelp before she rolled to her side and held her hands at her face to protect herself from further blows. Dent had no intention of hitting her again and was taken aback he'd hit her once. He turned away from her and closed his eyes tightly, regretting what he did. There were people who he wanted to fear him, but not those who were close. Finally, he turned back.*

*"My father was an asshole and my mother allowed him to be an asshole and there wasn't a damn thing I could do about it. Mitch took me away and was going to use me to leverage my father into doing something he didn't want to do, but that went to shit and Mitch took me instead. Back then, I hated Mitch and missed my father, but I was a kid, so I was blind to who the enemy was. There are truths in front of us that most people don't accept. Mitch is a criminal because of man made laws saying what we should and shouldn't ingest. You can watch a bunch of fat fucks eating fast food every day and killing themselves a bite at a time and that's okay, but getting a high for relaxation is taboo. Don't let the law and morality confuse you. There's a code I live by and it means deciding shit for myself, not just eating up everything they're telling you you should do and be. If I'd stayed back home, if Mitch had never taken me, I would have grown up to be another sheep, mindlessly following orders and eating up all the lies. I would have watched a piece of shit father be honored continually by the community while he physically and mentally abused my mother. I would have grown up to become one of the many mindless drones I see every day on the streets, in the shops, all over this city, that I despise. Say what you want about Mitch. He's opened my eyes. And if you don't have the loyalty that it takes to understand that, then get the fuck out of here…"*

...Night fell on Kern and as all the windows were covered in darkness, the blocks were filled one by one with cons as the guards marched them in and counted heads before leaving them to hoot and holler until they fell asleep. Dent lived on the second tier and always was in his bunk by the time the third tier started to fill. It was one of many routines in Kern—routines Dent once wanted nothing to do with, but had grown accustomed to. Every day was essentially the same for him. He'd learned to get along though, and at times, preferred the simplicity of routine.

He hadn't spoken a word to Stan and Stan seemed to have given up for the day, but Dent would have to be prepared for many days of objecting to plotting and persuasion. It would probably only get harder to ignore and at some point, Dent would either cave or be killed. Or he could work with them and find his way free of them later.

They both stopped and diverted their attention upward as some kind of argument took place on the tier above. There was a scuffle and shouting between guards and some of the cons but the whole block was in an uproar, encouraging the conflict and it made it impossible for the lower tiers to understand what was happening.

"This is right on top of us," Stan said. He stepped forward and tried to look up, but the upper tier completely blocked their view.

"He's going to jump!" someone above yelled and suddenly, a body was falling with a bed-sheet tied around the neck. The sheet pulled tight and the body jerked and the neck snapped and Wayne's body was suddenly swinging right in front of the cell. All curiosity faded and Dent stepped forward knowingly, staring into the face of a former enemy—a man who killed Ziggy but didn't deserve to die like this—not for Donovan's agenda.

No one would believe this was a real suicide, but somewhere in a filing cabinet, there would be a writeup stating it was and no one would ever answer for it. A man's life was so easily diminished here. Everything he was and everything he wanted to be were nothing the moment he was dead. Wayne's family and friends, everyone on the outside who even knew he existed, would hear only one story and it would be a complete fabrication of the truth.

Stan seemed unaffected, other than to look into Wayne's lifeless eyes with fascination. Dent wanted the body down as soon as possible, but was silent as a half hour passed. He stared at the ceiling and tried to block out the creaking as the body swayed back and forth, it's shadow swaying in the cell. Finally, the body came down and was taken away. After the commotion ceased, Donovan walked by, as if moseying past, and stopped.

"Sorry about that fellas," he said, but only spoke to Dent and gave him a nod before walking away.

Stan was pleased and by the look on his face, wanted Dent to understand the implications of whose side you wanted to be on. Instead of responding, he climbed onto his bunk and rolled toward the wall and stared at it, unable to sleep.

4

Tarek grew tired of being home because Aileen lingered everywhere he went. His place was spacious, but she was lonely, and though he was lonely too, hers wasn't the company he wanted. Being around Aileen made him feel too normal and down to earth. The time was coming that she'd have to find a place. He'd even give her money for a hotel. Being around her just wasn't an option anymore. Having a roommate didn't suit him well.

He told himself he'd done a good deed and she'd be okay. She wouldn't have the right to make him feel guilty or ask for more. He'd done enough, and he couldn't do it forever.

He'd just sent an email to his agent asking for a recommendation to study method acting, when he turned to find Aileen looking at him from across the room. She quickly diverted her eyes.

"Do you need something?" Tarek asked.

"I just wanted to talk to you about our arrangement," she said.

"Yeah, we should."

"I feel like I'm taking advantage of you and you're a really nice guy so you're probably just too nice to tell me I'm intrusive."

"That's not the case."

"Maybe not, but you've still done way more for me than I can ever repay you for, so I think I'm going to go tomorrow if that's okay."

"Where?" Tarek asked. He suddenly felt bad for her again, and worried about what she'd intended to do.

She hung her head a little and he barely heard her speak. "I might go to Victor's home."

"You're breaking in?" Tarek asked with a smile.

"No." She held up a key.

"How could you possibly have a key to his place?"

"I've always had it."

"Then why the streets? Why not just do that in the beginning?"

"It's illegal."

"So is…" Tarek cut himself off before saying prostitution, but Aileen's eyes told him she knew that's where he was going. "Sorry."

"I had a key to the back entry since I lived with Victor and I never gave him a reason to think I'd use it. I think I actually copied it once so I could hide one outside in case something ever happened, but I held onto it. Later, I wanted it for Jason."

Tarek didn't understand.

"Victor didn't let me see him. He told my son I was dead. But I liked to watch him get on the bus or play outside, so I would drive past or be down the street. I know. Stalker right?"

"Well, he was your son."

"Exactly. Something Victor never really saw importance in. Anyway, it was in case of emergency. Victor was hands off as a father. I just needed to know that if I ever needed to get in the house, I had a key. He didn't realize I had it. I wasn't going to use it maliciously. Only if Jason needed me."

"Again, I think you would have been better off staying there than on the streets."

"It won't be empty forever and it's not exactly a good memory. I hated that man. I didn't want him to do me any favors. Even dead."

"Then what's changing your mind now?"

"I realized he'd probably hate knowing I'm staying there, so if he's a ghost or something, I'll just piss him off for a while."

Tarek laughed, which pleased Aileen. She liked that he smiled on her account.

"Why don't you stay here a few more nights and think about it?" Tarek said. Aileen smiled and for a moment, looked as if she was going to start crying. She thanked him and walked in her room and moments later, the lights were out. Five minutes ago, Tarek couldn't wait to be rid of her. Now, he wished she was back.

*What's wrong with you Tarek? What are you looking for?*

He went back to his email and his agent had already responded and given him the name of an acting coach who worked with method actors. He stared at the email for a long moment. His agent offered nothing other than names and contact information. There was no optimistic encouraging words. Tarek suspected no one would see him as capable of such a thing, but doubt was the one thing that had always driven Tarek. While others used negativity as a reason to give up, Tarek had always been fueled by it.

He looked up at his wall where posters of The Marx Brothers and Abbott and Costello were hanging. His desk was filled with treasure trolls, a slinky, and newspaper comics he'd cut out over the years. A guy like Tarek was a born comedian—at best a comedy actor. What people had always, and would always expect of him, was that when Tarek Appleton was on the screen, they would see Tarek Appleton. He was the nice guy, the funny man, the life of the party. He could do magic and hypnosis and every party trick imaginable, but he wouldn't leave behind a legacy and he would never be remembered for being talented. The people who were remembered for being talented were the people who could transform themselves and create memorable characters.

His eyes stopped at the coffee table and he noticed Aileen had left the key behind. He turned away but his eyes kept coming back to it.

Victor Stone was the darkest man he'd ever known. He was a formula of things Tarek had never been able to understand. He was always serious, never smiled, never cared if anyone liked him, and stooped to ruining the lives of people who he didn't like. Tarek had always made a point to steer clear of all those traits. He'd respected Victor because Victor made him, but Victor and Tarek were on opposite ends of the spectrum.

*Maybe I have something to learn from Victor.*

He quickly snatched the key from the table and stuffed it in his pocket. There was no sound coming from Aileen's room and even if she came out, she'd probably dismissed the key from her mind by now.

As he drove through the rain, Tarek tried to decide what it was he was looking for. Maybe it was as simple as stepping into a new environment that made him believe he'd transform. Maybe the art on the walls would be a long way from The Marx Brothers and Abbott and Costello and he'd be absorbed by the atmosphere. Maybe just basking in it would make Tarek feel different. People changed with their environments and wasn't that what method actors always did? They'd blend into whatever role they were supposed to play and get a feel for what it was like to actually be in the skin of someone else.

Victor's estate was enormous. Tarek had no idea what one man and his kid could have wanted with so much space. Tarek liked a flashy life, but never understood the need for twenty rooms per person. Victor thought differently and Tarek would think differently, so maybe eventually it would all make sense—if he basked in it enough.

The neighborhood was quiet and the gates were low enough to climb. Tarek was in good enough shape to clear any barricades and was in the back of the mansion in minutes. Then, he tried the key, and it slid in the lock without a problem. Tarek and Aileen had never discussed alarms, but if she felt that she could get in without a problem, she must have known it wouldn't be an issue.

When Tarek was safe inside, he let out a breath of relief. He walked through the dark, observing the craftsmanship of the home. He was surprised at how little had been cleared out. It looked as if Victor was only on vacation. He'd been dead almost nine months and his house still sat in limbo. He supposed someone was taking care of it and all the expenses until only one remained. He hadn't thought about it before, but they'd inherit a mansion too. Property taxes would be a bitch, but Victor's riches would last forever.

He stopped thinking to himself and began talking out loud to break the silence. "What kind of man wishes for death on his enemies?" Tarek said. His voice sounded louder than usual in the silence. "I win people over. That's what normal people do. You're a billionaire and you held grudges unlike anyone else. That's not normal Victor."

He walked up a staircase that wound around the wall and to the second floor. From there, he followed a hallway, peaking into mostly empty rooms as he moved. Finally, he found Victor's study. "Let's see what you held onto." Tarek still was unsure of what he'd find but Victor's study was as good a place as any. He'd already felt something new creeping into his bones. A guy like Tarek had no business in this world. Just being there made him feel a little less funny—a little less likable.

On Victor's desk, a typewriter sat covered in dust. "You actually used a typewriter? You were a walking cliche Victor." At its side were crumpled papers with half pages filled. "Computers have backspace you pretentious asshole."

Then he found the stack of pages, haphazardly arranged in a pile that could easily topple with a light shove. He looked at the top page and discovered he'd come across the unpublished memoirs of Victor Stone. "You pretentious asshole," Tarek said again and turned the page.

Victor had never been much of an open book. In fact, he was more enigma than anything, but Tarek had just tapped into more information from Victor's brain that anyone in the world likely had. He sat and began to read.

5

Warden Sunjata came down to the cell block and rounded up everyone on tier three and interrogated them. Everyone's story collaborated, which was to be expected. Another full day passed and Donovan left Dent alone, but he was awoken at four in the morning the next day to find Donovan in his cell and Stan hanging back in support of whatever was happening. Dent stayed on his back with his head turned.

"This it?" he asked.

"Depends on you," Donovan said in a whisper. "I've given you some time to think about it. I think I've proved that no one is going to get in your way here. Now it's your turn to be gracious or continue to disrespect me, but I'm not waiting on an answer from you. You're all the way in or not."

"I'm not doing anything for you," Dent said.

Donovan stood there motionless for a long time. The only sound in the cell was Stan's frustrated breathing and suggestions that they give Dent more time. Finally, the guard spoke. "Tomorrow in the yard, a fight will break out. You'll take a stray bullet. I'm not bluffing. You have until then. Only you can call it off."

Dent barely slept the next two hours. His mind crept toward tossing the idea in his head of going along with their plan, but he forced it out every time. He wasn't going to work with the enemy. He would rather be dead and his mind worked toward preparation for that instead. He played his life in his head. No one would ever say it was ordinary if they bothered to remember him. He'd be buried and forgotten just like everyone in Kern was.

He wanted to write a letter or send a message, but he'd have no ability to do so and no one to send it to if he did. He refused to feel sorry for himself. He wasn't going to beg. Maybe Donovan really was bluffing, but he was tired of talking to him. He didn't want to play by their rules anymore. If the last thing he did in this world was spit in Donovan's face, that was satisfactory enough. He only hoped Donovan would live out his life in misery working in Kern. If so, Dent would always be in his head— the time he learned what one of the inmates could have been worth and that inmate stubbornly preferred death over compromise. Maybe Donovan would end Dent and regret it forever. He could only hope.

The morning routine stretched out. Time seemed to slow down, even in anticipation of death. Dent was fully prepared and wanted it over before his mind started working again. He could think of multiple ways out of this problem but he'd only prolong the inevitable.

When exercise finally arrived, Dent walked through the yard to his favorite spot and had a seat. He was about as far from where any action could happen as possible. If Donovan had a gun trained on him, he'd probably have to explain such a wide misfire later. His mind kept creating more wishes of Donovan's misfortunes that Dent would never be around to see to fruition. Dent stared at the sun and tried to block out the sounds around him, but when a fight started to break out in the yard, conveniently located near him as if some of the cons had repositioned, he closed his eyes and tried to find his inner peace.

He wasn't sure who he was talking to, but in that moment, felt he had something to say.

"I'm sorry," Dent said, and waited…

*…He'd never forgive Mitch.*

*His partner had disappeared every night for a week, out on business and always persuading Dent he was stepping out for a smoke, but the money kept rolling in and Mitch always returned early the next morning with a crew of men who had somehow imprinted themselves in the business. Dent wasn't being protected. He was being shut out completely, and for the first time since he was young, he felt like a prisoner again.*

*He rolled over in bed and watched Marlena sleep for a moment. Five minutes later, he was dressed and quietly left the room. He walked through the halls and out onto the patio which overlooked the Atlantic. He listened to the waves crash until he spotted a dark figure standing on the docks, smoking a cigarette. He walked in that direction until he was close enough to make out the figure as Mitch.*

"*What are you doing here?*" *Mitch asked when Christian was within range.*

"*I stepped out. What are you doing here? I thought you were out on business.*"

"*Yeah, I've been out on business, but I couldn't tonight.*"

"*Tell me what's going on.*"

"*I don't have to tell you shit. You're just a hostage that won't leave. You're free to go Chrissy. Get the fuck out of my sight.*"

*Dent swallowed hard and clenched his jaw with anger. Anyone else would have been given a beating by now.* "*Have it your way. I'll go tomorrow. And you know what? Fuck you. You're right. I am a hostage. You took me in, made me a part of this shit, and threw me to the curb. You owe me a hell of a lot more than this.*"

"*I'm giving you what you need!*" *Mitch shouted.* "*Because you don't need to pay for what I've done!*"

"*What have you done?*"

"*I'm dying kid. This cancer shit has given me another year at best. Incurable. I'm on my way out.*"

*Christian fell silent.*

"*I can't keep doing this and the new guys are hardcore. The business is being overtaken by foreigners who have no business sense. They just take what they want and kill everyone else. Five miles down the coast, a dozen killed. All Rocco's guys, and they're on the up and up. Used to be a handshake was good enough and the merch exchanged hands without a thought of betrayal or skimming or any of that shit. Nowadays, you gotta watch your back because the new guys...they just show up, kill everyone in the room, and take what you got. That's what it's coming to.*"

"*Great,*" *Christian said.* "*I told you I'm going.*"

"*Yeah, get in your boat and get out of here. I made a mistake taking you this far. I should have left you in the woods and let you go then.*"

"*Maybe I prefer this.*"

"*Yeah, we all prefer the hand we're dealt, but you don't know what would have been of Chrissy Dent if he'd gone to school every day and flipped burgers in High School. You think you stumbled on an adventure, but you're in a shithole. Go live an honest life and look back in ten years. I'll tell you what you'll be thinking. You'll be thinking about how much you regret that you stayed. You'll hate me and you'll hate this life and you'll wish me dead. Just go and see.*"

"*I'm getting Marlena.*"

"*Don't even bother,*" *Mitch said.* "*She's just a souvenir of all this. Your boat's got a full tank of gas. Get out of here now.*"

*Suddenly, sirens blared in the distance. Christian's eyes went wide, but Mitch didn't move. He expected it.*

*"We have to go," Christian said. "Come on." He ran for the boat, but Mitch stayed in place, only now he had a gun in hand.*

*The Coast Guard will be all over these waters soon. I'll hold them back while you get out of here.*

*The flashing reds and blues surrounded the compound and shouting and gunfire filled the air. Then, before Christian could say anything more, Marlena stepped out of the shadows with a gun in hand. "Drop your weapon!" she shouted, her gun trained on Mitch.*

*Christian desperately needed a gun, and as he watched his girlfriend hold a badge up for them to see, his teeth ground into each other. "Biggest mistake you ever made, you bitch," he said, his eyes burning into Marlena.*

*She ignored him and carried on. "Christian Dent, taken as a boy and forced into a life of wealth and drug running. No one will blame you for staying, but you need to make the right choice now. You've done nothing wrong. You were kidnapped and did what you thought was right to survive. There's no case against you here. The story I'm going to be telling is that you never had a choice."*

*Dent backed away toward the boat, while Mitch stood in place, his eyes on the gun.*

*"If you run now, you're a criminal. Do you understand that? You either come back with me and I help you through this, or you become a fugitive, but if you get on that boat, there's no turning back."*

*Dent kept backing toward the boat and suddenly, Marlena aimed the gun in his direction. "Christian Dent, you are under arrest. Anything..."*

*A shot rang out and Marlena turned, her eyes wide in terror. Mitch held his gun on her, watching as blood spread across her shirt. She fell to her knees and turned to Christian one last time before she fell to the ground. Mitch turned to Christian but stood his ground. A thousand words passed between them in that moment but neither said anything at all. As the voices in the distance grew louder, both men knew what they had to do.*

*Dent didn't stick around long enough to learn of Mitch's fate. He powered up the engine of his boat, which was stocked full of money, supplies, and gas, and he took off into the night...*

...His eyes opened at the sound of his name being shouted by one of the guards.

"Dent, get your ass off the ground. You've got a visitor."

Dent looked around and saw no evidence that his life was about to end.

Somewhere, Donovan was looking at him through the scope of a rifle and probably cursing that something got in the way. "Visiting hours are over."

"I know that," the guard snapped. "It's police business and time sensitive. Let's move."

Dent rounded a corner and his eyes narrowed with confusion as he spotted Trish Reynalds sitting on the other end of the glass partition, her hand resting on the telephone. He sat but didn't pick up his end. She waited patiently until he finally reached for the phone and put it to his ear. Trish looked tired and humorless, and any sense of disdain she had for Dent wasn't visible. Instead, she looked like she was in a confessional. Christian reflected on the last months. It had been a long string of meaningless days, but suddenly, his life had become very eventful.

"I've only got five minutes," Trish said, but choked up and said no more. Dent waited, forcing her to say what she had to say without any prompting from him. "I want to start by saying I'm nothing like you."

Dent almost laughed. Trish had done something bad and was going to tell him. She was justifying her actions in advance. He saw the whole conversation playing out before it did and began to think about how he would taunt her.

"You took lives because you were angry...because you wanted to live large."

"What are you getting at?" Dent asked.

"I need one thing from you, and I don't want you to laugh or play games or string me along, or act like we're no different than each other because that's what you'll do. I want you to sit here and tell me you'll do something for me if it means everything. If I can make things right for you and save you from this place, just tell me you'll do one thing."

Dent was surprised to find himself concerned. He hadn't seen Trish so vulnerable before. He no longer wanted to taunt her. He only wanted to hear what she had to say. "I'm listening," he said.

"You know of Victor's will. You almost succeeded in having your cellmate kill us."

"Until you killed him," Dent added. Then, Trish said the last thing he expected to hear.

"I wish I hadn't."

"Why?" he asked, leaning forward.

"Shiloh is dying. She needs surgery and I don't have the money to do it."

Dent leaned back again and put the pieces together. Trish needed money—and by the sound of it—lots of it. "You can check under my mattress Reynalds but I've got nothing."

"You don't now, but you will." Tears formed in her eyes and her lip quivered. "I've tried everything I can Christian. This is all I have left."

"What can I possibly do?"

"You met Shiloh. You held her in your arms."

"I remember. What can I do?"

"Soon…very soon…I will be dead, along with every name on that list. When that happens, the inheritance is yours to take. Only, you're going to be in here. My attorney will have you sign some papers, and overnight, you will become a billionaire."

"And I'll still be here."

"You will then release whatever amount is needed to pay for any treatment Shiloh needs. If you do, when she's alive and well, my attorney will release a video confession I've recorded…"

"One minute!" the guard at the door yelled as a warning. Both diverted their eyes for a second before continuing.

"It will state that I planted the murder weapon, that I never heard a dying confession…it will have enough content to have you taken out of Kern. Not only will you be free. You won't be on the run and you'll have whatever remains after Shiloh is saved."

"Why me?"

"You're the only person who will understand why I'm doing what I'm doing. You're the only one who wants something as badly as I do."

"And you die?" Dent asked with doubt.

"Another perk for you." Their eyes met. Her eyes begged for him to accept the offer. "I want to know that you'll do it. I don't care what you do, who you hurt, or if you go on to be the scum of the earth outside. I want you to use that money to save my daughter. In return, I'll save you."

"So you're just going to…" He looked up at the guard who was within earshot and didn't finish, but Trish nodded. "You know Reynalds…you say you're not like me, but I never killed a man without a good reason. Most deserved to die. It's too bad you'll never understand why things happened the way \ they did. If you understood, you might not have been so eager to lock me up. If you even knew why I went there to kill them that night, we would've had a whole nother conversation. I'm not the monster you think I am, and for all the bad I've done, there's been an equally good reason to do it. Suddenly, you're the judge who says one life is more important than a dozen, and you come to me with your whispers and telling me we're not the same. We're exactly the same Trish. We just have our own motivations. That's all. This isn't me taunting you. This is a fact."

The guard started to move toward them.

"Say you'll do it," Trish said. "Please. Time is running out."

"Yeah, I'll do it," Dent said, as the guard was close and the conversation needed to be discontinued. "I take it this is the last time I'll see you?"

Trish never answered. She was too busy expressing endless gratitude. As the guard escorted Dent out, he turned back once to see Trish wiping tears from her eyes.

*This is the last time I'll see her*, he thought, and was disappointed it hadn't been different. There were too many things she'd never understand, but he supposed that was life. Trish's opinion of him didn't matter—especially now that she'd die, Dent a hero in her eyes. But also…a monster.

Dent was taken back to the yard and he wasted no time in finding Stan. The fight had broken up and the day went back to the usual Kern routine. It wasn't half an hour ago that he thought his life was over. Now, the truth was far from that.

"You change your mind?" Stan asked.

"Yeah," Dent said to Stan's surprise.

"You going to work with us to get this done?"

"I will. Talk to Donovan and call off whatever plans you had. I'll do it. I want all the protections and privileges previously offered.

"Not up to me, but he'll agree. Donovan wants this to go smooth. No grudges and shit between us all."

"I won't be a problem," Dent said, and left Stan there while he walked back to his spot in the dirt. He sat and looked at the sun, wrapping his arms around his legs and plotting how it would all go down. Somehow, he'd stumbled upon two ways out of this mess. Both offered freedom and wealth and Dent saw no reason Shiloh should die. He just needed to string a couple of guys along a little longer without getting himself killed in Kern. Stan was a free man in two months and Donovan was a hothead. When Dent was free, he wouldn't be free from their existence, but he'd deal with that later.

Until then, all Dent could do was let the days pass. By the time he was visited by Trish's attorney, everyone would be dead. As he spotted Stan walking around the yard as if he was invincible, he hoped that day would come soon.

## *Chapter 6*

### *1*

She moaned and screamed as Tarek took her in Victor's old bed. Tarek picked her up easily and had been bolder than usual, cutting right to the chase and asking if she wanted to come back to his place. He offered her a drink and she was only one sip in before he was behind her, his hands running up her body and his mouth on her neck. She was having it and went along for the ride, but Tarek lost control of himself while he was with her. He approached her as a release, and nothing more, and when he was done, he kicked her out. She called him an asshole, but it rolled off of him.

At least that was what he told himself, and it was becoming more true by the night. The first night, he'd taken the time to talk to the girl and explain himself. By the fourth night, he'd been able to tell her to get out and ignore the slew of insults she slung at him.

Then, he was alone again, wrapped in sheets that clung to his body where his sweat had been.

"You just want someone to cuddle with," Tarek said, accusingly, though she was long gone. He'd mastered talking to himself in the last four days. At first, it was to fill the silence. Now, he used it as a way to vent his annoyance.

He checked his email through his phone and found his agent had set him up a meeting at noon with an acting coach named Uta Growtowski. Part of him wanted to cancel because he was starting to think he was on the right track. He wasn't feeling funny these days. He'd spent a lot of time in the dark, reading Victor's memoirs, drinking, and picking up women in the evening. He reminded himself that he was only isolating himself from the world…that when the time came to face the audience, he might crack and become fun-loving Tarek once again. He needed all the help he could get and hopefully Vance had something to teach him.

He grabbed the stack of papers from the nightstand by the bed and tucked it under his arms before leaving the property. He'd already moved a suitcase of his clothes in and bought groceries once. Eventually, the fun would have to end, but not until he'd submerged himself enough to adapt.

When he returned home, he found Aileen in a white nightie that hugged her figure. He knew he should look away but couldn't help but admire her figure. When she looked up, it didn't bother her that he was standing there.

*She's gotten comfortable with me. I'm her roommate.*

"Have you seen my key?" she asked.

"What key?" He knew what key.

"The one I showed you the other night. I think I left it here then and I don't think I've seen it since."

Tarek reached in his pocket and came out with the key and handed it to her. She frowned, confused, and tried to sort in her head why he had it. She was too timid to ask, so Tarek offered her the truth instead.

"I went to check the place out," he said.

"What? Why?"

"Just wanted to see how Victor Stone lived. Not every day you walk in a place of that size."

"Is that where you've been?"

"What do you mean?"

"You've been gone lately."

"I've been there a few times, but I don't have to explain myself to you because you're not my mother."

Aileen looked wounded by his remark and her facial features seemed to sink all in.

"Sorry," Tarek said. "I did hang out there a little, but only because I've been reading this." He tossed Victor's memoirs on the table. "You know Victor was having this written?"

"What is it?"

"Autobiography. It's really awful. Guy couldn't write worth a shit. But the events in it…his life…it's fascinating."

"So you're a fan of his now?"

"No, actually I like him even less than I did, but when you see where he comes from and why he is how he is…"

"It sounds like he just made up a bunch of excuses for being an asshole."

"No, it's not that. Feel free to give it a read. Just don't lose my place."

"So you're just reading his biography in his home every night?"

"Yeah. I figured it gives you some breathing room too."

"Tarek, I don't need breathing room in your house. I told you I'd move out and I would have moved out yesterday, but I couldn't find my key and you weren't around. It's not you who has to leave. It's me."

"You don't have to go."

"Tarek, I'm so thankful for everything you've done but…"

"It's helping me to have you here."

She fell silent for a moment. "How?"

"I don't know how to explain it. It just is. I like your company and now that I'm reading Victor's memoirs, I want to know more about him. I'm working on something Aileen. It's something you can help me with and if you did, I could credit you and you could have a cut. Depending on what you offer, maybe you can have a big cut, and this would pay out low six figures. I've stumbled on something huge here."

Aileen looked down at the stack of pages with doubt and shook her head. She wouldn't be able to open those pages.

"I have an appointment, but all I ask is that you give this a read. At least try. And if you absolutely disagree with me, I'll…

*…sell my soul to the devil."*

*"Nah, you might have helped the devil a little," Brandon Wood said, "But Cindy made the choice to date the guy. She likes him."*

*Tarek and his one of the stars of his show stood watching as Victor Stone and Cindy sat backstage talking. She smiled and leaned into him and Victor had a hand on her knee. And Tarek hated it.*

*Tarek ran lines with his other co-stars, Deke, Margie, and Brandon. They'd been waiting for Cindy, but she'd been sucked into whatever conversation Victor and she were having. Cindy didn't usually need to run lines. She rarely messed up during rehearsals. The others liked having her there for a sense of her presence, but they'd make do without if they had to. From the beginning of Victor and Cindy's relationship, Tarek had assumed it was nothing and would be short-lived, but somehow Cindy saw Victor on a regular basis and it hadn't faltered. It didn't seem to be serious. Just ongoing. The longer she stayed with Victor, the less Tarek saw her as part of the group.*

*As his co-star, Tarek felt a certain need to protect Cindy, but he refused to speak poorly of Victor. Tarek had used his fair share of women since fame had taken off, but it had always been mutual. Victor, on the other hand, seemed to be everything Cindy shouldn't like in a man. He was humorless, arrogant, controlling—it frustrated Tarek to watch two people in a relationship, who had no business being with each other. Cindy could have just about anyone. Why be with Victor? If Tarek were to answer that question honestly, he'd only be disappointed in Cindy.*

*Cindy finally finished and approached the group.*

*"We're going to The Belvedere," Deke said. "You want to join?"*

*"No thanks," Cindy said. "I don't understand how you guys can even eat meat after everything I've told you about what they do to them."*

*"I don't like the taste," Brandon said. "I just hate animals."*

*"You've gotta come," Tarek said. "I have to ask you guys something."*

*"Ask us now," Cindy said. "I really have plans."*

*"Okay, so Jo told me tonight that I broke the fourth wall twice in the last taping, which I know. I do it all the time. Always gets a laugh."*

*"Okay..."*

*"He said to stop breaking the fourth wall."*

*"Then stop breaking the fourth wall," Deke said.*

*"I always thought it was funny. Some great sitcoms have done that."*

*"You might be overdoing it," Deke said.*

*Tarek looked around and no one objected. "You guys think I do this too much?"*

*Brandon spoke first. "Well, the show is a show within a show, so I always assumed when you looked into the camera, it was supposed to be the camera within the show."*

*"He doesn't just do it on show segments," Deke said. "If you look into the audience when you're taping a scene outside of the show, it doesn't make sense. Takes the viewer out of the show."*

*"They laugh though."*

*"Yeah, but you're overdoing it. Just play the character. When you look in the camera and smile, your comic personality spills out of the parameters that the show is built on."*

*"The show's a comedy."*

*"Yes, a comedy with a plot about a character. Not Tarek Appleton."*

*Finally, Cindy chimed in. "When I was little, I was doing a commercial and I happened to walk into a sitcom set that I really liked and I felt like I was witnessing the exposure of an organizational complex lie. The sets that were familiar and comfortable, once I was standing in them, were crampy and flimsy. I touched the door and the walls shook. The carpets all turned raggedy where the camera didn't reach. Behind every wall was chicken coop fencing stapled in place, and dark narrow passageways with asbestos. So someone will say, for the purpose of lining up a shot, to lose the wall, and suddenly half the set is folded on undetectable hinges. The area between the sets and the audience seating was an alley and what little floor there was happened to be dotted with inscrutably marked pieces of tape."*

*"Okay..." Tarek said, waiting for the point.*

*"Our sets are the same and I'm much smarter now," Cindy said. "But*

*the live audience is here one night only. At home, viewers number the millions. Add DVD sales and syndication from the box at home, and you see none of that. And there's a reason we hide it and that's why there's a fourth wall. It's the side of the room we don't want them to see. When you break the wall, you've exposed the illusion and you take them out of it."*

*"So I shouldn't break the fourth wall…"*

*"I could go without it," Cindy said. "And Victor hates it too."*

*"What does Victor have to do with the show?" Tarek asked. He was sick of Victor showing up everywhere. It was one thing to hook him up with an agent, but the constant feedback and the power Victor somehow held over a sitcom were unsettling. It was far from Victor's niche, but it seemed he had to have his finger in everything.*

*"Victor doesn't like the direction or the tone at all and what he says makes sense."*

*"What's he say?" Tarek asked. The tension grew thick as everyone realized Tarek was angry.*

*"The anticipation of the love story between our characters. He says it's too drawn out."*

*"We're only in season two. It will ruin the plot. The story hasn't arched there yet."*

*"Victor says there's no arch at all. No one ever learns from their past on this show. At the end of every episode, we supposedly have learned something, but the next, we're making the same mistakes. It's this oddly purgatorial form of entertainment. The same characters appear week after week, displaying the same tics, and having the same arguments, in the same rooms, hallways, stairwells, and offices. There's always complications but rarely solutions, and rarely triumphs. He wants new writers. I told him no way. Those guys are your friends. So now he wants to bring in more."*

*"All this is how sitcoms are done."*

*"But TV has evolved and the days of people looping the same mistakes over and over again are old. The characters only make very small, incremental progress but never really change. And the jokes are getting predictable. So when you break the fourth wall, we're just keeping it dumb."*

*"I write most of the jokes," Tarek said, and a long silence ensued. "Wow, so in the course of five minutes, I pretty much just learned that everything about the show sucks."*

*"It doesn't suck," Cindy said. "It just needs to be reinvented."*

*"You know, in real life, most people actually don't learn from their mistakes. Alcoholics, drug addicts, sex addicts, hot tempered people—all relapse. And if they don't, it sure as hell eats them alive trying not to. The*

*shows depiction of the lives of our characters is fairly accurate, only with toilet humor. Hell, even a chronic womanizer who somehow even conned you into bed, should be able to get behind that logic."*

*Before he could say more, Cindy slapped Tarek and walked away…*

…Uta Growtoski was far more intense than Tarek expected her to be. The world of serious actors frowned on outtakes, canned laughter, and the concept of the fourth wall. In fact, Uta didn't believe in walls at all. Only the self, and that great acting was a reflection of universal truth. He tried to coach Tarek into tapping into his emotions, but Tarek was unable.

"I've had a mostly unemotional life," Tarek said. "I've barely dealt with loss or heartache. I've never had much stress."

"You were kidnapped by a fan," Uta said.

"I wouldn't say kidnapped. Now, that guy, he was an emotional wreck. I've never understood people like that though and maybe that's why I can't act. I usually just mock people but have no idea how to get in their heads. Stan Kline was too insane to understand."

"All of us in many ways are born insane. As babies, our emotions are unregulated, our moods are explosive, we are consumed by irrational fears, erupt into manic happiness, dissolve into inexplicable tears. It takes years, sometimes decades, for an internal emotional governor to fully turn on, and in that time, young minds can be prey to all manner of disorders and pathologies. You developed a resistance early in your life, long before you ever experienced trauma or heartache."

"So how would I tap into my emotional side?" Tarek asked.

"We break down that defensive system. Everyone experiences pain. As a comedian, you must have experienced pain to have found pleasure in mocking what you couldn't comprehend. That was your wall Tarek and I'm going to tear it down."

Tarek gave Uta a run for her money. It seemed it was harder than expected to bring the inner monster out of Tarek. He didn't even seem to have one, but what Tarek had never asked himself was how he got to where he was—why he was sitting in a club with a ventriloquist dummy on his lap in the first place. It wasn't a typical career path and something put him there, even while he was failing.

"You've always been Tarek Appleton, and the traits you displayed on camera were the traits assigned to you," Uta said "Most great performers have PA people who are paid well to glorify their image. You've learned to give people the good and the bad of Tarek Appleton, and you've done it without shame. But you have managed to mask your sadness."

"I'm not sad."

"Tell me about the fourth wall," Uta said, and Tarek was struck with silence. He hadn't thought about the fourth wall since the day his cast-mates expressed their opinions about it.

"You don't know what the fourth wall is?"

"You used to break the fourth wall."

"It's just a term for when someone breaks the scene and gives a nod to the camera."

"Why did you do it?"

"It was funny."

"But that's not why you did it."

"Why'd I do it?"

"Because as a comedian, you were a failure."

"I did well."

"You grew up in an unloving environment."

"That's untrue."

"Your father was military. So was your older brother and sister. But you weren't."

"I was born with an irregular heartbeat. I tried to join the Guard but failed the physical."

"And so you never fit into your environment."

"I didn't mind."

"Sadness is an almost universal trait among comedians. They hate it when their peers become successful. They grow positively apoplectic when success comes to someone they consider unworthy. The bigger the success, the bigger the resentment. You've attained a level of fame that most comics only dream about. Even more unforgivable is that some view that success as undeserved—the result of a bribe."

"I didn't bribe anyone."

"You were offered a series to keep you away from a man you'd been harassing."

"Victor saw potential in me and hooked me up with an agent. That was where it ended."

"And you were given a show and you played a character."

"That's right."

"And then you broke the fourth wall."

"For laughs."

"You wanted people to laugh at Tarek Appleton. Not the character you played. You desperately wanted them to like you for you because you didn't feel good enough growing up, and you didn't feel good enough on stage, and you were reciting lines from a script that you didn't write and the audience was laughing and you said to yourself 'I want to be Tarek Appleton for just a moment and I want to hear them laugh'."

This time, Tarek only opened his mouth to speak, but nothing came out.

"You need that. You couldn't stand that your character was so likable when you weren't sure if you were."

"It was my name on the fan-mail."

"You didn't earn those fans though, did you?"

The message was sinking in and Tarek wanted to say something in defense, but it was something he'd never heard and wasn't sure how to digest. He even started wondering if there was a fraction of truth behind it.

"Then, your show is canceled and you're given an actual talk show. You get to be yourself, but then that show is canceled, so now you're finally seeing that to be someone important, you have to learn to be someone else."

"Will you be the only one roasting me today or is Carrot-top backstage?"

"It isn't only you Tarek. As a society, most of us sing in front of the mirror our whole lives, only to discover the mirror can actually see us. And if we're really lucky, it likes what it sees and we get a TV series."

"I don't think this is going to work for me." Tarek got to his feet but couldn't stop listening.

"It's a hard truth but that's what it comes down to. You never truly succeeded on your own merit. You never evolved. You were tricked into believing you had some success for awhile, but now you know the truth. You want the role of a lifetime, but you're afraid because you have to face a possibility that you've never had to face before: That you might not be good enough."

2

In six months, Brian Van Dyke had dropped forty pounds. He still weighed in at a hefty two hundred and seventy, but his loss was noticeable and some of the regulars at The Wasp would bring it up every so often. Brian brushed off the compliment because he didn't realize he'd been dropping weight and especially didn't understand why.

He had William Lamone to thank. At William's side, he was a fun guy and learned how to go along to get along. William was one of those guys who could hold a conversation with anyone and often would introduce Brian or tell stories of things Brian had done at work and Brian stood by quietly, happy for the recognition. As the night would progress, Brian always became more outgoing. William would hand him a joint or wave him over to a table where a line of white powder was separated for him and Brian would do it without restraint. Throughout the day, William would give Brian something to relax and Brian took it without question. He didn't want anything to change. All pain and insecurities faded when Brian did what William asked him to do. There had never been a better role model for Van Dyke.

He was able to keep up at The Wasp. He'd grown too obnoxious for Guy, who switched to working nights and no longer had to deal with him anyway. Emily and Eve were still the usual night waitresses. Emily was cute and bubbly but was good friends with Eve and therefore, off limits to Brian, who'd learned to have fun working with his ex, as long as he didn't spend time with her outside of work. Their banter through the window that divided the kitchen and the lobby was filled with wisecracks and friendly ribbing, but Eve still held a grudge against Brian and Brian's pride wouldn't allow him to ever look at her the same. She'd stomped all over him and when he tried to have a clean breakup with her, she'd called him out on his mess of a personality in front of everyone.

What everyone but Brian saw though, was how much his personality had changed since then. It was hard to walk all over a guy who didn't take anything seriously. Brian would either be moody at work or not there at all. He'd stand and do his work and when someone spoke to him, he'd shut them out and do what he knew how to do. Some believed he was containing too much while others just thought he was acting like an idiot.

William and Brian manned the morning shift by themselves, with their boss Bob in the office on the computer. The waitresses were always a revolving door of girls who worked a part time job during high school until they found a better one. Brian did his work but never took on a leadership role. Instead, he left that to William, who ran the kitchen like a machine. He'd clearly become Bob's favorite and was even given employee of the year. Brian didn't mind that he was overlooked. He looked up to William too much and stayed loyal to him.

What Brian didn't notice was how much William had changed too. He was worn down and withdrawn. William had a mission of his own that he'd embraced in the beginning. Now, as he was told he would be employee of the year, it hit him just how much he'd been sucked into a role that was supposed to be short term. Brian was still alive and Toby had been holding back for a long time. Henry was in a similar boat—now married—and they often discussed backing out of the whole thing and saying screw the money. It didn't feel like the money could even exist and at the pace Toby had them moving, they'd never see it anyway.

He hated working at The Wasp and Brian's loyalty was an annoyance. He didn't like finding parties and didn't like using. No one noticed that he barely drank at night. He'd stand by and watch and pressure Brian into consuming too much. He secretly hoped that Brian would eventually do himself in. Maybe one night he'd get in an accident driving home drunk or just overuse and never wake up. It was the scenario that Toby had envisioned, but it was Toby that was in idle. William could have pushed Brian to the limits at any time in the last four months, but Toby never gave the go ahead, and the more Henry and William discussed it, the more they started to realize that Toby was holding back for a reason.

The day that it all took it's toll started with Bob sitting in his office and detecting an unusual smell. He searched for an hour before opening a floor safe that had been built into the floor but never used. When he opened it, the smell overwhelmed him and he found the culprit to be a mutant potato that had been in there for some time. It was blackened on the outside and had sprung branches that had run out of space to expand. He had to cut it in half to pull it out and when that was done, he grew angry that someone had put it there in the first place. He asked a few questions until he found the guilty parties to be Brian Van Dyke and William Lamone. William he could forgive. In the beginning, William had a mouth on him, but he eventually shaped up. It was Brian who was wearing thin on Bob and this gave him a reason to terminate him.

If only William would be okay with that.

"Where's my order?" Eve asked from the window.

"Going through a process called 'cooking'," Brian said, carelessly. His hair was uncombed, he had days worth of stubble, and deep lines sat under his eyes.

"It'll be a second," William said, overriding Brian's answer with a serious response which satisfied Eve. She thanked William and went on her way.

Bob entered the kitchen in that moment holding the potato in a plastic bag. "What the hell is this?" he asked.

"Looks like a potato," Brian said.

"Did you put it in the floor safe?"

"Shit, I think so. I forgot about that." Brian laughed as he observed the transformation the potato had gone through.

"Sorry Bob," William said, his face serious. "We did that a long time ago and forgot about it."

"For one thing, you're not allowed in the office. For another, do you know what would happen if the health inspector showed up?"

"I don't think a health inspector would check a floor safe," Brian said. "It was just an experiment."

"An experiment?" Bob put his hands on his hips. "What were you trying to learn?"

"Uh…what would happen to a potato in a floor safe."

"I'll tell you what happened. It rotted and now the office stinks."

"Sorry Bob," William cut in front of Brian. "We won't do it again."

"I know you won't. It's Van Dyke I'm worried about. Do you know how much waste we already have?"

"Why don't we just serve it?" Brian asked. William shot him a look, but Brian didn't care. He was still trying to win William's approval and hadn't noticed that William left him behind a long time ago.

"I've given you a verbal warning already. Consider this a write up. After this, any more incidents and you're done."

After Bob left the office, William shook his head in disbelief. "Are you trying to lose your job?"

"You did that with me," Brian said. "We laughed about it."

"Things have changed. You need to take everything out of the ceiling tiles, whatever is taped under the counters…"

"Okay, fine Dad."

"Fine. Get fired asshole. I'm through helping you." William went back to cleaning the kitchen and Brian stood speechless.

"What the hell's your problem?"

"You're out of control."

"Oh, right. First I don't stand up for myself enough. Now, I'm…"

"I tried to show you how to get some respect, but this isn't the way. Going around destructively ruining everything is worse than being too nice. All I suggested was taking control of your life. Not burning every bridge you have."

"You think I care about this job? If I lose it, I'll find another easily."

"Good luck passing a drug test," William muttered.

Brian tried to face away but watched William with a sideways glance. His hero was angry and Brian had no idea what he wanted. Whatever middle ground William was looking for wasn't territory Brian was familiar with.

Emily appeared in the window and nodded toward the lobby. "She's here again," she said to William. Brian glanced into the lobby where a hefty woman waddled into the diner and found her own seat. Emily grabbed a menu and filled a water for the woman.

"Great," William said.

"Who is she?" Brian asked.

"Her name is Nellie. She's been coming in lately and she fills her plate with chicken strips and tears them to shreds. Then, she tears a napkin into shreds and mixes it all together in a big pile and leaves."

"Why?"

"After she leaves, someone clears her plate. Then she comes back in an hour and throws a fit because we threw her food away?"

"How come no one told me about this?" Brian asked.

"It's not that interesting. It's just an annoying customer who's trying to game us."

"If she leaves, we should just leave her plate there instead of tossing it."

"We already tried. She'll just sit outside and wait until it's clear. She's apparently got nothing better to do."

Brian tried to get back to work, but he couldn't stop watching the table with the plate filled with chicken strips and napkins, sitting there waiting to be picked up. The woman sat outside in her car. She looked like she was sleeping.

"She's just waiting out there," Eve said.

"How about we bring it back here and she'll come in thinking we threw it away, and when she comes back in, we bring it back out to her?"

"She'll say we did something to her food. She always has a complaint."

"Eve, this is ridiculous."

"Why don't you just stock for the rush and ignore her?"

"We can't have someone like her in here."

William appeared around the corner. "Brian…stock," he commanded.

Brian obeyed and watched William out of the corner of his eye. He wondered if this was a test—or if he was just having a bad day. *Just be a good friend*, he told himself. When he finished stocking, he narrowed his eyes at the plate in lobby, waiting to be picked up. He didn't understand why they were so accommodating to the woman. She wasn't the kind of customer they should have wanted to return. He wanted to give her a piece of his mind, or spit in her food, or do anything but give her the luxury of a refund. To submit was to play dumb, and the last thing Brian wanted was for the woman to think she'd outsmarted them.

He walked away and tried to forget the woman. Bob was just about done with Brian and William would no longer be so quick to defend him. Brian suspected his days were going to be numbered if he didn't shape up, and kept telling himself to go along to get along, but the pull of Nellie and the plate etched itself in his brain, and as his eyes kept coming back to it and the ticking of the clock as the woman waited in her car, Brian felt a rage from somewhere deep within.

3

Tarek grabbed the mail coming into his building and stopped on an invitation, addressed to Aileen and forwarded by the post office to Tarek's address. He rolled his eyes, annoyed at how intrusive it was that Aileen's mail was coming there, yet, he didn't want her to go anywhere. She was one of the ways into the mind of Victor. He turned the invitation in his hands and the words PLUS ONE were where his eyes focused.

It seemed Aileen's son was set to be married in two weeks. She'd never mentioned it to Tarek and tended to shy away from conversations that made her address that she was a mother. Whatever qualms she had with Jason, he hoped she'd set them aside and attend. He also hoped he could be the plus one, but he doubted she'd ask.

When he reached his suite, he found Aileen in her usual spot on the couch. He handed the invite to her and watched her reaction. She looked stunned.

"If you need flight money, it's on me," Tarek said.

"No…" she said, but never offered a reason why.

"You're going right?"

"I don't know."

"I think this is one of those things that you either do, or you don't and he resents you  forever."

"He doesn't really want me there."

"How would you know that?"

"I didn't even know he was engaged. I never met her."

"I know you're not close with him but he sent an invite because he wants you there."

"He knows I wouldn't have the money to fly to Hawaii."

"My offers good if you change your mind."

*Damn*, Tarek thought. *I could learn something about Victor through Jason.*

He left it at that and went on his way to meet with his agent. He wanted to tell Levi Katz some of his plans and how the coaching went. He wasn't sure he knew how it went himself, but had submitted to his teacher completely. If there was a way that Tarek could detach from his true self, he didn't have the key.

Half an hour later, he hurried into his agent's office, late from the mid-day traffic rush. Levi didn't even notice the time. They smiled and shook hands.

"You hungry?" Levi asked, and another ten minutes later, they were sharing a table and ordering Thai.

Tarek relayed some of what he learned and as he repeated what he'd been told, it started to make more sense.

"What'd I tell you?" Levi lit a cigarette. "Uta's the best, isn't she?"

"Meeting with her will be beneficial."

"I got more good news for you. I got you a gig."

Tarek straightened up and raised his eyebrows in anticipation. The news of a gig wasn't what it once was though. Now, Tarek had a fear, and it all stemmed from what he didn't want to be anymore.

Levi exhaled a cloud of smoke. "That series Rhonda and Gene… highest rated show in prime-time…they want you to guest star."

"Rhonda and Gene? No shit?" Tarek asked. It was a sitcom...a popular one. "You got a script?"

"Not yet. They've got an upcoming episode where Gene tries to get onto a talk show with this talent he's got and they want to use your show."

Tarek sighed. "So I'd be playing myself…"

"Yeah, but on Rhonda and Gene."

"Pass."

"What? I told them you'd do it."

"Without talking to me?"

"I didn't think it was necessary. I thought you were trying to get back into the game."

"I'm trying to recreate myself though."

"Recreate yourself after this. You can't turn this down. Especially now."

"I'm looking at film Levi. I'm going to put together an on-line fundraiser to make an independent film. I'll have the script written and delivered and I'll play the lead. I don't need jobs handed to me. I'm funding my own career now."

"Well then what the fuck you need me for? Is that what you're saying?" Levi shoved the half smoked cigarette in the ashtray and twisted it into a pile of ash.

"I'm not saying that. I'm saying I'm taking on more mature roles. I don't need comedic material. I've been there. Done that."

"Oh geez." Levi looked down and shook his head.

"You got something to say to me?" Tarek asked.

"Yeah, you're not an actor. You're a personality. You know that."

"That's blunt."

"Don't act like this is a big newsflash. Surely you've picked up on this."

"I've never had a real shot. If I land on my head, I'll go back to this goofy shit, but I'm giving it a go."

Levi said no more. He changed the subject and they only spoke of the weather and Levi's kid's softball tournament. Now and then, someone would pass and recognize Tarek and whisper something to whoever they were with and they'd both look in passing, psyched to see a semi-celebrity. They'd laugh about something and move on. They saw Tarek the funny guy, Tarek the entertainer. He hated being recognized that way. He wanted to be left alone...left alone until people saw him as a talent... as the guy who should be the next comic book hero or James Bond. Until then, he just wanted to be left alone...

*...God it's great to be recognized, Tarek thought after an elderly couple insisted on taking a picture with him at the Citiwalk. He could get used to going out in public and smiling as people told him how great they thought him to be. He'd been stopped buying groceries, getting coffee in the morning, and just about everywhere that Tarek showed his face in public, people would recognize him. They were accommodating and full of questions, and it never got old.*

*Life was better now. If Tarek wanted something, it was his. The days of financing for large items were over. Everything was cash, and the banks wanted his business and gave him the best rates. He was able to donate to organizations and they'd praise him, though it was very little of what he had. There were few things to complain about.*

*One of those things was his relationships.*

*He'd never been attracted to his costar Cindy. She was about as attractive as a woman could be, but they'd started working professionally and that was the only way he knew her. Now and then, there would be a cast party or they'd find themselves in the same place, but Tarek considered Cindy to be like a little sister to him. He wanted to make sure she dated the right guys and didn't drive home drunk.*

*What really bothered Tarek about Cindy was how dismissive she was of him. He'd always believed that under the surface, she believed herself to be the star of his show. In some ways she was. She was all glitz and glamor and when fashion magazines featured a spread of what to wear and what hairstyle was in, it was Cindy they called. Tarek was happy for her, but sensed she didn't take his career all that seriously. It was great to be loved by the public, but he hoped to be loved by his peers.*

*After Cindy gave him her opinion about breaking the fourth wall, Tarek was distraught. Everyone told him it was no big deal, but if they'd withheld one opinion until he asked, what else were they withholding? Did they even find him right for the role?*

*His co-star Deke asked Tarek to play wing-man that night, but Tarek did what he always did when he was in the dumps: He went drinking alone instead. Sometimes, he needed the attention of a stranger to boost his ego. Deke was clearly talented and had studied acting for years before landing a spot on the show. On the side, he was landing roles in films and his career was seemingly headed in a good direction. Tarek needed to be a big fish that night and so he drove to West Hollywood and spent the night in the VIP room of The Rainbow. He smiled to himself as he recognized a couple members of classic heavy metal bands and even another TV star. There was something about The Rainbow that was a hell of a lot of fun, but dark and depressing at the same time. It hit the spot.*

*After a few drinks and short conversations with women he didn't find himself to be all that interested in—but would settle for if nothing better came along—he stumbled to the bathroom and joined a line a dozen men long. He turned to make a comment to the man who'd lined up behind him, but tensed up as he recognized Victor Stone. Victor was standing right at his back but hadn't recognized him yet. Maybe he wouldn't...or maybe he'd ignore Tarek.*

*Tarek's mind traveled to Cindy. She had said Victor was working, hadn't she? Tarek couldn't remember now.*

*Victor spotted Tarek and gave a slight nod and half smile. It was apparent that Victor was still displeased with their last encounter. They had a few minutes and Tarek figured it was worthwhile to smooth over, especially if Cindy was going to be dating Victor.*

*Tarek smiled wide and pretended as if they were friends again. "Hey Victor. Good to see you. How have you been?"*

*"Very well," Victor said. "Yourself?"*

*"Life is chaotic," Tarek said. "But in a good way."*

*"I'm pleased to hear that."*

*"Listen, Victor, I don't know what happened between us but whatever impression I've given in the past is just stupid because I actually have nothing but deep respect and admiration for you. Things happened fast for me and I'm just learning the business and I lost sight of some things for awhile."*

*Tarek was surprised he'd been so blunt, but it paid off immediately. It seemed as if Victor's whole body loosened by his confession. He made a mental note that Victor was a man who only needed to be shown some respect. That's all it really was. Disrespect the man and he'd hold a grudge forever. Call yourself stupid for doing so, and all was well. Tarek didn't mind letting go of some pride to keep his relationships healthy.*

*"I hadn't even been upset," Victor said. Tarek almost laughed at what was clearly a lie.*

*"I didn't peg you as a guy who would come to a place like this," Tarek said.*

*"This isn't my scene. I'm here with a friend." Victor nodded toward a woman at the bar, who wore a strapless dress that boasted her cleavage and a tight black dress that hugged her hips. The way she sat, the way she waited for Victor...she wasn't just a friend. At least that's not how she*

*saw it.*

*"Are you and Cindy no longer…"*

*Victor cut him off. "Cindy and I are fine. What we have is very open."*

*Tarek sensed Victor's discomfort and realized to ask him accusatory questions was another sign of disrespect. He almost apologized, but the realization that Cindy had been talking Victor up and thought they were a real couple set in. He wanted to give Victor a piece of mind, or plead with him not to hurt her, but Victor was the one man he couldn't fight. "Do I need to keep this between us?" It was a respectful enough question, but Tarek was fishing. He had to know.*

*"That would be best," Victor said. "Cindy could misread the situation."*

*"What's the situation?" Tarek asked.*

*"You of all people can understand that when you're in the shoes we're in, we can have almost anything we want. I would like very much to settle down one day Tarek, but I have yet to find one woman who makes all other women disappear."*

*"But you're a big deal," Tarek said. "She'll hear it from someone, if not the tabloids."*

*"The tabloids tell me every day that you and Cindy are a coupling, but that's not true, is it?"*

*"Right, but…"*

*"Things will happen how they happen, and that will be between Cindy and I. You have no place in this Tarek."*

*Victor was irritated again and Tarek backed down. A thousand words went through his head. He wanted desperately to tell Victor to fuck off and call Cindy and tell her where her beloved Victor was, but Victor was to be respected, and if Victor wasn't respected, Tarek sensed he would regret it.*

*"No worries," Tarek said. "I won't say a word…"*

…Deke did go on to star in some major motion pictures. He was the costar of two blockbusters, a war epic, and had brought home various awards for his work. As important as Deke had become, he still responded to Tarek's call and told him to come right over. Deke's house was one of the most impressive mansions Tarek had ever been inside. After Deke gave Tarek the tour, and made him a drink, they sat at the edge of Deke's pool and let their feet dangle in the water as they chatted.

Deke talked upcoming projects and Tarek expressed his desire to get into film—to become a serious actor. Tarek studied Deke's reactions and wasn't surprised to see doubt in his eyes. He tried to sell himself the best he could—to convince Deke that he wasn't going to be the same Tarek

Appleton that he once knew.

"People come to expect things of actors," Deke said. "You become reliable as a certain type."

"But not everyone. Look what happened to you."

"I was a stage actor before the sitcom. Studied at Julliard. I moved out here with high hopes and took the first thing I was offered."

"So you regret the show?"

"Not at all. In hindsight, I wouldn't be where I am without it, but I look back and it was foolish. It was me reading bad jokes. It wasn't a showcase of my talent, but it was visibility, and that mattered then."

"I've been there," Tarek said. "People know who I am. And maybe I'm reliable, but people will complain and say I can't do it and then I will and blow them away."

"Why now? What's been happening all this time?"

"What do you mean?"

"Word is that you had a breakdown on your show. You did the thing with the reporters and that pissed a lot of people off and made everyone else question your sanity. You escaped that fan who tried to kill you. I must have missed something somewhere along the way, but your whole life seems like a movie."

"Don't forget I ruined the sitcom."

"You didn't ruin it." Deke polished off his drink. "After that day with Cindy, you stopped liking each other and it showed. You lost your chemistry. The public knew your relationship was in the dumps and everyone stopped caring whether your onscreen characters would become romantically involved or not. But it was just a sitcom. It was a stepping stone. What mattered was what you did after…a talk show…more comedy…negative publicity…"

"To this day, people always reference the sitcom. Everyone loves the sitcom."

"It was about a talk-show designed to help people, and every episode featured the who's who of lowlifes and in every episode, you broke through their wall, only to have a new freak sitting on your couch the next day. And what happened to the characters? Nothing. No one grew. No one overcame their flaws. It was canceled before they had the chance. It may be that the sitcom's constant avoidance of any final, dramatic catharsis is its accidental strength. That would make this the least lifelike form of entertainment, but the most comfortingly like real life. We're born. We die. Their love for you will never live forever. Friends, family, women…all disappear in time. Everything you've done has come to an abrupt end. You've left nothing great because you refuse to step outside of your comfort zone and you've avoided that because you want those hallmark things: love, acceptance…"

"Is it too late to bounce back?"

"I couldn't tell you. That's for you to figure out. But I'll tell you one thing Tarek, and this is what used to bother all of us: You were the show, and you wanted it that way. And if you bring nothing to it other than your name, then you're abusing the kind of fame that millions of people are lining up to have a chance at. There are plenty of people far more talented than us that are never given a shot and what do you think they're thinking when they watch us read lines that anyone could deliver as well or better, a few months out of a year and make millions of dollars doing it? The trades are telling them you sleep with hookers, mess around, drink and party too much…they're dying to be in your shoes and they see what you do as a form of art. But you're here because you met the right guy at the right time. Have you earned it? Can you earn it? Or are you famous because you want to be famous and being likable is more important than being respected?"

Tarek nodded and between Deke and his acting coach, he was beginning to piece together and make sense of all perceptions. "So how do you do it? How do you step outside of yourself?"

"Well, I've been studying my whole life, but I'll share this with you, because it worked for me: A few years back, when I got the world war two picture, I suddenly woke up one night in a sweat. I realized I was in over my head—that I lacked the depth it took to play the part. I grabbed at it because it was everything I wanted, and then later I asked myself if I was even capable. So my agent sends me to this celebrity therapist who is supposed to dig up emotions and teach me how to control them. You know what he tells me to do?"

"What?"

"He said I needed to interrupt myself. I had to do something in life I would never do—something I was afraid of. So ever since I saw Jaws when I was a little, I've been deathly afraid of sharks. I wouldn't touch the ocean. I'd go out on a boat, but never in the water. So I decide I need to be in the ocean, but I can't bring myself to do it. At the same time, filming starts and I'm hung up on all this shit and my mind is cluttered and my performance sucked. Finally, I decide I'm going all in. In one weekend, I fly to Honolulu just so I can get in one of those touristy shark cages. They put you in this thing and lower you in the water and you get to see these beasts up close. I was deep in the darkness of the ocean and all I see are black shadows passing in the distance. Then, one comes right up to me. I swear this fucking shark passes by and nudges the cage as if testing it, because it looks like it wants to check me out…see if I'm something good to eat. It passes a second later, but I couldn't sleep for a week after that. But you know what? I was reborn Tarek. My mind was completely clear of all the clutter in life. I interrupted myself by doing what I don't do. And after that, everything was easy."

"So that's it?"

"Try it and see."

"I don't know that I'm afraid of anything."

"Everyone's afraid of something Tarek. You've always tried so hard to be the perfectly manufactured celebrity. I've never seen stubble on your face and I've never seen a hair out of place. A man as compulsive as you must be afraid of a little chaos. Interrupt yourself Tarek. Once you do, you'll find a kaleidoscope of shit that you never believed possible."

## 4

Brian's eyes fixated on Nellie, as she sat in her car waiting. She would waste half a day at their expense, just to get a free meal. Eve, Emily, and William were easily able to ignore her and go about business, but her plan latched into Brian's mind.

*There's something wrong with me. I can't be normal.*

He couldn't overcome the bitter feelings he had toward freeloaders. His hard work in life had gone virtually ignored, but he still believed in hard work. He would never sit in a casino or play the lottery because he wanted every dime in his pocket to be the earned. It was people who put band-aids or hair in their food who demanded a refund that repulsed Brian more than ever, though lately, those feelings were more apparent than ever.

If they let Nellie get away with this, she'd be back tomorrow and the next day and forever until someone put an end to it. If Brian dropped food or broke an over-easy egg when he flipped it, or dipped a fry in alfredo sauce while the boss was looking, he'd hear a lecture about shrinkage and the cost of supplies.

*I'd be doing them a favor.*

His mind was made up in that moment, and no matter what they would say, Brian was the one who was always told to man up. He'd embarrassed himself time after time for not having the balls to get things done, and if he was able to do what no one else did, they would never have the right to talk to him like he was a pushover again.

He walked straight to the lobby and to Millie's table. He could see her in the car perking up, ready to pounce once her lunch was in the garbage.

Time stopped for Brian as what was only a fifteen second journey slowed to every step, broken into every moment. What he was doing was a simple act, but it felt like one of the most important of his life. He hadn't been taking much shit lately. He didn't argue with people but he took a careless approach. He never offered the luxury of a reaction when being yelled at and he refused to show any kind of learning curve. He'd promoted himself as someone who would do what he wanted and was unaffected by other opinions. It hadn't really gotten him anywhere, but it also hadn't hurt him, and people at least backed off. The skunk had its scent, the porcupine had its quills. Brian Van Dyke's defensive weapon of choice was his lack of attention to anyone and anything. The only opinion that mattered was William's and even though William had been brash with him lately, this would show William once and for all that Brian was no pushover.

He grabbed the plate and with one swift motion, he dumped everything into the garbage. Moments later, when Nellie walked in and pretended to search for her food, Brian interjected. "It's in the garbage if you still want to eat it."

"I only left for a moment," she shrieked.

Bob entered the lobby. The waitresses froze in place. William's head appeared through the window, watching intently.

"We're not stupid lady. You think this scam fools anyone? You're not welcome here anymore."

"Brian, what are you doing?" Bob asked. His voice sounded calm, as if he was trying to talk Brian off a ledge.

"This lady sits in her car and pretends to leave and then we throw out the rest of her food and refund her when she comes back in."

"We don't know that."

"Everyone knows it!" Brian shouted. Now, the customers stopped eating too and all attention was on Brian. Even Nellie backed away with widened eyes. "We can't act like this is okay." His voice shook and Brian realized he was emotional—far more than he should have been. "Dammit..." he said and wiped a line of sweat from his forehead.

"Why don't you come sit down?" Bob said, as if Brian was a child.

"What about her?"

"Emily will take care of the customer. Come sit down."

Bob placed Brian in the office and repeatedly asked if he was comfortable and okay. Brian shook his head and was left alone. Bob entered the kitchen and waived William over. William approached, all color drained from his face. He had no idea what he was in the middle of, what he had done to Brian, or when it would end.

"What's going on with Van Dyke?" Bob spoke at almost a whisper.

"I don't see him as much outside of work," William lied. "He's been tired and pretty careless. I've suspected he's into things he shouldn't."

"You're a great employee here William. I think you're going to go far. I don't know what to do about this problem with Van Dyke."

"Fire him," William said and let out a deep breath. To say it was to unload a heavy burden.

"And what about you?"

"You would have fired him a long time ago if not for me. I've tried to be a loyal friend, but I agree. He's only getting worse. It's not good for business. You can do what you need to do and there will be no hard feelings from me."

Bob nodded and clapped William on the back.

After Bob had a long talk with Brian in his office, Brian walked straight through the kitchen to the back door. He passed William on the way out and before Brian hit the exit, a thousand thoughts flowed through William's mind. What would happen next? Would he still have that connection to Brian? Without William's influence, would Brian undo all the damage done? He hurried to catch up to him.

"I'll call you when I'm off," William said.

Brian spun. "Why?"

A pause. "Because we're friends."

"Sure we are. Stand up for myself. Stop standing up for myself. I can't win with you."

"What you did out there wasn't standing up for yourself. That was an unprovoked attack."

"On a worthless freeloading bitch."

"On a woman who very likely has a rough life and has to deal with that and is causing us to lose an average of two dollars a day."

"What? So you guys are ignoring her out of empathy?"

"It doesn't matter why we're doing it. It wasn't your problem. You don't lose that money. The company does, so if management is okay with it, you need to be too. This isn't about sticking up for yourself Brian, cause that's not what you're doing. You're just lashing out at everything. It's when someone is treating you as less than a human being that you should be making that injustice known."

"What are you gonna do?" Brian asked. "You hated it here. You just gonna stay?"

"For now."

"That's great," Brian said, sarcastically.

"Actually, it sucks," William said. "Because half my check is going to child support and I can barely pay my rent as it is. It really sucks that I gotta do this. Meanwhile, you're living large and working here just to have a job. You have plenty of money. You don't have the expenses I have. Maybe that's why you treat your life like it's just a toy to swat around. You don't know real hardship Van Dyke. You're a silver spoon child who was given an incredible job opportunity and a shitload of money before your boss died."

"You don't know anything about me."

"I know you ruined this and it had nothing to do with me, so stop blaming me. You're lucky you didn't get fired months ago like Bob wanted."

"Ah, so you did give him the go-ahead."

"Damn right I did," William said. "Because you suck at this."

"I agree," Brian said. "I'll just get something better."

With that, Brian disappeared through the door.

William shook his head. Toby would be pissed, but William was done.

## 5

*Think like Victor. Get in his head.*

It was the phrase he repeated the whole way to Kern and the only thought that comforted his nerves. It was Stanley Kline that had occupied Tarek's thoughts for months after he kidnapped him and it was reliving that day that ultimately caused Tarek, and everything he had, to crumble. Following his kidnapping, he'd had nightmares, in which he'd wake up in a cold sweat, breathless and trembling.

Stan was someone he hoped he'd never see again, but Deke had told Tarek that he needed to confront a fear, and no matter how much he tried to ignore it, there was no greater fear for him than Stan. He'd called Kern and learned when he could visit and what that entailed. He asked how close he would be to the prisoner and he was assured that there would be a glass wall between them. It was good news, and yet, defeated the purpose. He was supposed to be afraid, but just seeing Stan would slow his heart.

Everything Tarek did from that moment forward took a great deal of persuasion. He would stop and consider every movement, from driving to the prison, to getting out of his car, to entering the building. Everything was a series of decisions he had to talk himself into, until finally he sat on a wooden chair, staring at a glass wall and a telephone, waiting for the seat across from him to be filled.

A buzzer sounded and a door opened and a guard escorted Stan in. Stan looked like he'd lost a little bulk, but his hair was longer and his face was covered with patchy stubble, and his eyes looked darkened, as if being locked up had take a toll on him. When he saw Tarek, his face didn't give away any expression. He fell into the seat across from Tarek and picked up the phone. Stan didn't look up at Tarek. He only held the phone to his ear and waited for Tarek to make a final decision.

*Think like Victor.*

The manuscript gave Tarek an endless amount of information as to how Victor handled conflict. People, quite simply, answered to him. Victor feared no one because he had the money to buy his way out of problems, or buy his problems away. Tarek had money too—and much more power than Stan. He tried to tell himself that there was nothing to worry about because with his power, he could take care of a problem like Stan, but as he stared through the glass, his voice was caught in his throat and he wasn't sure what to say.

*Think like Victor.*

He picked up the phone.

"Yeah?" Stan asked, carelessly, as if he'd answered a call from an unknown number.

Tarek choked on his words, aware he was not channeling Victor at all. "I have something to…"

Stan seemed satisfied by Tarek's fear. To think about Stan was bad enough but seeing him in person made Tarek sick.

"How's Anthony Freeman?" Stan asked. "I hope he's eating plenty of vegetables."

Tarek looked up, and understood the joke while staring into Stan's cruel face. He was no different than a child with a magnifying glass, burning ants. He wanted the money, but he had a cruel way of enjoying what he had to do to attain it. "How do we take it out?" Tarek asked, bluntly.

"You mean no one has bothered to take a look at it?" Stan was genuinely surprised.

"He know if someone cuts something or tries to trip it…" Tarek's words broke apart again.

"There's nothing to trip it, but the circuit is completed by the flow of blood. While he's alive, he will be fine."

"Then how do you take it out?" Tarek asked.

"If you bothered to look at the bomb, you'll find a pad which has no numerals on it, but resembles the numeral keypad of a keyboard. It is activated and deactivated with a code."

Tarek sensed Stan was proud, and saw the smile begging for approval on his face. He was showing off—making it clear just how easy it would be to shut the bomb off.

"What's the code?" Tarek asked.

"If I gave you a code, would you even believe me?"

"Give me the right code."

"Why would I do that?"

"Because what you did to him…" Tarek couldn't think of the answer that would persuade Stan.

*Think like Victor.*

"Because if you don't, I'll make sure you never get out of here." It was better, but Tarek still wasn't feeling it. His tone was wrong, and Stan was laughing. Tarek couldn't keep him here and Stan knew it. "And if you get out of here, I'll kill you." The threat sounded unnatural, and Stan laughed harder.

Tarek closed his eyes and thought about Victor's home…sitting inside at a typewriter with the manuscript in his hand, swallowed by the darkness and the smell of rotting wood and dust coating the walls. The dark consumed Tarek on some nights, and on those nights, he'd step outside feeling like a different man. He'd smoke a cigarette, have a drink, pick up a woman, bring her back and have rough sex with her—sex that wasn't Tarek Appleton sex…the next day he'd read some more and go to the library to read articles about Victor Stone and men like Victor. He would read about the mafia, the cocaine wars in the 70s and 80s, the current news of bombs and religious killings, and the fathers who would murder their family because they couldn't handle separation and failure. On some nights, the light of the world was swallowed by the dark if Tarek only allowed himself to see it, and funny Tarek was consumed by someone else entirely.

"You think I can't kill you, you piece of human shit," Tarek said, leaning forward with darkness in his eyes. Stan smiled, but the humor was gone and replaced by curiosity. "I've got millions of dollars you dumbass. I can pay anyone in here to stab you any time I want. I'll provide the weapon. How many of these guys in here have wives and kids waiting for them? You think they won't kill one piece of shit like you if they think I can give their families a little something to get by a little easier? You have no leverage over me Stan. You've got nothing. You sit in here and smile and laugh like this is all planned and you're winning the war, but you had a plan once to kill everyone in a room, and I ruined that for you. I beat you then. You have no control, because as smart as you think you are, I've already beat you every time we've gone head to head, and if I don't FEEL like watching you walk out of here, I'll simply have you murdered. And I won't make it fast Stan. I'll make sure that they tear you apart limb for limb and feed them to you."

Stan's smile was gone and replaced by a stunned expression. He shook it off, disallowing Tarek the satisfaction. "I've seen you in action Appleton. You couldn't hurt me."

"Wasn't I the reason Victor got rid of you?" Tarek shot back, and though Tarek felt out of body, everything he said felt great. "Didn't you come and threaten me when I was still doing open mics and shortly after, Victor canned you? Yeah, he told me that when we first met. I forced you out. I've beat you twice. You're not a man Stanley. You had a family, right? You lost them because you couldn't provide because you're uneducated and worthless. Isn't that right? Where's your daughter now Stanley? I bet her mother only talks about what a horrible man you were. I bet that little girl could use a father. I bet when your ex talks about you, she makes jokes and laughs and she brings men home and talks about what an inadequate lover you were. I might have to look her up. I'll pleasure her while someone's sticking a fork in your skull."

That was what set Stan off, and when Tarek would look back later, what he would be the most surprised at, was that he didn't flinch. He stared through the glass as Stan threw the phone at the wall. The guards reacted immediately but Stan managed to struggle free of their grasp long enough to hit the glass partition a couple times. Tarek never lost his smile and kept his eyes glued to Stan's as Stan shouted every obscenity and threatened Tarek's life. Tarek stood, assuming the conversation was over, but then Stan whispered something to a guard and after he'd calmed down, they let him return to his seat. Tarek found it peculiar, since Stan should have been dragged out. Both men sat again and Tarek picked up his phone. Stan took a deep breath and picked up his end.

"Go ahead Appleton. Do what you think you gotta do. I'll be out of here very soon."

"All I'm asking for is the code," Tarek said. "Give me that and I won't have to humiliate you again."

"You never humiliated me," Stan said, slowly, his jaw clenched."What the fuck is wrong with you? I really screwed you up, huh?"

"We're not here to play mind games with each other," Tarek said. "I want the code, and I want it now, and if you don't give it to me, I will see to it that you never get out of here alive and long after you're gone, I'll make sure your family gets to know me and I'm sure my celebrity will go far with them. I'll pay your daughter's way through life. Maybe she'll call me daddy. And one day I'll tell her that you once put a bomb in a man and tried to kill a dozen people and what a psychopath you are. Or you can give me the code. It's up to you, but I have places to be, so I'll count down from ten. If you don't start talking, that's going to be the end of you…"

*…Tarek blocked Victor and his infidelities from his mind and minded his own business, which seemed like the only logical thing to do. Then the day came that Cindy figured it out for herself and she became intolerable*

*to work with. It was hard to make people laugh when someone toxic was around and though Cindy had always been a professional, she couldn't hide her anger toward Victor.*

*The crew made it through taping and Tarek attempted to carry the show with Cindy out of commission. It wouldn't be an episode for the "best of" lists, but it was good enough. It was a "filler" episode as they called it—an episode that didn't move anything along. It stood on it's own. In the sitcom world, most episodes were fillers.*

*They hoped it would blow over, but every time Cindy came to work, she was in a salty mood, often talking poorly of Victor and laughing at his misfortunes, while rolling her eyes when she saw he was in the news with a new woman. Finally, it came to a head and an intervention took place. Tarek didn't plan on being a part of it, but Deke sprang it on everyone after curtain call one night and Tarek got sucked into the conversation.*

*"We've all been patient," Deke said, not bothering to hide his frustration. "But if you can't be professional, it impacts all of our performances and the show itself. We're all going to lose this gig because of you."*

*Cindy turned and immediately began apologizing. Tarek expected rage, but she genuinely felt bad and told them there were things she needed to work through.*

*"We're here for you," Deke said. "But we need you to do this in a more private way. Just forget the guy. He's just a guy, and he's way older than you. What were you expecting?"*

*"Well, he's way older than his new girlfriend too and you know what he told me? He told me he was going to marry her. So not only was he cheating on me, but he was carrying on a relationship with a girl he met at the DMV two months ago. And for all I know, there's more than that."*

*"I saw him with a girl at a club a few months back," Tarek said, before sticking his foot in his mouth. He'd only been stating something matter of factually, but everyone stopped and gave Tarek their attention.*

*"You saw him with someone and didn't tell me?" Cindy looked wounded.*

*"I thought it was platonic. He's always been a serial dater and I told you that."*

*"I can't believe you wouldn't tell me you saw him with a woman."*

*"He's a business guy," Tarek said, growing defensive. "He probably has to be in all kinds of places with women. What difference does it make now?"*

*"I could have not been with him the last few months. That's what difference it makes."*

*"Except, if I had told you, you would have just been pissed off at me. If*

*you're blind to the public opinion of someone, then you're not going to believe me."*

"It doesn't matter how I would have reacted. You still should have told me."

"Whatever Cindy. I don't even know why you care about other women. You were with him for money, and that's what you got."

"And you're loyal to him because he got you an agent."

"Yeah, so what? That's not a bad thing. The guy got me a job. Believe it or not, I still don't like him. I can be loyal to him without liking him. It wasn't a preference of him over you. You're a hundred times better as a person. It's that I owe him and I figured you'd see it eventually anyway and I didn't think you two were that serious. And, you know, I'm a guy." Tarek shrugged off his last point, but it somehow felt like the most important point of all.

"What's that mean, you're a guy? What is that?"

"Guys don't tell on other guys." The other guys began to back away from the argument, making sure they weren't part of Tarek's circle.

"So guys can just go around and fuck anything that says yes and it doesn't matter if it's their mother or their sister who's a victim…they just have a pact not to tell on each other?"

"It's not quite like that, but for the most part, no. A guy shouldn't tell on another guy. It's up to the girl to figure it out. You've gotta grow up sometime Cindy. If you're dating a rich womanizer twice your age, he probably has the ability to bring lots of women home. It's not my job to expose that. It's your job to see it."

"We're done," Cindy said, and walked toward her dressing room.

"Done what?" Deke shouted.

She turned in a huff. "I'll come do the show. I'll set my emotions aside. I won't, however, have anything to do with Tarek beyond that."

A few mutters from the crew condemned Tarek while he stayed on the defense. "No one here disagrees and you know it."

Everyone disagreed and Cindy almost disappeared but turned again to give Tarek the last words she would ever speak to him while they were out of character. "You're a weasel Tarek. You'll step on anyone and anything so you can be famous and it works now, but someday everyone will see that you're not actually talented and when that happens, you're going to need friends and you won't have any left. But hey, at least you'll have Victor…"

…Tarek's Camaro was out of place as it drove through the woods on a winding dirt road while the weeds at its wheels parted and the leaves from the surrounding trees were brushed aside as it made its entry to lot

70. Tarek stopped and observed the large Winnebago that sat in the lot and the flames from a fire reaching out into the air as a man sat nearby to gather heat.

Tarek exited the car and approached. The sound of his footsteps caused Anthony Freeman to turn, an alerted look on his face until he recognized his company and a welcoming smile covered his face. He stood and greeted Tarek, invited him to sit by the fire, and after half an hour, both men were eating trail mix and catching up. Finally, Anthony looked up from a long silence, saw something in Tarek's eyes, and asked, "what brings you here?"

Tarek took a deep breath. "I went to see Stanley Kline." Anthony was suddenly all attentive. "He gave me a code that would deactivate your bomb."

"How do you know it's the right code?"

"I don't."

"Why did you go to see him?"

"I felt the need to confront him."

"Why?" Anthony asked, searching Tarek's eyes.

Tarek thought for a long moment. "I lost my show Anthony. I'm a has-been. I want to make a comeback, but I want to do something new. Something shocking."

"And what would that be?"

"Victor's ex-wife has been staying at my place. It's completely platonic. I don't know why I did it. I ran into her one night and she was on the street with nowhere to go, and I knew she was a fan of mine, and I guess I probably was trying to remain relevant. She still has access to Victor's home though and I broke in and I found his memoirs and you wouldn't believe his story Anthony."

"I assume you want to tell it?"

"I don't just want to tell it. I want to live it." Anthony frowned and Tarek quickly covered his tracks. "I don't mean really live it. I mean that…"

"I know what you mean, but you're treading in a dangerous territory."

"You know, in my High School yearbook, I was voted most likable, and up until then, I didn't know what I did to earn that. People just liked me. Then, as soon as I became aware, I felt like I had to live up to that, and in trying to be likable, I think I became more unlikable. It was at my five year reunion that all the people who once voted me likable—they all had stable lives: spouse, kids, career…and I just wanted to have fun and show off. I made a fool of myself. I've set this tone in my life and I can't just forget it. Maybe it's because it feels like it's too late to turn back and do the wife and kid thing. I've already set a course for myself. When you get off course, you don't turn around. You find your way back."

"You know what I learned in AA?" Anthony asked. "To be an alcoholic, you don't have to drink yourself into blackout every night. You don't even need to drink yourself into a buzz. You can have one drink a day and be an alcoholic. You see, an alcoholic is a patterned drinker. If at dinner, I have to have a beer instead of a cup of tea, I've created a pattern and I've become an alcoholic, but you see, we all live our life in patterns according to our priorities. In the same way I would always like a drink, you will always chase the height of your fame. It's the same way Victor Stone always resorted back to his bitter nature, even if he tried to fight it, and the same way your friend Aileen will always pursue security over pride. The problem with patterns is that we continue to make the same errors over and over and we never learn from them."

"I'm breaking my pattern. I'm done with comedy and light-hearted goofball jobs."

"No, Tarek. You're still following your pattern, because you're still trying to find your way to be loved by the masses, but you won't find happiness in that kind of fame. It will never be enough. And sensationalizing the life of Victor Stone is not something I am eager to see in my lifetime."

"You've given me something to think about." Tarek was annoyed that Anthony didn't support his ideas. He'd already made up his mind and nothing was going to change. "What about you? You're going to need someone who can enter the code."

"I'm not entering the code."

"Why not?"

"I have no assurance that Mr. Kline provided the right code."

"Then what are you going to do?"

"Why do you think I'm all the way out here? I rented the adjoining lots on both sides. I make a trip for groceries once a month."

"You're just going to isolate yourself until you die? It could still be decades Anthony."

Anthony rolled up his sleeve and showed Tarek the spot where the bomb rested under his skin, which was discolored a bright purple and blue. "You see what's happening here?" Anthony asked. "My days are numbered. Whatever is inside me has poisoned my blood and infected me beyond repair."

"You need to get to a hospital."

"That's just poppycock," Anthony scowled. "I'm a liability to the lives around me wherever I go. You shouldn't even be sitting with me now."

Tarek felt numb. The thought of Anthony dying all alone, a bomb tearing him apart from the inside, was too tragic to fathom. "What can I do?" Tarek asked."What can I do to help?"

"There is one thing," Anthony said, his mind spinning. "I refuse to allow myself to die in this way. If I'm to be burdened by this device, I'd like to settle a score in the process."

"What score?"

"The man who stabbed me…"

"He's dead."

"He's dead, but not the beneficiary who set up the lottery. I can't go to him, but you can help bring him to me."

"To do what?"

"To be with me when I die."

"Who set up the lottery?" Tarek felt squeamish. He suddenly wanted to get as far away from Anthony as possible, but another thought came to him. The darkness inside…his desire to surprise the world and do something different…something unlike the Tarek Appleton the world knew.

"I was able to obtain a list of beneficiaries, you and myself included, who the men in Gelatin Steel were to bet on. Logic would have it that the name left off the list is the name of the person who created it."

"Who was it?" Tarek asked, and then Anthony said a name that convinced Tarek to join forces with him—someone who as of recently, Tarek had wished he could get to know.

"Jason Stone," Anthony said. "It turns out the apple didn't fall far from the tree after-all."

Aileen Thick looked up from her position in the kitchen, where she was searching for any belongings to pack into an open box nearby. Her suitcase was full and she'd gathered everything she owned in the world, but was finding reasons to stall so she could thank Tarek for his kindness and be on her way.

"What are you doing?" Tarek asked, holding the door open.

"I told you I was going. I don't want to be a burden to you any longer."

Tarek closed the door and walked a wide circle around her. "I don't mind if you stay."

"Well, I do. It's hard to feel good about this. You've been very kind, but I have a place to go."

Tarek stopped at the kitchen, standing in the doorway, leaning in toward her, effectively creating a barricade. "I think we should go to your son's wedding," he said. "I'll front the tickets and hotel. It wouldn't be a problem. You should be there, and you shouldn't be alone."

Aileen shook her head and smiled, but couldn't hide how enticing the offer was—how much she clearly wanted to go. Tarek let go of the door-frame and entered the kitchen, walking slowly toward her. She backed away from him until her back was against the wall. Tarek was uncomfortably close. She could smell his cologne, feel his breath on her, and see deeply into his eyes, which appeared to be glazed over, but deep blue and hypnotizing.

"You can't walk out now," Tarek said.

"I don't want you to try to make a movie about Victor."

He stepped closer and they were almost touching. Tarek lifted his arm and rested it against the wall behind Aileen's head, leaning in to her. "We don't have to be alone," Tarek said and he watched her melt. Before she could say anything, he leaned in further and met her lips. He kissed her slowly at first and she resisted giving in, but suddenly, her hand was behind his head and her lips parted and their bodies pressed together. As Tarek pulled the shirt over her head, he knew he was going to have his movie. He was going to meet Jason Stone and bring him back for Anthony. He was going to make sure Stanley Kline never touched him again, that no one was ever going to call Tarek a hack, that Aileen wasn't going to stand in the way of his success. No one would. As Anthony Freeman had said, and he never believed it to be more true: no matter how hard he tried, patterns can't be broken.

# *Chapter 7*

### *1*

*Anthony Freeman hovered over a room filled with students and addressed them with his usual passion. Early in his career, the passion was always there and Anthony was consumed with connecting to his students. It was hard to tune out a man whose voice boomed like Anthony's and so as a professor, he thrived.*

*"Pretend I'm bringing in a guest lecturer tomorrow and I give half of you a bio of this lecturer describing our speaker as cold. The other half, I give you a bio that praises him for his warmth. You read this bio before our lecturer speaks and afterward, I ask you to write down your impressions. This is a very real experiment that was done and do you know what happened?"*

*Eager silence.*

*"Those who read the bio saying he was cold described him as distant and aloof. Those who'd been tipped off he was warm, related him as friendly and approachable."*

*Anthony's response was a mix of amusement and chuckling.*

*"What they had done, and what we all often do, is go along to get along. They had seen the mismatched lines as equal. Their senses had been swayed more by the views of the multitude than by the actuality. Peer pressure had squeezed their vision out of all whack with reality. In judging a fellow human being, students replaced external fact with input they'd been given socially."*

*His eyes wandered the room and everyone was glued, except for one fat student who was doodling. He dismissed the student, but after the lecture, found he'd stayed behind to talk to Anthony. Anthony hurriedly gathered his things, avoiding the student. He didn't want to make time for someone who couldn't give his full attention.*

"Mr. Freeman," Brian Van Dyke said, trying to steal his attention. I need you to sign something."

Anthony looked up and Brian held a paper in front of him. He scanned it with his eyes and was suddenly very interested in talking to Brian. "Why do you want to drop Mr...?"

"Uh, Brian."

"Why do you want to drop, Brian?"

"It's an interesting class, but it's not really what I'm supposed to be doing and I just never get it, so I'm switching to abnormal psych."

"Did you misunderstand the curriculum when you signed up?"

"Yeah. Well, I was taking business classes and was just trying to fill in a couple credits."

"This is an easy credit and if you switch now, you'll be lost. Stay in the course."

"K," Brian said, timidly. He hesitantly held out the paper. "Can you just sign it though?"

"Without thinking, give me three words that describe you," Anthony said.

"What?"

"Don't think. Three words."

"Um, nice I guess. Hard working and..."

"Did I hear you right? You say nice?"

"Yeah, why?"

"That's a cheap answer. Everyone believes they're nice."

"K," Brian said, confused.

"Business is about people. Nothing else."

"Not the kind of people you talk about really."

"What kind of people do I talk about?"

"Mostly criminals."

"We all are born naked and confused. We begin in the same arena. We're shaped by circumstance. In all your life, everything you've done and everything that's happened has led you to the conclusion that you're nice? Is that all?"

"You said not to think."

"What's the worst thing you're capable of?"

Brian spoke slowly. "I'm not sure."

"How will you work with people when you don't know yourself?"

"I do."

"What's the worst thing you're capable of?"

Brian shrugged again.

"Disloyalty? Anger? Violence? Murder?"

*"No."*

*"Because you're nice?"*

*"So could you sign it, cause…"*

*"Hitler was nice once. He wasn't born evil. He became evil. The benefit of this class is relevant to everyone, everywhere. Knowing yourself, knowing people, not just on the surface, but deep down, finding what they desire, what's missing from their life, and filling voids…that's business. Now describe yourself in three words. Don't think about it. Go."*

*"Nice. Hard working…"*

*Anthony dismissed his answer with a wave of his hand. "Find value in yourself as an individual. I'll sign when I have three words."*

*"I'm trying to think of a third."*

*"Your first two don't count. I need three. Nice is a nice word that is nicely used in a nice convenient way. It has no meaning to me."*

*"Can't you just tell me what you mean because I seriously don't get it."*

*"Did you ever watch Smurfs?"*

*Brian closed his eyes, unable to keep up with Anthony's rapid firing random logic. "Yes."*

*"It's a lot like smurfs," Anthony said.*

*"K."*

*"The widely accepted smurf theory of the world: We're all basically just the same people, doing different jobs. Papa Smurf, Carpenter Smurf, Happy Smurf, Pimp Smurf, Wife-Beater Smurf, et cetera. You can be a Republican Smurf, a Democrat Smurf, a diehard hockey-loving Smurf, or an effete elitist Smurf who adores ballet, but when it all hits the wire—no matter who you are, you're still a Smurf. All the trivial details washed away, erased by the common thread of Smurfidity that binds us all."*

*Brian laughed and shook his head in disbelief. He understood nothing, but liked how it was presented.*

*"Aside from the fact that the Smurfs were small blue genetic mishaps created as a PR effort for a Dutch oil company, I actually don't believe in Smurf theory."*

*"Then what do you believe?"*

*"Pay close attention because this is the last help I'm giving you. I believe that for every drop of rain that falls, a flower grows. I believe that people are distinct individuals. Think about it. Every man, woman and child on this Earth possesses a horrendously elaborate combination of billions of DNA, all working in conjunction to make them as different as possible in order to maximize the propagation of the species."*

*"K, well I believe that too."*

*"Now multiply each of those physical differences time millions of life*

*experiences that makes us mentally different from our peers. Let's be honest: Hoping that you'll find your partner and that you will fit together like a key going into a lock is like trying to find two snowflakes that, when placed together like jigsaw pieces, make a silhouette of Ronald Reagan. It's not going to happen."*

*"I agree."*

*"To know the differences between you and I and everyone else is the single most useful bit of knowledge you will ever gain. If you drop every business course you're taking and understand what I'm saying, you will be light-years ahead of everyone else."*

*"Okay, but if I give you three words that describe myself, I can drop?"*

*"Absolutely not."*

*"Now you're taking it back?"*

*"It's a trick question. There are no three words that can possibly describe you. If you understood what I was saying, you wouldn't want to drop."* Anthony gathered his books and shut the light off, leaving Brian in the dark. *"See you tomorrow…"*

"…Today's the day," Brian muttered to himself, staring up at Stone Enterprises for the first time in awhile. The doom and gloom were no longer within his head. It seemed life without Victor actually made the streets seem busier and the parking lots a little fuller. He had been prepared to beg Bernard Bell for a meeting, but Bernard happily penciled him in, which made Brian uneasy. Bernard was never really nice to him. Mostly, he was just dismissive, but he'd welcomed Brian's call and Brian sensed mockery in his tone.

Brian dressed up as well as he could, but his clothes were rather loose on him because of his drastic weight loss. He looked disheveled and no matter how hard he tried, he couldn't get rid of the bags and redness under his eyes. He hoped Bernard wouldn't notice, but he sized him up immediately with eagle eyes and looked like he almost even laughed at the sight of him.

Bernard stood to greet him. "You look like you've lost weight."

"Yeah, some."

"It looks like a lot. What's your secret?"

"No secret. I just cut back. I'm not really trying."

"Well, that's no help to me." Bernard patted his own stomach for affect, as if to say he needed to drop a few pounds. Brian couldn't see where though. "What can I do for you Brian?"

"K, well, after Victor died, I talked to Jason Stone and asked about employment and he said he'd look into it but never really did."

"That was nine months ago."

"Yeah, but I thought he'd get back to me and I had been working somewhere else at the time."

"What happened to that job?"

"It's just below what I'm looking for."

"You were his driver."

"Yeah, and if you don't need drivers, that's okay, but Victor had promised to help me along here and I even took college courses specifically cause he asked."

"What job title are you seeking?"

"I…I guess something big. I told Victor I wanted to be like him."

"Ah, so you want to be CEO."

"Someday. Not now, but if there's an internship or something that can start me at the bottom, but put me on my way. That's what Victor was going to do anyway."

Bernard leaned back in his chair and looked as if he was considering. Brian thought it looked fake, but he had told himself to be respectful no matter what Bernard said.

"I'm not looking for a driver," Bernard said. "And we do only accept online applications. I'd be happy to pass a resume to our recruiting department though."

"I tried online and…"

Bernard's eyes narrowed as an idea came to him. "How would you like to run an errand?"

Brian's eyes widened and he held a tight grip on his seat to control his excitement. He hadn't expected to get very far, but this was promising."Yeah, of course."

"Victor owned a piece of property a block down 2nd avenue and he was allowing a small business owner to use the property to run her own psychic thing."

"Yeah, I know who she is."

"Oh right," Bernard said, as if remembering. "You two were at the reading of his will together. I'm putting you in the same room, so make sure to behave. Should I pat you down?"

Brian turned red at the accusation, though Bernard was clearly joking. "I wouldn't…ever…"

"I'm kidding Brian. Relax. I just need you to deliver a form to her, but she's no longer on 2nd avenue. She's in Hancock Park now with a much larger office, and that's the problem. The shop wasn't hers to sell and it seems she made some profit off of it which she is going to have to pay back. You don't have to explain that to her. Just drop off the form and if she has any questions, she'll have to call my office. I tried to fax it to her, but the damned thing won't go through and it needs to be in her hands today."

"Do you have an address?"

"On the envelope," Bernard said and handed it over.

The job seemed easy enough, though somewhat unfortunate for Maria. If Brian had heard the amount she was due for, he might have realized the extent of trouble she was in, but his job didn't deal with the details.

"When you're done, give me a call. We'll talk more. I apologize but this is time sensitive and if you're willing, it would be a great help."

"Yeah, no problem," Brian said, and stumbled out of his chair. After he was gone, Bernard's smile faded and he shook his head.

While Brian was starting his day delivering an envelope, Toby O'Tool was ending a long night at the casino. He had been on his way out and stopped to place a few bets on the horses from the casino lounge, where he nursed a Jack Daniels and watched the screens from the bar.

William Lamone had been messaging him the night before and Toby had ignored the texts, but finally responded, and when he told William where he was, William insisted on seeing him. Toby told him not to come, but the next text came back and hour later. William was in the parking lot.

Toby met him outside and they smoked cigarettes and leaned against Toby's jeep.

"Brian got fired," William finally admitted. He wasn't sure how Toby would react, since he was unsure of whether or not it was good news."He lost it on a customer."

"Wow," Toby said, with raised eyebrows. "I like what you've done. What Picasso was to art, you are to turning people into assholes."

"If he's fired, then what next? Do I finish this?"

Toby closed his eyes and exhaled a cloud of smoke. "You been crashing at his place much?"

"Yeah."

"The job wasn't the only thing holding you two together."

"Then I'm going to quit."

"Wait until Brian's done."

"What does working there have to do with Brian anymore?"

"It's all in the presentation. He knows you have a kid and have child support to pay. You're going to quit for what? What are you going to tell him?"

"Toby, Brian could walk by right now and see us together and still not be suspicious. He trusts people. He searches for people to trust. I can tell him anything and he'll eat it. But I'm quitting because I'm beat, I've become dependent on a job I hate doing, I'm in a tax bracket that makes me want to kill myself, all my money is taken for child support, and I'm still managing to get Brian blazed every night I can. I'm tired."

"So what?" Toby said with a shrug. "It's worth it in the end. No pain, no glory."

"We've got twelve people remaining and Henry and I have been stuck on two for half a year."

"When the time is right…"

"The time is right now. My guy can get me a tainted product that would be cut to kill if Brian consumed just a little. Brian never pays attention. He just takes what he's given. I put a needle in front of him or a line on the table and he'll do it. I could get a party going tonight, get Brian trashed, give him tainted product, and leave while the party is going and everyone believes he's just passed out. This is such a guarantee at this point, that holding back would be stupid. Brian's already out searching for work. Too much can change now."

"I'm orchestrating this and I know what I'm doing."

"I'm knee deep in this and you know what? I'm going to do it whether you agree or not. You can thank me tomorrow."

"No you're not."

"Yes, I am, because Henry and I are sick of waiting for you to get over Richard Libby."

"You don't know what you're talking about."

"You've been stalling for six months. You liked the guy, fine. But I'm not wasting another second wasting my own time while you grieve."

"I didn't give a shit about Richard. The guy drowning himself was the best thing that happened to our list of people."

"Good, then we have nothing more to talk about. Brian's done and I want a new name tomorrow."

Toby let William walk away without a word. He didn't want to confront the topic of Richard, but William was right about one thing: There was no better time to eliminate Brian. Henry was so close with Maria and Gregory Neomin wouldn't be able to continue the illusion he'd created for Trish Reynolds forever.

*Yeah, okay*, Toby thought. *Maybe William will kill Brian tonight. And if he does, I guess we just keep moving.* Toby was never happy about what happened to Richard, but it beat most alternatives. He only hoped he could have had closure. Richard had always thought Toby was helping…

*We move forward.*

Toby smiled at the thought. Too much time had passed. The next time he heard from William, Brian Van Dyke potentially could be dead. He smiled at the thought.

*2*

Royce Morrow ran his hand down the side of his face, feeling traces of scars that Manny left on him six months ago. Whenever he was stressed, or in deep thought, he subconsciously traced his scars, and when he'd learned that Charlie Palmer's home had been blown up and Charlie nearly died as a result, he traced those scars more often. His mind went back to his conversation with Charlie, which he'd had only a day before the explosion. He knew Manny and Adlar were biding their time and would strike eventually. It was right as he really started to stress about it that he heard the news.

Royce was supposed to be campaigning, but an uneasy feeling that the past was finally catching up kept creeping into his head and he couldn't focus. He was supposed to be walking through neighborhoods and meeting people, handing out fliers and giving speeches, but his head wasn't in the game. Bernard Bell was an opponent worth defeating, but even when he did, a whole new set of obstacles would present themselves and the struggle would never end.

He often spoke in favor of the poor, but the fact that he was rich was always an issue. He hated to sound like a hypocrite and upped his contributions to every organization that catered to the homeless and those who struggled, but every time one of his associates was arrested or morally questioned by the public, the heat came down on his head.

That afternoon, he stood in front of a crowd and addressed them with strong conviction.

"There's a chasm between the professional and the plutocratic classes, and the tax system should reflect that. A better tax system would have more brackets, so the super-rich pay higher rates. The most obvious bracket to add would be a higher rate at a million dollars a year, but there's no reason to stop there. This would make the system fairer, since it would reflect the real stratification among high-income earners. A few extra brackets at the top could also bring in tens of billions of dollars in additional revenue."

"We already have tax brackets for the wealthy," someone in the crowd shouted.

"Our system sets the top bracket at three hundred and seventy-five thousand dollars, with a tax rate of thirty-five per cent. People in the second-highest bracket, starting at a hundred and seventy-two thousand dollars for individuals, pay thirty-three per cent. This means that someone making two hundred thousand dollars a year and someone making two hundred million dollars a year pay similar tax rates. LeBron James and LeBron Jame's dentist: Same difference."

There was some laughter from the crowd and Royce smiled but his heart stopped a second later as a familiar face showed up in the crowd. He scanned back the path his eyes had traveled a second before and the face of Manny Quinny was gone.

His voice faltered and he cut two paragraphs from his speech before simply saying "Vote for Morrow for a better tomorrow." The music and crowd cheers overshadowed the visibly distraught look on his face. Six months ago, Manny had dragged him to the middle of nowhere to kill him and satisfy the debt left behind when Manny's right hand man had been killed. It wasn't Royce who killed Bedbug, but it was Royce who'd placed Bedbug in the line of fire, where someone else finished him off.

"Don't say super-rich," a man said, as he put his arm around Royce's shoulder and shook his hand. Stuart Wiley was as good a campaign manager as any, but he constantly bombarded Royce with feedback that Royce believed to be petty. Royce hated the political games. What you could and couldn't say. Stuart knew a thing or two though and Royce always digested his advice. "You're super-rich. Don't remind them that you're the very guy that you're fighting."

"I need a moment." Royce realized he hadn't fully caught his breath from his momentary sighting of Manny.

"Meet me at headquarters. Half an hour." Stuart hurried off into a group of people.

Royce tried to find a moment of silence but was interrupted at every turn. It wasn't until he got into his limo that he finally had a second to rest his head on the seat and close his eyes. Then, his cell phone rang. He would have ignored it, but Bernard Bell was on the other end and knowing what Bell was thinking was the most beneficial campaign tactic there was. He answered and before he could say anything, Bell was talking.

"You're going to rebuild the tax brackets," Bell said with a laugh. "Spoken like a practiced politician able to say things in a seemingly spontaneous manner, no matter how many times you've uttered them."

"What do you want?" Royce rubbed his temples as a headache came on. Talking to Bernard always did that.

"My central issues are jobs and budget," Bell said.

"I know."

"I received a proposal from your office today. Well…let me rephrase that: From you personally. Not interested in running anymore or you realize you won't win?"

"Neither. I'm asking for us to work together. I'm not asking you to change your issues."

"No, you're not, but you're suggesting oversight committees, programs to feed and shelter the homeless, restrictions on business development in certain sections of the city. Royce…some of this counteracts everything I'm doing, so while you're not asking me to change my issues, you are asking that I contradict my values with opposing values. Makes no sense."

"I think we can work together to make both agendas work."

"The homeless don't vote Morrow."

"But they have a voice."

"As for oversight committees, those are campaign donations down the toilet. Are you crazy? Did you really think I'd accept this?"

"If you don't, I'll win. I'm willing to hand you the election if you'll only meet me halfway."

"Hand me the…" Bernard laughed and disappeared from the phone for a moment before coming back. "You don't have to hand me anything."

"I'm giving you a sure thing if I step down. That's worth something."

"It's worth suspicion. It's worth knowing you're not really up for the job, but you're willing to go after it to spite me. And what's that say about you? You want the key to the city, but you're willing to hand it over if the other guy runs with your ideals. Let me tell you something else Morrow: I've heard what you have to say about law enforcement in this city and it's way out of line. You knew my brother was a cop I take it…"

"I did."

"And disappeared years ago. Probably dead. So when you say you want to spend taxpayer money to monitor and record all on-duty activity that guys like my brother respond to, who made the streets safer, and you tell me you want to spend more taxpayer money to extend benefits to the lazy, unproductive, filthy, dumpster-diving addicts, it truly makes me wonder where your head is. And again, it makes me suspicious."

"You know my past," Royce said.

"Yes, I do. And I have nothing but admiration for your rise in power, but you are one in a billion and you know that. You will never find another like you, no matter how many people you think you can inspire, because what you did, simply doesn't happen. You're sticking up for a group of people because you seem to think there is hope for them, but there's not Royce. You will see that the weak in this city are weak for a reason. They go in circles through the same revolving door that feeds their addictions and lack of motivation to change. It's guys like us that make things happen, and the longer you hold yourself down, the less you're going to be able to do."

"I guess we're done talking."

"Always nice to chat," Bernard said and the other end was released. Royce rested his head again, his head fully throbbing.

*3*

The last time Brian saw Maria was when they attended the invalidation of the will effort that Richard had launched. Brian had thought himself to be the swing vote that day, but it turned out no one really wanted to be excluded badly enough. The last time Brian had actually talked to Maria was at Victor Stone's funeral, and that had been an awkward encounter. Brian had been bawling and Maria was there to speak to the dead. Strange as that seemed, it was Brian who'd been the creepy one and he'd noticed Maria had edged away from him that day. It was the same reaction Brian got often. He usually grew nervous and fidgeted and looked at a woman's chest and she'd notice and he'd stumble over his words, turn red, and his voice would break.

Maria never seemed to have a positive reputation among those listed in the will, and Brian was one down from her. At least, that's how he saw it. .Even in the days of Victor, it seemed Maria was just Victor's hidden friend who he'd see but never talk about, as if he needed her and was ashamed of her at the same time.

Brian knew he was delivering bad news but was somewhat amused. He thought himself cooler now and she was about to lose everything and he got to deliver the news, as if he was the important messenger tasked with it. He was also down quite a bit of weight and on his way back into employment with Stone Enterprises. It seemed he was on his way up while she was on her way down. Maybe she'd even regret how she'd edged away that day.

He was impressed when he arrived at her establishment. It was three times larger than the shop Victor had set her up in. He walked in and waited for her. She didn't have a client but was busy in the storage area. The shop wasn't open. It looked empty, as if she was moving again. Boxes were stacked against the wall and the electricity seemed to be off. Finally, Maria emerged from a back office with the man who'd met Maria at The Coop on the day Richard died. Henry kissed Maria on the cheek and went on his way, nodding to Brian on his way out.

"Hey Maria." Brian paced, waiting for her reaction.

"Brian...I'm closed."

"I was just here to give you something." He handed her the form.

She scanned it with her eyes repeatedly until the content made sense.

"Is this an eviction?" She suddenly looked up at him.

"Not from me. Victor's attorney gave it to me to give to give to you. I'm just running an errand."

"Did he tell you what this is?"

"Something about ownership of your business. He said it wasn't yours to sell."

"Of course it was. My name was on everything."

"I don't know. I never talked to him about it."

Maria's face was white. She suddenly pulled out her cell and looked up Bernard's number. She disappeared in the back and didn't come back for five minutes. Brian tried to eavesdrop on the conversation, but behind closed doors, her voice was only muffled.

She walked quickly out the door, her face filled with worry. She wrapped a scarf around her neck. "I have to lock up," she said. "I have things to do."

Brian resented how dismissive she was of him, as if all this was his fault. He wanted to carry on a conversation. "I can talk to Bernard and see if he'll forgive this."

"He won't. I already talked to the prick. They're taking me to court if I don't pay back the entire amount of the sale."

"Well…can you not do that?"

"I can, but we moved our money after we sold this place."

"Why'd you sell this?"

"My husband works and I'm going through a career change."

"I didn't know you were married."

Maria tried to move him out the door, but Brian stood in place, his eyes taking in the shop. He suddenly felt bad for Maria and wanted to help. It seemed Victor always had all his ducks in a row. Maria shouldn't have been duped like this. She legitimately believed her shop was hers to sell. If Victor was alive, this form wouldn't have been drafted. Victor would never do that to her.

"I really have to go," Maria said.

"K, but I'll still talk to him and let him know you didn't know."

"It won't help."

"It might coming from me."

"Why?"

"I'm going to be working for him again."

"Are you going there now?" Maria asked, softening.

"Yeah."

"May I go with?"

"Yeah," Brian said. He'd once saved Anthony Freeman from Ira Moore and he'd shown up to be the swing vote. Twice he'd been the hero of the day and had been overlooked. If he could talk Bernard into forgiving Maria's debt, there's no way it would be ignored. "Come on. I'll drive…"

"…*Did I see you driving a limo last night?*"

*Brian turned as a girl from class approached. He'd never talked to her, but he'd fantasized about her plenty of times. In reality, he never believed he'd talk to her, and if he tried, he'd sound like a fool. A scenario in which Jasmine Bianca struck up a conversation with him never crossed his mind.*

"Yeah, probably me. Where did you see me?"

"Gas station."

"Yup, I gassed up."

"You're a limo driver?"

"No, personal driver to Victor Stone." *Brian said those words every chance he got, especially to beautiful girls.*

"He let you take it out for a drive?"

"Not for fun. It's business only."

"Ahh…" *Jasmine seemed disappointed, but perked up as two of her male friends approached.* "Guys, this is Brian from Abnormal Psych. Brian, this is Adrian and Hud."

"What's up?" *Brian nodded.*

"You're the guy who was sleeping in the bathroom stall," *Hud laughed and Adrian joined. Jasmine smirked.*

"No, I didn't."

"I saw you come out man," *Hud said.* "You were in there with your pants around your ankles and you were snoring. I'm not ripping on you. It was hilarious."

*When Brian learned that they were supposedly laughing with him rather than at him, he joined in and took responsibility.* "I was tired," *Brian said.*

"He's the one who drives the limo," *Jasmine said. Hud and Adrian perked up.*

"No shit?" *Hud smiled.* "We're looking for a limo."

"It's not mine though."

"He works for Victor Stone," *Jasmine explained.*

"You cool with your boss?"

"Yeah." *Brian gave an exaggerated nod.*

"Awesome. See if he'll let you use it."

"K," *Brian said, and promised he'd at least ask. The truth was that Brian didn't need to ask. It had never crossed his mind to just take the limo, but he could if he wanted. He'd ran multiple errands for Victor in the past. Sometimes he'd drive in the evening and when he'd eventually park it, he had the remote to the garage and no one was there to see him pick it up or leave it. It had never dawned on Brian how much trust was placed in him, and he'd never abused it. After some persuasion from his new friends, he saw no harm in driving a few people around.*

    *Adrian's older brother was having a bachelor party and they'd requested Brian take them from place to place. Brian made them swear they wouldn't spill anything in the car and that they'd leave nothing behind. He was happy to help up until later when the limo was loaded with people and all at once he realized he'd made a mistake. They were out of control and even when Brian tried to speak, they didn't hear him. As he drove, he considered telling Victor the truth the next day as if it was no big deal, but he worried about how Victor would respond. Victor was always calm with Brian and was either conversational or educated him. Brian wasn't sure Victor was capable of directing angry toward him, though he'd seen Victor angry at just about everyone else. Brian really never gave Victor a good reason to be angry. Their relationship was perfect. That was why Brian had a hard time coping with the fact he'd given in to peer pressure. There weren't even any girls to impress, though it had been a girl who had initially approached him. That was how they got him.*

    *He'd been duped. He just wanted to get through the night.*

    *At one o'clock, he told everyone it was time to wrap it up and he asked if they all could grab a taxi or find rides from the last bar. There was some grumbling, but most were agreeable until Hud took the lead in the group and had the "great idea" of driving around vandalizing property.*

    *Though inside, Brian was as angry as he'd ever been, he went along, parking on the side of the road and waiting as one or two of his new drunken buddies would run from the limo, across a couple lawns, and throw eggs at houses or smash mailboxes.*

    *Everyone laughed after each home sabotage and Brian went along, tired and afraid. Eventually, the laughter died down and the alcohol had seemingly made some of the guys start to nod off.*

    *"One more," Hud said as they passed a home with a bench swing in the yard. He almost pressed his face against the window, eager to tear it apart.*

    *Brian had the drill down perfectly now. He parked the car around the corner of the next block. Hud would exit and return within five minutes and Brian would just leave. Hud was taking longer than usual on the last house, probably because it was the last house and he really wanted to do a bang-up job. As Brian heard the sound of Hud running toward the car, he realized there was more urgency than usual on his return. Either he'd made too much noise, or the owner had seen him, or...*

    *"Cops!" Hud yelled and instead of getting back into the car, he ran by, giving everyone the warning. In seconds, they were all out of the car and running between houses. As Brian began wondering whether or not Hud was joking, blue and red lights flashed in the darkness, stopping right*

*behind him.*

*Brian turned to find empty beer cans scattered throughout the car.*

*He was angry, but there was nowhere to direct that. Especially not on the cop. He buried it deep inside and began thinking about how he was going to get out of this. After a fifteen minute conversation and search of the car, Brian was fashioned with a pair of handcuffs and taken away...*

...Maria stood at his side in the elevator but didn't say a word. She was in her own world, which was understandable, but it bothered and motivated Brian. Soon, he'd be the guy people sucked up to...the guy who was to be respected.

She walked ahead of him when they reached the seventh floor. He hurried to keep up and met her at the receptionist desk. She tried to make an appointment but Bernard was booked for the day. When she insisted, the door to the office suddenly swung open and Bernard stepped out. "No need to make an appointment." He stared at Maria with judgmental eyes. "Not for what will be a two minute conversation." He looked up at Brian as if disappointed. "Did she not understand?"

"I tried to explain it."

"Alright," Bernard directed his attention back to Maria. "You were residing in a venue that Victor gave to you on loan..."

"It wasn't on loan."

He continued, speaking over her. "You then sold that property for a large sum of money, of which you now owe Stone Enterprises, unless you want to take this to court."

"It wasn't on loan," she said again.

"I understand that Victor gave you the impression that the building was yours, but I assure you that he paid the rent in full and no certificate of ownership was ever signed by you."

"I don't remember what we did, but he told me..."

"The days of Victor's promises are eons ago. Victor is gone and I don't do business on verbal agreements. That little property wasn't yours to sell. I've got the city coming down on me now because they paid you a large sum of money and they still don't have the rights to the property. When they asked me to sign it over, I was confused because I didn't know there was anything to sign, but sure enough, your little shop is worth a fortune to the city who wants to put in a parking lot and thinks it is theirs to do whatever they please. However, since I haven't seen the profit from the sale, I refuse to release it."

Brian stepped forward. "But if you just sign the certificate of release, you can give it to them right?"

"Good one Van Dyke," Bernard said. "Would you hand over a property for nothing?"

"Maybe if it was a misunderstanding like this. Or if I had enough already."

"Ah, so you think this should be a charity case."

Brian stepped back, releasing himself from the conversation.

"To make a long story short Miss Haskins, you have until the end of the month to pay back the funds you received for the sale of that ghost business you ran. If I don't see that money, I will be seeing you in court."

Bernard turned to go and Brian stepped forward again. "Do you want me to stop by tomorrow or do you have some time to chat today?" he asked.

Bernard stopped and turned, a confused look on his face. "Talk about what?"

"Employment."

"Why would I hire you?"

"You had me deliver…"

"I specifically asked if you'd run an errand and that's what you did. If you find your resume matches any of the job descriptions within Stone Enterprises, feel free to submit online. I told you the same this morning."

Bernard disappeared a moment later, leaving two stunned people standing in the middle of the room with thoughts of their own misfortunes on their mind. Finally, Brian turned to leave, and this time Maria followed. "I need a ride back," she said.

"Fine."

Brian was quiet as he drove and no longer needed Maria's approval or admiration. Instead, he faced a hard truth: He would never work on the level he once did again. Eventually, his money from Victor would dry up and he would be begging guys like Bob to even let him work part-time at The Wasp. He had no skills—just customer service and a few college courses that he flunked out of.

"What is wrong with your eyes?" Maria asked.

Brian was bewildered, but assumed he looked like he was about to cry. "Nothing. I'm tired."

"They're red."

"They're red when I'm tired."

Maria nodded. "Well, I wasn't going to vote before, but Royce Morrow is looking good now."

"Yeah, me too," Brian said. "You know, I never knew why Victor liked working with Bernard so much."

"Maybe he didn't. Maybe he's just good at what he does."

"How can you say that?"

"Look what happened today. He's taking what he doesn't need. He probably does well by doing so. We don't like it, but his business does. Victor didn't like everything Bernard tried to do though."

"Yeah, I know," Brian said. "Yeah, Royce Morrow's a better man. So what are you going to do? Are you even going to be able to operate anymore?"

"I already stopped. That's why I'm going out of business. But the money was put into an account to invest. I'm going to have to empty it. My husband won't be happy. We're going to have to just work hard awhile."

"Then will you go back to being a medium?"

"No, I'm done with that."

"Why?"

"It's not the right thing to be doing."

Brian paused. "I always meant to ask, with everything going on with all of us, did you ever think about trying to see what might happen? I mean, I don't know if that's how it works, but can you try to see like…"

"The course of our lives?"

"Yeah."

"I tried. I thought I knew at times, but my premonitions were off."

"But they were close?"

"I believe so."

"Maybe you misread them a little. I mean, like what is it you see?"

"Have you ever used a quiji board?" Maria asked.

"No."

"There's a piece—the eye—and those who participate put a finger on it. When you ask questions, the eye moves and it hovers over letters which then spell what your spirit is trying to tell you. The eye is very sensitive and leaves you to wonder if you are subconsciously pushing it, or if it is pulling you. If your eyes are focused on a letter, it is easy to move toward that letter and not understand that it is you doing the work. What I do is similar. I look for signs. I listen for voices. If you close your eyes and put yourself into a deep enough trance, you can hear something or someone communicating with you. If you are open, and receptive, it is as if you alone are the gate between the living and the dead. But one day, I realized that the things I hear and see are there because I search for them. If you want to meet your soul-mate or live in a large house and you focus hard enough, you will be able to see yourself there, but it is not a vision of the future. It's just a vision."

"Did you ever see anything with me?"

"Yes."

"What did you see?"

"It was strange. Out of nowhere. It was the day Richard Libby died, but it was before he left. We were all waiting for the judge. You were seated near me. I felt a connection between us, but not a good one. I felt that we were both under the same dark cloud."

"What would that mean?"

"We were both influenced by the same demon, or that we would both see the same fate as a result of one person or entity. I could not be specific. It was just a dark cloud...an aura that linked us together."

"But why would you see that? It's not like you would want to."

"Looking back, I would guess I was feeling down. Maybe I didn't like something you did or said. Maybe we had something in common and I found a similarity between us that I didn't like. It's not easy to understand why I see what I see or how I interpret it. I had never thought about who you were or what you would do, but when I felt that cloud, I wanted to tell you to run away—to cut all influences from your life and walk your own path."

"Is that what I should do?"

"I still sense the cloud and it has grown darker." Maria closed her eyes, lost in the moment. She had tried to resist being that person she knew to be a fraud, but she felt something strong and until Brian had asked, she hadn't fully felt it. "Maybe this is the moment when our paths cross and we both begin to fall, but you and I are influenced by the same thing—by an unknown entity. We have weakened auras and every day is darker—closer to the end."

"Okay, stop," Brian said, abruptly. He'd felt chills on his arm, up his neck, and his hand was shaking. "We need to talk about something else."

Her eyes snapped open and suddenly the moment was gone. She looked in his eyes strangely, as if she was trying to make sense of what just happened.

"Should I be worried about anything?" Brian asked.

"No," she said, but he didn't believe her.

## 4

Royce spent part of his day being brought up to speed at work and delegating to his trusted associates. Campaigning was a full-time job and it left little room for work and family time. He missed Sandra. Sometimes they met for lunch and they would talk in the evening, but Royce was exhausted. His life was constant and sometimes, instead of taking on more, he considered retiring and taking it easy. He certainly could, but years before, when Royce started to build an empire from nothing, the goal had always been to keep going. He never believed he'd go this far and didn't know when the right time to stop would be. A millionaire was one thing. Running for governor was another. He didn't know where he'd go from there, but suspected Sandra was lonely, and without her, he felt the same way.

His business was thriving. It was in good hands and Royce compensated them well, taking very little in return. Coming from a life of nothing made it easier to appreciate anything he could attain. It kept Royce humbled and the company morale and reputation high. He told himself he'd never lose sight of that, and he had done a pretty good job so far, but he was taking on too much and spreading himself too thin and he wasn't certain that he wasn't in over his head.

He checked his messages and for the fourth time in two days, he had a two minute message of silence from a restricted number. He'd assumed it was campaign related after the first. Now, it felt personal, but silence was nonthreatening and he dismissed it. When his phone rang again five minutes later, he quickly answered.

"Royce Morrow."

There was a moment of silence as the person on the other end decided what to do with actual contact. And then a voice Royce hoped he'd never hear again.

"It's detective Manny Quinny."

Royce closed his cell and let it fall at his side. He'd hoped to never hear from Manny again. Royce had regretted hiring Manny from the moment he'd paid him to take care of Adlar. It was after he'd committed to it that he realized his actions and tried to back out. When Manny's number one man turned up dead, it was Royce who Manny held responsible. When Adlar contacted Manny, he assumed he was off the hook forever. Maybe he was. He wouldn't know because he refused to talk to Manny. In fact, when he became governor, part of his plan was to dispose of men like Manny.

Sandra was waiting for him when he came home. She had the remote in her hand and was intently watching the news, most of which covered election talking heads and details such as where Bell and Morrow liked to eat and what they wore in public.

"He's a handsome guy," Royce said, pointing to an image of himself on the screen.

"I would leave you for him," Sandra said, dryly.

They embraced momentarily and Royce pulled away before realizing Sandra wasn't done. She clung to him unexpectedly and he stayed with her a moment longer, understanding he'd been away longer every day. He immediately felt guilty for such a brief interaction. She was the most important person in his world and if he didn't remind her of that, she'd see herself lost in his busy life.

Sandra managed her wheelchair well but whenever Royce was there, he insisted on escorting her to where she needed to be. It was the least he could do for a woman stuck in a chair all waking moments of her life.

"I don't like what they're saying about you," she said they entered an elevator built in-house specifically to carry her from floor to floor.

"It doesn't bother me. It's to be expected."

"I don't care. Most of it is completely untrue. You have the right to defend yourself."

"Voters are smarter than we give them credit for. Most people can see the difference between fiction and reality. If Bell wants to campaign on rumors and lies, eventually people will see his hostile nature. I will continue to talk about my proposals to improve this city and people will see a man with ideas—not insults."

"You already have my vote Royce."

"I'm going to leave a flier tomorrow just to be sure."

"There's something you should know, but you're going to be mad and I want you to stay calm," Sandra said. The door opened and Royce pushed her into the hall but came to a stop.

"Go ahead," he said, confused as to what could possibly be wrong.

"Manny Quinny called me."

"What?!" Royce shouted. Manny was crossing a line that Royce would not allow. The next time Manny called, they would have a discussion. "What happened?"

"I told him I didn't want to talk and hung up."

"What did he say?"

"He said you had a debt."

"Oh for crying loud. That man is psychotic."

"I know, but this was all ironed out, so why is he bugging you now?"

"Something must have happened with Adlar. Either they didn't work out or he wants my attention because of my status. This debt thing is ridiculous. We shouldn't all pay because he can't move past his friend's death."

"You have nothing to worry about."

"I'm going to make a call tomorrow and make sure we have whatever top of the line security exists…"

"You don't have to worry about me. I can take care of myself."

Royce's thoughts were distracted by Manny as he took Sandra into the bedroom. The last thing he needed was another thing to worry about—especially someone as dangerous as Manny. With Royce under the microscope, he was careful not to go near Manny or have contact. It would become increasingly difficult if Manny was planning on intruding into his life though. Even if Royce were to confront the man, it wouldn't do much good. Manny was clean on the outside with the reputation of a hero who kept the streets safe. To go head to head would certainly mean Royce would lose and probably end his life or reputation in the process.

*What the hell did Adlar do?* Royce thought. *What does he want with me?*

He wished he hadn't hung up when he did. He knew he'd be hearing from him again and whatever Manny wanted, whatever it took to keep him away from Sandra, Royce was prepared to do.

He helped his wife get dressed and into bed, kissed her goodnight, and rolled into bed with her. His mind was cluttered with worries, not just of Manny, but of the loss of control he was experiencing in all things. He was losing his grasp on his business, on his family, on his own life, and it was all for a campaign he wasn't expected to win. He thought about asking Sandra if she wanted to move to Europe and adopt children and live off the fortune Royce had built. It seemed so easy, and with a simple decision, it was possible, but there was only one thing holding him back: The possibility of beating Bernard Bell. Until he won or lost, all he had to do was keep himself and his wife safe.

Or maybe he could just drop out and they could leave right away and never be found again. As the thought started to sound good, he drifted off into sleep.

5

William Lamone spent a lot of time regretting cutting ties with Brian Van Dyke. Toby gave him an earful but William dismissed his ranting and talked himself into the benefits of following through on his plan. William was living outside what he had and had been for quite some time, always thinking eventually he'd get ahead of some bills. Paying child support took most of his money, which would have been okay if only he was allowed to see his kid. He was supporting a child that very likely hated his guts. The rest of his money went to ever increasing debt his nights out at the bars.

It was playing poker where he met Toby and at first, he'd been impressed. Toby won when he wanted to and lost when he had an ulterior motive. William began playing poker with him and eventually, played his right hand man when Toby had it in his head to pick up a girl or swindle someone. William saw Toby as his way into learning the skill of persuasion, of improvising to get by, of having a little more in life by doing a little less. In theory, it worked well, but William didn't take to making victims of people in the same way Toby did. It was okay sometimes when it was just a drunk scumbag on a bar-stool, but Toby often took from people who clearly needed what they have with the simple creed of "suckers get what they deserve."

When Toby had approached William with news of the will and asked for his help, William struggled a little but the price-tag was too high and he quickly agreed to help. Along the way, he learned that to help meant to get his hands dirty. He never intended on murdering anyone, but Toby presented the mission as leading people to the ledge and then talking them off. For Brian, that walk was driven by his need of a mentor. That part was easy, but as they approached the ledge, William had a hard time giving him that extra push, and Toby wasn't encouraging him either. It seemed the mission was at a standstill. Billions of dollars sounded great in the beginning, but eight months later, it seemed impossible. Brian could be pushed to OD at any point in time, but when that was done, then what? Inject himself into the next beneficiary's life and start over again?

Actually, that was exactly what he was supposed to do, and as the bills piled up all around him, he no longer needed Toby's go ahead. He could finish this now if he wanted, and instead of struggling with it anymore, that's exactly what he decided to do.

William had the contacts to get whatever he wanted: Pills, powders, needles, bags. He'd gone through his dealer, who informed a man whose street name was Sanjay, that William was legit. William met Sanjay at his apartment, which was a cluttered mess of art and bongs. Sanjay was decked out in shorts and a colorful button up shirt. He wore sunglasses, though it was dark, and his hair fell over his shoulders in dreadlocks.

Sanjay hurried William along, barely acknowledging him, and took him to bedroom, where he pushed against the wall until a secret door swung inward and they entered a room that was filled with boxes and briefcases. Sanjay opened a suitcase where needles and vials of heroin were neatly displayed.

"You know what you're doing?" Sanjay asked, sizing William up with doubt.

"Refresh me."

"Inhale or in the blood?" Sanjay asked.

"In the blood."

"Then you wanna cut it."

"With what?"

"Nutmeg, sucrose, starch, caffeine, chalk, powdered milk, flour, talcum powder, local anesthetics such as lidocaine or porcaine, even laundry detergent…"

"What happens if I don't cut it?"

"You'd be a dead man. Even if you had built up tolerance, you don't inject pure, chief."

"Good to know," William said, realizing just how simple this was going to be.

After their transaction was closed, William walked down the street with a bag under his jacket. It was strange knowing that he blended in with everyone else with these kind of substances on him. He wondered how many times a day he passed people carrying the same. He arrived at Brian's apartment and rang the buzzer at the intercom. A moment later, Brian's voice tiredly asked who it was.

"William." He left it at that, waiting to see what Brian would do. A second later, he was buzzed in.

When he was inside Brian's apartment, he looked around, observing the mess. A box of pudding pops was empty at his feet, two pizza boxes, empty soda cans. "You go on an eating binge last night?"

"Yeah," Brian said. "I get it. I'm fat."

"I didn't say that. I just know you haven't been eating like this awhile. You're a stress eater."

"I guess."

"Well, it probably helps to know that. Eliminate stress."

"I wouldn't know how," Brian said, falling onto the couch and laying his head on the pillow. If William didn't know any better, Brian was willing to fall asleep in front of him right there.

"Sorry about yesterday," William said. "I don't have a good excuse. I used to tell you that it was just a job and I forgot that myself. I'm so in debt with my ex and everything else and I just don't have the power to be unstable, but I'd be willing to leave if you say the word."

Brian opened his eyes, appreciative of the gesture. "No, don't quit. Not if you need it."

"That's what I'm saying: I don't. Fuck it. I'll get something else tomorrow. We'll stick it to Bob and Eve and everyone else and just leave them hanging." William could say whatever Brian needed to hear at this point, since William intended on being at The Wasp on time without Brian's opinion, since he wouldn't even be alive.

"Up to you man," Brian said, with a smile. Their fight was forgotten.

"And you need to find something, and if you need help, I've got your back. I say tomorrow we just drive around and apply everywhere. Tonight, we are just a couple unemployed assholes and we should celebrate the end to that place."

"I don't know."

"I'm not talking a big party or anything," William said. "You and me, right here in your apartment. A couple beers, a little weed, whatever... We'll call it a send off to our irresponsible days before we start building our own empires. We're not going to be working together anymore. We probably won't see a lot of each other. Clearly we were getting on each others nerves. Let's revive our friendship and go our own way. It might make it easier for you to call me in the future instead of hating me."

"I don't hate you." Brian sat up. "Not at all. You've helped me a lot."

"Good." William reached into his goody bag and tossed Brian a lighter. "You got beer in the fridge?"

"Not very many."

"We'll need to go on a beer run then."

"I don't know if I should get too drunk."

"I won't have that kind of talk," William said. "Tonight is the end of an era, which means we go big. No holding back."

Brian laughed and it was all William needed to see to know the idea was sold.

Four hours later, Brian was easily more drunk and stoned than he'd ever been. William wondered if he'd even need the needle. Brian could drink himself to death, but William wasn't going to hold back either. For every beer William drank, Brian drank three, completely oblivious to the fact that William was nursing it. William had started to act drunker than he was, but Brian couldn't spot the lie either way, and when Brian was drunk enough, William just walked around with a buzz, feeding Brian more booze, more caffeine, and eventually Brian was drinking straight from a bottle of Tequila. William pretended to drink, but back-washed everything.

Finally, long after dark when William could see a hint of light where the sun would soon rise, he fell into a chair facing Brian, who was sitting on the floor against the couch.

"You ever try heroin?" William asked.

Brian fought to stay awake. "What's it like?" he asked, but William could barely understand his slurring and the whispers in his voice.

"Gives you a high. You'll feel like you're floating." His hand suddenly held a needle up and Brian looked at it as if it was the second coming.

"Have to stop," Brian said.

"Me too," William said, and deep down, there was a lot of truth in that statement. "I have to stop, so this will be the last thing we do. Then we're done." William didn't know if it was the beer, but he grew highly emotional. This was the end of the line that he'd waited for so long. If Brian injected, William could leave and never come back. Brian would soon be found in his apartment, surrounded by alcohol with a needle in his arm. He was almost at the cliff and William had held his hand long enough. If Brian only took the needle...

"Give it to me," Brian said, leaning forward...

*...in his cell, almost falling forward as his eyes grew heavy. Brian had never felt as out of place as he did in that moment. He thought back to when he was just a goody-two-shoes kid, always in church every Sunday, being kind to his teachers while the other students would sometimes bring them to tears, obeying his mother...he would have never believed he would ever see the inside of a jail-cell and it was every bit as horrifying as he would have expected it to be. The bench was hard and impossible to sleep on. They were given a sandwich but it was mashed together in a plastic wrapper, only a piece of ham squeezed between two stale pieces of bread, and his company was three other guys who had gotten in a fight earlier in the night—all drunk. Brian needed to use the bathroom, but only one toilet sat out in the open and there was no way he was going to use it in front of company. He kept his mouth closed though, because his cellmates were big and the guards were brutal.*

*His mind kept wandering to how he'd ended up here. It would only be for the night but every second became less tolerable. Just as Brian was about to ask a guard to please let him go, two familiar faces rounded the corner. Brian had been afraid of whatever Victor would say, but Cory and Jones were even more frightening. Neither looked thrilled to see Brian and Jones hadn't even bothered to change out of his shorts and white shirt that he slept in. A guard pointed them in the right direction and Brian looked down with shame as they approached.*

*"Let's go," Cory demanded. A moment later, a guard appeared with a keyring and just like that, Brian was free. His cellmates caused a stir, demanding to be released too, but their pleas fell on deaf ears. As Cory and Jones escorted Brian out, both standing at either side, Brian had a moment of panic. He'd heard rumors and he'd seen the way Cory and Jones worked and he knew that there was another man named Stanley that was paid under the table and didn't really work for Stone Enterprises, but most definitely worked for Victor Stone. Brian had pretended not to notice that there was always something shady about how business was done, but he'd never been the one that was in trouble either. Surely, Victor was pissed off about what happened, but to what extent would he go? He was always polite to Brian, but Brian saw how Victor looked at people he didn't like and Brian had always assumed he'd never be one of those people.*

*"I'm so sorry," Brian said. Neither responded. "How mad is Victor at me?"*

*"Not mad at all," Cory said, and Brian believed him, but what he could see was that Cory and Jones weren't happy about the fact that Victor gave Brian a free pass. Brian sensed it from the beginning: Victor*

*saw something in him that no one else saw, and Victor was going to take care of him, no matter what he did.*

*"What'd he say?" Brian asked.*

*Jones stayed silent throughout but was visibly pissed off. Cory did the talking. "He said to pick you up, get the limo back, and take you home. All those things aren't going to be happening though."*

*"What do you mean?" Brian asked, but Jones fell silent. Instead, they drove him through the city to a destination unknown. They passed Hollywood, Sunset, Santa Monica, and eventually were driving down Vine in a darkened area where all shops were shut down for the day and traffic was scarce. Goosebumps covered Brian's arms and he tried to speak but couldn't find the words.*

*Finally, to confirm his fear, the car pulled into an alley between factories and stopped in the dark.*

*"I won't do it again," Brian said, barely able to squeeze the words out.*

*"Damn right you won't," Cory said and was out of the car in a moment and had Brian's door open a second later. He grabbed Brian under the arm and swung him out, his 300 pound frame sent him to the ground with a thud. He grunted and turned to find Cory on one knee looking down on him. He grabbed him under the chin and held his head in place so he had no choice but to meet Cory's eyes. Jones stood over them and watched wordlessly. "You know Van Dyke," Cory started, squeezing Brian's face with one hand, "You've managed to fly under the radar because we don't have to deal with you all that much and we've got bigger fish to fry. We've got a fuckin disgrace working on the sixth floor that we've been putting our efforts into and your fat-ass has gone unnoticed, but you're a joke. You're not headed anywhere, no matter what you think. Victor likes you because you'll kiss his ass no matter what, but he's not preparing you for leadership or greatness. You get that, right? You're useless. He's got you taking classes to buy time, because he doesn't plan on getting you ready for anything. Let's entertain the notion that you're going to one day move up within the company though. I honestly can not wait for that day to come, because once you have a little bit of visibility, everyone will be able to see you for the fat piece of garbage that you are."*

*Cory stood and looked down at Brian, burning him with his eyes. Brian started to stand, but Cory gave him a shove with his foot and Brian fell to his side and didn't dare to move. "Next time you pull something like this, you're going to be in a lot of pain, and if Victor hears of this, I'll fucking kill you myself."*

*Cory and Jones got back into the car and the doors slammed. They left Brian sitting on the ground, covered in gravel and his face stained with tears.*

*Two days later, Brian walked into Professor Freeman's class early in the day while Anthony was reading the newspaper. He set a paper in front of Anthony and this time his face was all serious. He wasn't timid and he wasn't in the mood for Anthony to give him a lecture about Smurfs.*

*"Sign this," Brian said, "Or I'll go above your head. You can't make me stay in a class I don't want to stay in."*

*"I was only offering a perspective," Anthony said, clearly disappointed.*

*"Yeah, well I didn't ask you. You can't just play these games like everything is so black and white."*

*"What are you referring to?" Anthony asked.*

*"Describing myself in three words. I can in one: useless, and when you're useless, there any other words left."*

*"Mr. Van Dyke…"*

*"Just sign it," Brian said. Anthony raised his eyebrows and grabbed the paper and signed…*

… "What did you say?" William asked, his interest suddenly perked as Brian positioned the needle over a vein.

Brian looked up slowly, with heavy eyelids and a world out of focus. "You can stay here." William fell silent and the world was still for a long moment as he considered what Brian was saying. As if to make him feel even more conflicted, Brian continued. "I got money. I can help you out with child support or whatever and you save on rent cause you crash here with me."

Brian looked down at his arm again, ready to do the deed, but the extent of everything that was about to happen hit William too hard, and suddenly he moved across the room and grabbed the needle before Brian could finish. He fell into a recliner to Brian's side and let out a deep breath in relief.

"I thought we were doing this," Brian said.

"You've done enough."

Brian lay back instead, submitting to his urge to close his eyes. William watched him from the side, unsure of how to proceed. He couldn't for the life of him, figure out how he was supposed to kill a guy who valued his friendship so much that he was willing to pay his way through his financial difficulties. "Brian…" William said.

Brian's eyes slowly opened. "William…"

Will knew that there was no truth serum in the world that was as effective as being fucked up. Brian was too far gone to form coherent thoughts, but there was no better time for William to dig in deep and find out once and for all who Brian was.

"What are you going to do with your life?"

Brian let out a short laugh as if the question was silly, and then clumsily shrugged. "I dunno. I don't have life left."

"What do you mean by that?"

"I might be in trouble. I dunno. I know this one lady who is a psychic and today she told me there's a cloud over my head and you know what? I think she's right." Brian's words were heavily slurred and the words he spoke were the kinds of words the sober version would never speak. It was as if a truth had been unlocked in his worst state and once he sobered up, it would be locked away again. "I think I'm going to be murdered by a ghost."

William smiled. He didn't have to ask what Brian meant, but he did anyway.

"Victor. He did a thing…" Brian trailed off. He couldn't find the words.

William leaned forward and studied Brian as he took a chance at something that he hoped would never come back to bite him in the ass. "I'm not who you think I am Brian."

"You're William," Brian said, his eyes closing again.

"I am, but I'm not a chef and I worked at The Wasp to ruin your life… to make sure you ended your own life. I'm friends with Toby O'Tool."

"I know Toby," Brian said, softly. "Toby O'Tool."

"That's right." The moment frightened William, but it also consumed him. Everything he had done with Brian had led to this moment and he could say or do anything. He could kill Brian or let him live, but what really had to happen was that William needed to unburden himself. He'd carried the secret of all secrets for too long and faking a partnership every day was exhausting. Brian wouldn't remember this conversation tomorrow, but it had to happen. "I only know you because I'm supposed to see to it that you die."

"Dark cloud…" Brian mumbled.

"Maybe," Willliam said, as Brian's head fell to the side and he nodded off. "Or maybe you'll be the last one…"

Brian had completely drifted away, but there was a hint of a smile on his face.

## *Chapter 8*

### *1*

The hustle and bustle of downtown Los Angeles was tamer than the usual. It was a slow news day and the weather was perfect, with clouds in the sky shading the sun and a slight breeze. The beaches on the coast were full and the shows on Sunset were bringing in business. Tourists weren't packing Hollywood Boulevard, the Metro was a quiet ride, and the traffic flowed faster than usual.

It was the kind of day that nothing bad could be happening. The positive vibe was simply too strong.

In a rented office building on first street downtown, the campaign headquarters of Royce Morrow, filled up as the day began and a countdown on the wall passed the 1 month until election day mark. Royce's crew began their day, printing fliers and sending his supporters out on foot through the neighborhoods to ask for votes. Royce's campaign advisers, Stuart Wiley and Ronald Wycleff, stood with their hands on their hips, looking at the timer.

"Crunch time," Stuart said.

"Yeah, and where the hell is Morrow?"

"He's volunteering this morning, followed by a public works and gang reduction meeting, followed by a budget and finance meeting, followed by a housing committee meeting. He'll be tied up."

"He needs to be on foot, in the neighborhoods visiting homes," Ronald said, his irritation rising.

"He has been."

"He's been knocking on doors on Normandy and past Pine. He needs to set aside his own agenda and start knocking on the doors of homes with multiple registered voters who actually vote. Not poor people who don't. I have eleven blocks in Los Angeles with homes of four or more voters and he's gone to one, and only because it fit his agenda. If Royce wants to win, he needs to start acting like it."

"I'll talk to him again," Stuart said. "I have before. He wants to show people he's a hard worker, so he doesn't campaign on foot."

"In the meantime, Bell does and reaches five times what we're reaching. He also attends ribbon cuttings and public celebrations. It doesn't matter if Morrow is working his ass off if nobody actually knows it. Bell is someone people recognize."

"Royce has an hour blocked off today. I'll meet up with him and let him know it's crunch time. He'll understand."

Stuart's voice was wooden and he was tired of arguing the dos and don't of campaigning with Ronald. They had always been on the same page in campaign strategy, but Ronald wanted to push Royce along while Stuart understood that Royce was too stubborn, and likely couldn't be persuaded.

"Here's the other thing," Ronald said. "Morrow doesn't want to run a smear campaign, fine. Good. But what's he doing giving speeches and speaking against politics?"

"What specifically?"

"He said, and I quote: Politicians are an omnipresent species of parasite known only to feast upon the vitality of human begins, and, alternatively, governments and corporations. Its long, fattened evolutionary history has produced in the politician a propensity for an unsavory activity called campaigning. Most human beings are so understandably averse to campaigning as to leave the politician with a lucrative monopoly with his hand in societies' business. When Royce talks like this, it sounds like he doesn't want to win."

"You think he wants to lose?"

"No. I think he doesn't want to win. I find that concerning considering we printed five thousand fliers this morning, most of whose life expectancy is the duration of time it takes to walk from the front door to the trash."

"He's telling the public the truth and it's not being received poorly at all. Not according to recent polls."

"He's criticizing campaigning while campaigning."

"Most Americans loathe politicians," Stuart said. "They love a candidate who hates the game. He's the kind of electorate this public wants. He's the anti-politician."

"And soon he'll be a hypocrite because he's creating an image of himself that he won't be able to fit."

"When he's elected, we'll work toward fitting that image. How about we cross this bridge first? I'll talk to Royce, but he's being honest, and that's refreshing. He's working hard for the public and we need to make that fact known. He's not running a smear campaign because he's not stooping to the opposition's level. The better man will focus on being the better man…not lessening his opponent. Aren't we all tired of candidates talking about what the other guy can't do instead of talking about what they can?"

By then, Ronald had zoned out and instead, had his eyes glued on the television set in the corner. The story was breaking news and Royce's face was on the screen next to Manny Quinny's face.

"Turn that up!" Ronald shouted to a nearby intern. They shushed the room and watched as the story played out, alleging Royce had been working with the mob, dealing with a crooked cops, and ordering a hit on an enemy. By the time the story had finished, the whole room was silent. No one could believe any of it was true, but there it was, a rumor that would raise questions and distract people from who Royce really was.

Ronald picked up the nearest thing—a calculator—and threw it at the wall. The small machine hit the wall and fell to the floor in one piece. It was underwhelming, considering Ronald's reddened face and blazing eyes. "Get Royce Morrow back here before he talks to anyone," he said as the crew began to scatter. He turned to Stuart. "So much for honesty…"

*"…I'm not lying," Royce told Judd as they walked with their hands in their pockets along the riverbank. "Paycheck over a thousand dollars, two raises in six months, and the guy is nice. He's real nice. I never told him about my situation, but I think he knows."*

*"What situation is that?"*

*"He wouldn't have hired me if he knew how I live."*

*"Can't hide who you are forever Rocky."*

*"I can change who I am."*

*Judd laughed and the conversation turned. Rocky stopped trying to convert his friends, but knew he had what it took to improve his way of life. Maybe some people really weren't driven enough, or capable. Most of his buddies scared people off on their looks alone. Judd was missing his two front teeth and his skin looked as if it was made of leather. Even if well groomed, he would still have the look of a man most people didn't want to get to know.*

*The sun was bright that day and Rocky didn't have to work, so his plan was to spend some time in the library and find a bank where he could start putting his money. He hated to let it go, but knew it made sense. The easiest way not to spend it was to put it out of sight. Then, he could get a bank card, start building his savings, and eventually, find a place to live. From there, life would be about working hard and building.*

*He spent hours in the library, learning everything he could find about his trade and even researching beyond it. He'd heard to dress for the job you want, but it didn't make a lick of difference if he knew nothing about the job he wanted. Education at a big institution would never be a part of the big picture, but all those places still housed information that could be found. All Rocky needed was his brain to be successful, and if he had that, he didn't need a piece of paper saying he sat through classes.*

*Afterward, he was off to the bank with two paychecks in hand. One he'd saved from two weeks before and one was given to him a day ago. He dressed up in the nicest clothes he had, which made him look as if he could live anywhere. He paid for a day membership at the gym so he could take a shower and freshen up in their bathrooms. He paid for a day pass every other day, just so he could work on grooming and have a place to hang out awhile. After he had a checking account, he could have a regular month to month pass and go there anytime he wanted.*

*He entered the bank and asked the greeter at the door if he could set up an account. He was pointed to an office and entered, coming face to face with Sandra Morrow for the first time, seated at her desk. Then, she was Sandra Thompson, and when Royce met her for the first time, he hadn't felt chemistry or attraction. The fact was, dating, or even liking someone, had been out of his life for so long that his mind never went there. He hoped down the road to have all the things other people had, but he was far from relationship-ready and though Sandra was pretty, he focused only on what he was there to accomplish.*

*"So you want to open an account," Sandra said with a smile.*

*Rocky nodded. "Yes ma'am."*

*She handed him a paper which displayed the types of accounts and went over them in great detail with Rocky. When he picked one, she began filling the paperwork and started a conversation he was uncomfortable with.*

*"Have you been just cashing your paychecks until now?"*

*"Yes. I don't have a lot of expenses but nowadays, it's getting harder to pay cash everywhere."*

*"That's very true," she said and looked up long enough to smile. "I don't know how you've done it this long."*

*Rocky shifted uncomfortably.*

*"You're definitely ahead of the curve though Mr. Morrow. I'd like to live credit-free one day. I wouldn't recommend burying your money in your mattress though."*

*"That's good advice. Thank you."*

"*Did you want to do a personalized picture on your debit or one of our designs?*"

"*I won't need a debit card,*" Rocky said.

She looked up. "*There are a lot of establishments that won't accept checks.*"

"*I'm just looking to deposit the money. I won't be using it.*"

"*Do you have other accounts?*" She spoke slowly, trying to get a sense of what Rocky's objective was.

"*I'm just saving. I have other sources of income and I use those to take care of what I need.*"

"*Okay, well it comes with a debit card, so I do have to have one sent to you, but you can always just store it in a safe.*"

"*That sounds good.*" Rocky shifted again.

*Rocky finished the paperwork, filling out his address as a PO Box he managed and his primary phone number as his employer. He'd managed to create an email address, and so everything was filled out as if he was just another Los Angeles resident, working, paying bills, and sitting with a beer in hand at the end of the day. Sandra and Rocky shook hands and she smiled again, but this time, her face reflected some doubt, as if she could see there was something awkward on his end.*

*Rocky left the bank and let out a breath of relief. It was later that he realized there was no shame in her knowing his situation, but he didn't want to lose the way people smiled at him or called him "Mr. Morrow" as if he was someone. His true self wouldn't have been treated with respect, the same way Judd never was, but the closer Rocky came to a normal life, the more he wanted to detach from life on the streets.*

*He was almost there, and every day, he obsessed over what he should look like, how he should walk and talk, what words he should drop from his vocabulary, what he should add, and finally one day, he thought about his birth name: Royce Morrow. He'd taken Rocky long ago, but Rocky was...rocky.*

"*Royce,*" *he said as he looked at his reflection in the mirror, his hair neatly parted on the side. No one would ever guess he'd slept on a mattress last night. It sounded so much more respectable. "Royce Morrow," he said, and smiled at himself, knowing he was well on his way...*

...His life was over.

Somehow, someone had spilled details of his business that Royce had hoped would always be locked up. His name even being associated with Manny was bad news. Not long ago, his heart stopped every time he thought of Manny and he'd panic every time he thought he saw him.

Now, he had no choice but to confront the man and find out what was happening. He had a full day ahead of him and Stuart was blowing up his phone with texts and calls. He couldn't stall for long, so instead of waiting for Manny to finish his shift, he went straight to the precinct himself and asked for Manny, but Manny was out on short term disability and when Royce drove past his home, he could see a car in the driveway and smoke coming from the back yard. The setting was good enough for a private talk. Surely, the media would be trying to capture pictures of the two men together.

Manny never turned. He just tossed another log into his fire and sat back. "Sit down Mr. Morrow," he said. It wasn't inviting. It sounded to Royce like a demand, but he sat in a lawn chair at his side. "You want a beer?"

"No." Royce nodded to Manny's arm, which was in a sling. "What happened?"

"I took a shot on the job."

"You okay?"

"You don't give a shit if I'm okay. Let's move on to why you're here."

"You've seen the news?"

"Yeah, I've seen it."

"Someone leaked something."

"I leaked it Morrow."

Royce frowned and tried to find words to say. "Wh...I..."

"I've been trying to contact you, and you're not returning my calls."

"You incriminated yourself for that?"

"Relax. All I gave them was a rumor among a dozen other untrue rumors. A couple will be invalidated and they'll all lose credibility. Probably even help you in the long run."

Royce stood and turned to go.

"I'm not done talking to you Morrow. There's still a debt."

Royce turned back, angry. "We've already done this. You took me to the middle of nowhere to kill me and Wilcox took over what you thought I owed."

"Wilcox is gone."

"What do you mean gone? Dead?"

"I don't know. We had some qualms. He ran off. I shot him. Body hasn't turned up anywhere but there's been nothing on the grid from him."

"So...he's dead?"

"Yeah, probably. We'll see. That leaves you."

"I'm not doing anything for you."

"Relax," Manny said. "I'm not going to ask you to fill the role. I'm making you an offer. I have some important contacts in this city. I want to help you win the election and if you've got me on your side, it will be handed to you. Trust me. My business goes higher up than you'd believe."

"And what do you expect in return?"

"Favors here and there. I just like knowing guys in good positions. It's all give and take Royce. I won't ask you to do anything that will compromise your integrity. You still owe me for Bedbug. I'm going easy on you here."

"I honestly don't give a damn whether I win or not. I wanted to do some good, but I'm not going to win because a criminal helps me, just so he can have free reign to be a bigger criminal."

"I think you lack perspective Morrow. I wish I could give you a list of the lives I've saved and the good I've done as a detective. It would take too long. Let's keep in mind that you hired me to do something you knew to be illegal to cover up something you did that was illegal. Enough with the holier than thou shit. You want me in your corner or not? If not, I still have another prospect."

"Another prospect for what?"

"To fill the debt."

"Would you quit with this debt shit? No one owes you anything Manny. You take lives all the time. You dabble in something that is high risk and you paid for it. Bedbug died because you sent him into the middle of a conflict. Pay your own debt."

"Charlie Palmer, since you asked."

"Charlie Palmer may never walk again. What's your problem? You haven't ruined enough lives?"

"You know, between you and Wilcox and Palmer, I'm not surprised Mr. Stone wanted you all dead. I've been doing this job for years and I've never dealt with this many pains in the ass."

"Then let's go our own ways and forget each other exists."

"No Royce, I don't think so."

"Decent people have died because of us. I made a mistake when I hired you. I admit that. I wanted to protect everyone from someone I believed was a threat. I don't want the money and neither do most of the others. The people we've destroyed have families, friends… The starkest reality of who you are is that your victims are never really monsters. Never inhuman. Warriors used to reduce their foes to subhumans to prop up their denial, just as you try to justify death as business. The fact is that your enemy is someone who dreams, someone who loves, someone who just needed a job, someone who is just waiting for a break to take a leak or eat his supper, a full fledged human, just like us."

Manny set his bottle down and struggled to his feet to face Royce. His words slurred and he stumbled a bit, only able to prop himself with one good arm. He winced in pain as he stood. "You want to lose the campaign, then lose. Give in to Bell. But let me tell you something. About ten years ago, I get a call about a breaking and entering and I'm off duty, but I'm nearby and I have a piece on me, so I respond. I'm looking around, no idea where this guy is, and suddenly I hear a gunshot. This guy was at the end of the hall, the only thing between him and the door was me. And he was going to kill me, but a random guy in the building knew what was happening because he picked it up on a police scanner. This guy comes to the scene—average citizen—and brings his own gun and shoots the guy and saves my life. You know who the guy was?"

"Bedbug."

"Very good."

"And so you turned a hero into a killer."

"Guy had nothing going for him. Had a bad past. Wife had just left him with the kids to raise them on his own. I owed him my life. Then, you took it."

"I'm sorry about what happened to Bedbug. It wasn't deliberate. It was bad timing. Palmer is already paying enough. Wilcox has paid enough. We all have. It's time to let it go."

Manny took a step forward, the bottle of booze dangling at his fingertips. "Do you accept this debt?"

"For the love of..."

"Do you accept this debt?"

"Don't come near me again," Royce said. "Or I'll spill everything myself. I have connections too and if you come near me, I'll make sure you're put down. I'll have security throw you out of my building and out of my home..."

"Security won't stop me."

"We're done. Get over your shit. Take some responsibility."

"You don't wanna win, maybe I'll talk to Bell."

"Then do it," Royce said. He turned his back and walked away, the rantings of a drunk maniac thrown at his back as he got in his car and drove away.

2

Toby O'Tool awaited word from William that Brian was really gone, but nothing came.

He probably backed out. Toby shook his head in disbelief. He'd been holding back and suddenly William had grown ambitious only to have backed out. Toby would rub it in his face later, but had other things to think about at the moment.

He'd had many things simultaneously in motion and they were all coming to a head. He was ready to execute, but that moment when everything was supposed to work as planned felt all wrong. There was a nagging feeling that Brian wouldn't really take his nightly habits to the extreme he was being pushed, that Maria wouldn't pull another fake suicide, only to find no one would save her. But the biggest itch of all was Trish Reynalds. Would she really go on a killing spree if the clock counted down to her own daughter's death?

He was ready to give the go-ahead on all three…to create uncontrollable chaos that would inevitably lead to the fall of twelve people.

It was Trish though…who could never know the truth. It hadn't been easy pulling it off. First he needed the family doctor on his side, which turned out to be easier than he expected. He found very little to blackmail Dr. Neomin with, but it turned out that Neomin was almost as greedy and his eyes turned green when Toby told him the millions to gain. Neomin knew he could give Shiloh the symptoms, make her sick when he wanted, and put it in her mother's head that she had an inoperable tumor.

Getting around the hospital was much harder. The first problem was obtaining x-rays and running tests that would diagnose a problem that wasn't there. To do that, Neomin had to make a false tumor appear on the x-rays. He administered the drugs that prompted the drowsiness and vomiting, but to create a pressure buildup of fluid within Shiloh's skull, he went to the deep dark Internet and paid for counterfeit x-rays and test results manufactured to his liking. At the moment he took blood tests and x-rays, it was just a matter of using the data he'd paid for, and he kept it coming as needed, but there would come a time when he could no longer stall.

It had almost ended when Charlie Palmer began running tests on his own, but fate stepped in and took Charlie out of the picture, but not before Neomin called Toby and could barely breathe as he begged him to finish this. Toby was going to make the call, but then Charlie's house blew up, and Charlie was in a hospital bed incapacitated. It bought plenty of time—until the next person began asking questions as to why Shiloh Reynalds was still a sick little girl on a waiting list. The tumor was outside of what Trish's insurance could pay. She could barely afford the experimental drugs, which ironically, were the same drugs keeping Shiloh's symptoms in play.

As twisted as Toby knew it was, he also knew Shiloh would be okay in the long run. Of course, her mother and those she was supposed to kill wouldn't be. He just needed to give the go head—a final determination by Neomin that the time to operate is now. At that point, Toby had no doubt she would do whatever it took and he'd hide out until it was done.

He'd even produced a copy of a death certificate for himself—though it was a real copy of the death of another Toby O'Tool, who Trish would be told was no longer a beneficiary because he'd "cheated his way off the will," a rumor which Bernard Bell was supposed to spread any day now, eliminating Toby as someone who needed to be killed. Of course, that certificate would never be submitted and Trish would believe she'd inherited everything until it was too late. At that point, Toby could just pay someone to eliminate her.

Everything had gone as planned, but as the clock counted down, Toby began doubting his streak would continue. The plan was just too big and dependent on too many perfectly executed things to be flawless. On top of that, it seemed his crew no longer had the enthusiasm they had in the beginning. William was ready to be done and fed up at how long he was tied to his gig. Henry was in the middle of a moral dilemma. Gregory Neomin was scared shitless. As Toby began to lose them, his consideration to finish the job continued to grow stronger.

"Toby?"

A small voice from behind had said his name and before he even turned, he knew it was someone he didn't want to see. The last time he'd seen Joshua was when Richard was alive and mentoring him. It was Josh who Richard had gone to see and Richard drowned shortly after. Toby had never heard what came of the boy and would rather not know. It would have been better than having to see him in person.

"Hey kid," Toby said and went back to his drink.

"I came to talk to you."

"I'm busy."

"You don't look busy."

"When someone tells you they're busy but they don't look busy, that's just a polite way of saying they want to be alone."

"This won't take long. I've tried to get a hold of you a bunch of times since I got back."

"Back from where?"

"Haiti. I went. Two months. Changed my life."

"Good for you." He didn't sound the least bit sincere.

"I wanted to know what happened." Josh fell into the booth across from Toby.

"What happened with what?"

"The will. Richard was trying to invalidate it. I never heard anything."

"He didn't get a majority. It didn't work."

"How many short was he?"

Toby took a deep breath and smiled. "What difference does it make?"

"He came to get me. If it was short because he wasn't there…"

"It wasn't. He didn't even come close."

"So has anything happened?"

"No. Richard was paranoid over nothing."

"It meant a lot for him to end it."

"If it meant a lot for him to end it, what'd he go chasing after you for?"

"To stop me from making a mistake."

"Well…then if you're looking for someone to blame that the will is still valid, you should blame yourself. You're the reason he left."

"I know." Josh spoke with comfort, any guilt long gone. "I blamed myself for a long time, but Haiti fixed everything. I got some perspective. When I got back, I talked to Richard's parents and to some of the members of his congregation. I told them what happened and no one was angry. They told me instead that Richard would have been content."

"That he died?"

"How he died. One of the last things he told me was that what happened with you all didn't matter. That you all could make your own choices. He'd made his—to be there. And I'll forever be grateful to him for it. I'll carry on with what he started."

"You won't invalidate the will. It's too late now."

"I'm not going to try. I just mean carry on my life the way he lived his."

"You trying to sell me religion? I'd rather tickle a tiger's balls in a phone booth."

"I'm not selling you anything. I was curious to know what happened. I'm glad to hear no one has hurt anyone else. I hope it stays that way. I don't think the existence of the will is important at all. I just think how you deal with it is. I don't really care. I don't plan on coming back here. I just wanted you to know that in the end, Richard was okay with it, and I'm okay with it. He knew he was going to die. He was at peace."

"Why would I care?"

"Because he liked you and you liked him. And even though you act like this now, I'm sure you wondered. So you don't have to admit that you wondered. I'm just telling you."

"Why?"

"So you can be at peace with what you did to him."

"I'm perfectly fine with everything and if I wanted to dig into my psyche, I'd watch Dr. Phil."

Josh slid out of the booth and looked down on Toby for a moment as if memorizing his face for the last time. Toby couldn't help but notice how grown up and mature he seemed—how at peace he really was. Josh was just a bystander to events and had no influence over the money. Toby didn't think it was so bad that he was slightly relieved at what Josh had to say.

"Have a good life Toby."

"Yeah," Toby said, looking into his mug of beer. "You take care of yourself."

Josh exited, leaving Toby to go back to his thoughts of the plan…the money…Richard. He tried to shake it off. Richard had been passionately on a quest to get the will off their backs forever. In the end, he'd set it all aside for one kid and supposedly been fearlessly swept away into the sea. Toby felt a little less grumpy, a little more upbeat, but especially motivated. He set his cell phone in front of his face and sent a text to Bernard Bell:

**Spread the word that my name is off the will.**

Once he had confirmation from Bell, he'd give his crew the go-ahead.

3

There was only one place Royce knew he could turn when he needed real advice. His advisers and campaign managers knew everything about how to maneuver through the business world, but only Sandra Morrow understood who Royce really was. He texted her and she told him she was at the mall. He asked if he could meet and they had lunch at the food court, Royce with a plate of Chinese food and Sandra with a sandwich. He made small-talk until Sandra finally asked him what was happening.

"I don't have what it takes to win," Royce finally admitted.

"Sure you do."

"Bell is running a smear campaign, which I'm fundamentally against, but seems to be what people respond to. He has more money to campaign with. He's squeaky clean."

"So are you."

"We both know that's not true."

"What happened to that man…he deserved that."

"And it will forever haunt me and follow me wherever I go. You can call Bell a lot of things, but he's running against the man who took his brother from him and he doesn't even know it. Don't you think I've done enough harm to his family?"

"Royce, the past has nothing to do with now, and you did what you had to do and I think you'd do it again if the circumstances were the same…"

"Of course I would."

"Then don't be ashamed of your convictions. That man has done far worse than you've ever done and if he wins, it will be a disaster."

"And the fact that I won't win?"

"Why not?"

"I told you why not."

"So he's making fun of you and spreading rumors. None of it's true. You just need to show everyone you're the better man. People respond to what he's doing but they don't respect it. Come that time when they have to put a check in a box, the better part of their brain is going to tell them that Bell isn't the guy."

"You watch the news today?"

"Yeah, and I've dodged reporters all day too. Who cares?"

"It's just that simple for you, huh?"

"Do you remember what we talked about that day that we met?"

"It was the second day we met."

"And what did we talk about?"

"I know."

"Rock, it's amazing you've built all that you've built but now is the time to take everything you've done and give something back—to leave your legacy. You doubt yourself because you think because a few things forced you to do things you feel guilty about, that you don't deserve success. This is different though. If you win, that's not success. It's going to be more difficult than ever. Half the city is going to hate every decision you make. You aren't running for glory. You're running to make real change, and to block a bad man from winning and making things worse."

"Yeah," Royce said, consumed in thought as he sipped through his straw. He suddenly looked up and smiled. "I love you Sand."

"I love you too Rock…"

*…Rocky learned accounting through books at the library, computer programs designed to teach the fundamentals of math, and by scribbling in a notebook. When he'd first started working for Earl Harrington, he was given the chance of a lifetime, and in the beginning, he faked his way through. He suspected Earl knew he wasn't qualified, but Rocky evolved day by day and was willing and eager to learn. If not for his learning curve, and his passion to know the job, Earl may not have held onto him, but soon Rocky was good enough to do the work and eventually, better than average.*

*Eventually, Royce was confident in his abilities and began asking himself the question of what was next. He'd been with Earl only six months and was contemplating the next move—something to a bigger company with benefits. The cost of living in LA was still outside of Rocky's reach and before he started applying for bigger and better, he would have to rid his life of the lie. He wasn't an average Joe with a big education and a house with a wife and kids. His background would close too many doors and so he needed something to show.*

*He was afraid that one day, inevitably Earl would start asking questions. He suspected Earl knew and kept quite, but then the day came that Earl had sent a W-2 to the address Rocky had provided and it came back. At the end of the day, Earl handed it to him in person.*

*"This still your address?"*

*Royce took the envelope and was ready to lie as he had from the beginning, but he'd grown too much respect for Earl and he couldn't do it. "I'll have to update it for you," he said.*

*"Rocky, do you have a home?" Earl propped himself up on his desk.*

*"I'm afraid to say."*

*"It won't change your position here, but if you tell me your situation, I might be able to make it easier for you. This is one piece of mail that you don't want to lose. I'd rather just hand it to you in person if we don't have a good address on file."*

*"Thanks," Rocky said, looking down. He was ashamed that his cover was blown. Earl didn't seem to mind but Royce knew he'd be looked at differently after this.*

*"You never talk about your family," Earl said. "No wife. No siblings. Are you sure this is where you want to be?"*

*"I came out here to play baseball," Rocky said, tracing his finger along the edge of the desk. "Had this idea in my head that I'd try out for the Dodgers because I was a big fish back home. The tryout was an embarrassment and I gave up on that, but was here and..." He shook his head as he reflected. "I never tried much in school. Didn't get good grades because I was all about sports. When I was here, reality sunk in."*

*"Why didn't you go home?"*

*"My father is a pilot. My mother died when I was young. I was left to take care of myself most of the time because Dad would fly from place to place and disappear for weeks at a time. I got to be pretty good at taking care of myself. Well, when I got through High School, I found out the mortgage wasn't being paid. He had the money, but he was just leaving it to be taken by the bank. I don't even know if he has a home, but he travels and has money, so he lives well. Not exactly the kind of thing you can take your kid along for. I didn't have grants or scholarships, but I was pretty good at baseball...thought I was anyway. And I'm a Dodger fan all the way so I came out here, but I've got nothing to go back to, even if I did."*

*There was a long silence as Earl considered the situation, a saddened look on his face. Finally, he spoke. "How long have you been living on* the streets?"

"About four years."

"Wow. And you just walked in here one day and talked yourself into a job..."

"I knew I could learn what I had to learn," Rocky said, suddenly afraid he was about to lose it all. "I'm really sorry but no one would take a chance on me. I..."

"No worries," Earl said. "You're a trusted employee. I'm just trying to grasp your plan here."

"My plan is to continue to build my life."

"To what?"

Rocky shrugged.

"I don't think most men on the streets could have gotten this far."

"They're good guys, but they've got problems. Some mental, or addictions. I know a couple guys who can't work because they owe back taxes and child support and they make any money and it's gonna be taken by the government. I just don't have those problems. I met this guy, back when I was out panhandling. He gave me fifty bucks and told me I could spend it on booze or I could use it to make fifty more. Something about the encounter really stuck with me. People don't just believe in guys like me in that way, but he said it as if...as if anyone could do it...as if doing well was as simple as wanting to do well."

"Sometimes it is," Earl said. "I can't speak to mental problems or addiction, but we all start out with the same amount of knowledge. We're all capable of learning what we need to learn to become who we want to be, so whatever it is you want—pipe dream or not—you have to keep moving Rocky."

"Would you be angry if I started looking for work that pays more?"

"I'd be a reference Rocky, and I wouldn't speak of anything you've confided in me about."

"Thank you Mr. Harrington."

"Do you have anything in mind?"

"Not yet. Just looking."

"Make sure they validate your parking."

Royce leaned in, admiring Earl more than ever.

"A company that doesn't validate parking is not financially stable," Earl said. "They should offer a drink or bathroom break during a lengthy interview, or they don't care or provide for their employees. If they're late for the interview and they're looking over your resume for the first time, the company is somewhat hectic and unorganized. If they're not enthused about the company mission, how can you be? If the interview is too easy, they don't set high standards and anyone can get the job. A brutal *interview on the opposite end, means they might take pleasure in trying to stump you with questions you wouldn't need to know to be successful at the job."*

*Rocky nodded and smiled. "I'll remember that."*

*"It's good advice. I promise." Earl hopped off the desk. "I'm done for the day."*

*"Thanks again," Rocky said.*

*Earl stopped at the door and turned, as if a thought formulated in his head. "I have a foldout couch at home. I'll have it here tomorrow in meeting room B. We never use it anyway. The streets are dangerous. You should be okay to stay there."*

*Rocky couldn't speak, but tried desperately to thank Earl. No one had ever done anything this nice for him before and he couldn't express his gratitude. Earl saw it on his face and gave him a nod as if to say he understood. He grabbed a hat from the hat rack and put it on his head. "Continue to evolve Rocky. There's nowhere to go but up..."*

…Royce spent some time at campaign headquarters, watching the latest rumors in the news. Already, most of the previous rumors were being dismissed as lies, but winning still meant there were rocks that could be turned. Royce dedicated the day to walking through neighborhoods and talking with people. He pretended to go grocery shopping to show how in touch he was with the people in the neighborhood, shopping where they shopped so everyone could see the regular man he was. He gave a speech at a school and granted an interview to a local publication.

When his day was nearly complete, he realized he'd been enjoying the process. When politics weren't weighed down by games and lies, at their heart was a guy who wanted to change the city for the better. The obstacle was always the other guy and if the other guy hadn't been such a horrible man, Royce might have been willing to lose.

It was on his way out of the bank that he spotted Bernard Bell sitting on the couch in the lobby, flipping through a magazine. He approached Bernard with high spirits. Bernard seemed like a very small man in person. He wasn't sure why he'd assigned so much power and ability to him. If they were head to head in the public eye, even Royce knew he was the more likable of the two. "Job searching?" Royce asked, and Bernard chuckled.

"Might be after the election."

"Nah, you'll always have your tower."

"Something tells me you're going to try to tear it down if you win."

"I'm going to put an end to corruption in this city if I win. If Stone

Enterprises is on the up and up, you'll always have a job. What can I do for you?"

"I was visited by a detective Quinny today."

Royce shook his head with disbelief. If Royce wasn't going to work with him, he'd contact everyone attached to Royce. "What did he have to say?"

"You know him?"

"I don't."

"He's the same Quinny who was linked to you in some of the rumors I heard on the news. I figured he'd be pissed off about that, but he wasn't. He actually offered to work with me."

"What did you say?"

"I said no. I don't know his qualifications and I don't know if being seen with him would hurt or help me."

"Why are you telling me this?"

"When I said no, he told me to ask you about my brother."

Royce knew the day would one day come that Bernard Bell's brother would come into the picture, but not like this. Not in the lobby of the bank in the light of day with no preparation. "That man is a liar and I don't know what he's referencing. I will tell you that some time ago, he and I had a disagreement over some things and he's been trying to wedge into my life since. Trust me when I tell you that the best thing you can do is stay away from him."

"How are you connected?"

"Is this off the record?"

"Of course."

"He's a crooked cop. He's threatened by my stance on corruption and knows if I win, his days are numbered. He offered to work for me and in return, he wanted my protection. I turned him down this morning, and so he's going to try to get the same from you."

"He knew about my brother," Bernard said. "Not many people do. Lucas used another last name after our father died."

"He's a detective. He has access to information."

Bell seemed desperate for answers but Royce withheld the truth, all the while thinking about what he was going to do to put an end to Manny. At one time, Manny was just a problem, but no matter what he did, he wouldn't go away. Manny would forever want vengeance for what happened to Bedbug and he was constantly in Royce's way. After he escaped Bell's grasp, the first thing he did was call Manny. After a dozen rings, Manny picked up.

"What do you want to make you go away?"

"You know what I want."

"You don't have my services. You don't have my loyalty. How much?"

"Royce, you don't understand that for the universe to be fair and balanced, wherever there's a loss, someone is responsible to fill it."

"Cut the bullshit Manny. You're supposed to be better than this. You wear a badge and you've probably seen a hundred homicides in this city go unsolved. There's no balance and there's no justice. We do the best we can. You're holding yourself back and you're holding me back. We can be doing more productive things, be helping more people, fixing problems instead of creating them."

"You're right Royce. I think you've shown me the way here today. I only wish we'd had this conversation ten minutes ago."

Royce's words were caught in his throat as he thought about Manny's words. "Why?" he managed to say.

"You'll know soon enough, but I have to get out of here. You'll understand."

Click.

Royce's knuckles were white and he nearly crushed his cell-phone. Manny had done something bad as a repercussion of Royce's rejection, and there was only one thing that Manny understood would ruin Royce. He immediately called Sandra and listened to her phone ring until the voice-mail picked up. He called twice more but with no response. Sandra never ignored his calls. The color drained from his face and he fumbled with his phone as he shoved it in his pocket and grabbed his car keys. He ran to his car and drove home, ignoring all traffic signs and stop lights. He hit the brakes in the driveway, creating a fresh tire-mark and hitting one of the bushes on his property with his car. He ran up the driveway, fumbled the keys into the lock, his hand shaking uncontrollably. The door swung open and he looked inside with horror.

"Oh God…"

## 4

Toby O'Tool was in high spirits, but his run-in with Josh kept returning to him. He'd been trying for a long time to escape the memory of Richard. If Richard could see what Toby was doing—what he was about to do—he would be highly disappointed. Toby tried to laugh off the notion and label Richard as just another religious nut, but his mind kept returning to Richard the man. Richard, who was sensible, kind, and even clever.

If the ghost of Richard was following him around, he was very likely pissing him off every time he walked into Banner to meet with Dr. Gregory Neomin. He could hear Richard now: *It's wrong to fake a child's illness to push her mother into mass killing.* Toby smiled to himself, unable to shake the thought of Richard chasing him down the hallway to stop him from moving forward. But Toby hadn't really moved forward much in awhile and that was because of his awareness of Richard's opinions about what he was doing. Those days were done though. He'd been pressured by his partners and Neomin couldn't stall any longer. It was time to execute and if the ghost of Richard was disappointed, he'd just have to get over it.

But why, of all days, had he run into Josh? He shook it off again as he rounded a corner and caught Neomin off guard with his presence. "You find the cure for syphilis?" Toby asked.

Neomin frantically pulled him aside and led him into a quiet room. Neomin hated when Toby popped by for a surprise visit but knew better than to argue with him about it. There were things Toby was just going to do, and being panicked or angry about it just seemed to make Toby want to do it more.

"What do you want?" Neomin asked.

"It seems like Will has dropped the ball on his assignment. We're spinning our wheels. Put the pressure on Reynalds and I mean full pressure. Give her as little time as you can muster."

"I already have."

"And what's she doing about it?"

"How would I know that? Have you considered the fact that she won't actually kill for her daughter?"

"Of course she will."

"And what happens if she comes to you first?"

"After today, everyone will believe I'm not even on it anymore. That's very considerate of you to be worried about me though." Toby mocked Neomin and Neomin hated it.

"Shiloh Reynalds has been telling everyone she's dying. There are social media pages raising money for the family. How are you going to escape this lie when it's over? Toby, the girl sits and cries through every appointment. She's in a room crying now."

"Well then she'll be relieved when she finds out she's going to be okay."

"Except that about that time is when she learns her mother is a murderer."

"What room is she in?" Toby asked. He didn't know what he was doing, but suddenly he felt like he was being controlled. *Fuckin' ghost of Richard* he thought.

"Two-o-two, why?"

Toby didn't bother to respond. Instead, he navigated the halls until he found the room he was looking for and walked right in without hesitation. Shiloh looked up suddenly, her eyes wide, and stared at Toby. She had the remote in her hand and had been watching the television. From the looks of it, it was a fashion reality show. Toby scowled at the people on the screen, hating them immediately.

First Josh. Now Shiloh. It was as if the whose who of lives Toby liked to ruin were all making an appearance just for him.

"Hey," Toby said, trying to sound cool.

"Hi?" she said, suspiciously.

"I'm not here to coax you into a van or anything. I'm a couple rooms down. I've got the big C." She stared at him, confused. "It's an expression. It means cancer is eating my insides."

"Oh," she said.

"I figured I'd get to know the neighbors. I'm bored as hell down there and none of the nurses here are attractive enough to hit on." Shiloh looked afraid, so Toby toned it down. "What about you?" he asked.

"Tumor," she said. "I'm dying too." Her lip started to quiver and as she thought about her situation, he could see she'd start crying any moment.

"Please," he said. "That's horseshit. They can fix that."

"Not without an operation."

"Then get one."

"My mom is trying," she said.

"Yeah, well no one ever dies from a tumor."

"That's not true."

"Yeah, it is. That's an easy fix for these places. They just gotta do it and they will."

"That's not what they're saying," Shiloh said, but she'd brightened a little, as if he was giving her a sliver of hope.

"It's like when you order a pizza, they always tell you it's going to be an hour even though they know it will be forty minutes. If they tell you the best news, you expect it, and that way if they screw up, you don't know it."

"So you think they lied?"

"They're not lying. In my experience, they prepare themselves for the worst, but that's never what happens, and I know some of the doctors in this place. Believe me when I tell you with a hundred percent certainty that you will not die. What the fuck you sitting in here watching this garbage for, like all you can do is give up and die? You ever hear stories about kids with diseases? People always talk about how brave they are and how they carried on like they were invincible. There's a kid across the hall with rickets who looks like he'll have his license soon. You need to get off your ass and try to pick him up or something."

Shiloh smiled and hopped out of her bed, suddenly interested in everything Toby had to say. "Are you sure? I mean, why would everyone say…"

"Adults always lie about this shit. Most diseases heal themselves. Tumors are caused by self inflicted stress. You just need to walk around knowing you'll be fine and you will be. I'm not making this shit up. You just will things to happen and they do. In fact, I vaguely remember this vapid little moron that everyone called Wheels. He was a standard self satisfied industry asshole, handing pain killers to a bunch of college kids. He had this stunning girl named Bella Cinco, a glamorous Vassar freshman interning for him. Drug dealer or not, I wanted her. You know how I made that happen?" She shook her head no. "I tried everything. Phone calls, flowers, literally sabotaging Wheel's business and publicly embarrassing him in every way I could. Finally, I won her over because I willed it to happen. I looked her right in the eyes and she saw it and knew she had to be with me. She called me the one."

Shiloh smiled sweetly and awed at him.

"So I bagged her," Toby said, proudly. "Got her sister too. So stop sulking. Get up, go across the hall, flirt with the ricket-boy."

Toby saw how relieved Shiloh looked and decided his work here was done. He'd effectively patched up the same bad feelings in the children who he'd caused pain in. He didn't know about Josh, but Shiloh certainly felt better. Neomin was right though: Shiloh was going to find out she was fine about the time a whole new set of problems started. Toby would have an endless amount of money though. He could make sure Shiloh saw some of it, or he'd at least find a way to repair some of his damage when this was over.

*That's the best I got for you Richard,*  Toby said as he walked out of Banner with his hands in his pockets.

5

Sandra Morrow lay on her side at the bottom of the staircase, her wheelchair about four feet from her, turned on it's side with a bent wheel. He called for an ambulance as he ran to her side, falling on one knee and dropping his phone while the operator asked who was there. He put a hand under her head with his fingers ending at her neck to feel for a pulse. He closed his eyes and moved his finger, trying desperately to find a sign of life.

"Sandra," he whispered but his breath was cut off as it set in that Sandra wouldn't be opening her eyes. He shifted into sitting position and pulled her body up toward his chest, wrapping his arms around her and burying his face in her hair. "Sandra," he said again, but her body was still and he immediately started to weep, holding her tightly. He sat there for an endless amount of time. Responders eventually came to his home but his cell never moved from the floor. When they arrived, the police were called and eventually, when Royce's name was spoken, the media arrived.

Outside his home were flashing lights and a small crowd of people, all wanting to know what happened. All Royce could say was that he'd come home and found her at the bottom of the stairs. It looked to be an accident, but Sandra never used the stairs. She never went near them. She'd always used the service elevator.

Royce had a state of the art alarm system in his home which appeared as though it hadn't been tampered with. The police drew the conclusion that she lost control of her chair and free-fell. Her neck broke when she hit the ground. Royce started to say more—to talk about Manny—but thought better of it. What good was it going to do to make an accusation that wouldn't stick? He had no time to worry about Manny now. He wanted to sit with his wife and he did for as long as he possibly could. After she was taken away, the police stayed behind, asked more questions, offered assistance in any way possible, and finally left him alone in his home, sitting in the middle of the wide entry, a blank expression on his face.

After he finally came out of his daze, he got in his car and drove to Manny's home. All the lights were off and Manny wasn't on his back patio. He drove to his work next and entered, walking like a man on a mission until he stood outside Manny's office. Manny was inside on the phone and looked up at Royce with a friendly smile, as if he had no idea what happened.

"Someone needs to arrest Manny Quinny," Royce said, speaking to anyone who could hear him. He walked through the office, receiving confused looks by Manny's staff. "He's a murderer. He is a contract killer. He makes everything an accident but he is a murderer and he murdered my wife tonight."

A detective gently put his arm on Royce's shoulder. "Mr. Morrow… let's sit down."

"I don't need to sit down. I need someone to take a statement from me. I'll give you all the information you need."

By now, Manny had opened his office door and stood in the frame, seemingly confused. "Royce…what's going on?"

Royce didn't speak to Manny. Instead, his voice projected to the whole office. "Manny Quinny murdered Sandra Morrow tonight in our home…"

"Whoa Royce, what are you talking about? I've been in the office all night."

"Please…" Royce said, growing desperate. He looked around from face to face, but no one was eager to react. "You have to take my statement. He can't get away with this."

"I heard what happened," Manny said, stepping toward him slowly and putting his hand up as if to calm Royce. "I heard it was an accident."

"Accidents always happen around you, don't they?" Royce asked, addressing Manny for the first time with vile, and when he found Manny's eyes and the innocence Manny was feigning, it enraged him more. "Let's talk about Bedbug, and Adlar Wilcox, and when you dragged me into the middle of nowhere to put a bullet in my head!"

Everyone watched the exchange curiously, all ready to jump in if it got out of hand. Manny stepped forward. "I have no idea where this is coming from."

Royce lunged at Manny but suddenly three detectives were holding him back. Manny stayed in place and took another step, nearly meeting Royce face to face. "You and I don't have any business," Manny said, quietly enough for only Royce's ears. "Your debt has been paid."

Royce tried to lunge again. He shouted names and accusations, most of it coming out as gibberish. Manny walked back to his office and Royce was dragged outside and shut out of the office. He pounded the door, screamed accusations, and finally fell to a bench where tears formed in his eyes again. It wouldn't be until later that he could think straight and begin working out what he was going to do about the situation—how he would fight back. That night, everything was blank, except for the memories of Sandra…from the last time he saw her all the way back…

… *"Is it Rocky or Royce?" Sandra asked, looking up with bright eyes and a polite smile.*

*"It's Royce," he said. "I went by Rocky when I was younger. Sorry for the confusion."*

*"No worries," Sandra said. "Your ID is all I need. I was just curious."*

*Sandra moved on with the deposit, taking the slip and Royce's paycheck. She matched the amount on the paycheck to the amount to be deposited into his savings. Royce detected the slightest shake of her head and smiled to himself, understanding that to her, he was an enigma.*

*As Sandra silently typed into her computer, Royce broke the silence when he read from a box on her desk, which was filled nearly the brim with dollar bills. "The Children Aid Society."*

*"Yup. Feel free to make a donation. There's a fundraiser on Friday and anyone that makes a donation can also have their name thrown into a raffle. You can win gym memberships, movie premiere tickets, passes to*

*the fine arts museum, Universal…"*

*"What is the Children Aid Society?"*

*"It's a home for children who have lost their parents due to death, imprisonment, or taken away because of parental addictions. They provide education and housing and see to it that children have their needs met until they're provided with a new home."*

*"Why this of all things? Is it personal?" Royce was trying to make small talk, but his curiosity got the best of him. Of all the diseases and unfortunate circumstances in the world, he didn't know why the woman at the bank cared so much for this.*

*"It's just my thing," Sandra said with a shrug. I wanted to find a cause and make it mine, ya know? Everyone has a soft spot for something. Mine is children born into an impossible circumstance. Some people just give a few dollars here and there, and who knows where any of that money really goes? A few years ago, I found out I was donating online to a cause that I later found out, mostly just used the money for their own staff. This is something I've thoroughly researched and believe in and I want to see how far I can take it."*

*Royce admired Sandra and in that moment, he wanted nothing more than to be someone who actually had money to give. He desired to be well off enough that he could give something back.*

*"You really should find a cause if you haven't already," she added.*

*"I haven't, but equality. I know that's broad, but fairness."*

*"Fairness for who exactly?"*

*"Everyone," Royce said. "Some kind of balance in the world, where we all understand other needs and respect them."*

*Sandra smiled. "Good luck with that Mr. Morrow. You might be aiming a little high."*

*"Probably," he said, coyly. Then, he had a thought. The woman behind the counter was beautiful and Royce liked her passion for people in less fortunate circumstances. He'd put his last four checks into a savings account and surely, they were adding up nicely. It would be a matter of time before he had what he needed to take his status up a notch. Right there, in that moment, he wanted nothing else but to make her happy. "You can give me cash this time," he said.*

*She looked up, surprised to hear it, but changed the course of the transaction, until Royce had eight hundred and twelve dollars in his hand. He then put it in the donation box.*

*"Whoa, what are you doing?" Sandra said, and to Royce's displeasure, she wasn't happy. She was panicked.*

*"Helping your cause."*

*"That's too much."*

*"There can be too much?"*

*"Well, no, but that's your whole check. You need something, don't you?"*

*"This is an account I'm only adding money to. I'm not using it. It is only two weeks of my life and I was getting by just fine with very little for a long time."*

*Sandra didn't know what to say. She stared at him with a blank expression, as if at any moment, she would either throw the money back at him or hug him. "I can't believe this," she said. She appeared to be looking for an angle and before she could say something embarrassing like that she would never sleep with Royce, he headed for the door.*

*"You talked me into it," Royce said over his shoulder. "Bring it to the auction."*

*As he almost reached the door, he heard her call his name. He turned to find her standing behind the counter. "Would you like to go with me?" she asked...*

... "The answer is yes!" Royce's voice boomed in front of an audience, who for the first time, saw a Royce Morrow they had never seen before. He was passionate, aggressive, almost standing in front of the microphone as he worked the crowd. "I will make it a priority to wipe corruption from every level of this city, from your elected officials to law enforcement."

A few blocks away, Bernard Bell was oblivious to what was happening until his campaign manager called to tell him to turn on his television. When he did, it was Royce, with a stark jaw and the gallant look of an adventurer in a movie serial—a throwback to an earlier age. Bernard's first thought was that Sandra had died two days ago. This would be a disaster, but the Royce on his television was a new Royce. It was a man who was playing by Bernard's rules now.

"The things Bernard Bell tells you sounds good, but you can sculpt a pile of horse manure into a shape that is pleasing to the eye and it's still horse manure. You have to have substance."

Scattered laughter filled the crowd. Bernard leaned in.

"He's just an image folks. He will do anything in his power to have me step aside, to guarantee himself an easy victory. I will not deride though. Brilliance must be respected, but not when it involves marketing in an era where image almost always passes for substance. Bell claims to have all the expertise of someone who has done nothing to earn that expertise."

A "hell yeah!" resounded from the crowd.

"I don't claim to always get it right, but I will always try to strike a balance between doing what is right based on what feels right and doing what is right because I can see that it will eventually cause more good than harm. My opponent couldn't make that claim on his best day. He disposes of ethics at a faster rate than—as hard as this is to believe—wives."

The crowd laughed again, followed by applause.

"I will beat Bernard Bell. I will take this city back, fight corruption, clear the streets and put an iron fist on law enforcement corruption. The days of committing the crimes that you pay them to prevent will be over!"

Cheers for awhile, followed by silence as Royce hangs his head for a moment. Bell watched closely, hoping he would fall apart as he undoubtedly thought about Sandra.

"Bernard Bell has gained strength by mobilizing the resentments of alienated voters. He will not be the only purveyor of extreme ideologies to spot opportunity in our fraying social fabric. If this great state is to regain our confidence, our tolerance and humor that marked it long after its influence declined, it needs to rediscover a faith in human nature. The mainstream politicians who did so much to dent that faith, may not find it easy to lead its restoration. There is a deep-seated belief that this city is approaching the eve of its destruction. Peruse the Web, listen to public discourse. Disastrous wars in the streets, uncontrollable deficits, shootings at universities, corruption in business and government, and an endless litany of other problems—all of them quite real—create a sense that the American dream has been shattered and that we are past our prime. They will assure you that our best day is behind us, but the key to prosperity is within you, and within your leaders. When I began charting this course, I believed I had the power, and the courage, to make a difference. It didn't take long to realize that no matter who you are, no matter what you do, there will always be an uphill battle, and the strongest among leaders will always do the right thing, even at their own expense. I have not lived up this standard every step of the way."

Silence in the crowd.

"Power and prosperity are illusory. Unless we change our ways together, we will pay a price. Both sides believe that reason is powerless to answer the most important questions in human life. And how a person perceives the gulf between facts and values seems to influence his views on almost every issue of social importance—from the fighting of wars to the education of children. So how do we square the circle? We must honor the tensions between two strains of the American dream: the rugged individualists who respect those who make it on their own, and those who revere the Americans who help their neighbors, fight our fires, and wage our wars. Both are central to the American character. Drift too far toward radical individualism and you risk changing our national motto from "From many, one," to "dog eat dog."'" But if you swerve too far into overweening communitarian-ism, you risk crushing the entrepreneurial dream that drives so many to excel. It's more important now than ever that we find that unity, and I will never lose sight of that!"

*I created a monster.*

Bell sat with his feet on his desk, running his hand stressfully through his hair, taking an inventory of all the things Royce could potentially dig up or say. Royce had committed a crime when he hired Manny, but something told Bernard that Royce didn't care—that he had nothing to lose—that to win the election now was completely about ruining Bernard.

*Plan B.*

It wasn't what he'd wanted to do, but there was too much heat on Manny, and Bell couldn't afford to screw up. He had an ace up his sleeve...something that fell in his pocket two days before and kept circling his mind.

Manny Quinny entered the office with Toby O'Tool at his side. "Sit down."

Bernard watched Manny for a moment, questioning his judgment by working with him. He hoped he wouldn't regret it, but he knew it would be the best way to get at Royce. They were going to play his emotions because the city wasn't likely to trust a man who threw out the accusations Royce had been spouting...even if they were true.

Toby sat in a chair across from Bernard, reading the anger on his face. "Did I do something to piss you off because usually I keep track of those kinds of things so I can laugh about them later."

"I don't have time for this. Let's cut to the chase. I..."

"Did you really just say "cut to the chase"?"

"I gave you a box with valuable information on the other beneficiaries in the group."

"Yes, it was good reading."

"I don't think my implication was all that subtle."

"It wasn't. I took it as you wanted me to kill a bunch of people for you."

"And what have you done?"

"Mostly just wondered why you want me to kill a bunch of people for you."

"You're not as valuable as I expected you to be. In fact, you've been disappointing every step of the way."

"If I were the soul survivor of that will, you wouldn't see a dime anyway," Toby said.

"You won't be the soul survivor."

"You bring me here to kill me?"

"I don't need to. I have your death certificate."

"You don't have to be dead to get one of those?" Toby asked, feigning curiosity.

Bernard pulled an envelope out of his desk drawer and opened it. He handed Toby a form. "That's just a copy you're holding."

Toby's eyes scanned the death certificate. "Great, let's spread the word."

"Maybe we don't just say we submitted this. Maybe we submit it..."

"What would the point of that be?"

Bernard stood. "Toby O'Tool of Charlotte, North Carolina, died three weeks ago. The guy stepped outside to have a smoke and got hit by a bus."

"There's a surgeon general warning on those things for a reason."

"I liked your idea to spread the word that this was submitted to keep the heat off yourself. It was a neat little trick you had planned."

"Well, thank you."

"I'll draw it out for you if you're going to play dumb. If I give this to my secretary, she can fax it within a minute."

"Why would you remove my name? There's no incentive in that."

"I didn't want to remove your name, but like I said: you've been useless. I'll give you 24 hours to change that though."

"I can tell you of some things I have in motion if you'd like."

"I don't care about the others. Only Royce Morrow."

"What? The highest profile name on there? What do you expect me to do?"

"I want him dead. And before you make any smart-ass remarks, we both know this time you can't win. I'd end this for you in a heartbeat, because frankly, I'm sick of you and your bullshit. You were a pain in the ass when Victor was running the show and you're a pain in the ass now. I thought you might be of some use, but you fucked that up too. This is your chance to redeem yourself and keep your name on the list."

"What's going to stop you from sending it anyway?"

"I guess my word will have to do."

"Well that won't work."

"You don't have another option. Trust that I'm a man of my word."

"You're actually a bastard in a bastard suit with a corrupt bastard cop buddy, which is why I'm going to go ahead and play that scenario out for you. If you don't live up to your end, I'll release everything I have on you, the pharmaceuticals, the cover-ups, and don't think I won't be able to dig up anything on Manny, because I will. Then, when you're governor of this state, I'll dedicate my time throughout your term to really embarrass and annoy the shit out of you. I'm talking some really creative accusations that you'll be defending left and right."

Toby walked to the door, but Manny stood in his way, his chest out, as if to intimidate Toby.

"Excuse me. I only have a day to do Bernie's dirty work."

"You better watch yourself." Manny's voice was deep and his eyes pierced Toby, but Toby wasn't intimidated.

"You wouldn't hurt me," Toby said. "I'm not an innocent, defenseless, woman in a wheelchair. Real stand-up move by the way. Especially coming from a homicide detective who's probably killed more people than actual murders you've solved. I don't know if you buy into the whole ghost thing or not, but I'm pretty sure Sandra Morrow is in your home right now, waiting for you to go to sleep so she can take a spirit shit on you while you sleep."

Manny stepped aside slowly, his eyes never leaving Toby.

Toby smiled and walked past, glancing at the clock as he exited: 6:00.

He kept his composure as he walked across the floor. It was only when he was alone in the elevator that his shoulders sank and he let out a deep breath. Twenty-four hours to murder Royce Morrow. If this were to happen, there would be no process. Just clean and simple murder.

"Damnit," he whispered. Bernard Bell had finally gotten the best of him.

## *Chapter 9*

### *1*

To Toby O'Tool, the downside of being the smart-ass who always had to out-talk, outwit, outdo everything everyone did, was that people were always looking for opportunities to beat him. Bad fortune was always wished on guys like Toby, which he didn't mind, but every so often, some insect like Bernard Bell, would find a way to beat him. Toby was convinced that with a little thinking, he could beat Bell at his own game. Bell wasn't even supposed to be a part of the game and he constantly had to deal with the man.

He first tried to stop the death certificate from being submitted by visiting the second executor of the will.

All death certificates of the beneficiaries were sent to a third party, also the other executor of Victor's will: The law offices of Benson & Parras. The Benson was Tyler Benson, a man who had only talked to Victor about the will and kept a copy in a safe, only to be looked at when fourteen faxes were received in his office. He'd gotten two and according to Bell, a third was on the way. Toby set up a meeting and Tyler squeezed him in for ten minutes in the morning.

"My name is Toby O'Tool," Toby said before he even sat. "Do you know who I am?"

"I do," Tyler said. "You're a beneficiary."

"Yes, and very much alive, as you can see."

"I would agree," Tyler said.

"Later today, you will be sent a death certificate that names Toby O'Tool, but it is not me. It's a mistake and I want to give you a heads up. I'd be happy to come by tomorrow and show you my birth certificate so you can see for yourself."

"What are you asking?" Tyler folded his hands in front of him.

"I would like the mistaken death certificate shredded. Clearly with a lot of money on the line, there are efforts being made for others to cheat and someone is clearly cheating."

"Mr. Stone entrusted Mr. Bell to submit death certificates as the other candidates pass. No one else is to do this. Have you talked to him?"

"Yes, I have talked to that asshole and he's the one who is cheating. He's trying to remove my name because he doesn't like me."

"Is that so upsetting? I was under the impression being on the will was supposed to be a curse."

"For some, maybe. I feel safe and would like my name to remain. There must be some kind of fail safe that prevents those with the same name from being submitted. That's a little too simple."

"Not when one person is entrusted. Mr. Bell's job is to be sure he submits everything properly with those intended to be removed."

Toby couldn't hide his frustration. "And with me, he won't do that."

"Then you need to talk to him."

"Talking to him is what got me in this mess to begin with. He doesn't like when I talk to him and I don't like talking to him."

"Then maybe you should consider how you talk to him." Tyler smiled.

Toby sat back with a realization. "You're in on this. You two are in bed together, aren't you?"

"I don't know what that means."

"You're both cheating."

"I'm doing what was entrusted on me."

"So I just have no options here?"

"You'd have to talk to Mr. Bell about that. I'm the executor in the case that the executor can not fulfill his duties. My only task is to accept death certificates and cross the names off as they come in and see to it that the last remaining inherits the money."

Toby stood. "Well, this was clearly a waste of time. I've told you that a mistake is going to be made and you're going to do nothing about it. I'm including you this year when I mail out holiday cards."

"I'm sorry Mr. O'Tool. There's nothing I can do for you."

"No problem," Toby said with a waive of his hand. "I'm one of those vindictive assholes who will annoy the shit out of you later for it. Very likely for the rest of your life. What I lose financially, I more than make up for with obnoxious gestures. Victor was worth 3.6 billion…let's see…" Toby pretended to compute in his head. "That's going to be a lot of holiday cards. We'll be in touch..."

*…Toby O'Tool.*

Bernard Bell repeated the name out loud as he drove to work, parked his car, and rode the elevator to the seventh floor of Stone Enterprises. He'd gotten the name from a private investigator he'd hired after the night a briefcase was stolen out from under their eyes by a stranger who'd conned a receptionist into giving someone authorization into the building on the same night an important deal was being made.

The name sounded familiar, but he was told Toby was just a local bar-going skirt chasing, amateur poker player. He hated that such a no-name could have taken such an important item.

When Bernard had Victor's ear that afternoon, he mentioned the name.

"I know Toby," Victor said. "I played poker with him a long time ago. He had a mouth on him, but we left the game with no qualms. I don't think you have the right man."

"My PI was able to place Toby in the laundromat where our receptionist was picked up, but he doesn't live in that area. We showed her a picture and she said it was him."

It was simple, but was good enough for Victor. "How would you like to approach him?"

"We send Stan."

"We're not starting there. I want you to ask first. If he denies, tell him we are calling the authorities. See what he wants. If he's looking to blackmail or bribe us, we have to consider. We need that suitcase back and we need it fast."

"I'll ask," Bernard said. "I'm not giving him a dime."

"We can afford whatever he offers. It will come from my pocket."

"I won't pay him. He stole from us. We don't owe him a thing."

"I don't care what he did," Victor said. "I want a resolution. Swallow your pride on this one. It won't be about money with Toby."

"What's it about?"

"His ego. He doesn't care about money. He only values winning."

"I'll see him."

"I'll send Cory."

"No, I'll see him." Bernard was irritated. "I'll do what needs to be done. I don't have much of a choice. I was contacted by a woman named Rurik. She wants it back by the time her flight lands on Friday or the whole deal is off."

"Maybe that's for the best," Victor said.

"We've come too far. You just have to trust me. You don't have to do a thing Victor. When I have the case back, I'll talk to Rurik and make it right. I'll see the whole thing through. All you have to do is sit back and wait until profit skyrockets. I'll talk to her."

Bernard made a promise to Victor he intended on keeping, but when he met Toby O'Tool, he had no intention of bending at his will. There would be no demands. Only compromise.

He'd never met Rurik but knew the name well. She was the one running the show and he was surprised she'd come to the states, but it would give him a chance to win her trust. He had many weapons in his arsenal when dealing with Toby, but he hoped this would be over fast. He didn't like being seen in hole-in-the-wall bars like the ones Toby frequented. Bernard believed a man could be defined on his choice of bar and the drink he held in his hand. Bernard enjoyed the atmosphere of the casino. He'd play a few hands of blackjack and spend some time at the bar nursing a cocktail. Toby was a man who liked a darkened dive and a glass of Jack Daniels in his hand. The bar maketh the man, and Bernard was much higher class than Toby. This whole thing should be easy.

After some examination of the bar, he finally settled on a man who acted as if he owned the room. He was the personification of who he'd expected Toby to be: Loud, brash, and dominating the conversation at the poker table in the corner. He'd talked down to the girl at the bar and made an unprovoked jab at some fat guy on a bar-stool. By the time he approached the table, he had no doubt in his mind that he was facing Toby—and he didn't like him.

"Mr. O'Tool..." Bernard said.

Sure enough, Toby looked up and sized Bernard up, mocking his demeanor with his eyes. "Don't know him," Toby said, but he'd already exposed himself and suddenly changed his mind and laid his hand on the table. "Alright, yeah, what?"

"May I have a word with you somewhere private?"

"I don't even know who you are chief. I'm not getting in your van."

"It's business. You took something from me and I would like it back."

The color drained from Toby's face and immediately, he knew he was in trouble. He also was surprised he'd been found. What had started out as a boring day, might become interesting after all. "You can talk in front of my friends. In fact, have a seat. You play?"

Bernard looked at the table with disgust. "I play, but I won't play at this table."

"You sure? I believe you said you wanted something from me."

"I did, but I didn't ask. I'm telling you that you took something from me, and I'm here to take it back."

"Sure...take it then."

Bernard paused and looked from side to side before he shrugged. "Where is it?"

"I don't remember. It looked like nothing, so I probably just tossed it *somewhere.*"

*"It wasn't nothing."*

*"Oh yeah?" Toby dealt an extra hand. "What was it?"*

*"None of your business. I told you I'm not playing."*

*"You beat me and my memory will likely improve."*

*"How about I just make you an offer instead?"*

*"What's the offer?"*

*"Two hundred and fifty thousand. That's worth more than a game of cards, wouldn't you say?"*

*"That depends. Let's say I win and you triple that."*

*"Let's say you lose."*

*"Then I take the two fifty."*

*"Sounds to me like you'd win either way."*

*"Yes," Toby said with a Cheshire cat smile. "My favorite kind of game."*

*"How about this?" Bernard took a seat and placed his hand on the cards. "Two hundred fifty thousand dollar buy in. I spot you to play. If you lose, you see nothing. If you win, you win the pot."*

*"Five hundred thousand to win? Nothing to lose?" Toby pretended to think. Bernard was taken aback at just how unaffected Toby was with so much money at stake. The man had a chance to win half a million dollars on the spot and he was playing games. "I'll do it because my three companions here are drunk and can't bluff worth a shit. You work for Stone Enterprises, so I assume you must be a decent poker player. You guys lie all the time out there."*

*"I suppose you would be the expert on spotting liars," Bernard said.*

*"I am," Toby said. "And I think you're going to be the best opponent I've had in awhile…"*

"…I think he beat you," William Lamone told him as Toby nervously tapped his fingers on the table.

"He didn't beat me. Bell isn't even supposed to be a part of this. You know he came to me right before the will was read? He gave me all this information on most of the beneficiaries. A lot of it was useless, but he wanted me to know who they were and expose some of their secrets. Bell wanted me to manipulate them. He wanted me to get the ball rolling."

"Why would he want you out of it now then?"

"I don't know. We've never liked each other. I've offended him in the past and I offended him six months ago. He decided he doesn't need me anymore."

"Unless you kill Royce."

Toby stopped tapping his fingers and thought hard. "He gives me an out that's impossible."

"Royce is heavily protected. There's no way you could get to him in one day."

"So the question is: Does he really want Morrow dead this desperately or to get to me?"

"It's both," William said. "He gave himself a win win. Either you fail or his biggest opponent is eliminated and if you do kill Royce, because he's high profile, you wouldn't get away with it."

"So I fold or I call his bluff…"

"If you fold, he's probably going to have you removed from the will. There's no good reason not to. The way I see it, you have to call."

"I would need more than half a day to eliminate Morrow. Much more."

"Yeah, no kidding. You've had us working ours for seven months and we had the easy ones."

"Give it a rest. I've got a real problem here. The only way you could be less productive right now is if you were the actual beer you're drinking and even then, you'd at least be providing me with a way in which I wouldn't have to get up to order another."

"I don't need to be productive. This is your problem."

"Unfortunately William, this is going to have to be something you do."

William stood and made his refusal known. "No fucking way Toby. I couldn't get him alone, which would be the only way. He's in the public eye. It would have to be one on one. You at least know him. This one is on you."

"I don't know Morrow any better than you do."

"You've been together on enough occasions that he knows who you are and how you're linked. You're going to have to use your Victor connection to get what you need. I've got nothing."

"I can get him alone and you can do what needs to be done."

William put his hands on the table and leaned in. "Except…" he said, all seriousness, "…this is as dirty as it gets, and I'm already tasked with Van Dyke. Someone has you in a corner Toby and this is one hundred percent your problem. You're lucky I'm even brainstorming with you. You have all this shit going on behind our backs and you haven't had to do anything other than pull strings, while Henry is married for your cause, Gregory compromised his whole career and life for you, and I'm constantly forced to hang around a loser while he vomits sunshine everywhere. This one is directed right at you and it's your problem, and realistically, a problem only you can solve. No one's throwing themselves in front of this bus for you. I'm going to lay it out clear for you though and then I'm done with favors. You either do nothing and hope he doesn't submit the Toby death certificate or you kill Royce and hope you don't get busted."

William turned to walk away.

"William…" He turned back. "When this is done, and I have Bell by the balls, you guys will need to step up your game."

"You're the only one anyone's been waiting on."

"And when I finish today, we're moving forward with full force."

"If you fail?"

"I don't fail. Be ready."

2

The best investment that Jason Stone and Erica Drake made was in a speed boat which they took out almost daily. They were housed on a peninsula with steep hills in every direction and a beach that stretched the coast as far as the eye could see. There were huts in the distance but Jason's home had its own plot in the middle of nowhere. On the beach was a large dock and tied to the dock was the boat, and what had once been a conversation piece (Do you think we should get a boat?) had turned into the smartest decision they'd ever made. Sometimes Jason would take it out, sometimes Erica. Sometimes they invited Todd Mason along or just Todd and Jason would go fishing. They'd had the boat for a month and already made it worth the money they'd spent on it.

Today was the day all three took it out into the waters. Erica was at the helm, staring out into the vast blue sea as Jason and Todd reclined on the leather seats with a cooler of beer between them, which was already half empty.

Five months earlier, Erica Drake came home distraught one day and tearfully told Jason that they'd lost the baby. They cried a lot and Jason yelled at her for going to appointments without him. After a month, they reconciled but the sadness always returned and the conversation always steered back to the baby. Jason had heard that many couples didn't survive a traumatic experience like that and he wanted to make it work since he'd fallen in love with Erica in that time. He proposed to her on stage at the Waipa Kalo Festival and she cried and clutched onto him with so much love that Jason and Erica both knew in that moment that they would survive together. The topic of the baby never came up again and instead, they began planning a wedding and bought a house. The boat was an afterthought.

In the six months that Jason and Erica fell in love, Jason and Todd also built a friendship. They got to know each other and the lives they'd led, and ultimately, became inseparable. Jason was an open book and Todd would talk about everything, only omitting Cynthia and his kids from the conversation. Jason wanted to bring it up often, to talk Todd into going back to LA, but he could see it in Todd's eyes. He wanted the same thing. He just didn't think he could.

When Jason got engaged, he asked Todd to be his best man. Todd graciously accepted and life couldn't be better, other than those moments that Todd thought no one was watching, but Jason could see the pain in his eyes as he thought about his wife. Todd would stare into the sky, lost in his memories. The more time passed, and the more Todd had to be third wheel to a couple in love, the more he zoned out, until the day Jason could no longer stay silent.

"Erica and I think you should fly them here."

"Sorry?" Todd said, snapping out of his daze.

"We know you won't go back, but that you want them here. I was thinking we can fly them here. I don't know if it would work, but at least fly them here long enough to talk to you so you can explain everything."

"No way," Todd said.

"Fly them out for the wedding. I'll back up what you're saying. She may not be with you, but there's no reason she has to hate you or feel abandoned. You left with good reason. Why not at least offer her the truth?"

Todd didn't respond and Jason never brought it up again and Todd tried to conceal his loneliness, but he didn't hide it as well as he thought.

That night, Jason and Erica went through the guest list. They wanted to keep it small, which was easy since neither had a lot of friends. Erica brought up Jason's sore subject, not unlike how Jason had brought up Todd's.

"I think we should fly your mother here."

Jason almost laughed at first. It was truly a day to open all cans of worms, but Jason knew he wasn't going to be as stubborn as Todd. Aileen had already been on his mind. "I don't think she would."

"Come on. What's so bad about your mom?"

"Nothing. Nothing that's her fault anyway. Victor ruined her, but she's still ruined. She can't move on. I don't blame her, but she needs to move on."

"I think you and her can relate."

"I don't make excuses not to live my life. She's unhappy, reliant on other people. I've tried to help, but she refuses. Like I said, she probably won't come. I don't even know where she lives."

"But I'm sure you still have her number."

"If her phone's not shut off."

"You'll call her tomorrow," Erica said. "Don't forget the time difference."

"I'm telling you: She won't come."

"Good. That's a win win then. You don't have to offend her by excluding her,and you still won't have to see her."

"It's not that I don't want to see her."

"Good, then we'll insist she comes."

Jason laughed. "You're not going to give this up."

"No, I'm not." She kissed him. "Because I want to meet her and I don't want you to live the rest of your life without her in it."

Jason called Aileen the next day but she didn't pick up. Erica made him call again and leave a message, which he did. It was later in the evening that Aileen called him back. They had an awkward conversation until Jason told her he was getting married. There was a long pause, and then Aileen spoke excitedly, but there was a distance in her voice that sounded as if she was hurt she wasn't invited. If not for that, he may not have gone through with asking her to come. When he did, the distance faded and genuine excitement came through. She didn't hesitate to say yes, and all Jason could think about was how Erica was going to rub it in his face that he was wrong.

Instead, she was proud of Jason. They made love that night and bought a plane ticket a week later when Aileen told Jason she had a plus one. He wasn't excited to meet her new boyfriend, but preferred she didn't feel out of place at the wedding. When all was said and done, Jason had no regrets and was happy he invited her. He didn't know what he was worried about in the first place and wondered if he'd just had a habit of assuming the worst out of Aileen. Maybe she was different. Maybe she was happier.

"What are you going to do Todd?" Jason asked weeks later as they took the ferry to Honolulu the morning Aileen's flight was set to arrive.

"That's a loaded question."

"It's really not. We're friends and nothing matters to you more, so what are you going to do and how can I help?"

They stared out the back of the ferry, leaning on the rails for a long moment while Todd considered the question. "I'm thinking about going back."

"Good."

"You want me out of here, huh?"

"I want you to go back. If you want safety, I can help you."

"I don't need charity. It's something I'm working out in my head. I don't need to talk about it."

"Why is this such a hot topic?"

"Because I screwed up and it's not easy to face. It's embarrassing. Let's drop it."

Jason let loose a loud sigh, frustrated that such a large chunk of Todd's life constantly had to be unspoken of.

"You nervous about seeing your mother?" Todd asked.

"No. I'm hopeful. I'm always hopeful when I see her."

"What, that she's changed?"

"Yup."

"A lot of time has passed."

"Yeah, but she's at a point of no return. She knows she's no spring chicken. She knows her best days are behind her. She thinks she needs a man to validate herself."

"You never know," Todd said. "If she meets the right one, he might fill her head with confidence and good thoughts."

"I've seen her date a few decent guys. She doesn't stay interested long. I'm not worried about it. I'm over it. I spent most of my life worrying about family problems. I'm at a point in life where I just need to build my own family. If she's interested in being a part of it, good. If she ends up drunk and acting like a floozy on the dance floor, I'll just say good riddance and hope in a year or two when I run into her, she's changed. It's the dance her and I do. She hopes I'm someone I'm not. I hope she's someone she's not. We both re-discover nothing has changed and go our separate ways."

"That's kinda sad," Todd said.

"That's funny. This is the happiest I've ever been."

As the island appeared in the distance, Todd thought about what Jason said and a thought hit him that he kept to himself. This was the loneliest he'd ever been. *When they're married*, Todd thought. *I need to start thinking about how I'm going to get my family back.*

3

Of all days Toby could have been propositioned to murder Royce Morrow, it had to be on the day of Sandra Morrow's funeral. Assuming Bernard Bell knew of that fact, Toby couldn't decide if it was extra cruel or if in some odd way, an act of mercy. To see how heartbroken Royce was, sitting in the front row of the church, the world around him invisible as he only looked at the casket and a picture of Sandra's smiling face placed aside it, it seemed as if Royce would happily join her.

Toby searched the church for signs of any other beneficiary but he was the only one, which Royce would understandably find to be odd, since

Toby would ordinarily have been the last to attend. He'd only been to two in his life, and threw up after both. If alcohol wasn't served and women weren't taking off their clothes, it wasn't the scene for Toby O'Tool.

He watched Royce throughout the service, replaying approaches to take that would pull him away from the world he knew. He thought it was once impossible, but Royce might welcome the honest words of a stranger rather than the usual crowd of people offering condolences and competing to see who could be the highest in Royce's good graces.

He suffered through the music, the traditional chanting and prayers and watched the attendees instead, disgusted at how predictable and cookie cutter they were. When it was over, Toby discovered it wasn't really over. Next, the congregation attendees were to walk to the cemetery to watch the casket get lowered into the ground.

*When does this end?* Toby thought. He wasn't sure getting close to Royce was worth all the trouble but reminded himself if this door closed, another wouldn't open by the end of the day. As the priest read more boring prayers and the people repeated the same things, all sounding like robots, Toby edged toward Royce slowly until Royce looked up and spotted him. Toby wore a fake smile and gave Royce a waive of the hand. Royce frowned and looked down.

When the funeral was over, the crowd lingered a long time, talking to friends and family. Toby was starting to believe that there would never come a time when Royce was alone. He took advantage as soon as it ended, to catch Royce on the way to his car. Toby pushed through the crowd and extended his hand. "My condolences," he said.

"Thank you." Royce shook his hand and looked surprisingly grateful. "Did you know Sandra?"

"No, but I know you. I'm here for emotional support."

"Well, thank you again." Royce began to pass and the door was about to close.

"Was this truly an accident?" Toby asked. It was so blunt and bold that not only did Royce stop in his tracks, but he whispered to the men around him one at a time and they all left him there with only Toby.

"Was this an accident?" Royce repeated. "I don't know. Why don't you tell me?"

"I wouldn't know."

"Then why are you asking?"

"Because you're running a campaign against an evil man who would wipe out this city if it meant more money in his pockets. Because you're on a list of people who benefit from your death."

"Only it wasn't me who died," Royce said. His voice cracked a little and Toby realized Royce wished it was him who died. Not because he had a death wish but because Sandra didn't deserve to die. Especially over Royce's relationships.

"What do you say we grab a drink?" Toby said. "You've gotta be dying to get away from these drones."

"And what makes you think you're the company I need?"

"Because everyone else tells you what you want to hear, whispering delicate words in your ears with kitten mittens. You won't get that from me though. You see, I'm going to talk to you about what we can do to ruin Bell and anyone else who had their hand in this. We have a common enemy Royce and so while I understand most of you don't like me, you also must see how I'm an asset."

Royce stepped forward and spoke under his breath. "Do you know a man named Manny Quinny?"

To Toby's surprise, he had no idea who Royce was referring to.

"No, but the list of people I want to piss off can never be too large. I promise you Royce, I may not have all the pieces in this puzzle, but I bet you anything that there are things that I know that you don't."

"What's in it for you?"

Toby tried to tell a lie, but what came out sounded more truthful than he'd believed it was. "Because I've struggled too. Richard was a friend of mine, and he believed bad things were going to happen and I believe he was right, and right now, you're in the thick of it." It was all true, except Toby's intentions.

"Let's have that drink," Royce said…

*…He sipped from his Jack and Coke and studied Bernard Bell across the table, who held his cards casually. It was hard to call his bluff because Bell wasn't invested in the game. He just wanted the hands to play out so he could have his briefcase back. Toby's friends gave up their place in the game, uninterested of playing with a man of Bernard's stature. Only Toby and Bernard went face to face, though Bernard made a call and a woman named Suzy joined him within half an hour.*

*Suzy rounded off Bernard's persona nicely. She was half his age and looked like she was made of plastic. When she tried to form an expression, Toby could see her injections fighting her face to stay in place. She gave Toby a whole new way to make fun of Bernard, but Bernard seemed unaffected by Toby's commentary throughout the game.*

*Every time Bernard won a hand, he used it as a teaching opportunity. "Your weakness is your pride," Bernard said.*

*"Thank you Yoda," Toby would say, mocking him.*

*"You never fold."*

*"I rarely lose."*

*"You just lost to me."*

*"That's because there's a degree of luck involved in every hand and luck is in your favor. Unless your Barbie doll is signaling you and letting you know my hand."*

*"Why don't you stop being an asshole?" Suzy said. "Stop picking on him." Even her voice sounded high pitched and fake.*

*"It's fine Suzy," Bernard said.*

*"No, no, no," Toby said. "Bernie's mommy has made it perfectly clear she doesn't want her little Bernie picked on. He's a delicate flower and we should all be super-nice to him."*

*"I'm standing up for him because I'm a good girlfriend," Suzy spat the words, defensively.*

*"And I'm sure he finds you wonderful, which is why you'll still be together when he's 70 and you're 40 and your face is 35 and your boobs are 20."*

*"Like you could do any better."*

*"Suzy, stop!" Bernard commanded. She did everything Bernard made it a point not to do.*

*"What?" she said, defensively. "He couldn't do better than me."*

*"I wouldn't want to," Toby said. "Slightly defective chicks are the way to go. I once went with this girl with a baby arm. She was insane in the sack. Defective chicks compensate for their shortcomings by being wild in bed. Your face fights you when you try to smile. I can't imagine how you can do anything else."*

*"Just deal," Bernard said and Toby dealt, but he kept his eyes on Bernard and smiled the whole time. Bernard refused to meet his eyes, turned away and staring at the bar instead.*

*"So what's the deal with the contents of the suitcase?" Toby asked.*

*"You looked?"*

*"I did."*

*"So you broke it open..."*

*"I did."*

*"I assume everything is still there?"*

*"It is."*

*Bernard looked at his hand and sighed. "Stone Enterprises has been cornering the pharmaceutical industry. It's no secret."*

*As they talked, the hand played out and cards were turned, both men wearing their poker faces throughout. "A briefcase filled with medicine is hardly worth this much money and trouble, unless you've got the cure for cancer in there."*

*"It's an experimental drug in the early stages of testing and you're holding the only samples in existence."*

*"What does it cure?"*

*"None of your business."*

*"You didn't call the police. You never reported a crime. You know who else doesn't call the police when their merchandise is stolen? Drug dealers and other criminals."*

*"We wouldn't be in business if we were breaking laws."*

*"Maybe you should rephrase that to you wouldn't be in business if you were caught breaking laws."*

*"Do you think I'm going to discuss company policies with you?"*

*"I just want to know why what I have is worth so much money. I walk away from this game a rich man whether I win or lose and you clearly don't like me, which means you're setting aside all your disdain for me because you simply want your merchandise back, which means it's worth a lot of money and this is the only way you can get it back."*

*"I could also send a couple guys to break every bone in your body,"* Bernard said. *"Which will happen if you don't hold up your end of the bargain. You're lucky I'm a reasonable man. All in."* Bernard pushed the remainder of his chips to the center of the table.

*"You know, all the money in the world doesn't affect the outcome of a poker game. The better man usually wins and that's usually the guy with more brains."*

*"You going to set your cards down?"*

*"You offer me half a million right now and I won't finish this game and you walk away with your briefcase in hand."*

*"Are you calling or folding?"* Bernard was out of patience.

*"If I call and win, I want a million dollars."*

*"Deal."* Bernard didn't hesitate. *"And you get nothing if you lose."*

Toby thought for a long moment, tapping his finger on the table. *"Deal,"* he finally said.

*The cards dropped...*


...Royce looked up over a beer he was downing faster than Toby expected. "Why are we really here?" he asked.

"I thought you could use a beer. Looks like you can use a few."

"Are we friends?" Royce asked, thick with suspicion.

"I don't know," Toby said. "I thought you might want to step outside of the craziness of your life and we could drown our sorrows."

"Richard Libby..." Royce said, deep in thought. "You know I meant to be there that day?"

"What happened?" Toby was one of many who had been curious as to why Royce wasn't there to support Richard's cause.

"Got tied up with some people," Royce said, his mind returning to

Manny. Toby was an unlikely bond to make but he wanted others to hate Manny. He wanted everyone to know who he was and what he did. "This guy...he knows about our situation with Victor. He wanted things of me and I refused and he believes I owe him something."

"Your wife..." Toby said, slowly.

Royce nodded, confirming Sandra's death was not accidental. Suddenly, Toby's predicament became even more clear. In his right hand, he held a small vial with a minute amount of powder that if dropped into Royce's drink, would dissolve. The next drink would make him sick and kill him. It seemed so simple and it made Toby think about the months they'd spent trying to ruin unimportant people like Maria Haskins and Brian Van Dyke with no progress and now Toby was tasked into killing one of the most high-profile people on the will within twenty-four hours and could easily deliver, but it was sloppy. Surely, witnesses would say they saw Royce having a drink with a mysterious man in a bar. If foul-play was determined, Toby would go down.

Bernard Bell had effectively gotten the best of Toby and it consumed his thoughts.

"How did Manny even come into the picture?" Toby asked, trying to distract Royce with questions and waiting for his moment to drop the vial into the drink. He was genuinely curious about how Manny got sucked into all this. It seemed there were things going on behind the scenes that he wasn't behind. Royce never answered the question though and reflected on his late wife instead.

"You know, Sandra was involved in the community in many aspects. Shortly after we met, she helped found six youth source centers. These young adults would walk through the door looking for training and education. Eventually, after she would spend countless hours working teenagers through their addictions and helped support them through employment options. She helped almost a thousand high school dropouts return to school. The U.S. Department of Labor awarded her with a Workforce Innovation Grant of twelve million dollars to expand the city's dropout recovery system, which helped another twelve hundred dropouts. The program expanded to twelve centers citywide."

Toby didn't know what Royce was trying to say, but Royce certainly liked talking about Sandra and the more he spoke, the more he could see the adoration in his eyes.

"Sandra was a hero," Royce said. "And she never walked around expecting a hero's welcome. In fact, most people instead didn't appreciate, or hardly remembered, her sacrifices. She won no medals, no monuments...but she was satisfied just looking at the world around her, at how greatly it had changed and she knew she helped to make that happen. For her it was gratifying, but in all modesty, I can't help but wonder if she deserved more than that. You see Toby, the best of people will still be cut down by assholes like Manny Quinny and Bernard Bell and those are the guys winning the awards and being revered as the heroes in this city."

"You're preaching to the choir," Toby said. "Saying Bernard Bell is an asshole is like saying the Grand Canyon is just a hole in the ground."

"And there's not a damn thing that can be done."

"Why not?" The vial was forgotten. Bell's ultimatum was in the back of his mind. Everything was coming together now. Royce Morrow was a real threat to Bernard and that's why Toby was being forced to kill him. Royce knew he was defeated and that Bell was too powerful to go up against and Toby suddenly didn't want to play along. Maybe it wouldn't be so bad to have his name off the will. Maybe there were loyalties that couldn't have a price-tag. Teaming up with Bell wasn't worth any amount of money.

"Because when you threaten to expose the awful truth behind powerful people, they will ruin you or end you. That's why no one ever stops these types of guys."

"Yes, but that's why you're a secret weapon," Toby said. "You're a powerful person and there's no one better."

"I'm not sulking," Royce said, rather abruptly. "Sandra wanted me to rise above these people. She believed the paradox of wrath is that it makes men dependent on those who have harmed them. For me to beat Bell, it means lowering myself to his level."

"I disagree," Toby said. "I've played poker with Bell. I'm playing with him now and it seems you have a game that you think you've lost too. In fact, Bell even gave me an ultimatum: Call or fold. And in either case I lose and that's where you are Royce, but you and I both failed to remember the objective of poker: To have the better hand."

*Have the better hand.*

*Why did I forget that was an option?*

Bell had thrown such a heavy threat his way that he'd been blinded by it. Toby never had only two options. He had a third, and it was the most important option of all. For any game with a finite number of sequential moves, there exists a best strategy somewhere. It's just a matter of finding it. Toby assumed Bell had the dominant strategy—one that outperformed his own.

The day before the will was read, Bernard Bell came to Toby in a bar and gave him valuable information on the other beneficiaries. Bernard always hated Toby, but clearly he had an agenda and was using Toby to fulfill it. That was how Bell always worked and Toby was too interested in what Bell had to gain from this to ask more important questions, like what else had Bell been doing to throw gas on the fire, but those were questions worth asking.

Toby let the vial slip between the seats, knowing he wasn't going to use it. Royce was his enemy's enemy and the time to call Bernard's bluff had come and as Toby thought about the events that occurred since the will was read, theories started formulating in his head and connections began coming together until Toby had put together truths that no one had even bothered to consider, simply because no one's eyes were on a man who wasn't even written into the will.

"Holy shit," Toby said to himself, as he had a revelation. Royce looked up with curiosity. "I have to go," Toby said and quickly slid out of his seat. "Listen Morrow, you got my vote, okay? But you need to start playing the game or you're going to let the biggest scumbag in this city have control over it. If you don't believe in vengeance, that's fine, because I do, and I'm going to destroy Bell and if I'm in the mood, I'll ruin Quinny too just for fun. You have one job and that's to get off your ass and use the memory of your wife to win the election, no matter what you have to do to win."

"Any ideas on how to do that?" Royce asked, doubtfully.

"Play a better hand," Toby said with simplicity. "Was it ever established who arranged the lottery that resulted in the attack on Anthony Freeman?"

"It's Anthony's belief that it was Jason Stone."

"Why?"

"The list of beneficiaries to bet on excluded him."

"But we don't actually believe it was Jason, do we?"

"I have a hard time with it."

Toby's mind began spinning until he came up with a theory. He paid for the beers and quickly apologized because he had to cut the meeting short.

"What is it you think you know?" Royce asked.

"It's a personal thing between Bell and I," Toby said. "You've got your own Bell problems. Let's attack him from two angles. Cheer up a little Royce. I'm going to ruin that fucker's day."

4

As the sun set on the island, Jason Stone, Erica Drake, Todd Mason, Aileen Thick, and Tarek Appleton entered a clearing and were welcomed by two Hawaiian girls who put leis over their heads and offered to take pictures with them. The group declined and entered a widespread area with multiple shops, activities, and shows. In all their time on the island, Jason and Todd hadn't bothered attending a luau, but having guests the night before the wedding, they decided to have an unofficial rehearsal dinner, which they would be eating with a thousand strangers while watching a fire show.

The group broke off into separate pairings and trios throughout the night. Jason, Aileen, and Erica watched people fishing with nets while Todd and Tarek drank mixed cocktails by the stage, waiting for dinner to be served.

They all met up for dinner and sat far in the back so they could chat while the audience watched the show. Everyone had let loose and gotten to know each other, with the exception of Tarek and Jason. Tarek kept trying to get close, but Jason gave him the cold shoulder. It was obvious and created tension in different moments, but for the most part, the conversation ran continually and as everyone drank more, they laughed more. By the end of the show, Jason had a strong buzz and sat back to watch everyone interact. He hadn't expected his mother to show up and was disappointed to see her there with Tarek, but when she smiled and laughed, she looked young and vibrant, as if the real her was always hiding and waiting to resurface.

Todd noticed Jason's silence and leaned in. "So what you think of the boy-toy?"

"It won't last."

"I don't know. They seem pretty happy."

"She seems happy. You notice he keeps leaning away from her?"

Todd looked over at them and observed. Sure enough, Tarek didn't seem invested, but it wasn't noticeable unless you looked for it. "So what? What are you thinking?"

"I don't know," Jason said. "But I don't like so many of us together in one spot, getting so close."

Todd nudged Jason and dominated the conversation, directing all attention to Aileen and Tarek. "So what brought the two of you together?" he asked. Jason smiled to himself as Todd pursued the answer to questions on Jason's behalf.

"I'm sure you heard that Tarek saved my life," Aileen said. "He saved everyone's life that was there the day that Richard…" She looked around, nervously, afraid the conversation was too depressing for the group.

"I did hear," Jason said. "You've been together since then?"

"Actually," Tarek cut in. "I ran into her just a few weeks ago. We had a drink and hit it off."

Jason studied Tarek's face. He didn't believe him, though Tarek was a good liar.

"Is it the real deal?" Todd asked.

Aileen looked as if she wanted to answer in the affirmative, but when Tarek shrugged off the question, she turned away with disappointment that she didn't hide very well. Jason noted all her reactions and the way Tarek was so passive about the two of them. He also noticed that Tarek had taken interest in him and Victor, asking a variety of questions about his childhood and his relationship with Victor. Jason gave him one word answers and redirected the conversation. Other than those few awkward moments between Jason and Tarek, the evening turned out to be a blast.

More drinks were ordered. They all shared some laughs. They enjoyed the show. When it was over, they stuck around, sitting at a bench while the area slowly cleared out. They had no intention of leaving the luau until they were kicked out, and for the next hour, they grouped together, sharing their opinions of Richard, their theories about what happened to Abby Palmer, and eventually, of what kind of influence Victor's will would have on them, if any.

Erica became disinterested and sat at a distance with Aileen. The men didn't know what the women talked about, but they seemed to hit it off. Jason kept his eyes on his fiance and his mother, pleased to see that they genuinely seemed comfortable around each other.

"What do you think Jason?" Tarek asked and Jason was pulled from his trance. "You knew your father better than anyone. He want us all dead?"

"Does he want us all dead?" Jason asked in disbelief. "Why are we talking about that?"

"Todd doesn't even know why he's on it," Tarek said. "You're his son and you're on it. I've almost been killed once because of it."

"Why are you on it then?" Jason asked. "What did you do to him?"

"Doesn't matter what anyone did to him," Todd said. "His will was bullshit no matter what. Everyone has enemies. He can't just throw his money around to ruin people's lives. It's evil."

"So was he evil? Was there any good in him?" Tarek asked. Jason thought his interest went beyond casual conversation.

"He made your career, didn't he?"

"I like to believe he sped up the inevitable." Tarek shifted uneasily, but Jason saw that Tarek didn't like to talk about his own relationship with his father.

"He helped people at times. At other times, he didn't. Do I agree with his final wishes? No. I did see his frustrations though and I've experienced them first hand. Victor believed in loyalty first and I saw him take a lot of chances on people who would squeeze whatever they could from him. Maybe he shouldn't have let it get to him so much and he definitely shouldn't have wished death on everyone, but the people I saw

Victor surround himself with weren't so great themselves. Evil has roots. Victor was born as innocent as everyone else. What happened to him shaped him."

"What happened?" Tarek asked in fascination, though he held much more of Victor's life story than anyone could possibly guess.

"I don't know," Jason said. "I just know people hurt him too. Including me."

They all fell silent for a moment before Todd attempted to lighten the mood. "That got serious there for a second."

The conversation turned to sports, music, dirty jokes, and finally, security asked the group to leave and they all dragged their feet to the parking lot, barely awake enough to be able to walk straight.

Erica and Aileen took the rear, watching the men as they laughed at something Todd was saying.

"What do you think?" Erica asked. "Did your husband's will turn everyone against each other?"

"That's what he wanted," Aileen said, her eyes moving from her son to Tarek, and back to Jason. "I think it backfired though. I think it's also bringing people together."

5

Bernard checked his watch and then checked his phone. It was almost six o'clock and there had been no word on Royce Morrow or about anything related to Toby's proposition. He shook his head in disbelief as he cashed out at the blackjack table and entered the restroom to make a call, free of background noise.

The day before the will had even been read, he'd given Toby all the information he could gather on the other beneficiaries. A lot of it was useless—just articles and pay-stubs and information on how they were linked to Victor. The idea had been to move Victor's agenda along by giving the biggest scumbag on the list a nudge.

When Richard Libby was putting together a case against Victor, Bell did it again. He approached Toby and gave him a time-line and Toby had somehow stopped it from happening. What Toby hadn't done, was effectively kill anyone. Bernard knew there was no way it was Toby who shot Abby Palmer. It wasn't his style and it had been too messy. All he knew was that Toby had pulled some strings, but almost a year after the will was read, though two had passed, Toby hadn't been effective at all. In fact, he'd turned against Bernard and that was no good for Bernard's ego. The time had come for Toby to be an asset, or lose out on the opportunity.

The digital display on his cell now read 6:00.

Bernard shook his head, disappointed Royce was still alive, but relieved to rid himself of such a pain in the ass.

"Mr. Bell," his secretary said, after he called. "It's chaos up here."

He leaned into his phone. "What? Why? What's going on?"

"I can't send your fax. The fax machine won't stop receiving faxes."

"Use the one on the north wing."

"They're all receiving faxes. They have been for the last ten minutes."

"How's that possible?"

"I don't know. It's an attack. The whole page is black ink and now all the cartridges are dry, but the faxes won't stop coming. We're working on tracing the source so we can have them stop sending."

Bernard ended the call while she was still talking, grinding his teeth as he thought about the joy Toby was getting. An attack on all the fax machines in Stone Enterprises wasn't enough to stop him. He'd hand deliver the death certificate himself. He hurried back to the building and when he entered, the lobby fell quiet. No one wanted to be the one to strike up a conversation about the issue, but judging by the looks on their faces, it was still happening. He walked past the receptionist and scowled at her. "It's just ink," he said.

It was more than ink though. It was an assault on communications coming in and out of Stone Enterprises. Hundreds of faxes were sent and received daily and any interruption in the flow of business,was money lost. Bernard guessed that Toby didn't care whether or not he was costing Stone Enterprises money. He was only trying to irritate Bell and create unwarranted chaos. Bell still knew he had the upper-hand though. Royce was still alive and the time to remove Toby from the will had come. Eventually the faxes would stop. Stalling was useless. What concerned Bernard was what would happen after Toby's name was removed. He wouldn't walk away quietly. He'd inflict his brand of warfare in retaliation. There was no doubt about it. Bernard still had a trick up his sleeve though: Manny Quinny.

Maybe the time to get rid of Toby for good was coming. It had never crossed his mind, but why the hell not? Toby was a thorn in his side for as long as he could remember.

As Bernard entered his office, his eyes narrowed at the sight of Toby sitting across from Manny in front of his office desk.

Manny looked up. "I invited him in," he said. "I figured we'd end this bullshit between you now so we can all move on."

"As I'm sure you know," Bernard said, "We can't fax a death certificate at the moment, but we can make a copy and deliver it in person. You willing to make a run?"

"Not a problem," Manny said, smiling.

Toby didn't flinch. In fact, he had a smile on his face too and it didn't appear to be a bluff. Bernard prepared himself for the game he hated to play. Sparring with Toby was old, and the truth was, Toby was good at it.

"You think you're calling my bluff, but I wasn't bluffing," Bernard said. "I'm having your name taken off immediately."

"I have the better hand."

"Sure you do," Bell said. "I know what you're going to accuse me of already but unfortunately, you need proof."

"Oh, I'm not talking about your pharmaceuticals here. I'm talking about the things I know that you don't know I know."

Manny was frozen at the door, the death certificate in his hand. He waited to validate the legitimacy of Toby's claim before proceeding.

"What is it that you think you know?" Bernard asked.

"You've got a friend in Hawaii," Toby said...

*...The reveal played out in slow motion. Toby tapped his finger on the table and held is cards with a tight grip, a deep concentrated frown on his face. Finally he set them down and revealed the better hand. Suzy gasped in shock, but Bernard didn't react. He crossed his arms and leaned back.*

*"Why sit through a game of poker for two hours if we could have decided this with a coin flip?" Bernard asked. "You didn't gain a damn thing from this game."*

*Toby leaned in, fixated on Bernard's eyes. "Because I wanted to know who you are...and now I do. Also, I'm a millionaire now."*

*Bernard's face hardened and in that moment, he knew a rivalry was born...that their relationship wouldn't end with one game of poker, and he refused to lose. Not against this scumbag...not one game...not one hand.*

*Toby got to his feet. "Game's over. If you're a man of honor..."*

*Then the door burst open and two men Toby had never seen before, entered the bar and approached the table quickly. One had his hand tucked into his jacket.*

*"You gotta be kidding me," Toby said, but the next words caught in his throat as he observed multiple things at once. Bernard talked to the bartender off to the side, handing him a wad of money. Suddenly, it was just Toby and two men in the bar. All other patrons wanted nothing to do with what was going on. "Come on guys," Toby said. "This was just a friendly game between Mr. Bell and I."*

*"Where's the suitcase?" the man with his hand in his jacket asked.*

*"What suitcase?"*

*Their hands were on his shoulders and he was being led into a room in the back of the bar. They effortlessly tossed him onto a billiards table and held him down. He kicked and struggled, but they were strong...they were the muscle. "Where is it?" he asked again.*

*As the struggle progressed, Toby held out as long as he could, but an hour later, Jones and Cory walked away with the briefcase in hand, all it's contents secure. Toby ended the night on the floor of his apartment, with two fractured ribs and a bloody face. He didn't have a dollar in his pocket and the only leverage he had was gone. The door closed as the men exited and as he began to fade, he heard it open again, followed by the footsteps of one man and a dark shape hovering over him.*

*The last thing he heard before he passed out was Bernard chuckling and muttering. "Stupid piece of...*

...shit was about to hit the fan for Bernard and his buddy and Toby was only a moment away from showing his cards and winning the hand. Bell had a smug look on his face and Toby basked in it, preparing himself to diminish his upper-hand. He stood in a room with one of the wealthiest men in the city and a decorated homicide detective who was also one of the most prominent serial killers of all time. Playing games with John Q Public was one thing, but Toby was ready to take some important people to school.

"I had Morrow within seconds of death. I'm not here because you tasked me with anything I couldn't handle. It would have been easy."

"What changed?" Bernard asked, grinding his teeth harder.

"I got to thinking about all our secrets and I came to the realization that I underestimated you. I never pegged you for a plan D kinda guy, but you've got layers upon layers of shit in motion. You have so many plans plotted that I'd admire you if you weren't such a ball-sack."

"This isn't going to work for you. You can't stop this from happening, no matter how much you stall."

"You're right. I'll cut to the chase. It's no secret that I've set things in motion that were manipulative by design, but there have been other pies I haven't had my finger in that could only have come from someone like myself. I asked myself who among the beneficiaries would have the same thought process that I had...the patience and time...and I kept coming up with nothing, but we know you've got a pony in this race somewhere; otherwise you wouldn't have fed me so much information. You wouldn't have showed up the day of the invalidation acting as the opposing voice to what we were doing. You want the will and the repercussions to have life. I didn't know why, but you wanted to keep the ball rolling, to see us all die one by one. You might want it to happen more than anyone, but since you're not a beneficiary, you've always had the luxury of being denied a suspicious eye. You have money and you have resources and that's why I know you're the guy who set up the lottery that almost claimed Anthony Freeman's life. You failed there, but blowing up the factory was a big mistake and you most definitely don't want that traced to you because it would make you a mass murderer. Among those dead, one of LA's finest, and you know what will happen when everyone finds out you're a cop killer. How am I doing so far?"

"You've got the floor Toby." Bernard sat patiently, waiting for Toby to finish.

"Even the lottery is just a tactic though. You never really believed a group of ex cons would kill the whole group, but you were hoping that at least one would die because if that happened, all the dominoes would eventually fall. Everyone believed they were safe until the first died, so you're really just trying to start the ball rolling. You also have drawn so much attention to what's happened that you're hoping we'll all be blind to the bigger picture…the story that hasn't ended in tragedy but that raises some valid questions."

"And what would that be?"

"Jason Stone left the company and ended up in the same place as Todd Mason."

"What could I possibly have done to make that happen?"

"Todd Mason is easy. You threatened him and bought him the plane ticket."

"Jason Stone left by choice."

"Did he?"

Bernard sat back, his jaw clenched. He crossed his arms and fell silent as Toby went on.

"I have resources too," Toby said. "It's hard for a person to travel without leaving a digital footprint. A month before Victor died, you took a trip to Vegas."

"I take half a dozen a year. So what?"

"On this particular trip, you got sloshed and met a girl. You woke up in her bed and the two of you hit it off. You saw each other a few times after that. I don't know when it happened, but you brought her in on something because you knew she loved money."

"Get to the point." All humor was gone in Bernard's voice and his mind was searching for a way Toby could possibly know these things.

"You knew Jason's desires. You also knew he was suffering from the loss of his father. You wanted the company but you also want the money on that will of which you're not a beneficiary on. You could have tried to team up with someone. You even made it seem as if you teamed up with me, but you're a lone wolf, aren't you? Jason Stone's name wasn't even on the lottery list because he doesn't need to die. You need him to be the one to inherit the money."

"Alright, we're done here. Your time is up Toby."

"Because your girlfriend conveniently met him in his hotel and told him all the things he needed to hear to fall for her while he was at his most vulnerable. She even convinced him to run to her in Hawaii and if I'm not mistaken, they're getting hitched soon. Tomorrow, right?"

"It looks like we have a stalemate," Bernard said.

"No, I've got checkmate. You can take me off the will if you'd like. I can ruin everything in your life. I can put you in prison with what I know, you'll lose everything you've worked for and be the running joke of this city. You'll lose your political aspirations, every dime that you have, every ounce of credibility. You think faxing a piece of paper and removing me from the will is a stalemate? You're not just the loser here today Bernard. You're not walking away from this without begging me for my silence."

"You win. Is that what you want to hear?"

"What's the plan? Kill us all while Erica Drake sets herself up as the beneficiary of everything Jason has?"

"That's on the nose," Bernard said, staring out the window. He didn't bother to object or even try. He was a man who knew when he lost a hand...

*"...He'll be sore for a while," Bernard said, watching Victor from across a conference table, the briefcase displayed in front of him. Victor stared at it with relief, but behind his eyes, he couldn't hide how troubled he felt with the way business had been done.*

*"Put a GPS in this and guard it with your life until we hand it off."*

*"We're back on track," Bernard said. "Cost us nothing."*

*"Except there's a witness out there who likes to cause trouble. He saw the contents."*

*"We scared him silent. I promise. We're back on track Victor."*

*As if further assurance was needed, Jones walked in on cue and gave the group a nod. "Rurik is sending an associate now. They want a quarter-mil for the trouble."*

*Victor and Bernard exchanged glances. Toby O'Tool wasn't going to pocket a dime, but he'd cost them their reputation and a pretty penny.*

*"The payoff will be greater," Bernard said. "This was nothing more than a small setback."*

*Victor diverted his eyes to the window, thoughtfully.*

*"Don't have second thoughts on me now."*

"Have Cory and Jones take care of this," Victor said after he regained his composure.

Two hours later, the briefcase was back in Rurik's possession and between the men, they'd taken a major financial hit that they paid for out of their own pockets. No money for the deal could be tracked through the Stone Enterprise pipeline. Bernard never offered to cover a penny.

The room filled with Victor's inner circle. Bernard sat at his side as if they were equals. Across from them was Jones and Cory who sat silently as if they'd been violated. The truth was that no one in the room wanted to talk about the security breech that had caused the mess. "Maybe we should take care of O'Tool," Jones finally said.

"What would that do?" Victor asked. "It's over."

"Maybe," Jones said. "Maybe he learned his lesson. I'm sure he probably did, but this is a guy who came after you unprovoked and wouldn't give up without a fight. His bones will heal and maybe he's just one of those guys."

"One of what guys?"

"A guy who doesn't like to lose. I mean, if this was about money, he could've walked away with plenty without challenging Bernard. He wanted to prove something."

"That he could win?" Bernard asked and let out a single spontaneous laugh. "Doesn't hurt my ego that he beat me. He didn't walk away with shit."

"I'm just saying…"

"What did Rurik say about all this?" Victor asked.

"She didn't say anything other than she thanked us and said you should have accepted her first offer."

The men in the room searched each other for an indication of what that meant. After a long moment of thought, Victor leaned in. "There was no first offer."

"That's just what she said."

"I want to know how Rurik contacted us. I want to know when and what was said." Victor turned to Cory. "Get on the line and find out where Rurik is now."

Cory ran off and for the next half hour, Victor stood in the conference room silently with Bernard at his side. Bernard was calm and sure that they were reacting to nothing. He changed his mind when Cory returned, his shoulders sulking and all color drained from his face. "I made a few calls and it's not good."

"Rurik told you she hadn't contacted us yet." Victor finished for him.

"Uh…yeah. We were contacted by an imposture."

"And no one looked into who was contacting us?"

*"No one but the people in this room know about this."*

*Victor's knuckles turned white as he grabbed the edge of the table and leaned in. "The people in this room and Toby O'Tool."*

*Toby stood in the shadows of the docks and watched as a car pulled up. He slowly got to his feet, grunting as every muscle in his body pulled along his bruises and fractured bones. His face was almost completely red from the swelling and he held his right arm in place just to keep from crying out in pain.*

*The headlights turned off and the door opened. A high-heel emerged and then the body of Aileen Thick, carrying a briefcase, which was filled with two hundred and fifty thousand dollars. She also had the other briefcase.*

*She approached. Toby could see her hands shaking as she neared him, still nervous about her encounter.*

*"All go well?" he asked.*

*"They seemed afraid of me," she said with a nervous laugh. "They gave me the money and the briefcase and apologized."*

*"Apology accepted," Toby said, with no humor in his voice. He opened the suitcase and the money displayed in front of him in neat stacks. "You tell them what I told you to say?"*

*"Yes," she said.*

*"They'll know it was me," Toby said.*

*Aileen was unsure but accepted it when she saw his confidence. Aileen had worn a wig and sunglasses, along with makeup that softened her skin tone. She still wasn't sure Victor wouldn't suspect her involvement but his associates would say there was a woman. She prayed he'd never know it was her.*

*"As promised..." Toby began counting money and setting a stack aside for her.*

*"Help me with my son," she said suddenly, realizing that Toby could actually make things happen.*

*"I don't solve domestic problems and if I were you, I'd get out of town."*

*"You said he won't know it was me."*

*"I'm not talking about that. I'm talking about what's in the briefcase," Toby said. "When it went missing, they didn't call the police or the FBI. What we're dealing with is the under-the-counter dealing done at Stone Enterprises."*

*"It's medicine though."*

*"Medicine that hasn't hit the market. A cure for a disease which doesn't exist. They're operating on a side project behind closed doors*

*and it's something they don't want anyone to see."*

*"I don't understand. Why?"*

*"Have you looked at their stock lately? They're teetering on the brink of collapse and they know it. They're creating a product that everyone will need…a cure. Do the math Aileen, and when you figure it all out…if I were you…I'd get out of town…"*

…Her eyes opened and her first conclusion was that she was dreaming. Then her senses kicked in and a pearl of smoke was in her face, bringing her off the guest bed and to her knees on the floor in a coughing fit. She tried to understand what was happening but all she could remember was the events of the day which led up to the group back at her son's home. The guest room was in the basement. Erica Drake had prepared the room for her. She had traveled that morning and spent the rest of the day with friends and family, talking, laughing, and drinking. When her head hit the pillow, she'd fallen right asleep. Between then and now, she had no sense of the time that had passed. All she knew is she didn't have time to think about how tired she was or what was going on. The room was filled with smoke and the heat of flames burned her skin. She turned from one direction to the next, unable to locate the door or a window. The room was completely full.

She pressed her body against the ground and told herself she'd catch her breath for only a second before she got up and tried to find the door.

A coughing fit overtook her body and her eyes began to sting. She squeezed them shut and wheezed as another plume of smoke hit her face.

Sirens filled the night sky as Aileen began to breath it in.

# Chapter 10

*1*

*Jason Stone was 20 the first time he fell in love. Her name was Pamela Maxwell and she was everything he wanted in a woman: Vivacious, charismatic, a wide smile and eyes to get lost in. Her hair was curly and two strands fell in front of her face and when the snow fell on her head, the flakes would pepper her dark hair and slowly disappear. She was a former clumsy, geeky girl, who had grown nicely into a young woman who didn't even know yet how beautiful she was.*

*Two days earlier, he'd finally said he loved her and for a moment, he didn't think she'd say it back, but only because she swallowed hard and held her emotions in long enough to pause and scare him into thinking it was over. Finally, with a whisker above a whisper, she said she loved him too.*

*They hadn't left each others side since.*

*In Laguna, an ice skating rink had been built and manufactured snow fell from the domed ceiling as couples held hands and skated below. Some were experts and others tumbled and often took their partner with them. Pamela took to skating fast, but Jason kept falling and she'd fall on top of him and they'd kiss until someone came upon them and told them to get out of the way. They'd find their footing and hang out at the edge of the rink and kiss some more before giving it another try.*

*It was in the middle of a lap around the rink that Pamela said the words Jason knew were inevitable but he hoped to never hear. "I think I need to meet your family."*

*"Just me and my dad."*

*"Then I should meet him."*

"He's not warm. He won't even pretend. You're just going to feel awkward."

"What if we set up an accidental meeting?"

"We can talk strategy all night long, but I say we just rip the band-aid off. Besides, if you're looking for funding for your product line, eventually we need to win him over."

"Really? I was hoping you'd just ask daddy for a few million dollars in start-up money."

"I don't think either of us really want your success to be the result of nepotism. I'll set up a dinner. I'll ask him to be nice."

"If he's not, does that mean he hates me?"

"I honestly don't know if he likes or hates anyone. He's basically a cyborg."

"On a business level, he kinda needs to like me."

"He needs to see a presentation and be able to project a rising profit margin. He won't care if you're the Prince of England or a twelve year old raised by wolves. He looks at charts and invests in what looks like it makes sense."

"Will us dating affect anything?"

"No. He doesn't care what I do."

"Are you sure you're okay with me doing this? I don't want to make things worse between you guys, or make you uncomfortable by asking your dad for help."

"I want you to succeed and it just so happens, he's the best connection we've got. I can separate my personal issues in this…" He stopped mid-sentence as he saw a familiar face in the crowd. It was a face he'd seen many times before, only he'd see her at random places and she always watched him.

"In this…" she asked, before she saw his expression. "What? What is it?"

"There's a woman sitting on the bleachers by the concessions. I've seen her before. She's watching me."

"Like, a stalker?"

"Yeah, it does seem that way, but she's a little older."

"She's all yours. I'm not fighting for you."

"No, seriously. It's starting to creep me out. This is like the fifth time I've seen her."

"Where is she?"

Jason scanned the crowds but couldn't see where she went. The snow and the people skating by obstructed his view and he'd lost his line of vision to where she'd been standing. "I don't see her now."

"Well, what do you think she's doing?"

*"Maybe someone Victor has watch me for some reason. I don't know. She doesn't seem…She seems harmless…or curious."*

*"Should we call the police?"*

*"And say what?"*

*She shrugged. "Let's go. I'm getting cold."*

*Jason grabbed her hand and they skated the remainder of the way to the gate. Jason kept his eyes on the crowds of people the whole time, looking for the woman, but she never appeared after that. Jason memorized her face and though he was sure he'd never known the woman, she was familiar. She looked kind, and somewhat beautiful, and she looked like she cared for him. What he really couldn't forget was how sad she looked.*

*He decided that if he saw her again, he'd walk straight toward her and ask who she was. He thought he was crazy before, but the woman really was following him…or checking in on him. The woman was…*

…Aileen Thick ducked under a plume of smoke, but sucked enough in to go into a coughing fit. She heard shouting but it was coming from two different directions and she couldn't see a foot in front of her. She fell to her hands and knees to escape the thickness of the smoke but realized it was worse on the ground. She'd never understood why people couldn't just run from a fire—why smoke slowed them down—but now she got it. She was suspended without direction, without sight, and weakening by the moment. Her eyes stung and she was forced to close them tightly as tears formed in the corner of her eyes.

The shouting was closer. She could hear Jason somewhere in the room and he was communicating with Tarek. She felt a last moment of hope, but then breathed and sucked in a stream of burning smoke. She tried to cough, but spit a string of saliva instead. She reached out to grab onto something, but her hand only found air.

And as she felt her last breaths come out with a whimper, a wet blanket suddenly fell over her back and draped over her body. She felt two hands on her back at either side and she was being pulled away. The moments in which she was taken from the house lasted forever and when she was outside, her eyes remained glued shut, stinging from the tears and heat that still burned.

She lay on her back and every voice she knew constantly asked if she was okay. She nodded and tried to speak, but only breathed heavy breaths instead. By the time she regained her vision, Tarek was laying at her left side and Jason on her right. They watched the house burn with an odd fascination. Todd Mason stood with his hands on his hips and Erica Drake at his side, her eyes sad as she watched everything she owned go up in flames.

"What happened?" Aileen finally managed to say.

Jason answered by shaking his head. Everyone was equally confused. "It happened fast," Jason said. "All at once."

"You suspicious?" Todd gave Jason a sideways glance.

"No," Jason said, but he was lying.

They waited for the fire department to arrive and put the blaze out. By then, a small crowd of locals had gathered to watch the show. It took some time before help arrived, but the fire was contained because it had nowhere to go. Erica and Jason's home was perched on a private peninsula overlooking the clear waters of Honolulu Bay and Mokule'ia Bay in Kapulua, situated on a 6.5 acre conservation zoned rocky bluff. Nearby, there were grass huts, but not within reaching distance of the flames.

Jason thought about the home he'd grown to know and love...the living area, the media room, the guest wing, and the master suite...all designed so the natural Pacific breeze effortlessly ventilated the whole house. They would be forced to uproot and find another home, but it had taken Jason awhile to adjust when he'd moved to Hawaii, and just when he thought he had, everything was gone. "Dammit," he whispered to himself. There was nothing that wasn't burning.

By the next day, the fire was put out and the investigators had asked questions and did a once over of the foundation, searching for the source. Jason couldn't help but remember the same process had occurred after his father died. Fire followed the Stone name.

"The fire started low and worked it's way up. Don't know the cause just yet, but looks like it started on the lower level."

"There's nothing down there though," Jason said.

"Well, you've got your electrical. You have any smokers in the house?"

Jason almost said no, but remembered Aileen was a smoker. "I doubt anyone had a cigarette," he said. "You can ask around, but she wouldn't have." He wasn't convinced of the accuracy of what he was saying.

"Here's the deal," the inspector said. "Fire burns upward, so if the fire started on another level, your mother would have had more time to escape. The most common reason for a fire to burn downward is the presence of a liquid accelerate already in place before the fire originated. Now, I have no reason to believe any of this is the case, but you said your mother's boyfriend discovered the fire first and you ran to them. That's reason to believe it started there. If it does happen to be a cigarette... you're going to have to take that one up with whoever smoked it and your homeowners insurance. I'll certainly keep you posted as we learn more."

"Ma-halo," Jason said and the investigator went to work. Todd offered to take Aileen and Tarek home with him and Jason and Erica went to a hotel for the night.

"It's possible Aileen tossed a cigarette," Jason said. "I hope not, but I've seen her smoke indoors before."

"Yeah…" Erica said. Jason turned to her as they drove through the windy landscape.

"What? What do you think?"

"Todd…he had already left. Why was he even there?"

Jason frowned as he thought about the question. It wasn't long after Todd left that the fire started. Why would he even come back? "You think Todd did it? Why?"

"I don't want to make you angry."

"Just tell me."

"I mean, I guess I just don't know him. And everything you say about your history with him makes it seem like he doesn't like you…that you two only hang out because you're both here, but you also said he threatened your life back in LA and that he left his family and…I guess…"

"Go ahead," Jason said, but she didn't need to finish. He already knew what she was going to say.

"Maybe it's not a coincidence that he's here. Your mother…Tarek Appleton…you…there were three people in one house on your father's will. What if Todd was trying to kill them all?

2

The next morning, the group looked back at the night before as a surreal memory, each replaying the events and anxious to hear more. The wedding was still going to happen, though they'd talked of postponing it. It seemed there was no reason not to proceed, though thoughts of the night before were the perfect distraction to rob everyone of their excitement.

Erica invited Aileen along to help with the day of planning. Aileen stood in the shadows but was made to feel like a part of it. Todd and Jason grabbed an early breakfast before Jason asked Todd if he'd pick up some toiletries since he had nothing from the fire. Todd saw Tarek lingering and invited him along and the unlikely duo set out on a road-trip, which Tarek was eager to be a part of. Tarek had hoped for more time with Jason but had surrendered the notion when he saw how busy the wedding planning was. He didn't want to come across as pushy but he was intrigued. Todd was the next best thing. His best friend would surely know some of the most intimate details about him and maybe even shine some light on Victor.

"Why here?" Tarek asked.

"Why Maui? Why not?"

Tarek laughed. "I'll give you that."

"Truth is, that's something I wondered myself. Someone wanted me out of Los Angeles. They bought my plane ticket and gave me an address. Everything was set up for me and to top it off, they put me in paradise. They threatened my life. It seems like for someone to want to kill me but also put me up in Hawaii…it doesn't make a lot of sense."

"Then you must have believed the threats were real…" Tarek said, watching the scenery as they drove through the deep hills of the island.

"Real enough. I wasn't going to take my chances."

"I imagine if you ever tell your wife, she'll be pissed you ended up in Hawaii. I mean, she's not going to believe the truth."

"That's why when I go back, I won't go straight to her."

"Where you going to go?"

"I'll find out who is behind this."

"You know what Anthony Freeman thinks?"

"The author? The guy who was stabbed?"

"That's him."

"What's he think?" Todd asked, curiously. He didn't realize until now that Tarek might hold some of the answers.

"He thinks Jason is behind it all."

"Why?"

"After he was stabbed, a guy showed up at his house and killed himself, but not until after he confessed that he was the attacker, but the guy had a criminal record and he worked for a company that employed ex-cons. Well, he tells Anthony that someone came to their place of employment one night and gives each person a name and they were to bet on who would be the first to die. People do it with celebrities all the time. I'm sure I've made lists…it's just a prediction, as morbid as it sounds, to guess who might die. The winner is offered a large sum of money. It sounds innocent, but remember, these are hardened guys so it's not completely unrealistic to believe that they might take matters into their own hands. That's what happened with the guy that attacked Anthony. He had some debts to settle and thought he'd take it upon himself. When Anthony survives the attack, the man is riddled with guilt and kills himself. But he gives Anthony a tip and Anthony follows up on it. Everyone there was given a name, but the person behind it logically would exclude themselves from the list. So guess which name was excluded."

"Not Jason," Todd said in disbelief.

"Yup. I wouldn't have guessed it either, but look at the facts. Jason could fund that kind of deal. Jason also left town shortly after."

"I don't believe it. Do you believe it?"

"I don't know him well enough. Anthony's not shitting me though and the logic adds up."

"Yeah, it does," Todd said, deep in thought.

"Anthony wanted me to come here and see for myself. Last night at dinner, I was convinced there was no way. Then, the fire."

"No," Todd said. He shook his head with exaggeration. "No way."

"I haven't made up my mind at all but I'm cautious. There are four of us in one place and if one of us is a killer, they're in a position to off three and if that's the case, they're definitely going the accident route."

"Well, I'll tell you this," Todd said. "There have been no incidents, no close calls, nothing, until you and Aileen arrived."

"Me and Aileen were in the most danger."

"So none of it makes sense."

"A legitimate accident makes sense, and maybe that's what it was."

"What will you tell Anthony?" Todd asked.

"He and I are friends and he deserves an honest opinion. I believe Jason is harmless but I don't believe in coincidences to begin with and if Jason showed up here after you were forced to come here, that's a little too 'it's a small world' for comfort. By just talking to him, you'd never know it, but since every other person on the will seems equally harmless, and we know that can't be the case, it makes me wonder who really can be trusted."

"And why should we trust you Tarek?"

Tarek turned to him and thought about the question. He didn't care if they trusted him, but he knew he didn't start any fires. What he wanted to know was whether or not Jason was as deranged as Victor was—to establish a relationship that would translate well into a story. He desperately wanted Jason to be as dark as his father, but he didn't see it in Jason's eyes. "I'm not saying Jason had anything to do with the fire," Tarek said. "I'm saying I don't believe in coincidences. We all know why you're here, and Jason chased a girl, but that doesn't mean it's a coincidence. It means an outside influence led you to each other. Why? I don't know. But I don't believe in coincidences and on this scale, neither should you."

Todd focused on driving and played events in his head again, from the moment he took a flight to Jason spotting him on a park bench to the fire that almost killed three beneficiaries. And then a thought occurred to him and ridiculous as it was, Todd's mind tossed a theory around and after some time, he realized it was worth looking into. "Shit," he said to himself.

"What?" Tarek asked.

"Nothing," Todd said, realizing it was ridiculous.

3

Jason couldn't shake the fire from his head but tried to focus on Erica and the day ahead. Everything was going as planned. The chairs were set up and the band was in place and practicing. The caterer was stocking the kitchen and Erica's family was decorating while Aileen offered to help in any way possible. Jason watched his mother, who was offering whatever she could to make the day go smoother. She didn't seem to be dwelling on the fire at all. Maybe because she started it and didn't want to face that fact, but as Jason watched her help out, he saw something in her that he'd only gotten glimpses of in the past. She seemed to fit in, to have some confidence, to know where she belonged.

"Your mother's great," Erica said, joining Jason at his side and laying her head on his shoulder.

"She seems to be doing okay."

"And she's dating a celebrity. Good on her."

"I wouldn't call Tarek Appleton a celebrity and I doubt they're dating. You know the guy's been caught picking up girls on Santa Monica, right?"

Erica put her arm around Jason. "She's an adult. If he's no good, I'm sure she'll see it."

"You're giving her too much credit."

"Let's just focus on today."

"I'm trying. You doing good?"

"Of course."

"You shaken at all about last night?"

"I'm not worried. We'll be okay. I lost a few things but nothing I can't replace."

They stood and watched the decorators progress a few more moments before separating for the day. Two hours later, Todd and Tarek arrived with the tuxedos. Tarek tried to get Jason's attention but Jason brushed him off, aware that Tarek appeared to have an agenda of his own. The man was different in person than what Jason had seen on TV. In fact, he was different than Jason had remembered at the reading of the will. He'd heard Tarek was a hero—that he'd stopped a bomb from going off and saved nearly every beneficiary in the process. He wanted to give credit where it was due, but the hero he'd heard about wasn't visible in the Tarek he'd encountered. That Tarek was darker, humorless, self-centered.

He didn't seem to have much interest in Aileen at all, but had taken interest in Jason—and especially Jason's father.

*Tarek was a hero once, but had something changed? Could Tarek have started the fire?*

Jason dismissed the notion, unwilling to entertain something he didn't really believe. Tarek hadn't hesitated to help Jason pull Aileen from the flames. He'd spent too much time thinking about the fire and who was at fault and eventually he'd find it was just an accident. It was his wedding day and he couldn't escape his thoughts about everything else. He wanted today to be perfect—to be the day that separated the first part of his life from the second. He'd grown up under the influence of everything his father made him and everything his mother didn't do. He'd come a long way in escaping his past and found a woman to start over with, but the same influences that had always been there were haunting him on this day.

Todd caught up to Jason on his way to the reception hall, where Jason would start to dress for the wedding. "Hey…got a sec?"

"What's up?" Jason kept walking.

"I spent some time with Tarek."

"How was that?" Jason asked in a tone, indicating it couldn't have been good.

"He's alright. He's smart. Put some ideas in my head that I've been thinking about."

"Yeah? Like what?"

"That maybe you and I meeting here isn't a coincidence at all."

Jason stopped and turned, curiously. "Okay?"

"I think with the fire and everything that's been happening, maybe you should consider holding off a few weeks on the wedding."

Jason laughed and patted Todd on the back. "See you later," he said with a smile and started walking again, but Todd kept up.

"People almost died last night, coincidentally when a bunch of us are in one place. For someone who wants the money, that was like the jackpot of beneficiary kills in that house. I've been worried because I was the only one who wasn't in the house last night and I thought that would look bad on me, but your mom and Tarek don't see it that way at all. The thing is, I still do."

"So you're saying you started the fire?"

"No Jason. I'm afraid to say what I think because I don't want to compromise our friendship."

"Too late to turn back now. Just say what's on your mind Todd."

"Did Erica sign a prenuptial agreement?"

Jason was speechless. He stared his friend down and searched for what to say. "You've gotta be kidding."

"You told me you were going to leave and that you stayed because she was pregnant. Then she suddenly loses the baby and doesn't tell anyone. Did she even have proof of that? Did she ever even show at all?"

"She lost the baby early."

"It was all too convenient, as if she was saying what she had to say to keep you here. She didn't even love you in the beginning. She…"

"If you don't support the wedding, just don't go," Jason said.

"That's not what I'm saying. I just think we've spent a lot of time wondering about why we're both here and whether or not it's a coincidence and we've ignored the one influence that could have brought us both to the same place. She's the only person who could have done that."

"Maybe you should spend more time with Tarek Appleton and the two of you can conspire on more ways to shit all over my life. I don't have time for this."

"Wait Jason…" Todd gave up the fight and understood he wasn't going to be able to stop the wedding. He wasn't sure what he even really believed, but one thing he knew was that the wedding was going to take place and when they both exchanged "I dos", everything that was Jason's was Erica's too. Todd turned and watched Erica from a distance, trying to catch her in a moment when she believed she wasn't being watched. Instead, she turned and faced him for a long moment, as if trying to decide what was on Todd's mind. Finally, she gave him a smile and walked away…

*…Pamela sat across from Victor Stone, trying to hide her nervous habits, but she wore it in everything she did. Victor didn't make it easy. He sat at the table as if neither was there, letting them hold a conversation with each other across the table and only chiming in when asked.*

*Finally, Pamela asked Victor if she could pick his brain. She pitched her idea and the more she spoke, the more attentive he became, until to Jason's fascination, she was completely on-board. Then, Victor began asking questions and when Pamela answered them without hesitation, he was seemingly impressed. Not only did Pamela fit in, but Jason was completely outside the room.*

*"Do you have a two year plan with financial projections?"*

*"I do," she said.*

*"How long until you see a profit according to your plan?"*

*"Nine months to a year, but I'm still adjusting the plan while I'm in the development and testing stage."*

*"How have you been able to fund this?"*

*"Friends and family and a couple angel investors. Eventually that will dry up though and when we start production, we'll be knocking on doors and possibly launching an online campaign. We need to be on a self sustaining level where retailed earnings can fund future projects."*

*"I think you should set up a meeting at Stone Enterprises. Make a presentation. Allow myself and my associates to look at the numbers. At the very least, we can coach you through the process."*

*"That would be great." Pamela beamed.*

*Suddenly, Jason was uncomfortable. Hoping for Victor's approval was hard, but seeing his approval and becoming a third wheel in the process was another animal. He cut into the conversation. "Pamela spent two years touring Europe."*

*"Where in Europe?" Victor asked, his attention on her.*

*"I studied art and architecture in Paris."*

*"I'm thinking about traveling this summer," Jason said, but was ignored as they carried the conversation without him.*

*"I stayed at the V-rue De Levence," she said and Victor nodded his approval.*

*"What's your Thursday night look like?" he asked.*

*"I've got nothing I can't cancel."*

*"How about I look over your slides and proposal in depth and help you prepare?"*

*"Absolutely," Pamela said. Jason watched the exchange with a sense of doom.*

*When he drove her home, he couldn't get dinner out of his mind and tried to decipher just what had happened in there. Pamela talked his ear off, but Jason stared silently forward.*

*"It's crazy how much you hear about a person," she said. "Like all the stuff the news is always saying and you never really know for sure, but then in person they become so real, ya know? Like, who cares if he's one thing or another? He's not like that to everyone."*

*"What have you heard in the news? What are you referring to?"*

*"I don't know. Same stuff as all business tycoons. Greed and paying themselves bonuses while the guys at the bottom barely scrape by."*

*"So you don't care if any of that is true or not?"*

*"I'm sure some of it probably is." Pamela sensed Jason's bad mood and her perkiness faded. "Why?"*

*"You can't just assume he's a great guy because he might help you get your business off the ground. He's a smart businessman, but that doesn't make him a great guy. And if you can't separate my dad as a person from my dad as a businessman, then you're in trouble."*

"*How so?*"

"*Because you can't just ignore the people scraping to get by. They're on the front-line, selling the product and taking the abuse.*"

"*Well, business-wise, I like him. That's all I'm saying.*"

"*Good. Me too.*"

*They fell silent for most of the ride back to her place. When Jason parked, she invited him in but he declined, which made her realize the seriousness of his attitude tonight.*

"*What's your deal?*" *she asked.*

"*Victor has a thing with women. You know that right?*"

"*So what?*"

"*So do you think he'd be asking you over on Thursday night if you were a man?*"

*Pamela rolled her eyes.* "*I'm half his age!*" *she said with a laugh.*

"*True,*" *Jason feigned consideration.* "*You are a little older than his usual type.*"

"*Wow Jason. That's a pretty low thing to say about your own father. I'm interested in his help. That's all. Is it even possible in your mind that he was interested because I have a killer presentation? It's not like he was all that interested in me until he saw I had some business sense.*"

"*I get that, but I just want you to be careful is all. If he has an ulterior motive…*"

"*Then I'll shut it down the same way I would anyone. Do you not trust me?*"

"*I do,*" *Jason said. As much as he tried to see her point of view, he couldn't shake the dinner. It came down to one simple fact.* "*I just don't trust him…*"


…Todd disappeared for the afternoon and Jason replayed their encounter through his mind, wondering if he should have forced the conversation to happen later. With Todd out of the picture, the wedding was shaping up to be an awkward moment in his life. He would have his mother, who was a stranger to him, and her prick celebrity boyfriend on his side. Erica had a group of friends who were attending and her side would be ten times Jason's side. He realized that was what he had always wished for. He was anonymous. He was so anonymous that his own wedding was empty, even void of the only person who had been somewhat of a friend for the last half year. Even Todd Mason was forced upon Jason though. Their first face to face meeting started with Todd threatening Jason's life.

Even though they'd been thrown together in one place and only had each other to befriend, Jason had grown to like Todd quite a bit. He'd usually bit his tongue on the topic of Todd's family, hoping one day he'd talk sense into Todd or convince him to open up, but that day never came, and it seemed the end of their friendship was coming.

"What can I help with?" Tarek asked from his side. Out of sight, Jason closed his eyes for a moment and told himself to be civil. He turned, but his annoyed expression hadn't changed much.

"We're fine, thanks." Jason started walking away, but Tarek followed.

"No, really. Everyone's pitching in. I can help."

"Go away," Jason said.

"Wow," Tarek stopped. "And I heard you were the nice Stone."

Jason turned to him and sized him up. "And I heard you party, pick up hookers, and are now dating my mom. Draw your own conclusions from there."

"And I heard you offered a million dollars to a room full of ex-convicts to the one who guessed which one of your contemporaries would die first. Apple doesn't fall far from the tree, huh Jason?" Tarek hated to be so blunt and he knew Anthony wouldn't have approved, but more than anything, he couldn't stand how much Jason couldn't stand him.

"I don't even know what you're talking about," Jason said.

"You know Anthony Freeman was almost killed at the University, right?"

"I knew that."

"Then I suppose you know that the man who did it confessed to Anthony before taking his own life. He worked for a company called Gelatin Steel which employed men out of prison work release programs. They were approached by a man with money and given a list of names so they could place bets on longevity of life."

"I'll call Anthony and confirm this myself," Jason said, but it was news to him—bad news. If it were true, there was much more going on than he'd anticipated. "He never said a word when I talked to him."

"He had other things going on, and he doesn't trust you."

"Just because I'm Victor's son..."

"No, because he was able to get a hold of the list of names. Yours wasn't on it. Everyone else is though. He asked me to come here and check you out for myself and my impression of you has always been pretty positive, but sorry Jason, you've been a prick to me since I got here, and so I guess I don't make very accurate judgments of people and since you weren't even a candidate to bet on, I think I will just draw my own conclusions like you asked."

Jason didn't know what to say. He wanted to clock Tarek in the face, but Tarek clearly believed what he was saying and if what he was saying about the list was true, Jason really did look like a suspect. He had been far away all along and no one bothered to confront him. "This is my wedding day," he said.

"Yeah, and I asked if I could help with anything. You can give me some silverware to place or we can talk about the fact that someone shoved a butcher knife in Anthony's back because of you…"

"It wasn't me!" Jason said. "I don't know how to explain what you're claiming, but I had nothing to do with that. I didn't even know about it. I'm not going to defend myself to you. I'll talk to Anthony myself. You can go back to treating my mother like one of your whores."

"That's not what's going on," Tarek said, but now that he was on the defense, it didn't feel so good. Especially because he was using Aileen—only it wasn't for sex. She had been great in bed, but what Tarek really wanted was permission to be consumed by Victor and intimate details. He'd hoped for the same for Jason, but Jason had his own judgments and Tarek clearly wasn't going to be breaking through any barriers. "It's easy for you to make assumptions from far away, where you don't have to deal with anything. You took your father's money and ditched everyone and everything and that's fine Jason. Really…that's your call. But your own mother was one of those people and I found her on the streets without a place to even rest her head. You don't have to like me, but she's your mother and while she's got nowhere to go, you're living it up in Hawaii. I gave her a place to stay because I felt sorry for her. If that makes me a prick, then what does it make you?"

Jason was awestruck by Tarek's words and had nothing to say in response. Even if Tarek was only using his mother, it was hard for Jason to pretend like he was any better. In fact, what Tarek had said was true, only Tarek could never fully understand the relationship between Jason and Aileen—how little Jason had ever been able to do to help her and how stubbornly she'd refused when he tried. He didn't need to be fighting —not now—and what was left of his wedding party had almost dwindled into nothing already. Maybe that was how it should be though. For Jason to truly start his life anew, it required being reborn without all the influences he'd once had, including his mother.

"Look, you don't understand everything between us," Jason said, his tone tempered. "I invited her to be nice. I didn't think she'd come. I'm sure she's told you we're not close. I didn't expect her to show up just because she's with a guy who could buy her a plane ticket. You overstepped Tarek. If you need something to take home, all I can give you is my word that I had nothing to do with what happened to Anthony Freeman, and if your intentions are honorable, then keep seeing Aileen, but you don't know her. Her life is a wreck and she's going to sabotage everything you do. Whatever you have now may seem alright, but that feeling isn't going to…"

He cut himself off as he saw her in the corner of his eye. He didn't know how long Aileen had been at his side, but judging by the hurt in her eyes, it was long enough. Jason opened his mouth to say more but she turned and walked away without a word. Jason turned back to Tarek, who lingered as if he wasn't sure what to do, but eventually, he realized he was supposed to follow her, and he did. Jason could see Tarek didn't truly care about Aileen's feelings, but he had nothing more to say. He knew he wasn't much better.

With all relationships successfully burned, Jason walked to the reception hall to be married.

4

When Todd was well away from Jason, he sat in a gazebo outside the reception hall and sat on a table, lighting a joint. He'd upped his habit recently as he found himself alone and bored more often. He preferred to be alone in the outdoors, sometimes reading the newest issue of Rolling Stone and smoking some hash. There was nothing in the world that was more relaxing, but when enough time passed, he'd become aware of how quiet everything became and it was in those moments he'd start thinking about Cynthia, Keith, and Jackson. He'd remember game nights and how hard his boys would laugh when Todd got a little goofy and he'd think about where they are now and where they would be in the future and he'd wonder if he would ever have a relationship with them again.

"Mind sharing?" Tarek asked, appearing from out of nowhere and taking a seat on a bench that lined the inside of the gazebo. Todd passed him the joint, happy to have a smoking companion, though he was unsure of whether Tarek was just trying to fit in or if he truly was a smoker. By the way Tarek sucked on the joint as if it was a lost love, he seemed to be no stranger to it.

Aileen lingered outside the gazebo, staring blankly into space.

"I think we're heading back," Tarek said. "Jason doesn't like me much and he pretty much told Aileen he'd hoped she wouldn't come. I thought we'd say goodbye to you at least."

"He's stressed over the fire is all. I've been talking to him and he's happy his mother made it. Just stick around for the wedding at least."

Aileen looked away, unwilling to participate because she was afraid her true sadness would show.

"Let me ask you something," Tarek said. "Between just the three of us: What's going on?"

"How do you mean?" Todd took the joint back and took a drag.

"Why did Stone come here? Why are you here with him? What was the deal with the fire? The shit going on back home? You guys aren't just two guys out here by coincidence."

"I'm starting to think that myself," Todd said.

"How do you think Victor knew you? You've gotta at least have a guess."

"Bernard Bell once told me that I probably wronged someone Victor knew. I don't know what I did or who I did it to. I've never tried to be a malicious man, but Victor could have known someone who hated me and maybe he took it personal. I don't know what I did. I know I didn't personally know him or ever encounter him. Why I was singled out and chased out of town, I have no idea. I'm actually safer here from what's happening back home. I can't figure out what the motive involving me is at all."

"Maybe you don't have to die for someone to get that money," Tarek said. "Tell me something else Todd, and this one is for you too Aileen: Was Victor an expert tactician who put something in place that he knew would inevitably ruin us all, or was he just insane?"

"He was insane," Aileen said, but the question lingered in her head. She hadn't spent a great deal of time being worried about the will, but for the first time since she had been at the reading, all the incidents began adding up. Could Victor truly have knocked over a domino, knowing it would start something bigger?

"Like I said: I didn't know him," Todd said. "But I don't care anymore. He's gone and I can't think about what he wanted. I need to think about who is responsible for me being here. I need to know why I had to abandon my life and who was threatening me."

"I'm making a movie loosely based on Victor's will," Tarek said. Aileen and Todd both stared at him, surprised.

"It won't have his name on it or anyone else. It's a thriller slash horror film…a whodunnit."

"What?" Aileen asked. "Is that why…?"

"I'm trying to understand why Victor did this…what he was trying to accomplish. No one seems to know or care about Victor anymore. Everyone ran away from it or is pretending like it's not happening. I was held hostage by a crazy man who tried to kill everyone in one shot. I came out unscathed, helped to put the killer in prison, but time has passed and it's like none of it happened. Instead, my show got canceled…"

"Are you feeling sorry for yourself?" Aileen asked, stepping toward Tarek.

"No, not that," Tarek said. "But when the press was hounding me to give up everyone's names, I was the one under pressure and I didn't cave.

And when Stanley Kline held a gun to my head and told me to push a button, I refused. I got away. I've been involved in this. I've lost a lot for it. The rest of you just moved to Hawaii or live in the woods or who knows what else? I've been a target and it sucked and when all was said and done, I had nothing to show for it, but it's a good story. It's something my agent is interested in and something I can be a part of. Victor's will ruined my career. I have no problem using it to get my career back."

"I don't care what you do," Todd said. "As long as I'm not in it and as long as you don't make Victor out to look like a saint."

Tarek fell silent. There were sides of Victor he'd identified with, and the more he consumed himself with Victor, the more he'd understood him.

"That's why you wanted to come here, isn't it?" Aileen said. "You just wanted to see Jason…"

"Aileen…"

"Guys, let's cut this shit for now," Todd said. He threw the joint to the ground and squished it under his shoe. "Jason's getting married in less than fifteen minutes and if we don't go back now, he'll never forgive us." Todd looked at Aileen and she knew he meant the two of them—her more than Todd. "Let's just do this and I'll take you to the airport afterward. We're all alive and I doubt anything will happen in the next couple of hours, so let's do this and talk about these things later."

Tarek looked to Aileen and she nodded agreeably. Todd led the way as they headed back to the beach, where a line of chairs and some decorations had been placed. Tarek reached out and he offered his hand to Aileen. After a moment, she took it and turned to him. He smiled as if to say everything was going to be okay and as they walked, she rested her head on his shoulder. After she found a seat, she looked up to see Jason standing in the distance in a tuxedo, his eyes on the trio. As the music began to play, all their problems were forgotten.

## 5

Jason caught the group returning out of the corner of his eye and felt relief. He didn't know who he could trust or what any of their real intentions were. His family and friends were less than what he'd hoped for in life, but they were what he had and he wanted them there. As he waited on Erica Drake to walk down the path drawn in the sand, his father joined him at his side. He showed no surprise that the apparition appeared on his wedding day. He'd expected it.

"Don't try to talk me out of it," Jason said, but to the small crowd of people, his lips weren't moving at all.

"We both know I'm not here," Victor said. "You can't use me as a crutch this time son. This is a mistake and deep down, you know it and you don't need me to point that out."

"You're saying what I know you'd say. That's all this is."

"But you know I'm right. You don't know this woman. You only know she's been a convenience. You think you have commonalities that matter, but you know it's not enough."

"And what's your suggestion?" Jason said. "Go run a global corporation and be like you? Never give a relationship a shot? All work and no play?"

"I enjoyed life."

"You had meaningless sex and bought big things, but you were miserable inside. I'm not going to be happy only on the surface. I'm not you."

"That's apparent," Victor said. "You're trying very hard to make it known you're not me. You're trying so hard to do what I wouldn't and it's given you tunnel vision."

"Well, hey, you already ran off all my other girlfriends all my life, so explain to me why you should give your stamp of approval on this one."

"I'm dead now," Victor said. "You can be whoever you want to be and you can do whatever you want to do. You don't need my influence anymore. You're already being influenced by everyone else around you."

"I'm marrying Erica."

"You still have some hard truths to face Jason. You're always going to come back to certain realities, like that you never saw proof that Erica was pregnant. Was there ever closure on the bar owner she was sleeping with on the side? How about all the times she just disappeared and left you home? Who's paying for the luxurious lifestyle you now have? Most importantly, who really started that fire?"

"It was an accident."

"Was it?"

"You're not going to poison my mind."

"Like I said: I'm dead. These are your thoughts. You're just disowning them so you don't have to feel guilty. There's too much of me inside you. You're unable to trust and that's how it should be."

"Not all people are bad. I don't walk around assuming the worst of everyone and I certainly wouldn't prompt people I don't like to try to kill each other. You didn't see the good in people? Great. Take a look in the mirror. You were worse than anyone you tried to screw over in the end."

Victor shook his head, disappointment in his face. "My will is so much more son. People will die, but it's so much more. Bigger things are happening…things you should be preventing. Instead, you gave the keys to the kingdom to Bernard Bell, which will result in the death of so many more people, and you're living in paradise. I'm gone Jason. It's too late for me to prevent what I started. It has to be you, but you can't do it here and you can't do it with Erica Drake."

Jason's eyes narrowed as he took in the words. If they were coming from his own head, he couldn't decipher what he was trying to say. "I don't understand…" He trailed off as he realized he was talking to no one at all and music began to drift from the speakers as Erica Drake appeared at the end of the line of chairs, a smile on her face. She looked beautiful, but he couldn't appreciate the moment. Words streamed through his head and at the most inopportune time of his life, he wondered if he was making the biggest mistake of…

*"…my life," Jason said. "My father is seriously ruining it."*

*Bernard Bell leaned on his desk and considered the moment. His partner's son seemingly had nowhere to go but needed to vent. It was a unique glimpse into the family life of Victor and he invited Jason into his office and poured him a water, ready to hear more. "What happened?" he asked.*

*"I'm seeing this girl. She met Victor and pitched an idea. Victor never made an effort with girls I was seeing but suddenly, they're spending time together. I come home tonight and they're having a business meeting, but they're both drinking and laughing. He's acting the way he acts with women he sleeps with. You get what I'm saying?"*

*"Why are you telling me this?"*

*"You're his friend. I was hoping you'd talk to him."*

*"You're uncomfortable asking your father to stop flirting with your girlfriend?"*

*Jason fell silent.*

*"You must have a very interesting home life," Bernard said.*

*"He's grooming me for this," Jason said. "I don't know if I want it, but I know he's preparing me for it and how am I supposed to want it when I see the way he is?"*

*"There will come a point in your life, and it's coming very soon, that you will be allowed to say no to him and there won't be a thing he can do about it. I will say this though: Most people would do anything to have the opportunities you have. The world is yours for the taking."*

*"Yeah, and then I become just like him…"*

*"Is that what you think?"*

*"Yeah, all the time."*

*"Jason, you don't want to do the things he does, don't do them. Victor's*

*money doesn't dictate his traits. He makes those decisions on his own. You can be wealthy and be loyal to one woman. You can have millions of dollars and still treat the panhandler on the corner with respect."*

*"The money makes it easier to be a prick."*

*"Of course it does. Hey, I have a reputation as a prick too, but that's because people tend to see the worst in me. And what they see is all real. I drink a bit much. I enjoy blackjack and bedding women. I'm at least honest about my vices, which is more than a lot of people can say. But what would people say if they learned that I gave over half a million dollars to children without running water in their village? What would they say if they learned I had a hard upbringing and worked three jobs just to support my brother and I when I was only fifteen? Maybe they'd change their tune. Maybe not. Everyone's got some good and some bad. People tend to only see the good in themselves and those close to them and ignore the bad. They also happen to see the bad in people that don't affect them in any way and ignore the good. Your father came from a tough place too. Have you ever asked him about his childhood? Do you even understand the pillars that hold him up and what they're made of? Yeah, he's doing a shitty thing. Maybe he even knows it and his intentions aren't honorable. Doesn't mean there's not some history there. Something drives his decisions, the good and the bad. I think your father isn't as sure of himself as he lets on. He ever tell you that he and I built this place together? This was an equal investment…and still more my idea than his."*

*"Why aren't you equals here?"*

*"His name sounded better. That's just how it happened. He wanted more. He took what he could and pretty soon, I found myself with a law degree and he was running the show. We both had equal value, but his name was the branding behind the business. Could it have been different? Probably. But it wouldn't have been enough for him. He always had something to prove but I knew when to quit."*

*"Maybe I should heed the warning."*

*"Hey, you know yourself better than I know you. I don't know shit. I just think you need to understand the field before you make any decisions. You've got a lot of options."*

*"What do I do about the girl?"*

*"Whatever you do, don't talk to her about it. Talk to him."*

Jason set out to take Bernard's advice. After driving around the city and contemplating how he would approach his father, he finally ended up sitting outside the gates of his father's mansion, staring at the one bedroom light that was still on in an otherwise dark home. He didn't *know if Pamela was with him. He didn't want to know. It could forever change the course of his relationship with Victor and he was afraid of the unknown future that would bring.*

*When he was finally able to bring himself to get out of the car, he worked his way slowly to Victor's room, listening closely as he approached the bedroom. There was no noise. A good sign. He knocked once quietly and a couple minutes later, a little louder. Victor could be sleeping with a book at his side. It happened often. He'd come too far though. He demanded an answer. He slowly turned the doorknob and entered the room. Immediately, Victor turned his head. He had the book in his hands but was wide awake. No one lay in bed with him. Jason breathed a sigh of relief, but only for that one detail. It still didn't mean much in the scheme of things.*

*"Dad..." Jason said.*

*Victor set the book down, looking at his son. It was uncharacteristic of Jason to interrupt him in his bedroom and Jason hoped he wouldn't come across as petty.*

*"Where's Pamela?" Jason asked. It came across as more of an accusation than he would have liked, but once the tone was out, he continued on. "You know she's my girlfriend, right?"*

*The concern left his father's face and instead, he spoke with a cold voice. "She left an hour ago."*

*"Can you do me a favor?" Jason asked, thick with sarcasm. "If you're helping her out with the business side of things, can you do it at work or through conference calls, like you do with everyone else?"*

*"What am I being accused of?"*

*"I'm your kid and she's my girlfriend and I know how you are with women and I know you're not interested in people unless you're trying to sleep with them."*

*"That didn't take place and it wouldn't have. I was coaching her and I took interest only because she is your girlfriend."*

*Jason lost the breath in his voice. He hadn't considered what should have been obvious, and his father's face was all serious. Suddenly, standing up for himself became the most embarrassing thing he'd ever done. Bernard's words echoed in his head. His father wasn't all bad, all the time. Jason refused to see the whole field. He only acted on disdain for the things he didn't like about Victor.*

*"What was I supposed to think?" Jason asked, but his voice was shaky, his confidence gone.*

*Then, Victor gave Jason a look that sent chills up his spine. It was a look Jason had seen before but had never seen directed his way. He'd seen it when he watched his father read criticisms or when people* wronged him. His eyes would narrow and Jason could see wheels spinning in his father's eyes, as if he was contemplating just how badly he wanted to see them in pain. Then, in a monotone voice, he told Jason "I'll take care of it."

"There's nothing to take care of," Jason said, but he was speaking to no one at all. Victor was back to his book and acted as if Jason had already left the room. He'd offended Victor and maybe there was no recovering from this.

The next day, he walked to class with a weight in his stomach. He wanted to say something to Victor to make things right, but the only thing he could do is wait until the incident was well in the past. Until then, he'd avoid his father. He also wanted to avoid Pam, but she was in the first course he had. He hadn't heard from her, which was rare, and he assumed the worst. Whatever Victor had planned on doing, it wouldn't make Jason look good.

Then she passed him on her way to class, walking quickly. "Great" he thought. This was going to completely fall on him.

"Pam!" he shouted and hurried after her.

She never turned. "You're a bastard."

"Tell me what I did."

"Your father cut me off. When I asked him why, he told me you were uncomfortable. I thought you supported me."

"He read way too much into something I said. I'll talk to him."

"You've done enough."

"I asked him not to treat you the way he usually treats women. That's all."

Pam threw her hands up dramatically and rolled her eyes. "He was giving me business advice!"

"Business advice? Conducted by the fireplace and drinking wine?"

"It was platonic, asshole! He was my best chance at getting my ideas off the ground!"

"I'll talk to him!"

She wiped her eye with the back of her hand quickly. She wasn't just angry. She was mourning the end of what she believed was a real relationship. "Don't call me or bother me again."

"You're dumping me over him? How can you not see my side of this? You don't know him at all!"

"No, Jason. I'm dumping you because you're letting him get in the way of who you really are. You're great when you're you, but the second your father's around, you cower."

"It's a little difficult not to."

*"No, it's not. He's just a guy."*
*"You're taking his side."*
*Pam stepped forward and her voice softened, but she spoke clearly to give him some hard truth. "See? You don't even hear me. That's why we can't be together. You have issues. If you can't separate yourself from who your father is, then that will always be in the way of whoever you're with...."*

...His memory of Victor was gone and all that was left was him and Erica Drake standing on the beach as the sun set behind them. The small crowd only saw their silhouettes and the words of the preacher were drowned out by the tides and the seagulls in the distance. The chaos that had surrounded the day faded as Jason fixated on the woman he loved. As Todd Mason and his mother made their way back to the wedding and sat in the second row, he forgot why they had been fighting at all. None of the past mattered.

Only now.

He caught his mother's eyes. Something that looked as if she was proud shone through. That and sorrow. He knew her intentions were in the right place. He supposed they were both broken in different ways—both trying to fix each other—unable to carry their own crosses.

He turned back to Erica and in moments, they read their vows and sealed the deal. He finally had everything he'd ever wanted in life. He'd detached from a life he always knew would be wrong and he'd found a stage to build new relationships. He'd found unlikely friends and a woman who understood him. His circle was small. The applause as he walked past the audience was sparse, but it was real. No one was kissing up and asking for a favor. Tomorrow he could have a beer with a buddy. He could make love to his wife and maybe have another try for a child. He could ask his mother to come back and see him sometime.

This was only the beginning.

The reception was held at Sugar Beach. It started with an ocean front, sunset, cocktail reception with the Pacific as a backdrop. A band played a mix of reggae and folk music, and a couple of Hawaiian girls taught the guests how to hula, embarrassing Erica's drunken volleyball friends in front of everyone on a stage. As the tone in the room lightened, Jason found himself at a table with Todd and Aileen. He leaned back and watched Erica mingle with guests, admiring everything about her. No one said anything. They just sat quietly, a mutual apology exchanged in their silence.

"Jason Stone?"

The table turned and the police chief sat at the table with them. The group exchanged glances as a result of the awkward encounter. "Yeah?"

"I don't want to take you away from the party but this has to be done now."

The group gathered Erica and met the chief outside where he held up an Ipad and scrolled through a couple of pictures of a man on the beach with a single bullet-hole in his forehead. "You recognize this man?"

Everyone shrugged. "Who is he?" Jason asked.

"The arsonist. Your home wasn't his first. Got a good-sized record. He had pictures of your home burning on his phone. He stuck around and watched."

Jason opened his mouth but no words came out. The events hadn't played out at all as he'd expected. Fingers were pointed all around, but at the end of the day, it was all just a coincidence, which was a concept Jason was learning to embrace.

"I didn't want to interrupt," the chief said. "He's done this at random in the past, but I had to ask. Get back to your fun, and congratulations to you both. You're a very lucky man."

The chief turned and walked off. Jason shrugged it off and went back to the party. Aileen and Tarek followed.

Todd hung back, watching the chief and feeling as though the meeting felt far too contrived. Everyone else just seemed to think his presence at the reception was weird. In fact, there were very few details as to the convenience of what had just happened. The arsonist had done this before and he'd chosen homes at random. Someone clearly murdered him and the police found pictures on his phone of Jason's home burning.

"Wait!" Todd hurried after the chief, who turned and raised his eyebrows. "That's it? Who killed him? How did you even find this guy and link him back to us?"

"Who are you?" the chief asked, as if Todd had no right to know police business.

"A friend who had been in the house and could have died."

"Anonymous tip."

"You know who killed him?"

"No idea." The chief walked away again and Todd didn't stop him. Another thought occurred to him in that moment: Why were they not suspects?

Todd walked back to the party, thinking hard. Unlike Jason Stone, Todd couldn't believe in coincidences and he'd been forced to believe in a few. Jason was a good man. That much he knew. Aileen wasn't a suspect. She was the one who almost died. Tarek helped save her. In fact, Tarek had saved others in the group on other occasions. No one who was named on the will could have possibly tried to kill everyone.

*Maybe it was a coinci...*

His mind kept going to the same place.

He walked back to the party. His knees felt like rubber and he took his time, afraid of how he could possibly approach such a heavy suspicion.

He looked into the hall where a slow dance had started. In the middle of the room, Jason and Erica were in a tight embrace. Couples danced around them. The music filled the room and alcohol flowed freely. Everyone was wrapped up in the music and calming rhythm in the room. Only Todd watched the Stones from afar. He squinted his eyes to sharpen his vision. The couple turned on the dance floor. First he saw Jason's face.

His eyes were closed, his body was at ease, and a smile sat on the corners of his mouth.

The turned and Erica came into view...Erica Stone, who unknowingly had only Todd's eyes on her at the moment.

Her movements were forced, her hands rested on Jason's back, barely embracing, but it was her eyes that took him aback. They were lifeless, loveless, and stared blankly at the wall.

Todd ducked outside again and stood against the wall, watching the waves crash on the shore as the last of the sun disappeared behind the endless ocean.

It was too late.

# Chapter 11

## 1

"Tread carefully," Todd told himself. He stared at himself in the mirror and let his mind replay the last few days. It had been a reunion of sorts— a bunch of Victor's enemies in one place and a near death experience for three of them, which had turned out to be classified as arson. It didn't add up. The story had no holes, but Todd was discovering that he didn't believe in coincidences. He always knew what brought him to Maui and Jason chased a girl he'd spontaneously met who came here first, so he'd decided it truly was a coincidence, until Erica's stories didn't completely hold water.

Todd found he was in a tricky situation. The problem was that either he would confront Erica and be wrong and forever shunned, or he would be right and have to convince Jason—or ruin Jason's life. He could see that Jason had found real love with Erica. What had once started as a rocky relationship had transformed into something real. If Todd were to call Erica a fraud in front of Jason, there was no way Jason would take his side, and Todd wasn't even sure he wanted to call her a fraud. He wasn't sure what her story was. He only knew there were holes.

The couple didn't go on a honeymoon because their lives were a honeymoon. They took in a luau and spent a few days traveling the island alone, but after feeling the effort was useless, they came home.

"To go anywhere else would be a lesser day than where I am every day," Jason had simply said. They immediately began house hunting and had spotted a location an hour down the coast. It would no longer be a walking distance from where Todd resided, but he didn't complain. He'd always been a third wheel and his presence here had always been temporary .Jason's presence was convenient, but Todd had serious decisions to make about what to do next. It was probably time to go back to LA and see what had been happening and check in on his old life.

He'd been threatened a year ago and run out of town, but being so far for so long had made him feel unafraid. He could hide forever and feel empty or risk his life to be where he felt fulfilled. His wife Cynthia and his boys Jackson and Keith would probably never forgive him, but he hoped the truth would do something for him. He hoped to win them back.

He thought about going back while Jason and Erica were touring the island, but questions kept coming up about Erica and even though he was going to leave Jason behind, it bothered him to know he may not be safe if he was with a dangerous woman. He hadn't decided what part she played, if any, in the lives of the beneficiaries, but if she was helping one of their contemporaries, Jason was in a prime spot to die. Or maybe she wanted Jason to inherit everything, and then she would have rights to half. It bothered him too much to bail.

He waited two days after they returned to catch her alone. She was at the dock, gassing up the boat.

"You going somewhere?" Todd asked.

She shielded her eyes with her hand and smiled when she saw him. "Nowhere specific. Just out in the middle of nowhere to get some sun."

"You do that a lot?"

"Actually, never. I thought I'd give it a try. You're welcome to join me."

"What's Jason up to?"

"He's in town in a meeting at the bank. Investing and a whole lot of garbage I don't know about."

Todd thought about the offer. She probably didn't actually want him there, but it was exactly the opportunity he was looking for. If he happened to offend her, she had nowhere to go. She'd have to sit through the conversation and by the time they returned, Todd was certain he'd know what she was all about. "You sure you wouldn't mind the company? I figure with the two of you moving, I won't have much of a chance to see you."

She waived him over. "Hop on"…

*...It wasn't long before Todd Mason lost track of time. It was easy to do when always shrouded in darkness. In reality, it had been a month since Todd was captured and thrown in a dirt hole with three others. Only one spoke. He was a former pilot who'd been shot down and captured and other than Todd, was the newest of the group. The pilot, Irving, was also working on a way out which only he believed would work. Thomson, Duffy and Danson were his other cellmates and were both nearing death. Both had been interrogated until their spirits broke, but neither caved.*

Todd was afraid to know, but his day was coming and wanted to be prepared. It was stupid for him to believe a person could ever be prepared for torture, but Todd had nothing else to think about.

It was a mistake to be here. He knew it the moment he was off to training. He'd passed a point of no return and he'd hoped to get through his time without any action. Not only was that wish unfulfilled. Todd was in the worst position a soldier could be in. All this because he wanted to seem noble to his girl Helen back home. How stupid it all was. She'd likely never even know what became of Todd.

No matter how many times Irving was taken, he'd return hours, sometimes days, later, and though he was always in pain and exhausted, he'd wake up the next day with hope. Todd couldn't wrap his head around it. He knew when the day came that he was taken, he would break. It was Irving, who never broke, who prevented that day from coming, and Todd hoped he never would. At least not until they were all rescued.

Irving had told Todd they would never be rescued—that even when the fighting was done, they would remain—that the enemy had no good reason to release them. They would probably shoot them and claim they had tried to escape. Better to risk their lives trying to escape than be killed and told that's what happened anyway.

Then, one day, shortly before Irving would be taken again, he muttered something that Todd would have expected from anyone else in the cell. "Kill me," Irving said.

"No," Todd crawled toward him. "You can do this."

"Do you believe in God?" Irving asked, and closed his eyes, resting his head against the wall.

"Of course."

"No, not believe because you were told to believe and were taken to church every week."

"I don't know," Todd said, and he meant it. "It was easier when I was younger. I want to, but if in my whole life, there is one time when I need to be saved, now is it."

"If you believed, then the only thing left to look forward to is death."

"I'm not going to kill you."

"Today's the day Todd. They're going to take me and today's the day I snap—push them to end me."

"Please don't do it," Todd said. "You were going to get us out of here. I'll help with whatever you need."

"You don't believe we're getting out of here anymore than I do," Irving said. "You're just counting the days and hoping someone's trying to get us. End my life so I can meet my maker Todd."

*Before Todd had a chance to even think about it, sunlight fell upon them and two men fell into the hole and pulled Irving out. Todd wanted to shout out to him, but didn't want to draw attention to himself. Instead, he watched and hoped that Irving wouldn't crack, but it was useless. Irving was on the verge and if it wasn't today, it would be tomorrow, and then Todd would be next.*

*That day had been the longest of all. Todd could hear screams in the distance, but it didn't sound like Irving. There were other prisoners in other places, all suffering the same torment. Maybe if they really could get out of their cell, they would have enough of an army to overpower their guards, but if every cell was like their own, there was little strength between them. If the others were free to walk away, Todd wasn't certain they even could.*

*Irving was gone until the next day—another bad sign—and when he finally was thrown back into the cell, it took Todd five minutes to determine he was even alive. "What happened?" Todd asked, noticing the others in the cell were more alert than he'd seen them. It seemed the little bit of life they all had left was hinging on Irving's spirit.*

*"I denounced America," he said. "I signed papers. Couldn't read any of it but signed." His voice was parched and most of his words fell into whispers. "That's all you have to do Todd. You don't have to mean it but you have to say it and do what they tell you."*

*Todd knew he would. He would confess whatever they wanted before they even had a chance to hurt him. When the day came that Todd was willing to do so, he found it harder than he believed as he was dragged from the hole. There was power in words that he couldn't understand— denouncing his country was the most cowardly thing he could think of, even if it was only to a couple of guards with guns who had no influence over the war. Todd suspected that the government, and those back home, understood that under duress, a person would say almost anything. These were certainly circumstances that one would understand why he'd do what he would do.*

*"What is your name?" a voice said from behind him. He spoke English well.*

*"Todd Mason."*

*"What is your service number?"*

*"Four, seven, eight, zero, eight, zero, four, zero, nine."*

*"Thank you," the voice said. He sounded pleased, and somewhat amused that they had such a cooperative captive. "What does your father do?"*

*"He's a teacher and a football and wrestling coach."*

*"No, he is not."*

*Todd looked up suddenly and tried to turn, but hand forced his face forward. There were certain realizations he was going to have to face, such as the fact that it wasn't only going to be his country he would have to denounce. His captors understood a certain truth and Todd would have to learn that truth and align his story to it.*

*"What does your father do?"*

*Todd wanted to ask what they wanted to hear and would willingly tell them what they needed, but had no idea. "He's a teacher," Todd said. "My mother is too. They teach at Garfield High in San Bernadino. I swear that is true."*

*There was muttering behind Todd and he closed his eyes tightly, praying that the answer would suffice.*

*Then, a flash of pain shot through him as the back of a hand hit his face hard enough to cut his lip. His captors were silent as the voice walked around the table and sat face to face with Todd, leaning forward, his eyes piercing Todd with a hatred he'd never seen. "You're going to tell me what I need to hear, or your father and your mother will die. What does your father do for a living...?"*

...Todd's father was a teacher but he was also a wise man in general, sometimes spouting off platitudes that sounded like they belonged in Lifetime movies, but that Todd took to heart when he was just a boy. Barney Mason was an avid reader and had a bookshelf filled with literature on how to coach and inspire. He used those lessons when coaching High School sports, but carried them around as life lessons in his head, passing them on to his son whenever he had the chance.

When Todd wrestled in his junior year, his father was his coach, on the mat but also in the time that spilled into life at home. According to Barney, his son was going to be the best, and that meant wrestling would be on top of his mind at all times.

"Endurance," Barney would say as if it was a complete sentence. "Endurance Todd."

He'd say it whether it was wrestling, test-taking, or dog training. Todd was impatient and his father would quote from his go to list of Barneyisms and teach Todd to be consistent and fight through every moment and to evolve and he'd look Todd in the eyes and say "endurance."

If there had ever been a more relevant word in Todd's life, and in the moments that mattered, that was it.

As Todd sat on the boat, looking out into the ocean, he reminded himself of what his father said. He'd been running away from one problem, but a new one presented itself out here and only Todd was capable of confronting it. He hoped he was wrong, but before the Stones and Todd parted ways and before he went back to Los Angeles, he had to know.

"Beer?" Erica asked, twisting the cap off a bottle for herself and handing Todd another.

"Yeah." He drank and it went down smooth. It calmed his nerves and he asked for another. Confrontation was never Todd's strong suit and in this instance, he would likely lose his only two friends on the island.

"You and Jason thinking about having a baby?" Todd danced around the subject, making small talk that revolved around the subject that Todd wanted to address. Erica answered everything just like anyone would. It was hard to see her as evil, with a carefully constructed strategy to get the money, but Todd sensed it in her very presence. The more he thought about the timing of everything, the more it made sense.

"We'll give it some time."

"I'm sure it was hard after you lost the other one. Sorry. I know it's a sensitive subject."

"Yeah," she said.

Todd watched her. She looked as if she wanted to say something more, but looked away instead. In avoiding a discussion, she looked like she was lying. The more sure Todd became, the more aggressive he was.

"What do you think about this business with Jason's father?"

"What about him?"

"Guy had a lot of money. Jason should have been set to inherit it, but the guy was crazy. You ever worry that Jason's life could be in danger?"

"We're pretty far away, so I think he'll be okay." Erica answered the questions but her mind was a long distance away. Todd realized she'd realized he was on to her.

"The fire was scary though."

"Of course."

"How were you able to move out here? It's not cheap."

"Big divorce settlement."

"Oh yeah? What was your ex husband's name and what did he do?"

His test worked. Erica couldn't formulate a believable lie in that moment and she didn't bother to try. Instead, she turned to Todd and let out a deep breath, pushing the boat farther into the Pacific. "Do you have something to ask me Todd?"

"Who from the list tasked you with this?"

"I don't know what you're talking about."

"I know I was placed in this exact spot and so was Jason and you're the only reason he's here. You're working with the same person who took everything away from me and I'm giving you a chance to come clean before I talk to Jason myself."

Erica turned again, staring into the distance. Todd thought she looked defeated and when she finally turned back, she looked as if she was ready to spill it all. She stood and grabbed the railing for balance. "It's a long story," she said. "Another beer?"

"Please, and we've got nothing but time."

She grabbed a beer from the cooler, her hands shaking as she struggled to twist the cap off. She was afraid, and Todd knew he would go easy on her when this was over—that he would direct his anger at whoever had propositioned her in the first place. The bottle slipped from her grip and hit the ground. She stepped back and buried her head in her hands, her body trembling.

Todd reached for the beer. "Look, I'll make sure Jason understands that you were only…"

Suddenly, Erica had a grip on Todd's arm and pulled him forward, in the direction he was already leaning. The force of the pull and his body's momentum sent him over the rail and into the water. Todd started to sink, but he started to kick and push himself back to the surface. By the time his head was above water, the boat was already slowly pulling away from where he was floating. Erica stood at the controls and looked out to where Todd was positioned. He looked around in all directions and couldn't see the island. He cursed himself for being fooled and realized he'd been weakened by her demeanor while all she had been doing was buying time.

"You and Jason are here because you're the only two on the list who didn't have to die!" Erica shouted.

"How's that possible?" he shouted. "Let me up and we'll talk about it and work something out."

"There's nothing to work out. You were brought to Hawaii to keep you out of the way. That's all. All you had to do was stay out of the way. You did this to yourself."

"Come on Erica. You're not just going to leave me here. I won't make it back."

"That's the point," she said, a smile on her face. Todd realized then that she really was evil…that she wasn't just tricking everyone to inherit some money. Erica Drake was a truly awful person.

"Erica, please. If anything, I need to know why me. I never knew Victor."

"I agree," Erica said. "And he never knew you. But you've already asked too many questions, so you've got more important things to be thinking about."

The motor roared to life and the boat started moving. He tried to swim and shout for help, but it was futile. Within minutes, the boat was long gone and Todd was left in the middle of the sea, with nothing in sight.

*2*

Anthony Freeman splashed water from the river over his face and let it fall in droplets, staring at his reflection, trying to decide if today was the day he was looking at a dead man. He decided against it since he felt a little more upbeat than usual. The sun was shining between the trees and the sounds of nature were amplified. It was a perfect day and Anthony spent most of it outside his Winnebago watching the movement of the forest. He watched woodland critters going about their routine. He reached around his side and massaged his back, trying to prod at the circuits inside him.

As the sun began to set, he pulled out a book and set out to enjoy some reading as darkness grew. Maybe he'd sleep outside tonight. H

He turned at the sound of tires coming his way and another Winnebago pulled into the lot next to his. Anthony had paid for both lots but suspected the time was running out on his reservation of the parallel spot. Seeing a new neighbor approach, he realized he should have called the front office sooner.

Anthony knew he probably still had a lot of life in him, but he'd taken cautions not to take any chances. If he were to have a heart attack, he wanted it to be in the middle of nowhere, far away from the population. Hopefully, his neighbor was only staying a night or two.

When the Winnebago parked, a man about Anthony's age stepped out and gave Anthony a friendly waive. "Evening," Nick said.

"This your site?" Anthony asked.

"According to my directions it is."

"For how long?"

The man seemed confused. "Weekend. Maybe longer if I like it."

Though Anthony wasn't pleased to put another man in danger, it was nice to see some kind of human life again. "I'm Anthony."

"Nick. Nice to meet you. Don't worry about me friend. I won't be in your hair."

"It doesn't bother me," Anthony said. "I've got a steak bigger than what my stomach will hold going onto the fire in a bit. You're welcome to join me."

"Sounds great, friend," Nick said. Anthony liked that Nick called him "friend" and decidedly liked him on the spot. "How long you been here?"

"Six months," Anthony said. "I'm retiring in the wilderness, far away from the hustle and bustle."

"Holy shit," Nick said. "I'm impressed."

They made small talk until Nick had to set up. Anthony offered to help, but Nick preferred doing things himself. Anthony ducked inside to call the front desk and learned from the front office manager that his time hadn't expired but that his money was refunded for the adjoining spot and that they changed their policy so he couldn't buy up the lots without using them. Even when Nick left, Anthony was bound to have neighbors down the road. Someone would always be at risk.

*Or I could have someone enter the number Tarek gave me.*

That night, Nick did stop by and the two men got to know each other by the light of the fire. Anthony realized he'd missed bonding with people more than he ever thought he would—especially strangers. He'd always felt like there was something to gain in getting to know someone you knew nothing about. As if their friendship couldn't be more in Anthony's favor, Nick was a retired firefighter who'd also served as a paramedic for forty years. The man was a trained medic. Anthony expressed concern about his own deteriorating health and next thing he knew, Nick was in and out of his Winnebago, finding the necessary equipment to run blood tests. What he saw concerned him.

"You need blood thinners," Nick said. "You're going to clot. You have high levels of mercury in your blood. Have you been on any medications?"

"Pain medications for my back."

"What's going on in your side? You keep touching there like there's a tumor or something."

"Not a tumor," Anthony said. "You wouldn't believe me if I told you."

"Try me. I've seen plenty in my life."

"A crazy man who wanted to kill a room full of people decided to use me as a weapon. He wired me up."

"What do you mean? Is this a military thing?"

"No."

"Terrorists?"

"Just a disgruntled man who used to work with cadavers. Met him in a bar and he knocked me out and put a bomb inside me. He wanted to see if he could kill a group of people by stopping only my heart. My blood completes the circuit, like any electronic device, such as a light, you can break the circuit with the turn of a switch. That's why I'm all the way out here. No offense to you Nick but I bought out the lot next to my own so innocent bystanders weren't exposed to this. I hate to tell you, but sitting here with me is suicide."

Nick scooted back as if Anthony was poison.

"You need to see a doctor," Nick said.

"This man is in prison. I've been told it can only be stopped with a code, which I have, but I don't know if it's real. A doctor would open me up and a bomb squad would try to deactivate the bomb. If anything went wrong, if my heart stopped for just a moment, they would all die. It's a nearly perfect predicament to be in. You might want to think about packing up and driving far away."

"You don't scare me friend. I'm dying too. I've got stage four cancer and I don't have another month. You've got yourself the right neighbor. Might as well occupy the spot with someone whose on his way out too. I'll probably go long before you."

"I don't know about that. The metal components have contaminated my blood. I'm dying Nick. I don't know how long I've got, but I'm dying."

"Geez, if I believed in this kinda thing, I would say the stars aligned perfectly by putting us together. But I'll tell you something else friend. I have a nephew whose a medical student now but he worked with the bomb squad in New York for a couple of years. He knows a lot and could look at that and we could keep it private. He's a good friend and I can promise you if you want to keep this under the table, I can make sure he understands that."

"I don't need help," Anthony said.

"He's the real deal. Not saying he could take it out of you, but he could tell you what you're dealing with."

"I know what I'm dealing with. I don't need false hope. No one can do this with any kind of guarantee."

The steak sizzled on the fire and soon the men were eating and Nick had a beer in his hand. Anthony told him his story, from suicide to alcohol and Nick listened intently to every word. When Anthony was done, Nick didn't object to any of his reasoning and accepted Anthony was there to die. He only offered Anthony an enticing offer that Anthony couldn't refuse.

"I'm on my way out," Nick said. "Doctors told me to stay in the hospital until the end but I told them to fuck themselves and left. I've got two boys and they both told me they wouldn't come to my funeral. To their point, I cheated on their mom and ruined their lives. Tried to get forgiveness a few times but they wouldn't have it. No one will shed a tear at my funeral, so why should I be in a hospital, going through the life saving motions and costing the tax payers to keep me on machines. I created the loneliness in my life and that's how I figured I'd die, but you and me here friend…this makes me think there's something to it all, like maybe no one deserves to die alone. Maybe you and I did a bunch of stupid shit in our lives and our creator is here now to tell us that even the worst of the worst deserves to have someone with them when they die, well I think that might be the case.

Let my friend take a look at you Anthony. If he can confirm that the only way to deactivate that thing is to punch in a code, then I'll be your guy. I'll put it in. I'll either be saving your life and die knowing that, or we'll go together in one big explosion in the middle of nowhere. My boys and my ex wife won't have to identify me. We'll just disappear in one boom and let the park rangers clean us up. What do you think friend? What do you say we take care of all our problems like that?"

Anthony couldn't find a reason in the world to refuse Nick's proposal.

3

Todd watched where the boat disappeared for a long time, trying to get a handle on his reality. He was off the coast of Maui, probably about three miles. The island was probably miles away but he was in the middle of the Pailolo Channel and the tides were strong and choppy. He knew he was being pulled away every second. Swimming against the tide would be useless and only waste energy, so Todd stayed still, trying to develop a plan and understand the geography.

It set in that this was really the end. That's what Erica had intended and she wouldn't have just left him there if she believed he had a chance of survival. There was too much at risk. His father's voice rang in his ears, telling him to start swimming.

Endurance.

But it was no better than swimming upstream. In the end, he would get nowhere. He tried to calculate his position in the water. A few miles off the coast, somewhere north of the island. They'd been docked in Kapalua. There was still some hope, and it wasn't a feat that had never been done before. In fact, a few dozen swimmers in history had gone from coast to coast between the Hawaiian Islands before. Todd wasn't a professional swimmer, but he had the advantage of starting somewhere in the middle. Of course, he was sporting shorts and a t-shirt, which was hardly swimming gear, but between the current which was headed toward Molokai and the fact that Todd couldn't be more than four miles away created something to strive for. Maui was roughly eight miles from Molokai. It was something that could be done and Todd wasn't a bad swimmer, especially when his life was on the line. He counted the problems that could arise: Jellyfish, sharks…

*Oh God please don't let there be sharks.*

He looked up at the sun which was bright in the sky, then turned in all directions to find the other island. Erica would have assumed he'd head back to Maui. She hadn't taken time to think through his options. She only knew he couldn't get back to their island.

*I can do this.*

He had to do it. He wanted to see the look on her face when he showed up in their home and told Jason that she was conspiring—that she was probably the cause of every bad thing that had happened to the beneficiaries. If he could expose her, Todd would be free to go home and take back his life. The only thing the stood in the way of the solution to all of his problems, was four miles of water.

*I have to do this.*

He started on his back and let the current take him on a trip. He could paddle along with it until he was tired and turn over to swim when he was closer. Right now, the most important thing was that he conserved as much energy as he could. He would need it when he was closer to the shore and needed to swim. He would float more than he'd swim, his mouth above water but little else. Water washed over his face constantly, but he kept paddling toward Kapalua, focused and determined, reminding himself that if there was ever a time to stay on task, this was it. His father's voice whispered in his ear as he swam and the more he heard the voice, the more real it felt, until he was sure his father was right alongside him. As a child, it had been an annoyance, but he needed it more than ever.

He felt something brush up under his back and his eyes went wide as what had only been a possibility in his head became very real. He waited to feel teeth, but whatever it was had passed harmlessly. He paddled a little faster and closed his eyes, telling himself to swim or drown…swim or drown…

*…Speak or die…speak or die…*

*Both options were the ruination of everything he was, but there was no other way out.*

*Todd was cooperative but he couldn't figure out what the answers they wanted to hear were. They certainly weren't the true answers he gave. Todd gave his captors his life story, only eliminating Helen from the account. He wasn't sure why he excluded her. He didn't want them believing there was someone he so badly wanted to return to. He'd once lost Helen to another man because he refused to fight for her. Joining the army was his way of showing her that he was a fighter. He felt foolish now. He was going to die to prove a point to her. She'd probably never even know what he went through. He'd be declared MIA and she'd move on. Todd had no one back home to mourn him. He had no wife…no kids. Now, more than ever, he realized those were the things he wanted. He wanted to be average, with a day job, a family, a house and a couple friends to play poker with. It was his own stupidity that ultimately put him in front of men who would torture and kill him, while so many others simply accepted what they had in life and appreciated those things.*

*"I don't know what you want me to say," Todd said. "I have no reason to lie to you. I have no loyalties, no patriotic duty. I don't want to kill and I'm not angry. I came here to prove I'm not a coward."*

*"Then what are you?" His captor asked, sitting on a chair backwards, his arms wrapped around the back. "Are you brave? Why do you wear this uniform?"*

*"I thought I'd go to drill...maybe across seas to stand on a post. I'm not a killer. I wouldn't have fired my weapon in combat."*

*"Then you admit you are a coward."*

*"No sir," Todd said. "I don't believe that war and killing people are brave. If you were born in America, you'd be wearing my uniform and the same goes for me."*

*"That is not true," his captor said. "I stand for ideas. I stand for my people."*

*"Your ideas and your people would have been different if you were born where I was," Todd said. "That's why both sides are always only composed of soldiers from their own homeland. We're all just victims of where we landed and we all landed in the middle of a fight that never ends. None of us understand the fight and we don't understand each other."*

*"You seem like an intelligent man."*

*"I'm not. This is common knowledge."*

*"Then you would have no problem denouncing America's involvement in our affairs?"*

*"I denounce everyone's involvement." Todd hated what he was saying. He was giving them a reason to torture him, but no matter how badly he didn't want to be harmed, he couldn't bring himself to speak the words they so badly wanted him to speak.*

*"Are you hungry?" his captor asked.*

*Todd slowly looked up. His captor was smiling, but he knew it was a trap. No more questions were asked though and he was instead escorted through the prison to another building across the clearing where he was led through a long hallway into a cafeteria, which looked similar to a mall food court back home. The aroma hit Todd first and soon he was watching as burgers and chicken was thrown on trays and groups gathered throughout the cafeteria, laughing and telling stories. Throughout the room, Todd spotted a handful of Americans who seemed to be enjoying their meals. Todd wasn't sure what set them apart. Did they answer the questions correctly? He thought about his cellmates and how over the last month, he'd watched them slowly die—slowly lose hope—and fifty yards away was a cafeteria where half eaten meals were being dumped into the trash when chow-time was over.*

*"Private Mason?" another soldier said, approaching and extending his hand with a smile. "My name is John Henry, second Lieutenant. I heard you were brought in some time ago and wanted to meet you."*

*"Why am I here?" Todd asked, mesmerized by his surroundings.*

*"How bout you grab some grub and join me?"*

*Todd filled a tray full of chicken and rice and a plastic cup with soda. After he sat, he forced himself to eat slowly. It had been a long time since he'd had a good meal and he didn't want to waste the chance. John watched him for five minutes before he finally cut to the point.*

*"They had me in a hole in the ground too. Four months down there. Barely asked me a question the whole time."*

*"Where do you sleep?" Todd asked, between bites.*

*"I've got a bed, roof over my head, about a mile uphill from here. They escort me and some of the others daily. We eat, we have a basketball court, tennis court..."*

*"How? What did you do?"*

*John leaned in and grew quiet, as if there were really secrets no one was allowed to hear. "You're doing something right Todd, or you wouldn't be with me now. You're telling them what they want to hear, but what they're going to ask you to do is sign something that basically calls the president a war criminal and denounces our involvement."*

*"They already mentioned it."*

*"What did you say?"*

*"I said I denounce both side's involvement."*

*John laughed for a moment and nodded his approval at Todd. "We're all stubborn in the beginning. I spit in my interrogator's face the first day. They left me in a metal cage for four days on my belly. It was so small, I couldn't get my hands from out under my body. Almost got eaten alive by insects."*

*"Then what?"*

*"Told myself I don't want to die here. Not like this. Don't get me wrong. I resisted a long time, but finally I said I'd do what they wanted. I videotaped a statement, read straight from a notebook and never heard anything more. That's all they want to hear. I don't even know if these things reach back home, but if they do, our government knows I said what I said out of duress. It's the truth."*

*"It's the worst thing we can possibly do."*

*"It's a label. I'd take any label in the world over being eaten alive by*

*ants, my friend. And I don't see any rescue choppers flying overhead, do you? Fact is, we may never leave here. I'm going to get what I can before this whole thing is either over or they eventually decide to put a bullet in my head."*

*"Is that why I'm here?" Todd asked. "So you can talk me into it?"*

*"I'm not going to lie. Of course it is. It's win win. Who loses? We have no influence over anything when we're in cages. Our words don't change anything and your opinion…" John tapped his temple. "What you love, what you believe in, is all in here. They'll never tap into your brain."*

*"What do I tell them?" Todd asked.*

*"Continue to be cooperative. They're deliberately making it harder than it has to be, but that's all for show."*

*Todd nodded, setting his spoon in the remainder of his rice. He wanted to take it with him in case he never came back to the cafeteria. If John was telling the truth, there was no reason that would have to happen, but Todd needed to work through this in his head. He thought again of his companions who were sitting in a hole. All of them likely had been given this same ultimatum and passed. He couldn't understand how a person could slowly die in the name of pride. Todd knew he was going to do it. He would never have what it took to be wrapped in a wire cage or sit in darkness, starving to death.*

*Todd Mason joined the army to prove he wasn't a coward, and it was during his service that he finally admitted he was…*

…not going to die.

*I am not going to die.*

Todd spoke the words as he paddled, occasionally tilting his head to see if the island was anywhere within his sight. Nothing.

He kept moving, occasionally feeling something brush against his leg. He refused to take a break. No one could survive the middle of the ocean for long. He wasn't even sure he was floating in the right direction anymore. There would come a point in time, and that was coming soon, that there would be no hope remaining. Every second that passed, he grew to accept his death. His mind began thinking about whether he should let himself drown before he could possibly be eaten by a shark, but he'd ultimately refuse to accept the reality of his situation.

No one would ever know what happened. Only Erica Drake.

Erica.

He found the energy to paddle faster as the sun beat on his face. After another object brushed against his foot, he began to cry. He reflected on his life. He'd tried to be an average Joe, but he'd been a prisoner of war, he'd lost a woman, found another, was placed in a situation to inherit millions, lived in Hawaii, and eventually…murdered. It wasn't the life he'd hoped for. He'd wanted to be invisible…lay low…stay neutral to the drama. Instead, it'd followed him around until it finally got the best of him.

Later in the evening, Erica would have dinner with Jason Stone and talk about her day as if it was just another day and they'd fall asleep in each other's arms, Jason clueless of the fact that Todd would either be at the bottom of the ocean or swallowed alive.

*I can't let that happen. I can't.*

He paddled faster, scared that he was giving his all just to be going in the opposite direction. He was able to hang onto his momentum for another twenty minutes, but all at once, exhaustion overcame him and he couldn't move. He repositioned his body and searched every direction, squinting into the distance in the hope of finding a sign of the island. He suddenly wished he'd swam in the direction Erica's boat had gone. At least he had a sense of direction at that time. He no longer had any idea which way was which and there was no sign of anything in the distance. A few yards away, a dark shape passed.

He forced himself to think about Cynthia and his boys.

*Why did I leave them? What the hell was I thinking?*

A visual of his family entered his mind as he closed his eyes and let go.

4

By the time the sun was setting, Anthony and Nick had become close friends. There was something to two old men dying coming together in the wilderness that turned them into open books. In the end, they would share their last moments with another stranger—someone who might have altered the course of their own lives if they'd only met sooner.

They spent the day fishing and rehashing old stories, laughing and growing serious as they talked about the ways their lives were broken. Nick hadn't talked about the bomb since he'd brought it up earlier, but it was on both of their minds throughout the day. By the time the fire was burning, Nick was six beers deep and offered Anthony a drink for the third time. Anthony passed and reminded Nick that he had an alcohol problem.

"Does it really matter anymore?" Nick asked. "Isn't alcohol a problem when it affects the people around the alcoholic?"

"That's one way of putting it," Anthony said.

"Enjoy your last days then."

"We don't know yet that they are and I don't enjoy drinking. I never did. I drank to forget. I want to die with a clean conscious."

Nick laughed. "I gotcha. You want to be clean and sober when you meet your maker."

"What do you believe?"

"That we're all destined to be dirt. What do you believe?"

"A friend of mine died some time ago. He was a preacher so he would talk about God and what we should do while we're here. We'd go around and round; Logic against faith. I liked what he had to say, against all reasoning, I liked it. I suppose I wanted to and that was enough for me to buy in for a while."

"What changed?"

"He led the charge to invalidate Victor's will. He was the driving force. The day I learned of the bomb inside of me, the same day the will was to be made invalid, he gave his life to save someone else. I don't know what to make of that."

"Sounds like a decent man."

"His lack of presence is what saved my life. It's also the very reason he's gone and the will is still valid."

"Then what are you saying? There's a god or there's not?"

"What happened to my friend was a self fulfilling prophecy. If you believe you have a purpose, you find a purpose. Because he believed that to be decent, you should sacrifice yourself for another, he did. Just as many people with evil intent fulfill their own prophecy. Where does God fit into that?"

"Sounds to me like you need to think about what you want. Your buddy, unlike most of these cardboard cutouts in the world, was someone worth listening to. Don't matter if he's right or wrong. He died being the guy he wanted to be. If you want me to put the code in and roll the dice, I'll do it, but don't do it so you can commit suicide out here with no one around to mourn your passing. You must have some relatives or a mentor or someone you can talk to."

"I keep telling myself I shouldn't still be here. I've tried to die, I've abused my body with booze for so long that I should have gone naturally by now."

"Nah, heavy drinkers live longer than non-drinkers. You know that drinking lubricates social interaction, which is vital for your physical and mental health? People who don't drink never allow themselves to join the party."

"I'd love to hear your source on that fabricated statistic."

"I don't remember where I got that, but makes sense, doesn't it? It's the addiction that will kill ya, but if you have the will-power to know when to quit, it ain't a problem."

"What do you think I should do?" Anthony asked.

Nick broke into a coughing fit and for the next five minutes. Anthony patted his back and asked if he was okay. Nick held his chest and caught his breath before asking where they were again. By then, the seriousness of their discussion was gone, but Anthony repeated himself. "What should I do?"

"I don't got a lot of time left, so if you want to take me up on my offer, the expiration is coming, but if you've got some loose ends to tie up, you gotta do it. What do you have to lose?"

"I've already talked to my parents, who are both in their nineties and will outlive their children," Anthony said. "I have a sister in Maryland. She's in hospice and wouldn't even remember she had a brother. I wrote to a few students and friends. I've had my closure. The only loose ends are things I can't put closure on."

"Like what?"

"The lottery."

"You said the man who stabbed you is dead."

"He is, but I never got an admission from the man who put it in motion."

"You know who did it?" Nick leaned into the fire, the shadows of flame and light dancing across his face.

"I was able to look at the list of beneficiaries to bet against. There were fifteen of us when it all started, but only fourteen names were on the list. I presume that the missing name is the one who started it all."

"Why haven't you talked to him?"

Anthony let out a single laugh to showcase the obvious. "The guy moved to Hawaii right after the reading."

"Yup, sounds guilty as sin," Nick said.

"I can't," Anthony said, and he was speaking to himself. "I just can't ignore what he's done. I either die alone or I take someone with me. I want that person to be someone who deserves to die—whose non-existence can save lives. I want to do as my friend did: sacrifice myself to save others. Then, I will know that my prolonged life had a purpose."

"Well, you ain't flyin with that thing inside you."

"No," Anthony said, leaning in close so the heat hit his face. "But I can bring him here. If I can bring him here, he can enter the code, and he can be the one who rolls the dice with me."

"Sounds like a plan," Nick said. "What can I do to help?

5

For a long moment, Todd Mason believed he was dead. Darkness swallowed him as he sank below the surface and let himself fall. The light from above grew dimmer as his body cut through the water. He felt himself fading as he took in a mouthful of water. Flashes of light streaked across his eyes and he saw images flash in front of him. Cynthia Mason, his boys, the moment in High School when he caught the tie-breaking touchdown that won homecoming. He was a hero that year.

*This is my life flashing before my eyes.*

But it wasn't. It was only the highlight reel and the common theme he kept coming back to was his wife and boys.

He had run away from home to protect them and in the end, he would disappear into thin air, forgotten in a decade. Forgotten now.

His foot hit something hard. He was on an outcropping of stone on the ocean floor, surrounded by tangles of reefs. Tropical fish dodged his body as he fell into a crouching position on the ground.

He didn't know where the burst of energy came from, but something lit a fire under his ass in that moment. He gave himself a push and suddenly he was on his way up, clawing at the water, angled to the surface. He had to be close. The water was shallow here. The ground wasn't far from the surface. He only needed a few seconds to rest his arms from keeping afloat and after that, he found the strength. He found his father's voice telling him to be resilient and to fight for what's yours.

Todd's life couldn't end with so many loose threads. Erica Drake, the threats against his family, watching his boys play ball, taking them fishing, making love to Cynthia. He'd never desired his wife—or seeing her again—more than that moment, and later, he'd realize it was that desire that brought him to the surface with barely a breath left in him. When he emerged from water, he sucked in air with a gasp and went into a coughing fit. It was uncomfortable, but his senses were heightened and he had enough energy to do twice what he'd done all day. He started swimming, periodically letting himself fall under the surface and paddling below the water. Dark shapes passed his eyes but nothing came near him and that fear was gone. Once he'd invited death, everything after was just bonus time. It wasn't just about his life. It was to see what he could do. It was nothing more than a challenge that he could have volunteered to attempt.

He still wasn't certain he was headed in the right direction, but that thought was dismissed within moments when he saw the shadow in the distance. It was high in the sky—mountains. The base was surrounded by fog and he'd missed it, but when he stopped and took it in, he realized he was closer than he'd believed. He swam faster and it all became visible. The beach in the distance, a sailboat miles to his right. He was going to make it. He would come back from the dead.

He thought about the look on Erica's face. What would he say? How would she react?

When his feet found the ground, he began running. He realized how tired he was again but now it didn't matter. He was safe, assuming nothing pulled him back in or he didn't have a heart attack in the next fifteen minutes. The remainder of his swim was easy. He bobbed through the water, his toes hitting the ground and pushing him forward leap after leap. Soon, his chest emerged, and then water was falling from his shorts.

Then he hit the beach with a thud, falling forward and letting his hands dig into the sand. He momentarily savored his victory before drifting to sleep…

*…The final moments in which Todd was transported from the housing facility for cooperative prisoners and back to the hole in the ground were the most stressful of his life, yet he wished the moment would last forever. On one hand, it seemed so simple. Cooperate, make life easy, live in a home instead of a hole and be fed instead of beaten. Yet, everything he'd ever seen on television and movies proved that the way to be a man was to stand up for your beliefs, no matter what the consequences.*

*He wanted to blame that fact on the film, but he'd been living with a group of people who refused, no matter how much they took, to say they disagreed with their beliefs. It didn't matter whether it was true or not, or whether they would bend with enough pain—they simply wouldn't say it. When Irving cracked, it made Todd feel like he had permission, but it wasn't that simple. The fact that it seemed simple was what complicated the matter. Were his beliefs not strong enough? Was he unable to withstand pain?*

*He was a coward, but he just wasn't so sure why that was such a bad thing. It was actually foolish to live your life on your convictions if your life was only going to be cut short. It was the others in the hole that refused to go home and raise their kids and build new generations that could contribute in positive ways in society and far outweigh a few meaningless admissions. In fact, it was dumb and Todd was growing to resent them.*

*He spent the ride back convincing himself he was right and by the time he was back in his interrogator's hands, he was ready to cooperate, and hopefully, he'd never even have to face the hole again.*

*He was escorted back into his room and for fifteen minutes, he sat quietly as a conversation carried on behind him between his interrogator and two other soldiers.*

*After a long period of contemplation, he initiated the conversation. "I will do whatever you ask me to do," he said. They didn't hear him the first time, so he repeated it. Then, silence, and that moment was the most frightening of all. Was the option truly an option or was John in the right moment in time? Maybe they didn't really need Todd or want him to do anything. Maybe he was made to be an example, or was being psychologically tested and failed.*

*"I mean it," Todd said, his voice pleading. "I don't care what it is. I'll do it."*

*Before an answer came, he heard shouting in the distance. Both men stopped and walked to the exit to see what was happening. Suddenly the shouting was closer and the soldiers ran from the area. Something was happening. Todd prayed it was allies coming to their rescue, but there were no gunshots and the sound of helicopters and tanks was void in the air. This was an internal problem.*

*Todd stood, his knees shaking as he looked through the doorway. About a dozen men surrounded an embankment where two emerged with one of the prisoners in their arms. The prisoner screamed and pulled away from them, but they held firm. It had been an escape, and the man hadn't gotten very far. Todd could see the pain in his eyes, the desperation to be free.*

*"Don't do it," Todd said to himself, unsure of whether he was talking to the soldiers or the prisoner. "Please don't..."*

*One soldier raised his machine gun and a short burst of shots in rapid succession rang out in the air as the prisoner's chest and neck exploded in a splatter of blood. The prisoner slumped in their arms shortly before they dropped him to the ground. One soldier said something and they all laughed.*

*Business as usual.*

*Todd numbly walked back to where he was seated and fell to the block of concrete where his eyes were wide open in shock and he realized he had no control over his arms or legs. He threw up in that moment, mostly dry heaving as the little bit of food he was allowed hit the ground at his feet.*

*Then, shouting behind him as a pissed off interrogator saw what he did, grabbed him by the arm and dragged him back to the hole.*

*Todd was thrown to the ground without mercy. He landed on one knee and heard a crack. He let out a cry and the hole was covered, masking the group in darkness. After he was able to sit up, Irving came to him and tended to his knee, wrapping a strip of clothe around it.*

*Todd looked up at the group, ready to tell them they all needed to wise up and cooperate. It was the man who tried to run who lost his life. He'd be buried in a hole and no one would hear from him again. In a year, his name would never be mentioned by those who knew him. As Todd caught his breath slowly and looked at the others, he saw their own pain, their own inner turmoil. They knew the simplicity of the decision, but unlike Todd, some people cared more about holding onto their values than anything else. Todd couldn't understand it and they wouldn't understand him. He wished he could be above, saying what needed to be heard and sitting at a table, eating a bowl of soup.*

*Downey came up close to Todd and sat at his side and whispered. "One week from today, in the middle of the night, we go."*

*"What? How?"*

*"We've got footholds carved into the wall all the way to the top. We will kill the guards and run."*

*"And go where?" Todd asked, panic in his voice. He would surely be interrogated again, but what was he supposed to do now?*

*"Anywhere but here."*

*"We're safer here than up there. Do you know what just happened?"*

*"We would rather try," Downey said. "We will not die in a hole. If we die, it will be for freedom..."*


...Erica Drake had never killed someone and she was able to justify her actions by convincing herself that Todd really wasn't killed. All she did was leave him somewhere. He was alive and well when she left him in the ocean—it wasn't technically murder. It was just abandonment with the possibility Todd wouldn't survive.

She tried to shake the incident from her head. Todd was a pretty good guy. In another time and place, she might have even gone for a guy like him, but he was really just a minor setback in the whole production. He'd really done this to himself. He never had to die. His death certificate had already been drawn up. The only way that could come undone was for him to resurface and he inevitably would have. It was his curiosity that had gotten him where he was. Erica didn't have a choice. If Todd would have had sufficient time to prove who she was, it would be over for her.

Now wasn't the time to quit. She'd gotten so far with Jason. She'd positioned herself to inherit half of what was his and by the time he passed away, he wouldn't know a thing. She'd never have to be exposed to anyone and that's how she liked it. She didn't want fingers pointed at her. She didn't want to be villainized. She was uncomfortable with the way Todd had come at her from out of nowhere. She didn't want to believe herself a bad person. She just wanted some money and to make Bernard Bell happy and all she was required to do was make a man fall for her and marry her. That was it. Todd Mason had been unexpected.

She had to push him over.

Of course, there was also the fire, but that was just too tempting. Her understanding of the deal was that the living beneficiaries wouldn't be alive for long, but from everything she'd heard, no one had died in quite some time. She loved Hawaii, but she wasn't sure what Bernard was doing back home. She knew he was gambling a lot and she knew he was wealthy and lived large. She wanted to be there with him. She wanted him there with her. She wanted to stop faking, especially if she was going to have to start getting her hands dirty.

"Penny for your thoughts," Jason said, turning away from the television that night. She hadn't even realized just how much she'd zoned out until he shook her out of it.

Erica brushed him off and as he constantly badgered her about why she was so quiet, she couldn't take it anymore. "I feel sick," she said, not entirely lying. "I'm going to bed."

"Alright, is there anything I can do for you?"

She shook her head no as there was a knock on the door. She froze in place, first looking at the clock: 10:00 pm. There was no reason in the world that they would have a visitor at this time. She knew at once it was the police. Someone saw something or someone reported Todd missing or...

Then a thought occurred to her. Maybe the Coast Guard saw him, or another boater. Maybe it was...

"I got this if you want to go to bed," Jason said, equally concerned about why they had a visitor this late. He walked to the door but Erica stayed behind, standing in the hallway which led to the bedroom, fixing her eyes on the door.

She heard Jason say "what's happening?" in his chummy way and she knew before she saw Todd standing there that she was going to have to answer for what she did.

*Or not.*

She couldn't be exposed. It wasn't even an option. She had no choice but to put on her game face without preparation or a plan. No matter what happened, Jason had to see Todd as the bad guy.

Todd entered and stared straight at Erica, never taking his eyes off of her. "Can we talk outside?" he asked Jason quietly.

"Yeah, what's up?"

"No," Erica said, abruptly. "I know what he's doing."

Jason turned, surprised to hear her desperate tone and looked between them momentarily, as if trying to comprehend what happened between his wife and his friend.

"He came onto me," Erica said. "Today we went out on the boat for some sun and he came onto me."

Jason turned to Todd for an answer.

"That's bullshit. Jason, we need to talk outside because I need to tell you this without being interrupted."

"Did you come on to her?" Jason asked.

"No."

"Yes he did and I shoved him over the side and left him. We were about half a mile from the docks and I knew he could drown but I was scared."

"You threw me over and we were over six miles from the shore!"

Erica feigned laughter. "If that were even true, how would you have gotten back?"

"I swam!" That was the moment both Todd and Erica could see it in Jason's eyes. He believed his wife. Todd had managed to pull off the impossible and because of that, no one would believe him. "I swam to the other island and took a ferry back."

Only Erica knew that to be true and inside, her stomach was turning because of Todd's will to survive and the problems that created for her.

"I'm your wife Jason. You know me. I thought I knew Todd. I thought he was a decent guy, but I was driving the boat and he came up behind me and put his arm around me. I tried to break free but then he held me tight and I could barely move so I pretended to give in and he kissed me and I only kissed him back because I was afraid, but the moment he let go of me so he could get his shorts off, I shoved him over."

She sold it, and Todd asked again if he could talk to Jason outside. Jason denied him the opportunity and told Erica to call the police. Erica ran off and Jason turned to Todd.

"You don't know what you're doing," Todd said. "Think about everything that's happened. She met you at the right time and said the right things and then brought you here. Man, you know me."

"I made every decision," Jason said. "And you better get out of my house before the police show up."

"Just stay calm and hear me out. Let me give you my side of this and if you want me gone, fine, but I think you need to pay close attention to her."

"What's her plan Todd? Who is she and what's her plan?"

"I don't know who she's connected to, but her plan was to make you her husband. That's all. She doesn't love you and she's a murderer. She left me in the middle of the ocean. She's probably the one who started the fire…"

Todd could say no more before Jason lashed out and grabbed him by the neck and slammed him hard against the wall. Todd fought back but was still weakened from the day's events. Jason shoved him outside and moments later, they were tangled up with each other, trying to grab at each other's limbs and throat, but Jason held the advantage, effectively pinning Todd to the ground and holding his hand to his throat.

"Don't ever come back here. If I see you again, I'll get a restraining order. You touch her again and I'll kill you."

"Jason..." Todd could barely talk and his face was red. "Please listen..."

Jason let go as the light of sirens flashed in the air. Jason slammed the door on his way in, leaving Todd in the sand.

## *Chapter 12*

### *1*

Anthony Freeman accepted the fact that he was going to die. It was a long time coming too. He'd wanted to kill himself multiple times throughout his life and failed and now death had been sneaking up on him and was whispering in his ear that the inevitable day was upon him.

His arm was infected and was a blotch of purple where the blood was evidently poisoned by the bomb inside of him. The end of his life would be an explosion in the wilderness that would baffle whoever came to investigate when it happened. His body would be torn apart and investigators wouldn't be able to make sense of any of it. Anthony could leave a note, send an email, even write a book, but the truth of his demise wasn't enticing enough to bother. What Anthony did desire was to use his misfortune to his advantage.

His refused for it all to end with an explosion in the night. He'd believed for too long that his survival had served a purpose and if in the end, his life had been delayed only to be ripped apart from the inside. What was the point of any of it?

There were clearly enemies. There was Stanley Kline, who had actually put the bomb inside of him. There was whoever murdered Abby Palmer in the middle of the night. There was the person who put the lottery in play that had gotten Anthony stabbed. When Anthony discovered that only Jason Stone's name hadn't been in the list of names to place bets on, he quickly accepted that the Stone name in which he hated when Victor carried it, had been handed down to the next generation. Jason was innocent on the outside, but he was his father in disguise. Anthony could end him with a simple act: Bring Jason to the same place and finally end his own life, ending Jason's in the process.

It wasn't easy to plot Jason's return to the states. Jason had no business with Anthony and there was nothing Anthony would be able to say to bring him home. He couldn't get on a plane because the bomb inside of him would set of any detector in the airport.

*I may just have to die. No purpose. No glory. No open casket.*

The bottle was all that was left when everything else was gone, but though Anthony had stocked up bottles of his old companion, he could only hold the bottle in his hand and feel comfort in the bottle's presence. To drink would be to end an era in which divided the era in which he was grateful to escape. But life had tricked Anthony Freeman. The things he believed he'd escaped from by tossing the bottle had come back to haunt him, even without having taken a drink. Alcohol had never been his poison. It had been in the air he'd breathed, in the life he was given. It was in being Anthony that the problem lived and to end the problem meant letting the explosive run its course—to let it take Anthony.

All he had was a number code to deactivate—something he couldn't trust, but couldn't ignore. What if Stanley had told Tarek the real number? He would have liked to ask himself, but Kern had metal detectors too and he wouldn't even have a chance to see Stan. He was perfectly isolated in every way.

His last attempt to bring Jason home was simply going to be to ask him. He told himself he'd leave it up to fate. If he could bring Jason home, he could end the Stone name. If he couldn't, there was no point to life. There was no purpose. There was no higher calling that was carving a path to some kind of meaning. Anthony was, and always had been, a pointless existence.

He sat on a picnic table with the bottle in one hand and his phone in the other. He dialed the number and took a deep breath…

*…Brock Dalton was somewhere between anxious and nervous to be meeting the author of the bestselling book Goodbye Cruel World. Ever since he'd heard the story of the author who once tried to hang himself but not before writing a suicide note turned bestseller, he was hooked on Anthony Freeman's career. When he received a message on his voice-mail at work for the LA Times from Anthony, secretly implying scandal, he jumped at the opportunity and called Anthony back.*

*They met once for coffee and didn't discuss business because Anthony wanted to test Brock's character and determine whether or not he trusted Brock with whatever he had. The conversation went well and Brock was certain he'd earned the story but two weeks passed before he heard back from Anthony and he'd given up by the time he received a second call.*

*Their second meeting was more discreet and Anthony was more paranoid this time around, looking over his shoulder every chance he got. They sat in the corner of a hole in wall pub, a thick wall of cigarette smoke between them.*

*"You can trust me Mr. Freeman. I hope you know that."*

*"I know I can," Anthony said. "Except I don't have a full story yet. Only pieces. I have attempted to put it together myself, but have had no luck. I'm reaching out because at this stage, I've exhausted my options."*

*"Start from the beginning and I'll see if I can help you."*

*Anthony started slowly, working his way toward the fateful night that he stood on a nightstand in a motel with a rope around his neck. He spoke of the mysterious stranger who talked him down and tricked him into believing life was worth living. Brock leaned in, anticipating the part where Anthony had a secret, but Anthony spun the tale with full details. Whatever Anthony had to say, he believed it to be the truth and looked deeply concerned.*

*Anthony spoke of the doubt that was shed on his story and the accusations that Anthony was only trying to profit off an engineered story that would relate to troubled people. He told Brock of his attempt to have his story collaborated by the witness at the motel, but Victor Stone denied being there that night.*

*"Victor Stone of Stone Enterprises?" Brock asked, to confirm the name.*

*"That's correct."*

*"Go on."*

*The name didn't faze Brock, but when Anthony carried on about the motel having no record of him from that night and the belief that someone really was murdered, Brock's full attention was on Anthony again.*

*"Why murder? You have no reason to believe murder."*

*"That's the story Victor gave me when he entered the room. He asked me to carry out the murder since I would die anyway and to sign a confession in my suicide note. I believed him and still believe that is what he wanted of me. You see Mr Dalton, there was no reason for Victor to be there that night. For him to have seen me drop a note on my doorstep, for him to have picked it up, he would have had to have been nearby watching. The fact that there is no record of he or I in that motel proves that something is being covered up."*

*"And you agreed to confess?"*

*"Yes."*

*"What changed your mind?"*

*"He left the room and in the moments before I was going to carry out my own death, I decided that I couldn't go through with allowing a man*

298|Tontine: The Scales of Justice

to die and for a lie to be carried out. I ran to stop it, but Victor was alone in the next room."

"Why do you think he was there?"

"Same reason he told me. I believe a man was murdered that night and that Victor's intent was to use my suicide to cover up the murder. When I didn't go through with it, they dismissed my part in it, but Victor bought my silence by doing me a favor...by having my manuscript published."

"That's deep."

"I've researched all disappearances and murders the night of. No body was found in the following days, but there were disappearances in Los Angeles. Most were runaways or gang related. There was one: A man named Gerald Wentworth. He worked for the police as an informant. Victor told me the man I would confess to was an officer."

Broke wrote down the name and looked up. "I'll start there. No record of him since?"

"He just disappeared from the earth that night. We've all heard whispers of corruption within big business in this city and Victor's name has been brought up more than once. On one hand, I owe this man my life and my success, but I'm alive because of a lie and if I stumbled onto a murder that has been covered up, then I need to know the truth."

"For your reputation or because it's the right thing to do?" Brock suspected Anthony was jaded by accusations of the legitimacy of his suicide.

"Both," Anthony said. "My career has thrived because I was shamefully honest in my manuscript and my honesty has been called into question. What sold books was raw and brutal honesty and without it, I may as well be dead."

They talked for another hour and Anthony ran up a tab higher than he ever had. He was a stranger to excessive alcohol but the booze flowed freely that night, releasing him from the constant ricocheting of theories in his head for the last year. It was nice to finally tell the truth to someone and form a partnership again, to move forward in his life, and to walk a line toward the truth. By the end of the night, he felt like he was released from a burden and though that burden would resurface along with a headache the next morning, that was the night Anthony first realized an escape from his problems that would be the first of many escapes.

"I'll see what I can find on this guy and cross reference to Victor. Sound good for now?" Brock walked Anthony out and called him a cab.

"Yes," Anthony said, his words long and drawn out when he spoke.

"You've been carrying this around Mr. Freeman. Take a vacation from this burden for a bit until I get back to you. Enjoy yourself."

That was exactly what Anthony intended on doing...

...The other line rang repeatedly and Anthony closed his eyes while he waited. It couldn't end like this. Jason couldn't just dodge...

"Hello?" Jason's voice on the other end came across as cautious. Anthony didn't like it and sensed talking to the man who'd almost killed him wasn't going to be easy.

"Jason Stone. This is Anthony Freeman."

A pause. "Is everything okay?"

"I've been doing some investigating into the lottery."

"Lottery..."

"The lottery that resulted in my attach," Anthony said. He couldn't hide his irritation at the game Jason was trying to play.

"I've been away awhile. I knew something happened to you but I didn't know the details. Tarek Appleton told me you were accusing me of this."

Anthony chuckled and shook his head in disbelief. "I would like to see you in person," he said when the laughter subsided.

"You know I'm a thousand miles away, right?"

"I do know that. Why is that Mr. Stone? Why would the man with everything just up and move to Hawaii?"

"You just answered your own question. Because I can. Have I done something wrong?"

"You've been working behind the scenes to have us all killed," Anthony said. "I have proof."

Another pause. "I don't know what you're trying to do or what you think I did, but I've been gone a while. I'm married now and I want nothing to do with LA."

"I'd like you to come and see me."

"No thank you."

The phone clicked and Anthony started to redial but thought better of it. He let the phone fall to his side and buried his head in his hands. If Jason was ever going to come home, he certainly wouldn't come near Anthony. He considered the fact that he could always spot a liar and Jason's confusion seemed genuine, but he reminded himself he was dealing with Victor's son and that Victor could be charming and persuasive but was really a monster on the inside.

"What's happening friend?" Nick shouted as he emerged from his Winnebago for the morning with a beer in his hand and some metal pots in the other. "I'm making omelets over the fire. You in?"

"Of course." Anthony spotted the beer in Nick's hand. He'd never wanted one more than in this moment. He'd started talking himself into believing it didn't matter anymore if he drank. When the end was near, who cared what bad habits he picked up? His drinking before had been tempered because he ruined other lives with it. In the middle of the wilderness with a buddy, it was just a drink. Nick had gotten drunk the night before and behaved as bad as Anthony usually did. They were driving anywhere and they weren't getting kicked out of bars. The worst he could do was take a piss in the river and the rangers had stopped checking on Anthony after two months. It was still early. He'd make up his mind later.

Then he realized something so jarring that he almost fell off the picnic table he'd propped himself up on.

*This may well be the last day of my life.*

He'd exhausted his options. Jason was far away and safe. Anthony wasn't leaving these woods. There was nowhere left to go, nothing left to do, and the only friend he had in the world had a mutual death wish. Neither would have to die alone.

Anthony watched Nick as he walked to the river and started coughing heavily.

"You okay?" Anthony asked. He saw a stream of blood fall from Nick's lip and he ran to help. "What can I do?" Anthony asked.

"Nothing." Nick began coughing again and Anthony stood back but patted him on the shoulder. It was hard to watch, but Nick had been doing this awhile and had accepted his own fate. Anthony looked in the man's eyes, which were sunken and red.

"Tonight," Anthony said.

"Tonight," Nick repeated. His voice sounded small and tired.

"You take care of breakfast. I'll cook up the best dinner you've ever eaten. We'll do some fishing, play some cards…"

"We'll drink," Nick said.

"Yes," Anthony agreed, but his voice was shaky. Even on the last day of his life, he felt as if he was betraying himself. He reminded himself that it didn't matter. "We'll drink, and when we're good and tired and ready to retire, you can enter the numbers and we'll let fate take it from there."

Nick looked up with exhaustion. "Sounds like a deal."

## 2

Charlie Palmer was consumed with pain, both physical and mental. It was all he could think about when he finally woke up. For the first few days, it felt like a dream. To see and feel nothing below the knees was something he could have never believed possible. He would fall asleep, sure he'd wake up again and be sitting in front of the television before joining Mindy for dinner. Or maybe he would wake up and find Abby there, or maybe he'd learn he never even met Abby Patterson and everything that had ever happened had been in his head.

His brain had been damaged at a young age when he flipped over the front of his bicycle. His parents were scared that whatever damage was done was permanent, but Charlie pulled through and the opposite happened: He became smarter, more driven, with something to prove. Before his bicycle accident, he didn't care much for school. He only cared to skateboard and go to baseball games with his friends. When his head was damaged, he studied instead, as if putting information into his brain would fix it. In a way, it did, but only because Charlie's transformation was mental. Physically, he would forever-more have headaches and lack focus. Life was about the brain, how the brain worked, how the brain was supposed to think.

Having no legs was something new entirely. It was a chapter of his life that should never have been written. Somewhere in life, about the time the will had been read, there no longer existed such a thing as normalcy. So much had happened in such a short time, in fact, that he couldn't even remember why he was here. He tried to trace time forward as far as he could remember, but he stopped at the day Richard Libby died. He had been waiting to see if Adlar Wilcox would arrive to support Richard's cause. He wasn't sure what he would have said if Adlar had been there, but he wasn't, and in time, the days just blended together.

Charlie and Mindy, spending their evenings together, falling for each other and creating a life together. The old insecure Charlie had become a thing of the past. He'd sat outside the bedroom door while his wife died behind it, and after that day, there was no such thing as character flaws that Charlie needed to hide. Being him had been easy because he was too consumed with masking the truth about Abby's death to worry about insecurities. Just as an accident had once fixed his brain, Abby's death had fixed his insecurity. He was suddenly confident and grateful for everything he had. In becoming a stronger person, Adlar Wilcox had been forgotten, but somewhere deep in his head, Charlie knew that Adlar had something to do with why he was here. And Royce Morrow.

He spent hours answering police questions and working with doctors and nurses. He had many visitors but when he was alone with his thoughts, he tried to fill in the blanks, always unable to hold his concentration. When he tried to think about Adlar, his mind only traced back to the night Abby died and refused to think forward in time. Adlar Wilcox had only been there once in his life and his mind would forever hold onto that moment.

The police told Charlie it had been an explosion and that someone clearly had been in the home. He didn't give them anything they could work with, and once again, Charlie had left Adlar for himself. All he needed was confirmation that Adlar really had tried to kill him, but every time he thought about Adlar, his mind redirected to the night Abby died.

One day, as he was staring into the dark as he usually did, he realized he'd been staring directly at Mindy, who stood in the doorway with her arms crossed. It was the first he'd seen her since he woke up and there was no love in her eyes. He'd expected this would happen eventually.

"Everyone says I should leave you," she said.

Charlie didn't have the energy to make an excuse, but refused to apologize. He only gave her a blank stare, realizing his lack of love for her too. It might have been there once, but Charlie had no love for anyone. He didn't want to see his family or friends. He didn't want compliments or prestige. He wanted to sit in the dark until he could move again and then walk out and never turn back.

"Did you hear me?" Mindy asked.

"You made a statement," Charlie said, his voice parched and deadpan.

"And how did you feel about it?"

"What are you hoping I'll do?" Charlie asked. "Give you a reason to stay with me? I don't want you. Get out of my life."

Mindy began to tear up but found the strength to say what she really had been there to say. "You burned our home to the ground and you're telling me to get out of your life?"

"I didn't burn your house down. It wasn't yours."

"It was your shit!" she shouted. "Just like with your wife and everything about your life! You're responsible!"

"The guy who killed Abby and the guy who did this…I did nothing to him!" Charlie shouted back. He wanted to get out of bed and walk away from her, but he couldn't even do that. Instead, he was left to face her until she walked out. "He just picked me and Abby. No reason…just picked us!"

"And you've sat on this without doing anything," she said. "You want to refuse to tell me who he is and why he did this, fine, but you could have told the police. You could have done something about it. Instead, you did what you always do: Nothing. You didn't stop him, you didn't save your wife, you didn't discuss it with me so we could have figured something out. Instead, you just did that thing where you sat on it all by yourself and hoped it would go away."

"Are you enjoying kicking me when I'm down? I'm sorry you lost a place to live, but I lost my fucking legs! Get the hell away from me!"

"I moved here for you."

"Then move back. Can't you see I'm toxic? Can't you see that everything around me dies!"

Mindy backed into the door-frame and Charlie breathed easier. He wanted her to go away and never come back. He wanted to be alone.

"You're going to get better someday," Mindy said. "You'll learn to live with this and you'll pick up where you left off, but when you do and you start feeling guilty, don't bother apologizing. Don't even come near me. You're a talented surgeon, but you're a broken man."

She left him there to dwell on words he already knew to be true, but he didn't care. Of course he was broken. He'd always been broken, but there were some things that could never be fixed, and never would be. Charlie's day in the sun had come and gone. He'd loved and been loved by a beautiful woman. He'd had a career in which everyone believed he was a hero. For awhile, he'd been an amazing man doing miraculous things. Those days were over and would never be revived. Charlie was young but the good part of life was over and all that was left were dark days.

He could kill himself now, but there were loose ends that needed to be tied. He wasn't going to give Adlar the luxury of going quietly. There were things that needed to be done and his mind was beyond caring about what was illegal, immoral, or how he was perceived in his actions. All that mattered was finishing what he should have finished when Abby died. He needed to be repaired and when he was repaired, he needed to draw Adlar out and make him suffer. As he thought about everything he'd had and lost and what he was going to do about it, the blanks began to fill in until he remembered everything.

## 3

Nick brought his nephew Brice to meet Anthony. Brice was a junior studying medicine and was hired by Anthony and Nick to do some research as well as borrow a few instruments that would be needed to get a good look at the bomb. Brice came through for them with flying colors. Everything needed to numb the pain, cut him open, and restitch the wound was there. The stitches may never be used, but in the case Stan had provided the real number, they would be needed.

The second thing Brice had been tasked with was researching code. Stan had told Tarek that the deactivate code was 12211988.

Anthony's first thought was that it was a date: December 21st, 1988, but there was nothing that linked the date to Stanley Kline. Tarek told Anthony that Stan spoke the numbers as if they were memorized, that it didn't seem as if he'd made them up. Stan could have changed a number or transposed a couple and Anthony wouldn't have any way of knowing.

Regardless, Brice was tasked with finding birthdays of everyone in Stan's life. None came close to the date. Stan had been married in March, his kids Birthdays fell in February and July, his own was December 10th, but the year was off. The date had no significance that could cross reference to anything related to Stan. It could have been a badge number, it could have been lotto numbers he played, he could have just made the whole thing up. The first five numbers were all ones and twos, which led Anthony to believe that Stan may have just been spouting off a number. If he were forced to guess, Anthony would say he was 80% sure that the number Stan gave Tarek was made up on the spot.

Brice had been helpful in researching code and supplying them, but there was too much uncertainty as far as the code went.

"I have an idea," Anthony said. "But it will have to be you because I couldn't get near him."

His idea involved Nick making a trip to Kern and confronting Stan himself, which Nick willingly did. He admitted that Stan gave him the chills when it was over, but when he'd asked Stan for the number, Stan gave the same eight digits without hesitation.

"The number means something," Nick said.

"He could have memorized the number. We have no way of knowing for certain."

"Well, I'm willing to put it in," Nick said. "It's worth a try."

"Is it worth your life?"

"Damn right it is. This could be the most exciting thing I've ever done. I either save your life or I get blown to smithereens and save myself the slow death. That's a win win."

Anthony pulled his shoulder forward and flinched at the pain it caused. His flesh was bright blue and he was starting to feel numb all the way down his back. "When?" Anthony asked. "When would we attempt to rip this band-aid off of me?"

"You said tonight," Nick said with enthusiasm, which was followed by uncontrollable coughing.

"You don't understand this man," Anthony said. "I don't believe the numbers he gave us will deactivate the bomb."

"You don't understand me," Nick mocked. "I don't care. Unless you want to live to see another day, I vote tonight. You just let me know so I can go blow the rest of my life savings on a woman and some booze."

Anthony chuckled as Nick disappeared into the trees to relieve himself. He watched the river, his eyes following every leaf and piece of debris that sat on the surface of the water. There were no loose ends he was interested in anymore. Jason Stone, Stanley Kline, Bernard Bell...all were just people who like Victor, would always be free of consequences.

He couldn't get his hands on Jason. They were an ocean apart. If Anthony was a man who believed in following the signs, there had been no clearer indicator that now was the time to let go. The world had never been fair. Quite frankly, the world was shit to Anthony. It was time to make his departure.

Nick emerged from the trees, zipping his fly.

"We'll need to make a run to the market," Anthony said. "Grab a bottle of the best that money could buy. I don't think I'll be able to do this sober…"

… *"Fourth night in a row you're in here drunk. Are you okay Mr. Freeman?"*

*Anthony looked up from the bar and nodded at the bartender, who went on his way with a shake of the head. Anthony finished the drink sitting in front of him and fixated on the rows of bottles at the bar. He had been out a lot, but it was the perfect cure for boredom and it helped him think. Interacting with other bar patrons gave him ideas, conjured fascinating conversations, but also made Anthony forget about Victor.*

*Until he'd wake up the next morning, covered in sweat and a migraine eating at his brain.*

*It was a Tuesday night, so the bar was nearly empty, except for the bartender and a couple in the corner. Anthony was about to call it a night when Dan Nottebart entered the bar, already drunk, and ordered a whiskey and Coke at the bar before stumbling to the billiards table. Anthony stood and approached.*

*"You want to play?" Anthony asked.*

*"You any good?" Dan asked.*

*"Not at all."*

*"Good. Me either." Dan inserted a couple quarters in the slot and set up the balls. He broke and immediately proved he wasn't an experienced billiards player. The game went on for awhile and by the time it was over, both men were sick of playing and had a seat at the bar together. The bar had a few more patrons and Anthony and Dan sat backwards on their stool, taking in the atmosphere and people watching.*

*Dan nodded toward a drunken guy in his early twenties, trying to talk to two attractive women, who clearly weren't interested. "I can hear the conversation in my head as it happens."*

*Anthony chuckled.*

*"You know," Dan continued. "People like to give me a hard time because I come here a lot, but I tell you what: I never see more clearly than when I've got a good buzz and I get the chance to watch people interact."*

*"Why's that?" Anthony asked.*

*"It clears your brain of all the bullshit. All the distractions floating around in your mind are gone and there's clarity. I look at people and I see who they really are. Not who they're trying to be on the surface, but who they are in their core."*

*"How do you know your assumptions are correct?"*

*"I just do. It's not a guessing game. I just see it."*

*"You drink because it makes you smarter?"*

*"You could say that, dumb as it sounds."*

*"You got me pegged?" Anthony asked, turning his attention to his new friend.*

*"A little. It's not hard to see you're here to escape some shit going on in your life."*

*"Everyone is. What else?"*

*"You're an artist."*

*"Now I'm impressed. I'm an author, but close enough."*

*"I knew it," Dan said. "Crossed my mind. And it's not working out how you hoped."*

*"What's not working out?"*

*"You're not getting the glory you deserve."*

*"You believe aspiring to be a writer means you do it for the glory. That's a myth that needs to be debunked."*

*"Still impressive to get yourself published."*

*"Authors are a dime a dozen. In fact, because the cost of printing and marketing usually supersedes profits, most authors never see profit. That never mattered though. I write for the reason I believe all authors should: I have something to say."*

*"Except you're here because you're blocked, right? Which means you have nothing to say, but you want to say it anyway."*

*"How truly profound. There's a glimmer of truth to that. The truth is that I'm looking for clarity. Unfortunately, unlike you, I'm not finding it in the booze."*

*"Then you're not looking hard enough. Let it clear your mind." Dan nodded back to the bar where all the action was happening. "Look at the playing field Anthony. See, drunks always get a bad rap, but we're at our most honest after a few drinks. We get moody, hungry, horny, violent—all the things we already have within ourselves but they come out in spades. It's our innermost evil surfacing and it's not pretty. Honest, but not pretty. Just look around."*

*Anthony observed the room, trying to find what it was that Dan claimed to see.*

*"Our senses are heightened here. I can see every lonely loser trying to*

*pick up every girl who comes here to reject men, to feel good about themselves while they secretly hope they're going to meet prince charming. If you watch closely, you can hear every word coming out of their mouths."*

*As Dan speaks, Anthony is hypnotized by the moment, his vision blurring, taking away the details of their faces and replacing them with characters he could have written himself.*

*The couple in the corner was no longer speaking. Both were on their cell phones, engaged in other conversations. The bartender was leaning against the bar, seemingly waiting the clock out. The drunken man was still talking to the girls while they exchanged looks at each other, telling each other with their eyes that he was pathetic. Anthony saw them from the inside out, knew everything about them without really knowing anything.*

*"You wanna blow your mind?" Dan said, leaning in. "Have a few more drinks, go home and write until you pass out. Read what you have tomorrow. You'll be amazed..."*

…. Brice swore secrecy, but after seeing Anthony's condition, he stood back with deep skepticism, seemingly afraid to be too close to a man who could die and take them all down with him.

After a long discussion, when Brice was comfortable enough to help, he edged closer and took a look at the skin around the bomb. It looked to be pulsating and Brice couldn't imagine the pain Anthony must have been feeling.

"I can numb it and cut you open," Brice said. "I'll expose the keypad for you and you do what you need to do."

"What happens to him if it works?" Nick asked.

"I'll leave my card. Just give me a call and I'll stitch it back up. Then, and I'm not kidding around on this, you need to go straight to the ER so they can take it out. Even when the bomb is deactivated, you'll need to treat the infection."

They set to work. Anthony winced as Brice stuck a needle in him and numbed the area. Anthony knew the next hours wouldn't be pleasant, but this was all that was left to do. Nick stood back and watched Anthony, his face muscles tightening as he clenched his jaw. When the incision was made and the skin pulled back, Nick felt as if he could faint, but held strong for his friend. It wouldn't be long until Nick had his own hand on the keypad. He knew he had no choice other than to fight whatever queasiness the situation brought on.

"Unbelievable," Brice said as his eyes scanned the bomb. "The guy wasn't kidding with you, but how he got this in you is beyond me."

"What do you see?" Anthony asked.

"Not much. It's just a few wires but there's definitely a circuit here. Problem is that most of it is attached to the muscle. Usually to deactivate a bomb, you have to detach the circuit from the explosive component. In your case, we'd be stopping your heart, so it's lose lose. Your only bet here is to have the right code."

Anthony looked to Nick, who only shook his head. "Well, I suppose we're going through with it then."

Anthony stared off into the distance and considered his situation. He knew the code couldn't be right, but all that was left was one last roll of the dice. This was going to be the last day of his life and he found he wasn't fully prepared. He'd wanted to end his life so badly in the past and only failed, but he didn't want this to be it. It wasn't on his terms. He left nothing behind—only a mess. His body wouldn't be recognizable. The plot of land was in his name and that would be the discovery that put his name on the front page, shrouded in a mystery of just how a man burst from the inside out. It would spark rumors of spontaneous combustion, or the worst case of acid reflux on record.

Brice pulled Nick aside for a private conversation. It was likely that he was telling his uncle that what he was doing was crazy…that Anthony was a stranger and that he was going to die. It was nothing Nick didn't already know and though Anthony appreciated the old man's loyalty, he felt regret that he was taking him from his nephew, who seemed like a good guy. After the conversation ended, they returned. Brice had quietly accepted Nick's final wishes. They hugged and Brice reminded Nick to call him immediately if the code actually worked. Then he gave Anthony a nod and told him "good luck" before disappearing on the trail back to his car. When he was gone, reality set in and Nick and Anthony sat quietly for a long moment. Neither wanted to be the one to suggest they get started, but Anthony knew it was he who had to initiate it.

"When do we do this?" Anthony said.

"We should get the fire going. Have a hurrah and celebrate life. We don't need to make this a bad experience."

Anthony liked the idea and as the sun set, the fire began to burn and Anthony and Nick talked about their good memories. The more Anthony relayed stories, the more he realized that the good overshadowed the bad —that life never was really the way he'd described it in his head. The shame, the rivalries, the rumors and lies about who he was, what he was, what his intentions were. None of it mattered. Everyone would be gone and forgotten in a hundred years and all the things Anthony had always moaned about would be trivial for only a fragment of time.

And then Jason Stone came into his mind and he grew quiet. Nick saw

Anthony's face and knew the time was closing in. Then Anthony did something he believed he'd never do again, but in the moment, nothing mattered anymore.

"I'd like a drink," he said.

Nick coughed into his sleeve for a moment before looking up with tired eyes. "You sure about that?"

"I am," Anthony said. "I need it."

4

No matter how hard he tried, Charlie couldn't shake the events of the last few weeks. He had and endless amount of time to sit in bed and relive everything on a loop. Abby's death…the day he became a murderer…the explosion that crushed his legs and ruined him forever…

Even if Adlar appeared now, Charlie couldn't catch up to him if he slowly walked away. He'd never been so helpless in his life. It was time to accept that he could never do this on his own. His mind spun a sea of possibilities, from Royce to Trish…even to Adlar's parents. He could hold a gun to them in their home and draw Adlar out.

He shook the idea from his head, ashamed of what he'd become.

*I had no choice. He did this to me.*

It was a completely unprovoked attack.

*It was retaliation.*

Charlie had moved on. He'd gotten past it all.

*Karma caught up to you.*

He closed his eyes and whispered "I deserved this," but it didn't heal his pain.

Manny Quinny was the only person in the world who could really help Charlie. If there was a price, Charlie would pay it. He'd give Manny anything he wanted as long as he took Adlar down. Royce believed Manny was a conspirator and Charlie knew it was probably true, but that didn't matter. He was all he had.

Charlie used his phone to find the number for LA's homicide division. He called and asked for Manny but was told Manny was usually out or busy and couldn't take calls on the business line. Charlie asked for a better number and he was told no one would give Manny's personal number to a stranger.

Finally, Charlie said, "tell him Charlie Palmer called."

After the call, he felt a burden lift from his shoulders and he fell asleep within minutes. Charlie had been exhausted but his mind kept spinning and every time he'd come close to falling asleep, his eyes would snap open as if he needed to retain what he'd been thinking about. When he did fall asleep, it would always be a nightmare that awoke him. Once, Abby had been there with him in the hospital. She held a leg in her arms and though in normal context it made no sense, in the dream, he knew she would attach it to his body and become a part of him. Just as she was about to connect the pieces, a wound formed in her stomach and a bloodstain spread. She fell back and Adlar stood behind her. Charlie tried to go to his wife but he only fell from the bed, unable to reach her.

After calling Manny, there were no nightmares. He slept well. He woke up the next morning to find missed calls on his cell phone throughout the night. All had been from an unknown number, so he waited for the next call, which didn't come until early afternoon.

When his phone buzzed, he fumbled with it and with a shaking hand, answered the call. "Hello?"

"You're awake."

Charlie had never heard the voice but knew who was speaking. "Are you the detective?"

"You shouldn't have called me."

"I know who was behind what happened," Charlie said. "I only have issues with him."

"That may be," Manny said. "But it's not that simple. You killed my guy."

"Excuse me?"

"On the rooftop. You killed my guy. Now, that may not mean much to you and I already know you thought you were after Wilcox, but all things in life have consequences Dr. Palmer. It seems that Mr. Morrow and Mr. Wilcox have been paying your debt for you and I tell you what, I shouldn't have allowed that because if there's a god in the sky that's balancing the scales, he's blocking everyone else's effort to pay your debt."

"I'm paying it every day," Charlie's voice was cold. "I can't walk. I lost my wife."

"You shouldn't have called," Manny said. "I figured you'd be toast… didn't think you'd make it. I wasn't coming back."

Charlie's voice caught in his throat. "Wh…"

"My life's been a mess Dr. Palmer. I'm usually someone who can keep things buttoned up but this has been out of control. It's time we put all this to rest, don't you think?"

"I will pay you anything to bring me Adlar. He's to blame for everything."

"Your bullet. Your debt. We'll be in touch."

Charlie tried to say more but the call ended abruptly and he was left regretting his decision to call. The man didn't care that Charlie was suffering. He was too angry Charlie killed his guy. He'd be in for another sleepless night and as if to prove his point, every noise in the hall, every member of the staff that walked past his door, caused him to freeze up. The pain in his body, from his lower spine to the nubs that were his legs, ached. A migraine began to form as the stress of the situation built in him. He not only would never avenge his wife's death. He would soon be dead too. He thought about leaving the hospital. Why not? What's left but to roam around the city in a wheelchair and let fate have its way with him? He had no career, nowhere to go, no one in his life. All that was left was rage and fear.

He struggled into the wheelchair and went to the hallway. He hurried to the water faucet, nearly running into an orderly on the way. "Watch it!" he said angrily. He found water and leaned in, letting it splash in his face as he drank. When he finished, he caught his breath and turned the wheelchair, letting his head rest against the wall and gasping for air. When he opened his eyes, in the distance, he saw Dr. Neomin standing with a clipboard and taking a patient into a room.

*Neomin.*

For the life of him, he couldn't remember what business he had with Neomin. His mind could only go one place, but as he caught his breath, he knew there was something he was missing and there were things undone.

## 5

The buzz was far more guilt-free than Anthony had ever remembered. Even when he was an alcoholic, the first few bottles were only the preface for a night that he knew he'd later forget. The regretful words and anger he'd displayed in his darkest hours, the way he'd risk his own life and others as he got behind the wheel on his way home, and the intolerable headache the next day, only curable by drinking more and doing the dance all over again.

In the course of the night, Anthony and Nick learned all the intimate details of each others life stories. Nothing was held back and both men had enough mistakes between them that there was no shame. When the night was at it's darkest and the bottles were nearly dry, both men fell silent, except for Nick's fit of coughs every few minutes.

"You ever think about what might have been if our paths crossed much earlier?" Nick asked.

"We would have had nothing in common," Anthony said. They both fell silent, thinking the same thing. Anthony said it first. "We should do this."

Nicolas positioned himself behind Anthony, with easier access to the circuitry.

"Please keep talking," Anthony said.

Nicolas let out a wheezing cough before going on. "My brother works for an insurance company. Did you know that a lot of the time, fatality rates involving sport utility vehicles actually save insurers money? By killing people who might otherwise have survived serious injuries, money is saved because severe injuries produce larger settlements than death. It's not just the poor and the maniacs who are cheaper dead than alive. It's actually almost all of us."

Anthony liked Nick's random musings, but at the moment, nothing could shake his fear of what would happen next. "Tell me something nice," Anthony said. "What was the best moment of your life?"

"I stole my first wife from a marine. It's harsh, I know, but he wasn't right. Just some mindless jerk so taken with her looks that he wouldn't even recognize how much this miniature woman in front of him was in need of consolation and repair. My frathouse threw this party and my friend at the time was making out with some other girl. Catherine caught him and started drinking. Then she started dancing and I noticed. When she danced, I thought she was quite beautiful, so totally lost in the majesty of music. The sound took her away and I admired her for letting it. I knew that what I saw in her face was what Id see if we'd make love. She had what cops called a getaway face. So beautiful it would always be a shield, no matter what she did or what was done to her, that face was her ticket. It would open doors for her close them behind her. It would let her get away."

"What did you do?"

"Picked a fight with my marine friend. Told him he had no idea what he had. He kicked my ass all over the place, but then Catherine told him to get lost and he left with that other girl. Catherine took me home and took care of me while I healed for two days. On day three, we made love. One month later, we were married. Now, it's your turn."

"I've never been in love," Anthony said, flatly. "I was told at a very young age that I was a genius. That came with a sense of responsibility. A woman would have hampered what I believed was going to be a spectacular life. I was either oversold my gift or I underused it. I spend most of my time looking back at life and wondering where, if at all, I might have traveled another path. For any game with a finite number of sequential moves, there's always one best strategy. Of course, that strategy is nearly impossible to find when looking at your own life. Just as you were taken away by a pretty face, you'll never know the endless alternate lives you'd have lived if you'd married another girl, if you'd decided to go into the military or moved to Europe. I do know that there are very likely some paths that feel as if they are perfect and others that are utterly wrong. I've made too many mistakes Nicolas. I've allowed my ego the driver's seat and I've shunned many good people who I believed were beneath me. If I had truly been a genius, you would think I'd have known better."

"By most accounts, wasn't Sir Isaac Newton a narcissistic, misogynistic, egocentric curmudgeon?" Nicolas said. "Yet, his light, gravity, and the structure of the cosmos stand on their own and would be no more or less if he were a saintly gentleman. When our past pain becomes our present identity, the shame cycle claims another victim. Stop picking at the scab or you will always live a life of unhealed pain."

"Words to live by if I'd heard them forty years ago."

"I've got this thing in front of me now," Nicolas said. "I can key in the numbers and you may live to see another day. You're no spring chicken, but if this thing doesn't go off, and you can get yourself treated, you've still have some years in you. Most great things that happen boil down to one day in time."

Anthony tossed the last of the bottle onto the dirt and watched it roll on the ground. "I'm at the mercy of the numbers."

"I'll do this then," Nick said. Both men paused a long time, and didn't acknowledge that so far, nothing happened. Anthony's eyes grew heavy and he let himself fall asleep, thinking it wouldn't be such a bad thing to prolong the inevitable. After some time, Anthony's eyes opened again and he realized that too much time had passed. He wondered if it worked or if his friend fell asleep at his side. He turned to find Nick sprawled out on the ground. His first thought was that the man had a little too much booze himself, but the coughing had ceased, the wheezing was gone, and Anthony listened closely but found no evidence that Nicolas was even in a deep sleep. He leaned down and felt for a pulse.

Nothing.

He let out a shaky breath and without weighing all that had happened, he lay across from his friend and stared at him for a long moment before closing his eyes and passing out...

*...What started as a way to focus turned into a nightly habit. He'd grab a few drinks at the bar and go home and sit in front of his typewriter. Every morning, he would wake up and reread his writing, which wasn't good, but there was more content than he could provide sober. Sober Anthony would then edit drunk Anthony's work and it wasn't half bad. It did bruise his ego to know that it wasn't until he turned off his brain that he was able to think.*

Pretty soon, it became habitual and there were nights when Anthony came home and fell into his bed without typing a thing. He would wake up the next day and curse himself for a day wasted. He'd try to write sober but came up with nothing, so he'd reread previous days and tweak what he could. As this routine imprinted on his life, he found himself writing less and less, but the thing that didn't change was his nights in the bar, mingling with strangers and putting back booze until last call. In Anthony's mind, last call would come sooner and sooner and the tab at the end of the night would routinely increase.

A month passed. Then another. Soon, Anthony didn't read his work. He'd set it aside for another day. Eventually, there was no desire to write at all. He called it "time off" from his craft. He told himself he'd come back to it when he felt like it, but that day kept getting pushed out.

The days blurred together and Anthony didn't remember much substance day to day, other than the sun comes up and the sun goes down. Somewhere in-between, he cured his boredom with a drink in the hand. He never felt more comfortable, more himself, than when he held a glass and sat on a stool, staring at whatever the bar had to offer. He would people watch and think about what other patrons were thinking, confident he had them all pegged. It was a lesson in psychology for him, and he'd proudly jot mental notes in his head, sure he'd created a character or had a deep insight, but by the time he woke up the next day, it was forgotten.

He didn't realize what was happening to him at the time. He believed he was in a controlled environment, immune to the consequences of his habit, but when Anthony was sober, he would tell people that all bad things eventually came to a head. He would have warned himself if he believed that he was doing something destructive. Instead, he lied to himself night after night and disguised his new-found habit as stress relief.

It was a Tuesday night, which was the night the bar was emptiest, that he arrived early and stayed until the end. He didn't know what it was that made him desperate for more alcohol but he tipped the bottle to the last drop that night and for the first time, he felt no joy. He sat at the bar and gazed at the bottles across from him, lined up in front of a mirror. He caught his reflection and realized how old he looked.

"Randy..." he said, and the bartender turned, kindly indulging him. Anthony couldn't see the knowing judgment in the bartender's eyes...eyes that had seen more than their fair share of depressed people drinking themselves stupid.

"What's happening Anthony?"

"Tell me a story."

*"I think I've told you every story I got."*

*"Then I'll tell you one."*

*"I think you've told me every story you got too."*

*"Son, you don't have the years in your bones to have heard every story I got."*

*"Yeah, well last call is in five minutes and I'm doing the work for two tonight, so you'll have to tell your story another time. Can I call you a cab?"*

*"Don't need one."*

*"I think you do. I think you may have broken a record and I'd like to see you leave here in a cab."*

*"No thanks," Anthony grumbled.*

*Randy sized him up, feeling sorry for him. He'd watched Anthony's fall, from a man just trying to find the words in him to this. "How's the book coming?"*

*Anthony waived his hand dismissively with an exaggerated gesture. "Humbug. I'll let you know when I get a good start."*

*"Why is writing so difficult? Shouldn't you be just itchin to say something?"*

*"Let me tell you something about writing. It is the only art form that is not sensual. You can see the colors and strokes of a painting, feel a sculpture, and hear music, but every writer uses the same letters on a piece of paper. You have twenty-six letters that combine to form words, which are the building blocks of your sentences and paragraphs. Everyone has the same words and when I write that word and you write it, that word goes into the senses of the reader in the same way. It's how we weave them together that impacts in the conscious and subconscious mind of the reader that makes all the difference in the world. To write well, you must get it right every time. We've all got the same letters." He trailed off and took another swig of his drink.*

*"Well, I hope you work through it. I've heard good things."*

*Anthony stayed as long as Randy allowed, trying to negotiate his way to another drink, but he refused to budge on the taxi. He told Randy it was a five minute drive and he'd done it many times before. Finally, Randy made him leave and Anthony stepped into the night, savoring the feel of a crisp breeze blowing through his thinning hair. He walked to his car in an uneven line, his mind on what to do next instead of going home to bed.*

*After he got in his car and drove past the bar, he began to wonder why this night had seemed different. Maybe it had been the lack of people in the bar but Anthony felt a depression starting grip him. He'd been suicidal in the past, so he made a mental note to make sure he contained whatever negative emotions he was having. He reminded himself that he was on vacation.*

*He noticed he'd left his phone in his car and that he had a message from Brock Daltan. It had been a long time since he'd talked to the reporter. He'd been forgotten, just as Victor Stone had been erased from his memory for some time.*

*He listened to the message.*

*"Hey Anthony, this is Brock. Sorry it's been a while but I was following up on some leads. Anyway, we need to talk. Long story short, I looked into Gerald Wentworth and you were right. Last time he was seen was the night you met Victor. But get this..."*

*That was when his car crashed into a bicycle and sent a teenage girl rolling onto the hood. He slammed the brakes and gasped at once, his eyes wide with terror. When the car was stopped, the body lay on the hood, barely moving but eyes wide open, staring back at Anthony through a cracked windshield.*

## Chapter 13

### 1

*Wedding planning wasn't up Charlie Palmer's alley, but he went along with it because he knew Abby's father wasn't fond of him and her mother wouldn't be if the real Charlie came out. What he wanted to do was talk about how shitty the taste testing went and how disappointed he was in the band. He also had hoped to steer away from a traditional church wedding, but Abby insisted and said it was too important to her. She didn't say it out loud, but he knew it was a deal-breaker.*

*It just so happened that most of Abby's family was in attendance a week before the wedding started, offering their services and going above and beyond to make sure the wedding was a success. One week before the wedding, Charlie would work his last day at Banner General for a month. He was bummed he'd have to take a break.*

*Charlie loved his job. It wasn't the staff or the environment that made him look forward to going to work daily. It was the prestige. He'd been labeled as a miracle man. His surgical skills were polished and he was sharp and worked with precision. His reputation fueled him and he was always ready for the next surgery, anticipating the accolades he would receive when finished. There could never be too many cards, baked good, and letters to the chief in gratitude of the work Charlie did.*

*Home life was where Charlie held less confidence, but he'd accepted that, Abby was with him for the long haul. The things he'd always believed were red flags in his character were all overlooked by Abby and she believed him to be the perfect man for her. He'd lucked out. Finding a woman was supposed to be the challenging part of his life, but Abby Patterson had made it easy because no matter what Charlie did or said, she still loved him. He was ready to marry her, but was constantly annoyed by the company that surrounded her.*

*Charlie was feeling insecure leading up to the wedding, expecting her family to detect all his flaws and give Abby a last minute warning to run away. Nobody seemed to see the Charlie that only Charlie saw though. Instead, they'd been hearing about his reputation and were impressed by him. Abby's cousins bombarded Charlie with questions about his chosen career and asked if the nurses were hot. By his last working day, Abby's family had made him out to be a celebrity and for the first time in all the time he knew Abby, he started not only to believe he measured up to her, but by some accounts, he'd surpassed her.*

*Charlie's temperamental ways didn't seem so bad when he put other qualities at the forefront of who he was. He could potentially become one of the most successful neurosurgeons in the country. Abby was a physical therapist and a personal trainer. In that department, she would never come close to the success Charlie had.*

*Charlie strolled into work and began his day, eager to get started saving lives.*

*Today, that life was Sarah Plano, who had a tumor growing at the base of her skull. Charlie had questioned whether it could, or should, be removed. The tumor was massive and was situated in the brain stem, which was a vital area. Left to itself, it would rob Sarah of her hearing, she'd lose the ability to walk, and eventually die, but surgery could leave her paralyzed if it didn't kill her. Her family had to decide and Charlie spoke with the family, projecting confidence in his abilities.*

*The family agreed and the surgery started at eight in the morning and Charlie would leave when it was done. It was expected to take at least eight hours and it would be the perfect way for Charlie to finish before a long break.*

*To Charlie, surgery was like diffusing a bomb. He worked through a microscope and used long-handled, fine-tipped instruments to pull the tumor away from the brain before removing it with a sucker. A quarter of the body's blood coursed through the veins and arteries of the brain. If one of them was torn, bleeding and stroke would result, so everything had to be precise or the consequence would be enormous. He was also in danger of removing important parts of the brain by accident because brain and tumor tissue looked the same. Unlike the rest of the body, the brain and spinal cord rarely healed. If Charlie made a mistake, the damage would be permanent.*

*Charlie queued the music, a combination of Beethoven and Greatest Piano Hits one through seven. The atmosphere in the operating theater was relaxed.*

*Most surgeons remembered all their errors and relayed them with generous spirit. Medicine was built on mistakes because doctors always learned by screwing up. Charlie wasn't interested in the usefulness of an error. To Charlie, an error was a confession, but when Charlie tore a branch off the basilar artery, a vessel the width of a wire, bright red blood started to pump upward and the severity of the error hit him at once. Charlie had cut an artery that carried blood to the stem that regulated the rest of the brain. It didn't take long for Charlie to stop the bleeding and he moved expertly and efficiently as if nothing had happened, but the oxygen deprivation was enough to do irreparable damage.*

*Sarah never regained consciousness.*

*Charlie didn't say a word throughout the rest of the surgery, though everyone in the room spoke of the accident and the complications of the procedure and reminded him that the family had been told of the dangers. Charlie wasn't fatigued or overworked. He was completely sober and at the top of his game. Sometimes, these things just happened.*

*Charlie walked out of Banner without a word and when he got stuck in traffic on his way out, he cursed the cars and drivers as if it was their fault Sarah would die. He shouted and stupidly hit the steering wheel with his fists and felt shame. Not just at his failure to save her life, but by the loss of professional detachment Charlie had grown accustomed to.*

*His phone buzzed and he looked down to its place on the passenger seat. Abby Patterson's smiling picture appeared. She was probably calling about something related to the food or their vows—something Charlie couldn't deal with now.*

*His foot pressed the gas and he flew through the streets without caution...*

...Charlie was out of forgiveness. Adlar would be dead when he could figure out how to get to him.

A week had passed and Manny Quinny hadn't contacted him or shown his face in the hospital. Charlie had calmed his nerves and mostly spent his days in limbo, his mind on nothing other than what was outside the window.

He was visited by Trish Reynalds, who spent a lot of time at the hospital with her daughter and would check in on Charlie from time to time. She never asked for his story. Charlie thought she already knew the truth and didn't care. She was different, but he didn't spend much time thinking about her. His mind was on his legs and what the rest of his life would look like. He would probably never operate again. His legs had been crushed, but he'd also fractured four ribs and his shoulder had been thrown out of place after the blast shot him into the yard. He'd landed on his chest and rolled onto the sidewalk, which was where he was found.

In moments, Adlar Wilcox had taken his career, his family, his home, and his legs. Charlie had fallen into a deep depression and spent most of his time thinking about Adlar and what he would do to him when he was free.

First, he needed to walk. The hospital brought in a biomedical engineer named Fredrick Vilisco to lay out his options.

"Prosthetic limbs are becoming increasingly sophisticated," Fredrick told him one day, though Charlie was barely listening. "But they can be difficult to control in a natural way. Patients control some motorized devices by flexing muscles where the limb was removed and the muscle movements are detected by electromyography sensors on the skin. The signals are translated into muscle movements by the prosthetic."

"What happens if my nerves translate my muscle movements wrong?" Charlie asked.

"There's a way to overcome that problem with motorized limbs. It's going to be costly but your insurance should cover you. There's a technique called targeted reinnervation, which involves rerouting the nerves that would have originally controlled and sensed the missing limb and connecting them instead to other parts of the body. By rewiring a missing arm's motor nerves to muscles in the remaining stump, shoulder, or chest, for example, and rewiring the arm's sensory nerves to the skin in these regions, a channel is opened to the part of the brain that once controlled the missing limb. By controlling and sensing the prosthetic using the same neural pathways and parts of the brain that once governed the real limb, the prosthetic can be made to feel and act like a genuine extension of your body. By stimulating the nerves in the legs or arms, nerves that have been cut off from the central nervous system, it's possible to create coordinated movement of great subtlety."

"I want complete control over my legs," Charlie said. "As close as possible."

"This would be it."

"Whatever it takes," Charlie said.

Eventually, Charlie would be able to walk, but for now, he was in a wheelchair and he hated it. He moved through the hospital almost all day, eager to be anywhere but his room. He hated when people looked at him —especially kids—and hated more when anyone offered to help.

He stopped in the corridor where Royce Morrow had come to see him. He wondered if anything would have changed if he had listened to Royce when he was warned in the first place. According to Royce, Adlar wasn't acting alone. Charlie had killed someone in Adlar's apartment and it had set a chain of events in motion that had made Adlar more dangerous than ever. Charlie didn't fully understand it, but with nothing left in life to look forward to, the one thing he could do was find and kill Adlar and Manny Quinny, once and for all.

He tried to set up a meeting with Royce, but Royce was in full campaign mode. It took sending a message through Trish Reynalds, who contacted Royce through campaign headquarters, to give him the message that Charlie was awake and wanted to talk. It was late in the evening when Royce finally came to see Charlie. Charlie was almost asleep, but knew Royce was a busy man and had to take care of some things outside of business hours.

Royce stared at the stumps at the end of Charlie's legs with sympathy, but his mind was somewhere else. Charlie thought again about Trish, whose mind was somewhere else too. Charlie's mind was always somewhere else. He wasn't sure how or when it happened, but the beneficiaries had all fallen on bad fortune.

"I was sorry to hear about your wife," Charlie said.

"I echo the same sentiment to you Charlie."

"Was it the same guy?"

Royce nodded.

"What about Wilcox?"

"I don't believe Adlar is working with him anymore. To be quite honest, I don't know what happened to Adlar. I suppose he must have been scared off by what he did to you. I can only assume this man was unhappy that you were left alive. My guess is Adlar is dead already and we'll never hear from him again."

Charlie let out a long breath, displeased to hear this. Adlar could be alive and well, but written off as dead, and then what? "Tell me again about Manny," Charlie said, regretting that he hadn't listened the first time.

Royce took a seat. "You and I, around the same time, had similar issues with Adlar. Shortly before your wife passed, I came home one day to find Adlar in my home. He threatened my wife, stole some of my property, and ran off. I considered him a threat to all of us, so I hired a man to take care of him. You tried to kill Adlar from a rooftop, but you killed the man I hired instead. It's his employer who wants revenge. He believes a debt is owed and he once propositioned me but I refused. Adlar accepted the debt in my place and until this happened to you, they were working together."

"He said shit like that when he called. Debts and balance and a bunch of nonsense…"

"He's dangerous and he's not going away. He has avoided capture because he kills using methods that are undetectable. He would not be an easy man to bring down, and if you did and you were caught, you would be labeled a criminal who killed a hero cop. It's not an easy path to travel."

"I'm willing," Charlie said. "Tell me what we need to do and I'm in."

"There's no we anymore," Royce said.

"You said he murdered your wife."

"And he's going to pay, but I'm going to do it the right way. This mess we're in, we're in it because we took matters into our own hands. We tried doing what we believed was necessary, but we have to stop now Charlie. We have to expose him in a legal and just way."

"I'm limited," Charlie said, pointing to the obvious. "I can't do anything Royce. I can't get anywhere. I don't care if this city hates me for it. I don't care what they call me or how they see him. You put me in the same place as this guy and I will kill him and if Wilcox is still out there, he'd dead too."

"I apologize." Royce rose to his feet. "I've traveled this path before and it's not worth it."

"And what happens if you can't expose him your way?"

"I can't think about that right now."

"You came to me Royce. You came to me when all you had was a premonition. Since then, I've lost everything and so have you. The only thing that's changed between now and then is that they've ruined us! How can you back out now?"

"I'm sorry Mr. Palmer." Royce stood and walked to the door. Charlie desperately tried to climb out of bed and find his way to the wheelchair, but failed and hit the floor instead. Royce rushed over and let Charlie put his hand on his shoulder for leverage. After some effort, Charlie was seated, but breathless and defeated.

"What do I do?" Charlie asked, catching his breath.

Royce was back at the door. "Find a cause," he said. "Find a reason to wake up in the morning."

Royce left Charlie in the chair, where he slept overnight, occasionally dreaming of Adlar and a faceless man pushing Charlie's chair from behind. All Charlie could do was try to reach around and shove the man away, but he his position left him helpless. He awoke abruptly in the night to the clashing of lightning and a cold sweat on his face.

2

Trish Reynalds stood in front of a mirror and observed the reflection looking back and wondering if when the time came, she'd be able to do what it took.

She knew Dent would come through. Even if they hadn't made a deal, he would have. There was a time when Dent really did care for Trish and Shiloh and though things had gone sour between Trish and Dent, Shiloh was innocent and Dent had a soft spot for kids.

Her next line of business was to have a meeting with Bernard Bell for a better understanding of the process of collecting and what kind of time-frame they were looking at to release the funds to the last standing. He was unable to give her information outside of what she already knew, other than to assure her that the process would be quick once all death certificates had been confirmed.

The next thing she did was grab her badge and go into work. She was assigned to patrol the neighborhood but drove far outside her jurisdiction to the territory her and Carlos worked when they needed information. She had contacts in the neighborhood and enough asking around eventually led her to a dealer who was new to the game and had a bad reputation as an amateur. One of her informants set up a meet and greet and within the hour, she was knocking on a door in an apartment complex. Jeremy Buchanan invited her in and she immediately saw why his competition didn't like him. He sold cheap and cozied up to his clients too much so they'd think it was an easy buy, but everything he had was recycled and recast. Once the pills were in front of her, she pulled her badge.

"Aww come on!" Jeremy said.

"I'm not here to arrest you."

"Then what you want with me?"

"I want to buy, but not that shit."

"Then what shit you want girl? I can get you whatever you want." He reached down to his crotch and adjusted his pants.

"I don't want your little pecker." Trish nodded at a door in the floor. "What's in there?"

"Just more of the same."

"I can bust you right now for twenty reasons, so let's see what's in the floor."

"Everything I got is prescribed," Jeremy said. "Thanks to the LAPD."

Trish opened bottles and dumped pills on the table. "This isn't prescribed. Everything is mixed."

"Bullshit girl. It's for my back."

"I don't think so." Trish ran her hand through a pile of pills, scattering them across the table. "I think you melt it and recast it. Oxy and Ambien."

"I don't know what you're talking about."

"Ambien's cheaper and once your clientele passes out, they don't care. They wake up and all they remember is the short high they had. You're recasting. I'm not here to arrest you because I already know nothing I charge you with is going to stick, but once I get word out that you're ripping off all your clients, I'm sure some of them won't be forgiving."

"Alright, alright, what do you want?"

"The door." She nodded to the door and Jeremy sighed and walked to the kitchen. A moment later, he came back with a key and opened the door in the floor. "It's just a good capitalistic business," he muttered.

"I don't plan to ruin what you've got going," Trish said. "But I will if you ever mention I was here." The door opened and inside was a plethora of weapons and ammunition."

"So what? You here to rob me?"

Trish's eyes scanned the cache as a lump formed in her throat. "Something like that."

3

Charlie barely slept and when he finally awoke, he felt hazy and worn down. His thighs were painful and he couldn't find a comfortable position to lay in. He hoisted himself over to his wheelchair and circled the room until his arms were tired. Then, he fell asleep in the chair for a couple of hours, this time waking up from a dream that sat with him for the next few hours. He couldn't remember the details, but he still had his feet and Abby was alive and adored him.

He closed his eyes and couldn't stop the tears from falling. Abby really had loved him. She was loyal, only had eyes for him, and he'd constantly accused her otherwise.

*What have I done?*

Charlie had always given Abby an out from the relationship because he assumed he would end up hurt, but it was Charlie who had been dangerous. It was Charlie who ruined her—not the other way around. That train of thought stuck with him a long time and whenever he thought of Adlar, his anger only directed back to himself. He knew now that Abby would haunt him for the rest of his life.

He felt numb. He had no desire to do or say anything. He was short with the nurses. He refused to watch TV—to watch fake people with fake problems. He looked forward to nothing—other than to have legs again. When he was able to walk, he would get far away from here, retire in a small community, talk to no one, do nothing. He would live with the pain and he knew he deserved it.

*And Adlar?*

He couldn't even muster enough energy to feel vengeful.

Later in the day, he tried moving again, this time working his way down the halls of the hospital without a destination in mind. He stopped and looked in on patients who were as helpless as him...people he'd always seen himself above. Others had warned him about his flaws in the past, but he'd ignored them. He wished he could go back and start over. Back before he became a doctor, before he met Abby, before he flipped over his bicycle and forever changed the way he thought about his brain.

He stopped outside the break room to grab a cup of coffee, but voices on the inside caused him to wait. The last thing he wanted was a conversation. The longer he waited, the more familiar the voices were, which wasn't strange in itself, but the voices he recognized were of two people who had no business being in a room together. One was Dr. Gregory Neomin. The other was Toby O'Tool...and they were arguing in secret.

Charlie didn't understand everything that was said, but the topic of conversation was Shiloh Reynalds.

*I never checked in on her.*

He'd gotten as far as confronting Neomin but that was the day shit hit the fan and Charlie had forgotten about Shiloh until now. It was a good thing too, because up until now, he'd only considered the possibility that Neomin was misdiagnosing her or that he wasn't taking her treatment in the right direction. He'd been consumed by his own life and his own hardships, but what he had been blind to, what it seemed everyone was blind to, was that the beneficiaries had some very real problems hanging over them. Two dead, people missing, attacked, hiring hitmen—it wasn't the kind of thing anyone could run from or pretend wasn't happening anymore. Charlie still had no concern for his own life, but Shiloh Reynalds, who was almost twelve years old...

The voices came to a stop and Neomin's frustrated tone reached the door as he said some final words to Toby. Something about not caring anymore and he can't do this. Charlie would reflect on the words later, but now he moved as quickly as he could away from the door and ended up across the hall in an empty room, his chair against the wall as the break-room door opened and Neomin stormed out, followed a moment later by Toby's measured footsteps.

Toby O'Tool, who allegedly messed with the Palmers shortly after the reading of the will by exposing their secrets—he'd always if Toby really believed their problems would escalate until something tragic happened. Toby could have been behind everything that had happened. Anthony's stabbing, Richard's drowning, even pulling Adlar's strings.

If even some of that was true, then Toby's very presence in Shiloh's life, was suspect. Her x-rays never made sense. The drugs, the side effects, the miraculous healing followed by the recurrence of the tumor—

was it really possible? Would any human being really do that to another? And how on Earth could he get Neomin to play along? Suddenly, Charlie had a reason to breathe again. He was probably the only beneficiary on the will who could see Toby clearly, but first he needed proof.

*I've got nothing but time to waste,* Charlie thought. *I need to find out for myself if Shiloh Reynalds is actually sick…*

… *"of course not,"* the chief of surgery told Charlie. *"You did everything you could to save her."*

*"I killed her."*

*"You went into a surgery that had a fraction chance of success. Sarah knew the risk. Her family knew the risk. There's no blame being placed. Don't ruin your career over something so small."*

*"How is this small?"*

*"You were performing a high risk surgery which required precision that maybe no one had. The patient was bleeding more excessively than was expected. It wasn't a mistake Dr. Palmer. It was a risk, to be expected even without human error. No surgeon worth anything never had a patient die on their table."*

Charlie couldn't accept that. He didn't know why though. He never cared much for the living but his job mattered…mattered enough to know that he preferred to fix broken people over the alternative.

*"I shouldn't have assured her,"* Charlie said, quietly.

*"Come again."*

He looked up. *"I told her I'd never had an unsuccessful surgery. I promised she was in good hands and I would pull her through."*

*"Dr. Palmer, in all my decades of medical practice, I've been a witness or a party to every imaginable mistake: Errors of commission, omission, errors unreported, errors of delegation…I once performed a simple spinal surgery and left the patient with a paralyzed foot. Now, I'm not going to lie and say it didn't bother me, but I will tell you that I get by because my intent is good. I'm skilled and bring a hundred percent to each surgery and I'm still the best chance they got. No matter who was in the room with you, she would have died, so you're not going to be in the room ever again? Think of how many more will die because you're no longer in the room. The world is deprived of a skilled surgeon because of one surgery gone bad. It's never the successes we remember. Only the failures. You just have to find a way to carry on."*

Charlie felt his cell buzz in his pocket and clenched his jaw, annoyed, as if Abby should know better than to be calling. Everything seemed different now, and somehow, that included Abby. Charlie wasn't sure his fate could be decided on the operating table anymore. It was well and *good when people treated him as a savior when something went right, but when it went wrong, they'd see him as a murderer. If Charlie could no longer control how surgery turned out, he was useless. He'd always refused to be realistic and even-keeled. He wanted to be the best, wanted to be impeccable and create a legacy.*

*"Why don't you take some extra time after the honeymoon? I'll make it work."*

*"We'll see."*

*"However bad you think this is for you, think of what Sarah's family is going through. You're about to get married. You need to focus and get your head straight. You don't need to be carrying this with you on the altar."*

*The chief was right.*

*Charlie left without a word to anyone that day. He supposed everyone would see him as an egotistical prick who couldn't handle dumb luck. Everyone had suffered through the same incidents but Charlie held himself to a different standard.*

*He felt his phone ring in his pocket outside the hospital and answered it quickly. "What? You don't know I'm at work?"*

*Abby paused on the other end before she spoke with concern. "Honey, are you okay?"*

*"I'm fine," Charlie said. "I'd be better if you didn't need to interrupt me over every little thing."*

*"This is important Charlie. I wouldn't be calling if it isn't. We have to pay for the hotel today. Like, before five."*

*"Then do it."*

*"I can't, because you have the card."*

*Charlie let out a sigh and closed his eyes. This felt so small, but to Abby, it was everything. "Why would you marry me?" he asked. "You know you can do better."*

*There was a long pause on the other side and what sounded like the start of Abby sobbing. Then, the line was cut off.*

*"Great," he muttered. A migraine started eating away in his head.*

*This was just another problem he didn't need and no matter how much he tried to dismiss how small these issues were, Abby kept coming back to his mind and his migraine worsened. He closed his eyes tightly, trying to block the pain.*

*The next thing he knew, he was on one knee, one hand on the ground, the other pressed against his forehead, wincing in pain...*

...Charlie waited for Neomin to go to lunch. His lunch was later than Charlie had the patience for, but when he finally did go, he didn't go to the cafeteria. He left the hospital, giving Charlie a wide opening. Charlie was familiar with most of the staff and he'd never given anyone a reason to be suspicious of his motives. Getting to Shiloh's files would be easy, but if he was wrong, he was going to have a lot of explaining to do with Neomin. Charlie didn't believe he was wrong though. The dots were fully connected. He only needed proof. With evidence of the truth, he could give Trish the good news, save a little girl from the stress of believing her life would be short, and ruin Neomin's career in the process. He could also effectively ruin whatever Toby had in the works.

The conclusion he drew was so simple that he couldn't believe it had taken this long. Toby was forcing Trish to kill them all. She'd vented that she didn't have insurance. Shiloh's tumor had unstable symptoms. None of it had made any sense, and every step of the way, every bit of information had come from Neomin.

He pushed his wheelchair quickly through the halls and to Neomin's office, which was locked. A white lie to the receptionist gained him the key. No one had a reason to distrust Charlie and so telling her that Neomin asked him for a second opinion on a case was all it took. When he was in the office, he went straight to the file cabinet and started flipping through folders. Shiloh's folder wasn't filed under R, like it should have been. Instead, it was far in the back, behind all the alphabetical files, sitting alone as if it was its own isolated case. He already knew what he would see and he allowed his disbelief to be confirmed. The file was filled with x-rays, no two consistent with each other. They didn't even all appear to be from the same person, but they all contained a tumor at different stages.

All eyes had been on Adlar Wilcox. Other than the murderer serving life in Kern, it was Adlar who everyone had been concerned about. He'd intruded in Royce's home and killed Abby. Adlar would get his in time, but no one had been paying attention to Toby. The general consensus was that Toby was an asshole. It was no secret that he wanted the money either, but Toby was clearly not a killer. Toby was dangerous though. He had another warfare in mind, prompting others to turn on each other. The Palmers had fought over the letters between Abby and Victor. Was that what Toby had really been trying to do? Was it all about friction and the hopes that lives would deteriorate to the point of desperation?

He flipped through the files, all confirming an illness, but not one proved to link the illness to Shiloh Reynalds. Shiloh had been having migraines and throwing up, but no symptom couldn't be faked with the right drugs. Toby was evil and Neomin was playing along.

Charlie wasn't sure where to begin. Confront Neomin? Call Trish? Go see her in person? Bring her in and have a confrontation with Neomin in front of Trish, Shiloh, and the whole Banner General staff? All he knew was that by the end of the day, everything would be exposed.

He left the room, taking the file with him and pushed himself down the hallway, wincing in pain as he moved faster than he physically was ready to move. When he was back in his room, he grabbed his cell phone and fumbled with the buttons. He realized he was shaking and was breathing in short gasps. He'd happened across a monumental revelation and wasn't sure he could find the words to say to Trish. She'd be relieved, but there'd be more emotion than that. She'd be on the warpath. Something of this caliber could potentially cause her to put a bullet through Neomin's head. He hoped she'd feel too much relief and not do anything drastic.

Her phone rang for a minute, never turning over to a machine. He tried again, but there was no answer. He sent her a text with an optimistic message that he needed to talk to her about Shiloh's treatment and there was good news. After a short while without a response, he called the police station and asked for her. After being placed on hold for five minutes, a voice came back and told Charlie she took the next few days off.

He set his phone on the bed and stared blankly at the window. His stomach turned as he considered the possibility that it was too late. He couldn't up and leave the hospital and track her down—not in his condition. He tried calling Royce but got no answer. It was the same at campaign headquarters. He tried to take an inventory of all the people he could trust—anyone that could check in on Trish and tell her to go see him immediately.

Finally, he called Trish again, determined to let the phone ring until she answered. This time, it didn't ring at all. Instead, it went straight to voice-mail.

*I'm too late*, Charlie thought.

The night he'd sat outside the door while Abby lay dying on the inside crossed his mind. The questioning after and the accusation that he'd called for help too late. She'd died because he was too late. He was in a special kind of hell, where his own sins were coming back full circle and taunting him, dancing in front of his eyes and chanting that he's too late…only moments too late. Forty-five minutes past the time that an ambulance could arrive and save her…hours past the time he could have told Trish that she was about to become a murderer because someone had tricked her into it.

He looked at the clock on the wall. An hour had passed. He had no idea where Trish was, but Neomin was back and he was going to answer for what he did.

## 4

Trish paid Jeremy out of pocket with funds she'd raised for Shiloh's treatment. It made her sick to spend charity like this, but reminded herself that there were no boundaries when it came to Shiloh's life.

*Soon it will be over,* she thought. *None of this will matter, except Shiloh will live.*

The thought kept morality in check.

She returned home and tried making dinner for Shiloh, but her daughter begged her to let her go back to school to hang out with her friends who would be leaving volleyball practice in half an hour. Trish reluctantly agreed and ate dinner alone. She would have liked to have spent as much time with Shiloh as possible, but she also needed alone time. What she was about to do was weighing on her mind and surely, Shiloh would see her condition was strange…that there was a certain darkness setting in that she couldn't hide.

The later it got, the more she regretted letting Shiloh go. Time was running out in more than one way. There was really only one thing left to do before she could actually execute her plan, and she'd put it off for last because it would be the hardest thing to do—aside from murdering a dozen people. There was never a better time than now and if she did it now, what did that mean? Tomorrow was the day?

*Yeah*, she thought. *Tomorrow will be the day.*

She sat at the table with pen and paper in hand and wrote a confession. It confessed to killing the people in the will and for framing Christian Dent for the murders of Jones and Cory. She cried as she wrote it and the writing flowed freely. It was done in one draft. It was the final nail in her coffin. She folded it neatly and put it in the pocket of her uniform. She would wear it tomorrow and move from one to the next until it was done. The confession would be found, Dent would be set free, and he would be a rich man. Then, his inheritance would pay for surgery, making him the hero and forever leaving Trish the legacy as a murderer.

She cried herself to sleep.

## 5

"Shiloh Reynalds was never sick."

Gregory Neomin turned to the voice in the dark of his office. He turned on the lights to find Charlie Palmer in his wheelchair, sitting patiently. Neomin smiled pleasantly, understanding the weight of what was happening and trying to soften Charlie up. "Dr. Palmer, how are you?"

"Did you hear what I said?"

"I heard you." Neomin fell into a chair in defeat. There was no point in arguing or trying to deny it now. Charlie had been onto this case for some time and even if Neomin could buy time, it wouldn't last long. He regretted ever making a deal with Toby. He knew at the time what being caught would mean for him, but Toby had been so persuasive. "You're positioned to inherit a large fortune."

Charlie nodded.

"Toby O'Tool came to me with this."

"I know."

"He had some dirt on me and offered a lot of money. I didn't think it would go this far. I wasn't even sure what he was doing at first. By the time I figured it out, it was too late."

"You were the one making her sick. You were poisoning her, keeping her sick."

"I hated every second of it. You have to believe that."

"I do, but my opinion doesn't change the consequences."

"What are you going to do?" Neomin leaned forward.

"Trish Reynalds is out there right now, not answering calls. How close was she?"

"To what?"

"How desperate did you have her?"

Neomin looked down and his demeanor seemed as if he was in a confessional. "She's been withdrawn. Toby was getting aggressive with the time-line. We told her..."

"You told her," Charlie corrected.

Neomin stammered momentarily and took a breath. "I told her that it was getting worse and that we needed to operate as soon as possible."

"You need to fix this," Charlie said. "I can't go anywhere, but you can. You need to stop her."

"I can't," Neomin said, shaking his head.

"If you regret this, you know what you need to do to stop it. No one has died. Make it right before someone does."

"The cop will kill me. I'll lose my license. I'll go to jail."

"That's going to happen anyway."

Neomin hung his head and let the tears fall. In that moment, Charlie saw a man who'd been pained by his actions. He knew they weren't that different, but while Charlie told Neomin he had to answer for his actions, he refused to allow his mind to travel that path that he knew was right. He could never turn himself in. He could never admit full fault, because there were too many variables.

*Just as there are for Neomin.*

Charlie waited for Neomin to bring himself together before asking again. "We don't have time."Neomin nodded and that was all Charlie needed to spring into action. "She won't ignore your calls. Not if she thinks it's about Shiloh. You need to call her immediately. Just tell her that she's made a remarkable recovery. Get her to come back here, whatever you have to say. Then, we'll tell her together. We'll hang this on Toby to whatever extent we can."

"He has stuff on me."

"You've got a choice to make Neomin. You can deal with whatever Toby has or you can deal with Trish. I'm not lying for you though."

Neomin nodded again and Charlie could see a weight lifted from him as he settled on what he would do. "My phone's in my locker."

"You've gotta hurry."

Neomin nodded and exited the room. Charlie followed and watched him walk down the hall. He wasn't hurried but he was cooperative, and Charlie hoped these last few moments of dragging his feet weren't going to make the difference between life and death for someone else. Charlie could kick himself for waiting so long. He could have made this discovery a long time ago if he hadn't been so self involved—if he hadn't been avoiding confronting Victor's will and those surrounding it. It shouldn't have come down to the wire—Neomin shouldn't have been able to get away with this for so long, but everyone was so preoccupied with their own and somehow, Toby O'Tool had turned a decent person into a killer.

Charlie began moving toward the surgical room, where Neomin's cell phone would be sitting in a locker. Some time had passed but Toby didn't believe he would run. He had nowhere to go. He might have been sitting in a room crying or pacing back and forth somewhere, or maybe he was talking to Trish Reynalds now. He was sure Neomin would do the right thing, but he kept pushing the wheels faster, dodging other people walking through the halls and ignoring a colleague who tried to stop him and ask how he was doing. A feeling of dread filled Charlie and just as he reached the surgery room, he heard a scream in the opposite direction, followed by a female voice calling for help.

Charlie followed the sound, but couldn't see over the crowd of people who'd gathered. What he could see was a plastic shower curtain that was tied over a beam on the ceiling and a suited man pulling out a pocketknife to cut it down. Charlie waited outside in the hall, listening closely for details. He heard someone say Neomin's name and moments later, the dreaded words. "He's dead…"

*…There was no lawsuit against the hospital or Charlie Palmer and*

*after a few days, it was business as usual. Charlie had a lot on his mind, especially blackout headaches he would have when he was stressed. He tried to remain calm, but his mind was always turning. He thought about Sarah Plano and her family, a wedding, Abby Patterson and the unlikely pairing of her and Charlie, but mostly he thought about his career and how he would handle the future of normalcy as a surgeon.*

*The chief recommended a counselor for Charlie and Charlie insisted they talk almost every other day, and though he was on leave for the wedding, he stopped at Banner to discuss the trauma behind errors, but what was really on his mind was the wedding.*

*Linus Krierman had a masters in Psychology and had spent thirty years in the field. He'd had six papers published and spent time counseling vets coming back from Afghanistan. He'd been around the block a few times and Charlie was nothing new. In fact, Charlie had watered down problems compared to most, but Linus also understood that Charlie had suffered a bicycling injury at a young age and a lot of his feelings weren't really his feelings at all. Sometimes, it was the pain that drove Charlie, that made Charlie's frustrations seem worse than they were. Charlie was as normal as people come and only Charlie didn't realize that.*

*"Dr. Palmer, you have a lot going on right now, don't you?"*

*"I do."*

*"Wedding in two days...death of a patient...that's two relatively significant moments for you."*

*Charlie scratched his head. "It feels like there's something bigger but I don't know what."*

*"You recently learned that there may be some after effects of a surgery you had years ago. You thought you were okay and you learned very recently that you may suffer from periodic migraines and other symptoms."*

*"Yeah..."*

*"A lot of people have trouble dealing with one crisis at a time, let alone multiple at once. You're at the apex of some large happenings, all coincidentally coinciding at a single time period and that time is now. Your life, most certainly, must feel out of your control."*

*"I would agree," Charlie said, nodding. "I need control. I think a lot of people do. I mean, isn't that really what stress is? Just the unknown and the fear of how it will turn out?"*

*"That's an interesting way of putting it. In fact, in a world where we all knew the outcome of all things, we probably would be stress free. If you know your chosen career, who you'll marry, how your marriage will turn out....there are no surprises."*

"Yes, surprises..." Charlie said, with a hint of disgust.

"I'd argue that we need stress though Charlie. I think not knowing the outcome is the fun in it all. There have been times in my life, for example, as a child, I knew where my mother would hide all the holiday presents. I'd sneak into that closet and she'd have them wrapped but I'd pull back a flap of paper and look at my toys and I was excited then, but feigning excitement on Christmas day wasn't the same as seeing my sister looking at her presents for the first time with wide eyes. Let's contrast that with the bad things that come out of nowhere...the death and the disease and the loss of homes and pets or watching the love of your life slip away because she fell for someone else...we need those things Charlie. Without them, everything is easy, and nothing was ever supposed to be easy. If you figure out how to control your life, please let me know the secret."

Charlie smiled and pondered. "This isn't anything I don't know or understand."

"Then why are you so eager to be here with me? What do you want to get out of this?"

"I want to know if I should..." He cut himself off there and recollected himself. "What if I'm not ready to be married?"

"Why wouldn't you be?"

"She's perfect, so I don't know. I used to think it was just that I couldn't measure up, but it's these plates I have to spin. Not a lot of plates, but big plates that require focus. Like, how will I be a great surgeon if I have to focus on her needs? Maybe a child's needs."

"Have you ever considered that what you think of as the problem is actually the solution? How often does your fiance hold you back in your career?"

"Never, but things change in time."

"She's going to be with you when you are victorious. She will mourn with you when you're defeated. A good woman will, anyway. Is she a good woman?"

"She's a great woman."

"You should let yourself off the hook Charlie. I think you'll find that in time, you won't be measuring yourself against her."

"I don't do that."

"You do. You don't want to let her down. You don't want to resent her. You are ever so constantly worried about Abby and what she thinks of you or how she'll impact you, but from what I know about Miss Patterson, and I know very little, she's happy to be along for the ride, just as you'll be along for the ride in whatever hands she'll be dealt in life. Good will happen to you. Good will happen to her. Bad as well. Some things you will experience together and some as individuals, but you *never keep score Charlie. If there's anything I want to impress upon you, it is to never keep score. There's no such thing as better than or too good for in marriage. You're simply compatible and you're both along for the same ride."*

*Charlie nodded and one corner of his mouth found a smile. When stated so simplistically, it made sense, and the weight of everything happening in his life was lifted.*

*"May I speak frankly?"*

*"Please."*

*"Not because I'm lazy and don't want to do my job, but go home. It's two days before your wedding and your fiance very likely wants you to be sitting somewhere with you."*

*"She's probably just watching TV or reading," Charlie said, dismissively.*

*"Maybe," Linus said. "But she still wants you there. You should go to her, tell her someone died under your care and it's bothering you..."*

*"She knows..."*

*"Tell her again. Tell her it's been hard. See what she does."*

*"She'll hug me. She'll want to talk about it."*

*"Good," Linus said. "Then I strongly recommend you marry her..."*

...He wasn't fast in a wheelchair, but Charlie was the only hope that was left. He hurried through the halls, cutting through people with only one goal in mind. When he got outside, his first thought was that he couldn't go back into that hospital again. He'd spent too much time there and he sucked in air outside as if he was free.

It took him even longer than he anticipated to get anywhere. Getting on a bus was a pain and clearly inconvenienced people around him. It made him suddenly aware of the way he once was when someone held him up. He'd curse and call them names and Abby would tell him to calm down and be nice.

When the bus stopped at his destination, he wheeled himself another six blocks just to get to the Reynald's house. He rang the doorbell and after a few minutes, Shiloh peeked her head out. It was a sad sight for Charlie to see that Shiloh was home alone, waiting for her mother. The child's life was about to be forever scarred and she didn't know it yet.

Shiloh recognized Charlie and gave him a nice smile. She looked like she had grown up years in the short time he knew her. She'd matured under the strain of the sickness she thought she had. She'd been deprived of months of time that she could have been thinking about her summer or hanging out with friends. Toby would pay for so many things when Charlie confronted him.

"My mom's not home," Shiloh said.

"I know, but I really need to get a hold of her."

"Is everything okay?"

"It's not. Everything is fine with you. In fact, Shiloh, I'm going to tell you something but I can't explain it now. I can explain it when your mom is here with us so just listen and know that I'm telling you the truth. You're healed. You don't have any kind of condition or sickness and you won't be having any symptoms or headaches or anything else related aside from your regular once a year flu."

"I don't understand…Was it the medicine they were…?"

"You were mis-diagnosed. You were getting the wrong medicine as a result and it was making you sicker, but you never had anything. The doctor was wrong and your mother needs to know that as soon as possible."

Shiloh looked like she wanted to jump for joy, but was shrouded in confusion and panic. She tried to understand, but knew that what Charlie was asking was important and immediately grabbed her cell from her pocket. "She has a sitter coming tonight and staying the next two days."

"Why? Where's she going?"

"She just said it was work related."

"She might her phone off." Charlie spoke quickly. "Just text her, call her, do whatever you have to, but tell her you're not sick and there was a mistake and Dr. Palmer needs to see her. Do you have my number?"

"I don't think so. Here…" She handed Charlie her phone and he quickly added his number to her contacts.

"If she responds, let me know. What I'm going to do is go up the street to the Sheraton and get a room. It's only four blocks away. She comes home or she responds, tell her to call me there and I'll come over immediately and explain in better detail."

"Yeah…" Shiloh shook her head quickly and couldn't help but smile as she understood she wasn't sick.

"Okay, call if you need anything."

Shiloh shook her head again and lingered in the door as Charlie turned and headed toward the hotel. He let out a breath and wiped a line of sweat from under his hairline, but he wouldn't breathe better until he heard back from Trish. He didn't expect she'd answer to him but she wouldn't ignore her daughter.

It might already be too late, but something told Charlie everything would turn out alright. It had to. Otherwise, Charlie's discovery and Neomin's death and everything they'd all been through to get here, would all be for nothing. At this point, all Trish had to do was look at her phone. It was such a minimal detail, but made the difference between life and death.

Charlie reached the end of the block and rested. His arms were shaking and he was winded from all the hustle in the chair. He looked down at the stumps where his legs used to be and let out a breath. Oddly enough, he felt revived. He wanted to make things right and be on a winning team for once. He'd been working toward vengeance and hiding the truth for so long that he didn't feel like there was anything good left, but if Trish could only check her phone then Charlie would play a part and maybe that would be the start of something new.

His wheelchair started moving, but it wasn't Charlie pushing the wheels. "Dr. Palmer," a voice said. He tried turning but only caught traces of the man behind him. Before he could scream, a knife was at his throat. "It's time we satisfy your debt."

Adlar Wilcox looked up as the door above opened and light shined into the cellar that he'd been sitting in for weeks. The last time he had been outside, he'd been trying to work his way up a river, only to be spotted by Manny and dragged back to his home. After he was caught, no matter how much Adlar kicked and screamed, Manny said nothing. He said nothing when he tossed Adlar into the basement and he said nothing every day when he delivered scraps of food and forced Adlar to sign into his server so that incriminating evidence of Manny's work wouldn't leak to the world. What Manny never did was ask Adlar to remove it, though Adlar repeatedly offered as the days dragged on. Manny was wearing him down. It was a game, but Adlar didn't know how the game was supposed to end. Knowing nothing, hearing nothing, doing nothing…it was torture unto itself.

Manny's frame filled the doorway, but this time, he had a large object. As Adlar's eyes adjusted to the light, he saw a body in a wheelchair being lowered down by a platform secured by a rope. The basement had no stairs, but even if it did, Adlar's hand was secured by rope to a metal beam in the middle of the room. Manny did nothing to secure Charlie to anything, but he didn't need to. A man without legs wouldn't go anywhere. Aside from that, Charlie looked like he might be dead.

"Charlie…" Adlar said, but Charlie didn't move.

Manny hopped down and positioned Charlie across from Adlar and set a gun at his side. Then, Manny turned to Adlar and finally spoke.

"He's going to be out for a while. You can spend that time looking at him, wondering what he's going to say when he wakes up, wondering how long it takes him to put a bullet in you. Maybe he'll give you a chance to talk. If he does, you can let him know there are two bullets in this gun. If he so desires, he can put the second in his own head. Whether he does or not won't matter because you're not walking out of here—neither of you are—and that's poetic Adlar. That's poetic because this is how we balance all things. You've all paid your debt now."

Manny started to climb back to the main level.

"If I don't sign into the cloud, you're going to be arrested."

"I took care of that. Hired a guy. I wasn't about to give you the satisfaction. Now you've got nothing. You're not the only hacker in this world kid. That's your thing, right? That's the thing that you embraced and made your own, but you're not that special. You never were. You're just a kid that constantly fucks up that everyone wants to kill."

"Please…I can do whatever you need. I can help you with whatever. There's still the money."

"I'll take care of it on my own. I don't need you. Never did. I regret teaching you what I did, but won't matter when Charlie comes out of that. Listen kid, this will be the last time you see me, but I've got nothing to say to you, other than not to forget who beat who here. Tell Charlie I said hi."

Manny boosted himself out of the cellar, using broken wood jutting from where the stairs used to be as support. Adlar begged, but soon, the door closed and he was back in the dark, with only the unconscious shape of Charlie Palmer to stare at.

## *Chapter 14*

### *1*

Trish couldn't tolerate another day passing with Shiloh no closer to surgery. Her will was updated, the confession was written and ready to be released, and she'd made her rounds to all her favorite hideouts over the years: The house she grew up in, the church she'd married Paul in, the pizza place parking lot she'd spent her High School weekends hanging out in, picking up boys and driving to the park where they'd make out.

The importance in all things in her past was magnified by the awareness that she was remembering everything for the last time. Everything in her life had led to one place though: Shiloh.

Trish was willing to go against everything she'd ever believed for her daughter. Every arrest she'd ever made, the suspect eventually would submit and make excuses. Many times, men would sit in the back of her squad car and break down in tears and talk about how bad they had it in life and how crime was their only option. She'd always tuned it out with the belief that crime was never the only option. It made her feel guilty to know how hypocritical she was, but she couldn't help but believe she'd fought the good fight and there was no other way to save Shiloh.

The business with the will had already gotten out of hand. Many people had died for the fifteen listed and while Trish's actions were for Shiloh, putting an end to Victor's revenge was satisfactory in itself. Surely, Victor never anticipated this route when he was drafting his will. Only Abby died in the way Victor had intended but Trish had always assumed Victor wanted them each to live their lives, ruined by the burden of his will—by the curse of having so much to gain without any real way to gain it.

The day before, she'd picked Shiloh up at school for the last time and while she drove her home, she fought back tears. To Shiloh, this was another day, but soon she would know things her mother did and she'd refuse to believe those things possible. She'd probably grow up hating Trish, but hopefully would one day understand why Trish did the things she did. She hugged her daughter and tried to give her some pieces of advice for life, without making it seem as if she was saying goodbye for the final time. Her daughter noticed nothing different but said the wrong thing to Trish instead—something Trish knew was going to haunt her for the next couple of days while she carried out her business.

"I was bored today in computer class and looked you up," Shiloh said. "There's tons of stuff about you Mom. Did you know that the newspapers are always calling you a hero?"

"I've seen the stories," Trish said, her brain a jumbled mess as Shiloh went on about how crazy it was that Trish had shut down so many bad people. Finally, Shiloh tore her mother's heart in two.

"I think I want to be a police officer, like you."

Trish hugged her daughter, clutching to her long and squeezing her tightly. She told Shiloh she was proud of her, who she was becoming, and told her that her mother wasn't perfect but that everything she ever did was for her daughter. Shiloh didn't question her mother's sentimental moment but did listen closely and absorb what she said. It all played out as Trish had hoped, but when she was finally alone in her car with her gun sitting in the seat beside her and headed to see the first on her list, she broke down in tears…

*…Trish watched the news, holding a six month old Shiloh in her arms. Time stood still as she kept up to date on the coverage of the arrest of sixteen high profile people, including Victor himself, within Stone Enterprises.*

*She handled the baby in one arm while dialing Paul's number with the other. She'd called him three times in the last hour and it wasn't until the fourth call that he picked up. Paul was in Northern California on business and his tone indicated she was bothering him. Or maybe he'd heard Victor was arrested and didn't want his wife rubbing it in his face.*

*"Paul…" she said, more dramatic than she wanted to sound.*

*"Yeah, what's up?"*

*"Did you hear the news?"*

*A pause. "Yeah, I heard. Nothing you need to worry about."*

*"Paul, we need to talk about what you know. You're at risk here."*

*"I know nothing. I'm a relationship manager. I travel. What's happening there is going to be restricted to accounting and to whoever is calling the shots."*

*"Victor."*

*"Victor will come up clean. I guarantee it."*

*"How do you know?"*

*"Because they're just trying to blame the top guy because it generates attention. There's probably some sour apples, but it's going to be a fraction of the staff. He's not dirty hon. I know you want him to be, but he's not."*

*"You couldn't know that for sure."*

*"I've had drinks with some of those guys. I know who's who. Bernard Bell...wouldn't shock me. Same with a couple consultants of his. Some of these guys get together and pull out hundred dollar bills, add up the serial numbers and the winner takes the stack. They toss money around like it's nothing. Victor is frugal. He constantly stresses over the numbers."*

*"All the more reason."*

*"He's not as confident in the future as some of those other assholes. Believe me, it's easy to see what's what there. Victor will come up clean. He's only under scrutiny because he's a big deal."*

*"If they didn't have anything, he wouldn't have been arrested."*

*"It's all for show hon. From what I hear, some of this info came from a disgruntled employee. It could all turn out to be nothing."*

*"You defend him a lot."*

*"You condemn him a lot."*

*"I care about your safety. What happens if the whole company comes down? Everyone even remotely tied to the scandal will go to jail."*

*"And I'm not. What, you don't trust me?"*

*"I'm a cop Paul. People know things they don't realize they know all the time. All they need to prosecute is sometimes a signature on a form somewhere."*

*"Well, I'll tell you what," Paul said. "You tell your cop friends to cut down on framing innocent people and coercing people into admitting guilt and innocent guys like myself won't have to worry about these things."*

*"Paul!"*

*"Every fucking day I hear about innocent people being shot by the police because the way they looked at them or the color of their skin."*

*"You're talking about one in a million one-off situations."*

*"Innocent is innocent and guilty is guilty. I know what I am and the fact that you have to worry about what's true or not really comes down to what kind of cop you are. If you don't really believe in justice, then why do what you do? I can answer that for you. Because your job isn't about justice. It's about keeping the peace and you guys don't care who goes down to do it. How much time and money was put into looking into Stone Enterprises? I'm going to go out on a limb and say that those resources*

*could have been put toward maybe the capture of high profile drug pushers, murderers, real criminals. Stone Enterprises employees thousands of people. That's the thing you're going to ruin?"*

*"Do you care if any of it is true?"*

*"Enough with the politics. The CII and the FBI and the LAPD should consider why they got into what they do in the first place and go after the people who ruin this city instead of counting every nickel and dime of the ones who make it better. Get over yourself Trish. Your department is a hundred times more corrupt than Stone Enterprises and to be honest, I don't single you out as innocent when I say that. I gotta get some work done now. Shiloh doing okay?"*

*"Paul," Trish said, her voice trembling. It was the moment she realized her marriage may not last forever.*

*"Is Shiloh okay?"*

*"She's fine, but Paul..."*

*"Great."*

*Click...*


"...She's definitely on the move," Henry said, watching from a parking lot across the street from the precinct. Things were happening fast and reality was setting in. Trish looked desperate and focused and even from across the street, Henry could see the sheer determination in her eyes. He realized Toby hadn't answered and checked his cell to see if he was still there. The line was active. "Toby?"

"I heard you," Toby said. He didn't sound enthusiastic. In fact, he sounded unsure.

"What do I do?"

"Try following her. Tell me where she is at all times. Eventually, she's going to come to me."

"She's moving." Henry started his car and followed at a distance. He'd never followed someone before and had seen enough movies to know that the experts always knew they had a tail. With Trish, and probably with most people, that wasn't the case. No one really checks their mirrors for tails...not even the police.

Trish was in uniform. If there were no witnesses and no cameras around, Trish could probably get away with just about everything in uniform. Toby had been smart about the plan to turn her into a desperate killer, but the plan had always been too intricate and Henry never actually believed he'd pull it off. Today was the day that Toby's brilliance would be fully proved to Henry.

"Turning right on Jefferson," Henry said.

"Heading west?"

"Yes."

"Stay on the line," Toby said. After another five minutes of driving, Toby finally shook his head in disbelief. "Well, this is horse-shit."

"She's coming for you first, isn't she?" Henry asked. "You're first on her list."

"Try not to sound too amused," Toby said. He began walking through his apartment, strategically setting the scene for Trish. A printed confirmation of a flight to Jamaica was placed on the dining room table. A suitcase of clothes would be missing, his mail piled up, and his car parked four blocks away. The only thing that could ruin it all is if she really did have that instinct that cops were rumored to have. Toby was smart, and he knew how police worked, but he couldn't predict how she'd see the room.

Henry confirmed they were headed right to Toby. He took an alternative route eliminate the possibility that she'd notice the tail. He already knew where she was going. He'd beat her there and wait. He wasn't sure what Trish would do—if she'd stay and wait for him or if she'd move on. Hopefully, she'd take the bait, eliminate all the others, and leave Toby.

"Alright, she's going in," Henry said. "I'll let you go. Be careful."

The call ended and Toby walked to the bookcase against the wall and pulled it from the side, opening up a hidden room that was invisible to anyone standing in his apartment. It was easy to build and would fool the average person, but the more time that passed, the more he wondered how average Trish was. He'd been fooling her for a long time, but this time she was on offense. For all he knew, she'd be able to smell him in an adjoining room.

He entered the room and slowly closed the door. He had no visuals of the living area, but a moment later he could hear knocking on the door. He closed his eyes and froze, trying to remind himself that he was safe here. He was a bundle of fear though—unlike anything he could ever remember feeling. He wanted her to leave quickly. He didn't want her to even be there. The thought of someone so close who was there to end Toby's life brought anxiety unlike anything he'd ever experienced.

The knocking stopped but the doorknob shook. A moment later, he could hear the metallic sound of steel on brass as she worked her instruments in the knob. He was suddenly sure he wasn't going to get away with this. He was positive he was going to be forced to come face to face with a monster he'd created.

She was inside his apartment. Everything fell quiet, but he could feel her presence on the other side of the wall. She was walking through slowly, looking at her things, probably with her gun drawn. Toby froze in place, a shiver traveled his body. He'd been proudly accused of talking too much in the past, but in that moment, silence took on a new meaning to him. He heard the sound of objects being moved, doors being opened, her hand running along counter-tops. It felt like she had been there forever and Toby continuously voiced *just go* in his head repeatedly.

He became aware of how many itches he needed to scratch, how badly he suddenly had to go to the restroom, how much he needed to cough. In regular moments, he released whatever he wanted, whenever he wanted. Restraint wasn't his strong point.

Finally, he heard her curse. She was at his desk where the flight information sat. She'd taken the bait and she knew Toby would have to wait for another day. She stayed a few more minutes, probably just going through his things, and finally, Toby heard the sound of the door close. He released a deep breath and ran his fingers through his hair. He would have to be cautious about where he went and what he did. If they crossed paths, he would be in trouble.

*Finish the rest*, he thought, still shaking from his near encounter. *We need to be done with this.*

2

Aileen Thick stared at her face in the mirror, admiring the last of her fading tan and searching for new sunspots or signs of aging around her eyes. Fortunately, today she saw nothing new. She'd expected to have been aging quickly lately as her stress increased and she spent most of her time worrying about Tarek Appleton. He'd changed so much from the Tarek she first met. Tarek knew it too but was satisfied with the change, since it meant he was accomplishing what he set out to do.

She'd grown numb to her life, to Tarek, to the fact that she was in Victor Stone's home. She'd spent time looking back at her life in disbelief, contemplating walking away from Tarek and begging her son for help. She wished she could start over, wished she didn't feel so much regret, but she was past her prime and stuck in a miserable life she couldn't escape.

She stopped as she passed the couch in the living room, where Tarek was sprawled out, his arms dangling from the side and his hair a mess. He was still wearing the clothes he'd left in the night before and his cell phone was in the middle of the floor as if it'd dropped. She shook her head in disbelief. If only the world could see the real Tarek right now, they would never believe it. She was a rarity—quite possibly the only person in the world who knew who Tarek really was. But maybe it was temporary and when Tarek finished his project, he'd become Tarek again.

Or maybe Victor's likeness had swallowed him whole and he was too consumed to turn back. Maybe Tarek liked being Victor more.

She didn't want to be there when he woke up, so she slipped out quietly and decided to spend the day reevaluating her life over a cappuccino. She could search job listings and work wherever would hire her. She could start at the bottom and try her best to still accomplish something with the remainder of her life. She decided she'd sell bagels if she had to. No job was below her. She couldn't continue to follow this same pattern of relying on a man, only to be disappointed in who he turned out to be. What she needed now, and for the rest of her life, was to learn to be self sufficient. She didn't want a boyfriend. She didn't even want friends. She wanted to travel the road she'd never gotten to travel.

She'd gotten into the habit of leaving home early and coming back late, wasting the day in every way she could find. She'd walk through the mall, sit at a coffee shop, go to the gym, or just sit in the park. She would have lunch somewhere new almost every day, always uncomfortable going to the same place twice. Today, she was downtown, wandering the streets and considering potential places of employment. She ran across a restaurant that she recognized, and suddenly memories of the man she'd killed resurfaced. She'd been in The Wasp to meet with an old friend of Sal Blovik's, but that day had been a nightmare. She supposed this was one of many reminders of Sal and always would be. She would have walked past, but she'd hoped to see his friend again, if only to see how he was doing and hear if he had anything more to say. She wasn't even sure if he was working, but she was hungry, so she entered and lingered in the doorway before a young woman with a name-tag that read Eve, sat her down. She chose a seat facing the kitchen.

*What am I doing? That day is behind me. Why relive it?*

She needed to relive it though. It was the same day that brought her to Tarek and as she kept revolving through the same hellish mistakes in life, she decided she'd reevaluate the decisions that got her to those places. She'd murdered a man. She'd suffered the trauma alone, desperately trying to learn who Sal was, only to run into the arms of the only person she could talk to, the only person who could take her away from the streets. Tarek had been kind that night and in the following days. In fact, she wasn't sure she'd made a mistake at all. It was only when Victor's manuscript enticed him that he changed.

Victor Stone, who ruined her life once, still had his hooks in Aileen, even in death.

*How the hell are you doing this?* She thought, but then a thought formed. It was foolish to actually believe Victor had any kind of influence over her life anymore, but it certainly seemed that way. Whatever she did, she couldn't escape his name and with Tarek successfully trying to channel her ex-husband, was Victor really even gone?

Voices interrupted her thoughts. It was the sound of arguing in the entryway that caught her attention. She looked up and had to do a double-take as she realized it was William Lamone, but he was with another person she recognized. It was Brian Van Dyke. The last time she saw him, he'd dropped about twenty pounds, but he looked like he was down fifty more.

She thought hard, trying to make sense of two unlikely people in one place. The friend of the man she'd killed and Brian Van Dyke, another beneficiary of Victor's will. It wasn't impossible that they just worked in the same place, but in the city of Los Angeles, it was hard to link people so easily through coincidence.

*What are you suggesting Aileen? What could you possibly be thinking?*

Was William lying to her? Was there some big conspiracy to inherit that money after-all? As she pondered these thoughts, Brian walked away from William, angry at whatever William had said. She watched as he got in his car and drove off. She ordered, her food arrived, and she sat for another hour, deep in her own thoughts, trying to connect people. Sal Blovik, to William Lamone, to Brian Van Dyke…Tarek Appleton, to Hawaii, to the fire…Anthony Freeman was stabbed…Abby Palmer was shot…Richard Libby drowned.

There was no common denominator. There were too many unconnected coincidences all under one umbrella.

*Truly Victor, how the hell are you doing this?*

Then another familiar face entered The Wasp. It was Henry, the man who had been with Maria on the day they met the judge. Henry and William met up in the lobby and had what looked like a serious discussion before going outside for a smoke break. When the break was over, William came back in but Henry got in his car and drove off.

Maria Haskins was even more connected to her list of coincidences. *No common denominator*, she thought. *Only Victor.*

Then she had a thought she'd never had before. It was what was she was supposed to believe about the will and what others had believed. What if Victor really did know what he was doing? What if his will wasn't just a threat but a real plan to create warfare amongst the group? If that was true, how many things were really in play and was the Apocalypse truly on the heads of those remaining 13 people?

As she counted their names in her head, she realized just how abnormal things really were. Anthony Freeman was drinking, Jason Stone lived thousands of miles away and was married, Charlie Palmer got his legs blown off. She'd been attacked.

*It's not random*, she thought.

She asked for the check as quickly as she could. She swore she'd never go to this place, but suddenly she realized she needed to know more about Victor and his intentions. She needed to know how he did business, what his feelings were for those he held in contempt. She held the key: The manuscript. She needed to read his manuscript.

### 3

Henry had come into The Wasp to warn William about what was happening. He'd been able to make the stop because Trish Reynalds had pulled into the parking lot and was sitting in her car, watching the restaurant. Henry didn't want to do the same because he knew she was going to be suspicious, so when Brian exited the restaurant and got in his car and drove off and Trish started her own car and followed, Henry let out a deep breath and stayed behind. He texted Toby and told him he lost track of her, which pissed Toby off, but Henry didn't care. He wasn't about to follow someone so dangerous, whose police instincts would recognize she was being followed all day.

William met him outside and got in his car for a talk.

"Shit's going down today," Henry said. "You think this will really play out the way Toby said it would?"

"No, because he neglected to plan around the most important thing of all: He has to die for her to feel like she completed her mission."

"Best case scenario: She pulls this off but can't find Toby. She gets arrested, goes to jail, and is taken out there. She's a cop…wouldn't last long."

"This is it." William looked at the restaurant with the realization that he probably wouldn't see Brian alive again.

"We should get out of town a while," Henry said "I don't want to be here while this happens."

William turned toward the street, watching in the direction Trish left. He wondered what Brian was doing in that moment. "I'm not going anywhere. I'm not convinced this is going to work the way he said. I'm seeing it through."

"Brian's next then?"

"Looks like it. I guess my job was pointless."

Brian blasted his radio and nodded along with the music, his eyes tired and his mind on one thing. He wanted to go home and get some rest. When Will was off work, they'd find a party in his building or at one of the neighbor's houses. He'd gotten to know a pretty big crowd of people and his cell phone was filled with contacts he could reach out to, but Will was still his guy. He didn't do anything without him. He watched over Brian and saw to it that he made the right decisions that always got him home. Brian's life was an endless cycle of nights where he'd black out at some point, only to wake up in bed the next day. Will hardly seemed impacted. He never had a hangover and he never needed a fix.

He wanted to stock his fridge with beers and grab a few snacks. His hunger had diminished in the last few months. He almost appeared to have a normal weight, but he didn't feel accomplished by it. Instead, he looked at himself in the mirror, his gut mostly gone and wondered when he'd lost such a burden without noticing. It'd seemed so simple. He never exercised and he didn't remember a time that he stopped eating. He just got too busy and had too much fun and suddenly food wasn't on his mind anymore. Instead, he wanted to get high, get lost in himself, and wake up in the safety of his home.

He made a stop at a gas station and when he exited, he looked up to find Trish Reynalds leaning against his car. She nodded to the case of beer in his hands. "Buying beer?"

"I'm twenty-six." He saw something in her eyes that scared him. She didn't care about the beer and she wasn't just making conversation. Her hand was on the butt of her gun.

"I need you to come with me," she said.

"K," he managed to say. "How come?"

"I'm arresting you for attempted murder."

From the moment she said it, he didn't believe it. There was something completely off about the encounter. He wasn't even sure she could bring him in, but he saw in her eyes that she intended to. "That wasn't me," he said. "He met the guy who did it."

"Someone paid that man to attack Anthony."

"K, but it wasn't me."

"I have evidence that says it was."

"What evidence?" He searched his mind for reasons this didn't make sense, trying to find a way to walk away with no repercussion. She hadn't read him his rights. She hadn't flashed a badge. She was ready to draw her weapon, knowing Brian wasn't a threat.

"You're coming to the station," she said. "If it wasn't you, you have nothing to worry about."

Brian circled around her to the driver's side of his car, reaching for the handle. The door opened a little way, only to be shoved closed by Trish, who then grabbed his arms and forced them behind his back. "What are you doing? This isn't a real arrest," he said.

"Then you have nothing to worry about." Her voice cracked, and Brian heard it. There was something seriously wrong and Brian knew he wasn't going to the station-house. She shoved him in the back of the squad as he asked why she wasn't reading him his rights. She ignored him and got in the driver's seat, hoping he didn't see her face. If he did, she'd give away the pain. Brian was the first of many and she'd already approached him with her guard down. If she couldn't get through one, how was she supposed to get through another ten?

"I saved him, remember? I saved him at the hospital and I was there for you guys when we were going to put an end to the will. You left, remember?"

"Stop talking," Trish said. "Just stop."

Brian shut his mouth and watched out the window as Trish started driving. "This isn't the way," he whispered, too quietly for her to hear. He looked up and caught her eyes in the rear view mirror. She appeared tired and afraid, Trish didn't want to do it. She looked as if...

*"...hell froze over." Victor said, circling Trish like a vulture.*

*She sat in an otherwise empty conference room with only one light on. He took a seat across from her and crossed his arms. Trish swallowed hard and looked up, pleading with her eyes. "Something is wrong with Paul."*

*Victor digested her words. "I can't speak for your marriage. I can only say that Paul has proved to be an asset for Stone Enterprises. From my vantage point, there's nothing to be concerned about."*

*"I don't want you to hear me wrong when I say this, but I know you're kinda an all-work, no-play, kinda guy. I'm not judging how you live your life, but Paul was always a family man. It wasn't until he started working for you that he changed. I don't know if you're actually demanding too much of him or if Paul is just eager to please you, but it's putting strain on our marriage."*

*Victor considered her words for a long moment. He took a deep breath. "He puts it on himself."*

*"I'm not surprised," she said. "When we first started dating, he constantly tried to impress me, even long after we were together. He goes above and beyond."*

*"What do you want officer Reynalds?"*

*Trish blinked rapidly, taken aback. Victor still just saw her as an arm of the law. She'd come to meet him in the hopes of showing another side of her—the side with some humility—so Victor would see her as something more. "You can call me Trish and I don't know what I want. Maybe give him some time off or less work or just talk to him."*

*"I'm not a marriage counselor."*

"*I know, but if he's told he's doing well, maybe he won't feel the need to please you.*"

"*Have you talked to him about this?*"

"*No, he keeps shutting me out.*"

"*Well,*" Victor rose to his feet and approached the door. "*I'm not indebted to you officer. If my memory serves me, you came after me maliciously.*"

She looked up and found his eyes again. He stared at her with a smug expression and the door was wide open for her. "*My God, you hold onto grudges like no one else.*"

"*There are no grudges officer. There are people who have something to offer and there are people who waste my time. Our first encounter should have been our last, but you took it upon yourself to force me into your life. Now, I've brought us even closer by graciously offering your husband employment and you're asking favors of me. I don't remember hearing an apology and I don't remember hearing any bargaining.*"

"*Bargaining?*"

"*Yes, you're sitting in what we call our Central War Room. This is where we meet when we have decisions to make and we're out of sync. When I sit here with a colleague or a client, we form a give and take partnership because in this world, nothing is free—not even advice.*"

She was almost afraid to ask. "*Then...what do you want?*"

"*I'd like to discuss the terms over dinner.*"

Trish closed her eyes an shook her head in disbelief. "*So you'll make Paul's life easier if I fuck you?*"

"*That's not what I said.*"

"*How many women have you taken to dinner and finished the night with a handshake?*"

Victor nodded and sat patiently for a moment. She put the ball in his court but he denied her the pleasure of a response.

"*You're unbelievable,*" she said. "*I can't believe I asked you for anything and Paul isn't going to be happy about this either.*"

"*Officer Reynalds, when you're done flattering yourself, I'd like to make a proposal.*"

"*Oh, so you're able to negotiate outside of the bedroom?*"

He went on, ignoring her. "*There are people who make themselves appear to be very successful by putting large businesses under scrutiny. The more successful Stone Enterprises is, the more eyes are on me, regulating what I do and auditing my every move.*"

"*Good. You deserve that.*"

"*I'm not a criminal, but every day, there are people who attempt to prove that I am. I have enemies, big and small, but I have many.*"

*"Why are you telling me this?"*

*"Paul tells me another year or two and you could make detective. I've also seen your name in the news lately. In October, you put yourself in harm's way to negotiate with a suicidal man who was holding his wife and child hostage. The following month, you found a truckload of cocaine coming in from Mexico."*

*"That was dumb luck," she said. All she did was pull over a trucker for a busted headlight and picked up on facial signals that made her call for backup. In the end, they'd opened the bed of his truck to find it filled with cocaine.*

*"Regardless, your record is respectable. What I want Trish, is for us to be friends."*

*Alarms went off. He'd said her name this time and as she connected the dots, he watched her knowingly. "You need me to turn my head to you," she said. "You...you want to buy my loyalty."*

*"I haven't, nor do I plan on, doing anything illegal. I'm simply wanting you in my corner as these people try to regulate..."*

*"If you don't know what kind of cop I am by now..."*

*"Except we both know you've cut corners before. I've proved it and when you needed my silence, I remained quiet."*

*"You want information..." she said. "You want to have an inside man."*

*"Call it what you will. You're making this much larger than what it is."*

*"Never." She stood and grabbed her purse. She turned back to him, her face a jumble of shock and anger. "You've gone too far."*

*"Trish..." he said, calmly. She stopped and turned and Victor was no longer civil. "You've heard my terms. I want to remind you that while I could pull some strings and bring Paul back to you, I can also do the opposite."*

*"Are you serious right now?" She was exasperated.*

*"More traveling, surround him with beautiful women who love American men, put him in casinos and business trips in gentleman's clubs. He may be a decent man, but a man's atmosphere can shape him."*

*"Then you've been living in a trash can."*

*"You can insult me, or you can accept my proposal. You came to me officer Reynalds. You made an offer. I counter-offered. That's business..."*

...He began to shake as he saw the look in Trish's eyes. She was different than the last time he saw her. Whatever was happening, she wasn't the one driving. Something had changed her.

"I always meant to thank you for saving us that day," he said.

"What day?"

"When I saw Anthony at the hospital. Abby was there and that guy came to kill us and you showed up and saved us just in time. It seemed just like the movies, the way it was so last second and all."

"You did thank me for that."

"I don't think I did."

"You thanked me at least twice already."

"I just wanted to be sure." But that wasn't it. He was nervous. He was testing her. He knew it and so did she. Her responses were short and cold and each time she spoke, it further validated that she wasn't just there for no reason.

"We're going to your apartment," she said. "I need you to stay calm. I'm only going to want to have a talk with you."

He didn't know her angle and he couldn't keep putting his feet in the water. It was time to jump in. "Are you wanting the money or something?"

She was silent and just as he decided she wasn't going to respond, she spoke up. "About nine months ago, my daughter got sick. What needs to be done, I don't have the money for."

"I've got money."

"Not this kind of money."

"Wait, so you're saying you do it want it?" Brian was ready to start bouncing around in his seat, kicking the doors and windows until he was free. He knew he wouldn't get far though.

"I don't want it. God no. I would never have even considered that. I need it."

"So you're killing us…" Brian said, his mouth dry.

"Don't take it personal." He couldn't help but notice just how carelessly she'd said it.

"Who's all left?"

"Everyone."

"So I'm first?" If he wasn't so afraid, he might have gotten around to being offended, but right now, all he could think about was how close he was to his apartment. They were within blocks and he had to talk his way out first. "I have a lot of money and there's on-line things where you can get people to donate money. I'll start one. I'll seriously help."

She sat in silence the last couple of blocks while Brian went through begging, crying, and offering help in every conceivable way. Finally, they were parked and she turned, annoyed with him. She wished she hadn't said so much, but she needed people to know she wasn't evil. She needed them to understand that this was for her daughter. "Stop crying," she commanded. "Look at you. Do you think I can't see what you're into?"

"I'm not into anything," he said, a fresh stream of tears falling from his eyes.

"You were high the moment I picked you up. You look like you've lost fifty pounds. You're tired, unemployed, worthless… What do you do Brian?"

"I saved them too you know? At the hospital, I saved them. And then I showed up to vote against the will even though Victor was my friend."

"You already said that. Let's go."

"No."

"If you don't get out of the car and take me to your apartment, I will kill you right here."

Brian slowly exited the car, shaking and sweating so much that he could barely grip the handle. He led her inside, searching for a way out or hoping someone would approach. "I'll pay you anything," he said, his voice a whisper. "I'll sell my stuff. I can talk to Bernard Bell or Royce Morrow. They have money. Or what about…"

"Go," she said, giving him a shove.

He led her up to the third floor where he resided. He hoped William was there, but then wondered if he would be killed too. He couldn't stand the thought. He pulled his key from his pocket, but before he could put it in the lock, Trish had another idea, which was only a relief because it might give him another three minutes to think.

"Where's the stairs to the roof?"

## 4

At the same moment that Trish was ascending the stairs to the roof of Brian's apartment, Aileen had her mind on their last encounter. When Aileen had almost been raped and killed, there was no one she believed would identify and sympathize with her more than Trish Reynalds. When they met, Trish had been cold toward her and distracted by her own thoughts. At the time, Aileen thought she was just being a bitch, but her perspective was changing and what she was really starting to notice was the transformation in everyone. It wasn't just Trish or Tarek. From what she knew, it really was every single beneficiary.

She'd looked each name up, searching for news stories and had found a couple things that set off alarms. Royce Morrow's wife had died in what the media was calling an accident, but Royce Morrow said otherwise. Adlar Wilcox had fallen off the face of the earth. Charlie Palmer's house blew up. Some of it was new and some she knew, but it confirmed certain suspicions that were starting to feel like doom. Could a man truly orchestrate all of this from beyond the grave? He couldn't have done it to precision, but maybe Victor understood the chaos that would come of his will.

"I'm taking the book with me tomorrow," Aileen told Tarek when he arrived home.

"I need it though."

"You don't need it. You've read it twice. I haven't read it at all."

"Well, why do you even need it?"

"I want to read it."

"Why?"

She wanted to scream. He was talking down to her, treating her like she had no right to anything. Tarek didn't need it. He just carried it around protectively. "I'm looking into some things."

"Like what?"

"Like why all the people from Victor's will have changed so much."

"Probably because people change."

"Not in the ways I've seen. It's not natural."

"Well, we already know there's been some sour apples, but Stan Kline is locked up and the only other criminal is behind bars."

"Two weddings, two deaths, an attack, alcohol, disappearances…and I'm only counting what I know."

"What are you?" Tarek said with a smile of thick mockery. "Are you a detective now?"

Aileen wanted to cry, but it would be emotions that would turn this into a fight and it really was simple. "I just want to read it. I want to see what it says about everyone and what everyone did to be added to his will."

"He doesn't talk about the will. A lot of us aren't even in it."

"But I am, right?"

Tarek raised his eyebrows. "You don't know why you're on it?"

"I know why I'm on it. What I don't know is what happened years before he hated me. I want to know why he gave up on me." It wasn't until she spoke the words out loud that she realized them to be completely true. As much as she'd avoided reading the pages that discuss Aileen Thick, it had grown unavoidable. To understand Victor was to understand what his dying wish was capable of.

"I'll give you those pages."

"Give me the whole thing," she demanded. Tarek stood in place and smiled at her, seemingly amused by her attitude. "Or I'll take it with me and leave and you'll never see it again."

"What the hell's wrong with you?" he asked.

"It's one day. You'll get it back."

"I better." He walked away and came back with the stack of pages, dropping it on the table. She noticed he'd bent multiple pages back and even highlighted select passages.

"Tarek…"

He slammed the door to his bedroom and she stared at it for a long time, fully accepting that the days of Tarek and Aileen were getting shorter with every moment. She hoped she could open his eyes to the reality in front of them, but Tarek didn't want his eyes opened. He wanted fame and that meant stepping to the side and changing. The real Tarek cared about people and privacy and the lives of those he was associated with. This Tarek was shutting down that part of him, but when this film, or whatever it was, was finished, would he be able to turn it back on? Was the funny, charismatic Tarek Appleton the world knew and loved, completely dead and replaced with this guy? It dawned on Aileen that he really might revive his career and he'd ride that wave forever if it did. Or he'd be laughed out of Hollywood. She wouldn't be there to catch him when he fell and she certainly didn't want to stick around while this darkness consumed him.

He was the closest thing he had to a friend, but he was distracted, just as her son was distracted, and Trish Reynalds was distracted. Aileen was no hero and she would never be the leader or the influence that the group needed, but she feared she was the only one who was fully awake.

If shit really were to hit the fan, she didn't know how she could relay the danger to everyone else.

*It doesn't have to be me*, she thought. *This isn't something you're good at.*

5

Trish closed a large metal door behind her and pulled her gun, holding it at her side. It was only Brian and her alone on the roof. She started to feel sick as she prepared herself to force him over the edge. If she showed weakness, he'd play to that, so she stayed strong, putting on a stern face but weeping on the inside.

Brian hovered in the middle of the rooftop, staying as far from the edge as he could. She raised the gun and he backed a little, but stayed far from the edge. "Jump," she said.

"I can't…" His face wrinkled and a flood of tears fell.

She opened her mouth but could say no more. She'd tried to predict what this moment would be like and in her mind, it had been so simple. She didn't want to shoot him and she didn't want to push him. She wanted him to jump. She knew it was foolish. Her partner, Carlos, used to say that the guy who gives the gun to a man who he knows will definitely kill a person and doesn't care and allows it to happen, isn't as guilty as the man who pulled the trigger and commits murder, but he's damn near as close as you can get.

Brian wouldn't stop begging, and soon he weakened at the knees and fell to the ground, shaking uncontrollably. She lowered her gun and watched him with pity. It wasn't too late to turn back, but she needed her daughter to live. If she could get past Brian, she'd be unstoppable, and even his pathetic ways couldn't tempt her to pull the trigger. Laying on the tar of the roof made it seemingly impossible to get him to the edge. All she could do was to put a bullet in him now and walk away.

Trish stepped toward him, closing the distance, and trained her gun on his body, which was curled in a ball, shaking as he sobbed. If anyone deserved this, it was Brian. She could see the track marks on his wrist, and the deep lines under his eyes. He wasn't functioning well and would probably never contribute much to the world, but he was just a guy who wanted to live, sobbing uncontrollably because he believed his life was as important as Shiloh's and from a faraway distance, looking down, wasn't it?

She took another step and pressed the gun against the back of his head. He jumped and repeated "please" and "I'm sorry" as if he did something wrong in her eyes.

She closed her eyes and imagined squeezing the trigger, but told herself she should have waited longer. She should have prepared more. She knew she wasn't a bad person, but she'd also been part of many arrests in which the murderer, chained in handcuffs, spouted off excuses which fell on deaf ears. A killer's a killer and there was no good reason. That was always her belief, but here she was.

She pulled the gun back and put her hand to her temple, trying to think. *Shiloh would live.*

But…

*What would Shiloh think of me? What happens today is forever going to be burned into her memory.*

But…

*Shiloh would live.*

She desperately searched for a rescue, or some kind of hope from Gregory Neomin or Charlie Palmer. She wanted to reach out and beg them to give her news. She pulled her phone out of her pocket.

And held it there, afraid to open it.

She'd have missed calls…missed messages…people she didn't want to face or answer to. Yet, she needed one last ray of hope.

She powered it on…

*"…I assume you've made a decision?" Victor asked. He sat with his feet reclined as Trish walked through his mansion, looking up at the*

*ceiling and down the halls. She knew he had a lot, but being in his home truly brought perspective to his situation.*

*Trish and Victor squared off. Trish tried to read his thoughts but his face wouldn't betray him.*

*"We need to figure this out," she said. "You have so much already. Why can't you just be a corrupt individual instead of asking everyone else to be put at risk with you?"*

*"I have never done anything worthy of the law coming down on me officer. Not one thing."*

*"Have you directed people to do those things?"*

*He fell silent long enough that it answered her question. "We do need to figure this out. I am unwilling to lose Paul and I'm not going to continually answer to you. If you want to play super-cop, then find a real criminal. There are plenty. Anything you do to me from this day forward, I will retaliate with full force."*

*She left his home in a hurry, needing to be away from him so she could breathe. When she was outside, she walked toward the street, tired of this cat and mouse game she'd been playing with him—tired of trying to protect her husband, who was an adult and could take care of himself. "Screw it," she said to herself. The whole charade was trivial at best. Who cared if Victor was the criminal she believed him to be and who really cared if Paul was in on it and brought the law on himself someday? She found herself wanting to say "told you so" to him and hopefully, if shit did hit the fan, it would knock some sense into him. Maybe this problem would eventually fix itself. Paul would grow tired of Victor or Victor would give him the boot. No matter what happened, as long as Trish and Shiloh were safe, that was all that mattered. Paul had changed, and she wasn't going to sit around and try to convince him to be the man she married. He would either fix himself or it would work itself out.*

*She looked up at the sound of a car starting its engine and driving away. She recognized the car and the driver and her breath stopped in her throat. Paul had been watching, but why? And what conclusions would he draw?*

*"Great," she said.*

*Paul drew the conclusion she was afraid he'd draw. It was the only thing he could think. She entered the kitchen to find him doing the dishes, making a show of how angry he was by slamming drawers and nearly breaking plates as he put them away.*

*"Knock it off," she said. "I wasn't there for the reason you think and you probably know that since all I talk about is how much I don't like the*

guy."

"Oh, no, I know why you're there and you're going to stop now."

"Why was I there?"

"You're trying to get me fired. You're trying to bust him. You think that thing with the DII meant he's guilty, even though they cut him loose."

She was somewhat relieved that Paul didn't think she was cheating on him, but also disheartened to hear the truth out of his mouth. It was almost worse. "I've only asked him to look out for you, to not drag you down when things go bad."

Paul laughed and shook his head. "Things go bad..." he repeated, finding it funny.

"You think you're invincible but he's already coming under fire for some of his practices. If you look him up on the Internet, or look up Stone Enterprises, you'll find a lot of people who make some strong claims. Some are people who used to work for him who couldn't deal with the company ethics. Can't you consider the possibility that not everything is on the up and up?"

"I already know it's not. That's why you need to back off! What happens if you help bring the company down? I go down with it!"

"Not if you're not doing anything..."

"Except I am."

The statement hit her hard and she tried to register it for a long moment. A thousand questions ricocheted in her head, but nothing came out. Only a plea. "Then you need to stop."

"Stay out of my business."

"I'm your wife. It's our business. I'm not going to have Shiloh come visit you in jail."

"The shit we're talking about is small potatoes that won't even see the light of day. I'm talking off the books."

"Why are you freely admitting this? Do you want me to be pissed at you?"

"Maybe I do, because you've been pissing me off for a long time, so there you go. All the terrible things you don't want me to be—I'm those things."

"Great way to set an example for your daughter..."

Paul struck her so hard and fast that she saw a flash of light and when she recovered, she was staring at a wall mindlessly. She turned back in anger, unable to believe what just happened. Before she could speak, he was wagging his finger in her face.

"Don't talk to me about being an example for my daughter. I stay home with her every night, helping her with her homework, reading her stories before she goes to sleep. You're on the streets, trying to make a widow of *me, while I'm raising our daughter. I'm making the money. I'm paying the bills. You haven't done anything for this family. You've only done for yourself."*

*His words hurt, especially since she felt the same way toward him, but she didn't feel like calling him a hypocrite, or listing everything she had done for the family. Instead, she only focused on the fact that he hit her. She stepped close to him and though he was bigger and more intimidating, she raised herself to his level and looked into his eyes with a seriousness that she never thought she'd need with Paul. "If you ever hit me again, I will file charges and leave you so fast..."*

*"No need," he said, and turned his back to her to walk away and pack a suitcase. "We're done..."*

"...Trish, this is...this is Greg Neomin,"

She pressed her phone against her ear, listening intently and praying there would be some hope restored in his message.

"I'm calling to tell you that I made a mistake. I misdiagnosed your daughter..." For a long moment, he said nothing as if he was trying to gather himself. "I didn't misdiagnose her. I...I lied about her diagnosis and I can't keep living with this weight. Please know that...I'm so sorry and nothing will ever make it right but Shiloh is perfectly healthy. That's what you need to know. Just...be with her and...I'm sorry. I can't...I can't explain. Talk to Dr. Palmer...please. I deserve to answer for this but...I can't."

His voice broke and the message ended. She tried calling him back, but no one answered. She tried calling Charlie, but that was silent too. She tried them both again and it wasn't until she gave up trying to contact both doctors that she let it all register. She couldn't comprehend how what he was saying could even be remotely true, but she think she understood the point of it all. Shiloh's tumor had been falsified. To further confirm this, Shiloh had texted her saying the same, and left messages of her own.

She couldn't bring herself to listen to them. Instead, she turned back to Brian, who was looking up at her from where he lay, his eyes begging for mercy. She had been moments away from doing something she wouldn't have been able to take back, but as she readied herself to hurry off to Shiloh and search for answers, she still had Brian left to face. She crouched to his level.

"You know I can see you're using illegal substances," she said. "Yes or no?"

"Y...yes..." he said, his voice trembling.

"I'm letting you off the hook, but I can throw you away for a long time for this."

"I d...I didn't h...hurt..."

"Keep it that way," she said, her voice stern. Inside, she was just as afraid, but Brian had to believe everything that happened was by design.

Brian nodded his head and she backed away from him, trying to determine whether or not she'd delivered a blow that he wouldn't recover from. He'd already put himself on a bad path but the last thing she wanted to hear about was that he'd completely spiral after this encounter.

She drove home at a fast pace, needing to see her daughter. She called Charlie again and again and then Neomin. Neither picked up. While she'd turned her phone off, it seemed a lot had happened, but no one was around to answer her questions. Instead of pursuing them further, she ran to her daughter, who was crying when she saw her mother. They both hugged each other tightly and Shiloh scolded her with real anger, asking where she had been. She told Trish that Charlie needed to talk to her. She gave Trish the information about the hotel but when she called, she learned Charlie had never checked in. She didn't know what was going on but as badly as she wanted to know, all she was able to focus on was how relieved she was, how happy she was that Shiloh was fine. Answers and anger would come later.

She called the station and took the next week off. She argued with the chief of police over all the time off she'd been taking lately, but assured him that when she was back, she wouldn't have any needs and that Shiloh's treatment had been working. After the call, she kept her phone nearby, the volume way up in case anyone called. She learned later that night that Dr. Neomin had committed suicide. She tried to enjoy her time with Shiloh but kept asking herself the obvious question: Why had he done it in the first place? Charlie Palmer had the answer to that question, but her phone never rang.

As Trish fell asleep with Shiloh laying against her on the couch, Brian hid in his apartment. He took two tablets Will had given him to calm himself down. He drank a couple beers and called Will, begging him to do something. Will came over and watched Brian spiral, smoking and drinking and trying to calm his nerves. By the end of the night, Brian fell into his usual coma. Will got to his feet and walked to the bedroom he'd been staying in, turning back to look at Brian. Any day, he wouldn't wake up. What happened with Trish had set him into a deeper depression. His perceived stress level was high and he wasn't coping well at all.

"Idiot," he said, realizing just how much he'd grown to despise Brian. He closed his bedroom door and opened his phone to find his son had sent him a text: **Hey, Mom said you fucked her on child support this month. That true?**

William closed his phone and fell back into the bed. "Yeah, it's true," he said to the ceiling, watching the fan turn. "Just die already," he said out loud, hoping tomorrow would be the day Van Dyke didn't open his eyes.

# Chapter 15

1

*She believed that life was perfect. Though they'd met by happenstance and were forced together by a drunken night that resulted in her pregnancy, and though he was much older than her and different in every way, life together had become a rhythm and it dawned on Aileen Thick that she was happy.*

*When Victor committed, he became a different man. Maybe it was because he refused to be forced into anything—the decision had to be his —but when it was, he was supportive, loving, and available. He invited Aileen to social gatherings and took her to nice restaurants. He bought her clothes and jewelry and supported her while she took classes. He introduced her to other artists and gallery owners, giving her every opportunity to showcase her talent.*

*She started to fall in love.*

*She never saw it coming. They were of two different worlds, but when they synced, she was truly happy. When she was within a week of her delivery date, all fears were gone. She would raise the twins and give them everything a child could want. She'd offer unconditional love and Victor would provide generously. It was something completely different than how she grew up and she never expected to break away so completely. Memories of her parents were far in the past and all she could do was look ahead.*

*They'd decided on names, but neither told each other the name they'd picked. Aileen picked the name for the boy and Victor for the girl. They would decide later if the names didn't match well and re-evaluate if they needed to.*

*Victor preferred Aileen to be home. He was old fashioned and believed that's where she should be. At first, it was offensive, but she'd learned he had a soft spot for women—that he simply liked to accommodate them. Whether it was someone he'd dated or a woman in his office, he preferred their company. She'd noticed his lack of excitement at the prospect of raising a boy. He'd wanted a girl and he'd settled on twins, but his excitement was for the girl. Aileen could only hope he'd love the boy equally. She wondered what it was about women that moved Victor so much. It wasn't just attraction. He held himself differently in the company of all women.*

*He never talked about his mother and she knew he had respect for his father. Wherever it was rooted, she assumed she'd never know, but Victor had handled life well enough so far. She wasn't worried about his biases.*

*Her belly made her miserable. She was twice the size and felt more kicks than expected, each day growing more painful. The babies wanted out and she was more than happy to make that happen, but she carried them past the due date by a week before her water broke.*

*Victor had a pager and he was ready to go the moment it beeped. Aileen was to carry hers on her at all times, but it just so happened that when her water broke, she was outside talking to a neighbor. The neighbor called an ambulance and the pager sat on the dining room table indoors. It was one of two times Aileen didn't happen to have it on her. She'd walked out to get the mail and assumed she'd be indoors within two minutes. Instead, the chatter lasted an hour and by the time Aileen was at the hospital, she remembered the pager and asked someone to call Victor quickly. Calls were made, but Victor never answered, even through his business line. He sat in meetings with his pager in his pocket, waiting for it to beep.*

*If only he would have known she was going into labor that day, the perfect life may have gone forever…*

…She walked toward his memoirs slowly and stared at the pages, harmlessly stacked, daring her to open and read. She refused, afraid of what she would find. She wanted to read everything from beginning to end, but when she skimmed the pages, she skipped ahead when she saw her name. She tried reading from the beginning, but found herself uninterested in the early and teen years. She was disgusted that Victor even considered himself interesting enough to write about.

She suddenly straightened the pages back into a neat stack and with solemn eyes, just stared at the cover page for a long while.

Finally, she grabbed the stack and carried it in her bag to the coffeehouse on Larchmont, where she could sit outdoors, sip on a coffee, and try to find some will to read. She didn't know why it was so hard to know Victor's feelings of her. Maybe because she never fully understood what changed so many years ago. Things had been going in a good direction and then Victor hated her—wanted nothing to do with her—blamed her for things she never had control over.

When she had her latte, it didn't seem to help the mood. She stared at the stack of papers without turning a page. It had been such a long time ago and she had tried getting answers from Victor for years until it seemed possible. Now, suddenly his whole life was in front of her and understanding could be so simple.

She flipped past the Aileen pages and settled on a passage. She read.

**Business is a generic term to describe a number of processes involved in production of products and services. The process in which these activities occur is neither linear nor organized as a game of chess. Business is war and there are many events occurring simultaneously and at different speeds. Despite this difference, the stories told by a chess game are similar to those that can be told in business. For example, the idea of sacrificing material to gain compensation in the form of an attack on an opponent or positional advantage is something companies do all the time. There is also the concept of an overloaded piece which can occur if a company expands too quickly and spreads resources over a number of areas.**

**In the 70s, there was a lot of discussion about the Japanese incursion into American automobile markets. The Japanese knew they would not be able to clear a profit during their ascent, so they sacrificed profits to gain market share with their energy-efficient and cheaper cars. Through meticulous production and total quality management techniques, the quality of these cars improved rapidly and combined with higher gas prices, American consumers began buying the Hondas, the Toyotas, and the Datsuns (now Nissan). When the American auto companies reacted with cheap substitutes, it was too late. The Japanese were able to increase awareness, grab market share and have never looked back. Japanese cars now command a lion's share of the American market and its cars are popular worldwide and synonymous with quality.**

Aileen knew that most of what Victor had to say was above her understanding, but what she read stood out and somehow brought together a whole sequence of events. She'd refused to believe that events were unfolding just as Victor had intended in his will. She'd always thought he was just insane and bitter, but the question kept arising: Did he know what he was doing?

She read on…

**One of the most important aspects of business is preparation for battle. Prior to an inevitable clash, a manager has to have a plan and**

launch pre-emptive tactics to deter competitors from entering a market. This also comes with an understanding of the competitors, their strengths, weaknesses and vulnerabilities. We often enter a tournament game thinking about our opponent and perhaps we've studied their previous games or have encountered them before. Based upon this intelligence, we develop a strategy that will hopefully help us to meet a strategic end.

This however is ancillary to the preparation that one has to do on their own set of skills. Despite the gathering of intelligence, one does not go into a tournament without some basic preparation of opening strategies and without developing confidence in one's abilities in tactics and strategies. In addition, there is also the idea of establishing a good frame of mind for battle. Perhaps physical fitness becomes a part of this equation... proper rest, diet and meditative techniques. Likewise, companies have to provide some internal support to motivate their employees and provide them with the environment to compete at a high level. Companies such as Microsoft and Google have become famous for their corporate culture which allow their company to stay motivated and prepared to take on competitors at any time.

The parallels between business and chess are striking in a number of obvious ways. So much that there are countless company ads that elevate chess to a loft status due to its perceived connection to making intelligent decisions. Of course there are many other characteristics that make chess an attractive pitch. The purpose of understanding the game of chess is not merely to express a connection to the prestige of the game. Chess involves foresight, which is a quality I've always valued above all others. Foresight to see two, five, twenty moves ahead—to position yourself and your opponents in such a way that you see their future long before they do.

Aileen set her coffee down and reread everything. She'd forgotten her interest in what Victor had to say about her. Her mind was back to the connections, to the tragedy that had struck many beneficiaries in such a short period of time and the significant life changes, that on the surface, seemed to be individual events. Could everyone have been positioned?

She continued turning Victor's written words in her head and randomized images appeared. Abby Palmer, Anthony Freeman, Richard Libby, the lottery, the fire, Stanley Kline, Tarek Appleton's descent into darkness. Now, William and Henry. Henry who was linked to Maria Haskins. William, who was linked to Sal, who tried to kill her. She considered the possibility of a coincidence, but reread the passage one more time.

**...to position yourself and your opponents in such a way that you see their future long before they do.**

"No one sees it," she whispered to herself. She went inside to order another coffee, knowing she had a lot more reading to do.

2

It took a great deal of persuasion, but Anthony Freeman was able to talk Tarek Appleton into visiting him at his campsite. Tarek was tired and not in the mood for company. He had always liked Anthony and considered him a friend. As he drove to the site, he suddenly resented Anthony, though he was unsure as to why exactly. The light that shone on Anthony had somehow changed and he was no longer a talented, intelligent, author. Now, he only thought of him as a drunk.

He drove onto the gravel road and wound his way through the trees until he came to the river that drew a line from one site to another. He parked and got out, irritated to see that Anthony wasn't outside waiting. He knocked on the trailer and only a moment later, Anthony emerged, his eyes bloodshot and some extra fatigue in his movements.

"Are you okay? Tarek asked.

"Never better," Anthony said, not bothering to even sound as if he was lying.

"I can't stay long."

"It won't be necessary. It's just a proposition."

"Is it something that couldn't have been discussed over the phone?"

Anthony paused and sized Tarek up. "Have I done something to upset you?"

"No, let's just get on with it."

"Very well. I want to talk about your recent trip to Hawaii. I want to talk about what happened."

"The fire?"

"Yes. I want to know your theory."

"Todd Mason or Jason Stone. Wasn't me or Aileen."

"Let's talk about Jason."

"What about him?"

"Shortly after Victor died, his son walks away and starts over on an island. This is also shortly after I was stabbed because someone with money and ties to Stone Enterprises set up a lottery where our lives were bet against. Jason wasn't in the room to help invalidate the will and when you vacationed there, it was Jason who was well away from danger, correct?"

"Jason came to the rescue."

"You came to the rescue."

"That's not how I remember it," Tarek said. "I got there after Jason. We hauled Aileen out."

"Maybe you were the intended target."

Tarek's patience was thin. "Alright, alright, I get it. You think Jason Stone stabbed you. It sounds like it's all worked out in your head, so what'd you bring me here for?"

"I've got weeks, maybe days before this thing inside kills me. I don't want to just die out here for nothing. I'm not supposed to."

"Yeah, whys that?"

"Because I was willing to die and fate stepped in."

Tarek laughed, resenting Anthony more with every word. "What do you want?"

"Get Jason back. Any way you can. Tell him something happened to Stone Enterprises. Tell him something happened to his mother. It doesn't matter what you say. I just want him alone with me."

"You're not a murderer. You wouldn't do it."

"If it means preservation of the remaining in the group, I will."

"Sounds like you don't have a sure thing there," Tarek said, walking back to his car. "Good luck."

"What the hell's wrong with you?" Anthony shouted.

Tarek turned back. "Do I owe you some respect? Is that what's happening here? Maybe you've forgotten history Anthony but I haven't. If not for me, you would've been scraped off the pavement for weeks. I stood up to Stan when…"

"He kidnapped you. You had no choice."

"Okay," Tarek said. "You're welcome."

"I've been grateful."

"Of course you have. You're sitting alone in the woods for the last six months, getting trashed and plotting a murder over someone who had nothing to do with your problems. It's pathetic."

"That's not what I'm doing."

"It's always what you're doing. Ever been married Anthony? When was your last relationship? Oh, right. You're so super smart and you don't have time for anything or anyone. You just strive to prove yourself constantly and when you fail, you try to kill yourself. What kind of accomplishment is it to be famous off of a suicide note? Wasn't it Victor who saved you? And what happened? You treated him like shit."

Anthony was enraged. "He deserved it! You have no idea!"

"Oh, I do. I'm on his will too, remember? But the difference between you and I is that I actually regret what I did to him. I did it because I was selfish at the time. You're just ungrateful, pissing on the grave of the man who gave you the breath in your lungs today. What's so damn important about fate and dying with a purpose and all that other shit you try to sell? If you want to be dead, then stop making excuses. Fate intervened? Well then try something else. Just don't come to me asking me to help you murder someone who may or may not have anything to do with your conspiracy theories. You just want to blame him because he's your enemy's son."

"His name wasn't on the list."

"I don't care about the list!"

"You weren't stabbed."

"I've had my share of problems due to Victor's will, but I protected your names when everyone was asking and I prevented most of your deaths. In return, my career was ruined. Don't try to drag me into your bullshit. What you're doing isn't noble."

Anthony put his hands up in surrender. He wasn't sure what to say, and was certainly thrown off-guard having been out-talked by Tarek. Tarek was a personality most of the time. He was easy-going and liked to mock the world and crack jokes. The Tarek he was with was tired and frustrated. Anthony regretted asking him for help.

"Can I go?" Tarek asked.

"Yup," Anthony said, looking down. Tarek walked to the car, but Anthony stepped forward with his hands in his pockets. "Tarek…" Tarek looked up. "This is probably the last time you will ever see me alive."

"You want some last words as a souvenir?" Tarek asked.

"I'd like to offer a few."

"Make it quick."

"I've lived with a lot of regret in my life. It sounds like you have a few of your own. Don't let what happened between you and Victor eat at you. You were eventually going to be famous with or without him. Just don't lose sight of who you really are. The world grew to love Tarek Appleton. Not a character or your net worth."

"Yeah," Tarek said and stopped to give Anthony one long look. He really did look sick. He knew they probably never would see each other again. "I'll remember that."

He entered his car and drove away, catching a glimpse of Anthony in his rear view mirror as he pulled a flask from his inside pocket.

3

She heard Victor's voice speaking as she read the words in his manuscript. A lot of it wasn't relevant, but she turned page after page, reading it all, looking for an indication of what he really wanted from the group. Here and there, he would mention someone she knew, but it was always in relation to a story that had nothing to do with their personal relationships. A girl cleared her table and said something to her, but Aileen was deep in the manuscript.

She looked up suddenly and allowed herself to run events through her head again, hoping this time she could connect them all. A man attacks her in the middle of the night on a busy street, with the intent of raping her. This man was friends with a man who worked with Brian Van Dyke and also happened to be friends with the man who married Maria Haskins. Aileen drew a diagram on the back of a blank page, connecting person to person. They could have all connected as a result of the will. Maybe there was no coincidence at all.

Then, she wrote the names, one by one.

Jason Stone
Todd Mason
Tarek Appleton
Trish Reynalds
Brian Van Dyke
Maria Haskins
Charlie and Abby Palmer
Richard Libby
Toby O'Tool
Christian Dent
Royce Morrow
Anthony Freeman

She wondered about the remaining few that she hadn't seen or heard from. She thought about Trish Reynalds, who she'd called after she was attacked but the Trish that had appeared had been different than she remembered.

One by one, she thought about each beneficiary and how Victor had wanted to create an environment that no one would enjoy being a part of. Sure, there had been some initial hope that maybe she would end up with the money, but after the reading, the ramifications of surviving the longest began to set in. She knew it wouldn't be her. Even if there had been no foul play, she wasn't young anymore and she certainly didn't have it in her to even think about bringing death on any of the others. She also never felt her life was in danger. The death of fourteen people was too complex. When she'd looked around the room, she had just seen people like her...people who would have liked the money, but wouldn't resort to something drastic to have it. Christian Dent was the exception, but he was incapacitated. Trish Reynalds was a cop, and her presence had made her feel safe. Now, she wasn't so sure.

Anthony Freeman had been the voice of reason, but he currently seemed out of his mind.

Tarek Appleton had proved to be a protector...a hero even...now he personified the very man who set it all in motion.

She realized she'd been reading but hadn't been paying attention. She backtracked and stopped, her mouth dry as she came across a passage that was leading up to another Aileen reference.

If she hadn't stopped for gas that night, if she'd picked another gas station, if they'd been there five minutes sooner or five minutes later, her whole life would have been on a different course...better for her...but without Jason. Even if she hadn't gone back to his house. Her friends had drunkenly flirted with Victor. She'd played the role of the responsible friend and when Victor stood up for her in front of her friends, the moment stuck in her head. She dropped them off and went back to thank him and apologize.

*That's not why I went back.*

She'd initiated the kiss. She'd undone his pants. It had been all her.

Victor never pushed her to do something she didn't already want to do.

His chronicles would probably tell the same story.

As much as she'd hated him, as much as he'd ruined, as off-kilter as her life became because of him, she had started the whole thing that night. It was Aileen's moment of weakness, her actions that led her back to him. It was the same reason that deep down she'd always hated herself for that moment.

Yet, she had gotten Jason out of the deal. And maybe things would have worked with Victor if not for the moment that changed everything. Her life was defined by mere seconds...by moments that if had been a little to the right or left, a little later or earlier, moments that created...

*"...complications."*

*"What do you mean?" Aileen asked, doctors and nurses working at her bedside as the drugs began taking effect and Aileen's eyelids grew heavier. "What complications?"*

*Half an hour earlier, when Aileen entered the hospital, everything had been running smoothly, except that Victor Stone couldn't be contacted. She'd hoped he would check his messages and was ready to hop in the first taxi straight to wherever she was when her water broke. She'd learned not to expect much from the man. He'd always been honest about who he was and what she could expect from him, but she'd hoped he'd only set those expectations so that she'd never use them against him if he couldn't live up to them.*

*Now, more than ever, she needed comfort, and the only person she could think of was Victor. Before she'd even made it to the gurney, she began coughing and had a hard time breathing. One doctor turned into six and the next thing she knew, she had a tube down her throat. The doctors worked urgently and her own doctor leaned down and spoke softly as she started to grow hazy.*

*"In pregnancy," her doctor said, "...large blood vessels from the mother feed into the placenta and some of them are veins. If there is a tear in the amniotic sac around or through the placenta, the amniotic fluid enters the mother's blood stream."*

*"Okay," she said, barely able to speak. "What does that mean for me?"*

*"We had to put a tube in you because the embolism set off an anaphylactic reaction, constricting the bronchial tubes and shutting down your airways. At the same time, a phenomenon known as disseminated intravascular coagulation occurred. Your blood is losing its ability to form a stable clot and so you've suffered a profound drop in blood pressure. We've stabilized you, but a relatively large amount of amniotic fluid is not supposed to be in maternal circulation. If it goes to the lungs, it can cause an immediate reaction from a mechanical obstruction perspective. Now Mrs. Thick, we have a couple options, but..."*

*She didn't hear the rest. Her heart-rate rose and she passed out again for what felt like days, but in reality, it was two hours later that she opened her eyes, still pregnant, closely monitored, and the room filled with doctors and the chief of obstetrics.*

*Her doctor, who had the job of being the compassionate voice in the room, sat at her level and met her eyes. "Have you picked out names yet?"*

*"My husband wanted a girl and I wanted a boy. Since we're having both, we agreed we'd both name one but we didn't tell each other. I know that the names may not match well, but we're going to discuss that when we do the reveal."*

*Silence. Compassionate doctor looked up at his colleagues and then back to Aileen.*

*"We don't have a lot of time right now Aileen. You're going to have to undergo an emergency procedure to stop the internal bleeding. Your kids are at risk right now. The heartbeats have slowed."*

*"What do I have to do?"*

*"We have two options. We can do a C-section, but your babies would be at risk."*

*"What?" she asked, trying to sit up, but she grew dizzy and her head hit the pillow.*

*"You need to stay calm Aileen. We're going to go over this."*

*"Why would a C-section put them at risk?"*

*"The anesthesia we would use to save your life would kill the babies."*

*"We're not doing that."*

*"The other option is to do the same surgical procedure, only you stay awake. You would put your own life at risk."*

*"What the hell is wrong with me? What do I have? I was healthy yesterday."*

*"You are healthy. You have what's called AFE. Sometimes the fluid surrounding the baby will penetrate the blood stream and put you at risk for a pulmonary edema or heart failure. The amniotic fluid in your blood stream will eventually kill you. You've lost twelve pints of blood and you've had a transfusion. The fluid in your blood is filled with foreign cells from your babies. Sometimes, that can mean some hair or fingernails from your unborn child enter your bloodstream. When a large amount of amniotic fluid from the sac around the baby enters maternal circulation, there is often a high mortality rate. You need to understand this before you make a decision."*

*"Where's my husband?" she asked. "Have you called my husband?"*

*"We've called and left messages."*

*"I need my husband," she said, her voice breaking into a cough."*

*Suddenly the machines at her side were beeping and the doctor was speaking urgently again. Aileen lost all focus and was unable to understand what was happening around her. The room began to spin. She heard the doctor tell her she had to make a decision now. She couldn't remember her options. She only saw flashes in front of her eyes: Her parents, her friends, Victor. The flashes moved in time toward the future, to the life she wanted that was slipping away. All she fully understood was that she was going to die.*

*"Please God, save the babies," she said as darkness swallowed her...*

...The light hit her face as the sun peaked out between the trees. She could barely see the manuscript, but she needed the break. Reading his words was tantamount to sitting with Victor and listening to him speak.

A lot of what Victor had written was uninteresting or went over her head. She didn't care much about his feelings for business, but often found passages that spilled over into how he felt about people. Many times, she got the impression that worlds overlapped for him—that his philosophy about the man sitting across from him with a pitch was not far removed from the woman lying next to him in bed.

**Business can be a lot like chess: there are surely principles that generally apply, but they might admit of important exceptions. If you**

want to play good chess, a principle like "Don't lose your Queen" is almost always worth following. But it admits of exceptions: sometimes sacrificing your Queen is a brilliant thing to do. Occasionally, it is the only thing you can do. It remains a fact, however, that from any position in a game of chess there will be a range of objectively good moves and objectively bad ones.

Aileen had never played chess, but had a good understanding of how the game worked. Victor had been analytical in all things. He'd spend a good deal of time in a restaurant, staring at a menu and adding the cost of a rib-eye versus the cost of a porterhouse, adding the sides at cost and searching for the best bargain. Aileen understood that while some people told Victor he was rich and didn't need to be frugal, that the truth was that he was rich because he was frugal. She found hints of this throughout the manuscript.

**Parents still think that their wealth can automatically transform their children into economically productive adults. They are wrong. Discipline and initiative can't be purchased like automobiles or clothing off a rack.**

There were passages she admired and passages she rolled her eyes at and when she came to a point in which Victor was going to talk about being a father, there was about a page where she caught her name throughout, which is what made her close it and order another drink. Now considered skipping ahead.

She reconsidered. This was why she picked it up in the first place. Hadn't she always been curious about just what it was that caused Victor to turn on her? Had it really been in the hospital, or was there more to it? She backed up and read the preface to the section where her name was peppered throughout.

**Imagine that you're looking at an ocean and you see many waves today, but tomorrow you see a fewer number of waves, and it is less turbulent. Are you looking at the same ocean? People are actually patterns of behavior of a universal consciousness. There was no such thing as Aileen, because what I saw as Aileen was a constantly transforming consciousness that appeared as a certain personality, a certain mind, a certain ego, a certain body. There was a different Aileen when she was a teenager and a different Aileen when she was a baby. Who was the real Aileen?**

**There is an old proverb about three blind men and an elephant. The first blind man grabs hold of the elephant's ivory tusk and describes the smooth, hard surface that he feels. The second blind man grabs hold of one of the elephant's legs. He describes the tough, muscular girth that he feels. The third blind man grabs hold of the**

elephant's tail and describes the slender and sinewy appendage that he feels. Since their mutual descriptions are so different, and since none of the men can see the others, each thinks that he has grabbed hold of a different animal.

Aileen Thick pretended she was content, but deep down, she knew I'd taken her away from something more. I gave her the opportunity to continue on her path. I even offered her help and I'd ask her what she wanted and she would pretend everything was perfect but would say 'I just want to be happy.' That statement: I just want to be happy, is a hole cut out of the floor and covered with a rug. Once it is stated, the implication is that you're not. The 'I just want to be happy' bear-trap is that until you define precisely, just exactly what happy is, you will never feel it.

Aileen closed the book again and stared straight forward, unable to be angry or feel anything at all. The only thing she wondered was how it was Victor understood her so much, but never relayed any of this to her.

What made her angrier than anything was that he was right. The same thing she'd resented him for, he had understood.

She opened the manuscript again and looked down at the page. Her name was plastered all over it. She was afraid to move on, but everything was honest. It told of how they met, how she'd come back to his place that evening, and the course of events that led them toward marriage, toward the babies, and toward that fateful day in the hospital. She'd never relived it so vividly in sequence, and so much of it, she'd forgotten until she reread it. To someone else, it was an interesting read, but Aileen's mouth was dry, her insides heavy, as if she could heave up her coffee at any moment. She reminded herself this was a long time ago, and all this was, is what happened. She needed to face what she knew to be true. It could be the only way she'd ever fully understand Victor.

She read on.

4

Tarek thought about what Aileen had told him the day before. She'd tried to point out the difference in beneficiaries in the last year, and though at the time, she'd upset him, he couldn't deny his surprise at the fact Anthony Freeman was back on the bottle. There had been other incidents in his face, but he didn't have the energy to think about them anymore. He was on a different kind of mission which required great focus. The thing was, even if Aileen was right, it didn't change anything. Tarek wasn't built to be any kind of savior. He stuck his neck out for the group twice and he wasn't even sure they cared. He'd done his job. If they were too weak to avoid their actions, it wasn't his job to play guidance counselor with them.

He brushed it all out of his mind as he sat at an outdoor diner eating sushi by himself. A couple tables away, two teenagers spotted him and laughed and made gestures. He'd seen their kind time and again. They weren't starstruck by celebrity. They got their rocks off mocking celebrities and hoping to be famous for being the person who threw a water balloon at Tom Cruise or got in a fight with Dustin Diamond in a bar. It made for good news and stood out from the swarms of fans who just wanted an autograph. Tarek hated their type. Plenty of people knew Tarek was among them, but sat and enjoyed their lunch instead of calling attention to the fact. It was the tactful thing to do, but these guys were clearly too immature not to call attention to being near him.

He pulled out his phone and scrolled his contacts, looking for a girl he could meet up with for drinks and a nightcap.

His thumb scrolled the screen and the contacts spun nearly to the bottom where he came across Tony Tadesco, who he hadn't thought about in weeks. The last time he thought about him, it was because he wondered how he was doing and considered reaching out to Tony, apologizing, and seeing if he'd want to meet up for a chat sometime. Now, the passing of time had changed his feelings entirely. The name gave him a sour taste in his gut. Tony had stabbed him in the back, gotten another friend murdered, and had leaked information about the other beneficiaries that ultimately fell on Tarek's head to protect. He scolded himself for ever feeling like he wanted to forgive Tony. Instead, he wanted to give him a piece of mind, right here and now with a couple of assholes nearby giggling at whatever they thought was so funny about being near Tarek.

He pressed call and after a couple of rings, an old familiar voice was on the line, the tone sounded anxious, as if this was a long overdue conversation that he believed would never happen.

"What you doin, you prick?" Tarek said. His anger was driving. There was no foreplay. No questioning his old friend. He was just angry.

"Wow, Tarek. Did you call just to ask that?"

"No, I've got more. You killed Rick."

"What are you, drunk?"

"Perfectly sober. You're a murderer Tony."

A long pause on the other end. "You know that's not true. I know the part I played and I've spent a lot of time feeling like shit and I'll always feel like shit, so if you need to hear that I'm miserable, there ya go."

"I heard you're writing political satire now."

"Yup."

"So you just keep working like nothing happened."

"Six months ago, I called you, you remember?"

"I remember…"

"I took full responsibility and I told you if you want to file charges, I get it…"

"You should have turned yourself in…"

"You said you weren't filing charges and then I talked to an attorney for some advice and you know what my attorney said?"

"That you're a murderous prick."

"My attorney pointed out something that I didn't even fully grasp until then. I didn't actually do anything illegal. I gave a guy who hated you some information. It didn't come from a very good place when I did it. It wasn't innocent, but it wasn't illegal. Now, what Stanley Kline did with that information, well that's why he ended up in jail, but I did nothing illegal. My crime was that I was a bad friend, but you were a shit friend first and you know it. You're the least grateful person in this town, which is why you don't work anymore. You were a big fish in bumfuck, Missouri and you got the lead in a bunch of small-town plays that entertained a few dozen blue-haired ladies, and you came to Hollywood with a huge sense of entitlement and somehow, you made a name for yourself, but that shit expired now Appleton. You were outed for being the fraud that you are. Don't call me and start name calling because you're too bitter at how shit turned out. I don't need you telling me how I should feel guilty."

"You've got a career because you're a good writer, but you're a shitty person. I stood up to Kline and you cowered and got someone killed. I don't know how you can write funny material, sitting around in a room laughing with a bunch of writers…"

"Where's this coming from? What the hell Appleton? Don't call me again."

"Don't hang up…"

Tony did hang up and Tarek tried calling again but it went straight to voice-mail Tarek had been boiling during the conversation, but Tony had pushed him to his limit. Before he even had time to think twice, he was on his feet and turning the table with the teenagers, screaming in their face, oblivious to those around him. "It's so fucking funny that you're near someone who had some success in this town, you pieces of shit?"

A few people nearby laughed, assuming it was part of a sketch, but most started texting and taking pictures. No one captured the incident on video, but a few caught Tarek storming away and got a shot of the overturned table and the teenage boys laughing off the encounter.

Tarek got in his car and started it up. Before he put it in reverse, his hands gripped the wheel tightly and he realized he was catching his breath.

*What the hell just happened?*

It was a disaster, but it was exactly what he wanted. This was beyond creating a character. He was in his character's skin. He'd get some bad press over this and in the days and incidents to come, but he would create art and people would forget he was just a goofy comedian at one time. This was different, but it was good. When he caught his breath, he drove away, passing the restaurant he'd been sitting in. Eyes watched him as he passed. He stared back until they were out of view, and he headed home, desperate to write.

5

**I walked in to the hospital that day and my instincts kicked in. There was something dark about the atmosphere, as if news had traveled throughout the hallways of something tragic, and without the slightest consideration that it had happened to someone else, I knew we lost one, or both, babies.**

**It felt like I was walking through the hallways in slow motion, but I was actually carrying myself with an urgency I'd never felt before. I needed to know who was okay and who wasn't. The doctor caught up to me and told me there had been a problem. I went to see Aileen and learned she was in surgery and that one of the twins had died. The doctors told me Aileen had been given a decision—that she could have been awake and saved the baby but chose...**

She closed the manuscript and squeezed her eyes closed. That wasn't the way it happened, but somehow, in the mess of it all, between her fatigue in the moment and all the doctors who had caught wind of what happened and how things were relayed, translated, and understood, Victor had believed that Aileen made a choice. If she would have fully understood in that moment what was happening, she would have saved the babies. It was miraculous that Jason pulled through. The mortality rate for mothers was 70%, but Victor lost the girl he wanted and had come to believe that Aileen chose her own life over the baby.

Victor left her over a misunderstanding.

This time, she did skip ahead, past the incident in the hospital and to the section that closed the chapter on Aileen, forever forgotten to Victor but forever damaged Aileen.

**She refused to change her life, without realizing that you only need to perceive it in a different light. What you "see" in your mind is what you ultimately expect. What you expect is what you ultimately**

get. **There are no magic powers at work that make some people successful and others failures. "Average" people are average because they think "average" thoughts. "Exceptional" people are exceptional because they think "exceptional" thoughts. Life gives you whatever you ask for. Aileen lost in live because of something called sunk-cost bias, which is the tendency to believe in something because of the cost sunk into that belief. In business, we hang onto stocks, unprofitable investments, and failing businesses because of what we've put into them, even as they fail, we're blinded by our own sacrifices. Aileen Thick was in an unsuccessful relationship, blinded by what she'd lost to be in it and even when I told her we would never work, she was unable to move forward, forever held back because she was consumed with what she gave up, without even the smallest belief she could have it again...**

*...She wanted the moment back. She fully understood her options now, but now was too late. She held only one baby in her hand and though she thought he was the most beautiful thing she'd ever seen, he was incomplete. He was supposed to have a sister, but she'd gone too long without oxygen. The doctor said this was a best case scenario—that she was lucky because usually the mother doesn't survive. She wasn't sure what that meant. At the beginning of the day, everyone survived. How anyone could call this a best case scenario made her want to hit them upside the head.*

*She caught a figure in the doorway and did a double-take. She felt relief when she saw Victor standing there, but took it back when she saw his face. His eyes were without joy and his countenance was cold. She felt immediate guilt but didn't understand why.*

*"Where were you?" she asked. Inside, she was angry, but she spoke softly, hoping Victor could be happy with the result of the day.*

*"I was up north on business. You went into labor early. You were supposed to page me."*

*"There were complications."*

*"I know."*

*"I'm sorry Victor. I stepped outside for a minute and I didn't have my pager..."*

*When he saw her grow emotional, he didn't move. His face didn't change and he didn't have words of comfort. "You had options," he said.*

*"I know but I wasn't aware of what was happening and I passed out and I'm so sorry. They told me I'm lucky to be alive under any circumstance."*

*Victor stayed frozen in the doorway, looking at his child as if Jason was nothing. He never even asked what name she chose. He walked to the window and looked out at the parking lot below.*

"*Victor, please say something. Are you mad at me? I didn't know what was happening. If I did, I would have told them to keep me awake, but if they have to do something and there's no one to say otherwise, they save the mother's life first. They said it's priority.*"

"*We believed this was real,*" *Victor said.* "*Everything had fit into place for both of us. We called it fate.*"

"*I know. It's going to be hard, but we have to do this together. They said that if we don't talk about this and grieve together…*"

"*What are you talking about?*" *Victor turned and she saw disgust in his face—disgust directed at her.* "*What do we have?*"

"*We have each other and we have Jason.*"

"*We don't have anything. You threw yourself at me and you wound up pregnant with my child. Very convenient for you Aileen. It worked out well having you…*"

"*You think I did this all deliberately? Are you insane?*"

"*We used protection.*"

"*That's never a hundred percent!*"

"*Do you think I haven't grown accustomed to women like you, who try to find a way to make me owe them something?*"

"*I gave up everything for you and this child. Do you think that I wanted to live in a big house and have everything paid for?*"

"*You grew up in a trailer.*"

"*So what? I was trying NOT to be my parents. I was working my ass off to get out and do my own thing.*"

"*Yet, you walked up to my doorstep in the middle of the night…*"

"*I made a mistake! It was dumb. If I could do it over again, I would've stayed home. I wouldn't have gone out that night at all.*"

"*That's my point Aileen. It was a mistake.*"

*There was silence, except for a murmur from Jason. She repositioned him and quieted her voice.* "*Look…no matter what happened that shouldn't have, here we are and we have a child. I don't want anything more from you than what it takes to make sure he has everything he needs growing up. If you want to move into an apartment, or even a trailer, then that's okay with me. I just want to make sure he grows up healthy and happy.*"

"*He can have those things,*" *Victor said.* "*But you and I…we are through.*"

"*I can't believe you're doing this on today of all days.*"

*Victor walked to the door. Aileen wanted to shout but she didn't want it to be the first thing Jason heard in the world. She wanted to tell Victor what an asshole he was and that he was just doing this so he didn't have to settle down. She knew it was all true, that this wasn't really about her or what she did, but she couldn't say it. She hoped he'd see it on his own and come back to her later. If not, she'd take everything she had and find them a place and work toward the best life possible. She didn't know how she'd work and raise a baby. Her parents were deceased. She had no aunts or uncles or close friends. She'd been a recluse for so long that Victor had built the walls around her. Without them, there was nothing. Just her and Jason. She couldn't believe she'd reached a point in her life where she was completely dependent on someone else.*

*"How can I raise a baby on my own?" she asked.*

*"You won't have to. You'll only have to take care of yourself."*

*He walked out, leaving her on that note and left her speechless. She hugged Jason tighter, refusing to believe Victor would ever have a chance at taking him away from her…*


…Aileen walked into Tarek's bedroom, the pile of pages in her hand. He opened his eyes and let out a sigh of relief upon seeing that they were safe. He'd been laying there bored, waiting for the manuscript or trying to channel evil, or whatever it was he spent so much time on anymore. Aileen had been with men with all types of bad habits and she'd accepted a lot of them, but she couldn't watch a nice guy turn into Victor Stone.

"We need to talk," she said.

His eyes were glued to the pages in her hand, as if he was possessed by them.

"Tarek," she said. He finally made eye contact. "The thing with Victor's will is about to blow up."

"What are you talking about?"

"I spent some time today reading this and thinking about what Victor wanted from us and what he was able to do. I know this sounds stupid because I know he's not like, controlling us now or anything, but what he did is working. It's working Tarek. Obviously that woman who was shot was probably a victim of it. I know Richard seemed like an accident."

"It was an accident. There were witnesses that said he climbed down to help a kid."

"Okay, I don't know, but there was the stabbing and the guy with the bomb…"

"I have a lot to do and you're home a lot later than you usually are and I needed to be reading…"

"Tarek, you need to stop with this movie. I need you to focus on this because I can't do it. I can't talk to the group about this but you can."

"Talk about what?"

"Someone needs to show them all how much things have changed. I mean, the types of things that are happening are big."

"Yes, marriages and moving to tropical islands…happy events Aileen. You're reading way too much into this."

"It's not all happy Tarek. It's not. Even the happy stuff…it's just odd is all."

"Give me the manuscript Aileen."

"Someone's going to die. I just know it."

"So what? We're safe. They're not our problem. I've done more than my share for them."

"I know, but the more that die, the less safe we all are. What if there was only two people left? One would for sure kill the other. The less of us there are, the more likely someone is to do something."

"So let them."

"Tarek, I'm not crazy."

"You are crazy. Now hand it over."

Aileen stood frozen, unable to hand over the manuscript and once Tarek started reading it, he would be consumed with it and continue to grow darker every day. She couldn't watch it happen anymore.

She suddenly turned and ran back to the living room and straight to the balcony, which hung far over the city below. She heard Tarek call her name and jump out of bed to chase her through his suite, but she was far ahead of him with only one objective in mind.

Tarek turned the corner just in time to see Aileen toss the pages into the night. They broke into hundreds of sheets, each flying it's down direction and drifting into the air like pieces of confetti. Tarek watched in horror as his obsession flew out of reach forever. He could hurry to the streets and collect a good amount of pages, but he'd never have the manuscript in its entirety again. He ran to the balcony and watched as the pages grew smaller and smaller, falling onto an on looking crowd of people curious about such a massive amount of littering.

"I'm sorry," she said. Her breath caught in her throat.

"What did this even have to do with them?" he shouted.

"Everything. Everything I read…everything I know…everything I've seen tells me that he wanted everyone to turn on each other…that they eventually would. Business was a succession of movements with one objective. That's what he said over and over. He said it's a slow boil and it's there but we don't see it until the line hits the ceiling or until it all falls. It's his analogy Tarek. It's there and it means everything because everything he did was for something and his will isn't nothing. You've seen that. You saved us and then everyone forgot that there were things that happened that no one was paying any attention to and we've all failed to pay attention. We've all been so distracted by other things and we're all spread out and so no one is looking at the big picture. Everything changed Tarek. Everything changed for everyone."

The wind from the balcony sent her hair blowing in waves, her shirt rippling in the wind as a heavy draft hit her. Tarek stood on the balcony, watching her with a venomous look. The last of the pages hit the ground and Tarek closed his eyes, his comeback fading from memory.

Aileen felt sympathy for him and approached with caution. She put her hand on her shoulder and apologized one last time.

His hand struck out and grabbed her hand. He spun her around and grabbed her by the shoulders, pulling her to the balcony, dangerously close to the edge. The only thing that stopped her from falling was his hand on her wrist. He leaned in.

"I took you into my home and away from being a whore, but we're done. Get out of my place and go back to the streets or live in Victor's home but get away from me!"

Her eyes were wet with tears. She struggled for the right thing to say but Tarek was too far gone. He only cared about one thing and she took it from him. He pulled her back and shoved her into the safety of the inside, but she stumbled and fell to the ground. She quickly got back up and gathered some things, glancing at his back as he looked out into the sky with distress. When her arms were full with everything she needed, she took a last look at him.

"If you want proof of what Victor did to us, look in the mirror," she said. "You're the worst of them all."

Tarek looked over his shoulder with ice in his eyes. "Get out."

She slammed the door behind her, but fell to the hallway in tears.

## *Chapter 16*

*1*

Only four days passed, but to Maria Haskins, they were intolerably long, as she wept constantly, and continually called Henry. He hadn't returned any of her calls, and it drove her mad. Henry, more than any man she'd ever known, had accepted her and positioned her to have all her trut in him.

The breakup was so out of the blue that Maria refused to accept it was real. Something strange was happening, but Henry was nowhere to be found. She couldn't find him at any of his usual hangouts. She would have assumed he'd had an accident and died if not for that one cryptic text telling her he didn't want to be with her anymore. There was also the fact that he'd changed the locks at home. Two nights in a row, she waited almost all night, but he never came back, or maybe he saw her and had to sneak in through the back door.

She could no longer go to the shop, because it was owned by the bank. Her place to run to was no longer there for her. The amount of money she still had to pay back was enormous. She felt guilty for thinking it, but sometime in the last year, she'd put all her trust in Henry. Without him, she had nothing. All her money was in his investments. She assumed he'd give that back, but her focus was solely on talking to him and fixing whatever was wrong and picking up where they left off. As the minutes ticked away, she grew sick and she couldn't focus on anything. By the fourth day, she was having panic attacks and trouble breathing.

She wondered if he was going through anything similar.

Henry's panic attacks came from processing what he'd done. Maria was walking right into the trap they'd set for her, but there was two steps that remained and the first was impossibly hard to do. The second, Henry wasn't sure he could possibly have in him. Today was the day to execute on the final steps and see if Toby predicted the outcome all along. All Henry had to do was send one message.

He was supposed to wait three days, but to Toby's objections, pushed the call out one more. It was hard to ignore every one of Maria's calls, harder to read her texts, begging him for an explanation. To his surprise, he found himself wishing he could have just killed her himself. If he could go back in time, he would have supported Sal Blovik's desire to just murder them all. Henry didn't know if he could ever be happy with the money. They'd all made a woman believe her child was dying, they'd faked relationships, friendships, they'd sold their souls for an amount of money that had lost it's appeal. Greg Neomin ended his life out of guilt. Henry wasn't the suicidal type, but if he followed through until the bitter end, he suspected he'd hate himself forever.

But there was no turning back now.

He closed his eyes and held his phone in front of him, sitting in the dark so he could maintain his composure throughout the call. He thought about his parents, his sisters, his best friends throughout life, the woman he married after college, the professor who told him he would do great things... No one could ever know the evil that Henry was going to do. He would be despised forever by everyone he'd ever known if they knew his true nature. He even despised himself.

"I'm tired of thinking about this." His voice sounded louder than expected in the dark. He scanned until he landed on Maria's number, his thumb hovering over the keypad while he thought about what he was going to say. He took a deep breath and started typing...

*...Victor listened to Maria tell her story.*

*She told him about how when she was a little girl, Matthew Chowder murdered April Lovelace and Maria's vision resulted in his capture. He listened intently and she searched for doubt in his eyes, but nothing indicated that he didn't believe she was telling the truth as she knew it. When she was finished, there was a long silence before Victor finally spoke.*

*"Is he staying in the city?"*

*"I don't know."*

*"Do you believe he will harm you?"*

*"I don't know. I haven't seen him since I was a little girl."*

*"Is there anyone you can stay with for a few days?"*

*"I..." she considered, but came up with no one. "I might be able to stay with a friend."*

*"Here's what we'll do," Victor said, commanding attention. It was like watching the man in a business meeting with his associates. "I will put*

*you in The Suites for as long as is needed. We'll close the shop for now and I'll have Mr. Chowder looked into and see if I can't use some connections I have to see if we can get him on harassment charges."*

*"Victor, you don't have to. This is too much."*

*"If your life is truly in danger, this is the least I can do."*

*She tried to withhold an emotional outburst, but she could feel the tears stinging her eyes. "I could never thank you enough."*

*"You've done enough for me Maria. You're a good woman."*

*"I'm not..."*

*Victor fell silent, looking down at her, her bangs covering her eyes. She finally looked up. "I'm not the woman you believe me to be."*

*"What are you saying?"*

*"I don't always know if I'm telling you the right thing," Maria said. "I sometimes cold read you. I try my hardest to tell you what I believe is right, but you have come to me with so many questions about your life, and I have given you my opinions. Not my visions."*

*The confession came out without thought and she looked down for a long moment, trying to avoid Victor's eyes. Finally, she looked up. He had a look of understanding.*

*"I'm not oblivious Maria. I understand this already."*

*"Then why do you come to me?" she asked, a mix of relief and surprise.*

*"I come to you for another perspective."*

*The revelation hit her hard and he said it so matter-of-factually, that she realized he didn't understand her values at all. He saw the hurt in her eyes and explained himself. "I've never known where I stand on what you do, but I do know that you're a genuine person and that you have always meant well."*

*"I've had real visions," she said, awestruck. "Matthew Chowder is proof."*

*"Maria..." he found her eyes. "Have you ever seen anything when you looked into my head? Have you ever truly had a vision of where my life was headed or where I've been or who I am?"*

*She thought long and hard, replaying every meeting she'd ever had with Victor, all the fear she'd felt in all the times she told him what she thought he wanted to hear or what she believed he needed to hear. In all their visits, she'd never experienced so much as a blip of truth from the man's soul. She never realized Victor himself knew it to be true.*

*"I don't believe so," she said.*

*"I like you Maria. I don't always seek counsel from my associates. Sometimes, the opinions that matter the most come from the streets...from the people who are impacted by my business and what I do. I don't want*

*anything to change. Right now, I want to focus on your safety, and when you're ready, go back to work. Allow me some time to take care of this business with Matthew Chowder."*

*"Please don't do anything to hurt him. I just want him to leave me alone."*

*"You said he's murdered multiple women Maria. I will do what I need to do to prevent that from happening..."*

…Dark thoughts circled her mind as she tried to get a hold of her emotions. It had all been too out of the blue and out of character for Henry. Up until the moment he'd ended their marriage, everything had played out perfectly. Whatever had happened to Henry had happened fast and she prayed it would undo itself equally as fast. He'd come to his senses and realize he'd acted drastically. He'd come to the conclusion that he couldn't live without Maria, because Maria couldn't live without him and they were both on the same page—always had been. They were in sync from the moment their eyes met and he'd pursued her. Surely, he was just as distraught.

He'd changed the locks at their home. He wouldn't answer why, but she became aware quickly that if she were to try to get into the house through a window or break a lock, she would be trespassing. She'd moved in with Henry. He'd always covered the mortgage payments.

Her shop was locked up too, with a heavy chain wrapped through the handles of the doors and a sign proclaiming it was the property of the bank.

She had no money for a motel. Everything she had was in a shared account—or had been invested in stock options. Henry had talked her into it and made her completely dependent on his income. If her mind had been working rationally, she might have seen the set-up there and then, but she refused to believe there was no love. Henry loved her as she'd loved him. It was real. Her mind never wandered away from that arena.

She called him again. She sent a text. Another text. Another call.

There was only ringing. Ringing and a one sided conversation.

Maria was on foot. She had no idea where to go or what to do. Henry was the key back to everything. She'd never realized just how much of her life was in his hands. There was a time she always had a place to call home. When she wasn't there, she always had her shop. She never made a lot of money, but she'd never lacked either. She gave up her home, her income, her career, her everything…everything was in his hands. He was a decent man and surely he wouldn't leave her with nothing.

She had a thought. Maybe his investment fell through. Maybe he hadn't even invested the money. Maybe he gambled it away, or paid off some debts and was just too embarrassed to face her.

She sent another text: **Whatever happened, I will not be angry.**

It satisfied her. It had to be right. Henry probably was doing what he thought was best for her. She sent another text, and later, three more. They all suggested they talk…that she wouldn't be angry…that whatever was happening, they would get past it. She even told him she had nowhere to go. If he cared, he would respond.

But he never did. Maybe he'd lost his phone. Or maybe he was injured and helpless somewhere. He had to be. The alternative was that he simply didn't care…that he had no problem with a penniless, homeless, Maria Haskins wandering the streets, heartbroken and with nothing left in the world.

As the sun passed in the sky, she was left alone, sitting outside their home, waiting. He'd have to come home eventually. She'd confront him then. She'd ask if he loved her. She'd accept the answer, no matter what he said, but she'd need to know why.

No.

Tears formed in her eyes as she realized she wouldn't accept their separation. He would take her back. He would prove he loved her. If he didn't, she couldn't go on living. It wasn't a threat this time. She had nothing but Henry. If he was through with her, she'd be done in the world. She fell asleep on their doorstep, and dreamed dark thoughts.

2

Campaign headquarters for Royce Morrow were buzzing with less than one week until election day. The mood had turned as Morrow lost ground and the staff and volunteers prepared themselves for what appeared to be an inevitable loss. Royce was nowhere to be seen and when he did step onto the property, had very little to say to anyone. His words were uninspiring and his demeanor wasn't encouraging. The last man standing who was fired up was Royce's campaign manager, Fletcher Davis, who put his agenda on the back-burner so he could track down Royce's whereabouts and give him an eleventh hour speech to light him up. The time to stage a comeback had come and gone, but only days remaining, there'd be no miracles unless Royce was on-board.

Fletcher was able to look at Royce's schedule from their shared Outlook calendar and discovered Royce was volunteering across the city at St. Matthews, where breakfast was being served to the homeless in downtown LA. He rolled his eyes and straightened his collar before hurrying to the church in rush hour traffic. When he arrived and hour later and entered the church hall, he found Royce right where he'd expected to see him, in the front and center, dropping pancakes onto plates and chatting it up with the locals. He tried to draw Royce away from afar, but Royce didn't budge, even when he saw the frustration that Fletcher wore so outwardly.

Fletcher impatiently checked his watch and approached Royce. He interrupted Royce mid-conversation. "What are you doing?"

"What does it look like I'm doing?"

"It looks like you're trying to lose an election."

"My time is better spent with voters."

"These aren't voters," Fletcher said. "You'd already have their vote if they were voters. You refuse to send mail. You refuse to visit editorial boards. You've earned the scorn of newspaper editors around the state because the most prized resource anyone can have is your time and you won't give it to the voters that matter. You can't seek office due to strong feelings on a single issue. When the voters don't share that strong feeling, you need to be comfortable focusing on other issues. Likewise, decisions need to be made about comfort levels with negative advertising. You refer to Bell far too often in voter contact and it's not always constituted as fair game."

"There's no such thing as fair game when we're talking about Bell."

"That may be, but people are tired of mud-slinging without substance of your own. You could win if you shared who you are, give people a sense that you're here to serve. You can't offer ten-point plans when no one can safely say they know you and you're a good guy who cares about them. You used to be a public speaker but then this became a personal thing. You don't sound like you're talking to your audience Royce. You're talking to yourself. You talk more about what you're against than what you want to do as governor."

"I don't know how to do that," Royce said, his voice rising. He stepped aside, afraid to show emotion in front of the crowds. "I'm taking a few," he said to a man working at his side.

Fletcher led the way as they stepped into an empty pantry. "You don't know how to do this job for the people instead of out of spite? Is that what you're telling me?" Fletcher asked. "Is that what you're going to tell the four hundred volunteers who are out there every day saying that you're for the people? Because if that's not true, you've wasted a lot of peoples' time, including my own."

"You don't know what I'm going through."

"Of course I don't. I only lost a wife to cancer two years ago."

"I'm staring into the face of it every day," Royce said. "Not just Sandra but the men responsible for her death. I see posters that are designed to show how human and relatable Bell is and I see crowds cheering when he walks into an auditorium. I have to watch as this state applauds an evil man, who is partnered up with the man who killed Sandra."

"And if you continue on this path, he wins the election. You get that right? That your reaction to Bernard Bell is the very thing that will cause him to beat you?"

"Yeah, I get it," Royce said and ran a hand through his hair. "I can't control it."

"Let us help then. Let's get you through this next week and put our best shoes on every day. One week of you as a class act in this thing. Bell's defenses have gotta be down. They're beating you good and probably already popped the cork off their champagne. You want to give him that satisfaction?"

"Tell me what you think I should do," Royce said. Fletcher was relieved to see Royce submit and began speaking fast and excitedly.

"There are certain principles on which successful campaigns are built. We need to be guided by one principle: Talk to one audience."

"Which audience?"

"From the polling, we know we've got the right mix of talent, predictive analytic, digital marketing, media optimization, data management, and field operatives, but we're operating in silos. Television ads are bought based on Nielsen ratings. Direct mail is sent to voters with modeled attributes. Online ads target voters based on their interests and online activity and the field team knocks on doors of voters based on their past vote history. Everyone is talking to a different audience. Campaigns need to settle on a base-scoring system using predictive analytic and dynamic modeling that will serve as the common currency for all aspects of the campaign. It's this currency that defines the audience to whom paid media, digital marketing, and the campaign's grassroots communicate."

"Isn't it too late for a new marketing audience?"

"No, it's just the right time. Bell has a lead, but the Bell campaign settled on parameters based on their likelihood to support Bell and their propensity to turnout to vote early in the campaign that produced a universe of approximately fifteen million voters. Everything the campaign did communicated to those people or a subset of them. What we need to do is target voters whose attributes were most similar to those of our supporters, which we were continually refining based on data across platforms from various sources who were online, donors, volunteers, activists… Using ongoing modeling we scored and updated every voter in the state as supporters, persuadable targets or lost causes. This allows us to identify a large pool of persuadable voters. All field contacts and all our online advertising and even our television ads will target these voters. I'm talking about reaching a universe of thirteen million on-the-fence voters using predictive analytics. We predict if we start using video and Facebook promoted ads, we'll be about to reach up to 75 percent of our target persuasion audience, serve them an average of 22.51 ads each at an extremely cost effective average of thirty-four cents per voter."

Royce stared into space for a few moments, seemingly unaware that he was staring at a shelf filled with canned foods. It seemed they had a strategy, but what Fletcher couldn't do was breathe life into Royce. He didn't know how to speak passionately and how to shake all hands…not just the hands of those he respected, but those he didn't as well. Politicians were everyone's best friend before election, but Royce didn't have the energy to play nice for people who were responsible for murdering his wife.

"Give me the day," Royce said.

"We don't have any time left to waste. We needed you to give a hoot yesterday."

"If I come back to you by the end of the day and I tell you I'm in, I will do everything you say and more until the bitter end and when it's over, if we haven't won, I'll personally apologize to every person who so much as put a sign in their yard."

"And if you tell me you're out?"

"Then I'm not going to waste anyone else's time. This was different in the beginning Fletcher."

"I know."

"It was supposed to be about goodness and decency. What they did, it wasn't just a smear campaign."

"I agree."

"They deserve worse than just losing this."

"Well, when they lose, you can see to it that you lock them up, or whatever justice needs serving."

Royce nodded, his eyes rapidly moving as he thought. "Do you really believe I still have a chance?"

"You? No," Fletcher said. "The Royce Morrow who went from rags to riches in a matter of years…that guy would win for sure."

## 3

Toby found Henry at the corner bar, which was where he expected to find him. Once he'd changed the locks and broken up with Maria, Toby expected him to be drowning his guilt. He wasn't even sure Henry had it in him to go this far and to really pull the plug on her. To follow through until the end, that would be the hardest part. It had already taken a toll.

He'd spent so much time and energy on Maria. He'd probably grown somewhat bonded to her and seen the human being inside.

Toby found a seat across from Henry and ordered two drinks. Henry sat staring through his mug and didn't look up.

"She been calling?"

"Constantly. Texting, calling, probably at the house…"

"Probably."

"I tried to make the call...tried to send a text...just can't do it."

"You have to finish this."

"She's just absolutely desperate. Just like you said she'd be."

"Hey, once you've had Henry…"

Henry looked up and scowled at the joke. "Don't do that today, okay?"

"Once you start mourning, you're in dangerous territory."

"Doesn't mean we have to treat it like it's nothing either."

"Grand scheme of things, I don't think it is. If she does what I think she'll do, she doesn't value life enough anyway."

"What are you going to say about the others? Does Royce Morrow value life? Tarek Appleton? There are some decent people among this group and Maria's not all bad. In fact, she's not bad at all because she does mean well. What's so wrong about wanting to be accepted? Yeah, we can brush that shit off, but she's just a person who wants someone to understand her, and yeah, it drives everything she does, even in some pathetic ways, but her values are no different than most people."

Toby shrugged and simply said, "Look, I'm not going to go around with you every time you have a moral dilemma. You said you wanted in. You knew what it entailed. You want the money or you don't, but you can't have it both ways."

"Isn't there another way? Isn't there something we can do legally to just let them split it all up or something?"

"We tried that and when all was said and done, it didn't work out. If I didn't pick up my earnings or I was to ignore a check in the mail, eventually it just goes to the state. You have the right to not want something, but you can't change the law and a man's last wishes are set in stone. Look Henry, it's fine if you're out, but now is the time, so you're either out or you can text her back."

Henry shook his head. "Maria really likes animals. We need to get a notebook and write down an organization and a million dollar donation in her name."

"You need a notebook for that?"

"We do it for everyone. When we're done, a million dollars in the names of each we murder."

"It's not murder."

"Toby!"

"Fine, a million for each that we're actually responsible for. If it's not us, it doesn't count. Maria can have her animal shelter. We'll find some fat camp for Van Dyke."

"And no more talking about them like they're not people. Not to me at least."

"You're setting terms with me?"

"As long as I'm doing all the work, I am."

Toby gave Henry a long hard look, before nodding at his cellphone, which he noticed was still buzzing. "I'll send the text."

Henry didn't believe him at first, but saw Toby was serious, which caused him to take pause and consider. "What would you say?"

"To get lost."

"We need to talk about other options."

"We already did. Give me your phone."

Toby was serious and fed up with the game. Henry had been giving Toby a hard time from the start, but he was right. Henry had volunteered for this and even tried to go above and beyond to impress Toby in the beginning. Then, the weight of what they were doing hit him and he'd began resenting Toby, but here Toby was, the same guy with the same offer and the same methodology. He was right, and Henry couldn't send the text, so he slid his phone across the table.

Toby grabbed it, thumbed through the keypad, and slid it back within seconds. Then, he finished his beer and got up and walked away without a word.

Henry opened his phone and read the text, swallowing hard at the content.

**LEAVE ME ALONE. I DON'T LOVE YOU ANYMORE…**

*…Matthew Chowder weighed heavily on Maria's mind. She'd spent many moments throughout her life thinking about the day she caught him and in a strange way, those thoughts were happy. It was awful that so many girls died at his hands, but Maria had put an end to it. Whether she was psychic or whether there was something more to how she had known it was him, it was Maria that had pointed in the right direction. No matter what the story was, she was a hero.*

*She'd gotten used to believing that and it was true, but now she was facing a new reality and it brought pain to her heart. Chowder was free and he would kill again and he would challenge her to stop him. This time, she couldn't, because deep down, she wasn't sure how she did it the first time. She remembered it was effortless. There had been a vision, and she didn't know where it came from. She hadn't forced it, or meditated, or asked for it. It was just there one day. Years later and much more practiced as a medium, she'd never been able to force anything. She got what she got. Nothing more. Nothing less.*

*Not only was she afraid of what he would do, but she was afraid of him. She didn't want to see him or hear his name. It was all fine and good when he was behind bars but he was out in the city somewhere. Maybe he'd get a job and live an honest life, but he led Maria to believe otherwise and now, every murder she read about in the city, she wondered if it could possibly be him. She kept her eyes on the newspapers, trying to find someone who potentially could have fallen victim to Chowder. If bodies did start turning up, particularly younger women, she would find a way to stick it to him.*

*She never got the chance though. One day, while skimming the paper, she saw his name. Her first thought was that he got busted, but upon closer inspection, the article was about the murder of Matthew Chowder. It was logic turned on its head, except maybe this made sense. Chowder had ruined lives. He'd torn families apart and there were bound to be people who weren't happy to hear he'd gotten released from prison.*

*She followed the story for days until the trail of articles ended. The end result was that there were hundreds of people questioned, including friends and families of Chowder's victims, and there were no leads or arrests made. The more Maria obsessed over his death, the less she believed it was someone he wronged.*

*She tried to meditate. She studied the man and attempted to force her way into his shoes, but she felt nothing. It took her a week to realize that she'd refused to consider a practical possibility. She'd told Victor Stone of Chowder. He had been angry to hear what she had to say. He'd told her he'd take care of it. She hadn't seen him since.*

*Victor was a lot of things, but he was no murderer. He'd confessed immoral actions in the past, but that was infidelity and cutting ethical corners and terminating employees who had families to feed. This was on another level and she'd always believed Victor to have kind eyes—the type of man who made tough decisions sometimes, but ultimately struggled with them.*

*The murder was hard to ignore. Chowder had been found under the Santa Monica Pier. He'd been shot in the head and dumped over the side. No one wanted him found and from what Maria understood, that wasn't a crime of passion. That was premeditated with enough man-power to kill a man execution style and dump a body.*

*She wasn't going to bring it up with Victor but her curiosity got the best of her and her suspicions would be revealed if she said nothing. Naturally, she would have asked Victor if he ever talked to Matthew*

*Chowder, so that's what she would do. It wasn't huge news for someone to be found murdered in the city, so there was no reason she couldn't play dumb and see what he said. She'd be able to read him well if he brought it up and denied it in one sitting.*

*Maria tried to make an appointment that day, but Victor was stuck in the office and invited her up for a quick chat. It made her want to believe his innocence more in knowing that he had no problem letting her into his office without a second thought. There was no doubt that other associates found it odd and maybe they even gave him a hard time, but he had no shame in their friendship and she appreciated that quality in him more than any.*

*He smiled and greeted her when she entered, but he had a scattered way about him. He was busy, but he still made time. She knew she was acting crazy.*

*"Is everything okay?" Victor asked. She studied his eyes. They were innocent. He didn't have a hint of fear in facing her, even though he easily could suspect the reason she was here.*

*"I've just been anxious," Maria said. "I have not heard anything about Matthew Chowder and wondered if you talked to him."*

*"You know what? I never did. I apologize."*

*"You don't have to," she said, trying to pry information. "I think he was just trying to scare me."*

*"I'd like for you to always have your phone near you and keep your windows open. When you're driving home at night, make sure you check..."*

*"I'm sorry. I'm not being honest," she said. "Matthew is dead. He was killed. It's been in the news a little."*

*"When?" Victor asked, genuinely surprised.*

*"Sometime early last week. His body washed up on the beach in Santa Monica. He was shot."*

*Victor stared blankly at her for a long moment and then shook his head in disbelief. "Have there been any arrests?"*

*Maria couldn't put her finger on why, but the question was odd. It wasn't the right question. His voice and mannerisms were steady and controlled, but the question was unnatural. "No. Victor, I already know the answer to this but I have to ask because the last time we spoke, you said you would do something about it and then I didn't hear from you and it's just...the convenience is the only reason I have to ask but I already know the answer."*

*"Did I have something to do with his death?"*

*Maria looked down, ashamed to ask. "I wouldn't be angry. He's a dangerous man."*

*"Maria, you need to go home and get some sleep and stop thinking crazy thoughts." She nodded. "You've been stressed and this is no doubt a traumatic experience, but you're drawing the wrong conclusions."*

*Maria mentally noted that Victor never denied it, but dismissed the thought. It was foolish. Victor couldn't be the successful man he was, so highly visible, and get away with something like that. Matthew was in prison a long time. He'd probably made some enemies, or maybe he made them when he was out, struggling to find his way back into the world, no doubt an angry man who could piss off the wrong people. He'd probably never even been to LA and had no idea what it was like here. It might have been okay to sit in a bar back home and give a little push to the guy next to you, but here, you don't want to say or do the wrong thing if you're in the wrong place.*

*Victor put his hand on Maria's back and walked her toward the elevator, making smalltalk the whole way. It was in those moments that she decided she would put the matter to rest. It didn't really matter who killed Matthew and if they did what they did because he was a child killer, the killer deserved a medal anyway.*

*They reached the elevator and Victor pushed the button and waited with her. "I have a busy afternoon but I want you to call me if anything comes up. I'll try to stop in sometime next week."*

*She smiled and nodded, feeling better already. The elevator doors opened and she stepped inside. Victor held out his hand and she reached to shake before the doors closed. She was about to say goodbye, but when their hands touched, she felt a flash like she'd never felt before and it changed everything…*

...The text made Maria cry until her eyes were dry and red.

She didn't understand how it was possible or what it was that changed Henry so much in such a short amount of time. She'd given up everything for him. Her home, her business, everything she had. She not only needed him because she loved him. She literally needed him.

She began formulating plans in her head of what she would do if she couldn't have him back. Where she'd live, how she'd do it—but her mind kept coming back to a fact that she was forced to accept.

She didn't actually have any money.

Would she have to beg him to give her back what was hers? Talk to an attorney? She dreaded every option that didn't include Henry changing his mind. In every other scenario, she lost. She wanted her life back.

Henry just didn't know what he was talking about. She knew he loved her and was having a lapse in judgment. She just needed him to see the world without her.

She'd promised herself she'd never go to this place again, but this was every other breakup magnified.

Her sadness became anger and suddenly, she started having feelings she'd suppressed for years. Henry had really done her over. He'd messed with her emotions like no other man ever had, but what really confused her was just what was real and what wasn't. Was he genuine before or was he now? It killed her not knowing what changed, and this time, she knew it wasn't just a Maria thing. This was a feeling that she knew all people should have in a moment like this. They dated for six months, were engaged for another month, married, and a month later, he wanted nothing to do with her.

It seemed almost...deliberate.

He'd been acting strange, especially around the time her father died. He'd been wishy washy on what it was he wanted her to do—especially when he learned she could have been taken off the will. She couldn't find a motive though. There was no conceivable reason for Henry to have taken this course with her—at least not one that came to mind.

She wanted to meditate. She wanted to close her eyes and focus and see if the universe could provide answers. Now more than ever, she needed that, but she was certain that she wouldn't find answers. She'd tell herself what she needed to hear like she did to everyone else. She needed to move on.

*Not this time. What we had was real.*

She needed Henry to notice her. She needed him to run to her side, and if he didn't, well...then maybe it was all for the best.

Maria broke into the house through a basement window. Ordinarily, Henry would probably be pissed off, but under these circumstances it didn't matter. She still had things in the house. She had the right—though her name wasn't on the mortgage—but any judge would agree that she had the right. Fortunately, it wouldn't come to that. She'd said it before and hadn't meant it, but this time it was real. Without Henry, she wanted to be dead. She would give him a chance to see what he could lose and how deeply her loss would impact him. If he didn't, he'd have to live with the guilt forever.

She entered the bathroom and pulled bottles from the medicine cabinet. Among them was a bottle of antidepressants she'd stopped taking a long time ago, around the time she met Henry. He'd found them one day and told her she didn't need them—that a person chooses whether or not they're happy. She tried to adapt his attitude and it came easy, but only because he was in the picture. She never got rid of the bottle though. She never knew why.

Now she could only stare at it and tell herself that this was really happening, but Henry would come through. If he didn't, she'd probably never know.

*I'm not ready*, she told herself. *Henry will come through. He's the one. He loves me.*

It was that thought that caused her to swallow the pills.

4

There was only one thing Royce wanted to do before deciding his fate in politics. He had two problems to deal with but the weight of one was too important. Bernard Bell had always been a disgusting human being, but it was Manny who had murdered Sandra. Manny wasn't running for governor but he was in bed with the man who was and if only he could take Manny's power, even at the expense of his own win, he would do it in a heartbeat.

Bernard accepted his invitation and in front of forty reporters outside an Italian restaurant on Melrose called Osteria Mozza, they sat together for lunch.

"I'll pick up the tab," Royce said.

"You didn't have to bring me here," Bernard said. "I would've met you if you only bought me an Oki-dog."

"What's an Oki-dog?"

Bernard exaggerated disbelief. "Holy shit, you've never had an oki-dog? How long you been living in LA?"

"What is it? A hot dog?"

"It's a hot dog on steroids. What else you gonna eat after the bars close?"

"I'm not at the bars when they close."

"Oh, right," Bernard said. "Saint Royce."

"Is that how you see me?"

"That's how most people see you. Not me though."

"How do you see me?"

"You're the homeless guy who saved his money. You've got one story Royce and that's it. You'll never top it."

"Why should I stop there?"

"Because you're not a politician and you know it. You're not even running for the right reasons."

"Well, the way to beat you is less than honorable and I don't know how low I'd want to stoop to take a victory lap. I was hoping we could change the face of politics and do this the way they did it decades ago."

"You're the one that gets in front of a camera and calls me corrupt… calls me a murderer."

"Both factual statements."

"You know Royce, I know who your issue is with and what Detective Quinny does has nothing to do with me. He's just a drinking buddy."
"He's an associate. I'm not dumb."

"Okay, he's an associate too, but believe it or not, we actually spend a good deal of time talking about how to fight the war on drugs, how to get crime off the streets."

"I already know how he does it. He kills people, but not just criminals. He only needs to ask how much and if the dollar amount is good, the job gets done."

"Well, you can say that until the cows come home. I don't know anything about that."

"Sure you don't." Royce's eyes burned into Bernard's, but all Bernard could manage was a smile that seemed forced.

"Why you buying me lunch Mr. Morrow?"

"I'm here with a proposition."

"If you were leading the polls, would you be here with a proposition?"

"If I want to win, I'm going to win."

Bernard broke into a fit of laughter and followed with a drink of water to collect himself. "Cocky doesn't suit you. What's the proposal?"

"See to it that Manny Quinny goes down and I'll hand you the election."

"What's your definition of goes down?"

"Locked up forever."

"You know that's a jury's decision and not my own."

"I think we both know that police corruption is out of control in this city. It's been my issue from the beginning and I'm losing because I've neglected to talk about other things like budgets and city parks."

"Hey, I'm not running your campaign."

"Corruption and crime is, and always will be, at the forefront of what I care about, but I'm not asking you to change your position on anything. If you win, you'll do what you do. I'm just asking for one guy to go down. You didn't even know him a month ago. He has no real value to you. If you really knew him, you'd understand that he's a time bomb and when he goes off, it's going to reflect on you."

Bernard crossed his arms and nodded as he thought to himself. "He threw a tantrum toward a waitress last night because his steak was cooked wrong. Pisses me off too but tantrums are for children. It was off-putting."

"I'll step down," Royce said. "We put it in writing that the homicide division is put under investigation, every dollar in and out is tracked and a full audit on Quinny as well as a third party review of their practices and procedures…it will be all we need to take him down. You get in, it's as easy as giving a command."

"You realize I could agree to this and do none of it…"

"I realize that, and that's what Manny would do, but you won't."

"Why's that?"

"Because that's what a child would do. You wouldn't be a successful businessman if you had no honor."

Bernard nodded again, his mind taking an inventory of all the ways Manny could benefit him, or potentially hurt him.

"If you're in the spotlight with a friend like that, he'll eventually ruin you. He's going to ask a lot of you—more than you can give. His tantrums, the violence, the criminal record waiting to be exposed. He does what he does because he despises people. That's your associate… your drinking buddy. A human-race-hating murderer."

"I'm not a fan of most people either."

"I understand, but Manny Quinny is all bad things under a microscope and unfiltered. You'll boost your approval. You'll get rid of a guy who would kill you for a dollar amount."

"Tell you what," Royce said, turning his attention to Royce and sitting up in his chair. "I'll agree to this but I have one other condition."

"Name it," Royce said, confident he would be willing to do whatever was necessary.

"Tell me what happened to my brother. Show me where you put the body."

Royce fell silent. His stomach dropped and for the first time, Bernard knocked the wind out of him with mere words. "I don't…"

"If you finish that statement, we're done talking about this. I know where you were when he disappeared. I know where he was headed. I know all the key players in this story. I just don't know what happened and I don't know where he ended up."

Royce felt like he couldn't talk his way out of this. Bernard wasn't asking to stump him. For the first time in his life, he saw Bell as vulnerable—maybe even desperate for the answer to a question that had been nagging him a long time. He could see it cutting Bernard so deep that he almost told him.

"I suppose we're playing this out to the end," Royce said.

"I suppose we are."

"If I am elected," Royce started. "I'm going to bring Manny down, and I'm going to link him to you. Then I'm going to bulldoze your building."

"When I win," Bernard said. "I'm going to do the exact same thing to you."

5

Just as Toby predicted, Maria contacted Henry to tell him she couldn't go on and just swallowed a handful of pills. She had done the same thing twice before and in both instances, the man on the receiving end of the message had her taken to the hospital as soon as he could. It was the kind of bluff people called and Maria had always known that. In the two previous circumstances, it had been men that she'd been with for less than nine months. She was confident that if they'd come through, so would Henry, who not only fell in love with her but made her his wife and sacrificed everything to be with her.

When he showed up at the house, she'd already started coughing and vomited once. She looked up at him with swollen eyes and tears falling and though she only felt relief that he came, she hated the look he gave her.

"I'm going to get you to the hospital. What'd you take?"

She was disorientated and sleepy and tried to give him the answers but her world was out of focus. "Celexa, Tylenol PM, Unisome, Naproxen, Prilosec…"

"Jesus Maria…"

She heard him, but everything was in slow motion as she faded into another place. As she thought she was going to completely drift away, only to be awoken in a hospital bed with a tube in her throat, she started to feel stomach pains like she'd never felt before. Whatever was happening inside was a clash of chemicals that was causing great discomfort. She curled up and let out a scream. Henry hurried to her and picked her up. In her hazy state, she studied his face, which was filled with fear, but there was no concern. He wasn't afraid for her. She saw something else…guilt.

He carried her to the car.

"Call an ambulance," she murmured a line of spit on the corner of her mouth.

"I'll get you there faster."

She let her head fall back and tried to close her eyes but the discomfort kept her from passing out. Maybe she'd taken it too far and this time, she wouldn't wake up. Henry had done everything she'd wanted him to do, but it might already be too late.

She laid in the backseat of the car on her back, her hands to her stomach and her eyes rolled back, watching the world pass outside. Though she could barely think, she felt something was off. She struggled to sit up and saw they were moving slowly through the neighborhood, circling the block and taking random turns that ultimately didn't lead to where they needed to go. Her eyes narrowed and she found the power within to sit up enough to see his eyes in the mirror—eyes that were conflicted—eyes that she would have looked at in a cold reading and said "you did something very bad."

"What is going on?" she asked. The car took another turn and they were on the freeway, driving fast. He'd picked up on her suspicion. "What are you doing?"

"Just lay back and when you wake up, you'll be okay."

"No," she said. "You're…"

She fell back in her seat, unable to help herself. She felt copper in her throat and a tingling sensation on her skin. The world began to spin into a kaleidoscope of colors. She couldn't see outside and she couldn't feel the seat under her. It was as if she was floating.

There was only one thing she was fairly certain of and it answered a lot of questions. Henry wasn't who he said he was. It was all a charade.

*This was all deliberate. This was what was supposed to happen.*

She'd been blind to it but had seen it all along. She'd just chosen to shut down that part of her brain…the same part she usually tried to open beyond human capabilities. Love really was blind, and in this case, it was killing her.

Her pain was unbearable, physically and emotionally. She hated him more than anything she'd ever hated and she couldn't believe he'd manipulated her. She wished she had sandalwood oil or jasmine or Benzoin. Eucalyptus, thyme, mugwart, cinnamon, candles… She wanted to perform a healing ritual…things she'd studied but never tried.

"Mother Earth, fire, wind, water and spirit, I ask thee to free and heal my body from your negative forces," she said repeatedly, her whispers filling the car. "Mother Earth, fire, wind…"

"Stop!" Henry shouted. "Just stop!"

"…Guardians of the east, south, west and north, powers of the earth, air, fire, and water, join my circle and I ask for your blessings as you depart. May peace be between us now and forever."

Magic was a manipulation of energy just as thoughts were a form of energy. Visualization was an even stronger form of energy that she used to intensify and direct her will. She tried to control the energy she'd produced. She tried to see it…to feel it…direct it, but it was taking her. It was Maria Haskins who had given herself the poison that would take her. One of the most important elements in the practice was the universal law of cause and effect. Whatever you do, or don't do, will cause something to happen. The most important consideration was the universal law of retribution. No matter what you do, it comes back to you in kind. It is the nature of things that as you send something out, it gains momentum, so that by the time it comes back to you, it's three times stronger. If you do something nice for someone, someone will do something nicer for you. The same was true if someone were to wrong you. Maria believed this negative energy could be directed back at that person and it was the only weapon left in her arsenal.

"With all the negative things you imposed on me, it will find its way back to you three times three…"

"Shut up Maria," he warned.

"…With the harm that you will send to me, it shall return three times three. Mote it be three times three. Mote it be…"

*"…Mote it be…"*

*The elevator doors closed. Maria stood in shock, unable to press a button…only to reflect on everything she'd seen. She gasped for breath having seen the city as she'd seen it. It had taken her energy and left her breathless. She put her arm on the door for support and bent over, wheezing.*

*Maria gasped for breath and closed her eyes, letting it all in. She saw a busy intersection. A man walked through the street, a droplet of blood falling from his nose. His illness evolved in real time as months passed in a moment and the man's eyes turned red and face grew white. He coughed and wheezed and more blood fell and then so did he. She turned and all around her, the population shriveled and fell, their faces all presenting the same symptoms.*

*Everywhere she turned, the city fell. Death was in the air, sucking their auras and rotting the streets.*

*She looked up and at the top of it all was Victor Stone, standing in the window of his office on the seventh floor of Stone Enterprises, admiring his work below.*

*She closed her eyes, trying to shake the vision, but she could hear the coughing, the gurgling of blood and vomit as people choked on their disease.*

*She tried to close her eyes tighter. "What is this?" she asked to no one. She visualized herself walking through the city, trying to find a sign of life. She tried to walk away from the building but she transported inside instead. She walked through the offices of Stone Enterprises, continuously moving toward Victor's office. Light shone on the outsides of the door. It seemed to be the only light left in the world. She rushed to it, needing to find safety from the rot that formed on the walls around her. She grabbed the knob and pushed inward and as the door swung in, she saw the smile on Victor's face, his eyes plastered to his handiwork.*

*She searched for the light and found the source. It came from something on his desk, but it was too bright to see from where she was. She walked toward it, but suddenly Victor was trying to get to it first...to diminish all that was left that could bring light back to the world. He grabbed it before she could reach it, but she caught a glimpse...*

And her eyes snapped open, fully understanding the meaning, who Victor was, what he was doing.

The elevator had reached the ground floor, but she let it close while she stood inside. She pressed the button to the seventh floor and waited, her eyes wide and full of fear. She'd spent two years afraid to say the wrong thing to Victor, only to learn that he was pure evil. He wasn't just a bad man. He was the man with his finger on the button. He was the end of times.

The door slid open on both ends and she stepped out, walking through the offices without hesitation, directly toward Victor with a different thought in mind. She felt as if someone else was controlling her, but she knew it was the better part of Maria...the part that knew that darkness must be stopped.

When she was twelve yards away, she grabbed a scissors off a cabinet.

Six yards, he looked up with a smile.

Three yards and she exposed the blades and brought them above her head.

His eyes went wide.

She brought the scissors down.

Her arm was suspended, held in place by one of Victor's associates, just inches from his chest. Another grabbed her other arm and in a moment, she was on the ground, struggling to break free and yelling a curse that she would later say she had no recollection of.

Victor commanded to let her go and Maria was on her feet, struggling to get to Victor again. This time, she was held back but faced Victor.

"What the hell are you doing?" He was exasperated.

The seventh floor was quiet, all eyes glued to the encounter.

"You're evil," she said. "You're darkness and disease. You're the end..."

The men holding her, pulled her tight and kept her body in place. Only her lips could move and they cursed Victor again, speaking in a language she didn't even know. Victor watched her dumbfounded, unable to grasp what was happening. His concern soon turned to anger as she kept going, talking gibberish about dark energy on his head and wishing him a shortened life and a slow death. When she finally stopped, it was because she had no voice left in her.

"What do we do with this?" one of the men holding her asked.

*"Don't let her back in the building."*

*"Should we call the police?"*

*"No," Victor said. "Kick her out. Make sure she doesn't come back."*

*"That's it?" the man asked.*

*Maria looked up and her eyes found his, asking the same question: That's it?*

*Victor's face was twisted in a fear she'd never seen before. He knew there was something to her…something to the things she said. It triggered something in him and he couldn't stay angry. Instead, his face betrayed him and she saw he was afraid.*

*"Yes, let her go."*

*"From this day on…" Maria started to say, repeating more of the same, putting a hex on his life in front of fifty people in shirts and ties.*

*"You better hope this wasn't more than a moment of deranged weakness Maria. You better hope you haven't done anything here today that will bring anything on me."*

*"You kidding?" one of the men asked. Victor shot him a look that silenced him immediately. Most in the office saw a crazy person. Watching Victor fear her was a sight to see.*

*He turned back to face Maria and waived them away, his hand shaking and his mind spinning as he tried to comprehend what had just happened. He wanted to call her or sit her down, but the woman who'd struggled for years to impress Victor had just tried to stab him with scissors because she had premonition of something that Victor didn't believe was entirely impossible.*

*Maria was escorted back to the elevator, but watched Victor in horror, seeing him for the first time. If someone didn't intervene, he would be …*

…the end of her.

She was trapped, unable to move, unable to speak…

Even if he had a change of heart or someone came to her rescue, even if he got her to the hospital now, she felt that this time, it was really over. She couldn't reason as to why that would be, but knew it was the money. It was the will…it was their greed that really would bring the end.

She closed her eyes slowly. She stopped moving her lips and her energy dissipated completely. Her last thought was that Henry would get what was coming to him, three time three time over.

She took her last breath and was still.

When he was sure she was gone, Henry pulled over to the side of the road and rested his forehead against the steering wheel, It was almost hard for him to believe he could feel even shittier than he already did, but when it was done, he hated himself and he knew he'd hate himself forever.

"What the hell did you do?" he asked.

He couldn't bring himself to look at her body. Instead he held the wheel tightly and closed his eyes, hoping he'd wake up and it would all just be a dream.

The sound of cars whizzing by and horns honking resounded in his head and shattered the peace he tried desperately to find. Sweat fell from his pores and he struggled to maintain a regular breathing pattern. Just as he was going to start hyperventilating, he stepped out of the car and dialed Toby's number, ready to tell him to go to hell before he got back in the car and drove far away. The other end opened and before Toby could make a smart-ass remark, Henry began speaking in short bursts.

"I...she's..."

"Relax," Toby said. "You did it, didn't you...She's gone..."

"Toby...I..."

He'd lost track of his surroundings and stepped too far from the car in his distress. A horn blared and Henry looked up in time for a semi to pass, the side mirror smashing into his face and knocking most of his teeth out. The phone flew from his hand and his body got sucked under the truck, toppling head over legs as all tires crushed him and sent him rolling on the pavement. The truck cleared his body and slowed but Henry rolled once more and what was left of his shattered body sprawled out by the side of the road.

## *Chapter 17*

### *1*

"I thought I'd never see you again," Christian Dent said, staring at Trish Reynalds through the glass divider at Kern.

Trish swallowed hard, having dreaded this conversation for some time. She almost backed out of coming to see Christian completely, but one day, she would no longer be able to hide from it. She'd spent time with her daughter, cherishing every second. She felt no anger. She was too relieved for that. Whoever Neomin was and whoever he'd been working with, she was unable to determine, though she had her suspicions. Instead of going down a road of revenge that would turn her into the kind of person her daughter would have to come to terms with, she backed away from the whole incident on the roof with Brian Van Dyke and mellowed herself out.

She hadn't heard from Charlie and it seemed no one else had. She suspected the worst—that he was dead. If that was true, she may never know what he knew. Just as she was going to start asking questions about Charlie's disappearance, Maria Haskins committed suicide. Her husband had tried to get her to the hospital but got out of the car for undetermined reason and wound up spread across the highway. She would have looked further into Maria's death, but she refused to get involved. She only wanted to spend time with her daughter.

Shiloh was bored of her though and ran off with friends for the first time in a while. Trish saw her daughter smile for the first time in a long time and it overwhelmed her. When she was alone again, it forced her to think of what she'd almost done.

In hindsight, she couldn't believe how close she'd been. Her love for her daughter was so powerful that Trish could have easily crossed a line she'd never cross otherwise. Now, she felt regret. She felt like a fool. Most importantly, she'd accepted that if a beneficiary had been pulling strings, there was still danger out there somewhere. She'd started applying for jobs all over the country. She didn't care where they ended up. She'd take Shiloh and disappear, work in a small town and find a piece of happiness where she could put her actions behind her forever. She'd finally gotten an offer at a precinct in Texas. It wasn't exactly where she'd hoped to end up, but anywhere but LA was fine with her. All that was left to do was explain herself to Christian and walk away.

"This will be the last time I come see you," she said. She'd been juggling her opening statement for hours and that was all she could say.

"That's what you said last time. What changed? Are we still doing this?"

"Shiloh's not sick. She doesn't need surgery. She never did."

"How..?"

"My doctor was compromised somehow. He faked it."

A long silence fell between them before Dent finally spoke. "You have nothing to gain from my freedom…"

"Dent…"

"You selfish bitch."

"I'm selfish?"

"You staged evidence to make me guilty. You came to me asking for a favor before you plan a killing spree with a dozen victims and now you come here and back out of our deal because you no longer need me?"

"I get it Dent."

"I don't think you do. You're obligated. We've come too far."

"I'm not going to apologize to you. My daughter is more important to me than your freedom. I would do anything for her. I'd do it again."

"And I'll do anything to get out of this place. I don't need you Reynalds. I never did. Any bit of sympathy I had for you and your bullshit situation is gone. You'll be the first I come after and it won't end with you. I'll take your daughter. I'll make sure she's well taken care of. Maybe one day, she'll even call me her father and when she asks about you, I'll tell her you got yourself killed because you were a dirty murdering cop."

Trish's jaw clenched. Nothing prepared her for threats of this caliber. She'd expected Dent to be angry, but now she was afraid. He'd already made one legitimate escape attempt and it seemed as if he was making ties in Kern. She'd always told herself never to underestimate anyone. People with enough drive can do just about anything. It wasn't entirely impossible that Dent could one day be free. The thought of Texas calmed her down.

"You won't find me. I'm leaving. I won't have the same name and I will always have a badge and gun. I'm going to tell the guard about these threats and see to it that you're watched closely."

Dent leaned back with a sly grin. "I'm going to watch the life drain from your eyes."

Trish was sure he was just trying to scare her, but it worked. Any shade of doubt she'd ever had about his guilt was gone. In that moment, he looked like he was pure evil. "Sorry it had to be this way," Trish said. "My doctor lied about Shiloh. Probably the work of another one of you assholes who think money is worth your soul, but now I know the truth. She needed to be saved at any cost and now she doesn't. You were my last resort and I don't need you. I'm not letting a dangerous man go for nothing. I'm sorry."

Before he could threaten her further, she hung up the phone…

…*Dent drove his boat west for a while before landing in Baton Rouge. He worked odd jobs long enough to save enough money to go further. By the time he landed in Texas, he ditched the boat and stayed there another year, holed up on a ranch where a man named Percy Barnett agreed to let him work in exchange for food and a roof. Dent insisted on staying in the stables, which were rebuilt onto another part of the ranch and left empty. Dent worked to create something out of the space he was given. He had seating in the sun and a comfortable loft.*

*Percy would toss the remains of the newspaper outside the stables daily and Dent would stay in touch with what was happening in the world. For nine months, Dent didn't wander off the property once. He stayed hidden from the world, unsure of just where he was supposed to go next. After being a part of the biggest drug operation on the east coast, he walked away with nothing. The money he took with him he burned through quickly and he was left to fend for himself.*

*Most of his time was spent reading the books that Percy picked up for him, but the remainder of his time, he weighed his options. He hadn't made enemies and it seemed that with the ever transforming drug trade in Miami, he was forgotten. He was safe, but there was no place left for him. His mother was dead and he despised his father. Going home never felt like an option, but as the days passed and Dent came to terms with the hand he was dealt, he began to see his future as wide open.*

*It was on a rainy day that Christian sat in his loft with the newspaper spread out in front of him that he came across Mitch's name. He read one paragraph three times before resting his head and looking out into the rain. The man who'd kidnapped him, forced him into the drug trade, and then mentored him, was going on trial. Mitch had murdered many people that Christian had known of, but the trial focused on the kidnapping and murder of Christian Dent Jr. He'd sold drugs and participated in numerous offenses over the years. There would be no escape for him but Christian couldn't help but feel like he needed to be a part of it. Resurfacing could save Mitch.*

*He was numb for days and days turned to weeks. He kept telling himself it was time to go, but going meant being a part of the world again and what would the world say when they learned Christian Dent was alive? At his request, Percy gave him access to a computer for a few minutes a day. Christian followed the trial from beginning to end, as Mitch confessed to everything. Christian expected his friend to have some fight in him, but he was a man defeated. He hoped he'd made a deal or would come out with a job working for the FBI, trying to catch men like himself. Instead, it seemed that Mitch would be bombarded by witnesses and experts who were all set on taking him down. Family and friends of loved ones gone and the families surrounding victims of their products, rallied against a verdict of guilty. Christian never fully understood how large of a name Mitch had until then.*

*Then one day, Christian saw his own name in the newspaper blurb. The questioning revolved around his mother and father, the election Mitch was hired to rig and the kidnapping of Christian Dent, designed to keep his father in the running and steal votes. Everything was as factual as Christian knew it to be. Mitch had proved to be nothing but cooperative, but then his own name was written and with it a lie...the first one Christian knew Mitch told.*

**Son of city councilman, Christian Dent, Christian Jr...dead.**

*Mitch had confessed to his murder. He claimed he stuffed his body in a steel barrel, set it adrift in the Pacific, but not before blowing a tennis ball-sized hole in it. Mitch was shown to have no remorse as he talked of the boy he'd murdered. He'd only given an account and an explanation of "I didn't need him anymore."*

*Christian wasn't sure what to think. Was it for his protection? To give him the option to stay hidden? Or maybe Mitch was intent on dying. He was looking at lethal injection and the trial never strayed from a straight line to it. No matter what was happening, he knew Mitch was in it alone. Christian belonged at his side, but there was no way he could resurface without the story calling him a victim. He would be nurtured and used for entertainment. He wouldn't see or talk to Mitch at all. They'd tell him it was for his own good.*

*Christian stood outside with Percy one day and asked if he could finish working a month and head out. Percy didn't act thrilled but he accepted the decision and never tried to talk Christian out of it. Christian wanted to ask for money, or help, or even if Percy had a connection, but he never did. He left quietly and worked his way back to the west coast, following the trial along the way. By the time he was exiting Nevada, the trial was over, the verdict was guilty, and the sentence was lethal injection. Christian couldn't find it in himself to mourn. He wasn't thrilled to be going back to LA but he had no intention of anyone learning who he was. Instead, he plotted a return that would keep him under the radar, but that could get him some favors and important friends.*

*When he was ten, Christian Dent was taken and given no choice in how his life turned out. He'd learned some things, had some fun, but now his abductor was going to die. His time away had come full circle, but it wasn't over until Mitch was dead, and that wasn't going to happen until Christian had closure…*

…He sat on the sidelines of a basketball game in the yard. He leaned back with his elbows on a bench and soaked in the sun. After flicking a cigarette to the ground, Stanley Kline sat at his side and wrapped his large arms around his knee.

"Would you believe that the only thing that separates us from our freedom is a large gate?" Dent asked.

"It's not the gate really," Stan said. "We can bring down the gate. It's the guards, the judge, and the jury."

"I don't know how they do it," Dent said, watching the convicts throughout the yard, laughing, playing games, and gathering together in groups. "I don't know how they adapt."

"Well, most know they don't have a prayer to get out, but most prisons operate more sensibly than society."

"Yeah, except someone else is paying to keep us here, just like when we were children and our parents spoon-fed us."

"What happened?" Stan asked. "Why you talking like this?"

"Cop that put me here…she came to see me. She's a beneficiary."

"Trish Reynalds?"

"That's her. She propositioned me. Said her kid was dying and she wanted the money. She was going to kill them all. Then herself. All I had to do was save the kid."

"Well shit, that sounds like a great deal to me."

"There were other things at play. Her doctor lied. Someone lied. Her kid…never sick. She told me this morning."

Stan's brow creased deeply and he shook his head in admiration. "Charlie Palmer must have been the doctor. He's another beneficiary. I don't know much about him but looks like he almost used her to get the job done."

"Another name on the will," Dent said, fully understanding events.

"Looks like there's plenty of people after that money."

"Lying about a kid dying isn't fair play."

"Then you can tell him that before he dies."

"Yeah," Dent said, fully intending on doing just that. "I think we're ready to go."

"Go where?"

"I think it's time we start working the list."

"Just like that? I thought we agreed to wait for me…"

"I got something better."

"You mind bringing me in on whatever it is you're doing?"

"Donovan can get us wherever we want to go."

"But he won't."

"If he wants the money enough, he will."

"Right Dent, but when you walk out of here, you disappear. No one believes you'd keep your word. Wouldn't happen."

Dent sat up and spit on the ground. He looked out into the distance, past the gate. "You want that money or not?"

"I'm out in a month and I can finish what I started. You'll inherit everything and we can buy your way out of here. Whatever it takes. Get someone to look at your case again, pay another witness to come forward to throw a wrench in the story. You can walk out a free and wealthy man."

Dent chuckled a little. That had been the plan until Trish ruined it, but Dent refused to let four walls hold him in. "Not without the cop's confession I can't. Talk to Donovan. Tell him I want to make a deal. That money's no good if I'm here forever."

"I can't go with you if you do this now."

"I know."

"And I'm your partner here, so you can't just run off."

"I'm a man of my word. Set up the meeting."

"Damnit," Stan said, speaking to no one in particular. He looked up at Dent, who seemed at peace. He was confident and content. He had no worries at all. It was as if he knew something no one else understood.

*Oh well*, Stan thought. *If he gets himself killed, I'll just find someone else. Maybe Charlie Palmer.*

He wanted to do this with Dent. They had the same mind and with Dent, it wasn't so complicated. He didn't need to resort to blackmail or persuade anyone. Dent wanted the money and had no reservations about murder. When the time came to collect though, Dent would be on the run. Stan wasn't sure how that worked out in the end, but Dent was smarter than Stan by a mile and they both knew it. The notion of how a wanted man could pick up a check worth millions of dollars couldn't have been lost on Dent.

Dent wasn't thinking straight and there was no way he could be trusted. He would never be a free man. He could never collect the money. If he could, he wouldn't share.

"Yeah, I'll get this set up," Stan said. A plan was forming in his head. It wasn't going to work out for Dent after all, but fate had brought them together, if only because Dent had been untouchable when Stan was on the outside. He might have even been the hardest to kill for anyone that wanted the money. Stan realized that he wasn't here to team up with Dent. He was here to cross him off the list.

2

Darkness slowly became light and memories came back to him slowly. A breakfast burrito, a suicide, Shiloh Reynalds…an explosion. His memories were out of order and he tried to track them to the present… where was he and why did it feel as if he'd been out a long time? Pain and trauma were becoming friends to Charlie, as life dealt him more shit in the last months than he'd ever seen in his life. He'd started it and he had been willing to deal with some pain, but the fallout after Abby's death wouldn't end. Somehow, the house of cards was falling and there was no escaping.

He began to remember the last moments before he blacked out. He was going to stop Trish Reynalds from committing mass murder and he was taken by the man who'd helped…

Adlar Wilcox.

His eyes came into focus and his senses came back to him. At his side was a gun and across from him in the dark basement was Adlar Wilcox, bound to a metal pole with his eyes closed. Charlie couldn't make sense of the situation, other than to believe maybe he was dead and this was his hell, but what it really seemed to be was a gift. Since Abby died, it was Adlar he'd wanted to kill, but he could never get them alone in a room with an advantage. The scene was set more perfectly than Charlie himself could have arranged.

Charlie reached across his body with his right hand and grabbed the gun, inspecting it closely. It had been a while since he'd had a gun in hand. The last time he did, he'd spent hours practicing shooting at targets with a rifle. It had cost Bedbug his life and a simple act of revenge caused the walls to crumble in on him. This time, there were no long distances. There was no need to practice or hide under a tarp on a roof. It was only Charlie and Adlar, face to face.

He tightened his grip on the gun and held it up. "Adlar Wilcox," he said, his voice parched. He said the name again and Adlar stirred awake, unhappy to see Charlie was awake. Charlie didn't know how long they'd been together—it seemed as if it may have been a while—but Adlar likely spent a lot of time hoping Charlie wouldn't come to.

In the dark, Adlar's features looked sunken. He was always skinny, but he looked famished and his eyes were hazy.

"Who did this?" Charlie asked, noticing for the first time that there were no stairs leading up. They were trapped together. After Adlar was dead, there would be new challenges.

"Manny," Adlar whispered. "Detective Manny Quinny."

"Why?"

"He wants me dead."

"Why?"

Adlar shook his head. It was a question with a thousand answers, with a thousand different beginnings. "He just does," he said, his voice as parched as Charlie's. "He knows everything. What I did. What you did. All about the will and the money. I was going to work with him because he lost his friend. I don't know." Adlar didn't have it in him to say more.

"The man I shot from the roof..." Charlie said.

"Yeah. This is what he wanted. He thinks you'll kill me."

"He was right..."

"I know, but Charlie, listen."

There was desperation after-all. Adlar looked ready to accept his own death, but something was lighting up inside. "Don't bother denying..."

"I'm not," Adlar said. "I did it." His face fell and he looked at the ground, unable to look at Charlie as he confessed. "There's other stuff going on though. Manny will kill them all. He's probably going to use you to get the money but he'll kill you too."

"They might be dead already," Charlie said, thinking about the state of mind Trish was in before he was captured. Two strong forces were out there somewhere, shooting up random people in Los Angeles. "How long have we been down here?"

"Four days I think."

"Shit." Charlie lowered the gun so he could think. Maybe he was all that was left and killing Adlar meant Charlie inherited everything. There was nothing he could do with that money though. He never wanted it and he always knew the steep cost it would come at. Strangely enough, he probably had paid for more than anyone because of Victor's will and he was the one who wanted nothing to do with Victor. "I'll figure it out," he said, and raised the gun again. "You though...this finally has to be done."

"I know you think that," Adlar said, speaking quickly. "But if you want to stop Manny and you want to save everyone, you gotta think about this."

"There's nothing I can do."

"I know," Adlar said. "You won't even be able to get out of here if you kill me, but you can untie me and boost me up."

Charlie tried to feign laughter but it came out dry. "You're pathetic."

"I'll get help and we can get help for you and I can release everything I have on Manny. I can't do it dead."

"If we die, he just walks..."

"I swear. He's setting you up. Obviously this is what he wants to happen but he's using you to kill me. He did this to punish me, but all you have to do is the thing he doesn't want you to do, because I can stop things."

"You think I'd just let you walk out of here after what you did? I let you walk away once and look what you did to my legs!" As Charlie spoke, he screamed the words, spit flying from his mouth as he said them. The words echoed in the basement and everything fell silent.

"I'd come back for you," Adlar said, quietly. "I promise I would because things are different now. I'll go to jail or whatever. If you have to kill me then okay but let me out so we can stop him first. We can do this again later but this is more important."

Charlie shook his head in disbelief, partly because the situation sucked so bad, but mainly because he was considering it. After everything he'd done to track Adlar and the time he'd spent wanting to kill him, it was possible that the only way to prevent Manny and Trish from murder was to get out and see what the world around them looked like.

"I promise," Adlar said. "I'm tired of this and I screwed you. I know I did. I don't feel happy about it. I kept going to people to help. Manny was helping and that one guy Toby from the will was the one who helped me kill Abby."

"I knew it," Charlie said, his face blank. "He has Trish Reynalds believing her kid is dying too."

"See? So there's stuff to figure out but Charlie, if you kill me, he's not going to let you go, and then who's left? You and me are the only two who know this stuff. If I could boost you out, I would, but it won't work. If you want to stop that other stuff, then you gotta let me out. But if it matters to you more that I'm dead, then fine, but..."

"Just hang on. Shut up for a second." Charlie closed his eyes and rubbed his temples as he felt a migraine come on. Adlar was right, whatever his motives, he was right. The question now was whether or not he could trust Adlar to do what he promised. Revenge could wait, but if they were all dead, or if Adlar was ready to run and never be seen again,

Charlie could potentially make a regrettable decision.

Justice was long overdue, but if they weren't already, there were ten people who were about to be murdered, and only Adlar Wilcox could prevent it.

## 3

Maria Haskin's wake wasn't overcrowded, but the turnout was higher than Trish expected.

She felt guilty mourning the passing of a woman who not long before, she was going to kill. She tried to dismiss her actions as being not in her right mind, but she was. If she had gone through with it, a good number of people would understand and identify with the love of a daughter O5hers would call her an animal and say the lives of ten are more important than that of one. At the time, she didn't care what they'd say, but as an officer of the law, she'd almost disgraced the uniform.

All for nothing.

It wasn't her fault though. It was Neomin and whoever had compromised him. She tried to remember the beneficiaries and what made them tick but her mind drew a blank. She'd been distracted by Shiloh for so long that she'd lost sight of protecting the group. She knew that was the point...that and a crusade to kill every last beneficiary.

She looked around the funeral home, specifically to see if she could spot Brian Van Dyke, who wasn't in attendance. Maybe he was afraid of Trish and maybe he was too consumed with his own issues, but she would have to circle back on him too and explain herself—maybe even apologize. She didn't fear retaliation. He was too incapable.

She closed her eyes, ashamed to admit that was the reason she'd targeted him because she didn't like him. She had fewer moral qualms with his death than any of the others. She feared in herself a monster that she'd never been introduced to until she was manipulated into disappearing inside herself. It was so easy in the smoke and din to mask that something dark had taken root, but in the aftermath, she had experienced so much relief for her daughter's health that she'd pushed a reality back in her mind that was surfacing now.

She looked down at Maria in her casket, seemingly at peace, and she began to cry.

Royce Morrow made a short appearance, surrounded by his entourage of guards and his campaign manager. Some pictures were taken and he was asked sporadically how he knew Maria. He asked if he could be allowed to grieve and sat as far away from the crowd as was possible, thinking about how many deaths he had seen in such a short amount of time.

He noticed Jason Stone trying to sit discreetly, not far away. Jason turned and saw him looking. They both nodded mutually and Royce took the moment to join Jason and asked his crew to hover nearby and give them a moment.

"I heard you were married," Royce said.

Jason smiled and nodded. "One month ago yesterday."

"Congratulations."

"Thank you. I'm sorry for your loss Royce. If there's anything I can do…"

"Vote for Morrow," Royce said in good humor, but he barely cracked a smile. He looked solemn.

"Your opponent is the shot caller at my father's organization."

"Wasn't that supposed to be you?"

"Maybe if I'd wanted it."

"May I be blunt?"

"Please."

"If you don't want it, then fine. I can respect that, but you do have a responsibility to leave it in good hands. That much power and influence needs to be used in other ways. Bernard Bell's not a good man and from what I understand about you, you are."

"I assume that's the point of your campaign," Jason said. "To bring him down. Are you even up for the job? If you win?"

"I'll put the cities' best interests top of mind."

Jason leaned back and reflected. "Who has ever seen an election like this? You're both business conglomerates, running empire against empire in the business world, man against man in the political world. A lot of people probably don't see the difference between you."

"There's many."

"Maybe, but they don't know that. They know where you come from though Royce and that's your edge. At the end of the day, all these people who don't know this for that about the issues are going to lean toward you. You're one of them and they know that. You're proof that anyone can go from rags to riches if they make the right step. You're an expert on coming out of nowhere and building the American dream out of nothing."

"You should be on my staff," Royce said.

"Politics aren't my thing and if they were, I wouldn't run for the same reason Bell shouldn't run. We've never seen the other side of the line. I never worked a fast food job or picked corn in the summer because I didn't have to. Now, I'm an adult and most people struggle in ways I can't identify with. I can't speak for them. Neither can Bell. There's a saying that goes: You go pluck potatoes so that when you eat potatoes, it's very different. You know where they came from and what it means to have them from the ground to the plate."

Royce smiled and shook his head. "I'm going to lose Jason."

Their conversation was interrupted by a phone call for Jason from his father's security company telling him there was a break-in at his father's mansion. It was relayed to a secretary at Stone Enterprises, who didn't know what to do with the information and found Jason's name in the phone directory. Jason told her he'd check on it and cut his meeting short with Royce. Before he exited, he turned back. "I think you're going to win Royce. I'm talking to Erica about coming back. I have a bit of a deadline with Bernard about the future of the business and it's quickly approaching. I want to see what he does with this election—where he really stands. I'll oversee the business and make sure it's in good hands."

Jason started to walk away, but turned back at the sound of Royce's words, his voice cold and pained. "He's a murderer." Jason turned back. "I can't say more or prove anything, but you can't trust him. You need to remember that."


As Aileen Thick headed into the funeral home, Jason walked past her on the way out, turning in time to greet her. She tried to stop him, but he offered to catch up with her that evening. They agreed to meet for an early dinner near LAX and he hurried off to check on the alarm.

Aileen noticed Royce in the corner but steered clear. She paid her respects and was about to leave when Tarek Appleton walked in. They made eye contact immediately. She noted that he looked as if he was only there searching for her. She greeted him and he hung his head for a moment before making eye contact. "I owe you an apology. For a lot of things."

"No, I shouldn't have destroyed something I knew you cared about. The funny thing is that in everything I read, I couldn't find one thing that wasn't true. I just…the truth sucked. It sucked reliving some things."

"So everything about your pregnancy…"

"Yeah," she said.

"Sorry you went through that."

"It was a long time ago."

"Look at this," Tarek said, looking toward the casket. "You were right."

"She committed suicide. I wasn't right."

"You really believe that? She just got married. She was happy."

"We can't possibly know what was happening with her or what she was going through. I heard she's done this before though. Maybe she just had mental issues."

"Regardless, I think you should present some of what you told me to the group. Maybe you can point out some things they didn't realize about themselves."

"I'm the last person who should do that."

"Aileen…" She found his eyes and saw the kindness that she knew was the real Tarek. "It was you that predicted this. It's you that saw the significant changes. I think you're sharper than you know and I don't think you have to be afraid to make yourself known."

"You could do it. They'd listen to you."

"No, not me. I didn't believe you. I think you own this. Besides, the studio loved the script. We're in pre-production." Aileen didn't look thrilled and Tarek saw it in her.

"You're going to be a movie star."

"Who knows? The world thinks I'm a lovable goofball who occasionally has violent tendencies in public and picks up women on street corners. I'm not the most bankable person right now."

"I'm not that sharp Tarek, but it was just that guy…Sal Blovik. The day he attacked me, and every time I think about it, even though it all happened so fast, I saw in his eyes that there was this recognition. I think he would have raped me. He would have killed me. But it didn't feel random. It felt like he had been there watching and even though this sounds silly, I mean, is it possible someone hired him to do it? Do we trust anyone near us? For all we know, Maria's husband killed her. I don't know, but maybe someone somewhere is thinking about what we're going to do and how we're going to react and they're finding ways to kill us without…really killing us."

"Well, I think you're onto something and I think you should take credit. I think…" He spotted Trish Reynalds, who looked distraught, staring at the flowers that had been sent to the family. "I think you should talk to her."

"She hates me."

"Her opinion of you doesn't matter."

Aileen turned to Tarek. She wanted to put her hands on his arms. She wanted to wrap herself around him. He looked better than he had in a while. "Tarek…" she said. She could feel his breath on hers and he looked down at her as he struggled with his own desires. Then, he stepped back, denying her any kind of embrace.

"Thank you for everything Aileen."

She watched him pay his respects and hoped he'd come back after, but he walked out the door instead. Aileen turned to Trish, who looked like she was in need of a shoulder to cry on. She thought about the last time she'd seen her, how Trish had lectured her and dismissed her after she'd nearly been killed. Aileen wanted to help, but she didn't know who to trust. Even Tarek had let her down. She watched Trish for a long moment before going to the casket and looking down at Maria.

She swallowed hard at the sight of her, looking like she always had, looking as if she could pop up at any moment. Seeing Maria at peace made her feel at peace, enlightened, and invigorated. It wasn't the first time she saw death face to face, but this wasn't like all the dreadful experiences she'd had. Maria's hair was done up nicer than Aileen had ever seen her. The make-up on her face highlighted how beautiful she really was. The corners of her mouth tilted slightly upward, displaying a smile, or that look people had when they know something you don't. Aileen never knew Maria well. She hadn't thought about her much at all —just as Aileen assumed people never thought much of her. She'd never tried to make herself known. She wondered if anyone would have listened to Maria if she tried to open their eyes. Maybe Maria had tried. Maybe that's why Maria was here.

She turned back to the room and walked through the small crowd. She walked around family members and friends and some of Maria's clients, not knowing who any of them were or what their connections to Maria were. She passed Trish on her way out. Trish looked up briefly and their eyes caught, but Aileen turned away and walked out.

## 4

Donovan spoke with a guard, who passed a message to Donovan. An hour later, Donovan pulled Stan out of his cell under cover of being reprimanded. He dragged him through the cell block and out to the yard, where the act was over as soon as they entered a shed filled with grounds-keeping tools.

"What's happening?" Donovan asked, handing Stan a cigarette. Both men leaned against a wall and sucked in smoke for a long moment. Stan closed his eyes and savored the taste for a moment.

"Something lit a fire under Dent. He wants out. Says he's going to kill em all."

"Really?" Donovan said, incredulously. "That won't happen."

"That's what I thought too. This is the Dent we wanted, but he walks out of here and we never see him again."

"Yup," Donovan said. "He hates me. Maybe if I can get a hold of an ankle bracelet or some kind of tracker that he can't remove..."

"I'm going to make a suggestion," Stan asked.

"I'm not sure I trust you either," Donovan said. He took another drag.

"Well, I got a kid and a few relatives living in state that I'd very much like to keep safe. Threaten me with them and I'm under your thumb."

"Okay then," Donovan said. "I'll need their names. Let's hear what you got."

"I'll kill em all. I'll take care of it. Who needs Dent?"

"Dent's name is on it."

"Yeah, well so are others and some of them want the money. My guess is since they're not dropping like flies, it's not so easy for them to take care of. I can do it, no problem, and I'll share. I'm out in a month and I won't be running from nothing. I'm not hard-headed like Dent. I've got no beef with you."

"No, you don't," Donovan said. "But if you're getting out, what do you need me for?"

"Well, Dent's name is on the list. He wants out. Says he only needs access to the roof. Help him there and maybe that's the end of the line for him."

"I thought you and Dent were cozy with each other."

"I tried to partner up with the guy but he's not practical. He's making deals behind our backs with others on the list, now he's trying to break out and like he'll still honor his word. Makes no sense. He's playing us."

"Yeah," Donovan agreed and let the proposal sink in. "I'll need contact information and names of everyone you're associated with and I'm going to check it out. I don't need you double-crossing me."

"Not a problem at all," Donovan said. He had every intention of splitting the money. "We'll need a communication plan. I need to know you can do this right and quickly."

"I'll have it done in under a month when I'm out."

Donovan nodded and the men smoked another three cigarettes a piece before parting ways. The change of plans had been unexpected for Donovan, but he wouldn't be complaining. He'd hated Dent a long time and dreaded the thought of being dependent on him to be rich. Stan, he trusted. This was shaping up to be a great day. Donovan had stepped on the scale that morning and found himself down two pounds from a couple weeks ago, he'd met a girl online who agreed to have dinner with him on the weekend, and tonight he was going to be able to shove Dent from the roof of Kern. As a result, by the end of the year, he'd be a millionaire.

Life was going just fine for Donovan.

He arranged for Dent to meet with him after dinner while the inmates had a semi-celebrity guest speaker, who would tell them to hang in there and read your Bibles and inmates lives were as important as anyone else's. Donovan thought it was all bullshit. He'd soon have his reward for suffering in this prison with the rest of them, only he wouldn't be taking them with him. Long after he'd retire and spend his old age in a cabin in Montana, all these lowlifes would still be killing each other and reading scripture, repenting their sins while shoving homemade weapons in each other.

Dent would be a parting gift—the equivalent of a retirement cake—one last pleasure for Donovan before he could start counting down his days. He looked at his watch. Dinner was in an hour. He was anxious, but he'd bide his time. He imagined how it would play out in his head, trying to see the look on Dent's face as he flew through the air. He couldn't quite see the expression—not even in his daydream.

*Save that for tonight,* he thought. *I'll see it tonight...*

*...Travis Keegan covered Mitch's trial from beginning to end with high enthusiasm. He'd just gotten started at a career in journalism when the kidnapping of Christian Dent Jr. was news. He'd fought to report the story but lost out to senior reporters. After a decade of following the new of Mitch sightings, just as he was beginning to believe the case would be cold forever, Mitch was arrested in Miami and taken back to Los Angeles for trial.*

*Now, Travis had a lot more clout and when he demanded to be the one to cover the trial, his boss said yes without hesitation. Travis had no other assignment. He sat in the courtroom day after day and was even granted an interview with Mitch, which didn't get him much information other than that Dent was dead and the body would never turn up. He'd always secretly thought Christian Jr. was still alive and would one day resurface, but throughout the trial, the story never changed and deep down, Travis knew it had to be true. Guys like Mitch murdered everyone who inconvenienced them. Christian was just a child and would have been a gigantic distraction for Mitch when he was on the run, long before he fell into the drug trade.*

*The trial ended with a sentence of death. The state was happy to see him go, but a dozen authors jumped on the chance to write their version of the truth and a movie producer approached him. Mitch turned him away.*

*He acted like a man who had accepted his fate and was counting down the days, trying to find inner peace. At the same time, he was being treated for cancer so he'd live long enough to be put to death. The only quote Mitch would ever give the public was to tell them that his life's work had finally come full circle and the devil was coming for him.*

*The story faded from the public eye and Christian Jr. was forgotten.*

*Dent set up a meeting with Travis under the name Felix Patel. He passed a message through the assistant of Travis's editor. It was an anonymous tip that Felix knew the location of Christian Jr.'s body. It included a time and a place and Travis showed up without fear, though he positioned himself to be alone in an apartment on a cul de sac off the highway.*

*Travis stood in the entry. The apartment was dark and nearly empty, except for some old furniture and a stack of books.*

*"Shut the door and sit down please," a voice said from across the room.*

*"Nah, not just yet. I don't know you. Who are you and why should I believe your message?"*

*"I've been in Miami. I worked with Mitch."*

*"If you know where the body is, why haven't you gone to the police?"*

*"Because I'm willing to give you a story, but in return, there's something I want."*

*Travis sensed Felix didn't intend on hurting him. He sat in a chair across the room and looked at his watch. "I'm leaving in five minutes if you don't have anything to say that interests me."*

*"You will be attending the execution..."*

*"Yes, I will."*

*"I want to be there."*

*"Impossible, and you still haven't given me any substance."*

*"How can you get me in the room?"*

*"The only people invited to watch are family of the victim, family of the accused, select members of the press, the executioner, and the mayor."*

*"But you can get me in with you..."*

*"Yes, I could get you in with me, assuming you have credentials and I have a reason. That said, I have nothing more to say on this topic until you can explain to me why I'd want you there in the first place."*

*"If I prove to you beyond a reasonable doubt that I can provide the location of the body and I have enough documentation to show that I'm legitimate and have a degree in journalism, would you be able to get me in? Yes or no, or I will move on to the LA Times."*

*"Absolutely. You prove you have the location and you do it before the execution, and you tell me how you know and what your connection is, then we absolutely have a deal. If there's a shadow of a doubt, then we don't."*

*Dent leaned into the moonlight coming through the windows and made his face known. Travis had looked at hundreds of pictures of Christian as a boy, but he didn't recognize the face before him at first glance. Then, he looked into the eyes and found there was something more to this man. He wasn't a friend or an associate of Mitch and he didn't just want to watch an old buddy die from lethal injection.*

*His mouth was dry and numb as he suspected the impossible. "What's your real name?"*

*"I'm Christian Dent..."*

...Stan watched Dent from the corner of his eye at chow-time. Dent had been conspiring without him and it made him want to exact revenge, but that would be too messy and compromise his ticket out of Kern. He reminded himself to remain cooperative and be in favor of the other COs. Giving them Dent was the final detail, but he couldn't shake the fact that Dent had worked against them, even after agreeing to wait it out. His curiosity got the best of him.

"So why you doing it this way?" he asked. "Why not let me do it? It was a good plan."

"Some things just can't wait," Dent said.

"What's that mean for me?" Stan asked.

"I don't know," Dent said. He didn't bother to hide how little he cared about Stan's problems.

"Let's go," an officer behind Dent said. Both men looked up at him and thought the same thing. This officer was the next step.

"I guess this is where we part ways," Stan said.

Dent didn't say anything. He stood and let the guard lead him out. Any eyes on Dent assumed he'd gotten himself into trouble or he had an urgent visitor. He walked quietly through the chow hall.

"Where you taking me?" Dent asked as they stepped outside and walked along the wall. The CO didn't respond. He led Dent to a large metal door that went into Kern from the outside. Dent had never seen anyone come in or out of the door and couldn't even geographically place where in Kern this door would take him.

The inside was unfamiliar. It was a long corridor which long appeared unused. Lights flickered and pipes hissed far in the distance. The smell of copper was strong in the air. "Where are we?" Dent asked.

"This is the original layout of Kern. They abandoned the design a year after they started locking prisoners away. They were building below ground level, which for some convicts, meant just on the other side of their wall was a cave network. The real problem was the plumbing. After a rainy winter, they realized because all the rock was built around the walls, the water wasn't escaping so fast. This whole level flooded back in the forties and everyone locked up drowned. They had to clear it out and never used it again. It was a huge disaster. If you ever hear noises in the night, don't be surprised. People who know the history of this place tend to think it's haunted."

Dent had never heard ghosts, but he knew Kern had history and more people had probably died in the yard than drowning in the underground tunnels. It was unnerving to know that the prison was on top of all this and could collapse with one good earthquake.

The CO left Dent to wait in what looked like it was once an office. All that remained was a desk and a stool. Dent waited forty minutes, growing concerned at what would happen when he was found to be missing. As he was ready to explore, he heard footsteps, and moments later, Donovan Willis entered the room and looked down on Dent.

"You ready for this?"

"I need to know the plan. How do you get me to the roof from here?"

"There's a ladder on the inside wall on the east side. It takes you to the roof from the inside of the building. There's a lot of hollowed out area within the walls here. In fact, I've seen cons try to break through the wall, only to find there was another to break through. By then they're busted though. Breaking through walls is useless, but if you walk the edges and climb up, you can at least get to the roof. About a decade ago, we had some gang member almost get out of here because he figured that out and he was almost taken out of here on a helicopter that tossed a ladder down to him. He actually did get outside the walls but he was caught within days. Brings me to an interesting question Dent. What makes you think you're going to succeed?"

"Maybe I won't."

"We have a lot riding on this. My career, your life, all that money… We had a plan and you didn't stick to it. Give me a reason why this is better and we'll start walking."

"You've seen what I've done. The only thing that ever stood in my way was you. You take me to the roof and I will do exactly as I intend and you will never have to worry about me again. If I get caught, throw me in the hotbox and let Stan follow through."

"That's the better option Dent," Donovan said, shaking his head. "I'm not convinced I'll ever see you again."

"You'll have to trust me," Dent said.

Donovan didn't trust Dent and he was surprised Dent wasn't suspicious that he was going along with this at all. He only drilled Dent with questions to keep his suspicion low. He only needed to play along long enough to get him to the rooftop. He could have sent someone else to do the job but Dent was his pain in the ass and he was going to deal with him. He accepted Dent's proposition to trust him and led him through the corridor, anxious to rid the prison of Dent once and for all.

The convicts were finishing dinner and would be spilling into the wellness room and others would participate in leather-crafting or painting. The yard would be empty, accept for guards on duty. The sun was setting and as the day was coming to a close, Dent believed he was going to be a free man, oblivious to the fact that he would soon be dead. Donovan felt the cold slap of a hunter's knife against his outer thigh under his uniform. He wasn't going to make this quick. He was going to let Dent lay on the roof and bleed out awhile…give him time to think about who ultimately ended his life.

Donovan smiled in the darkness, eagerly awaiting the moment.

5

Charlie lowered the gun and let out a deep breath. Letting Adlar go now meant he may never pay for what he did, but if it meant saving everyone else, it was all he could do.

"You need to contact Trish Reynalds and you need to see if you can contact Royce Morrow, which might be impossible, but you have to try.

"I can do it," Adlar promised. He'd lost his cell phone when he'd tried to escape from Manny in the woods behind his house, but if he could get to a computer, he could get just about anything.

"Why the hell would I even consider this?" He was relieved that Charlie was able to wait for revenge and consider the circumstance. If Charlie would have killed Adlar, he'd help execute a plan Manny had carefully orchestrated. The only way to beat Manny was to get ahead of him, which they'd never been able to do. Unfortunately, with Charlie in a wheelchair and unable to even go anywhere and Royce busy trying to get himself elected to the governorship of California, Adlar was going to be on his own until he could recruit some kind of help.

"I don't know," Adlar said. "If we both die in here then we just won't be able to help anyone else."

"Since when did you care about any of us?" Charlie asked, his voice thick with emotion.

"I don't…I don't care like that. I just know what I did was dumb. I should have stayed out of it. I didn't want to start all this."

"It's too late to fix what you did."

"No it's not cause he'll keep going. He'll get away with it."

Charlie took a deep breath, unable to believe what he was going to offer. "If you run or if you don't come through on your end in any way…"

"I'm going to try my best. I'll find help for you and I'll try my best but I don't know how to beat him. I'm gonna need you guys too."

Charlie softened as he saw Adlar really did want to take Manny down. It wasn't for the other beneficiaries and it wasn't for his own safety. Adlar was filled with inner turmoil and it was his responsibility. He felt guilty for what he did and this was how he'd redeem himself. Charlie searched the area for something to cut the ropes with and eventually broke a pitcher of water that had been left for him. He approached Adlar with a shard of glass and cut him loose, fully accepting that Adlar could turn on him and kill him right there. When Adlar's hands were free, that didn't happen. Instead, he stood and walked to where the stairs should have been and looked up. He turned back to Charlie.

"I'll bring someone back and we'll get you out. If he comes back, just say I escaped or something or that I wasn't here when you woke up. When we come back, hopefully we can kill him."

Charlie felt sick. He didn't want Adlar to leave, but it had to happen. They had to do what Manny didn't intend on so they could finally get ahead of him. Charlie extended his hand and held out the gun. "In case you run into him."

Adlar couldn't believe what he was seeing. He reluctantly took the gun and gave Charlie a grateful look. He could see that Charlie was waiting for Adlar to turn on him, but that wasn't part of the plan. Instead, Adlar tried to climb without success. Then, Charlie gave him the boost he needed, allowing Adlar to step on his hands and climb to the main level. Adlar turned and crouched down, looking in on Charlie. "You gonna be okay?"

"Just come back for me," Charlie said, exhaustion in his voice.

Adlar disappeared for a few moments and came back with a box of crackers, two bottled waters, and a package of cookies. He tossed them down to Charlie and took one last look at him, hoping by the time he came back, it wouldn't be too late. "I'll make it right," Adlar said.

Charlie looked up slowly and found his eyes. "I hope you do."

6

The rooftop opened through a door in the ceiling, which swung upward and fell back with a metallic clang. Donovan watched Dent disappear onto the roof and hurried after him, the seconds closing in. He gripped the handle of the knife as he reached the roof, thinking about plunging it into the back of Dent's leg so he'd be unable to fight back. As he decided that was exactly what he was going to do, he surfaced on the roof and found that Dent was standing in front of five armed guard and warden Sunjata, who was unhappy to see them together.

Donovan's hand moved away from his knife and he panicked inside, trying to comprehend who had tipped them off. He'd only included a couple of guards that he fully trusted. Then there was Stanley Kline, who was walking out of Kern in a month and didn't likely want to bring Donovan in. The plan had formulated in such a way that Donovan was needed, but with Dent out of the picture, that wasn't true anymore. It was Stanley who'd told Donovan to kill Dent. He was working the list… trying to eliminate Dent so he could walk free and take care of the rest. Stan could eliminate both in one move. He'd underestimated the man.

Donovan needed to talk his way out of the moment so he could show Stan just who was in charge.

"Dent's trying to escape," he said, improvising quickly. "I've been following him. Wanted to catch him in the act."

All heads turned to Dent, but he didn't seem all that surprised that they were waiting for him. In fact, he looked like he'd expected it. The fact that he was up to something didn't register with the warden though, who stepped forward to confront Dent.

"We finally got you Dent. This time, you can't play dumb. This time, you walked right into a trap."

Dent put his hands up and lowered his eyes to the ground.

"What was the plan?" Sunjata asked. "Did you really believe you were going to get out of here?"

"No," Dent said. "I'm not trying to escape."

Eyes shifted from one man to the other as they pondered his objective. "Doesn't matter why you're up here. You can't make it any worse for yourself at this point."

"I can't?" Dent asked. "Well that's good to know."

In the moment it took for everyone to think about Dent's response, he grabbed Donovan by the collar and pulled him to the edge. Dent released him but the force of the pull was enough to send Donovan over the edge. There was two seconds of screaming and then Donovan hit the ground, his body folding as he landed on his head.

Every guard pulled a weapon and held it up to Dent. The warden looked to the ground with wide eyes.

Dent kept his hands in the air, indifferent to Donovan's quick demise. He looked up at the warden. "Like I said, I didn't come here to escape…"

*…Travis spent a great deal of time getting to know Christian and learning everything there was to know from beginning to end. Dent gave him all the details, only leaving out the what implicated him in crimes. He was forthcoming about his decision to stay and his friendship with Mitch. In the process, Christian and Travis befriended and a trust was formed between them. Travis kept his secret and Dent gave him the promise that the story was his and he would talk to no one else. This, for any journalist, was a story to create a legendary career.*

The date closed in that Mitch was to be executed. Dent wouldn't be able to meet with him, but Travis did, and he relayed a message from Dent—that he would be there and Dent anxiously awaited the response.

Travis met him on a bench near the farmer's market at the Grove. They ate sandwiches and sipped sodas while they talked.

"Mitch wants you to go straight."

"That's it? What's he think I'm doing?"

"I told him you haven't resurfaced yet. He was concerned about how you would react to the world knowing who you are and that you're alive. He asked that you do it after the execution. He doesn't want more delays."

"What else?"

"You sound like him. He just kept asking questions about what you and what you all said and what your plans were. I told him I didn't know but that I'd make sure you had a good attorney and that you were eased back into society with as little publicity as possible, but there will be a lot."

"I know."

"It's going to be hard for you Christian," Travis said, stuffing the last of his sandwich into his mouth. "When Mitch said he hoped you'd stay straight, I didn't think he had anything to worry about, but that's all you know. You've never had a normal job or worked toward an honest career. You're going to have to adapt."

"I know," Dent said. It scared him to think about normalcy. It wasn't just drug running he understood. He'd also seen many people murdered. He'd seen things that wasn't the kind of talk you'd have around the water-cooler. Dent didn't see himself in an office, pushing pencils and punching numbers into a calculator. The future was uncertain and he would be in for a lot of chaos once he was exposed to the world. When the seas calmed, would he even know where he fit in?

Another month passed and then came the night of Mitch's execution. His feet were heavy as he walked through the halls and into a room with a large window where only a chair and a bundle of tubes and digital displays jutted out of it. He fell into a chair and Travis squeezed his shoulder in a gesture of support. "You sure about this?" he asked.

Dent nodded and remained silent over the next half hour, as the room filled with people. His father sat two chairs ahead of him but never recognized Christian. He tensed up at the sight of the man and was filled with rage upon seeing him so relaxed. It seemed as if he was there to go through the motions...because he was supposed to be there.

He snapped out of it as Mitch was taken into the room and sat in the chair, which reclined all the way back. They attached the tubes and hooked it all up to Mitch with the same carelessness as assembling a

*DVD player. It made Dent sick to see Mitch so powerless. He was older and frail and looked as if he wouldn't survive another month on his own. He laid flat, seemingly at peace, staring at the ceiling. He was undoubtedly aware of the crowd that were there to watch, but he never turned his head.*

*"Do you have any final words?" a man who was running the show asked.*

*"Yeah," Mitch said. "The world is ugly and I don't wanna be a part of it. You shoulda let the cancer take me but finally I get to leave. The rest of you...you have to stay. Living this long...that was punishment. Stop wasting my time and end me."*

*Dent closed his eyes and refused to let emotions take grip on him. They proceeded with the process, simply hitting a series of switches which slowly pumped one tube after another into Mitch. His eyelids fluttered as he grew sleepy. He finally turned his head to get a view of the audience, but he only looked at Christian. Travis turned to see Christian's reactions, but his face was set, his eyes open and expressionless. Inside, he was fighting, but Travis couldn't see it.*

*A doctor watched a screen and turned and nodded. Mitch was gone.*

*Dent thought back to the day in the cabin when Mitch beat his wife to death with only his fists. He'd been dragged along after that and eventually he followed. Everything he knew came from Mitch and the books Mitch gave him. He was smart, and business savvy and could look at a problem and find a dozen ways to solve it, but he'd never paid a phone bill, or met a woman for coffee, or RSVP'd to a family reunion, and he knew he probably would never be capable of those things. The man who'd influenced his life and controlled his actions for so long was finally gone, but traces of him would live forever in Dent.*

*"You okay?" Travis asked. "You want to grab a drink?"*

*"I'm fine," Dent said, staring at Mitch's face, but only seeing his own, as if he was looking in a mirror...*

...They all waited in shock and their reaction to Dent was slow because of the sheer surprise of what he'd just done.

"You just got yourself killed," the warden said, grabbing Dent by the shoulder.

"About time," Dent said.

The warden let him go and looked into his eyes. Dent was ready to die. He hated Donovan and planned on taking him with. However he lured Donovan to the roof would be looked into later, but this was what Dent wanted. To affirm the fact, Dent nodded to his pocket where the warden fished out a note. "He touches me, shoot him," the warden said, unfolding the paper. He read the note, which confirmed Dent couldn't be locked away in Kern anymore, that he was ready to die and an apology to some people the warden didn't know.

"Well you got what you wanted," Sunjata said.

"Stop wasting my time and end me," Dent said, thinking of Mitch.

"Ah right. You're up here because you were hoping you'd make that fall with Donovan. Do you know the amount of shit you just caused me?"

"I didn't cause you any trouble. Donovan was going to kill me. I killed him first. You got here and shot me. That's your story. Put it on him."

"You're trying to make a deal with me?" the warden asked in disbelief.

"I'm asking to trade a favor for a favor. I'm giving you the story. I ask that you finish what I came here to do."

"That's the last thing I'm gonna do," the Warden said. "Oh yes, you'll die, but you'll die in the hotbox. You'll be there day and night until we take you out in a bag."

"Please," Dent said. "There's no reason..."

"How about you just murdered a correctional officer? How about the bullshit you pulled last spring with the tunnels and the gas? How's that for no reason?" The warden turned to the group. "Get him to the hotbox. Don't speak to him. Don't give him any food or water."

They obeyed, though somewhat reluctantly. The warden stayed on the rooftop and watched as Dent was dragged kicking and screaming in the distance. When he was thrown in the hotbox, he struggled but they forced him in. After they latched it, he kicked and screamed some more, but everyone in Kern would be instructed to ignore his pleas.

After some time, he climbed down the ladder and walked through the corridor and into the yard, making his way around to where Donovan Willis lay. He straightened the body and shed some tears. They'd worked together more than twenty years. They hadn't seen eye to eye on everything, but he was the closest thing to a friend he'd had. This incident would require a report and some heat was going to come down on him, just as it had when Dent had poisoned the prison ventilation systems and almost escaped. He'd been a problem for too long, but it wasn't going to go on—not on the warden's watch.

He looked up toward the hotbox in the distance. Reggie Sunjata kicked up a cloud of dirt and left the yard, the faint screams of Christian Dent, filling the yard.

### 7

Jason held his phone between his chin and shoulder while he tested the doorknob on the front door of Victor's mansion. He asked information for the number to FrontPoint Security and in moments, he was speaking to a representative.

"Hey, this is Jason Stone. I got a message about a break in at 12777 Northwest Willowick Alley. This is my father's home and he's deceased, but my name is on the account and I have power of attorney."

A long pause. "I'm not showing anything tripped at Willowick Alley."

"Everything looks normal to me, but I got the call from you guys."

"You sure it was us?"

"That's the message I got."

"Yeah, sorry, I don't see anything tripped or any calls made in regards to this. This alarm has been inactive for almost a year."

"Alright, thanks." Jason hung up and brushed it off as an error, but took a walk around the mansion just in case. Every part of the property brought back memories, good and bad. He remembered being told not to play outside on the property and that the groundskeepers kept finding his toys and muddy prints everywhere. Other times, as a teenager, he'd camp out in the back yard with a sleeping bag and look up at the stars. The front patio was the scene of his first kiss. In the back corner of the house, in the atrium, was the scene of his first broken bone, caused from an attempted climb to the top followed by a fall to the bottom. Memories came flooding in just standing outside. He didn't want to go in and take a trip down memory lane. He had other things on his mind.

He was about to leave when he noticed one basement window that had a light on. He inventoried all the people that may have been through the home and couldn't come up with a single person who would even have business down there. Maybe it was a light turned on by Victor himself shortly before he died, the only light left in the world shining for him.

Instead of going through the house, Jason made his way to the storm shelter. He walked down a small flight of stairs to a door, which was secured tightly. He punched in the code at the keypad and a steal lock unlatched.

Jason opened the door and walked inside, surveying the contents of the room, which was mostly unused.

*Why would anyone even have been in here and how did they get in in the first place?*

His question was answered almost immediately as the door behind him slammed closed and a shadow stepped in front of it. Jason's heart pounded as he realized the intruder had trapped him inside and the disposition of the frame in front of it suggested this wasn't going to be pleasant.

The shape stepped out of the shadows and Jason backed toward the wall as Anthony Freeman stepped into the center of the room, a bottle in his hand and a gun held at his side. His arm had splotches of blood on it and he walked with a limp that was prominent enough that he looked like he could fall over at any time.

A series of questions ran through Jason's hand. What was he doing here? What did he want? How did he get in? Instead, upon seeing his demeanor, Jason asked, "what happened to you?"

"You did this to me," Anthony said. "And now you're going to undo it." He tossed a paper on the table in front of them and Jason studied the numbers 12211988. His pupils moving rapidly with a panic. Anthony turned to reveal a piece of his back had been stripped away and underneath, a small circuit with a keypad, nearly masked in blood. "Enter the number," Anthony said.

"Mr. Freeman…"

Anthony's hand tightened over the grip of the gun. "Your lottery was your misstep. Ignoring me was a mistake. You won't hide from me this time though. You're going to disarm this, or we're both going to live, or we're both going to die."

# Chapter 18
## (Election Day)

### 1

*Three years, four months, and fifteen days after Lawrence Curtullo first put Victor Stone on his radar, he finally sat face to face in an interrogation room with him. Victor's attorney was present, but this moment had been a long time coming for Lawrence, who'd always been sure of Victor's guilt but had been told many times that Victor was immune to prosecution.*

*Victor looked smug and far more confident than Lawrence hoped he would be, but Lawrence would break him. Most people who sat in that chair attempted to wear that armor, but inside they were desperately praying for a break. Lawrence could expose those fears and hopes and hopefully get himself a confession in the process.*

*"You know I hate guys like you, right?" Lawrence said. "I know, kinda pathetic that a government agent has a personal issue, but I can't help it. I just hate guys like you. I saw a man who had everything and I listened to the chatter about you and it turns out that no one really likes you Victor. The women you've bedded are clearly bought. The ones you like don't like you back because they're genuine and see through your bullshit. Your business partners and the men under you don't like or trust you. Your family doesn't exist because you don't care for them half as much as you care about your empire. I guess, Victor, I just don't like you because you're an incredible asshole who deserves to lose everything solely because you have no grasp of what the rest of the world looks like."*

*"Feel free to be blunt," Victor said, leaning back for comfort.*

*"Good," Lawrence said with a smile. "I like that you're not going to make this easy. You see, some people break down because they're just*

*afraid and know we have what we need, but it's guys like you who have so much damn pride…you'll see this all the way through to trial and in your head, because you're used to everyone bending over for you, you're going to believe there's no way you're going to prison, but then you will, and even though you'll never lose your composure, I'll know that inside, you'll be furious that you couldn't buy your way out of this. And all those women, and all your associates, and the little family you have, will all be free and happy that you're gone—that you're probably some guy named Woody's bitch and that you have no power over anyone anymore. You think I want you to break down and confess in here Victor? Not at all. No way. I want this to go all the way. I've spent a lot of time on you and the last thing I want is to start cutting deals. We'll go through the motions because we have to, but I insist you claim you're innocence until the bitter end. I need to see that moment, you understand? I need to be there when the judge and jury puts you away forever."*

*"Do you have a family Mr. Curtullo?"*

*"Wife and three daughters, and I'm never late for dinner and I've never missed a student teacher conference."*

*"I see," Victor leaned forward and thought to himself. "And this disdain for me stems from your dislike of my personality? Of my relationships with people… Though I've provided jobs for thousands of people…"*

*"That shit won't work with me Stone. I don't care what you're going to claim you've done for this city. What you've done has always been for yourself."*

*"I see," Victor said."Then I take it you work for the DII for nothing…"*

*"I work to take care of my family and I'm not paid well. You're reaching Stone."*

*"I believe that's why you hate me, director. You have a family at home that you're bound to. You envy me because unlike you, I took risks. You hate me because I succeeded where you never even tried and because at the end of the day, I can have a drink or sit at home with the newspaper and I don't have to change diapers or answer to a nagging spouse, or temper arguments. You wouldn't hate me if you'd succeeded in becoming me, but when you look at me, the only thing you see are your own shortcomings."*

*Lawrence crossed his arms and reclined in his chair. "You done?"*

*Victor nodded.*

*"Good, because I'm going to entertain that notion for a moment, but remind you that while you and I are very different people, we're on opposite sides of the same coin. Where I'm tied down, you're lonely. Where I don't have a company bowling team, you have thousands of*

*people kissing your ass who hate you when your back is turned. That's right Stone…take everyone who has ever done anything for you and ask yourself if they weren't just doing it for something in return. Where I have to break up my children's fighting and listen to my wife nag, as you so bluntly put it, I also have people who will express their undying loyalty to me. I also work with a large group of associates who genuinely respect me. I imagine my funeral will be very nice and my eulogy will bring tears. Yours will have a larger crowd, no doubt. Everyone will be wondering if they're going to be moving up a notch in the company. Your partner will be thrilled to have you gone. Your ex-wife will probably piss on your grave. Your son won't shed any tears. He'll have a son of his own one day and he'll raise him nothing like you raised your own. You see Mr. Stone…you don't actually have anything. Money, sure, but as the saying goes: You can't take it with you. What you can have is a legacy, so even though I'm not bedding a new whore every night of the week, at least my death will be mourned while yours is celebrated. Did you have anything to add while we're critiquing each other?"*

*"How long have you been building my case?" Victor asked.*

*"You can get those details from your attorney."*

*"Will my attorney know the name of your inside man?"*

*Lawrence stopped suddenly, puzzled by the question. He'd framed Adlar nicely and it seemed Victor took the bait, but it was a strange question. "Do you need to hear the name?"*

*"I need to hear the name of who was working with you," Victor said. "Not who you wanted me to believe worked with you."*

*"And who do I want you to believe was working with me?"*

*"Adlar Wilcox."*

*"I was working with Adlar for some time while your case was being built and no longer needed his services when you were arrested."*

*"Did he give you anything on me?" Victor asked. Lawrence panicked inside but refused to let it show. He was suddenly very worried about what exactly it was that Victor knew.*

*"You'll learn all the details in time," Lawrence said and retreated from the room before Victor could say more…*

…Adlar Wilcox sat in a park, eating a sandwich and staring at the trees surrounding him. He'd spent a lot of his life in darkness, but without his laptop and a room to plug in, the world around him had a very different tone. To stop and sit on a bench and do nothing was liberating. He wasn't sure how long it would be until he got bored, but he'd been there every day since Charlie freed him and it was the only place he wanted to be.

He'd weighed all his options. He wanted to go to the police, to Trish

Reynalds, to anyone who would be willing to help, but he couldn't risk talking to anyone who knew Manny. He didn't know many other people, and so it left only Adlar to consider what to do about Charlie.

Trish wouldn't answer his calls, so the only man left who had investment in stopping Manny was Royce, but he was impossible to get a hold of. Adlar had stopped by his home, his business, and campaign headquarters. No one bothered to allow Adlar to even get close to him. Today was election day and every day that passed made a meeting more and more impossible. For all Adlar knew, Charlie was dead. Maybe that was for the best and the time had come to just walk away, but then what? Adlar couldn't simply disappear in the world, never to be heard from again, and if he tried, Manny would find him someday. He had two options: Win back Manny's trust or to kill him. Then there was Charlie, who Adlar no longer could kill but would kill Adlar the first chance he had. There were no good options. There was no winning scenario. Adlar had done too much damage and one way or another, he was going to have to pay for it. Running and hiding or fighting back was too heavy a burden to him. It had never worked before and it never would. Adlar wasn't meant to interact with people. He wasn't meant to be mixed up with the likes of the other beneficiaries. He wanted to go back in time and never do the job for Stone Enterprises. He wished he'd never been on their radar. He could have lived life without knowledge of any of the players he'd come to know—all more powerful than he ever could be. He'd tried to outsmart them, but in the end, he was just Adlar Wilcox, professional gamer.

He dialed Royce's number again but it came up as temporarily disconnected. He let out a deep breath and stood, his feet planted to the ground for another ten minutes, staring at a rabbit that didn't move at all, but seemed to have his eyes on Adlar. He walked down a running path with no destination in mind. He replayed events in his head, in disbelief at all the things he had done. It would haunt him forever. Without realizing he was doing it, he'd walked in the direction of his home and when he walked through the door, his parents were both shocked to see him. They hugged him, fed him, and asked him to stay. His father had cleaned the den up for him but Adlar had no interest in being there. He stood in the room but it felt small and depressing. He couldn't figure out when exactly he'd changed so much but the world had lost all color.

"What would Royce Morrow want with you?" his mother asked him later. Adlar only gave her a confused look until she explained he'd stopped by and left a number. When she gave him the number, he held it in his hand in disbelief. He wasn't one to believe in signs, but one thing he was realizing was that to be a better person and to make some of the right moves, he was sometimes rewarded in a round-about way. He was where he belonged and when he made the right move, his problem solved itself.

He borrowed his father's phone and ran to the den, wondering what the chances that Royce would actually answer would be, but after one ring, Royce's voice came across the line.

"Royce Morrow."

Royce sounded different. This was surely a big day for him, but a piece of him was gone and it was present in his voice.

"This is Adlar Wilcox. My parents said you came to see me."

A long pause. "Adlar...I came to see you because I'd heard you've come looking for me."

"Yeah, I have." Adlar swallowed hard.

"I'm sure you know this is a busy day for me." Adlar could hear people in the background, shouting out numbers, frantically trying to make things happen and evaluating every last detail that was either going in Royce's favor or against him.

"I know," Adlar said. "But today might be the best day. I mean, that guy Manny...he has Charlie Palmer in his house."

This time, the pause was so long that Adlar wasn't sure whether or not Royce had even stayed on the line. "Say that again..." Royce said, as if he was unsure he'd heard right, though the message was clear.

"I know a lot of bad stuff has happened and that it's my fault," Adlar said. "I feel bad though and Manny will kill everyone. He knows who we all are and he doesn't even want the money. He just blames us and the will and everyone for what happened to his friend. I think he's crazy. I know you hate me but I want to do something to get Charlie out."

"What do you want with me?" Royce asked. He sounded uninterested.

"I don't know. I mean, maybe I can just go there and get Charlie out at least, but I don't know. I..." He trailed off and the truth hit him hard and it felt good to say it out loud. "...I just can't do it alone."

"You have to. You made your bed Wilcox."

"You hired him to kill me," Adlar said. "I know you did. And I know you did it because of what happened between us, but Manny is mad at you more than me. If I go there and he gets me, he'll just kill us all. I just want to do something and if you help..."

"Today is the biggest day of my life."

"I know, but him too. He's working and he's helping Bernard Bell and so he won't be there. We could get him out and maybe wait for him in his home or something. We have to at least get Charlie out and we can think of what to do about Manny next."

"Do you really believe I have time to go to this man's home today of all days?"

"I thought it would be important to you," Adlar said. "I think he's probably the reason your wife died."

"I know he is," Royce said. "Which is why when I have some pull in this city, I'm going to expose him."

"It's not going to work like that," Adlar said. "I was working with him. He knows everyone. You can't call the police on him or even higher. He won't ever go to jail. He's said so before. He spent ten years just killing people in the city and everyone thinks they owe him something. People in city hall and on the force and in the FBI…everywhere."

"When are you going?" Royce asked.

Finally, he was getting somewhere. "Around two."

"Why two?"

"They're counting votes. I know he'll be with Bernard."

"I'll need to be at campaign headquarters at the same time," Royce said. "Sorry Wilcox. Best of luck to you though."

"Charlie is in a wheelchair and he's in a hole in the floor. There's no stairs or nothing. I can't get him out alone."

"Tell me something Adlar: After you walked in my home and threatened my wife and my life, after you blackmailed me, played a part in the death of Abby Palmer and countless others, burned Charlie's home down and deprived him of his ability to walk forever, why should I suddenly have to help you when you decide to do something good?"

Adlar wiped his eye as it grew wet. He didn't have a good answer and Royce was right, but Royce was his only hope. "It's because I did those things," Adlar said. "I have to be there because I did them. If you're not there, that's fine, but I will be, and maybe I can prevent more bad things from happening and so that might not have anything to do with you, but I know this is for me because of the stuff I did. All I know is that Manny has to be killed and I don't know if I can do it alone."

Royce fell silent again. "I'll think about it. That's the best you're getting."

2

Various realizations flooded Jason Stone's head as he stared at a crazed Anthony Freeman. One was that Anthony still believed he set up the lottery and didn't dismiss the accusation with a phone call. The other realization was that Anthony was drinking heavily. He wreaked of liquor, and though Jason didn't understand his story in full, he at least knew Anthony had struggled with booze before.

Behind Anthony was the only exit, but one look at the latch on the wall with a padlock looped into the door and Jason understood it for what it was—Anthony wasn't just asking questions. Jason was going to have to answer and pay for whatever misdeeds Anthony believed he did.

"What do you want from me?" Jason asked. "I told you I had nothing to do with what happened to you."

Anthony smiled. "Of course you didn't. You were thousands of miles away while we were being shot in the night, stabbed, had our lives bet against and explosives put inside of us. You had an alibi."

"That's because I wanted nothing to do with any of this. I met a woman who became my wife and that's where she went and gave me an open invite and one day I said 'why not?' I'm ashamed of the things my father set in motion. I don't have an explanation for what happened to you, but…"

"The men in Gelatin Steel, a company owned by Stone Enterprises, were offered a lot of money, which you have, to bet on the death of the next person on a list of people whose name you're not on."

"I can't explain it but I didn't do it. You can keep me here as long as you want, but I'm not admitting to something I didn't do."

Anthony took a seat on the stairs, blockading the way to the exit. Jason wondered if he could knock him out and search his body for a key, but the wrong blow to the head could potentially kill him and then Jason would be gone too. Anthony reached into his inner jacket pocket and came out with a flask.

"I thought that was in your past."

"It was," Anthony said. "When I believed life could mean something more."

"Who says it can't?"

"I've escaped death numerous times. Can't escape this though," Anthony said, tapping himself on the back with a smile. "This one is going to get me and it's not going to be pretty when it does. I would have liked to have passed gracefully. Instead, the newspaper is going to read of an explosion, and a lowly professor's brains splattered a mile away."

"Have you talked to anyone about this? A doctor or, hell, a bomb expert?"

"I have and wouldn't you know, I even had a plan. One last ditch effort to give whatever forces control our universe to give me an answer. Live or die. You see Mr. Stone, as it turns out, only Stanley Kline knows the real code and so it's not so easy to key in what he gave me."

"I'll talk to him."

"I met a man whose life was coming to an end. He offered to put in the numbers and we left it to fate. We would either force the inevitable or live another day, knowing that was supposed to happen, that all the talk of fate and purpose, and all the pishposh that Richard Libby once spoke, was all for something—that there really was a reason for every individual to be here. We're all just Smurfs though Mr. Stone. We're all just meaningless labels who mistake coincidences for something more."

"I don't understand. What happened?"

Anthony laughed, too long to be a sober laugh. "He passed before he could do it. If he had lived another minute, we'd have our answer."

"That sounds like more than a coincidence."

Anthony scowled. "I don't believe you buy into fate any more than I do. You were born the son of the great Victor Stone. You get what you want with the power you have and you've made the choice to follow in your father's footsteps."

Jason shook his head with disbelief. "I don't know how to convince you of the truth. I don't blame you for considering me suspicious with that information, but have you looked into my past? I don't have so much as a j-walking ticket to my name."

"Money can help buy your way out of anything."

"Then ask around. My father usually got what he wanted but people whispered behind his back. I need you to consider that there's more to the lottery than we know and follow up on other evidence, because if you do something to me now, you're going to regret it later. Whoever really set it up is still out there and surely has other tricks up their sleeve."

"We're wasting time," Anthony said, pushing the written code toward Jason.

"I won't enter it."

Anthony raised the gun and pointed at his own temple "There's more than one way we can do this…"

*"…What does your son think of what you do?" Lawrence leaned back in his seat, awaiting an answer.*

*"How does he feel about the fact that I run a successful global corporation?"*

*"How does he feel about the way you run it?"*

*"My son is aware of the spotlight that guys like you attempt to shine on me, if that's what you mean."*

*"All the money in the world and you're doing no good with it."*

*"Other than creating jobs and providing services to millions, what should I be doing with it?"*

*"Ever try giving to a cause? Have you ever rolled up your sleeves and gone to Uganda to dig a well?"*

*"I make those things possible."*

*"Sitting in meetings and eating rib-eyes?"*

*"You and I have different ideas of what making a difference means."*

*"Then enlighten me."*

*"Digging a well in Uganda is what you call doing good directly. I would argue that a greater difference can be made by doing good indirectly. You see, there's a term we use called replaceability, whereby you make a real difference only if you do something that would not have happened otherwise. So, while there are currently a large number of people who want to go into the charity sector to dig wells and so forth, there probably aren't as many bankers who would chose to donate a big chunk of their considerable salary to effective good causes. I don't suppose you audited my charitable donations, but that's another topic."* Lawrence shifted uncomfortably as Victor went on. *"If you were to become a banker and take a pledge, then you are literally making a difference, because that action would probably not have been taken otherwise, whereas digging wells, although you are doing good directly, you are not doing anything that wouldn't have been done anyway. That is not to say these people are not making a difference, but it is a smaller difference than they could have made by being irreplaceable as a rich, but altruistic, banker. Of course, if everyone took that argument to heart, there might not be anyone left to dig the wells that guys like me are paying for."*

Lawrence smiled. *"You're good, you know that?"*

*"I could go all day, but I think the time has come for you to let me go."*

*"You still don't believe I have anything on you..."*

*"I'm just waiting for my attorney."*

*"Your attorney is facing the same charges."*

*"Then I want another one."*

*"I can do you one better."* Lawrence rose to his feet and walked to the door. After he opened it, a minute passed before Adlar Wilcox was escorted in, almost by force. *"I'm going to give you some time to talk. Maybe you can work out some kind of arrangement, but we already have the data we need, compliments of Mr. Wilcox."*

Adlar looked down as Victor stared at him, ice in his eyes.

When they were alone, a long moment passed before Victor leaned back. *"Is what he's saying true?"*

Adlar slowly nodded, never looking up.

*"Why?"*

Adlar shrugged.

*"What a waste of intellect. It is indeed ironic that the gift of high intelligence can be an occupational handicap."*

Silence.

*"You have nothing to say to me? After everything I've given you, after*

*all the shit you pulled getting your hand in my business and I accepted you into the company and protected you, despite the way you composed yourself in all that time."*

*"I worked hard for you," Adlar said, quietly.*

*"You wanted more money? More attention? What didn't you have that you deserved?*

*"I don't know," Adlar said. "It wasn't you. It was everyone else. It was like, I was there and wanted to be there but no one acted like I should be."*

*"They were right. The people I employ have graduated from college with a degree and a resume. You were a hacker. That's all. And you think that because you were dangerous to us, that you were special? You were a threat Wilcox. That's all you were."*

*"My old life made me happy. I shouldn't have worked for you. I know that. I'm sorry."*

*"And the DII agent approached you and offered what? What are you getting?"*

*"I could have worked for them. I don't know. I also could have gotten in trouble because I saw everything."*

*"You saw nothing. There's nothing to see. Do you know how much good we do? My company could do 99 things right but there are always assholes like these guys who take that one thing and try to bury you with it, and guess what Wilcox: Thanks to you, that's what's happening. You confused the map with the terrain."*

*"I said I'm sorry."*

*Victor slapped his palm on the table and held himself together with every bit of control he had. He sneered at Adlar, who only cowered in his chair. This really was the end between the two, but Victor couldn't figure out how it was that such a small person could have ultimately gotten the best of him.*

*"I grew up on video games," Adlar said. "I liked computers. The games and the websites with information and all that stuff and I spent a lot of time just doing that and when your guys came to me that time and hired me to do something, I thought it was cool because my life was nothing and suddenly I was important. It was like the kind of stuff I read about...the kind of stuff I played...but it was reality. It wasn't a game. It felt like I was a spy or secret agent. That's why I made you guys hire me and then after a while, I didn't like reality anymore. It sucked."*

*Victor steadied his breathing and watched Adlar for a long moment. He hated him but also realized he knew no better. Adlar Wilcox had immersed himself in the world of computers, seeing them as an extension of reality and readily manipulated. For him, a computer was not something one read about or poured over lengthy manuals to understand. It was not an external device, like a refrigerator or a car, but a window into himself. He organically processed information the way a computer and its internal programs do. What really bothered Victor though, was that as he stared at Adlar, he could see that the boy was holding back— that there was something more to his confession. More importantly, why was he here? Why would anyone allow them to speak? Lawrence was certainly standing behind the two way mirror, watching and waiting for something, but what? It seemed the only reason Adlar was here was to make it known that Victor was busted. Victor turned toward the mirror with a frown...a realization...a ray of hope...*

*"It wasn't you," he said.*

*Adlar didn't react. He didn't look up at all. It was all Victor needed to see that he was lying.*

*"They're making you say it was you but it wasn't you."*

*"I wouldn't say it was me if it wasn't me."*

*Victor nodded, his head spinning as he considered all the possible ways things had gone wrong recently. He forcibly admitted to himself that it started the moment Maria Haskins tried to murder him and then put a hex on him...*

*"Did you know there's a comic book character named Victor Stone?" Adlar said, his voice almost a whisper.*

*"I did, but I don't know much about him other than he's called Cyborg."*

*"Yeah."*

*"Is he good or bad?" Victor asked, truly curious to know.*

*"Mostly good. Sometimes bad."*

*Victor nodded and wondered how the same question about him would be answered. "The Internet doesn't create lonely people Adlar. It's just where lonely people dwell."*

*Adlar looked up and found Victor's eyes, which were no longer angry. He just looked tired.*

*"Do you claim responsibility for my arrest?" Victor asked. "Did you hand them the evidence against me?"*

*Adlar nodded.*

*Victor didn't believe him, but this would be the end of their relationship and if Adlar wanted this on his head, then it would be Adlar that would suffer the consequences...*

...Sandra Morrow's plot of land at the cemetery was covered in sprouting blades of grass that had only recently pushed through the surface. With each evidence of time passing, Royce grew more conflicted in his feelings. He was the only person who knew she'd been murdered. He was in the rare position to gain a lot of power but to do what? As the days passed, an anger grew inside him of which he hadn't felt in a very long time. He tried to contain it for Sandra, but the city was blind to what really took place on their streets every single day. Good people paid the price for the sins of the powerful. Royce constantly reminded himself that he could be a secret weapon for good. He could be high in the ranks and hold strong against men like Bernard Bell and Manny Quinny. He could expose and end them and find more like them and show the city that money and power have no chance against righteousness.

Yet, he stared at the grass rising from the dirt and it tore him apart inside. He didn't know how to stand in front of a city and give a speech or rule with reason and democracy when he felt like if he were alone with Manny, he would kill him. His thoughts weren't the thoughts of someone who should have the office he was trying to hold.

He thought about his conversation with Adlar and the clock running out on Charlie. The timing couldn't be worse. Today was the day that everything Royce had worked for and everything he'd fought would come to a head. He wasn't expected to win. His unstable, emotional, unpredictable actions had cast doubt on Royce to lead the city. On the other hand, Bernard Bell was under a lot of scrutiny and there were rocks that could be turned. To put him in office meant to put him under a microscope. One way or another, Bell would get his in the end. Royce would dedicate his life to it.

There was a line Royce had tried not to cross. Since the day Victor Stone graciously gave him money on the street and told him to make it multiply, Royce had made his way by being honest and prideful in all he did. As a result, he'd won over his dream girl and built an empire. He'd stayed honest through it all and the line had never been fuzzy—not until Sandra was murdered.

"Sandy," he said, staring at her name on the tombstone. "I don't know what I'm supposed to do."

He fell to his knees and said nothing more out loud. The words only echoed in his head.

"I did a bad thing...a thing I should have never done. When that kid broke into our home, I thought to keep you safe, I had to act. The kid was a danger not just to us, but to a lot of people. I paid someone to scare him, but before I even realized what I was doing..."

He wouldn't allow himself to admit the truth, but he knew Sandra already knew. She would haunt him forever with the knowledge that it was Royce's actions—it was that line that he'd crossed—that ultimately led to her death.

"I don't know what to do," he said again.

Then he heard her voice. It didn't speak from beyond the grave, but in his head. It was a voice he knew and words he would expect her to say. "You've done all you can Rock. You've taken it as far as you can. The votes are cast and the outcome is no longer in your hands."

"I don't know if I can do it." His eyes flooded with tears.

"Take one thing at a time, just as you did when you had nothing. Pennies become nickels, nickels become dimes, dimes become quarters…"

"I can't start over."

"Of course you can, because this time it's important. You only wanted to make something from nothing and you did. Now you have a cause worth fighting for. Until we are together again, you can build in the same way you already have. You can take the goodness in your heart and spread it in the same way you built an a skyscraper from a rusty shopping cart."

"And Charlie Palmer?" he asked.

"The votes are cast. A man will lose his life if no one else is there to save him. You can go back and wait or you can be there for him."

Though he'd conjured the voice, he knew it was what Sandra would have said. Help the individual. Not the crowd. Eventually, the individual becomes the crowd, just as pennies eventually become hundred dollar bills.

He left flowers at her grave and drove straight to Manny's home. The driveway was empty, just as it always was during the day. It seemed Manny lived at the office or in a lawn-chair in his back yard. There was nothing to indicate he was home and Royce didn't expect him to be. It was election day and Manny was probably hovering around Bernard Bell somewhere, sinking his claws into a man whose influence and power could protect him forever. Manny was too dangerous of a man to live under Bernard's cloak. He couldn't control that anymore, but there were still people who knew who Manny was and those people were all the hope left of ending him. Adlar Wilcox and Charlie Palmer—they wouldn't work well together but they would need to—if only to complete this one task. Manny had to go.

Royce worked his way around the house, searching for an opening. Manny was too cautious to leave anything incriminating. He felt his phone buzz in his pocket. It had been buzzing all morning. He was wanted back at work. He was wanted at campaign headquarters. Everyone needed Royce in one place or another and the time to get back on track would come, but he focused on Charlie. If Royce was able to stop Manny from claiming another victim, he would do anything he could.

The back door was locked as expected. Royce gave up on an easy entry and searched the yard for a brick or a rock. They were everywhere. He just hoped when he broke a window, he wouldn't trigger an alarm. He needed to work quickly. Charlie Palmer was in a wheelchair and he was placed somewhere where he couldn't get out. He needed time.

He grabbed a chunk of landscaping from along a small garden and carried it back to the door. He brought it down hard on the doorknob and in three swings, the knob broke loose. Another two swings and it fell off the door. Even the slightest amount of damage to Manny's property brought Royce satisfaction. The man deserved every bit of bad fortune that life could bring him.

"Royce?"

Royce jumped at a voice from behind. He froze in place, sure Manny would be standing there. When the voice spoke again, he realized it was Adlar.

"You came to help me?"

Royce turned to face Adlar. His eyes darted to Adlar's jeans, where a gun was tucked. "If Charlie Palmer is here, we'll get him out and to a hospital. From there, Manny is your problem to deal with."

"He's everyone's problem," Adlar insisted. "He has plans for you all."

"If I'm elected governor, I will be sure to end his career. If I'm not, I will still find a way."

"We need to kill him," Adlar said.

*Yes, we do,* Royce thought, but kept it to himself. *I'm going to be the one to do it.*

Adlar sighed and walked past Royce into the house. Royce followed at a distance and watched Adlar open a cellar door that was disguised as a bookshelf. When it opened wide, Royce saw there were no stairs. Only a drop to the cement below. "My God, Charlie's down there?" Royce asked.

"Yeah," Adlar said. "But I left the door open and the entry too. Manny's been here. Charlie might be dead."

### 3

Warden Reggie Sunjata had less than twenty-four hours to make sense of the tragic loss of Donovan Willis and answer to the Executive Director of the California Department of Criminal Justice, a chairman of the California Department of Corrections, and the president of the state's correctional employees union.

Dent was clearly at fault, but he'd put a spotlight in a place that the Warden and COs didn't want it to be. This was why guards weren't supposed to injure the inmates. They were supposed to get another inmate to do it, or throw two men who had no being in a cell together. There was always racial tension in a maximum security prison. It would have been as easy as throwing Dent in with a violent offender or a rival gang who would kill him just for credit.

Instead, Donovan had to go and make things personal and the warden had turned his back while he did. Because they'd always been careful about their actions in Kern, they'd assumed too much. This time, it could bury them.

That day, a meeting was called, and the warden sat in a small room with a bunch of men in suits who were going to tell him how he screwed up. He would be lucky to keep his job, but he wouldn't go out without a fight.

The chairman of the Department of Corrections read the suicide note and set it in the middle of the table, for all to see. "It seems to me there was a breach in protocol regarding this correctional officer escorting a prisoner without backup."

"I can not give insight as to what was happening."

"Yet, you were there. You arrived on the rooftop within moments of Mr. Dent and your CO."

"I was told by another CO that Donovan Willis was pursuing what looked to be an escape attempt," the warden said.

"If Mr. Dent was on the roof to end his own life, why did he kill Mr. Willis?"

"You can talk to him about that."

"Oh, we will. Right now we're talking to you."

The warden sighed. "Mr. Dent has been a problematic inmate from the start. He's attempted to escape and he was in a fight that nearly got him killed."

"My report shows that fight was with Mr. Willis and that Mr. Dent was stabbed multiple times and almost lost his life."

"That was his story."

"What's yours?"

"I don't know what his beef was with Donovan. I just know they had problems with each other."

"He's not the only inmate who has had a beef with CO Willis. According to reports, a dozen inmates over the course of three years have died on his block, all who had filed grievances with CO Willis and claimed he had brutal tendencies. How closely did you investigate this?"

"I put him on leave for it."

"Right, in April of this year and he was back on cell D within months."

"I will not stomp on the memory of Donovan Willis. He had some complaints, but he also had a long history here and he felt the stress and strain of the job. We all do. Thanks to your state budgets, Kern is operating at maximum capacity. Staffing, which we've struggled to maintain, has played a role in attacks on correctional officers too."

"You believe CO Willis's blood is on my hands?"

"I believe prison conditions and the treatment of inmates are regulated at several levels, the highest being the U.S. Constitution."

"The Eighth Amendment states that no cruel or unusual punishment be inflicted. These treaties require that prisoners be clean, safe, and properly fed with access to adequate medical care. Records should be kept of their presence and status within the prison and all their basic human rights should be recognized to the fullest extent possible. Don't think because you're running this place that there are not guards and authorities, and even state bureaucrats in the Department of Justice, who don't belong in jail for very long stretches. For every death and every act of abuse, there are scores of guards, medical personnel, and prison administrators who actively participate or tacitly acquiesced in the abusive behavior. The list of crimes committed by prison authorities, and those who cover them up, is pretty shocking, and if the state of California is too cowardly or corrupt to investigate, then perhaps there should be a Federal investigation and prosecution instead."

"Mr. Dent was…"

"Forget Mr. Dent for now," the chairman said. "Mr. Dent wouldn't have had the opportunity to drop your man from the roof if protocol had been followed in the first place. It's going to take major housecleaning and correctional union cooperation to overcome what appears to be an ingrained and devastating culture of abuse here."

"You know…" the warden started. "I've done time in reform school where I was sexually assaulted and brutalized. I've spent time in the adult slam as a political prisoner for refusing to be drafted in the Vietnam War. I've covered cops and courts as a reporter and I wrote, decades ago, extensively about the brutal mistreatment of prisoners. I've also covered the failure of progressives to put prison reform anywhere near the top of their concerns despite the fact that our nation incarcerates people at a rate higher than any nation and despite the fact that the majority of those in prison are here for nonviolent offenses. And over the course of many years of such stuff, it's not hard to become a bit hardened by it all. From the inside looking out, I know what's required to keep Kern running like a well-oiled machine, but the guards aren't in charge of making the budget. The blinders are on for quite a few executive levels higher than that. You and our state leaders requesting constant budget cuts across state agencies aren't helping either, but the buck stops here. We just lost an officer. When will the questions be directed toward you and the rest of the suits who take our arms and legs from us and then tell us to work harder?"

"Let's move on," the Executive Director said, recognizing a situation that was only going to escalate further. "I want to go back to the question of how Mr. Dent had access to the roof and what his intent for being there was."

"My assumption is he thought he'd escape."

"How could he escape from the roof?"

"He couldn't. He'd have to jump an impossibly long way to clear the fence. It became clear to us that the murder of Donovan Willis and his own suicide was his motive."

"What did he have on him?"

The Warden looked up, searching for someone to answer the question, but it was only him. "Other than the note, you'll have to ask the guards."

"Was he searched?"

"He was taken to solitary confinement. I don't know if he was searched."

"Why wouldn't he have been searched?"

"We were all in shock. I was angry and emotional and had him taken there."

"Does solitary confinement go by another name in Kern?"

"A lot of people call it the hot box."

"Why?"

"Convicts sit in the sun in a metal box."

"Would you consider that to be cruel and unusual?"

"Give us the budget for something better and we'll use it."

Eyes glanced around the room and the Director brought the conversation back in. "Did Dent have any friends or partners he spoke with on a regular basis?"

"He had a cellmate, but he probably didn't know what he was doing. He's got a month left of his sentence. He also was talking to some of the merchants here."

"Is that allowed in Kern?"

"We don't police it unless we see weapons or drugs. Usually they just smuggle cigarettes, Playboys, or decks of cards. Keeps them quiet, so we let it fly. All prisons do."

"Alright, let's start there. Can we bring in his merchant and his cell-mate?"

"Why not just talk to Dent?"

"I want to be able to collaborate all stories, his being last."

"Yeah, we can get them."

"And warden…" The warden met his eyes. "I hope for your sake that Dent orchestrated this whole thing. If he didn't, CO Willis's blood will be on your hands."

## 4

At the same time the warden was rounding up the key players, fifty miles away, William Lamone was sitting on the stoop outside of his and Brian Van Dyke's apartment. He found it harder and harder to go home as the days passed and his conscience ate away at him. Brian had given William more than anyone ever had. Call him foolish and useless, he'd do anything for his friends, even friends who were positioned to manipulate his death. After Greg and Henry died, the objective felt too broken to carry on. Maria had lost her life, but Henry's death had been careless. William mourned quietly in front of Brian's eyes and Brian was too fried to recognize anything.

He'd talked himself out of killing Brian once, but when Maria Haskins died, it reinvigorated him.

Part of him resisted that kind of thinking. It wasn't William who took a life. It wasn't even really Henry. At the end of the day, options were presented and decisions were made. Maria chose to take a handful of pills. Brian chose to put a needle in his arm. Was guiding someone to die, truly murder? Or just a suggestion?

It was these unanswerable questions that kept William from coming home until late and stalling before he did. Every night, without fail, when he entered the apartment, Brian was there, all alone, high or drunk or both. William stopped getting him drugs. Brian was able to find them on his own. He was addicted. He cared about little else. His weight had dropped, but he didn't look good. No one acknowledged the drastic loss because he looked unnatural. He looked miserable and unkempt.

William hoped he'd be sleeping so he could avoid an encounter, but it never worked. It was as if Brian waited up for his buddy and every time William saw him, death seemed to be inching closer toward Brian, creeping up without William's provocation. He didn't have to do a thing to accomplish his task. For Brian, it had been as easy as getting the ball rolling, but as easy as it was to put things in motion, inside, William's spirit was eroding. Everyone who'd worked with Toby had gotten themselves killed.

Brian turned his head slowly when William walked in and there was only a hint of a smile on his face. He looked too tired to move, or maybe his brain was completely gone and there was only a ghost of recognition.

William tried to walk past, to go straight to his bedroom, but Brian pushed himself off the ground and tried to stand.

"Calm down there," William said. "Go to sleep."

"Can't," Brian said. "We should hang out."

"Brian, you can't even stand. Go to sleep."

"Man, I gotta get it together," Brian said. His words came out slow and slurred, and William knew that in Brian's state of mind, no matter what his thoughts and opinions were, tomorrow he'd wake up with no recollection and go back to only one thing: Seeking his next high.

"Yeah, you do. What you're doing isn't cool. You're going to lose all this. You get that, right? You'll lose it all, unless you die first."

"I don't care."

"Sure you don't."

"I don't."

William shook his head and stood in place for a long moment as he thought about just what he was doing. Talk Brian off the cliff or push him. He could go either way, but it wouldn't matter. The end was near. There was nothing he could do now but find a way to be at peace with it. "You really wouldn't care if your life was over?" he asked.

"No, man."

"Then what you always talking about the future for? Why you always after a girl or some success or talking about how awesome it is when someone laughs at you or smiles at you?"

"They don't laugh at me. I mean, they do, but it's *at*. Not *with*. I can't be witty or clever, ya know? People laugh *at* me...not *with*."

"So what? Funny isn't everything."

"It is when you're nothing else. I'm not smart or attractive or anything. You think I ever had a real relationship? I've never even had sex."

"Again, so what? You're to blame. Not me or the world or any of that. Yeah Brian, you're fat. Stop eating. Yeah Brian, you're not that smart. Pick up a book sometime. It's easy."

"No, it's not."

"Yeah it is, because the root of the problem isn't that you don't read or you eat shit all the time. It's that you're lazy. You don't have any drive. You wait for me to tell you what to do and you can do it, but you can't think for yourself. You never would wake up in the morning and go for a run without someone to tell you to do it. You'd read a book if I gave you one, but would you go to the library because you had a day off and thought it sounded like a good use of time?"

"Screw you."

"Yeah, screw me. Someone is telling you to do something other than sit on your fat ass, drinking and doing drugs. Screw him."

"Seriously, why do you hate me?" Brian asked. He was clearly trying to soften William, but he wasn't going to get that luxury this time.

"I just do. I hate you because I have to be around you and I hate you because you're the worst kind of person to be around."

Brian looked wounded, but William didn't care. He even reminded himself that Brian wouldn't remember this tomorrow, but he couldn't do it day after day either. "I'm just going to move out," William said. "It was nice of you to let me crash and pay for my shit, but you can't put a price on some things. I just don't care anymore."

"I don't either," Brian said, stubbornly. "I want to die."

"Then you probably will," William said, dismissively. He left the room and entered his own bedroom and bit down on his knuckle hard, as he tried to contemplate what was next. Not only did he no longer care, but suddenly the money really did sound good. He wanted away from all the trouble. He didn't want to work or drain himself on child support. He just wanted to be free of all the bullshit.

He turned and pulled his cell from his pocket and called Toby.

"Hey," he said. "Before you say anything else, Brian is just gone bro. He's on the edge."

"Can you get it done?"

"No," William said. "But you can come by and as a gesture that you're in this with me, you can take care of it yourself."

A long pause on the other end, before Toby finally spoke. "Give me an hour."

## 5

Royce and Adlar crouched down, looking into the basement of Manny's home. Royce stared at the remaining evidence that there were ever stairs in place. "Who would do this kind of thing?"

Adlar ignored the question and got on his stomach, searching for Charlie in the basement. They both said his name multiple time. It was possible he was dead, or maybe Manny got him.

Then they heard a raspy noise that almost didn't sound human, but both perked up at the sound. "I'll go down," Adlar said, and before Royce could talk out a plan, Adlar grabbed the edge and let himself fall, dangling for a moment to soften the landing. When he was on the ground, he let his eyes adjust to the dark and found Charlie under the stairs, as if he was hiding in the shadows.

"Told you I'd come back," Adlar said.

"Adlar!" Royce was at the top of the steps and had grabbed bottled water from the fridge. He tossed it down and Adlar tilted the bottle so that Charlie could drink. More water spilled down Charlie's chin, but Adlar could see him swallowing hungrily and let out a breath of relief.

Adlar looked up at Royce, and they consulted about how to get Charlie out. They found a rope in the garage and tied it around Charlie's waist for support. Royce pulled him up while Adlar pushed from the ground. When Charlie was safe upstairs, adjusting to the light of the world around him. Moments later, all three sat together in Manny's living room, catching their breath. Charlie had regained some energy, having consumed enough water and some cereal from the cabinet.

"Now what?" Royce asked.

Adlar's eyes darted to Charlie, who sat quietly to himself, with no motivation to do anything to Adlar. "I dunno," Adlar said.

"We can wait for him," Royce said, and then looked to the gun in Adlar's hand. "Is that loaded?"

"Yeah."

Royce nodded, his face turning white as he thought about what was next—what he was really here for. His mind traveled in time, back to all the things Manny had done, to beating Royce bloody in an isolated place, to finding Sandra at the bottom of his stairs. Today was election day. Was it really possible that one of two candidates to become governor of the great state was actually considering murdering a man?

*It's for the good of the city*, he told himself.

"Have others died?" Charlie asked, thinking of Trish Reynalds.

"Maria Haskins did," Royce said, prompting a surprised look out of Charlie and Adlar.

"How?"

"Looked to be suicide. Her husband was taking her to the hospital and got in an accident on the way. Both are dead."

"No," Charlie said. "It was murder. It will always be murder when it's one of us." Charlie's eyes found Adlar's and Adlar nodded in agreement. Royce fell silent, accepting the answer.

"Everyone else is fine, as far as I know."

"I need to contact Trish Reynalds," Charlie said. She believes her daughter is dying…"

"Not anymore," a voice said, standing in the doorway. They all turned and froze at the sight of Manny Quinny. "Doc who did it left a message on her phone. She knows the truth. Too bad though. Sounds like she almost took care of some business for me."

Before Charlie or Royce could react, Adlar stood and held his gun on them, joining Manny at his side.

"No…" Royce said.

"He gave me a call," Manny explained. "Said as a peace offering, he'd get you both in one place. You know, I've been going tit for tat with one or the other of you for a long time and our wires just keep crossing, but what we should have done in the first place is all come together and figure this all out."

Adlar held his gun on Royce and felt Charlie's eyes burning through him. He refused to look back, unsure he could face so much hatred directed at him. "Sorry," Adlar said. "He would kill me if I didn't do this. I meant to help you guys but I knew Charlie would kill me, so it had to be like this.."

"He's going to kill you anyway," Royce said.

"No," Manny said. "It seems to me like this has all been tied up in a neat little package for me. After all was said and done, it's only the four of us in this room that know what I do. I know Adlar is loyal, as long as he doesn't screw things up, but we won't be blowing up any houses anytime soon, right kid?"

"No way," Adlar said.

"This time around, after the two of you are gone, there will be nine left. It's been a long journey but it really worked out in the end. Royce, you would've been a hard man to get to, but you've wandered too far from safety. Tomorrow, the headlines will read that Royce Morrow disappeared on the day he lost an election. Mr. Palmer…I'm not even sure there's anyone left in this world who knows you exist after you either ran everyone off or killed them. You guys really set this up nicely for me."

"Adlar…" Royce said, his voice pleading.

"No reason to talk to him. I'm calling the shots today."

Adlar confirmed what Manny was saying by handing him his gun, which Manny now trained on Royce. "You, I'll have to put a bullet in, but Charlie, he'll be fun. I don't suppose you'd be a very good swimmer, would you Mr. Palmer?"

Charlie swallowed hard, knowing this was the end. Adlar had taken everything and beat him. Manny would walk away from this, a free man, Bernard Bell would run the city…no good would come of today. He wished he could go back in time to when he had one bullet and a room with Adlar. He wished he could make a different choice this time. He wished he'd made a different choice when Abby was dying. He wished he'd saved her. If only he could go back in time…

"Let's go," Manny said, waving his gun toward the yard. "We're going for a walk…"

"*…The whole thing fell on Wilcox,*" Lawrence Curtullo said, sitting across from Bernard Bell. "*Victor can do with that what he wants, but* *you're in the clear."*

*"I certainly appreciate what you've arranged," Bernard said, "but since you did this to Wilcox, what's to say you're not going to do the same to me?"*

*"Because we both have secrets we don't want exposed."*

*"What happened?" Bernard asked. "Victor's going to walk free. This was supposed to put him away."*

*"I can't convict something that's not there. Nothing's got his name on it. A few accountants will lose their jobs and go to jail. Probably some others who've put their John Hancocks on the transfers, but none if it can be linked to Victor. He's clean."*

*"Except, he's not."*

*"Hey, provide me with that proof and I'll put him away for you."*

*Bernard almost told Lawrence that to incriminate Victor meant incriminating himself, but for now, this would do. Victor had gone through some hard times over his arrest and he'd lost a lot of faith in people he trusted. Adlar Wilcox took the fall and would inevitably just go back home, where Victor might, or might not, ruin him for what he did. Nothing was lost and very little was gained, but Bernard didn't need Victor locked up to move on to the next step.*

*He only needed Cory Owens and Jones Mitchell. They met that evening at Bernard's place, where his third wife made dinner and served wine while the men sat in his study, where no one could hear them.*

*"Where does Victor stand?" Cory asked.*

*"Well, I assume he's going to be distracted by all this in the next few days, so let's not talk to him now, but we need more data. Stone Enterprises is hemorrhaging money right now. Our reputation stinks and I'm tired of being a cog in Victor's machine. I think we need to proceed with the virus and cut him out."*

*"I don't know how that's going to be possible," Cory said. "He started the whole thing."*

*"He's also the one who had a change of heart. He's had some moral hang-ups that he can't get past. As the time gets closer, he's bound to completely go against it."*

*"Of course," Jones said, not completely insensitive about what they were doing. "We're talking about a lot of people dying here."*

*"We're talking about a few," Bernard said. "We'll announce that we have the cure relatively quickly. I've already invested a good deal of money into medicine and pharmaceuticals and it won't be impractical for Stone Enterprises to move quickly once the virus spreads. We'll save lives, we'll be paid generously, and we'll buy our way out of here and start something of our own."*

*"And what's Victor do while all this is going on?" Cory asked.*

*"He won't implicate himself. He won't like it, but he'll have to watch it happen and he won't be able to object. His fingerprints are all over this."*

*"Well, remind me not to ever piss you off," Jones said.*

*"Victor didn't piss me off," Bernard said, matter-of-factually. "This is business. When it starts to bleed, you fix it. Victor's running his business into the ground. Have you noticed his decisions? He befriended a psychic. He hired a pizza delivery guy as a driver. Look at how much free reign Adlar Wilcox had around here. Then, the same idea he conceived, a brilliant plan to release a disease and then the cure, he backs out. Not before his lack of security caused a man off the street to walk in the building and steal the cure. I had to get it back. I've been watching our boss make a lot of bad decisions for a long time and I'm the one constantly bailing his ass out, but I come to work every day and I see Stone Enterprises written on the office pens and coffee mugs and I ask myself how it isn't me running the show, when I'm the one keeping it afloat. I'm not doing it anymore. Once this virus is complete, it will be my way out. People will die. Maybe a hundred, maybe a thousand, maybe the whole damn city, but I've worked too hard for too long to let him hold me back any longer. If Victor wants to stand in our way again, next time, I'll make sure we get rid of him for good..."*

...Bernard watched the coverage as the talking heads speculated who would win the election, but his jaw was permanently held open for the last hour as he watched Royce's numbers skyrocket.

Everything he'd come to understand about what the public wanted and what Royce's chances were, were being completely dispelled based on what he was seeing before him.

Supposedly, Bernard had secured his base far ahead of time, appealing to the people who knew they would back him from the start. Royce was winning all on-the-fence voters, who didn't really pay attention to the candidates, but knew Royce came from a place much more similar to their own backyards.

As the numbers rose continually in favor of Royce Morrow, dread set in. Bell had big plans for his win, plans that went back to the days when he believed he was able to release a virus onto the city and then save it, becoming a hero, becoming infinitely wealthy.

And then his associates were murdered by Christian Dent and shortly after, Victor Stone died, leaving him with a briefcase and an un-guessable password to bypass the security. He would never release the toxin because the only person who knew the code was Victor himself and so he had the key to fortune in his hands but there was nothing he could do with it.

"Come on Erica," he said through a clenched jaw and grinding his teeth simultaneously. The only thing that held Bernard up was the profits of a dying company. There was no saving Stone Enterprises, but if he held on a little longer and the other beneficiaries could be offed...

Manny was the key, but a Royce win meant Manny would be no more. He would bury the homicide department in audits and investigations that would send Manny to jail for life upon life. Manny was the ticket to a quick succession of kills, and in turn, Jason Stone would inherit the fortune he never wanted, but when Jason was gone, Erica Drake would take it instead and run off with Bernard into the sunset.

Todd Mason was just an extra plan he had in place, but a kind of ace up his sleeve back-up plan for if all other plans went south. Todd could be dead or alive. It didn't matter. He held the death certificate, unfaxed, for if the day came that he needed his ace. If only Jason and Todd were left, he'd fax Todd's in. If Todd were to be the last standing, he could go that route too. He had plans stacked up behind the scenes—more than Toby O'Tool could ever dream to have—but Manny was his quick fix. Manny was his way to paradise the day after tomorrow and Manny was about to become powerless.

Governorship was useless. Manny was useless. Toby O'Tool had been useless. The lottery had been useless. The virus was useless.

"Come on Erica," he said again, unable to fathom another failed plan, but coming to terms with the fact that when Toby had proved to not accomplish anything and Manny was about to leave the picture, the only person left that could get his hands messy was Bernard himself.

*I'm not walking around in the night with a gun in hand.*

He needed something more. He needed a new scapegoat, but he didn't know just what that was going to be yet.

He opened the laptop, which was just a giant carrot he'd never catch. The screen flashed on and the first thing that appeared was an impenetrable request for a password. He didn't know how long it was, whether or not it was a word, a set of numbers, or a bunch of random characters. He did know Victor though. The key inside was something meaningful...something from the mind of Victor Stone that he carried around like a tattoo on his mind...something that defined everything he was about.

Bernard typed slowly.

...P...A...T...T...E...R...S...O...N...

He hit enter.

Denied.

He knew he'd probably tried that before. He'd probably tried it a dozen

458|Tontine: The Scales of Justice

times, along with another handful of words that only Victor would use.

He turned back to the television. He'd gained a little ground. It wouldn't be enough. Nothing had been enough. Bernard understood what this meant. He would have to step it up.

6

"I can't do it," Jason said. "I can't put the numbers in. We both know they're wrong. I'm not suicidal."

"That's because everything was handed to you. Everything."

"That's a cop-out. If you can't handle your life, change it."

"I tried."

"You had a best-selling book and were a prestigious professor. You've had more than a dollop of prestige. You need to get to a meeting. This isn't you. It's the alcohol. I'll take you to one."

"Don't blame alcohol."

"It's to blame. Look at yourself. You're about to become a murderer."

"Someone has to do this."

"Do what? I had nothing to do with the lottery."

"Someone has to bell the cat Jason. Someone has to step up and eliminate those of you who are trying to eliminate us."

Jason saw the full impact the booze was having over Anthony. He wasn't hearing anything he was saying. He wasn't reasoning, which was his strength when sober. Jason wanted to keep him talking to gain trust. It was the only way to calm the man. "What do you mean by bell the cat?" Jason asked.

"There's a children's story about belling a cat. The mice decide that life would be safer if the cat had a bell around its neck so they could hear it coming. He problem was, who will risk his life to bell the cat? A problem for mice and men! Have you noticed that small armies of occupying powers or tyrants control large populations for long periods of time? Or how about a planeload of people powerless to a single hijacker with a gun?"

"I've noticed."

"In all cases, a simultaneous move by the masses stands a very good chance of success, but the communication and coordination required is difficult and the oppressors, knowing the masses have that power, take steps to keep it difficult. When this happens, or when fifteen people are put together and possessed to kill each other and some of those people are truly dangerous, the remaining in the group are left to wonder who is going to be first? What leader is willing to pay a very high cost, possibly his life? No one will bell the cat though Jason. Do you know why?"

"Because the costs exceed the benefits."

"Exactly!"

"Except you're belling the wrong cat. You're so intent on doing something noble in death and you don't even see that you're not eliminating an actual threat."

"Then tell me why it is that your name was not on the list."

"I don't know. Maybe for this exact reason."

"It was never premeditated for me to learn of the lottery and no one anticipated I'd see the list."

Jason shook his head, defeated. "I don't know," he said, quietly. "If I did, I would tell you, but you can easily go back and see my actions from start to finish and…"

"You're his son!" Anthony yelled, suddenly and unexpectedly.

"I'm not him."

"Enter the numbers."

"I'm not entering the numbers. They're not right."

"How would you know?"

"Because it's my Birthday. December twenty-first nineteen-eighty-eight is my Birthday. I don't know why he gave you that or why he even knew it, but it's not the code."

"Your Birthday," Anthony muttered, his face white. He set the bottle down on a table and walked in a small circle. "It all leads back to you Jason."

"I'm in the middle of it because I'm his son. I didn't do…"

"Victor didn't build the bomb! Stanley Kline did!"

"I didn't do it."

Then tell me who did!"

Jason shook his head and tried to focus, for the first time brainstorming scenarios that could be the answer to the riddle before him. The question was valid: Why was he excluded from the lottery? Why was his birth date being used as a deactivation code? Anthony wasn't in his right mind, but there was something to what he was saying. There was a cat that needed a bell and there were enough incidents now that at some point, someone had to stand up and fight back. There was an invisible enemy and to figure out who it was, everyone had to be a suspect. He had to set aside all opinions about…

He closed his eyes and his mind went to the places he'd kept locked. At Maria's wake, Royce Morrow had told him not to trust Bernard Bell… that he was a murderer.

Then he thought of Todd.

"Oh God," Jason said. He opened his eyes and Anthony was staring intently at him. "My wife…"

Anthony's face warped into confusion. "What about her?"

"There was a fire that almost killed three of us the day of the wedding. We were all eliminated as suspects but no one ever looked at her. We met right after the reading. Everything she said was exactly what I needed to hear. I was going to leave but I didn't because she was pregnant. Then she lost the baby. I could always see there was no love. I saw it from the start but she was so…" Jason fell to the ground and hung his head. "Todd Mason told me she tried to kill him because he learned something. She said he came onto her, but I've seen Todd pass on every woman he met. He's loyal to his wife. I never saw how unlike him it was…and I never saw how convenient and coincidental…"

He trailed off.

"Who is she then?"

"I don't know. She must be connected to Bernard or one of the others."

"Bernard's not on the will."

"He doesn't need to be. She married me. There's no prenuptial agreement. Of course I wasn't on the lottery because all the rest of you could die and I didn't have to. Not until after she had the rights to what was mine."

Anthony hadn't expected the turn of events, but he sobered up quickly, and joined Jason on the floor, sitting with his feet extended far in front of him. "You must leave her."

"It won't be that simple. Geez, how could I not…? Nothing anyone was doing made any sense and I just ignored it."

Anthony looked down, basking in his shame. "We need to start over. All of us. You, me, Trish…everyone we trust. I think there are forces at play that have kept us distracted and in the meantime, people have died. The rest of us are taking swings at nothing in the dark because we don't know what we're up against. We need to form the other side, and it starts here in this room, no matter what you and I have done."

"Start by sobering up then," Jason said. "We have a lot of people to talk to and a lot of questions to ask. You need to be healthy."

"This circuitry is attached to my muscle. It's contaminating my blood."

"I'll find someone to take a look."

"I can't be around populations of people until this is removed. I've been afraid just to buy milk. If I were ever to have a stroke or even if I sneeze hard…"

"We'll work on a bomb expert too. I'll talk to Stanley Kline."

"Thank you…" Anthony said, sincerely. "I can't express how sorry I am…"

"You don't have to," Jason said. They sat in silence for a while, Jason resting his head against the wall, a thousand thoughts ricocheting around in his brain. Everything was different now. He'd been blind to what was in front of him for so long. He didn't want to run back to Erica and start pointing fingers though. To expose what was happening was going to take a great deal of planning and Jason wasn't going to show his hand to everyone all at once. It would take time to heal, but when this was over, everyone would get what they had coming.

7

Adlar walked with Manny down a hillside, thick with trees, following Charlie and Royce, who made their way slowly down the hill. It was steep enough for a man on foot, but for Charlie, it took a great deal of mapping his way, using trees as leverage. Royce tried to help him but Manny forbid it and told them they march to their deaths like men.

Royce tried three times to reason with Adlar, his back turned to them, but Manny shut him up every time, telling him he would die slowly if he didn't stop talking.

"This can't happen," Royce said, under his breath so only Charlie could hear.

Charlie had no response. He was only frozen in fear, hoping that cooperation was his best chance for mercy, but deep down, he knew that wasn't true. Even a last ditch effort such as running away was no possibility. Royce wasn't a fighter and even if he were to go against Adlar and Manny, there was no way he'd win. There was nothing left, other than to do what Royce was doing—try to sway Adlar—but even then, Manny had the upper-hand, and Charlie would rather have died than beg Adlar to spare him. If this was the end, all Charlie wanted was to be alone with his thoughts. He wanted to scan his life and try to remember the good and if there was a god, he wanted to beg to go wherever good people go. He wanted to see Abby and apologize for everything and beg to be with her. He wanted to go back and do life again and do it different —appreciate what he had and be nicer to people and more patient.

"Charlie…" Royce said, but Charlie only focused on getting to the river. He wanted to get there faster, to end the inevitable so he didn't have to suffer this moment any longer.

"Stop talking," Manny said from behind.

"Why does it matter if I talk?" Royce asked. "The same thing happens either way. What are you afraid of?"

"I'm not afraid of a damn thing in this world," Manny said. "Just annoyed by most of it. I've ended lives for doing a lot less damage than the three of you have done. You've all been crossing your wires time and time again."

Adlar turned to Manny, uncomfortable about being grouped in with Royce and Charlie.

"This will be traced to you," Royce said. "If you think there aren't people that knew I came to see you, you're crazy."

"I might have bought that on another day, but it's election day. No one would have let you out of their sight. I thought you'd be impossible to get to for a while. Then Wilcox called me up and made me an offer. The two of you for his life and we go back to how it was before: I'm the trigger and Wilcox is the bullet. If we finish the list, Adlar was generous enough to offer seventy per-cent. I get the hell out of this city."

"How could anyone turn into someone like you?" Royce asked.

"Easy. Commit yourself to the betterment of the city like I did once upon a time. Fight for a cause and no matter who you convict, no matter who you take off the street, four people, twice as violent, replace them. Even that, you can deal with, but then one day, you find out some piece of shit broke into a home in the middle of the night. Raped and murdered two little girls while their parents were bound and gagged watching. Killed the girls. Killed the parents. Maybe you remember Buzzy Packard. They weren't the first he'd killed but thanks to cameras at the seven-eleven on the corner, we were able to identify the killer. I'm just a rookie cop at the time and I'm just out looking to bust a hooker or break up a domestic disturbance or something. I'm gassing up and who do I see ducking in a car? Buzzy Packard. So I make the arrest without any backup and I haven't even called it in because I'm shaking in my boots. I'm thinking I got this sick-in-the-head serial killer sitting in my car and I don't know how to process that. But then he starts taunting me, telling me all the details about what he's done and what he's going to do…how he's going to convince a jury he's innocent and come back and kill again, so I get emotional and I stop the car and drag him out and put a gun to his head. He starts crying and even wets himself and suddenly he's changing his story, saying he's innocent and he was just all talk. So we get back in the car and I bring him in."

Manny cut the story off there. Royce didn't know if it was because they were nearly at the river or if the story was over, but it was abrupt. "Then what?" Royce asked. "Is that it?"

"No, that's not it. You need to know what happens next if you want to really understand why we're all here. Same thing Buzzy said would happen when he was taunting me. Jury finds him innocent and he's free. Before Buzzy finally ends his own life, he murders three other families in nearly identical ways. Probably wanted to make it known to me that I had a chance that night and I didn't take it. If I'd have killed Buzzy, I think we'd all agree that the media and half this country would have tried to crucify me, because due process and jury of your peers and all that bullshit that we like to call justice, but it's not. There's a thousand loopholes for cops and criminals alike and if you even know fragments of how the system works, you can slip right through it. Those families that died, that was because I didn't have the balls to end a scumbag's life. Tax-payers keep guys like that in prison, where we like to think they rot, but prison's exactly what they've been looking for their whole life. They fit in, they form friendships, they work and they get fed for nothing and pay no taxes."

"If you killed me like Buzzy Packard, I wouldn't have much to say," Royce said. "But you end lives for a bounty. That's different."

"And you hired me."

"Biggest mistake I ever made. How can we undo it detective?"

"You can't."

They stood at the riverbank. Royce turned to Manny with a disappointed look in his eyes, pleading for another alternative. Charlie said nothing. He watched the river, only hoping he'd never hear the shot or feel the pain. He hoped he would just be gone without ever realizing it.

"Face me," Manny said and then he said it again, louder. Charlie slowly moved his wheelchair in an arc, facing Manny, but he looked to the ground. "Join them," he said to Adlar, who stood frozen, uncertain of what to do. "Did you hear me? I said join them."

"Why?"

"Because if any of you live, there's no balance."

"But…"

"Join them." His voice was stern and Adlar slowly walked to the bank, to the side of Royce and Charlie, trying to distance himself from them. "I'm not going to say much in parting because we all know why we're here, but Charlie and Royce, I'm going to allow you to be last because you both wanted Wilcox dead. I'm going to give you that satisfaction. I've only got two bullets, so I'm afraid you're going in the river upside down Mr. Palmer. That's the cost of murdering Bedbug. Then we'll all be squared away."

Charlie mumbled something.

"Excuse me?"

"I said go to hell," Charlie said, refusing to look up.

"You're not going to want to miss this," He raised his arm, gun in hand, at Adlar and pulled the trigger.

Charlie squeezed his eyes closed, but there was no bang and he heard nothing. He kept his eyes closed, waiting for the shot, but nothing came, only the sound of Manny cursing. When he opened his eyes, Manny was inspecting the trigger of the gun. "What the f…?"

Adlar stepped forward confidently. "The gun you gave me…that gun… I tampered with it." Manny looked up at Adlar, eyes wide, and the rest of the group could see that something was happening to his body. "I emptied the bullets but also jammed the trigger and wedged a needle inside. It was a trick I thought up back when we were partners. The anesthetic numbs the whole body but you're completely conscious. You taught me about a needle placed under a car handle, but then you gave me the gun and so I figured that would work too."

Adlar smiled at Manny and waited, as if he was searching for validation.

Manny tried to lunge toward Adlar, but his knees buckled under him. "I knew you would kill me," Adlar said. "I worked with you for half a year. I know your methods and I wanted it to be like this. You said it was poetic…yeah…yeah it is. This is how it should be. Royce and Charlie and me, because you keep saying we made your life hell, but that's what you did to us. You could've let up. Geez, Royce just wanted me dead cause I almost killed his wife and then Charlie just wanted me dead for the same reason but I got away with it and you just got in the way of it all and you didn't let up."

It was the most Royce and Charlie had ever seen Adlar speak and the first time they saw him speak with any kind of anger…with conviction. Though too much damage was done, Adlar had clearly made the right decision in the end. Neither knew what that counted for, but because of Adlar, they would walk away to see another day.

"You killed all these people. Where's the debt you owe them? Where's the balance in that? You just say that cause you think it sounds cool but it's the dumbest thing ever. But now it's your turn. You led us out here, where there's no witnesses and we all hate you, so this is poetic. What we just did is."

Royce could've laughed if the situation hadn't made him want to throw up. This had all been Adlar's handiwork. There was plenty of brain-power between them, but Adlar had executed flawlessly, manipulating Manny into unknowingly marching them to his death. He watched Manny's face as the muscles tightened in his body and he curled on the ground, unable to control his limbs. He tried to speak, but couldn't. He only spit up phlegm and drooled on the ground. Only his eyes were animated, trying to do all the speaking, but no one was listening.

Adlar picked up the gun from where it fell to the ground. He delicately found the needle and pulled it from where it was housed alongside the trigger. He then pulled two bullets from his pocket and reloaded the gun.

"I'll do it," Royce said, stepping forward. Adlar sized him up, but held the gun tightly. "Please let me be the one to do this…for Sandra…"

*8*

The inmates of Kern were in the exercise yard when six guards walked through, surrounding Warden Sunjata came storming through the yard, creating a pathway toward a man named Downtown. Another group of guards gathered Stanley Kline and they were both brought back inside where the warden brought them to his office and sat them down with four other correctional officers in the room, standing between them and the door.

"I'm going to make this short," the warden said. "I want to know everything you know about what Christian Dent has been up to."

"I don't know," Stan said.

"Don't even know who you're talking about," Downtown said.

"I know you're a mule," the warden said, directing his attention to Downtown. "I know you've been getting Dent what he wanted and Correctional Officer Willis was turning a blind eye to it. I'm not after you or your business. I only want to know what it was that Dent wanted.

Stanley's eyes diverted to Downtown, wanting to know too. It was news to him that Dent had been getting paraphernalia behind his back.

"Don't know what you're talking about," Downtown said again.

"Alright, then we'll try this another way. How would you like to lose all business overnight?"

"Wouldn't care."

"I think you would because you're just a little skinny pansy who's trying to get through a sentence unharmed and you figured out how. In Kern, wealth is power. It's probably the most powerful weapon anyone can have. You've built quite a status here and I can take it from you. Then who's gonna protect you?"

"Sorry boss," Downtown said. "No idea what you want here."

The warden sized him up. He knew that working with authority was suicide and he wasn't going to cave easily. "How would you like to lose the liquor?"

"Don't know what you mean boss."

"You think I don't know what happens here? You make bootleg liquor by mixing fruit juice, water, bread, and sugar in a plastic bottle and leave it to brew on warm pipes that heat your cell when it's cold. That's why everyone's so happy in the fall when we turn the pipes back on so you can brew your homemade hooch in time for Christmas. Who's to say I won't just shut off the pipes in your block this year? And how about I drag in a device that detects frequency so I can find cell phones? Or how about a ferromagnetic detector? Have you heard of this? The cell phone doesn't even have to be on or in use. It will pick up the electromagnetic field generated by any mobile phone, even if it's off and the battery's removed. I'll even increase the surprise dormitory searches."

Downtown couldn't keep listening. He knew he was beat. "You haven't asked a question. Maybe I can help but I gotta know what you want boss."

"You're not implicating yourself in any way and I'm not even going to ask you the name of any of the other guards who don't know which side of the bars they're supposed to be on, but I want to know what you were getting Dent."

"Two things: A razor, and nitric acid."

The warden turned to Stanley, who shrugged. "I haven't seen him with anything out of the ordinary. He was private…didn't tell me anything."

"Nitric acid…" the warden said. "For what? What's that good for here?"

"Maybe a weapon," Downtown said.

"Nitric acid will eat through metal," Stan said. "possibly an escape from the yard, but there'd be too many guards."

"How'd you get it in here?" the warden asked.

"I got a guy on the outside who usually just throws tennis balls over the fence between perimeter sweeps."

"For that, you've got a guard on the wall who turns his head."

"You said you wouldn't ask."

"I won't, but that's correct?"

"Yes, boss."

"What'd he say? How much did he get?"

"He got about four tubes of it. It had to be packaged very specifically, so I had it brought in through my contact."

"I'm going to contact the local state attorney's office. If you're willing to give up your main source for contraband smuggling, I'll push for a lighter sentence on charges of conspiracy to introduce contraband into a correctional facility, which is a felony."

"Come on man. That's bullshit. You said this wouldn't fall on me."

"You brought nitric acid into my facility. Do you have any idea the risk you've brought upon everyone in here?"

Downtown looked dumbfounded. "You think he'll use it as a weapon?"

"It wasn't even a year ago that the man gassed this whole prison through the ventilation system. Dent is off limits for you, assuming he ever sees daylight again." The warden turned to the guards. "We need to know where he's storing it and what he's doing with it, as soon as possible."

"Should we go now?"

"Get them back to the yard. Don't say anything about this to anyone. I need to finish this bullshit interrogation and then we're going to have a talk with Dent."

9

Toby O'Tool stood over the motionless body of Brian Van Dyke. His mouth was wide open and his body still.

"I can't tell but he might be dead," Will said, standing far back.

Toby leaned down and put his hand over Brian's mouth. He felt the faintest breath. He looked up. "He's still in here somewhere. Maybe won't be through the night though. If he does make it, if this is his habit, then…" Toby shook his head. Brian was toast.

"Maybe we should walk away and let it happen," Will said.
"I was thinking we could restrict his breath more. Turn him or put him face down on a pillow.

"Go ahead."

Toby looked up at Will and saw it in his eyes. He was done. He wasn't taking this another step forward and who could blame him? The targets they'd been working were supposed to be the easy ones. Henry had succeeded but got himself killed. Neomin had gotten himself killed and hadn't even accomplished a thing. In fact, it was a matter of time before Trish Reynalds came knocking at his door. If not her, then Charlie Palmer or Adlar Wilcox. Bernard Bell had proved to be able to stay ahead of him and they had barely gotten started.

"If Van Dyke dies, that will be a good distraction, for a little while."

"Yeah, great, now there's only two of us and you've got a nine month turnaround on success and that only happens half the time," Will said.

"Look, with Brian on his way out, it will shift focus a bit…"

"Not enough."

"We still know what Trish tried to do. We can use that to keep her under our thumb."

"But she didn't do anything," Will said. "She didn't break any laws."

Toby fell silent. He was at a loss for words, completely unmotivated. He'd lost half his crew and the one remaining wanted nothing to do with this. Toby shook his head in disbelief. He'd screwed up badly. He'd overcomplicated things. He wondered if he would have been smart to have just let Sal loose when he'd offered. Maybe what Toby really did need was a crazy man to run around killing people.

"I'm not doing anything to him," Will said. "If you want me to help you with anything else, you need to get your hands dirty because lord knows I have, and Henry and Greg gave their lives for that money and made very little headway."

Toby couldn't take his eyes off of Brian. He really did look like he was gone, and if he wasn't, he would be soon. All the right strings were pulled. He doubted Brian would ever find the motivation to snap out of this. *We created a drug addict,* he thought. *Deliberately.* This was never the kind of scam Toby started out with. He liked to win games and take money…this was above his head.

"Maybe we take a break and re-evaluate," Toby said. "We can just chill for a while, let everything set in and talk again later and see where we're at with this."

"What about Brian?"

"Let's just leave him. Quit that job and get out of here and let him do what he does. My guess is he won't last a week, assuming he wakes up at all. I'll understand if you back out. I liked Henry from the moment I met him, and Neomin didn't deserve what happened to him, but if you're in Will…if you do this all the way with me…"

"What? Then what? We're both rich?"

"Spare me your holier-than-thou attitude Will. Pick up the newspaper and you'll find five people who died yesterday over something dumb like a bar-fight or an elderly woman who ran a light. Senseless deaths happen by the minute in this country, whatever the cause, and those people, they get their funeral and nothing more comes of it. No good at all. You signed up for it. You can walk away when you want. You haven't killed anyone yet."

Will looked down at Brian. "Until he dies."

"Everyone dies. Proven fact that the number one cause of death is birth."

Will's face expressed a whole poem of restrained anger, disdain, and indignation. "This doesn't bother me like it did Henry okay? I wondered if it would at first but it didn't. This whole thing with Maria…it doesn't bother me. It's a relief actually. I'm pissed that Sal died. I'm pissed that Henry and Neomin died. We're putting ourselves out there for this."

"Any one of those guys would recognize my face. I need strangers because I can't make Maria fall in love with me or shoot up with Van Dyke. They would know what I was doing."

"I'm not saying you can. I'm saying that we haven't gotten very far and we've done more damage to our group than them. One gone Toby. One."

"It will be two soon."

"And you'll have to answer to the cop and maybe Palmer."

"You want to be in charge? Tell me what to do then."

"We need to link Neomin to Van Dyke. He's got money and motive and he had a great relationship with Victor."

Toby was surprised to see that William in the driver's seat wasn't half bad. "And how can you possibly link them?"

"He's you. It's that simple. He's the guy that blackmailed Neomin. It was all part of Victor's plan. Brian's been pulling strings all along. No one can question a dead guy."

"All we'd have to do is plant something in his apartment that shows Brian was in contact with…"

"Exactly."

"You're my new favorite."

"I'm flattered."

Toby saw something new in William that he liked. There was a confidence…a maturity. He no longer struggled with the mission. He just didn't always agree with Toby's vision. Toby knew he'd screwed up. He'd tried to do too much with too many, but the days of having a crew were over. Henry did a great job, but he was too conflicted and unlucky in the end. He did everything he set out to do and then got himself splattered across the highway. Neomin was a disaster from the start. He did what he was told but he tried talking his way out of it at every step. The days of babysitting were over. William had become a reflection of Toby, and in this game, two like-minded people were better than one.

"We don't need to take a break or regroup," William said. "We need to step it up."

Toby smiled. "Then let's finish this."

They hoisted Brian up and carried him to his bed, positioning him face-down on the pillow. It was no sure thing, but if not today, Brian would finish himself soon enough. As Toby and William stood on opposite sides of the bed, watching Brian lay still, they both knew that it was time to pick their next target…

*…Maria Haskins looked up as her door opened and Victor Stone walked in. She gasped at the sight of him, but he strolled in casually, determined to talk. After a few days to calm herself, she wanted to talk to him too. Neither spoke though. She waited for him and he stared at the wall, picking his words closely.*

*"May I sit?"*

*"Please…"*

*Victor fell into the seat across from her and leaned back. "Things got out of hand when we last saw each other."*

*"Yes…"*

*"But I know you and I know who you are. What you said…what you tried to do…sat with me. Maria, there's truth to some of your claims. I*

*don't know the future, but what you said, it's always been an outcome I've feared."*

*"Outcome of what?"*

*"Something we set in motion…some associates and I. It wasn't my idea. I went with along with it but had reservations. Now that I see it as a reality…"*

*"It's death…"*

*"I can stop it."*

*"No you cannot."*

*"Why do you say that?"*

*"What I saw Victor…was what you said. You created the cloud but you can't stop the rain. It's already formed and it's growing over millions of people. You no longer control it, but you've created it. I know your heart and I know your convictions, but it is too late."*

*"That's it? It's too late? That's not good enough Maria. There's always a way to undo damage."*

*"You've made many friends and you've become very successful, but you've surrounded yourself with the wrong people. Those who are your friends are your enemies and your enemies are your friends, but you do not see that…"*

*"I don't know what you're saying…"*

*"Have you made a list?"*

*He looked into her eyes, frightened of her, realizing the power and knowledge within such a small person. Most people didn't think much of Maria, but she'd cursed his life and saw things in a perspective he couldn't comprehend, but desperately needed to.*

*"I've created a will."*

*"Have you created a list?"*

*"My will contains a list. A list of enemies. It comes from a bad place but I don't intend on keeping it."*

*"Why your enemies?"*

*"They've used me. They've disrespected me. I gave them everything and they wanted more. I wanted to…" he trailed off and shook his head as if the whole thing was ridiculous. "After you cursed me, or whatever that was, I wrote your name on it. I'm not keeping it though Maria. I simply must swallow whatever urge I have when I'm angry. Most of the people I've written in…a man of God…you…my ex-wife…a man I never even met…good people… It's this piece of paper I have that I tell myself I will tear to shreds and throw into the fire every day and then my anger consumes me and the list grows."*

*"The list is your only hope."*

*He looked up and searched her eyes. "Excuse me?"*

*"Your friends are your enemies and your enemies are your friends."*

*"Can't you just tell me what you mean? I don't know how to understand this cryptic talk. I don't know what you're telling me."*

*"Your list came from a bad place but you're already who you are Victor. You are incapable of being anyone else. You will always surround yourself with the powerful and you will never see the evil you're a part of...the same evil that has conjured a darkness that will take the lives of millions of people, but you cannot stop it because you are one of them....but...you also have convictions and something within you that tries to reject this darkness. It is those who you hate, those you have been angry at, it is those people you will never understand, could never be... who hold the key to a light that you're unable to reach."*

*"I will redraft my will when..."*

*"No," she said abruptly. "The only light I saw...the only weapon against this cloud of darkness...was a list...your list. Like all good and evil things, a million events before them have to happen to get there. A million events were put into place so that you and your associates could create this darkness. A million events must happen for a light to shine through...a defense against it. That light is your list."*

*"Keep my will?" he asked. "Shouldn't I tell people what you're telling..."*

*"No. Victor, you must bring them together. If you try to influence what they do, if you try to set them on another path..."*

*"How can you possibly know this?"*

*"You have to trust me."*

*"Do you understand what this list really is? It's an invitation for each one to murder their contemporaries. You're on it Maria."*

*"I should not have told you what I saw that day because in telling you, I've led you to believe that you should take another path, but you must not bend yourself because of what I've said. You must be who you are... you must remain in that darkness but bring together this light, because there are bigger things happening and it won't matter who are your friends and who are your enemies. All that will matter is who will win in the end. You're our secret weapon Victor. You're on the side of evil, but the light in you creates the weapon against this cloud."*

Victor understood, but it changed everything. He knew that there was a part of him, a little boy, who didn't want to be so wealthy, didn't want to be so angry, or bed multiple women. That part of him was a family man, with a son and a daughter, who sat in a picnic table at the park while his children ran and played. Part of him had always believed that one day he may end up there and have those things, but the vision was fading.

He'd done too much damage and deep down, he'd always known she *was right. Bernard Bell, Jones Mitchell, and Cory Owens were ruthless businessmen. They always wanted more, no matter who was hurt, and they would inevitably unleash the virus to the city. Victor believed damage control was as simple as releasing the cure immediately, but if Maria was right, the casualties would reach far beyond what any of them had ever believed.*

*To prevent this, all Victor had to do was continue doing what he was doing. There was only one thing that nagged at him.*

*"These people won't be brought together until I die."*

*Maria found his eyes and gave him a long look. She didn't need to speak. He already knew what she had to say. His days were numbered. Everything would play out after he was gone. He smiled at her, letting her know he understood. "I should go," he said. She nodded and watched him approach the exit sadly, knowing their relationship was over. There was nothing more to say...nothing more for her to see.*

*He turned back. "Don't let anyone tell you you're not the real deal Maria."*

*Victor was a rarity. She couldn't profit off moments like this. "Only this..." she said. "In all the time I've known you, this was the only time..."*

*He smiled and nodded, showing he understood. He knew.*

*She watched him exit...*

*...On the seventh floor of Stone Enterprises, in a corner office, Victor opened a laptop. There was a flash of light and a screen displayed, asking for a password. With a quick typing motion, he was in and a screen populated—a screen which asked for another password and had an "execute" icon.*

*He wondered how it was that he found himself in a position to end everyone in the city, but here he was. He could shut it down now, but it wasn't built for one man to make a decision. It was built for two. Bernard Bell had the other laptop and to release the virus or to stop the virus, it took two.*

*He thought about what Maria said and came to terms with the fact that he wouldn't be behind the controls when that decision was made. It would be Bernard Bell and company, or according to Maria's logic, his enemies. He stared at the screen for what felt like eternity, alone with his thoughts, thinking about how he was going to be remembered when he was gone.*

*"She's a fraud," he said to himself, but he'd already accepted his fate...*

"…I don't think Wilcox should have the gun," Charlie said. "But you can't do this Royce."

Adlar looked wounded that he still hadn't gotten their trust, but he accepted it, willing to hand the gun to either man.

"I lost everything because of him," Royce said, extending his hand. "We all know what has to happen."

"Yeah, except it's not going to be you," Charlie said.

"Why not?"

"You're the only one whose hands are clean. You've got somewhere else to be."

"I've got nowhere to be."

"Wait…" Adlar said. He'd picked up Manny's phone and was scrolling through a page, his eyes darting from number to number. "You're going to win."

"Win what?" Royce was either playing dumb or refused to believe the election was his.

"You're killing Bell."

Everyone fell silent and all eyes ended on Manny, who tried to move but all he could do was choke out sounds. It was all they needed to hear to know he was in there, he could hear them, and he was begging for mercy.

"You gotta go," Charlie said. "This is just something that needs to happen and it will, but you're going to be governor of this city and you don't need this guilt. You don't need this to eat at you because trust me, you're not going to want to be in your right mind."

Charlie's eyes shifted to Adlar, who nodded his agreement. Royce was the only one who deserved to walk away from this. He'd made his share of mistakes, but he was the only one who could come out clean. Charlie and Adlar were forever damaged. It was their job.

Royce nodded and wiped away a tear. He crouched down to Manny and looked into his eyes. They were filled with fear. "You still owe a debt," Royce said with a trace of a smile. He stood and brushed himself off, gave Adlar and Charlie a grateful look. "Whatever I can do to help when this is over…"

"We know," Charlie said.

Royce gave them one last look and began his hike up the hillside, grabbing onto trees for support. The sun was beginning to set and the sound of insects filled the air. Charlie and Adlar stayed in place for long after he was gone, until Charlie finally spoke.

"How long will he be like that?"

"Hours."

"We should get this done before it gets dark."

They both turned to Manny, who they'd been afraid of for so long. He was helpless and desperate. Adlar couldn't help but feel sorry for a man whose whole life was about control. All he could do was manage to make a sound here and there. He couldn't protest or make his case.

Adlar raised the gun and pointed it at Manny's head. Manny managed to move his mouth, but he couldn't make a sound. Adlar had nothing more to say and Charlie was right. This had to be done. He squeezed the trigger and this time, a shot echoed through the woods as Manny's head snapped back and his forehead burst in a splotch of blood.

Adlar turned away and Charlie closed his eyes and when enough time passed and the sun began to disappear, Adlar found himself with a gun in his hand and no next move. Charlie watched him closely until he found the courage to find the words that were long overdue.

"You killed Abby."

"Yeah."

"And I let her die."

Adlar saw the pain in Charlie's eyes and how much the confession had unburdened him. "Did you even love her?"

"Yes," Charlie said and tears formed in his eyes and fell before he could wipe them away.

Adlar sat on a tree that had fallen in a storm, holding the gun at his side.

"What are you going to do?" Charlie asked.

Adlar slowly extended the gun, holding it so Charlie could take it. Charlie studied his face to see if it was a trick, but Adlar kept it held out until Charlie took it from his hand. "You can finish this. I just need..." Adlar shifted himself over the tree so he could sit facing away.

"Wilcox, I'm not going to do this."

Adlar didn't speak and Charlie knew he was probably crying as he waited for Charlie to fulfill his promise. Charlie considered his options and replayed the events in his head, but he couldn't find the anger he'd once had. Instead, he found a compassion he hadn't expected...a compassion he could never find when he needed it the most. Adlar had accepted death. There was nothing more for him to do. He couldn't go on living and if he did, he was too dangerous under certain circumstances.

"Adlar..."

"Just do it," Adlar said. "Or I'll do it to myself. I murdered your wife and took your legs. Just do it please!"

Charlie could hear his voice shaking and knew his face was wet with tears. Adlar was owning up and this was how Charlie always intended it would end between them. He just didn't expect Adlar to go so freely. There was too much pain...too much guilt...he could never live with himself. Adlar's body was shaking uncontrollably. He was afraid of what would happen next, weighed with guilt, feeling as if his whole life had just been useless and destructive. Charlie closed his eyes for a moment and found an inner peace, thinking about Abby, the day he first saw her, their first date, the first time they made love… He opened his eyes. Adlar was whimpering as he sobbed, unable to control his emotions. His body trembled, his arms twitching and his legs swaying whichever way his body was pulling. Charlie had never seen someone riddled with so much guilt and fear.

Charlie raised the gun and held it still for a long moment.

"Adlar..." Charlie said. "I'm going to tell everyone about Manny. I'm going to tell them you saved all of us."

He watched Adlar long enough to see he'd stopped shaking and no more tears were forming. Instead, Adlar's body was calm and in that moment, even though he was staring at the back of Adlar's head, .Charlie thought he could see Adlar smile at the thought.

He pulled the trigger and a flash of light filled the forest.

Royce Morrow stepped onto a podium as the crowd around him roared. He looked out into the sea of people in disbelief, raising his hands to keep the applause rolling. He wanted them to cheer. He wasn't ready to speak. He wasn't all that prepared to win. He wasn't supposed to win. In fact, his luck had turned in the course of the afternoon. He'd been punished from many angles during this election. Bernard had fallen from power and Manny would never hurt another person. It could potentially come back at Royce and maybe even ruin he legacy, but he would always know that on this day, more good than harm came into the world.

The applause lightened and he stepped up to the microphone.

"Wow…" was all he could manage before they started cheering again.

"I want to say thank you to everyone who voted. I want to thank my campaign managers Stuart Wiley and Ronald Wycleff, who hung in there when I resisted all of their advice. I want to thank the two hundred and forty folks who have been working on the Morrow campaign, tirelessly patrolling our neighborhoods and getting the word out about what I'm all about. I want to thank, most of all, my late wife Sandra, who once told me to pick a cause and stick with it. That advice has carried me through my life and I hope I can accomplish even a sliver of what Sandra did her in life.

Let's talk about us and what we need to do to make this state great. Fortunately, I no longer need to pick a cause. I will have the opportunity to serve you, hear your voices, and together, we'll re-evaluate and re-invent this great state.

From time to time, all establishments, all individuals, need to re-evaluate. I believe we grow comfortable going with the flow. We change with our influences and we lose sight of ourselves. What did you set out to do and what are you doing? Who did you want to be and who are you? I challenge each of you to ask yourself these questions every day. Are we fully awake, completely aware, or are we closed off to the suffering and pain that is in front of us every day?"

The crowd let out a series of "hell yeahs" as miles away, Jason Stone walked Anthony Freeman into a late night AA meeting in a church basement. Anthony fell into a chair and Jason sat in the back, watching and waiting until they could talk more. Jason thought about Todd Mason and Erica Drake and what he was going to say and how he was going to approach the woman who'd forced herself into his life in secret, and how he hadn't been able to see it.

"It's not the city that makes us great. It's us that makes IT great, but to do that, we must look deep within ourselves and find our shortcomings, our temptations and desires, and ask ourselves if those shortcomings define us or if we can rise above them and stand by our convictions…to make the difficult decision to give our time or our money so another less fortunate can have a hot meal, to set aside our greed and intolerance and know that the lifeblood of this city is the same blood that flows through all of us…"

Royce found his voice and as he spoke with passion, Aileen Thick waited anxiously for her son to arrive to join her for dinner. She picked up her phone to call but she couldn't bring herself to push the buttons, knowing he either forgot and didn't care enough or something else came up and he couldn't even give her a courtesy call. She thought about Tarek, who was off talking to the studio heads about his upcoming film and trying to rid himself of the guilt of the way he'd treated Aileen. She thought about Maria and everyone else on the list, wondering if they were all safe tonight. It was as she thought about them that Adlar took his last breath.

"…We all breathe the same air, we want the same things. We love our families and friends. We're all brothers or sisters, fathers, sons, mothers, daughters… We all want a roof on our head, a meal to eat, we want to be healthy, wealthy, successful, but is that enough? To be great, we must want that of each other that we want it in ourselves and we must demand it in each other—that your neighbor is respectful, kind, generous, just as we will be the same for our neighbor…"

As the crowd offered cheers of approval, in a strip club called "Girls, Girls, Girls," Toby O'Tool and William Lamone sat together, composing a new list and charting their way through it. They'd already linked Brian

Van Dyke to Gregory Neomin, leaving his number on a napkin and putting it in his phone, as well as calling his number and sending texts asking for a status update. It wasn't much but it was all Trish would need. Toby and William didn't believe he'd make it through the night. Brian did though. He slept on his face but his breathing wasn't restricted and as the night progressed and the liquor and substances worked their way through his system, he slowly began to breath more steadily, able to live to see another day.

"…And ladies and gentlemen of this great city, I promise you that better days are coming…that a lot of us have been fighting our battles for so long that we've forgotten the feeling of victory, but we can't win by ourselves. We must work together, and if we do, and only if we do, we will rise above our pain, we will rise above our demons, and we will be victorious, together…"

The crowd let loose an applause while fifty miles away, the warden of Kern marched toward the hotbox with a dozen guards at his side. They called Dent's name with no response and the warden grew sick as he knew the answer to what was inside. The hotbox was opened and it was confirmed. Every guard dropped their jaw at the empty space, on the opposite wall, a large eroded hole where the metal had been eaten through. An all out search began but Dent had been free almost twenty-four hours.

"…This will be the beginning," Royce shouted. "Right here and now, we wipe the slate clean. We stop making excuses, we refuse to be held back by who we think we are and we start becoming the city we wish to be. It is time that we collectively re-evaluate ourselves and re-invent ourselves, and as one, we will create a better tomorrow! We will start over! This, tonight, at this moment, THIS, is the beginning!"

The crowd roared and echoed in the night, reaching the outskirts of the surrounding neighborhoods and bringing comfort to Charlie Palmer as he stopped to catch his breath. He was at the corner of the block, not far from the skeleton of the home that he and Abby had shared, which was now just pile of burnt wood and police tape. He had nowhere to go, but that was okay because the night he sat outside the bedroom door while Abby begged him to come back, he sealed his fate. He just hadn't realized it until now. There was only one place he was supposed to be, but until recently, he hadn't realized how much the world would fight back when there was injustice.

It was time to pay. Manny called it a debt. Royce would have called it justice. Victor Stone would have called it vengeance. Whatever name he was to give it, he'd had it coming for some time and the more he fought it, the more he lost. With nothing left, his eyes were opened.

He pulled Manny's cell from his pocket and dialed a number and waited until the other end picked up.

"This is Trish," she said. She sounded happy. If Charlie had tears left to cry, he would have let them fall. Instead, he smiled and choked up.

"This is Charlie," he finally said.

She paused for a long time. Surely, she'd tried to contact him. She might have been the only one.

"Charlie, we need to talk. I got your messages. I know about Neomin. Where have you been? Do you know that he…"

"We can catch up Trish, but I need you to take me in. I killed Abby. I was part of it. I want you to be the one to arrest me."

A pause. "Where are you?"

"I'm at the house...Abby and my…"

He was suddenly cut off, but he didn't know by what and he didn't have time to think about it. He knew his neck felt like a razor blade was cutting into it but couldn't make sense of it. He felt hands behind his neck, tightening the wire. Manny…Adlar…It couldn't be…

He tried to breath, but the wire tightened and he realized his life was slipping away. The phone fell to the ground, still open with the faint voice of Trish saying his name.

Charlie's eyes rolled back as a figure leaned in, making himself known. Charlie had never seen Christian Dent until now. He never thought even thought about the convict on the will. He didn't know he was out of prison and he didn't know why his throat burned, other than the obvious monetary value that existed if he died.

"There are unspoken rules in this game," Dent said. "Just about anything is fair, except we don't use kids. You shouldn't have dragged Shiloh into this."

Charlie didn't hear the words. He only heard noises. If he'd been allowed to breath, he might have explained that he wasn't Trish's doctor…at least not the doctor Dent thought he was. It probably wouldn't have mattered if he could speak, but as Charlie's eyes turned red and his neck turned white, he tried to beg, to say he owned his mistake. He was willing to take responsibility. Whatever was happening was a mistake.

And then, Charlie's body went limp and the force of the pressure Dent was putting on him, pulled the wheelchair to the side where it fell to the ground and Charlie's lifeless body rolled onto the grass. Dent looked down at Charlie and then to the phone, still open, a concerned voice coming through the speaker—a voice he recognized.

He picked up the phone and put it to his ear. Trish must have heard the breathing or sensed the movement because she fell quiet. They both listened intently, trying to decipher the sounds of silence to know who was on the other end. Then, Trish felt it.

"Christian?" she said.

He pulled the phone away from his ear and held it in his palm, staring at the screen. She said his name again and he hit the end button, as if confirming her suspicion.

"I'll be seeing you," he said to no one at all. He stepped over Charlie's leg and disappeared into the night.

## From the Author

Upon finishing this book, it occurred to me that now is the time to tell you where Tontine stemmed from. Book one was my pilot. It was intended to seem like a bowl of water on the stove with the heat turned up. It was also very introductory and as the water heated, I asked you to remember a lot of characters that barely interacted with each other, all the while, the water getting hotter.

By book two, introductions were over and the water was boiling.

With book three, I turned up the heat.

Since you're still with me, I'm going to assume you will be until the end, and maybe as a loyal reader, you're asking yourself why I'm writing something so insanely long and where it came from.

At the time the first Tontine was released, a smart author would have been publishing a book about vampires or an apocalyptic world filled with zombies.

The evolution of Tontine has been with me since I was young and the way it's been shaped over the years has developed into a story I couldn't ignore.

For beginners, I've been a daydreamer for as long as I could remember. I was so unfocused as a child that my lack of attention was once attributed to a learning disability. I remember being taken out of third grade art class and brought to the hospital where doctors hooked a bunch of tubes to the top of my head and somehow monitored my brain by having me answer questions and telling me to think about random words they fed me. The end result was that I didn't have a learning disability. I was just too damn in my own head. At the time, it sounded like a bad thing and maybe if I had been different, I'd be a day trader or a doctor, but when I look back at the creative process and where and when most ideas come to me, it all begins with daydreaming. There was never a time that I had to sit down and say "Okay, think of an idea." The ideas have always been there and most of them were fighting to come out at a very young age, long before writing was even on my radar.

Which brings me to Tontine. I've always liked the elimination one by one story. Die Hard comes to mind. In the story, people are being held hostage by a group of criminals. One man is free to stop them and to do so, he must eliminate the bad guys one by one to even the odds. The "only one can survive" story has been done before. We've seen it in Battle Royale, Highlander, The Hunger Games, The Long Walk, and even in every reality show in which one person is eliminated per episode.

My only problem with all these stories, with the exception of reality TV (which doesn't count in my opinion), is that we already know the hero. We always know the last man standing from the very first chapter. We may not know how they'll get there and a lot of these stories surprise us in other ways, but we always know the hero. I've always wanted a last person standing story where we didn't know who the last person standing would actually be. I also wanted the story to be grounded in reality. The last man standing plot is often implausible, or at least couldn't take place in the world we know.

In the summer of 2002, I moved to Los Angeles to pursue a career as a screenwriter. I was writing about a screenplay a year and had a handful of ideas on the shelf to be written. I can't pinpoint exactly when and where I got the concept for Tontine, which at that time I called The Will. I think it was just my love of the last man standing concept, but where I failed was that at one time, *The Will* was shelved as my horror script concept. I was given advice that the smart way to sell a script was to write one in each genre and keep them all in the trunk of my car. The reason for this is that when you're sitting in a bar, you never know who you're going to meet and when you finally say "I write screenplays" and a big-shot says "What have you written?" you want to be able to offer him whatever genre he's looking for on the spot. The objective is that some big-name director or producer drunkenly asks for your script and wakes up the next day with a hangover and something to read sitting on their nightstand.

I didn't write to every genre, but I intended on doing so, and my will concept was my horror movie. It was going to be the same basic idea: jaded billionaire leaves everything to the last surviving in his will. One by one, ten people off each other until one remains. It was even going to be a whodunit. In hindsight, I can only imagine how awful that would have turned out had I written it, but life continued to be breathed into what would ultimately become Tontine.

Fast forward to 2005. Things weren't going so well for me in LA. At the end of the year, I fly home for the holidays with a round trip ticket that didn't turn out to be a round trip. Shortly before that, I had a buddy who worked in the movies and he gets himself a pitch meeting with a big name studio. He tells me he has no ideas but if I have any good television reality series ideas, he could probably get me a pitch meeting. I had nothing because reality TV wasn't my thing, but suddenly I'm searching my mentally shelved ideas for something that would work on TV.

I landed on The Will and all at once, the sensibility of a multi-character last man standing story on TV week to week made a ton of sense. I never went to a pitch meeting, but everything else I had planned was forgotten and I began outlining ten seasons of this story. I knew who would die in what season and how they would die. I knew every twist and turn along the way, saving the better ones for later in the series. My reasoning was that there were too many shows that were popular when they first aired, but by season 3 no one cared about them anymore. My opinion was that the writers gave the series their everything when starting but realized later there was no direction and they'd exhausted their best already. Remember Heroes? Prisonbreak? Ugly Betty? There were plenty of shows that were loved at first and canceled 3 years later. I was going to avoid this by saving the best for last, but keep the series strong throughout, which meant learning to pace myself. This is where the boiling pot comes into play. I never intended on having each beneficiary buy a gun in chapter 2 and start trying to shoot each other. There had to be a natural progression.

In developing characters, I first brainstormed every reaction possible to this situation and I came up with ten. I then built a character around each reaction, set them all in very different worlds, and let it play out as I outlined the progression of their actions. I also created 5 extra characters and built plots around them, because I needed people who would die early in the series. Throughout the years, some of those original 10 have died sooner than expected and at least one of those 5 who were created to die, will actually still be alive in book 7, so it's truly been a work in progress, despite my early outlined plans.

The next step was to write the episodes. My plan was to write the whole series, go back to LA, and start pitching an already finished television series. It had an ending, which gave it direction. It had plenty of characters and each episode was centric to one, so the same people doing the same things in every episode wouldn't get old. Instead, viewers would be treated to multiple plots and they'd only get them in doses. Throughout it all, characters are eliminated and without one distinct hero, no one will actually know who will live in the end (yes, there will be only one in the end).

I wrote 54 episodes, which equated to two and a half seasons. I was in love with the story. It was my baby. I knew it would be the one thing in my life that I had to complete and leave for the world to see.

So how did my 54 completed episodes, 10 season series, become a 7 book series?

Three events took place that made me realize writing books was a better path.

The first was one night, while I was working late at a coffee shop I managed in Des Moines, a car with a U-Haul attached pulled into the parking lot. The place was empty and though a customer would interrupt the writing I would secretly be doing where no one could see, the man who entered was intriguing. He asked me for directions and while he's ordering, I find out he's traveling to Los Angeles. After he sits, I get to thinking that he has a presence about him that makes me wonder if he's someone I want to talk to. So I force a conversation and tell him I'm an aspiring screenwriter and he suddenly brightens and tells me he wants to read something I wrote. It turned out that this man was the director of a popular 80s comedy, as well as a variety of other films and television episodes. I even looked him up online later and he was the guy. So I'm in Des Moines, Iowa, just me and this guy who probably can get things done and he's asking for a script. I tell him about one of the scripts I'm most proud of. He gives me contact information. He even later emails me and tells me our meeting was like fate and so in my head, this guy has seen me the same way I've seen him: A fateful meeting where suddenly someone is going to look at my script and read it and say "I want to make this movie."

Weeks pass, months…now and then, I'd email him. He's always going to get to it. To this day, every so often I get an email from him promoting a new film he's finished, but my script was never read. So that was that—my hopes were high and nothing came from what felt like a fateful meeting.

As if that's not coincidence enough in Des Moines of all places, one day someone I knew met a guy who knew a guy who was brothers with a guy in Hollywood who was one of the producers of a couple successful sitcoms and they are told about me—a screenwriter with a series and somehow emails exchanged and I communicated with this man's brother and he asked to read the Tontine pilot and I sent it to him. Weeks later, his brother and an entertainment attorney fly to Des Moines from Hollywood to meet me. They buy me a beer and some wings and we sit and talk about Tontine. They loved the pilot. They talked excitedly about all these ideas for things the characters could do and potential plot-lines and someone even asks "So when will Christian Dent finally get out of prison?" and I quoted the exact season and episode, which showcased how well I knew the series from beginning to end.

The meeting ended. A week later I get an email from the brother that says to contact them with anything if I ever have representation. The producer was busy with the sitcom at the time and couldn't fit anything else in his schedule.

Those were my two close calls, but at the end of the day, I don't know how Tontine could possibly be the right project for the producer of sitcoms or 80s screwball comedies. Still, I was discouraged. Successful people talk about how they met the right person at the right time, and somehow two impossible scenarios had happened in Des Moines, and both fell through. I was growing cynical and pessimistic about screenwriting.

Then, I read a book called Tales From the Script. The whole idea of this book was for screenwriters to talk about how much it sucked to be a screenwriter. Credit was rarely given to the writer because Hollywood always assigns their own trusted writers. Sometimes, the original writer didn't get any credit at all. Other times, the script was changed from something serious and great into something stupid that bombed at the box office. A script is usually good enough to earn the writer a payday but reputation and credit aren't to be expected.

Between what I read in this book and what I knew already, I realized that Tontine was too important to lose. A dozen 'what ifs' came to me. What if I ever achieved my goal to get this to TV and they changed the plot? What if they cut characters? What if they put a dozen writers on it and spit it out as something completely unlike what I envisioned? What if it did make it to TV but was canceled after six episodes? This was something I'd worked on for almost a decade at this point, and I suddenly had to ask myself: How do I own this? How do I keep this story 100% my own?

The answer was to publish it myself. No agent, no partners, nothing. I would publish my book as I saw it and though the odds of seeing TV diminished, I knew that whether Tontine ended up exploding in popularity, or was just a whisper among a small group, it would be my story as I wrote it, and I didn't have to depend on anyone to breathe life into it.

If you've made it this far, I assume you've stuck with me for a reason. What you're reading is from one guy who refused to hand the story over, and though I'm stubborn, I'm proud of that. There's a rule I live by, which goes: Write what you'd want to read.

No matter what happens, it is still my baby and whether it sees TV, thousands of sales, or is just something to be discovered here and there by readers who find it to be their cup of tea, it really doesn't matter. I put my blood, sweat, and tears into this series and it's exactly as it should be. It's my story to tell.

To the reader, thank you for sticking with me to this point. If you're reading this before the fourth Tontine is even published, you're the reader who took a chance on a name you didn't know. If at the end of my life, I've written fifty-plus books and someone were to ask me the most meaningful story I ever told, this would be the one. Tontine is impossible to put into a genre. To me, it's everything because there's a part of me in every character. It makes me smile, makes me sad, horrifies and delights me. It also makes me think I'm messed up in the head. I embrace that though because if I wasn't, I'd be writing books about vampires. This series is, and always will be, exactly everything I've ever liked about film, television, and reading, all in one story.

Tontine is the story I would have liked to have read, and the third book —the one you just finished, was the book I had been the most excited to write, but the pot will continue to boil and the biggest surprises are yet to come.

Thank you again for coming this far with me.

# *Acknowledgments*

Thanks to my mother for encouraging me, even when I'm in doubt. She's the first to read everything I write and is the encouraging kind of mother that I wish everyone could have. Thanks to Jennifer Darr who acts as my part-time editor and is a huge support. Thanks to Jason Darr who is about 95% in sync with me when it comes to taste in television and film. He liked my first two books and it was the best validation I could ever get. Thanks to Patrick Bertroche who helped me edit all of my books to date and has been a strong supporter of my work.

Special thanks to other people who have shown support: John Henning, Susan Glass, Travis Knobbe, Sean Beachem, Jason Hough, CJ Pace, Dawn Theilan, Katie Flannigan, Nick Konz, Mollie Guy, and Julie Darr.

And of course the man who makes this all possible: Dane.